RE:TRAILER TRASH

FORTY SIXTY FOUR

aethonbooks.com

RE: Trailer Trash
©2022 FortySixtyFour

1

AN UNCOMFORTABLE HOMECOMING

"You're *kidding me*," Ms. Tabitha Moore groaned, casting a wary look at the colossal old-fashioned MRI. There was something *familiar* about the giant thing. "This thing looks even older than I am."

"Almost!" The young nurse laughed, distractedly wafting and drifting holographic menu screens projected into the air from the ring on her hand. Her fingers danced as she navigated through the clusters. "She's about half a century old now. Don't knock her age, though—somehow or other, this old girl gives us more comprehensive scans than our brand new ones."

"Somehow, that seems... unlikely." Tabitha chuckled uneasily. She pointedly glanced around at the hypermodern fixtures and glossy white walls of the chamber deep within the University Hospital complex. It was the year 2045, and at sixty years old, she was petite and frail, with short gray hair and weathered skin lined with wrinkles. She'd lived a rather hard, unforgiving life, and *futuristic* medical breakthroughs in life expectancy had plateaued in the 2020s—life expectancy even slowly *declining* with each succeeding generation due to increasingly unhealthy modern lifestyles. Which she was as guilty of as anyone else.

Still, though... Looking at this huge old machine, Ms. Tabitha Moore was even more nervous to get her recurring headaches looked at for some reason.

"No, it's true!" the RN insisted, patting the giant old machine. "She's *special*. Reads extremely fine deep-tissue electrical activity, catches all the little individual neurons as they're firing. There's some big legal deal, with the patent-holder not releasing the rights to the technology, or... something like that. University of Louisville Hospital has some sorta loophole that lets us keep using this one for patients, though."

"And... it's absolutely safe?"

"Of course! It had some sort of issue, only like, *once*, forty-seven years ago, I think," the bubbly nurse assured her. "Do you have your PC on you? It'll have to come off before we put you in, sadly. Not because this machine's old! Even with the new ones, you can't wear your computer inside them."

"That's fine," Tabitha said, sliding her bracelet-style PC off a wrinkled wrist and watching it go dark. She set it on the offered tray and then caressed the unfamiliar absence it left behind. "It's just, I've had a bad experience in an MRI like this before."

"Oh, do you get claustrophobic?" the RN asked, flicking a finger through the display of light to summon Ms. Tabitha Moore's chart back up. "I think we can give you a sedative, if that'll make you feel more comfortable. It just makes the whole process take a lot longer."

"...No." Tabitha slowly sighed. "No, let's just get this over with."

"You'll be fine." The registered nurse smiled, helping the older woman up onto the examination table. "Take deep breaths and lie still, and this'll all be over before you know it."

With that, she slowly slid the exam table and its reluctant old passenger into the MRI. Leaning inside to check on her one last time, the young nurse crossed a safe distance away and opened the holograph for the device with a spread of her fingertips. Indicator lights blinked into existence as it began powering up.

"You still doing okay in there, Ms. Moore?"

"It smells like old lady in here."

"Hah hah ha, we'll have to see what we can do about that next time." The nurse laughed, shaking her head. "Alright, here we go!"

Deep breath, Tabitha, deep breath. Ms. Tabitha Moore frowned, squeezing her eyes tightly closed. *It's fine, that was a long time ago. And this is proven technology, this time. This machine hasn't had a mishap in... wait, forty-seven years? Forty-seven years... wasn't that—*

———

A terrible *screeching* resounded from the prototype MRI device in the Emsie St. Juarez Children's hospital. A noise like impossibly loud scraping glass, rising then to a high-pitched nails-on-chalkboard crescendo, before finally fading away with the disconcerting *pop* of an electrical breaker blowing out. Everyone within a quarter-mile of the facility visibly flinched, a stinging pain blossoming in their eardrums, and then the power went out across all of Jefferson County.

Thirteen-year-old Tabitha Moore was still screaming within the device when the hospital backup generators restored power to the MRI room—an enclosed space that had sharply risen over thirty degrees in temperature, and was rapidly filling with smoke. The fire alarm triggered, and the twitching and shuddering teenage girl inside the prototype MRI felt raw panic swelling up inside her just as an intense pain began to subside.

"Jesus *fricking* Christ!" The door set in the copper-lined wall shielding the room and its sensitive device from radio interference burst open. Tabitha's ears were ringing from the unearthly din, but she still heard a familiar-sounding male voice shouting out, *"Get her the frick out of there!"*

I'm never getting in one of these contraptions ever again, Tabitha resolved, quaking in fear and struggling with the hospital gown she found herself caught in. *Where the hells did this thing come from? I don't care what she says, or how bad the headaches get. These old things are goddamned deathtraps.*

Several people pushed through the billowing smoke to yank the sliding examination table out of the hulking cylindrical aperture of the scanner. It was unbearably hot now, and to her horror, in the waning light of the smoke-filled room, Tabitha discovered that her fingers now appeared *bloated,* looking like stumpy-looking sausage appendages.

In fact, she felt grotesquely swollen all over, her tissues... expanded, like a marshmallow microwaved for too long. Terror took over. Her breath hitched into tiny, useless gasps for air as she began to hyperventilate, and as the people were trying to help sit her up, she realized her entire body was now shrunken, *misshapen,* her center of gravity agreeing that something was terribly wrong with her.

Eyes stinging with frightened tears, Tabitha looked up, saw the worried face of her father, Mr. Alan Moore—and promptly fainted.

———

"No, I'm not in any pain," Tabitha insisted, scrutinizing the man who resembled her late father. Even her own voice sounded off, now, child-like somehow. "Mister...?"

"You sure don't seem alright," the man said, leaning in uncomfortably close and giving her a serious look. "Sweetie, you've never called me '*Mister,*' before."

Sweetie? Did she... know this young man? She seemed sure they had never met. A relative of hers? He was in his mid-thirties, and definitely from the paternal side of her family—a cousin, perhaps? The similarities to her long-dead father were simply uncanny.

"Did your goddamn piece of junk give her... what, *amnesia,* or somethin'?" The man turned to the doctor standing in the room again, his familiar-looking face filling with anger. "She's sure as hell never called me '*Mister*' before today."

"Mr. Moore, there's no, um, *obvious* indications of memory loss of any kind," the doctor shook his head, "and no way of knowing for sure, without taking her to the University of Louisville for another reading, on their MRI."

The first man snorted at that, clearly indicating that wasn't an option for consideration.

"But she's been through some... trauma with this whole experience, so if she *was* experiencing short-term memory loss, it would be understan—"

All of the myriad clues seemed to fall into place, and the breath she'd been taking seemed to seize in her chest as Tabitha froze up. *It can't be. I'm not shrunken, or misshapen. I'm... YOUNGER. I'm a fat and useless trailer trash little girl all over again. TUBBY fucking TABBY. You've got to be kidding me...*

"*Trauma?* Dr. Powell, that goddamned piece of junk almost had my ears bleeding, and she was stuck in there right in the ground zero of it!" Mr. Alan Moore shouted. "If you think—"

"There's no problem with my memory," Tabitha interrupted with a sense of finality, staring across the room with a blank face. "Just... with my comprehension of this current situation. Mr. Moore, am I to understand this is *not* the University of Louisville Hospital?" Her powers of observation had apparently flagged in the midst of this ordeal. She was only now wryly noticing that the hospital walls here were terribly outdated—sterile plastic panels, rather than the glass-like enamel resin typical of hypermodern medical establishments.

"Sweetie... sweetie, no." The man who seemed to be a younger version of her father blanched, looking at her with concern. "We drove to the children's hospital, St. Juarez. Remember, it has the big, pretty sculptures in the fountain? Emsie St. Juarez?"

"...I see." Tabitha nodded, struggling to keep disbelief from her expression. She turned to the doctor. "Then, may I ask what the current date is?"

"Thursday, May..." The doctor flipped the corner of a page on his clipboard and glanced at the date on her patient chart. "May seventh. Nineteen ninety-eight."

Nineteen ninety-eight. Having her ridiculous suspicion confirmed stunned her into silence, and Tabitha stared down at her small hands and their now chubby little fingers in incredulity.

Forty-seven years. I knew that hulking goddamned piece of shit machine looked familiar. IT WAS ME. I was the one who was in their precious multi-million-dollar MRI when it went haywire, forty-seven years ago. So, in 2045, it sends my mind back to... the past one that went berserk? Back to '98, when that infernal machine was at the children's hospital—when *I* was at the children's hospital?

Time travel seems so impossible... well, improbable. Nineteen ninety-eight. Dad's still alive... this is really, actually him. He's alive. Mom too, probably. I'm in, what? Eighth grade? Ninth? I hope to God this isn't real. That this is just some... electrical signals frying my brain into some death seizure in this MRI piece of shit. Please, ancient fucking machine spirit of the MRI, just let me die.

I don't think I have the strength to do this all over again. Please, don't make me go back to being this fat fucking useless trailer trash. I'm so tired of hating myself, I can't do it all again. I really can't. Letting out a choked sob, the overweight girl gripped the front of her hospital gown until her fists were shaking, and she rocked forward.

"Sweetie!" Mr. Moore leaned over her, alarmed. "Sweetie, what's wrong?!"

"No," Tabitha cried, shoving him back with flabby thirteen-year-old arms. "No, *please, no!*"

———

"I said I was sorry," Tabitha repeated, once again breaking the awkward silence within the cab of her dad's truck. "I was upset. I didn't mean to be... melodramatic." They were headed on the long drive home, after an ineffectual round of tests on her and some additional angry indignation from her father, who was threatening the staff with a malpractice lawsuit.

"You don't have to be sorry, sweetie," Mr. Moore said again. "I'm just concerned, 'cause you're still... talkin' funny. You've every reason to be upset. *I'm* still upset. I'm not gonna feel better 'bout any of it 'til I hear back from that lawyer. That piece of doo-hickey they shoved you in could've cooked yer noggin for good. Buncha psychos, is what they are, puttin' a little girl in a *prototype,* where anything and anywhat could go wrong. Buncha crooks."

"Do I still have to go to school, then?" Tabitha probed, trying to sound petulant.

Having been living forty-seven years in the future as of... just earlier this morning, her grasp of exactly *when* that original MRI mishap had occurred in '98 was shaky. *When* as in, what had been going on in her life at that point. She'd remembered that she'd hit her head taking a bad tumble off a friend's trampoline, way back then—the name of that friend had since then escaped her, but bruises on her head seemed to corroborate that memory.

Am I still in middle school, or am I already in high school? It being May would indicate that an academic term is concluding, and summer is starting. Right? Fortunate, because I'm rather unlikely to remember the names of any classmates. Or... even where my classes were.

"Well, I dunno, Sweetheart," Mr. Moore said, uneasy. "You've got yer finals left to do yet... and you seem to be up and about okay, thinkin' clearly. Tell you what, how 'bout I call yer counselor and have you off for tomorrow, and we'll see what kinda shape you're in come Monday morning?"

"...*Fine,*" Tabitha grumbled, genuinely unenthused. *Just finishing out middle school, then, I suppose.* The thought of having to repeat high school all over again, from the beginning, was a nightmarish prospect—all of her absolute worst memories were from that period.

Sighing, she gazed out the window at all of the antiquated-seeming models of car that seemed to fill the roads. *Nineteen ninety-eight. What happened back in 1998?* The only *major* event she recalled from those years was the big plane-hijacking, that terrorist attack on the twin towers. And, for the life of her, she couldn't recall if it'd happened in the year 2000, or the years just after that. It was, after all, a lifetime ago. The phrase *nine-eleven* stuck out in her head. *Maybe September, of 2011? That's further off than I expected.*

Not like I'd know where to even begin preventing that, she sighed. *Or if I even should. Let's see. I never memorized lottery numbers, and I was always too poor to pay attention to stock market trading. So, I guess getting rich quick is out of the picture. I'm not AMAZING at anything in particular, just... mediocre at dozens of things. Why ME? What's the use in sending ME, of all people, back to the past?*

She dreaded the thought of being forced to live it again, to be thirteen years old and be the fat, unattractive girl without friends all over again. Trailer trash, from the Lower Park. The social pariah, who smelled kind of funny, who wore yellowed T-shirts that never quite looked clean, and never really figured out how to take care of herself until it was too late. The dumpy young woman who forced herself on dates with asshole guys of the worst sort, simply because she was terrified of winding up alone. The Tabitha who made one, *single* genuine close friend in her entire life, a woman fifteen years her junior—a brilliant, talented young woman who wound up committing suicide.

Went to college to teach, but it seemed too difficult. Tried to become a fantasy writer instead, and published two books of a trilogy before they terminated my contract. Then, I just gave up on writing. Worked at the safety plant to pay the bills 'til I was out of debt from school, which took... most of my goddamned life. Julia killed herself. And then, I became a county clerk in Town Hall office for years... and that was it.

Tabitha held a blank stare, feeling hollow and disappointed. *Not much of a fucking life.*

She shook her head, turning to watch the profile of her father's face as he drove. *Dad, you look so young. I have to watch you die all over again. And Mom. I don't know if I can do this.*

"Almost home, Pumpkin," he said, misreading her concern. He pulled past a familiar liquor store, and his pickup truck made a turn down the hill, passing the sign for the *Lower Park*. There had been an *Upper Park* at one point, mobile homes filled with retirees and the elderly, but it had been bulldozed and replaced with convenience stores, a gas station, and parking lots. The already low property value of the Lower Park neighborhood plummeted even further as a result, more or less hitting rock bottom in their area. The truck lurched over the speedbumps ever-present throughout the narrow lanes of the park—a measure to keep reckless and impatient drivers from speeding through the confined spaces—and the familiar sight of their trailer came into view.

Her childhood home; a sunbaked and graying double-wide tucked into the rows of mobile homes. It actually looked less dirty and decrepit than she recalled. There were no gaps in the paneled skirting around their trailer right now, and the ugly hedge hadn't grown in yet either. The tree she'd remembered seeing last, back when she moved out in her late twenties, was still a scrawny little thing, not much more than a thin sapling. Uncle Danny's car wasn't there either—in her past life, it had been a permanent fixture of their yard for most of her time there, up on cinder blocks and wrapped in a faded brown tarp. *Wonder when he'll be dropping THAT little beauty off, so that he can go be in prison for the rest of his life.*

"*Are you okay?*" her father asked once again as the truck finally rumbled to a stop in front of their trailer. He gave her another look, and she guiltily stopped peering around at everything as though seeing it for the first time.

"I—" She froze when she met his eyes. *—Never appreciated how* *much I actually missed you. I don't want to lie to you, Daddy, and I don't think I can pretend to be a child. Wouldn't even know where to start.* "I'm fine."

"Uh-huh," he murmured doubtfully, reaching over to tousle her hair. He hadn't done that in—well, it certainly *felt* like forty years. Tabitha fought to keep her eyes from watering again.

————

Her homecoming was appalling, as she'd expected. Her mother, Mrs. Shannon Moore, was still fat in a fresh, plump way, only just beginning to bulge at the seams. Nothing like the bloated and gigantic obese mass she would become in a few years. Tabitha pondered what the most tactful way to ask if she'd been diagnosed with diabetes yet was. Still, her mother's knee problems didn't appear to have surfaced yet, and she was getting around under her own power right now, at least. Even if she didn't get out of her seat to welcome her daughter home from the hospital.

The trailer's interior was cut off from outside sunlight by both curtains and blankets over the windows, dimly lit instead by the yellow light of incandescent bulbs. It was cluttered with mismatched, tacky, and worn-out furniture, and it smelled. Body odor and greasy cooking. The carpet hadn't met a vacuum cleaner in well over a year, black mold was accumulating in the corners of the ceiling, and dirty dishes were everywhere.

Tabitha begged off dinner on the fabricated excuse of a nausea that was becoming very real, but rigid family tradition dictated she sit with them at the table while they ate all the same. Baked beans and toasted bread—*why toasted bread?*—was the fine meal that she passed up.

Nothing about the intermittent silence and small talk seemed *real* to her. Her stomach turned itself into knots as she warily eyed her surroundings in the trailer, because everything was half-familiar and half-horrifying. She could never determine which was specifically which either.

"Hope you've learned yer lesson 'bout those trampoline jumpers." Mrs. Moore finally shook her head. "Yer lucky you didn't break yer neck."

"Yes, Mother." Tabitha nodded politely.

"Yes, *Mother?*" the woman asked incredulously. She glared daggers at Tabitha, as if warning her daughter not to sass her.

"Yes," Tabitha repeated dispassionately. *What, did I normally say... 'Yes, Momma?' I may have never amounted to much, but I WAS an English major. I'm not going to be able to keep up some ignorant kid charade anyways. I have too many other things to deal with right now.*

"I've learned my lesson. I wasn't being sufficiently responsible at that time, and the consequences of my actions were unexpectedly severe. In the future, I will mindfully endeavor toward more appropriate courses of action."

"No need for attitude, Tabitha Ann Moore," Mrs. Moore warned with a laugh, forking more baked beans into her mouth.

Tabitha found that her mother *smelled.* Mrs. Moore was gross, disgustingly fat, and petty, and Tabitha was beginning to hate her all over again. *Mom, when you died, I came to terms with everything I could, and buried the rest. So that I could just focus on the GOOD memories, and leave it at that. Why am I being made to go through this again?*

"Kids're getting smarter every day," Mr. Moore joked, not looking up from his own plate. "Sweetie's so smart, she broke their brain-scannin' machine. Guess she was clean off the charts." No one had actually suspected anything of that sort. From what Tabitha had overheard, everyone was blaming the MRI's apparent failure on an electrical fault that came about from a surge during the power outage.

"Shame they never get any more respectful." Mrs. Moore frowned, pursing her lips.

With the wisdom and grace sixty years had given her, Tabitha kept silent, neither agreeing nor disagreeing. She stared instead at the yellowing floral wallpaper, and patiently endured the sounds of her parents eating.

Afterwards, she found her cramped bedroom was stuffy and strange-smelling, and she could only resign herself to accepting that some of the body odor this trailer was rank with belonged to her previous self. There was a brief but potent mixture of nostalgia at seeing all of her long-lost childhood toys, and repulsion, in really realizing her past living conditions. Taking a deep breath and steeling her nerves, she finally turned to face the mirror sitting atop her dresser.

She'd studiously avoided her reflection on the doors out of St. Juarez, and the windows and mirrors of her father's truck. She feared the impact this sight was going to have on her psyche, and most of all... she simply didn't want to believe. Because she already knew what she would find. She'd spent most of her life detesting and struggling with this.

A hefty thirteen-year-old girl scowled back at her in the mirror. Pudgy enough, at that age, to already have a protruding stomach paunch. Despite having just started puberty and growing taller, her breasts looked like *fat,* not like boob. They were the unappealing fleshy contours a fat man would have, *moobs,* not feminine assets she could push together to form cleavage. Her neck was fat, her chin—fat, fat cheeks, her entire face was wreathed in it, swaddled in layers of fat. She clutched the edges of the counter and dry-heaved. She pressed her eyes shut and took a deep breath.

Okay. Okay. It's not that bad. I knew I had a complex about my weight and my appearance, I just... well, nothing was ever going to make me ready for this all over again. Never thought I'd miss the OLD LADY physique.

It wasn't until her late fifties that she would drop all of the weight, mostly because of stomach ulcers that turned into a cancer scare. Not being able to eat certain foods without a trip to the hospital had finally transformed her into a rather normal-looking, even scrawny, gray-haired old woman. Her diet drastically changed, and on the orders of the nutritionist on her insurance, she enrolled in the local Taekwondo program for basic daily exercise. *And that was when I became a martial arts grandmaster...*

...Hah, yeah right, as if. Another prime example of her mediocrity. As the only elderly woman in that Taekwondo school, she'd been exempted from actual sparring, and never laid a finger on anyone. More often than not, she spent the classes corralling the younger ones, or resigning herself to practicing warm-ups, stretches, stances, and exercises with some of the girls who hated fighting. In the end, Tabitha felt about as qualified in Taekwondo as an amateur yoga instructor.

Although, I wonder if... Out of a nascent whispering of curiosity, Tabitha carefully—carefully set her feet into a forward stance. Then, she shifted into a back stance. Dropping into a horse-riding stance, rising up into a tiger stance. Crossing her legs in a forward cross stance. Twisting into a backward cross stance. *So, I CAN use future knowledge in my past body. At least that means those forty-seven years weren't some... absurd hallucination. Actually, these moves seem kind of... easy?*

She let herself fall forwards in the scant space of her room, keeping her back rigid and catching herself with only her palms. It was a loud crash and an ugly struggle, but she just barely kept her nose from violently meeting the floor—and even managed to do a single proper pushup, before her protesting arms seemed turned to jelly and gave out on her.

Okay... doing that was dumb. But also completely impossible, back when I was sixty. Guess it can be nice to be young. I could... actually get in shape. Not in my room, maybe. I could practice katas out in the yard?

I don't... HAVE to be fat, this time. I'm already disgusted at the thought of eating fattening garbage like my parents always did, here. I... know how to cook now. I can actually JOG now that I'm young again, basically whenever I want to! High school starts in, what, August?

September? I can be in AMAZING shape by then! Everything can be different! All at once, the idea of *changing* her life began to brighten her perspective, illuminating all of the opportunities she'd been too distraught to see earlier. Her skillsets from the future may have seemed unimpressive then, but couldn't she still apply them to the problems from her past? She'd had a lifetime to regret and dwell on all of them already, after all.

I can write my story all over again. GOBLINA, and GOBLIN PRINCESS. But with all the feedback and techniques I've learned since about the story structure and pacing. AND, I can get it out there and published before the market's oversaturated this time. Tabitha thought, her mind racing. *Julie... I can save Julie. I can fix things for her. Make everything right so that she never even THINKS about taking her own life. I can save Mom and Dad from themselves, somehow! I can... I can do ANYTHING.*

As night descended on the aging and worn mobile home lots of the Lower Park, the bright, beautiful laughter of a young girl resounded from one of the compact little rooms within.

"I'm never going to be trailer trash again."

2

CLEANING UP AND
CLEARING OUT

Tabitha woke up early and full of energy, despite having skipped eating dinner last night. Her father was gone already, having left for work at five thirty, and her mother was unlikely to rouse for at least another hour, giving Tabitha free range to re-explore the place.

Last night, she'd slept in her underwear, having tossed yesterday's clothes in the bathroom's communal laundry hamper. She began her day by opening her dresser drawers and sorting everything she found into neat stacks. Several dozen articles of clothing were immediately discarded into a trash pile: socks with holes, shirts too discolored to wear, pants that were ripped along the inseam—*who had bothered to wash and fold those?*—trashy T-shirts that had their sleeves haphazardly removed, and similar pajama pants that had been cut into shorts.

Diligently trying on all of her remaining clothes, Tabitha was dismayed to find that less than a third of them fit—she didn't even have a full week's worth of clothing to wear. Luckily, her bras and underwear were the newest of the lot, and all correctly-sized, likely purchased to keep up with puberty. She dressed herself in a pair of sweatpants and an oversized shirt, then carefully folded and returned the clothing she would keep into their drawers.

The Moore family weren't *packrats* like some of their neighbors, but they did seem to hoard things like bags. After a quick trip to the kitchen pantry, frowning at nearly everything she saw, she returned with two grocery bags to pack the clothes too small for her into.

They'll tell me to hang on to them JUST IN CASE, because of all the little cousins who could grow into them, Tabitha grumbled to herself. *As if any of them ever needed any more hand-me-downs. Need to convince them to take me to a thrift store so I can fix my wardrobe. Yesterday's pair of jeans, several pairs of sweatpants, and what appears to be a single value pack of cotton shorts is NOT enough attire for a teenage girl. Now I remember why I used to wear the same clothes so many days in a row.*

In the meantime, the scrunched-up wads of grocery bags were already spilling out the pantry door, so she collected them and made her way around the trailer, emptying out three small waste-cans into the grocery bags and then fitting one inside each as a liner. *Why were we collecting these bags at all, if we weren't going to use them...?*

She managed to fill another entire bag with garbage she found simply strewn about the trailer, before it dawned on Tabitha that she was cleaning house. She paused, grimacing. Keeping a living area free of trash and clutter was second-nature, something she now did without thinking. *Because it needs to be done. And, being surrounded with filth stresses me out. Might be a bit out of character to attempt doing ALL of the long-neglected household chores at once...*

But what else can I do? She scowled, collecting dirty dishes and piling them in the sink. *I can't live like this.*

Even after making a few trips to the bathroom hamper for the errant bits of clothing she found strewn in the corners of the living room, the place still looked... well, *dirty.* She pulled down all the blankets covering the windows, releasing clouds of dust to hang in the air just as dawn light was beginning to stream through the windows. All of those blankets smelled and they needed washing, so she folded them and arranged them in a giant pile next to the hamper.

Okay. Carpet. Now that the room was properly lit up, it looked terrible, and after a cursory search, she discovered why the floor hadn't been cleaned in ages. Their vacuum cleaner was outside, in the shed, caked in moldy dust and cobwebs—and it was *old*. A rather bulky independent canister-style motor and collecting bag, connected to the upright cleaner by an umbilical of electrical cord and ridged flexible hose.

Making three trips to carry the contraption and its attachments in and onto the kitchen tile, she then grabbed a bucket of water and one of the ripped socks she'd just thrown out and sat down to wipe the cleaner clean. The amount of time and effort she had to put into simple tasks like tidying up a room was beginning to seem absurd to her, but Tabitha gritted her teeth and fantasized about soon having a carpet clean enough to sprawl out upon.

The entire vacuum cleaner was a filthy mess, and the bag had never been changed whenever the thing was stored, so the contents inside had begun to rot. After a thorough scrubbing that turned the water in her bucket an unsettling shade of brown, she reassembled the thing and was ready to begin cleaning. Unfortunately, it was as loud as a leaf-blower, and Tabitha had only pushed and pulled the thing over three square feet of carpet when her mother stormed out of their bedroom, furious.

———

"Don't know what you thought y'were tryin' to butter us up for, doin' all of this, but whatever it is—you ain't gettin' it." Mrs. Shannon Moore frowned, blinking at the dishes all over the countertop. The drying rack had long since been filled, and the rest were being set to dry on a towel Tabitha had spread out. "How am I s'posed to eat breakfast?"

"With clean dishes," Tabitha answered with a deadpan expression, and she drained the sink water. She'd been doing dishes for forty-five minutes. As absurd a concept as it was, *all* of the dishes had been dirty. It was apparently custom for dishes to only be cleaned directly before use, oftentimes only rinsed, and then set down wherever afterwards, dirty and forgotten until they were needed again.

There wasn't even a place for the bowls, plates, and cups in the kitchen cabinet, a fact that managed to stun Tabitha. The cabinets were jam-packed with everything else under the sun, it seemed—flashlights without batteries, forgotten tools, empty tins, metal brackets, cheap Christmas decorations, and a dozen old plastic margarine containers, each filled with a mysterious assortment of rusting nails and screws.

"I'm going for a walk." Tabitha sighed, wiping her hands dry on her shirt. Last night's charged enthusiasm for tackling all of her problems in this new life head-on... was rapidly draining away as she realized that she'd be forced to fight for every inch to complete even what should have been basic tasks.

"A walk?" Her mother inspected one of the bowls. "Outside? And where do you think you're going?"

"I'm just going in circles," Tabitha said, wishing there was a way to explain the truth of her circumstances. "...Around the neighborhood. I just need to walk for a while, get some fresh air. After what happened yesterday, I really can't handle being cooped up right now."

She failed to put emotion into her voice like she'd intended, but her excuse seemed to hold up, and she was given permission to go outside. Which honestly surprised Tabitha, because it was still technically a school day—her mother would have had a fair argument to keep her from wandering about. *If she even knows what day it is.*

But, regardless, my plan's holding out so far, Tabitha thought as she put on her worn little sneakers and stepped out into the neighborhood. *If I seem unusual, it's because I was traumatized by what happened at the hospital. I have to keep all the windows uncovered all the time too, because I'm selectively claustrophobic now. I need sunlight, fresh air, and clean, open environments that don't have clutter. Or I'll flip out.*

Exhaling slowly, Tabitha started walking along the rows of trailers at a brisk pace. She couldn't wait until her body was ready for running.

———

She returned from the hour-long jaunt outdoors equally exhilarated and disappointed with her young body. The extra weight sitting on her was something she hadn't become accustomed to yet, a constant and obnoxious reminder of her unappealing image. On the other hand, joint pain didn't seem to exist at all for her at thirteen, and though individual muscles began to ache, she didn't actually feel *tired.* Youthful energy coursed and thrummed through her, ready for everything coming her way. Which was, of course, a miserable onslaught of problems throughout the trailer that required her immediate attention.

Their refrigerator, one of the few constants in Tabitha's life, was still the exact same one she would own for years in the future, all the way until she'd moved into her second apartment. When she saw her parents had crammed the freezer tight, she even felt indignant at what they were doing to *her* appliance. The fan circulating air throughout the compartment was completely blocked, so TV dinner boxes were frozen to the back of the freezer, while some of the bagged veggies in the front were practically thawed out. They'd turned the freezer knob to ten for some reason as well, so after adjusting the contents properly within, she set it back to where it should be, at seven.

Nothing within the fridge seemed remotely appetizing. An artery-clogging array of leftovers from various meals filled unlabeled Tupperware, one of the shelves seemed dedicated exclusively to various styrofoam take-out boxes, and the rest of the interior was a smorgasbord of mystery jars, condiment bottles, and cans of beer.

Going to need to beg, lie, and cheat my way into convincing them to get us to a farmer's market for some actual decent produce, some fresh fruits and vegetables, Tabitha made a face. *Haven't had a meal since 2045, and I'm famished.* Withdrawing a half-empty carton of eggs dangerously nearing their expiration, she put a pot of water on the stove so that she could hard-boil all of them. These would need to be set aside and rationed out over her first week, for whenever she couldn't stave off her hunger anymore and absolutely needed to eat something.

Need to dig out the hamper and see if I have any more useable clothes in there. Maybe sneak away a cup of detergent, and wash my clothes in the tub. There were just too many things to do at once, and Tabitha was feeling overwhelmed. Out of habit, her hand kept creeping back to her left wrist where she'd worn her bracelet-PC for years—she would kill for web access. It was dismaying to realize she was trapped all the way back in the dial-up era of internet. Sighing, she pulled her legs up in stretches while waiting for her water to boil.

I'll need a word processor over the summer if I want to get a head start on my novels. The library's over a half-hour walk from here, from what I remember. Decent for some extra exercise. I'll need a library card, and a... what, a flash drive, to keep the work on? Did they have flash drives back in '98? A CD? Maybe a floppy diskette?

She'd leafed through some of the miscellaneous worksheets and papers scattered around her room, and didn't think she'd have a problem breezing through middle-school finals without seriously reviewing them. High school calculus or physics would have been a different story, but she was eminently confident in passing coursework intended for children. *Also need to keep using 'big words' around my parents, even when diminutive ones would suffice. ESPE-CIALLY when diminutive ones would suffice. That way, they'll imagine my new vocabulary is some emerging teenage phase... and hopefully never stop to question how or why I know certain words that I likely shouldn't.*

"*What the—*" Her mother did a double-take as she stepped away from the living room TV for a moment to refill her sweet tea —a murky concoction Tabitha had long since concluded was more sugar than tea and water. "What, you're *cooking* now? Tabby, you've never cooked a day in your life. You're liable to burn down the whole trailer park."

Tabitha simply crossed her arms, looking unamused, and Mrs. Moore's expression faltered.

———

Having just arrived home from work, Mr. Alan Moore was first stepping inside the door when he was immediately waylaid by his wife.

"What in the—"

"*Honey,*" Mrs. Moore said in a furtive whisper. "Somethin's *wrong* with Tabitha. She went on this—this *rampage* today, and she's speaking all strange. She's not actin' her normal self at all."

"Rampage, what... ?" He stepped past her into the trailer, marveling in disbelief at the incredible transformation their home had gone through. "*Ho*—ly hells. I come home to the right house? Tabby did all *this*?"

"She's gone *weird*, weird in the head, honey," Mrs. Moore insisted, gesturing toward the kitchen. "She went and pulled out everything in all the cabinets, and moved everything around. *Everything.* When I told her she wasn't allowed to throw out any of those newspapers, she sat down with them and was... shuffling them around, looking all serious. I ask her *what on God's green earth she thinks she's doing,* and she says she's *organizing them by date.*

"She's not acting right, Alan. She's telling me she's *claustrophobic* now, that we have to keep all the curtains open. So that we're living in a goddamn fishbowl, and all the neighbors can gawk in and see whatever they please? I don't think so! She went out and about for hours, and wouldn't tell me where she went, says she was *going in circles.* She even tried to take half of all our canned goods outside, said *they were expired.* I tell her canned goods keep well on for years and years after their date, and she looks at me like I'm speaking Swahili! It's *canned food,* for cryin' out loud! She's always been such a *good* girl, I don't know what's gotten into her!"

Mr. Moore frowned. If a cleaning spree hadn't been strange enough, the thought of Tabitha opposing her mother was downright abnormal. His wife wasn't one to be crossed, and yet, right now, she seemed... downright spooked.

"I'll... talk to her," he assured her, still looking around the pristine trailer in dazed astonishment. It was his home, and yet he was wondering where it was okay to put his shoes now. The well-trodden gray of the living room carpet was now a light blue that seemed positively vibrant by comparison, and with all of the windows open and the curtains tied back, this cozy space he thought he was familiar with seemed to have opened up into something else entirely.

"Sweetie?" He paused, rapping his knuckle on Tabitha's door. Yet another strange thing—Tabby had never been in the habit of closing her door. *Hell, yesterday she'd of had to shove aside a big ol' pile of stuff to even close the dang thing in the first place.* "Can I come in?"

"Please do," her voice called out.

"Uh... yeah," he said uneasily, opening the door. Her room was even more changed than the rest of the trailer—it was as if she'd just moved in. Her panelboard walls, which had been littered with taped drawings and posters, were bare. The dresser was clear of everything, and she'd even cleaned the mirror, removing all of those Sunday School stickers she'd decorated the edges with. *Her bed was made,* sheets pulled taut with military precision.

"I'd like to have a discussion with you about our living arrangements," Tabitha said, coolly appraising him. "But, it doesn't have to be right now. You've just gotten off work, so you can relax and have dinner first. After that, we can speak at your convenience."

"That's very... considerate of you, honey," he managed. There was a strange *stillness* to her mannerisms that he couldn't quite put his finger on. She wasn't fidgeting, or slumping, or even breaking eye-contact with him.

"You cleaned the whole house," he grunted.

"Yes, thank you for noticing."

"Any reason in particular... why? There something you want?"

"A clean home," Tabitha answered curtly. It didn't look like she had anything else to say.

"Okay, then." Mr. Moore sighed. "Were you being smart with your mother?"

"We had a rather... animated discussion, on the semantic difference between a *best by date* and *an expiry date,*" Tabitha explained, choosing her words carefully. "Though I'm unable to concede my... apparently unique and challenging views on that matter, I've already taken the liberty to apologize to her for any offense I may have inadvertently caused."

"Sweetie—why are you talking like that?"

She paused, seeming to ponder for a moment, before answering, "Because I've had the time today to consider the things I want to express. Thank you for allowing me to stay home from school today. It's been very useful."

"Okay." He shook his head helplessly. "Fine. Get ready for dinner, then, I guess."

Plodding back out to the living room and removing his wallet and keys, he noticed that on the once-cluttered ledge where he normally left them—now cleared, a small tray had been placed for them.

"Well, what did she say?" Mrs. Moore asked impatiently. "What does she want?"

"I don't know," Mr. Moore replied, thoughtfully picking up the tray, a decorative metal stamped with the engraving of an Amish carriage pulling toward a covered bridge. *She really DID go through all the cabinets.* "Hell, she explained, and I still don't know what she said."

He placed his wallet and keys in the tray and carefully placed it back on the ledge.

"*That's* what I've been talking about!" Mrs. Moore exclaimed, looking uncomfortable. "You can't understand a word comin' out of her mouth anymore! What did they say at the hospital? Did getting knocked upside her head make her—I don't know, *autistic,* or something?"

"I dunno," he said, frowning. They'd given him a packet of papers to take home with them, and he'd set them down on the armrest of his chair yesterday. He didn't know where on Earth they were now. "But she *did* clean."

His wife shot him a dirty look, glancing around her as though she only found it unsettling and unnatural.

"What?" Mr. Moore shrugged. "You were the one home with her all day. She said she wanted to talk to me about something after dinner."

———

"Thought you hated green beans," her father grunted, forks clinking against plates as they all ate together.

"I do," Tabitha lied, looking down at her plate. They actually weren't bad, for frozen food. She'd drained, rinsed, and then steamed them just like she had when she was back in college. The flavor was weak, but they were the healthiest option she had to work with at the moment.

Her parents were eating yesterday's baked beans with today's jumbo hot dogs, the kind that ran eighty-nine cents for a large pack. The mere memory of that meat—bland, tasting like bologna, processed to the point of having no texture, and swollen with preservatives, was enough to make her stomach turn. No one had commented yet on why the parents and daughter were eating separate meals, so hopefully, they were already prepared to let some of her new eccentricities slide.

"And you're eating them because...?" Mrs. Moore asked, already sounding annoyed.

"I want to be healthy."

"You're plenty healthy, honey," Mr. Moore said, wiping his mouth with a napkin. "You're fine just the way you are. Did one of those Taylor girls say something to you?"

"Oh?" Tabitha looked up at him in surprise. "You didn't know? Everyone calls me *tubby Tabby*. They always have. I've been made fun of for being fat and smelling bad my whole life."

"*What?!*" Her mother threw her fork down into her plate with a loud clink. "*Who* said that?"

"It doesn't matter," Tabitha said, taking another bite of her green beans. "It's common knowledge, and they're right anyways. No one's quite as honest and cruel as other children."

"You're not fat," her father insisted.

"*Who* called you fat?" Mrs. Moore demanded. "I want their names, right now."

"I *am* fat," Tabitha said, an edge appearing in her voice. "And that's not something that scolding children or forcing apologies is going to change."

"You're not fat, Tabitha. Don't you dare call yourself that," Mrs. Moore insisted, sending a pointed look toward her husband. "*Well?* Tell her, Alan."

"How much more weight would you have let me put on?"

Tabitha interrupted with a glare she turned toward each of them in turn. Something dark was growing in her eyes, and Mr. Moore found his response was caught in his throat. "How far would I have gone before you addressed the issue? Are you fine with me being unhealthy? Are you fine with *tubby Tabby?*"

"*Tabitha Anne Moore.* Who taught you to talk like that?!" The table was gripped with a long, tense silence.

"...I'm sorry," Tabitha finally said, pushing aside her unfinished plate and leaving the dinner table. "I've lost my composure— please, excuse me."

"*Alan,*" Mrs. Moore hissed in a low voice as Tabitha retreated to her room. "Did you know about any of this?!"

———

"Tabitha?" Mr. Moore knocked on the door again. "You okay in there? You didn't finish your greens... and your mother said you didn't have anything else to eat today."

"Hunger is just the sensation of my fat reserves beginning to deplete," her strange words called out through the door. "I have sufficient energy to finish my exercises tonight."

"Sweetie..." He shook his head in exasperation. *Exercises now too? Looks like she's finally getting into that difficult teenager age.* "Can I come in?"

"Please do."

Please do? What happened to 'yeah,' or 'okay?' He slowly opened the door, to discover she was in the midst of stretches, legs spread out in a V on the floor and attempting to reach as far forward toward them with her hands held flat.

"Honey, we don't think you're fat," he said.

"Do you know exactly how much I weigh, or how tall I am?" she retorted. "Because the BMI *I* calculated indicates that I'm very overweight, well on my way toward obese, by *medical standards.*"

"That's not—"

"I know you're trying to comfort me, and I appreciate that," she cut him off, "but what I need now is *encouragement,* not comfort. I'm sorry for my outburst earlier at dinner. I understand that all of this must seem very... emotional, and perhaps overly theatric to you, but I assure you, I am very, very serious about this."

"Okay, okay." He held up his hands. "Just... well, you know how it seems." *Wait, does she? She actually does seem very... aware. Not to say she was stupid before, or anything, but this...*

"I'm thirteen years old, so I can't be considered a child anymore." Tabitha shrugged. "I'm a young woman now. That's what I wanted to discuss with you."

"Well, go on."

"I want you to teach me how to balance a budget," she began, sitting up and relaxing her legs. "How to plan and prepare meals, and how to manage my time and money."

"Uhh, well—that's..."

"I recognize that we don't have much financial leeway, but I'd like for all of us to agree on a fair monthly allowance for me. In exchange, I'll pull my weight by cooking for us every night, and regularly keeping the house clean.

"As you're both parent and provider, if you don't feel that is acceptable, I'm prepared to negotiate on your terms. I think that learning responsibility is an important aspect of my personal development, and that hard work should be rewarded with equal compensation. Do you agree?"

"Well, I... you want allowance money, huh?"

"Yes."

"Money's tight, sweetie."

"I understand that."

"I'll talk about it with your mother."

"Thank you. When do you think I can expect your decision?"

"We'll see, sweetie." He shrugged, raising his hands. "You've been acting... different, and your mother's in a mood."

"...I understand. Thank you again. I'm going to finish up, now, and then get some rest. Goodnight, Daddy."

"Sweetie?" He paused for a moment as he turned to leave, slowly reevaluating his daughter. "Don't you try and grow up too fast now, alright?" He didn't know what else to say to her.

"...Of course, Daddy," Tabitha promised, but she was wearing a bitter smile that had no place on his thirteen-year old girl. "I won't."

3
TESTS OF HER ENDURANCE

Soaked with sweat and panting from exertion, Tabitha stepped forward in the patchy plot of grass between trailers and punched out as hard as she could. Parts of her jiggled in a fleshy, unflattering way, but she could only grit her teeth and bear with that. For now. Planting her left foot heavily amid the weeds, she adjusted her stance and lifted her right knee up in the air. She pivoted her leg and round-kicked—clumsily, before dropping down, shifting her weight into another careful stance and raising her arms up into a crisp block.

It was hot out today. The sun overhead was relentlessly beat down across the tiny yard beside her mobile home where the young girl was toiling away through a series of memorized movements and positions. To her dismay, Tabitha had been forced to recover several of those redneck-style sleeveless tops from the trash simply to have workout clothes to wear.

Working through the familiar Taekwondo forms and katas... was hell. Normally, each series of stances and movements flowed with natural momentum from one into the next with grace and ease... but her thirteen-year-old body was *useless*. She felt awkward and rotund, all of the extra weight she was carrying constantly throwing her off balance and forcing her to consciously compensate for it, all the time. It was like trying to type a document while wearing heavy winter gloves, only that aggravation was joined with an ever-present aching burn throughout all of her muscle groups as they shrieked at her in protest.

Well, if nothing else, at least I know how to do proper stretches, Tabitha thought to herself bitterly, throwing a knife-hand strike and then lunging into a forward stance to awkwardly jab an elbow out into the air. Despite several years of regular Taekwondo, she'd only advanced as far as a yellow-belt. Stretches, warm-ups, a few drill forms, and the first thirteen katas made up the entirety of her knowledge. Most of the practical application, like sparring and actual martial arts, would have come later, after a certain foundation of basics had been built up.

But it's not as if I have to fend anyone off. If a burglar breaks into the trailer looking for money and valuables, I'll help them look. Hopefully, we'll turn up something. Tabitha snorted. *If someone tries to abduct me, I'll sigh with relief.* She snapped out a side-kick, and then held her extended leg in the air until it began to tremble.

My grasp of the fundamentals could be considered excellent... but basics will only get me so far. The Taekwondo school she'd attended in the future existed here in the past, as well—but enrolling wasn't cheap, no matter which time she was in. From what she recalled, in these years, the Taekwondo place in town was run by Mr. Lee Senior, while many years from now, he would pass it on to her instructor, Mr. Lee Junior. She did still intend to at least visit the place sometime in the next few years, if only to show off her mastery of the katas.

Gwwwwrrrwww.

Wincing at hearing her stomach growl, Tabitha lowered her arms and allowed her shoulders to slump down. She was *hungry*. It was Sunday, her third full day in the past, and all of the frozen vegetables were long gone. She'd had the last hard-boiled egg for breakfast, and although she was intent on starving her body of carbohydrates, options were running out fast. There was a single can of chopped spinach still, and then she might be able to cannibalize each of the frozen TV dinners for their small portions of assorted vegetables... but that was it. Her family didn't grocery shop until they were just about out of everything, and that was still days away, from the look of the fridge.

Tabitha frankly wasn't used to being without any form of agency. She had no money or resources of her own, little say in how her life was led, and required her parents' permission for virtually everything. Being a minor again was more stifling than she could have imagined.

Her parents had sat down with her yesterday to discuss the matter of arranging her an allowance... and rejected the idea outright. They simply didn't have the money to spare. She'd nodded, thanked them for the consideration, and retreated to her room without any further argument. There were plenty of areas where their spending could be reduced, but Tabitha was smart enough not to bring that up in this first confrontation.

Still, this lack of capital is going to grind all my other efforts to a halt, Tabitha exhaled slowly, readying herself into another combat stance again so that she could resume her practice. *A healthy diet may be fairly cheap, but it isn't free. I need clothes for school. A pack of floppy disks to store my work on, when I start heading to the library. Maybe laundry detergent too. The cheap stuff they use isn't great in the first place, and on top of that they're diluting it to make it last longer. I'm going to start high school, I need some basic things. Better deodorant. Conditioner. Foundation, and concealer.* The make-up kit she'd found in her room was intended for children: gaudy cheap eyeliner and several horrific shades of lipstick.

Unfortunately, she didn't own anything of value to sell for cash. Apart from her room's worn furniture, the only thing worth more than ten dollars was her dilapidated old stereo, and she doubted she'd be able to sell the thing. It wasn't like she could just find a job either.

She couldn't remember anyone who had kids she could babysit—looking after her cousins was a familial obligation and wouldn't be paid. She wasn't allowed to handle her father's small weed-eater to mow lawns for money. No one in this area seemed to maintain their landscaping, so prospects like watering plants or weeding for neighbors seemed... unlikely. Everyone seemed to have either tiny inside dogs they'd only let out into tiny fenced enclosures, or large, filthy dogs chained outside in the yards of their trailers, so even walking pets wasn't a viable option. *Everyone living here's as broke as we are anyways.*

What she *did* have was all the basic ingredients to bake cookies, which was... a start, she supposed. There were no chocolate chips or even raisins, but she estimated she could make several hundred plain sugar cookies with the materials on hand. If she could find a venue to run a bake sale.

I could beg for money along a busy street downtown, if only I wasn't fat, Tabitha rolled her eyes. *Nothing quite screams IMPOVERISHED CHILD like an obese kid, right?*

Front kick. Step forward and punch. Jump kick, barely getting off the ground and landing rather unsteadily. She kept bracing herself for sudden joint pain, but at thirteen, her body just didn't have any. Her overall stamina and recovery seemed to be several orders of magnitude greater now than they had been when she was sixty; the only limiting factor to her youthful energy seemed to be her skipping so many meals. In fact, Tabitha's body was struggling on pretty well, considering the thorough punishment she was putting it through.

I need a REAL plan, something more than just... scraping by slightly better than I did last time, Tabitha decided after long deliberation. Breathing heavily again, she pushed herself to thrust out her strikes faster, to snap her kicks up higher.

There's at least two years before Julia's even born. I definitely need to save her from everything that's about to happen to her. Maybe get custody of her, if I'm able. I'll turn twenty-one in... what, eight years? So she'll be six already by then. Clenching her teeth, Tabitha attempted the jump and twist of a butterfly kick, but achieved neither the height nor spin necessary to complete it yet. *Need to get* Goblina, *at least, on the market as quickly as possible,* she decided. *My writing may not have ever been much, and maybe Julie was my only real fan. But, if my story helped her through rough times like she said it did, it needs to be better than ever. It needs to be PERFECT for her.*

Then there's the shooting this October. Few other future events stood out to Tabitha. Later this year, a police officer would be fatally shot, down on the other end of the trailer park. That had been what really gave the Lower Park its horrible reputation, more than anything else. She'd always seen it in the way people in the area looked at her when they learned where she was from. The subtle, slightly different way they treated her, as if she was raised in a den of criminals. Ironically, the shooter wasn't even a resident —the officer had simply pulled that driver over to ticket them for something, and happened to do so from the road that went along-side that lower end of the park.

I know that he was shot, and that the officer bled out on the way to the hospital. She pressed her lips into a thin line. *But I don't remember his name, or the exact day, and I've no idea how I'd prevent it. Call 911 right beforehand? Shout out a warning just before it happens? That'd be tough to explain afterwards. 'Hey, be careful! That crack-head has a gun, and I don't want the office lady at the safety plant giving me constant dirty looks when I work there in the future!'*

Tabitha sighed. She really hoped circumstances would never force her back to work at the safety plant.

In the meantime, she needed to secure a source of food. Grandma Laurie—her grandmother on her father's side of the family, had an apartment across town. Perhaps she could be convinced to lend some aid; she should be only a half-hour's bike ride away. Unfortunately, they'd never had much of a close relationship, as her cousins—Uncle Danny's kids—seemed to have claimed that grandmotherly resource for their own exclusive use. They were even territorial about it, from what she remembered. *Little hellions. But, well... I am starving. Mike's around, and I can borrow his bike.*

"Hey, Mike!" she called down the street, finding a barefoot eleven-year old clutching a basketball and staring off into space.

"*What?*" he yelled back, indignant. Mike had always been a character, and she found herself wondering whatever happened to him in the future.

"I'll trade you all of my toys if you'll let me borrow your bike today." Aside from a few hand-picked sentimental keepsakes, she'd already collected all of the rest of her toys into a square plastic basket she'd found.

"Nah," he said after a moment's consideration. "I don't want stupid girl toys."

"I *mean it,* Mike," she pleaded, stepping closer and sending him a serious look. "Just this once. You can give them all to your sister."

"I hate my sister, and you smell. Why're you all sweaty?"

"Mike. Please."

"*Fine!*" he cried in mock exasperation, rolling his basketball with a crash into a pile of junk in front of his trailer. "But only my old bike."

————

"Grandma! Tabby's here! Tabby's here!"

"Tabby's here!"

As Tabitha feared, four of her cousins were running amok throughout her grandmother's apartment. She knew them to be Sam, Aiden, Nick, and Joshua, and remembered that they were all only a year apart. They sported identical buzz-cuts, and she had no idea who was who right now.

One of them was carrying a driveway marker, while the others each wielded sticks like a small mob. She hoped they were only hitting each other with them, and not chasing cats or looking for squirrels to hunt. Grandma Laurie was watching them from the chair on her porch, at least... so in theory, they were all behaving. She looked even more spritely than Tabitha remembered, probably only somewhere in her mid-fifties now. *Younger than me. What a trip.*

"Good afternoon, Tabitha," Grandma Laurie said, rising out of her seat. She had a very slight, almost frail stature, not unlike what Tabitha had in the future, with shortly cropped brown hair and crow's feet wrinkling the corners of her eyes. "This *is* a surprise. When did you learn to ride a bicycle?"

Oh. Whoops.

"You can't even ride a bicycle?" the youngest of her cousins asked, disdain in his voice.

"Uh, *duh,* she's riding one right now, retard," another cut in.

"Yeah, you're retarded," another agreed, swatting the youngest one with his stick. "*Duh.*"

"Ow! You can't hit me here. I'm out of bounds!"

"Hi, Grandma Laurie," Tabitha greeted, stepping off the borrowed bicycle. Realizing it didn't have a kick-stand at all, she gingerly laid it down beside the sidewalk and skirted around the stick-fight her cousins were suddenly engaging in. To her dismay, the young boys all too quickly lost interest and started following alongside her instead.

"Tabby *smells.*"

"Hey, I heard you hit your head so hard, you had to go to the *hospital,*" one of the cousins taunted. "Did you get *brain damage?*"

"Yeah, are you retarded now?" another asked.

"She was already retarded."

"But is she *brain damaged?*"

"She was already brain damaged. That's how you get retarded, duh."

"On the contrary," Tabitha replied with a serious face, sending the small group of boys into a rare silence, "acute trauma seems to have unlocked the higher portions of my brain, making me extremely intelligent."

"A cute drama?" One of the boys turned to look up at their grandmother. "What's a cute drama?"

"*You're* a cute drama, Aiden." Grandma Laurie stepped off the porch and bent down to pinch at his cheeks. "She means that she's real smart now, from hitting her head. Like a superhero."

"Oh yeah?" a cousin challenged, yanking at Tabitha's arm. "What's a thousand times a million, then?"

"One thousand multiplied by one million," she shrugged him off, "is exactly one billion."

"What's... uh, what's the capital of Albuquerque?"

"Albuquerque is a very large city in the state of New Mexico. *Santa Fe* is the capital city of New Mexico."

"Uhhh... how much does a T-rex weigh?"

"I would expect more than several tons, though the exact weight of any individual Tyrannosaurus Rex would vary greatly based on its age, size, and diet."

"Uhhhhh." The little boy stared up at canopy of branches spread out above the yard, tapping his lip as he struggled to stump her.

"You go on now and leave her be." Grandma Laurie shooed the brats away. "Well, Tabitha, what brings you here today? How's your head?"

"It's fine. Barely even notice it. I... came to ask for your help," Tabitha said, flashing her a guilty look. "I'll do anything I can for you in exchange."

"What do you need, honey?"

"I'm... fat," Tabitha said bluntly. "I want to change before I go to high school. I *need* to change, both my lifestyle and my eating habits. I need to eat healthy. I need to *be* healthy."

"Well, that's *good,* honey, good for you," Grandma Laurie praised, placing her hand on Tabitha's shoulders.

"*Pfft,* she said she's fat." One of her cousins erupted into laughter. "That's *priceless!*"

"Go on, get out of here." Grandma Laurie waved him off the porch. "Let us ladies talk."

"But..." Tabitha paused. "I've eaten all the vegetables and eggs at the house, all that's left is... food that's bad for you. They're not going to go shopping until all of that runs out."

"Ah," the older woman said, frowning. "Well, I'd love to help you, honey, but there's not much here, unless you eat cucumbers."

"I can eat cucumbers," Tabitha said, perking up. "I'm not picky at all, so long as it's healthy. *Please.*"

"Of course, let's see what we have!" Grandma Laurie said, leading her around the house toward the garden in the back. "I haven't checked on them in a few days, but I know there's a lot of cucumbers this year."

In no time at all, her wild cousins were tasked with enthusiastically pillaging all of the cucumbers and tomatoes in the kind old woman's normally *off-limits* garden. The tomatoes were still shades of yellow and orange, but Tabitha knew from experience that they'd continue to ripen if she kept them in a dry, somewhat enclosed space. She was also given a half-bag of lettuce from the fridge, and several cans of sweet peas her grandmother was more than happy to part with. *I should look into starting a garden at the trailer for next year.*

"Have you talked with your parents about being healthy?" Grandma Laurie asked, reinserting one of the driveway markers she'd sectioned off her garden with.

"...No, not really," Tabitha admitted. "Mom got angry when I called myself fat. Like, she doesn't want to accept... certain things. I don't think I can change their comfort food diet right away, but I am very, *very* desperate for change myself. I was the fat girl in middle school, Grandma. I don't think I can make it as the fat girl in high school."

Not again, at least. There's no way I could endure.

"I'll talk to your father the next time I see him. Let's get you a paper bag for all of these."

"Geez, no wonder she's so fat—she's takin' all our food!" a cousin remarked.

"Oh?" Grandma Laurie raised an eyebrow. "Are *you* going to eat cucumbers, then?"

"Ew, no way." The boy backed away, holding his hands up defensively. "I thought they were pickles."

"You thought those were *pickles?*" Another cousin guffawed at him. "They're two completely different plants, you retard."

"...Thank you so much, Grandma," Tabitha said, trying to keep her face from twitching. "It's been... it's been so hard. But I'm going to keep at it, and I'm not going to stop until I'm thin. I'm going to make you proud of me."

"Don't push yourself too hard, dear," she said, pulling Tabitha into a hug. "Stop by and visit whenever you can."

It was touching that Grandma Laurie loved her just fine the way she was... but also disconcerting when she realized how indulgent she was with Uncle Danny's kids, and how low her standard was for their quality of character. *Well... they ARE family...* Tabitha resolved to visit her every weekend over the summer anyway, because Grandma Laurie had always been good to her, and deserved the best company.

At Grandma Laurie's insistence, Tabitha was sent off with a startling amount of food to struggle home with, all heaped in a double-bagged paper grocery bag. She hadn't even remembered when shopping centers even still *used* paper bags, and found herself idly wondering when they'd gone obsolete. With a little bit of a struggle, she hugged the food against her body with one hand and pedaled home on sore legs.

After discreetly tucking her treasured vegetables in the fridge, hidden behind the take-out containers, Tabitha readied half a can of sweet peas for her dinner. She would still be hungry afterwards, sure, but she wouldn't *die*. True to the promise she'd made them, she set her parents places at the table and pulled out leftovers for them: ham loaf, baked beans, and scalloped potatoes. She wanted rid of the last of these leftovers, because she wasn't sure how much longer they would be edible. Also, she was actively working to empty the fridge in preparation for a new and healthy spread of groceries. She had just finished preparing for dinner and was tiptoeing to take a quick shower... when her mother rose from her position at the television and gave her a look.

"Let me guess. You're gonna take *another* shower? Tabitha Anne Moore, you *just* showered yesterday," Mrs. Moore griped. "I hope you don't think you're taking one every day after school. Do you have any idea what our water bill is?"

"A little over forty-seven dollars, not counting the sewage charges," Tabitha answered, keeping her composure as she continued down the trailer hallway and stepped into the small bathroom. "I organized all of our utilities. They're in the letter-holder, on the counter."

"Yeah, well, are *you* gonna pay that, Missy?"

"I would love to meaningfully contribute." Tabitha nodded, closing the bathroom door between them. "Please reconsider giving me that opportunity to do so."

"I've had it up to *here* with all of this attitude, young lady," her mother's voice barked. "I don't know what's gotten into you! *Alan,* did you hear the lip she just gave me?"

Releasing a deep breath, Tabitha turned away from the door and took a moment to regard herself in the dingy light of the bathroom mirror.

Yep. Still a fatty. She knew looking for any sign of weight loss after just these few days was unreasonable, but despite knowing that, her hazel eyes seemed to search all the same. *I just look... tired.*

Reddish-brown hair hung just past her shoulders, looking limp, stringy, frayed and without volume. She'd started carefully brushing her hair out the past several days, but damage from neglect had run its course, and she'd need to get her loose ends trimmed. Using shampoo that wasn't dollar-store brand and acquiring appropriate conditioner would probably be a great help as well.

Her forehead, nose and neck were beginning to turn red from spending each day out in the sun, despite the expired sunblock she'd applied. Otherwise, her face just looked so *fat,* her full, pudgy cheeks, deep frown and—

Tabitha purposefully turned away from the mirror to undress. Once she started criticizing her current appearance, there really was no end to it. Dwelling on the issue wasn't productive, and there were too many other things to do. From what she gleaned from one of the packets that had been strewn about in her room, her middle school finals were approaching in the coming school week. They consisted of a basic examination for the overall middle-school coursework for her various classes, as well as two high school placement tests, one for literature, and another for mathematics.

As a college graduate, Tabitha didn't imagine she'd fare poorly on any of them... but college *was* also a long, long time ago. She remembered the classes leading up to exams being non-stop review sessions to prepare them all, but it wouldn't hurt to read through all of the worksheets and papers in her room. The difference in score of even a few percent on her tests would affect whether she was placed in normal classes or honors classes in September. Her first time through, she hadn't been transferred to honors courses until after her sophomore year. From her recollection, she much preferred the more focused, quiet group of honors students as peers.

Still… school tomorrow. School, all over again, Tabitha shook her head as she started the water running. *What a joke. I'll do it again if I have to, if only for Julie. Even if it's just as bad as last time, because I'm still just trailer trash right now. But I can change—I'm GOING to change! I'm going to always get top marks, and I'm going to have both* Goblina *and* Goblin Princess *sent to a publisher before I'm out of high school, using a pen name if I have to. Somehow or other, I'm going to make all of this right, Julie…*

4

FINISHING MIDDLE SCHOOL

Laurel Middle School was a sprawling relic primarily made up of old-fashioned portables; small rooms hauled into place and assembled into *what should have been* temporary classrooms. All of the older, outdated structures, aside from the cafeteria, auditorium, and administrative buildings had been razed to make way for *new* middle school facilities, which were tied up in state funding and never seemed to appear.

All Tabitha had on hand for today's adventure, besides her backpack and some scavenged school supplies, was a handwritten note. She'd managed to prepare the names of her teachers and the class period for each, information gleaned from headings scribbled at the top of various old assignments she'd collected her room. Although the middle school *seemed* vaguely familiar, she only remembered the actual location of her last two classes with any certainty, so her first stop was the administrative office.

"Hello. My name's Tabitha Moore," she said, sliding her note forward across the counter there. "I suffered a severe head injury last Thursday. I was told to have someone write down the locations of each of my classes."

"You... don't remember where your classes are?" The administrative assistant behind the desk frowned, looking over the list with a doubtful expression. The lady was a spry woman in her mid-forties, quite a bit younger than Tabitha used to be, and Tabitha found herself wondering how similar working at a school was to working as a clerk in town hall. "Should you be here attending class at all then, if you hit your head *that* badly?"

"I don't know?" Tabitha shrugged, giving the woman a helpless expression. "Maybe not, but—my dad said, with it being this late in the school year, I might as well try to finish the year anyways?"

Just like that, her hastily-planned excuse was rewarded with a simple printed map that had her classes circled in highlighter, and she started her school day without a hiccup.

Okay. Here we go. Although Tabitha would be bullied severely later on in high school, here in eighth grade, she felt almost like a non-entity—she lacked any sort of presence at all. Not a single one of her fellow middle-schoolers tried to engage her in conversation on the way to her portable, even after waiting outside the boxy structure with several other classmates.

When their Language Arts teacher, Mrs. Hodge, arrived to unlock the door, Tabitha cautiously followed them all inside, pretending she didn't feel terribly out of place. She loitered awkwardly around the back of the room as the other students showed up and gravitated one by one toward their desks, eventually exposing a lone empty seat. Tabitha carefully sat down, trying not to seem as self-conscious as she felt. The bell rang, a series of tones over the loudspeakers, and class began.

That... worked?

"Tabitha—you missed a practice test on Friday." Mrs. Hodge smiled, and strode forward, wetting her fingertip with her tongue so she could separate the stack of papers she was preparing to pass out. "Here's the packet for this week. I understand you had to visit the hospital?"

You almost gave me a heart attack, Tabitha thought wryly, and she looked up from her own tightly clenched hands to take another look at the young woman who was her teacher—seemingly in her thirties, surely no older than thirty-five. *But I must seem like a child to her... I guess I'll see how far I can push the SLOW act.*

Tabitha had decided to keep answers to her teachers' questions short and perfunctory, so that she wouldn't give away that she was now a drastically different Tabitha. Since she wasn't sure she could portray a convincing *normal Tabitha,* she was going to be attending instead as *severe head injury Tabitha.* So she gave Mrs. Hodge a muddled look and forced herself to slowly count to three in her head before finally responding.

"...I hit my head," Tabitha answered after that long pause. "I hit my head really bad. Had to get an MRI."

"Er... are you okay?" Mrs. Hodge asked, appearing surprised.

"...I don't know," Tabitha said, looking back down at her desktop and then back up to Mrs. Hodge. "They said it wasn't good."

"Are you... feeling alright for class now?" Mrs. Hodge asked, her smile faltering. The young woman looked like she regretted bringing the topic up, and Tabitha felt a pang of guilt. "Do you think you're okay to work on review material, today?"

"...Yeah. Yeah." Tabitha nodded weakly, furrowing her brow. "I just feel kind of... dizzy... I guess?"

"Well." Mrs. Hodge stared, apparently hesitant to hand Tabitha one of the review packets. Finally, she let out a slight sigh and offered one. "If you have any trouble with the packet, then you can come see me, alright? This isn't due until the end of the week."

"...Okay." Tabitha tried to look confused as she accepted the small stack of stapled-together worksheets from her teacher. Mrs. Hodge lingered over her for a moment before moving on down the row to pass out the rest of the packets.

That was some of my best acting yet, Tabitha decided, slightly pleased with herself. *Didn't get nervous after all... except at the begin-*

ning. I think it helps really, realizing how young Mrs. Hodge seems to me now.

The *thoroughly concussed* charade would hopefully establish a believable change in her behavior, with any luck precluding unwelcome curiosity or questions from students. Tabitha really had no idea how she'd acted as a thirteen-year-old girl back then in middle school, and being among so many of her peers, someone would have been bound to notice discrepancies.

In some ways, it was convenient for Tabitha to not have any school friends—she wouldn't have known how to interact with them, how to maintain that appropriate thirteen-year-old facade. At the same time, however, it would have also been nice to be able to share a textbook with someone. All of her books were probably in her locker... which she didn't know the combination for. Or even where the blasted thing was located.

Turning her attention now to the first page of her work packet, she blinked in surprise at the coursework laid out before her.

8th Grade Language Arts Section 9, Vocabulary Terms

Match the following vocabulary words to their definitions:
1) Symbolism
2) Foreshadowing
3) Suspense
4) Theme
5) Setting

You can't be serious.

There were thirty vocab words, and definitions for each were printed out below, each with a blank space for filling in a word. Tabitha was forced to cover her mouth to stifle her laughter.

As an English Major, I could write a dissertation expounding and elaborating on any one of these terms. As a former aspiring author, I have personally worried each of those ideas down to the bone to comprehend every last nuance of profundity from the marrow therein! Look unto my knowledge and despair, Eighth Grade Language Arts Section 9 Vocabulary Terms, for you are not my equal!

Tabitha then hastily scrawled in all thirty correct answers—having read and solved all of the questions at a glance—and flipped to the next page. It wasn't an exaggeration to say that the work was far too easy to pose any sort of challenge to her, and she breezed on through the packet oblivious to the fact that someone was watching her.

———

"Oh my God—she's even more *stupider* than she was," Carrie whispered, letting out an amused giggle. "Elena, quick, look!"

"Who?" Elena asked, arching an eyebrow at her friend.

"Tubby Tabby," Carrie whispered, pointing out the chubby red-headed girl across the room with her pencil. "She was staring at the first page forever, *shaking* like she was about to cry, and then she just gave up and scribbled in whatever. Look, she's doing it again!"

"Wow. *Wooow.*" Elena laughed, watching as Tabitha moved down the next page, penciling in answers without more than a cursory look at the questions. "Least now we know *somebody's* not making it to 9th grade with us."

"Right?" Carrie snorted. "I heard she hit her head bad last week, and lost like, half the brain cells she had left. Like, look at her—can she even read anymore? I bet she's turned illiterate."

Many of the girls in their grade had long since decided that Tubby Tabby was, to anyone familiar with the cruelties of adolescence, an unfortunate existence. One that few would ever willingly associate with. She was fat, unattractive, looked like she rarely showered, wore gross clothes, and even often smelled distinctly *unwashed.* Now, apparently, the tubby girl was also mentally damaged in addition to all of that.

"Yeah, like you're any better." Elena rolled her eyes. "*I'm getting into AP English at Springton High.*"

"Fuck AP." Carrie rolled her eyes. "I'm not doing summer reading."

"See? *See?*" Elena goaded her friend, prodding her with the eraser-end of her pencil. "You can't read any better than Tubby Tabby."

"Uh, I can read; I'm just not ever gonna read books if I don't have to, thanks?" Carrie scoffed, turning to a guy several seats behind them. "Ethan. *Ethan!* Did you see what Tubby Tabby's doing?"

———

When Tabitha returned home from middle school, rather than relief, she felt strangely... *unsatisfied.* None of the middle school curriculum seemed specialized enough that she struggled with anything, and with sixty-years of knowledge somehow or other burned into her young brain, she'd been finishing everything well before anyone else in each of her classes. They were all simple review sessions leading into their finals, but everything seemed so terribly unorganized and inefficient.

With fifteen minutes between classes, and about that long again for each of the teachers to get any traction with what they were trying to teach, too much of middle school seemed like a blatant waste of time. Thankfully, each school day was short— actual class time in middle school only amounted to some five hours or so—time didn't seem to drag on and on endlessly like her work shifts at the safety plant had so many years ago.

Well, any more than that, and it'd interfere with my training schedule, Tabitha decided, hanging her backpack on the peg behind her door and pulling out the slightly musty clothes she was using for workouts.

"I don't want you doin' any of that runnin' around outside today 'til your homework's done," Mrs. Moore yelled. The large and fat woman had enthroned herself upon their battered and beaten sofa, and was nursing a pitcher of iced tea—idly drinking from it directly rather than pouring it into a glass—as commercials flickered by across their boxy old tube TV. "What homework have you got?"

"I was assigned a set of thirty algebra review questions, a worksheet in Social Studies, and I was given the final weekly study packet for Language Arts," Tabitha reported, already changing into one of those cut-off T-shirts so she could head out for her daily circuits around the trailer park.

"Did you hear *a word* I just said?" Mrs. Moore demanded in annoyance. "You sit your butt down at that table and get to work on all of that. You're not steppin' foot outside this house 'til then."

"My Language Arts class was on the way to the bus loop from my Social Studies class." Tabitha shrugged, pausing as she opened the front door. "All of my homework has been completed, Mother. I thought it expedient to turn in all of the outstanding assignments before boarding the bus and returning home. Now that I have your permission, I'm proceeding with my daily run."

"What a bunch of bologna!" Mrs. Moore scowled, twisting around to shoot a look after Tabitha. "Don't you think for one instant that I won't—Tabitha! *Tabitha!*"

Her daughter was already gone.

"*Un*believable!" Mrs. Moore swore, shaking her head in indignation. "That girl. I'm liable to call up her teachers right this instant. If she's so much as *a little* behind in her lessons, her sorry behind's getting tanned." But then, her sitcom came back on. The pale glow of the television illuminated her bloated and frowning face as one-liners were followed up one after another by the prerecorded laugh track, and her outrage and anger were gradually forgotten.

———

"Why're you always runnin' around, goin' nowhere?" Mike asked. The scrawny eleven-year-old boy was idly riding his bike alongside her as she jogged her familiar route around the circumference of the Lower Park.

"I'm... running away from something," she huffed between breaths. "Or... chasing something. I'm not sure yet."

"Weird," he said. "My Mom said you're tryin' to lose weight."

"That's another way... of putting it," Tabitha gasped. "Yeah."

"Oh. So, how much have you lost so far?"

"Not enough."

"Okay, what's your like—you know, your goal?"

"What... do you care?"

"I'm bored." Mike shrugged, lazily pedaling along with his bare feet. "You're at least, like, trying to do something. So, that's cool."

"My goal... is to lose fifty pounds. Before high school starts."

"*Jesus,* lady." Mike goggled at her. "Fifty pounds? That's impossible. That's like, almost as much as *I* weigh. I'm seventy-six pounds."

"It's *not* impossible," Tabitha struggled out, her breathing still ragged. "It's... the upper limit... of how much my body can endure. I was overweight... to begin with. Hundred and forty-eight pounds. I can safely lose... four pounds, every week. *I can do this.*"

"Yeah—if you don't die." Mike laughed. "That's not healthy. You're crazy."

"High school's... a cruel place, Mike," Tabitha panted, tilting her head as she ran to give him a look. "I think... I'd be crazy... *not...* to do this."

"Okay, okay. If you say so," Mike said, letting his bike coast to a stop in front of the turn-off for his trailer. He watched the chubby girl plod along ahead of him with no sign of slowing down or stopping.

"Well, good luck."

———

Her dreaded last week of middle school passed by without major incident. Tabitha immediately and impeccably dispatched any homework sent her way—her playing dumb act seemed sufficient for students to continue ignoring her. The most trouble her sudden academic ability aroused was Mrs. Hodge remarking on *how focused* she'd become. The exams for her classes ended up almost all being laughably easy multiple-choice sections, and she simply filled in all of the correct bubbles at alarming speed, racing through everything except for the essay on her Language Arts final. *That,* she worked and reworked until moments before time was called.

She's certainly going to be surprised when she tries to grade THAT one, Tabitha thought, smiling to herself with satisfaction. *I believe they'll all find my thoughts on how the growing advancement and availability of computer technology might affect the nature of all social interaction in the future... rather prophetic. They'll also realize that not setting a limit on essay length may be biting off more than they can chew.*

School was never my real opponent, though, now, was it? Grimacing, Tabitha, stretching from where she stood on top of the living room chair to reach the mildew on the ceiling with her wet rag.

"Are you even listening to me?" Mrs. Moore demanded, slapping the remote control onto the armrest of the sofa she occupied.

Tabitha paused for a moment, took a deep breath to calm herself, and resumed scrubbing away at the ceiling. Back when she was growing up, her mother possessed a commanding, authoritative presence. Mrs. Moore was one to be feared and respected—

and never disobeyed. Now, however, the woman seemed to irrationally be in direct opposition to every single task Tabitha set her mind on, without any logic or reason. *Was she always this way? Did I repress all of this?*

"I *said*, I really don't like all that karate you're trying to do," Mrs. Moore called over to her. "You're just askin' to hurt yourself, like you did on that trampoline jumper. And I don't want to ever see you trying to fight with people either!"

"It's not karate," Tabitha said, wringing brackish water out of the washcloth and into the waiting bucket perched on the window ledge.

"Karate, *kung-fu,* whatever it is you think you're doing." Her mother shook her head in apparent distaste. "It's disgraceful seeing you standing out there with your leg up in the air, where everyone can see you."

"I'm a practitioner of *Taekwondo,* a Korean martial art known for its emphasis on kicking techniques," Tabitha explained in a dull voice, wiping absentmindedly at the dirty water trying to trickle down her wrist before returning to scrub the paneling.

"*Martial arts, Korea,* listen to you. You're thirteen. You don't know a damn thing about *Korea.*"

"I may know more about Korea right now than anyone else alive," Tabitha muttered under her breath.

"Don't get smart with me," Mrs. Moore warned. "I mean it, I don't want you out there doing who knows what anymore. The neighbors are asking what on God's green earth you're up to, and I don't know what in the world I'm supposed to tell them anymore. So, no more. I don't want you leaving this house unless—"

"*Okay,*" Tabitha threw the filthy rag down into her bucket hard enough to splash water out across the clean living room. She stepped off of the chair and dropped heavily to the floor, turned, and finally glared at her mother.

"Fine. Okay. How do you plan on stopping me?"

"*Excuse me?*" Mrs. Moore heaved herself up from her indentation in the sofa.

"How do you plan on stopping me?" Tabitha repeated, her voice going cold as the last of her patience today ran out. "What consequences are in store for me should I refuse to obey? *What are you going to do?*"

"*Tabitha Anne Moore,* if you *ever* speak to me like that again, I'll tan your sorry—"

"Go ahead," Tabitha said, and the heavyset thirteen-year-old girl stepped forward. "*Try it.* Violence might just be the only leverage you have left. Let's just see if my will breaks before your hands do."

Stunned by her daughter's cold indifference, Mrs. Moore was flabbergasted, still deciding how to threaten Tabitha next when her daughter simply stormed out the front door of the trailer, leaving it hanging open behind her.

"*Tabitha!*" the fat woman exclaimed, stomping to stand in the doorway. "*Where do you think you're going?*"

"Grandma Laurie's. Again," Tabitha answered with a shout, not turning back. "Before either I do something stupid... or you do."

"You're thirteen years old; you're not walking the whole way 'cross town!" her mother bellowed. "Come back here, right this *instant!*" Your father's going to hear about this!"

———

Summer sun filtered through the trees overhead as Tabitha jogged along the city sidewalk toward Grandma Laurie's. Since receiving a talk from Grandma Laurie, Mr. Moore had provisionally agreed to allow Tabitha free rein in both planning their groceries and cooking meals for the family. As a result of that first batch of *real* food, Tabitha's energy levels had skyrocketed. Gone were the days of teetering on the brink of exhaustion from failing to scrounge up healthy food—now the fridge was fully stocked with a variety of produce.

All she'd had to do was keep the cost well under their normal budget, and promise they would get more meals out of the purchases, both of which were easy to achieve. The *quality* of some of the grocery store vegetables was debatable, but Tabitha planned to use even that as a point in favor of at least visiting one of the farmers' markets nearby.

The only problem was... once again, Tabitha's mother. The sudden and alarming change in their foodstuffs threw the woman into fits for more reasons than one, and she was perpetually on edge and irritable. As if being robbed of everything she enjoyed eating wasn't enough, the entire situation came about because Tabitha used Grandma Laurie to pressure Mr. Moore, which totally circumvented Mrs. Moore's household authority.

I never wanted to take sides in these stupid family squabbles, Tabitha fumed, gritting her teeth. *I just want to eat right. Is that so much to ask?!*

She knew that her impatience to reshape her life was at fault here, but as she rounded the corner into Grandma Laurie's familiar neighborhood, she just couldn't see any other feasible route to take. *I can't live that same life again. I CAN'T. Even if it earns me all of her ire, even if it turns Mom completely against me. I'm sorry, but that's how it is. Things were going to get bad between us once that blue album comes out anyways.*

Tabitha felt her shoulders start to reflexively hunch up at even the thought of that.

"I know I said I'd like to see you more often," Grandma Laurie called over. "But you've been coming by every other day now. Is everything all right?"

"No," Tabitha admitted honestly, trudging the last few steps of her journey across town and collapsing on her grandmother's porch step. "Had another argument with *that woman.*"

"...*Ah.*" Grandma Laurie sighed, easing out of her chair so that she could sit down on the steps next to Tabitha. "What was it this time?"

"It's always the same thing, I guess," Tabby said, staring across the yard. "I'm growing up, and growing up fast. I think I can manage to deal with all of the changes I'm going through. But I don't think that she can."

"It's hard watching your children grow up." Grandma Laurie nodded, stroking a hand through Tabitha's hair.

"Do you think I'll ever have kids?" Tabitha wondered out loud, leaning into her grandmother.

"Well, of course you will, sweetie." Grandma Laurie laughed, shaking her head as if it was a silly question.

...Huh? Tabitha blinked. *What? I know I'm still young now, but... did my relatives actually assume I'd ever find someone?* Tabitha had already long since stopped considering it as an option, years and years ago. *Well, it still isn't anything to think about now. Maybe if the right guy appears in my life this time. Then I'll think about it. After Julie's older.*

"I think I'm going to adopt," Tabitha said. "When the time's right. I want things to be perfect. I want to be able to give her *everything.*"

"Adoption?" It was Grandma Laurie's turn to be surprised. "That's always an option too, I suppose."

"Are the boys home?" Tabitha asked, standing up and brushing leaves off the seat of her sweatpants.

"I'm sure they're still playing their video games." Grandma Laurie smiled. "I was just about to take them to the playground so they could burn off all of that energy before I send 'em on back to their parents."

"Can I take them?"

"You want to take them to the playground?"

"School's out for summer really soon." Tabitha nodded. "I can look after them every other day, so that you can get some peace and quiet."

"Uh... that's very thoughtful of you, sweetie," Grandma Laurie said, surprised again. "But you don't have to do that. They can be a bit of a handful."

"You've helped me out a lot," Tabitha said, looking at her grandmother with a serious face. "I meant it when I said I'd find some way to return the favor. Can I do this for you?"

"If that's what you want." The older woman chuckled. "You can take them today. I'm not going to pass up a chance for some peace and quiet—why do you think I'm out here on this porch?"

"Thank you," Tabitha said, enveloping Grandma Laurie in a hug. "I'll have them back by dark."

"Oh, trust me—you're very welcome."

"Booooys!" Tabitha crossed over to the screen door and called inside, a grin spreading across her features. "Who wants to go play tag at the playground?"

————

"Huh," Tabitha's history teacher, Mr. Mann, grunted to himself as he graded the exams he'd given his classes. After going out of his way to make the thing obnoxiously difficult—and even throwing in several trick questions—someone had still managed to get a full score. He'd purposely made his test a nightmare to give those damned lazy eighth-graders of his a real kick in the pants.

"Well, s'only one out of all the classes anyhow. Let's see, who's our little prodigy... Tabitha Moore? Tabitha... Moore? Wait, isn't that... that chubby head injury girl from second period? SHE got full marks?

"That... can't be right...?" He flipped the paper back over with a frown, intent on double-checking all of her written answers again, more closely this time.

5
THE TRIALS OF SUMMER

As the pounds steadily disappeared, Tabitha found that *everything* was becoming easier. What began in her first days as a walk became a slow jog, and then a run. By now, her daily run was laced with sprints to get her heart rate up, and even that didn't feel like enough. Holes had worn into the crease of her sneakers where they bent with her step, and she had to superglue the soles several times as they were starting to peel off.

Over the course of her summer before high school, she spent a large fraction of time visiting Grandma Laurie, wishing only that she'd appreciated the woman more in her past lifetime. They had so much in common! Although she'd initially planned on making long treks to the city library to start writing her novels, *Goblina* and *Goblin Princess*, she found herself too distracted with stopping over every other day to chat, and then dutifully taking her four cousins to the playground.

There, they played the most ubiquitous game in existence across playgrounds everywhere: tag. Despite her initial overweight appearance, Tabitha had an uncanny ability to predict the timing of their lunges, and was able to outmaneuver her opponents into being cornered when she was 'it.' As time went on and her weight steadily fell, her increasing speed and stamina made her almost unbeatable. When they started playing team tag, she took only the youngest cousin, Joshua, onto her side to even the odds.

Eventually, the teams seemed set at all four boys against her; any one of the boys could tag her for a win, but then she had to tag out all four in succession. She never thought herself above playing with the children; the boys loved having someone to play with. Besides, scampering around in an energetic young body—one that became a little better-looking and more able with each passing day—was simply intoxicating.

What affected Tabitha's increasingly positive mentality the most, however, was seeing that new face in her mirror every day, trying out hesitant smiles. Over the weeks, as the fat began to recede from her face, a surprisingly lovely young woman was emerging somehow from within. A girl with features she could vainly admire for hours, if she didn't stop herself.

Whatever asinine genetic trait it was that had stored so much fat in her face had gradually been overcome by Tabitha's zealous weight-loss regimen. Her neck had gone from being a bulbous distraction to a slender thing, and her chin and the line of her jaw looked more defined and appealing to her every single day.

The incessant *burning* of every stored calorie her nonstop efforts could reach seemed to have a direct impact on every aspect of her body. Rather than her old toad-like blob of a nose, the center of her face was now adorned instead by a cute button nose. Her figure—not slim yet by any means, but definitely slimmer. Tabitha's eyes looked bright now, large and expressive now that her cheeks had slimmed down and the very proportions of her face were changed.

Unfortunately, Tabitha wasn't sure exactly what her current weight was at. Weighing herself twice a mere ten minutes apart had revealed a fourteen-pound difference! Which was, obviously, impossible.

To her dismay, she realized that accidentally shifting or nudging their beaten old bathroom scale at all would yield a drastically different result when next stood upon. None of the flooring in the trailer was level, the patchwork plywood and particleboard beneath their linoleum and carpets all uneven in different ways and angles. Which meant now she was no longer confident in what her *initial* weight had actually been, or how it would be best to calibrate the scale without something of exactly predetermined weight.

As much as the visual results of her tireless effort put a smile on her face, however, it wasn't *all* good news. She was constantly aching all over, and it was evident that the rapid weight loss was dangerous, because it was wreaking havoc on her young body. The first menstrual cycle of her new life had come and gone, and it was very irregular from what she'd ever remembered having.

Enough to send her into a mild panic. If she were to classify the periods throughout her past life, they would rank into simple *light*, or *heavy*. This one was a weird *thanks for trying,* or maybe a *reply hazy, try again later.*

Well, deal with it, body, Tabitha scoffed to herself. *I know what I'm doing isn't very healthy—but what about my mental health? I NEED to change. So what if it throws off my cycle? I don't have time for your bullshit anymore anyways, uterus. AT BEST, you were nothing but dead weight to me; an obnoxious monthly inconvenience that I lugged around for no reason for almost sixty years! Don't go thinking that I won't just go get those tubes tied this time through. I totally will. I'll do it, just try me!*

———

"Sweetie... I know you're going through a lot of changes right now," Mr. Moore began awkwardly, frowning. "But you don't have to try to do everything all at once, okay?"

"...Are you trying to discourage me from improving my life?"

Tabitha asked, pausing mid-pushup. She held herself there, waiting for his answer. An uncomfortable distance had formed between her and her parents. She didn't know how to act when she was around them, and in turn, they seemed to have no idea how to treat her. Mrs. Moore was caught up in following the explosive Monica Lewinsky/Clinton scandal that was dominating the news, and her father was... well, he was trying.

"Of course not, I—it's just—well." He sighed. "Can you sit up so we can talk properly?"

She completed her pushup, then rose to meet his eyes. She knew she was drastically thinner than he was used to seeing, as though she'd shrunken a size, all over, and it was obvious that it was worrying him.

"We... don't think it's healthy, you losing weight this fast," he said. "You've been at this for weeks now. You're working out, what, five? Six hours a day? You'll kill yourself, sweetie."

"Six hours a day," she admitted, sliding a notebook out from beneath her bed. "Which is another way of saying that I'm *also* resting the other eighteen hours every day. My exercises rotate through different muscle groups throughout the week to prevent excessive damage. I wrote myself up a schedule, if you'd like to take a look. It may ease your concerns." She passed the notebook up to him.

"I, uh... still don't think that—*holy* cow," he mumbled, looking at the fitness routines, repetitions, hours and numbers she'd crammed the pages with. "This is... well, sweetie, what are you—where are you going with all of this? Are you aimin' to become an athlete?"

"No," Tabitha said, looking away. "I want to be pretty, for just once in my life. I know all of this must seem... *impatient*, to you, but I'm done waiting for some fantasy dream world where I'm beautiful and things work out and I matter. Dad, I'm going to *make* it all happen."

"I believe you can too, sweetie," he said after a long moment of silence. "You know we love you just the way you are though, right? No matter how you look."

"I know what you think. And... I tried that. It didn't work out," she said in more of a brisk tone than she'd intended. Feeling a little ashamed of herself, she dropped back down and positioned herself to resume the push-ups. "I'm... sorry. I love you too, Daddy."

"How about I take you out this weekend, get you some new clothes," he offered. "Since you seem hell bent on changin' yer whole figure before high school."

"I'd... I'd love that, thank you." Tabitha heaved herself back up and rocked back to sit on her heels. "Thank you, thank you, *thank you!*"

———

As Tabitha leapt up into the air and snapped out a neat and precise jump-kick, the most she felt now was a slight, almost imperceptible *wobble,* rather than that unpleasant *jiggle* from several weeks ago. Landing steadily, she twisted positions and performed a low cross-hand block with both arms. Though she'd lost a significant amount of weight and was finally seeing it in the mirror, the pounds weren't exactly melting away. Rather, they were being *wrung* out of her, *exhausted* out of her through the rigors of her exercise and diet plan.

I feel like I need to be doing even MORE, though, Tabitha thought, unable to shake the anxious feeling that'd been plaguing her. She was working through her exercise rotation, she was practicing her katas, and running to Grandma Laurie's and then playing with the cousins made for good cardio in between. *What else can I do?*

Glancing up and down the street of nearby mobile homes to see no cars were coming and that no one was in sight, she took a couple careful steps and—attempted a handstand. Her palms planted on the concrete of the sidewalk, her legs kicked up into the air... and flailed. After a short, fleeting moment with all of her blood rushing to her head, she lost her balance and fell forwards, her shoes slapping onto the sidewalk.

Ow. That... wasn't as bad as I thought it'd be, Tabitha thought, lurching back up to her feet and looking around with an embarrassed expression. *Maybe I don't need to try it out here on the sidewalk, but... I can probably do flips. Cartwheels. Actual gymnastic stuff now.* Looking thoughtful now, Tabitha brushed herself off and resumed her Taekwondo forms.

Lately, her thoughts had begun to stray while in the midst of doing her katas, and even more so as she ran the loop around the lower park neighborhood. She couldn't stop thinking about *parkour.* Somewhere between a movement technique and a training discipline, parkour was a rather eye-catching method of traversing various obstacles along a course. Although here in 1998, it was more or less completely unknown, several decades in the future, it would feature prominently in almost every single action movie. Tabitha hadn't even actually learned parkour was the name for it until she was already in her fifties. During belt promotions one fall at the Taekwondo school, a few of the youngsters had set up a demonstration for everyone.

Damn my old bones. Should've at least tried their little obstacle course, Tabitha thought to herself in dismay. Now that the Taekwondo and running felt virtually effortless to her—a race against boredom more than an effort of exertion, her mind kept wandering. *If they could do it, I can figure it out. The cousins are going to get tired of tag sooner or later.*

———

A week later, Tabitha pursed her lips as she pushed hangers of clothing down the rack one by one, carefully working her way through the aisles. Even though she'd coerced her father into taking her to the thrift store rather than anywhere else for her clothes shopping... on the stated limit of ten dollars, there wasn't a whole lot she could afford to buy. Either one new pair of jeans and a shirt to go with it, or maybe several shirts. She needed much more than that, however. After asking the sales clerk for clearance items, she was told that items with certain colored tags were further discounted to half-off.

Which led her to her next dilemma: she didn't even know what size she *would* be by the time her freshman year started. Her waist-line was steadily shrinking, but she didn't know what size it would stop at. As if the issue weren't already complicated enough, she was also still growing in other ways—the ravages of puberty wouldn't complete her adolescence for another two years, at least. There were only three pairs of jeans that fell into her projected size range that were also half-off, so she picked the best-looking two and threw them over an arm to try on. She would likely just barely squeeze into them now, but by the end of the summer, she might have to pull them apart along the outer seam and re-tailor them to a smaller frame.

All of the preparation and planning for high school is finally starting to pay off, though, Tabitha thought to herself, absent-mind-edly stroking at her red hair. Some of the ingredients she'd budgeted into their grocery list had nothing to do with the meals she was cooking for them. It had taken some experimenting, as she hadn't perfectly remembered the instructions, but sifting a tablespoon of light rye flour through a tea strainer, and then adding it to a tablespoon of warm water made a hair wash that was supremely effective as a substitute for shampoo. She was now diligently scrubbing the oils out of her hair, every three days. After a few more weeks of care and treatment, her hair would be looking better than it ever had before.

I wonder if Grandma Laurie has a sewing machine. Tabitha paused, pulling a rather cute dress off a nearby rack. *The upper part of this is a lot like a modern-day blouse. Er, modern like they'll be in the future, I guess I should say. Hey, it's half-off.*

"Girls are all dumb and have big fat butts!"

"Sam, that's a rude and hurtful thing to say," Tabitha scolded. "Please behave yourself until we're at the playground."

"What're you gonna do about it, sissy?" Sam taunted. "Hit me like a girl?"

"I don't think you'd like that," Tabitha warned.

"Yeah right, like I'd even feel it," Sam scoffed, stomping toward her with his hands raised in a provoking way. "Betcha can't hit me! Betcha can't hit me!"

It was the middle of summer, when Sam, the eldest of her cousins, made that mistake of slapping a sharp spank on Tabitha's undefended bottom. All of his brothers watching were just about to shriek with laughter and join in on teasing and messing with Tabby...

But, unfortunately for Sam—Tabby *didn't* hit like a girl anymore. She hit like someone trained in the correct way to punch, like someone who spent time each day practicing throwing that exact strike over and over and over again in studious repetition. So the boys watched in surprise as their angry redheaded cousin pulled back her fist like an action movie star—and threw a punch into Sam with a twist of her entire body that put every ounce of weight in her body behind it.

She put Sam down in the grass beside the road, *hard.* Clenching and unclenching her hand, she then scowled and left for the day, without saying another word to any of them.

"*Jesus,*" Nick mouthed.

"Is... is he dead?!" Joshua prodded his eldest brother with the toe of his sneaker.

When the boys saw Tabitha again days later, she wasn't angry. She smiled sweetly at them and pulled Sam aside, apologizing for losing her temper. She then warned him to never, *ever* do that again. To her, or any other girl, *ever*.

"If I hear that you have, I'm going to hit you again, just as hard," Tabitha promised, examining him with deadly seriousness shining in her eyes. "But you're not a child anymore, so you're going to have to take it right in the face next time. Got it?"

She ignored the way Sam subconsciously flinched back, and then brought them to the playground and played tag with everyone like nothing had ever happened... but the social dynamic between her and the boys would never be the same again. Aiden sided with Tabitha—it felt to him like she was in the right, like she'd had a good enough reason, and to his surprise, both Nick and Joshua quickly agreed with him. Sam sneered and called them all wussies, but he never tempted fate with Tabitha again.

After all, over the course of the summer, the *tubby Tabby* they were used to making fun of was transforming into an angel of death. What seemed like a third of her body weight simply melted away, sloughed off beneath a relentless onslaught of physical activity that would have seemed *Olympian* to them, if they'd understood the concept. The girl wasn't just fast anymore—she was jumping, she was kicking off of the sides of playground equipment, she performed dive-rolls to avoid their tags, and they'd even seen her do a hand-spring to get away once. Tabitha was working out and improving every day, and the hours of playtime she spent with the cousins left all four of them completely exhausted.

She wasn't an ugly duckling anymore either, but despite how pretty she was becoming, they never thought to compare her to a swan. A hawk, or an eagle maybe. Some fierce bird of prey that had beautiful wings but also sported powerful talons, the kind that could rend flesh with ease. The cousins might have not grasped the finer nuances of concepts like respect just yet, but the fear and awe they felt when they looked toward Tabitha was becoming profound.

The bruise on Sam's chest was a deep purple for weeks before fading away in sickening yellows and faint greens, and they told their father, Tabitha's Uncle Danny, that Sam got hit with a softball. Everyone was warned to pay more goddamn attention, and watch what they were fucking doing.

This time, they did.

———

Tabitha had already set the table and was putting the finishing touches on their dinner when the phone call came. Turning the heat off the stove but continuing to whisk the noodles, chicken, and the pesto sauce in the skillet, she couldn't help but glance up with interest as her father received the call.

"Moore residence," he said, frowning.

She looked back down, giving the noodles and chicken one last stir—they were done enough. *Telemarketer, perhaps? We don't get a lot of calls.*

"She what?" Mr. Moore said, turning and looking directly at Tabitha.

She paused for a moment, but he was still listening to someone on the other end of the line talk. She scooped a portion of chicken pesto into bowls for each of them, gently dipped the skillet into waiting soapy sink water, and brought dinner to the table.

"I thought we were having *noodles* and chicken," Mrs. Moore complained, glaring at the bowl placed before them. "Noodles aren't supposed to be green, Tabitha. What is this, green pepper?"

"Honey—I'm on the phone," Mr. Moore said, throwing his wife a look.

"They're zucchini noodles," Tabitha whispered in a low voice.

"I spent almost an hour with the peeler preparing enough for us." *I wish you could understand how precious every hour of my time is.*

"*Zucchini?*" Mrs. Moore sighed, picking a slender piece of green out of her bowl with her fingers—which Tabitha found exceptionally rude—and examining it. "Tabby, you can't just replace noodles with zucchini in a recipe out of nowhere. How are we supposed to eat this?"

"I'd appreciate it if you tried, at least," Tabitha whispered, trying not to scowl.

"Well, of course you have Tabitha's permission," her father told someone on the phone, causing Tabitha's head to snap around. Narrowing her eyes, she took her seat at the table and waited for him to finish.

"Alright," her father continued, nodding to the person he couldn't see. "Uh-huh. Well, thank you. I'll let her know. Goodbye."

"Alan, Tabitha didn't make any noodles," Mrs. Moore pointed out in an accusing tone. "All she made was *zucchini.*"

"Dinner is chicken pesto, served with zucchini noodles," Tabitha calmly explained. "I worked very hard on it, and I'd like you to please try it."

"And what about those of us who don't eat *zucchini?*" her mother exclaimed. "What are *we* supposed to eat?"

"We still have steamed broccoli from—"

"*Enough,* Tabitha. I'm sure you think this is real funny."

"It looks good, sweetie." Mr. Moore sat down, clearing his throat. "We're very proud of you for making dinner every night. No matter how it turns out."

Unsure whether to thank him or object to the backhanded compliment, Tabitha bowed her head and led them in saying a simple grace. Both of her parents had been rather incensed the time she launched into a lengthy grace, insisting she was being disrespectful, so she kept her thanks short and sweet.

"That was someone from the school board, calling about one

of your essays," Alan said, turning the zucchini over thoughtfully with his fork.

"It's very thoughtful of them to call," Tabitha said, trying not to smile.

"They're going to send it to the *Tribune* and publish it," he said, looking up at her. "And they want to put you in AP English when you start at Springton High. They're recommending you. Do you know what all this is about?"

"*Aye-Pee* English, what th—"

"It stands for advanced placement," Tabitha elaborated, interrupting her mother. "I put a lot of thought into the essay on my exam."

"They said it was *seven pages,*" Mr. Moore said, popping a forkful of zucchini noodles into his mouth. He looked like he was going to continue his thought, but instead chewed distractedly. "You know... this isn't half bad."

"Thank you."

"They made you write a seven-page essay for your exam?" Mrs. Moore asked, still reluctant to taste her noodles.

"Oh, no," Tabitha said, relishing another bite of the pesto chicken she'd worked hard on. "It's a middle school Language Arts examination. They asked for a minimum of three paragraphs. Like I said... I just had a lot of thought to put into that essay."

———

"Hope you're all *actually* ready this time," Tabitha said, looking from cousin to nervous cousin standing in the playground with her. Sam, Aiden, Nick and Joshua eyed her warily but didn't speak —they were prepared to burst into motion the moment she made her move.

"Okay... and, *go!*" Smirking, she turned and broke into a sprint across the playground, and her four cousins dashed after her, chasing the now-familiar bob and sway of her bouncing red ponytail. She seemed to run on effortlessly, however, and the slim girl widened the distance between her and her pursuers in an instant.

The three-foot tall chain-link fence at the edge of the park looked like it would be an obstacle for the five-foot four girl, but she planted both feet heavily in front of that fence and *leapt*, launching herself up to land on the fence's top rail with both of her worn shoes. Her arms flashed out momentarily for balance, and then she *flipped*, twisting sideways through the air to land on the other side of the fence with what seemed like the natural ease of a born acrobat.

She called it *parkour*, and promised to teach them all how to do all of it—when they could keep up with her. As Aiden led the others in struggling to clamber over the park's fence, he knew that it wouldn't be soon—he knew from experience now that if she'd kept running, she wouldn't even be in sight by the time they all cleared the fence. She was waiting for them now on the other side, taunting them with her proximity—because none of her cousins had been able to tag her in days.

6

FIRST DAY AT SPRINGTON HIGH

Tabitha Moore didn't remember what it was like stepping onto the bus for the first day of high school in her past life—because nothing had happened back then. She'd been greeted with indifference and summarily ignored, never given a second glance. As she climbed up the steps within the large yellow school bus at the end of her neighborhood and first laid eyes on the rows of high schoolers seated there... she realized that everything about this life was destined now to be different from what she knew. Immediately upon stepping up into view, a guy sitting at the back of the bus let out a jeering *whooo* that was picked up on by several other guys. Everyone turned and stared at her, and Tabitha froze.

Her coppery red hair was worn down and falling in a deliberate tangle—very subtle use of her mother's curling iron and a little bit of product gave her hair some volume for that perfect slightly mussed look, an endeavor three weekends and quite a bit of research in the making. Tabitha's large, expressive hazel eyes were framed with a tiny bit of subdued eyeliner and her delicate, sweet features were just a shade pale of perfect.

Despite spending most of her summer outdoors, she hadn't tanned—with her genetics, she simply *couldn't*. Her skin was either Irish white or redneck red, so in the days before school started, she rearranged her schedule to put herself out of the sun. Running times were shifted to early mornings and late nights, and she'd even specifically skipped today's run to spend time going over her appearance, paying rigorous attention to every detail.

The white top she wore had once been a discounted thrift-store dress. It showed off her shoulders and neck without revealing any cleavage, had exquisite embroidery and generally looked great on her, but had been a little too *dressy* for school. So, it had been sundered at the seams, cut apart and then re-hemmed into a lovely blouse. The better-fitting of her two surviving pairs of blue jeans and her new shoes made it a decent outfit. Grandma Laurie had proposed making a school bag together out of the different shades of jeans they'd cut up—the straps of her bag were real belts, worked through actual belt loops on the bag and stitched into place.

Painfully aware of everyone watching her, Tabitha picked her way down the bus aisle looking for a seat. Conversations went silent as she passed, and guys were politely shifting over to offer her a seat next to them.

For a second, that would have seemed thoughtful, Tabitha scowled inwardly. Raising her guard, she stepped past them to instead situate herself next to a lone girl who was staring absentmindedly out the window. *But none of you were ever this thoughtful last time through. Nice try.*

"Good morning." The guy across from her waved.

"...Hi," Tabitha greeted back warily.

"You nervous?" he asked.

Do I look nervous? Tabitha wondered for a split-second, mentally re-evaluating the entrance she'd made. *No. I didn't make any expressions or show anything at all. Must just be his way of breaking the ice.*

"...About what?" Tabitha questioned.

"First day of school," he reminded her. There were one or two other conversations going on throughout the bus as it lurched into motion with a diesel hum, but for the most part, it felt like most of the passengers were listening in on them.

"Yeah, real nervous," Tabitha replied in a clear, steady voice. "You know, my palms are sweaty—knees weak, arms are heavy."

The guy gave her a curious look and laughed.

Halfway through chiding herself for not remembering the rest of the lyrics, Tabitha realized that it was still 1998... that particular Eminem song probably hadn't even come out yet. Mentally grimacing, she kept her composure and turned her head away to listlessly watch the scenery roll by outside the window.

Oh, well. At least I didn't say anything about vomiting spaghetti. Everyone could tell I was quoting something... right?

Before they arrived at the school's bus loop, another guy introduced himself, ducking forward from the rear of the bus into a nearby seat to tell her that *hi, my name's Kyle—how you doin',* and Tabitha began to understand that the attention she'd *thought* she craved after a lifetime of being ignored was actually... awkward and a little embarrassing. *I always hated being put on the spot. Why did I ever think I wanted to stand out?*

As everyone filed out of the bus and into the school commons of Springton High, Tabitha felt jittery stage-fright rise up within her. She'd hoped to have a nice moment, stepping off the bus and seeing her old alma mater once again, but it felt like she was being watched from every angle. Heads were turning as she passed, a guy in the distance elbowed his buddy and jerked his chin in her direction, people were looking over at her. It wasn't just guys either. Girls were sizing her up and evaluating her when she stepped into the school commons, and an older man—a teacher? Administrator? Principal?—nodded and said *good morning* to her.

Is this how normal people feel all the time? Tabitha wondered, struggling to not feel overwhelmed before she even made it to her first class. *Like they're the protagonists of their story? Was I not even the main character of my own fucking story, last lifetime?*

The thought made her a little angry.

Despite attracting interest in spades, Tabitha was in a strange mood for her debut and didn't want to chat with anyone or make new friends just yet. Following her written itinerary, she strolled past the clusters of high schoolers milling about throughout the commons waiting for first bell and headed toward her classroom.

"Hi." A pair of students were already there, both guys around her age. Her current age anyway. "Here for Mr. Simmons, Marine Science?"

"Mr. Simmons, Marine Science," Tabitha confirmed, waving her slip. *Everyone's just so friendly when you're not fat and unhappy-looking...*

"You new here?" the other boy asked.

"I'm a freshman, yeah," Tabitha answered cautiously.

"Cool. Awesome, me too."

She wasn't able to tell whether she was meeting these people for the first time, or if they were middle school peers who failed to recognize her because of her summertime transformation. However, she would have no excuse for not recognizing *them* if they were people she'd should have met before in middle school, which was an awkward situation just waiting to happen. *Don't want to seem like I'm putting on airs now.*

Unfortunately for her, forty-seven years had gone by, and she didn't remember any of her prior classmates at all. She'd become familiar with a few middle-school faces during the last few weeks of finals before summer started, but none of them had talked to her. She hadn't bothered remembering many names.

There is one name I remember for sure, Tabitha thought to herself, pursing her pink lips. *Alicia Brook. Brooks? I think it was Alicia Brooks. Fellow hometown hero.*

"Got any good classes?" The taller of the two guys interrupted her thoughts.

"I have classes." Tabitha shrugged. "Too soon to say what's good and what's garbage, isn't it?"

"I've got bus tech next," the tall one bragged. "*Business technology*—the whole first semester's learning how to type, and I already know how to."

"I touch type," the shorter one said.

"Hah, chicken-pecking." The tall one rolled his eyes. "You should transfer to bus tech. You'll need to learn how to type someday anyways."

"For what? I don't have a computer," the other one scoffed. "Probably never will. Computers are for nerds."

"Do you type?" The taller one looked toward Tabitha.

"Um... a little bit, I guess?" She showed them an uneasy smile. *A little bit as in, over a hundred words a minute. I'm a writer, and I clocked myself when I was looking into working data entry, right before Town Hall hired me. In THIS life, I bet my fingers are even faster than that.*

"You should take bus tech too," the tall guy said. "You can get a cushy job somewhere as a secretary, barely doing anything and getting paid for it. What're you planning on doing when you grow up?"

'When I grow up?' Tabitha struggled to keep a straight face. *Do people in high school seriously still use that phrase? I mean, I'm still thirteen until December, so I know I'm really, really young, even for high school, but still...*

"I'll be a hometown hero, I guess," Tabitha mused.

"What's that?" The tall one gave her a weird look. "Me, I'm gonna run a video store. I have it all planned out."

"What, like a rental shop?" the shorter one asked. "That's pretty cool."

"Yeah, I love movies, so that's always been my dream."

"...Good luck," Tabitha blurted out before she could stop herself. Neither of the boys noticed anything strange about the smile she wore.

"Yeah, thanks."

———

A lifetime ago

"Here you are! Voila!" A woman with closely cropped salt and pepper hair in a navy blue pantsuit stepped back and gestured toward the large glass display with a theatrical flourish. "Tabitha Moore; hometown hero."

"Aww, Sharon... I don't know." Tabitha shook her head and gave her boss a nervous smile. "It doesn't seem very... appropriate?"

"What's not appropriate about it? You're a *published author!*" Sharon exclaimed, rapping a knuckle on the smudged glass.

Springton's Hometown Heroes, the faded letters slipped into the signboard proclaimed, and the prominent glass case contained five different displays. This portion of the town hall normally featured seasonal decorations—but, in one of the long lulls between notable holidays, Sharon had come up with the idea of honoring the prominent locals residing in their tiny city.

Guess that explains why she wanted copies of both Goblina *and* Goblin Princess. Tabitha sighed, looking at the two paperback novels propped up beside a large, rather unflattering office photo of her that had been printed out. *Makes sense, though. For a while there, I thought she was actually interested in reading them. Silly me.*

If she were to be honest, the paperbacks weren't particularly flattering. either—cartoonish green goblins were baring their teeth on the covers of each of them. She'd never been satisfied with the artist her publisher commissioned, one of the many ongoing problems that had eventually destroyed their unsteady partnership.

"A published author—not a successful author," Tabitha protested weakly. "No one ever read those old things, Sharon. Besides, all the others are, you know... they're *real* heroes."

The three displays in the middle were very obviously military ones. Service medals were laid out in a neat display beside uniformed photos of veterans of the Iraqi war. Placing her photo next to these men and insisting she was the hero felt borderline sacrilegious.

"Well. Not everyone can relate to those kinds of heroes." Sharon dismissed Tabitha's concerns with a wave of her hand. "Besides, we have Alicia here, on the other end."

"Alicia... Brooks?" Tabitha leaned over and read from the placard.

A softly smiling African American woman wearing an over-sized pair of glasses was featured in a nice portrait on that side of the display. Beside the picture was artwork—in one, inked lines formed sorrowful faces, each bold black scratch and scribble forming understated gestures and figures. In another, the scrawled lines portrayed the naked back of a woman, each muscle and detail, every strand of cascading hair defined in light and shadow and rendered in stunning etched lines.

"Our *artiste*," Sharon said proudly. "She's drawn pieces for *Sports Illustrated*, *People* magazine, and even *Playboy*!"

"She lives in Springton?" Tabitha asked, enthralled by the artwork.

"She's... working in Chicago right now, but she was still born and raised here," Sharon explained. "I thought you might recognize her—I think you two went to school together?"

"School?" Tabitha echoed, wincing slightly.

"Yeah, Springton High—you both graduated in the class of 2002, right? I thought for sure you'd know her."

"I wish I had." Tabitha admitted sheepishly. "I, um, I didn't... talk to people much back then."

———

This Life

"John Stephens."

"Here."

"Kevin Matthews."

"Here!"

"Elena Seelbaugh?"

"It's pronounced 'EE-lay-nuh,' actually."

"Sorry about that. You're *here*, I take it?"

"Yeah."

"Kiersten Birch?"

"Here."

There's still so much to do, Tabitha thought to herself, staring vacantly off into space as Mr. Simmons did his first roll-call. She needed to start writing her book. Some source of income, no matter how meager, was also necessary for her to continue surviving. October was also looming closer and closer, and she had no idea what she should do about the approaching calamity. Try as she might, she couldn't remember what would happen in any more than the most basic details. *Police officer shot in the Lower Park. October of this year. Don't remember the day. He bleeds out on the way to the hospital—so, he must have been shot somewhere vital?*

I could prevent it. Somehow. But directly interfering with what will actually be a fatal shooting incident... isn't that just asking to get myself killed? Not interfering when she had foreknowledge was probably equivalent to letting the man die, but how could she prevent it? Providing first-aid after the fact seemed even more helpless for her. *I don't think I can deal with that much blood in person. Should I just stay out of it, after all?*

"Tabitha Moore?"

"I'm present," she answered out succinctly in her clear, lovely voice.

———

Tabitha Moore?...Isn't that TUBBY TABBY? Elena was curious and turned her head to see the girl several rows across from her who'd spoken up.

Frowning, she discovered instead a slender redhead girl with a bored expression. *This* 'Tabitha Moore' was gorgeous, one of the handful who could be considered peerless beauties throughout the entire school. Dressed well, wearing tasteful makeup, attention was paid to her hair—but she wasn't actively scoping out the rest of the class. She wasn't feigning sleepiness, wasn't fidgeting, wasn't sneaking looks at the boys, and she wasn't *presenting* herself in a social way, or making any effort to build a rapport with anyone. This redhead didn't even seem to be posturing—she really came off as entirely indifferent to their class.

What, think you're too good for us? Elena looked at this Tabitha Moore again with distaste. *Same color hair as Tabby. Same name. But... it can't be her, right?*

When attendance was taken and Mr. Simmons was passing out the syllabus packet and a worksheet for them, Elena took initiative to lean over and call out.

"Hey, Tabitha—are you *Tubby Tabby?* From Laurel Middle?"

"Yes." Tabitha turned to face her, not seeming irked in the slightest by her old moniker being brought to light. "That's me. Have we met?"

Yeah, right... That reflexive scoff died in her throat, however, when Elena realized with surprise that there was absolutely no recognition in the girl's expression. *What the hell?*

Elena always considered herself one of the elites of Laurel Middle School. She hit her growth spurt before everyone else, came into her boobs before the other girls. She knew how to dress well, how to wear makeup, and didn't ever take shit from any of the other bitches there. Elena had assumed her popularity made her well-known, that everyone was familiar with her name, or at least *aware* of her. *Guess... not?*

"Uhh, I'm Elena Seelbaugh? We've had classes together before...?" Elena said, racking her brain and trying to recall if she'd ever directly bullied this girl back then. She'd certainly seen others making fun of her, and definitely laughed along with them—but had they ever actually interacted individually?

"I'm sorry." Tabitha smiled at her. "I don't remember you."

Indignant, Elena was just about to give her a sarcastic retort when Tabitha continued.

"I hit my head, right before our middle school finals," Tabitha explained. "I don't know if you heard about that. So many names and faces feel familiar, but I still have trouble connecting them all."

That's right! Elena looked shocked. She *did* remember that, because Tubby Tabby—*Tubby Tabby the trailer trash girl*—had waddled into class one day back then with a weird head injury, looking even more unkempt than usual—almost like a zombie. They'd all snickered about it, joking that she was going to be put into the special ed class when she got to Springton High.

"Right! Yeah, I remember," Elena admitted, eyes widening. "Just—you, uhh, you look so different! I almost didn't recognize you!"

"Sorry." Tabitha gave her an actual apologetic smile that stunned Elena. "I—"

"C'mon now, save the chit-chatting for after class, you two," Mr. Simmons called out.

———

Although the deluge of attention to her now was unexpected, several classes through her first day of high school, Tabitha thought things were going very well. The coursework was vaguely familiar, and, as she'd expected, it only took a little bit of brushing up to refresh her memory on some of the subjects. The textbooks distributed to her were an unnecessary burden, in her eyes—thick, heavy monstrosities, last vestigial remnants of the era before digitalization, but the subjects themselves wouldn't pose any problems.

Dozens of students had introduced themselves to her, apparently based on her new appearance alone, which was both startling and well outside of what she'd anticipated. While the handsome young men seemed rather well-assured of their own unerring charm, in her eyes... they were still thirty years or so too young for her interest. In some ways, they were children merely masquerading around in the freshly ripened bodies of fledgling adults.

At the same time, Tabitha wasn't able to look down on them. This was her second try on this, and even then, she didn't feel wiser or more mature than them by an enormous margin—just a small one. She thoroughly considered her first life a miserable failure, so she couldn't bring herself to look down on any of these teens.

———

Alicia hated high school so far. She didn't sit near anyone she knew from Fairfield Middle, and those that did would rarely give her more than a passing glance anyway. Making new friends was absolutely the worst, most aggravating experience she could think of, and it didn't help that most of the school was made up of white kids. Her parents' idea of Springton High being a better choice than Fairfield High just because it mostly consisted of white kids was, in fact, fundamentally racist.

She'd planned on taking an 'eccentric and artsy' identity for this new school experience. However, looking in the mirror just this morning at the 'artsy' look she'd done up... it felt so contrived and fake that she wasn't comfortable with it. Instead, she was blending in with the background, as always. Hair pulled tight into a bun, glasses, polo shirt, jeans. *I'm just the bland black girl extra again in this scene too. No, I don't have a speaking part. Don't mind me.*

She kept her sketchbook out on her desk, the pad as much a security blanket as anything else she owned, and hid herself away in her efforts to draw. Anything rather than meeting her new classmates, really. Unfortunately, between the anxiety of being in a new place, being surrounded by fellow teens and a growing, untraceable frustration, all she had were senseless scribbles. Inspiration was especially elusive today—she had a page and a half of random cross-hatching, a few floating eyes with eyebrows hovering above them in the blank white void of her paper, and some random cube shapes.

Thankfully, it was all almost over—this was their last class of the day, and it was almost time to be back on the bus and off home to her parents, who would demand to know how great her day was, how many friends she'd made, what classes she liked, and so on and so forth. She couldn't help but make a sour face at the thought of running through *that* particular gauntlet, and her mood darkened even more.

"Hello!" a pretty white girl with red hair said, interrupting Alicia's thoughts.

"Hi...?" Alicia looked up in surprise.

"My name's Tabitha." The girl smiled at her, looking pleased to see her. "I noticed your sketchbook—do you draw?"

"A little." Alicia sat up straighter, now on alert.

Upon closer inspection, this wasn't just any pretty white girl. This was *the* pretty white girl, a thought driven home by the fact that all the guys in class were still discreetly watching her right now. She was young, thin, had a fairy-like face, perfect red hair, and was wearing a cool top—*Where'd she even get that? Looks expensive.*

"If it's not too much trouble, do you have any drawings I could take a look at?" Tabitha asked. "I'm starting a large project soon, and I'm very much in need of a talented artist."

"Uhh... I'm a no one," Alicia refused, trying to casually cover today's awful doodles with her hands while she spoke. "This is just for fun. I can barely draw anything."

"I very much doubt that." Tabitha laughed, a lovely sound. There was a strange, knowing look in her eyes. "If you ever change your mind, will you please come find me? I'm very interested in your work."

What was that? Alicia couldn't help but stare as Tabitha wandered back toward her seat and all the boys immediately pretended they hadn't been ogling her. *I don't... think she was trying to tease me, or bully me, or anything? But why come up and talk to me, of all people?*

Oh, well. Alicia returned to resting her cheek on her hand and scribbling geometric shapes as she waited for the final bell to ring. *She'll probably never even talk to me again anyways.*

———

"Well, how was it, then?" Mrs. Moore asked, a hint of irritation apparent in her voice already. Tabitha had come home from school without so much as greeting her. Instead, her daughter had traipsed right on over to the trailer's bathroom. The door was open, and she peered into the small enclosure to check on her daughter—her new daughter, the slight-figured and pretty one she struggled to recognize. "How was your first day of school?"

Tabitha *was* a whole new daughter, ever since the day she'd come home from the hospital after that head injury. Qualities Mrs. Moore hadn't ever thought the girl possessed were focused, sharpened to a point and thrust into a relentless drive that Mrs. Moore didn't understand at all. She wanted to be happy for her—her daughter was a stunning little beauty now, and just over a little bit

more than a single summer—but more than anything, she wanted
to feel like a mother again.

"Everything was copacetic," Tabitha reported. The redheaded
girl was sitting on the edge of the bathtub working on something,
now wearing only her jeans and a bra. Somehow now even her
posture seemed graceful, like someone out of a Renaissance
painting.

"*Copacetic,* huh?" Mrs. Moore frowned. "What're you up to,
then?"

"Grandma Laurie and I made this blouse," Tabitha replied,
gently rubbing along fabric laid carefully in the long basin of cool
water. "Out of a dress, from the thrift store. It's very lovely, but it
was never intended for casual wear. It will need a lot of special
care and attention if I want to continue to wear it every week."

"Sounds just like the new Tabitha," Mrs. Moore muttered.
Emotions roiled through the mother as she stood in the bathroom
door. Resentment at their current relationship, that Tabitha
always chose to spend time with her grandmother, rather than
her. Annoyance at the flippant way Tabitha treated her now. Envy.
No—not envy. She's just a little girl. She's MY little girl.

"That's an astute connection to make," Tabitha remarked,
looking up at her mother in surprise. "It isn't easy... you know?"

Tabitha held her gaze for several long seconds before turning
her attention back to the garment she was carefully hand-wash-
ing, and Mrs. Shannon Moore's discomfort intensified. Over the
summer, they'd been at constant loggerheads, and something
about this felt like they were forcefully trying to have a civil
conversation for once. She was alarmed at how frightened she was
of messing things up here.

"...Why?" Mrs. Moore asked, leaning against the door frame.

There was only the sound of Tabitha displacing water for a
while as Tabitha drew the blouse out of the water and turned it
over. Her cute brow was furrowed, and the girl seemed at a loss as
how to answer for once.

"*Why*, Tabitha?"

"Would you care to elaborate on your question?" Tabitha asked, an edge appearing in her voice. "Why, *what?*"

"Don't sass me right now," Mrs. Moore warned. "*Why* are you always doing all of this? Nothing you ever do is normal anymore! Ever since the hospital."

"Oh." Tabitha seemed to chuckle to herself. "You mean *that*. I've been waiting all summer for you to ask me that."

"*Well?*"

"The answer's in a box at the top of your closet. In a blue album."

Shock, anger, and then humiliation rolled across Mrs. Moore's expression, and she opened her mouth to berate her daughter for the invasion of privacy and blatant disrespect, but couldn't quite find the words. *No. She couldn't have. She didn't. She—*

"I'm old enough to understand why you kept it from me," Tabitha said slowly, pulling her towel down from the bar on the wall to carefully dry her hands. "If I hadn't stolen into your room and found your secret, I wouldn't have known any better for another two years. When Daddy stops you from throwing the album out."

"It's not a *secret*, Tabitha!" Mrs. Moore yelled, her temper exploding out. "I didn't want this—I just, I *can't*, okay? How dare you go into *my* personal things without any permission, *how dare you—*"

"Why wouldn't I dare?" Tabitha challenged, rising up from the edge of the tub. "You don't have to tell me that it's my fault. I *know* that it is. I know that having me made you lose your figure—made you give up on how you look. I know you wanted to do more with your life than *simply settle,* and settle in a trashy fucking trailer park like this, of all places. But you had me. And I fucked up your life."

Mrs. Moore backed up into the wall of the hallway, startled tears of anguish rolling unbidden down her face. All the bitter and hateful thoughts she'd swallowed down over the years were unhidden all at once like an exposed nerve, and it *hurt*. She hated the way she felt, hated herself, and knowing Tabitha somehow understood everything from just those last few old photographs she'd been unable to part with? It made her more ashamed of herself than she'd ever imagined possible.

She sank to the floor, crying hard enough into her hands to shake, covering her face and shaking her head. Regret and remorse flowed out of her in racking sobs as she completely collapsed, unable to keep up a stern face or motherly pretense. *She sees right through me. Right through me.*

"But now I know, Mom," Tabitha said, crossing to where her mother blocked the hallway and crouching down to take her by the shoulders. "And now—I'm going to unfuck everything. I just need you to give me some time."

————

Waiting outside on the grimy concrete steps up into the trailer, Tabitha was surprised to see Grandma Laurie arrive in Uncle Danny's old car. *Well. It's not his old car YET, I suppose.* In the next couple years, she remembered the thing would be here to stay with the Moores for good, up on cinderblocks and out of commission.

Which means Uncle Danny's probably getting convicted soon, Tabitha realized, noticing that the little faces of her cousins were peering out the car windows with interest as the car parked in front of her double-wide. *I didn't really get to know them, back then. Should I... say something to them? Warn the boys?*

"What happened?" her grandmother asked the moment she opened the door. "Is she okay?"

"We had our... confrontation," Tabitha explained, stepping forward to dutifully hug her grandmother. "The big one, I think. I'm really sorry for calling you over like this."

"It's fine, it's fine." Grandma Laurie gave her a quick squeeze. "It's just—I have the boys today..."

"I can look after them," Tabitha promised, gesturing for her cousins to get out of the car. "We'll put a movie on, and I can make dinner for everyone. Do they have homework?"

"Not that they've told me," Grandma Laurie rolled her eyes. "Where is she? C'mon, boys, inside."

"I gave her a sedative and put her in bed," Tabitha explained, ushering them all up inside the mobile home. "She isn't asleep yet, though. Can you...?"

"I'll talk with her," Grandma Laurie assured her, turning to throw the cousins a stern look. "You boys all be on your best behavior here. I mean it."

"What'd you do?" Sam asked, looking at Tabitha in bewilderment as their grandmother disappeared into the back room of the trailer. As the oldest, over the summer, Sam had grown a half-head taller than his three brothers awkwardly milling about the tidy living room. Although all of the boys were in a perpetual state of conflict with one another, they were uncharacteristically obedient today while in Tabitha's home. "What was the emergency?"

"I had a fight with my mother," Tabitha explained, sliding a tray of VHS tapes out from beneath the couch. "I'm sorry for dragging all of you over here. Sam, can you pick out a movie to watch?"

"You fought your mom?" Nick asked incredulously, looking around as if he expected to see broken glass and trashed furnishings from such a battle. "...Is she okay?"

"Women fight each other with their words, not their fists." Tabitha sighed, crossing over into the kitchen and pulling that unwanted pack of hot dogs she'd been longing to get rid of out of the freezer. "It winds up more damaging than physical violence, really. You'll understand someday."

"Ew," Aiden objected. "Those are the big gross hot dogs. We're not eating those."

"They're only gross because they don't have any texture or

flavor," Tabitha explained, putting two tablespoons of sesame oil onto her skillet and tilting it back and forth until the oil spread across the basin. She turned on the stovetop. "Joshua, could you turn on the television, but lower the volume? The VCR works on channel 3."

"Why'd you fight your mom?" Sam asked, more interested in that than any of the Moore family's small VHS collection—all of their movies were recorded from television onto blank cassettes, four or five to a tape, with the titles handwritten onto labels on the side. "Won't you get in trouble?"

"She... hid something very important from me, for a very long time," Tabitha said, looking a little troubled. She sawed the frozen jumbo hot dogs into quarter-inch medallions with a serrated knife, and then prepared a mixture of brown sugar and soy sauce to pan-sear them in, to give the pieces of meat some texture. *Then I can use up the last of that beef base to soak them in, while I put the noodles on. That'll be just about the last of the old pantry cleared out.* "She tried to hide it from herself too. But doing that was only ever going to make her unhappy."

"What'd she hide?" Nick couldn't help but ask.

"You'll be able to see it... once I'm able to reveal it to you," Tabitha answered cryptically. *Mom's weight gain plateaued when I took over all the meal preparation, but she's not going to actually lose weight until I can wean her off sugars completely. I'm sure everything else with her is going to become a struggle too. Ugh...*

"I'm a part of it," Tabitha admitted. "Did you notice how much I changed over the summer?"

"Yeah, you're like—almost a whole complete different girl than you was," Nick said.

"Than you *were*," Tabitha corrected, gingerly placing medallions onto the skillet one by one. "How is school going for all of you, by the way? Today was my first day."

"Starting our second week," Sam said, drumming his fingertips across the countertop as he watched her cook. "It's alright, I guess. The playground at recess is way better than the one at the park."

"No, it's not," Nick retorted. "It totally sucks."

"It sucks," Joshua agreed.

"Did everyone like, totally freak out when they saw you?" Aiden asked Tabitha with a fair amount of anticipation. "At school."

"No—why would they?" Tabitha laughed, giving him a strange look over the counter.

"You're like, totally different!" Aiden exclaimed indignantly. "You were fat and boring, and now you're like, uh... it's like from the ugly duckling to a ha—uh, the swan, you know?"

"They do treat me differently," Tabitha mused. "I'm not really sure what to make of that, yet. The reaction you were hoping for wasn't going to happen, though."

"What? Why not?"

"Because no one cared who I was, or even ever noticed," Tabitha said, pressing the medallions down onto the skillet with her tongs until they sizzled loudly. "When you're fat, ugly, poor, or you're fat, or smell bad, have no confidence, aren't attractive, when you're *fat*—"

"You're saying 'fat' more than once," Sam pointed out.

"As I should," Tabitha muttered. "My point is—no one ever cared about me, and that hurt. Deeply. I can deal with not having close friends. I'm... I'm used to it. But when *no one* cares about you, when you go to school with a concussion and no one gives a damn, when you realize no one will miss you when you're gone, fuck, no one *would even notice...*"

The boys exchanged glances before finally looking back at Tabitha, but none of them interrupted her.

"Sorry. Well. It starts to really affect you. Now that I've changed, people are actually just first starting to notice me. It's still shallow—I know it's an appearances thing, that it doesn't have any real meaning... but it's a start."

"*I* think you're really cool," Joshua said helpfully. "You can do flips, and wall-walk and stuff. And, you always play with us. Aren't we like your friends?"

"Hah, you are *not* my friends." Tabitha chuckled, starting to flip the medallions. "You're my cousins—you're family. You're friends I can't get rid of, even if I want to."

7

THE GOBLIN ARTIST

To her surprise, Alicia found that not only did Tabitha remember their conversation, the redheaded school belle of Springington High actively sought her out during lunch period the very next day. She was wearing another gorgeous top, this time an asymmetrical light blue blouse with only one shoulder—the neckline scooped down under her right arm at a diagonal over her chest, decorated with flowered white embroidery.

"Alicia! I'm Tabitha. I'm not sure if you remember me, from yesterday?" Tabitha began, standing hopefully beside the lunch table Alicia was sitting at.

"Uh... yeah, I remember," Alicia said. Against her better judgment, she courteously moved her backpack off of the adjacent chair so Tabitha could sit down. *Are you being sarcastic with me? Take a glance around. There's like a dozen guys scoping you out right now.*

"Oh, thank you," Tabitha said, taking a seat beside her.

"Can I ask where you got that shirt?" Alicia blurted out before she could help herself. *Stupid, stupid. Probably some rich white girl boutique at the mall.*

"This?" Tabitha looked down at her chest in surprise. "It's a bridesmaid gown. My grandmother and I've been pulling apart dresses from Salvation Army. We turn them into blouses like this. Everything beneath the bust was cut off of this one, and then split it into sections. That way, we could still use the trim of the dress as the shirt hem. Here, like this."

Tabitha leaned back in her seat and held out the hem of her shirt so that Alicia could see that same embroidered floral design circled the girl at the bottom.

"Wait—did you say you got this from Salvation Army?"

"Yes." Tabitha gave her a knowing smile. "I think there were still two more of the matching bridesmaids dresses up on the racks there too. Seven dollars each."

"Seven dollars...?!"

"Did you happen to bring any of your artwork today?"

"Yeah," Alicia admitted, pulling a small portfolio out of her bag. "Here."

I had my sketchbook with me yesterday too. I just... didn't think you actually wanted to see it.

Carefully opening the faux-leather portfolio, Tabitha laid it out and began examining each of Alicia's best drawings. After a few moments of study, the redhead set a notebook on the lunch table beside the portfolio—and began taking notes. The girl steadily made her way page by page through Alicia's artwork, carefully flipping each of the plastic-sheathed drawings and then jotting down a series of thoughts.

The hell? Alicia had been drawing for most of her life, and she knew she was talented. She'd proudly shown off her burgeoning collection of finished pieces dozens of times, and almost always, she got the same sort of responses from people. *Ooohs* and *aaahs*, some smiles, and then some politely-worded praise or expectations for her bright future. That was what Alicia expected when she'd presented the portfolio here; for the girl to flatter her and otherwise tell her how *gosh darn impressed* she was.

Instead, the lovely girl was staring at each of her drawings one by one with a strange sort of intense focus, as if she was *looking for something,* something in particular. Tabitha was so intent on the drawings, in fact, she seemed to have lost track of everything around her. In that moment, Alicia Brooks found the strange urge to do a quick sketch of this girl's expression. *It's like she's looking THROUGH the drawing, trying to make out something more. She's peering into the abyss.*

In any case, Tabitha seemed to be finding plenty, and Alicia couldn't help but peer over the girl's shoulder to see what she was writing.

5, figure study, female
    excellent posture
    good expression
    shaded, uses same light source as previous figure studies!
    no background
    6, figure study, female
    ¾ angle view
    excellent cloth detail!
    no expression
    shaded, uses same light source again
    background: vanishing point and line
    7, figure study, partial female
    face and hands
    size difference implies depth of field!
    excellent expression
    shading uses same light source again
    no background

"Uh... what are you doing?" Alicia couldn't help but ask. "Were you assigned to do critiques for some class...?"

"Oh! No, I'm so sorry," Tabitha hastily apologized. "Your work's phenomenal! I wanted to remember a few of these for reference later on. Do you have copies of any of these?"

"Look, what do you want me to draw?" Alicia asked, still bewildered. "You don't have to say all that. I can do whatever it is you want drawn, when I have some time. I've been in kind of a slump anyways, haven't had inspiration."

"I want you to draw..." Tabitha hesitated, giving Alicia a guilty look. "Many, many things. I'm preparing a large project, and I need a lot of help."

"A school project?"

"More of... a life project. I'd like to propose a partnership," Tabitha announced, settling a thick binder on top of her notebook. "In a project I've been planning for... some time now."

"Uh." Alicia blinked. "Okay."

"May I go on?"

"Yeah. Sure."

"I've been preparing material that I'll be writing into a fantasy story. It has a unique setting, and I have many, *many* ideas... but I want to collaborate with a capable artist, to help realize and improve upon all of them."

"You're writing a book. And you want... concept art?"

"It may not have to be limited to just a novel. Illustrations could become storyboards, for an animated project, or even a film someday."

"Okay."

"Okay? You're interested?"

"Um. No, I don't know yet. I mean, okay; keep talking."

"Alright, my first project is called *Goblina*. In the story, everyone has magic, but everyone who isn't able to *use* magic becomes deformed by it. They're considered goblins, and either cast out of society to live like savages, or they become slaves and servants. If you're a goblin, there's no way to escape a life of servitude and total inferiority, no way to oppose the Magi."

"Right. Magi. So, obviously, your story is *actually* about someone opposing and then overcoming them," Alicia deduced.

"Exactly!" Tabitha beamed. "It's the most suggestive theme I can sell to a young adult audience. I want to use allegory to illustrate the struggle of taking that final step of personal growth out of your parents' influence to stand on your own as a person."

"Uh... wow," Alicia admitted.

"Is it no good?"

"No, it's just—that's a lot to take in, all at once," Alicia said, not wanting to admit she didn't know exactly what 'allegory' meant. *I know what ALLEGATION means, thanks to dear old President Clinton, but...*

"Yeah, it's... more and more complicated, the deeper you get into it," Tabitha admitted, patting the binder full of notes she'd organized with a guilty look. "I have pages and pages of rules on how magic works, and the way the Mage's society and culture fits together, and... a lot of other things.

"Oh! I'm not going to dump all of the exposition on the reader like that, though," Tabitha assured her.

"Our protagonist will be the lowest of the low—beneath the slaves, even. Everyone refers to her as a goblin. She starts with nothing, and we learn bits and pieces of everything along the way as she does. By the end, clever readers will be able to piece it all together, but it should still be a compelling story, even for those who don't."

"Okay, the main character. She's a goblin?" Alicia asked, trying to figure out what Tabitha wanted drawn. "What's she like?"

"She's me," Tabitha said, giving Alicia a slightly embarrassed look. "She's, uh. She's always been me. I'm the goblin. I've always been the goblin."

"You're the goblin," Alicia repeated, giving the beautiful redhead an incredulous look. "In the story, you're the goblin, and you triumph over all these Magi?"

"I... I will," Tabitha gave her a strange look of resolve, for some reason, further confounding Alicia. "This time, I will for sure."

Sounds terrible. Alicia somehow stopped herself from making a face. *Like YOU of all people need some self-insert power fantasy, where you impress everyone and save the day.*

"It's neat and everything, but I'm probably gonna pass." Alicia turned her down as diplomatically as she could. "I'm not really into all that kind of stuff."

"Oh. I... yeah, that's fine. I totally understand. Would you want to... be friends, instead?" Tabitha asked, in what seemed a lot to Alicia like a shy voice. "I think it'd be really cool to hang out with someone my own age, for once."

Of course you don't hang out with people your age. For a moment, Alicia couldn't help but imagine this sophisticated-looking redhead climbing into the car of some college-age boyfriend that she surely had. Going to busy house parties, or bustling night-clubs, whatever it was girls like her did with their nights. *Are there even clubs anywhere near Springton?*

"I can't tell if you're messing with me or not," Alicia answered carefully.

"Messing with you?" Tabitha looked surprised. "No, I'm not. Not at all. Was it a weird thing to ask?"

"I don't know," Alicia answered honestly. "Why would you want to be friends with me?"

Is this part of your rich white girl fantasy, having a black friend as your little sidekick? I don't know you, I don't WANT to know you, and I'm not comfortable around girls that are like you.

"I feel like we could be... something like kindred spirits," Tabitha said. "Hometown heroes."

"Hometown heroes," Alicia repeated in disbelief. She'd had no idea what to expect from this conversation anymore, and found herself completely bewildered. "What does that even mean?"

"I don't know." Tabitha gave her a laugh and an exasperated shrug. "I never really knew. It means *us*, I guess?"

"Has anyone ever told you that you're an extremely strange individual?" Alicia asked, trying not to lose her cool. *Does she think her little quirky act is cute? Does it make all her normal friends laugh and fawn all over her?*

"No," Tabitha said, looking down. "I... um. Yeah, I shouldn't have said that. Sorry, that was a weird thing to say. If you ever want to talk, or hang out, or show me your drawings or anything, I hide myself in the library every lunch period. Corner table. Sorry for taking up your time."

"Yeah, bye," Alicia muttered to herself, watching Tabitha gather her things and get up from the table. *What the hell is her deal?*

I never bought in to high schools having that stereotypical social strata thing going on... but there are exceptions, and she definitely has to be one of them. Tabitha's the prom queen type, I'm sure she's gonna wind up head cheerleader or something—but she's pretending she's not. What's her sudden fixation with me? Why fantasy nonsense with magic and goblins? Does she think I'm a geek because I draw, or something?

———

"Tabitha Moore? Didja know they used to call her *Tubby Tabby?*"

Cheek resting in her palm, Alicia was gazing out the window, daydreaming, when she heard her classmates talking. It had been several days since that unusual talk with Tabitha, and she'd almost put it out of her mind. Snapping out of her reverie, Alicia glanced over at the other students. Three girls had turned away from the rest of the class and were caught up in their own conversation. Alicia turned her attention to her sketchbook, scribbling out a doodle as she listened in.

"Why, was she fat?"

"She was *so* fat. Apparently, she went and got lipo over the summer. I guess she used to be like, two hundred pounds heavier, back in middle school?"

"Two hundred pounds? *Christ.* Did she go to Springton Middle?"

"Nah, I think I heard it was Laurel. Carrie used to have class with her, she said Tabby was basically the class retard."

"Haha, *nice*. So, what, her parents bought her lipo and a nose-job? Damn, wish my parents were rich. Must be nice."

"Next time you see her, be all like, *how's it goin', Tubby Tabby?* Bet she hates that."

"She should've had them put all the fat they took out back into her boobs. I heard you can do that?"

"Damn, really? That's dumb of her, then, 'cause for how all high and mighty she's always acting, she's just *basic* now, you know? She's not all that."

"Well, you gotta consider she used to be all fat hog. I'd want all of the fat out for good too, if I was like that."

"Not me. I'd put it in my boobs."

"Betcha I know why she's nowhere to be seen 'round lunchtime. You know—she's gotta be all blueergh!"

"Hey, gotta keep the pounds off somehow, right? Haha."

"Bleeeurgh!"

Lunchtime? Alicia glanced up to see that one of the girls was leaning forward over her desk, miming a finger down her throat to induce vomiting. *Wasn't Tabitha supposedly hiding out in the library?*

"Cut it out, that's so gross. I heard when you do that, your breath's permanently like, *puke-breath*. Is it really so hard to just not eat garbage all the time?"

They were freshman girls, and Alicia wasn't particularly surprised to hear them being catty... but it did pique her curiosity once she realized they were talking about Tabitha. Which was fine. Alicia didn't particularly like that girl either. Oddly enough, though, there was no mention of Tabitha being eccentric, or pursuing strange interests—topics that Alicia felt would have bubbled to the surface of their gossip right away.

...Have any of these girls ever even spoken to Tabitha?

———

Later that day, Alicia found herself wandering away from the direction of the lunch line and over to the hall that led down toward the library. She wasn't *that* hungry, and the routine of waiting in line, getting her food, and finding a place to eat was starting to feel mechanical already, and they were still only in their first week of school.

Springton High's library center was large, the center area consisting of a small computer lab next to a series of long tables for students to sit at, which were flanked in all directions by tall rows of bookshelves. True to her word, Tabitha was hiding at the corner table behind a comical pile of books that had to be at over a foot high. The only other students in the library were a few kids playing *Oregon Trail* or solitaire on the computers.

"Oh, hi!" Tabitha seemed to light up upon seeing her come in, and she slid a small pile of books to the side and out of the way. "You came!"

There was something *off* between Tabitha's image and how she acted. She was putting off a friendly vibe, but it didn't quite have any of the confidence Alicia would have expected to it. With a twinge of guilt, Alicia had to wonder how many of the rumors flying around about this girl were based entirely on everyone's preconceptions.

"Hi," Alicia said, casually striding over. None of the books on the table looked like fantasy novels. "You really were hiding in here. Reading... uh... the *1996 Emergency Response Guidebook*? And, this here... Law enforcement field guide? *Practice and Procedure; the Police Operational Handbook?*"

"Er... yeah," Tabitha looked guilty. "I was doing a little bit of research."

"On what?" Alicia asked incredulously.

"If someone got hurt, and I had access to a police radio, I'll know how to call it in," Tabitha tried to explain. "You know. Just in case."

"...Wouldn't the police officer normally do that?" Alicia gave the girl a strange look. "I think they keep their radios like, on them. All the time. They have that little shoulder thing?"

"You're right." Tabitha winced. "That would be ideal, yes. Silly of me."

"Did you give up on your fantasy novel idea already?" Alicia asked. *She seems so... flighty? Maybe she just doesn't have a whole lot of common sense, and she latches on to these ideas of hers in a weird way. I think there's a name for people who're like that.*

"I... haven't given up," Tabitha said with some difficulty. "It's just. I can't focus lately. At all. There's too much going on."

"Like what?" Alicia slid out the chair opposite Tabitha, and decided to take a seat. *Hot white girl problems? All these people talking about you behind your back?*

"I think... no, I'm sure that my uncle is going to be sentenced to prison in the near future," Tabitha began. "His children—my cousins, I spend a lot of time with them, and I like to think they look up to me. I don't know what I can do for them, but at the same time, I can't stand standing by and doing nothing."

Huh, Alicia thought, surprised. *THAT certainly came out of nowhere.*

"Also... my mother and I haven't actually spoken to each other since the first day of school. We had an argument. I don't know what to do about that at all either. Then, there's this... uh. *Thing* happening, in October, and I can't stop stressing out over it."

"Wow," Alicia said, unsure of what else to say. *Definitely wasn't expecting all that.*

"But I'm not giving up on the story either," Tabitha affirmed, straightening up in her seat. "It's important to me too. I just haven't been making much real progress."

"Can I ask you a totally random question?" Alicia asked.

"Of course." Tabitha smiled.

"Is it true that you got liposuction over the summer?"

"No, it isn't." Tabitha chuckled. "Someone must have noticed my weight loss? I was a little over fifty pounds heavier earlier this same year."

"But you didn't get lipo?"

"Of course not," Tabitha answered. "Liposuction isn't for dramatic weight loss—it's more of a cosmetic surgery. They usually only remove about four to six pounds at any one time. Adjusting your eating habits is far more effective. As far as I know, there aren't any surgeons who'll accept patients for liposuction before they've finished puberty anyways, and regardless, I'm sure those procedures wouldn't be covered under my father's insurance."

"Oh," Alicia blinked. "Really?"

"Really. I changed my diet in a significant way," Tabitha said. "My summer was... extraordinarily active. I had to change, I really had to. I take it you've heard what they used to call me?"

"Yeah, I did hear about that." Alicia chuckled uneasily. "Girls can be mean, huh?"

"It wasn't hearing *Tubby Tabby* that hurt." Tabitha fidgeted with her tall stack of books, and then leaned forward to rest her chin on it. She didn't raise her eyes to meet Alicia. "Not that much. I was tubby, they were right about that. That was only the beginning, though. As time went on, someone started calling me... a goblin. More than that, I felt like they—well, a lot of people— actually began *treating* me like I wasn't even human anymore."

"Oh. *Oh,*" Alicia mouthed. "So, your story you're writing—"

"Yes." Tabitha nodded weakly. "Like I said, I'm the goblin."

That makes things a bit different now, doesn't it? Alicia thought to herself. At first, it felt a little too far-fetched for this knockout beauty to insist she was the goblin underdog. But, then again, she *was* holed up here in the library away from everyone else, and her white girl peers did seem to all be pretty rotten.

Laying her sketchpad on the library table, Alicia produced a pencil and drew a hasty rectangle, a little wider at the bottom than the top. The pile of books; she could pencil in the specifics later on.

Then, the oval of Tabitha's face, framed within a quick triangle that loosely represented shoulders slumping on either side.

Maybe Goblina or whatever could be kinda cool.

The drawing took definition inside those basic shapes as Alicia filled everything in with finer detail. Each subtle curl of her hair that fell over her face, the delicate curve of her eyebrow, the way her eyes seemed to tighten at some past memory, that slight, despondent turn that was the profile of her cheek down toward her lip... features scrawled into existence one by one with every steady flourish of Alicia's pencil.

"Ta-da," Alicia finally said, spinning her sketchbook around to face Tabitha and sliding it over. "There. I drew your goblin."

"She's... beautiful," Tabitha said, raising her head in surprise and then admiring it with a wistful smile. "It's so... somber. Almost tragic. I *wish* I looked like that."

"You do look like that," Alicia scoffed, taking her sketchbook back and comparing it to Tabitha again. "If I'm gonna be your concept artist, then you can't go dissing my artwork."

8

WHEN WHAT SHE DOESN'T
KNOW WILL HURT HER.

In Tabitha's first few weeks at school, she'd already begun to question her initial goals.

I knew, in an OBJECTIVE way, that simply being thin and pretty weren't all it took to make a bunch of friends. But I guess it really is completely different when you're experiencing it firsthand.

She realized now that in her past life, she'd associated all of her high school problems with her low-self-esteem and poor body image. Subconsciously, some part of her had attributed her past life's social estrangement and loneliness entirely to her weight and appearance—but several weeks into school, she'd only made one friend this time.

She'd somehow thought she would easily make friends, become more *important*, somehow; a component of the school's social paradigm. People would think about her, care about her, worry about her when she wasn't around. She recognized that it wouldn't be *that* straightforward, but the actual brutal truth of just how naive her line of thinking had been was disconcerting.

Even the positive attention was difficult to bear. It wasn't uncommon to catch a guy guiltily looking away from her breasts, which was an awkward situation she'd failed to mentally prepare herself for. *How does anyone prepare for that?*

Contrary to her expectations—or lack thereof—when her fat receded over the summer, teenage breasts emerged. This was, in some ways, Tabitha's first 'real' experience as a budding young woman. Her breasts weren't large—they were rather small B-cups, but because they stood out on her frame in a way she'd never experienced before, it was hard not to be self-conscious about them. She'd expected them to disappear with her weight and be unnoticeable—that was what had happened in her past life. No, they weren't the dream boobs that could form perfect cleavage like every girl wished for. But Tabitha thought they made pretty good shapes, and found herself a little proud of them.

"Yeah? Well, I heard she sucks a looot of dick," one of the nearby girls in her Biology class chuckled loud enough—purposely so—for Tabitha to overhear. This group of gossiping teenage girls were all sitting sideways in their seats partway across the class-room, with their backs to her. One of the less bright ones kept sneaking unsubtle peeks over at Tabitha.

"Nuh-uh, no you didn't," another freshman girl said—but in a goading tone, rather than a voice suggesting actual disbelief. "Who said that?"

"Fuckin' everybody *I've* talked to," the first girl replied. "Hey, you know where she's from... right?"

Stifling a wry smile, Tabitha ignored them, continuing to half-heartedly fill out her homework in advance.

She knew the loudly gossiping girls were inexpertly baiting her for a reaction, hoping to find a guilty conscience. A series of sexy rumors about her was making another round throughout Springton High, but she couldn't help but regard them with more amusement than annoyance. From the bits and pieces she'd over-heard, they may as well have been primitive precursors to clickbait media of the future: *These girls were STUNNED when they heard these seven secrets that TABITHA MOORE doesn't want you to know!*

As absurd and surreal as the whirlwind melodrama of high school politics seemed to her, she was *involved* this time, by apparent virtue of her appearance and persona alone. As the social strata among their freshman year solidified and matured, she discovered being a rogue attractive entity outside of the traditional cliques made many of Springton's upper echelon hostile by default.

I'm impressed, more than anything, Tabitha thought to herself, resting her chin on her knuckle as she reviewed her Biology questions.

While her fellow high school girls were without a doubt petty, they were in no way simple. Rather than a straightforward teen-movie hierarchy one could label *the queens of Springton High,* these girls were mapping out a full-fledged geopolitical landscape based somehow on popularity. A proving-ground arena, complete with power plays, counterintelligence operations, third-party negotiations, and of course—sabotage smear campaigns. Tabitha found herself approached more than once by what she began to think of as *investigatory commissions,* rigidly smiling parties asking which guy she was interested in, and what she thought of Heather, or Melissa, or Cassidy.

Tabitha's ignorance as to exactly *who* any of those girls were was treated as feigned indifference at best, and open provocation at worst. Tabitha's public stance on relationships—'I'm not interested in dating right now,'—was likewise treated with suspicion. Was she posturing in an attempt to inflate her own market value? Which of the Springton guys *did* she have her sights set on? Or, was the *other* buzz about her true? Was she a total lesbian?

Tabitha was an oddity; well-known by everyone, but not 'popular.' Spoken to her face, she was treated on friendly terms—for now—but never befriended. Because she didn't jump to make connections and associations, she remained an unknown—there was apparently no one to vouch for her, no one who knew for sure *what she was saying,* or about who, or *who she was after,* guy-wise.

Tabitha was, potentially, a high-value *girl that all the guys want* —in other words, an active threat, equal parts comparison and competition. She was an unwelcome complication for the many girls staking their claims on boys, the girls affirming their positions and affiliations—which girls they were besties with, which of them were trashy fucking whores that *if she gives me any shit, I'll flip the fuck out on her, swear to God!*

As if any of it actually matters, Tabitha mused, wanting to roll her eyes.

"Don't you think it's *weird* how nobody knows where she disappears to during lunch period?"

"Uh, *duh,*" another girl retorted. "She's fooling around with Mr. Simmons. He gives all his other Marine Sci classes a grade curve *except* the one I'm in with her. He even basically came out and told us she was his little beau; he waved around her test in our faces for like, twenty minutes."

"That's so fucking gross," a girl said, a little more loudly this time. "What a dirty old creep. I did wonder why I never see her around lunchtime."

"Pfft. Sure hope she *enjoys her lunch* today."

"Big ol' lunch."

"Ewww, I hope she brushes her teeth afterwards, like, gargles soap or something. Bet you can smell it on her breath afterwards."

"Oh my God shut up, I'm going to puke!"

"Geez, chill. Just offer her some gum or something." A girl laughed. "Maybe a tic tac?"

I'm... in the library every lunch period, though? Tabitha barely held herself back from turning and giving them a look of consternation. *It's not exactly a big vanishing act. There's plenty of other kids in the library for lunch that see me there all the time. Isn't there?*

———

Her time spent during lunch was turning a little more desperate each day, and a pressing *grim* feeling came down on her as she pushed open the school library's double-doors and walked through the metal detector. As usual, the computer lab there was full of students playing primitive computer games, but today, Tabitha made a point to make eye contact and compose a friendly smile for one or two of them.

They'll eventually notice that I'm always in here for lunch. Right?

Her normal corner table was vacant as usual, and even untouched—none of the books she'd collected there yesterday had been removed and put back on shelves. Having exhausted all of her other ideas, Tabitha was finally assuming a worst-case scenario in her current topic of study. She was now reading up on how to field dress gunshot wounds.

A hopefully not-too-dated ATLS—Advanced Trauma Life Support—protocol guidebook rest atop a small mountain of related material on field dressing wounds in emergencies, all heaped upon her familiar library table. Springton High's librarian, endlessly enthusiastic to help an eager young learner find sources of reference, had been sure yesterday that Tabitha was interested in prepping for medical school.

That would be the smart move, after all. Tabitha frowned, feeling her insides churn as she found her bookmark in the medical texts. *Lots of money in it, excellent career choice. It's just so... Ugh. So GRISLY...*

A severe bullet wound wasn't simple, and no amount of cram-studying was giving Tabitha any optimism for the upcoming situation. It was going to be bad—*of course* it was going to be bad. Last time through, the man had died. *Fatal gunshot wound.* Death. The horrifying thought that when worst came to worse, it could be *her* hands desperately trying to staunch the man's bleeding threw her into a panic.

She didn't remember hearing anything about a rifle, so she assumed the wound would be from a handgun—low-velocity ballistic trauma, in other words. Not that any of the knowledge related to that she was learning made things particularly any easier on her. Tabitha was supposed to very rapidly assess where the bullet penetrated and what specific dangers it posed, and then take the most correct action she could. But even narrowing it down to assume a chest or abdominal entry wound had Tabitha's hands shaking as she imagined *actually* being there and witnessing it all unfold. Because it was really going to happen, and dreadfully soon.

There's going to be a LOT of blood. And, I'm obviously going to have to be actively trying to stop the flow. Somehow. Tabitha grimaced, flipping into the sections of different respiratory compromise. *But what if it hits a lung? Maybe I'll stop up the blood loss—and then he ends up drowning in his own blood instead.*

Back then in her first life, she'd been watching TV when she heard the gunshot echo across her neighborhood. Specifics, like exact time of day, the officer's name, and precisely where he'd been shot, however, continued to elude her. *If I could just remember what freaking show I was watching at the time! Then I'd be able to match it up in the TV guide... aggh!*

Unfortunately, she *didn't* remember, not for sure—and the more she tried, the less sure of anything she was, progressively becoming less and less confident in any of the details she thought she knew. *The future never seems quite so nebulous as it does when you start second-guessing yourself.*

Did the bullet pass through too close to an artery? Did it fragment? The crux of the issue was that Tabitha didn't know *why* the police officer had bled out. *Was the call for emergency services immediate, or was there a significant delay?*

It wouldn't be as easy as simply tapping 911 into a bracelet PC or smartphone for another few decades, and she knew for a fact that several of their neighbors in the trailer park didn't even have landlines. *IF the cop was too incapacitated to radio in, IF there was never another officer in his squad car, IF no one in the Lower Park called the emergency dispatcher right away, if, if, if, if...*

There was also the sobering idea that nothing Tabitha might attempt would ever save the man. Maybe he was fated to die no matter what she did, and causality was locked in certain ways beyond her understanding. Unchangeable. *Would I regret getting myself involved, then, or would I once again begin to despise the hidden powers-that-be?*

I hate how much this terrifies me, Tabitha admitted to herself. *I don't want to form some sort of God complex, thinking I can do anything and save anyone. But, at the same time... I'll hate myself a little—maybe more than a little—if I know this is going to happen and remain indifferent to it.*

"Hey," Alicia interrupted her thoughts, giving a small wave to get Tabitha's attention. "You alright?"

"Alright?" Tabitha blinked, wondering when Alicia'd come in. Her only real friend at Springton usually didn't stop by to chat with her until after she'd eaten, but this was the first time she hadn't noticed the dark-skinned girl enter the library.

"Yeah. You look kinda... uh. You know." Alicia shrugged, pulling out the opposite chair and dropping her sketchbook onto the table beside the stacks of books. "Are they starting to get to you?"

"They? No, no." Tabitha shook her head with a chuckle. "No, fine. I'm just... stressed."

"Uhhh." Alicia's eyes went wide as she snatched an annotated military field dressing guidebook off of the pile nearest her. "...You wanna talk about it?"

"And how's school goin', sweetie?" Mr. Moore asked, punching his fork through the romaine and chicken of his salad.

Tabitha's high school debut and her first few weeks at

Springton High had come and gone with what seemed like little
fanfare. Whatever it was she felt like she expected didn't seem to
be happening. No sword of Damocles had descended to put an end
to her cheat-like second try at being a teenager, but nor was she
universally well-loved by everyone, like she'd idly fantasized about
while on her morning jogs.

And that's okay. Her staggering routine of waking up before
dawn to run, cleaning herself up before school, researching for the
future, and coming home to practice Taekwondo forms, and finally
make dinner for her family *should* have seemed a near-impossible
burden. *It's rough sometimes, but once I got into the swing of it, I can
manage. For now.*

Although the man ate with typical aplomb, Tabitha could tell
her father still wasn't enthusiastic about eating salads, despite the
extra effort she had put into this one. It was a grilled chicken fajita
salad, and his portion in particular was more slabs of chicken and
pepper slices than it was traditional greens. The chicken's marinade doubled as dressing, and with as liberally as it was applied,
Tabitha was forced to concede that the dish might no longer be
particularly healthy.

"Perfect," Mrs. Moore spoke without looking up, stabbing and
picking at her own meal in a petulant way. "She's doing perfect.
Perfect at everything."

"...I'm doing well," Tabitha said carefully. "Certainly not
perfect, but—"

"Nonsense," Mrs. Moore snorted. "You're just perfect at everything, aren't you?"

"I'm only human," Tabitha decided to say. "I make mistakes."

"Oh? *Well.* I'd sure like to see that," Mrs. Moore's fork clanked
against her dish a little louder than necessary, and flecks of marinade dotted the table.

"As you please. I'll endeavor to restrain my academic
perform—"

"What's goin' on, here?" Mr. Moore interrupted, a steely edge to his voice. "Does one of you wanna explain to me what this is all about? Honey?"

"Well, I think everything's just fine," Mrs. Moore replied flippantly. "We're all just perfect here. Aren't we, Tabitha?"

"*Honey.*"

"Please excuse me," Tabitha stood up mechanically. "I'm afraid I've had sufficient—"

"No. Sit down," her father commanded, pointing toward her. "Both of you are gonna sit right there, look me in the eye, and tell me what all this is about."

"Oh, I don't whatsoever comprehend what you mean," Mrs. Moore said in mocking imitation of her daughter's manner of speech. "Pray tell if—"

"This isn't the—" Tabitha began.

"Oh, did I pronounce something wrong? I'm so sorry; don't be shy about correcting me, dear."

"Both of you, *stop!*" Mr. Moore raised his voice in aggravation, shoving his plate toward the center of the table. "Goddamn. I mean it, what the hell is this? Tabitha?"

"...I apologize," Tabitha said. She clamped her mouth shut resolutely and stared off at their fading wallpaper, saying nothing more.

"You apologize," Mr. Moore repeated sternly. "For? You apologize for what, exactly?"

"My mother's immature behavior." Tabitha gave Mrs. Moore a sidelong glance. To her own surprise, she *did* feel responsible for the way her mother was acting. She'd hoped the small breakdown the woman had experienced after that first day of school would be a watershed moment—a sign that things were on the cusp of change between them.

"*Excuse me?*" Mrs. Moore roared. "My *what?*"

If only things could be that simple. Tabitha gritted her teeth. Instead, it seemed now that the moment back then had been nothing more than a tantrum. Her mother was just as irritable and on-edge as before, perhaps more so. She was volatile now, in a way that suggested the woman was indeed coming to understand the source of her own deep-rooted issues—but that it was only unhinging her more and more.

"Enough!" Alan Moore stood up.

He looked angry now, angry in a way Tabitha hadn't witnessed since seeing him lay into the hospital technicians at Emsie St. Juarez, and she found herself shrinking back in her seat. She'd remembered her father annoyed and frustrated throughout her childhood, but never *angry* like this. From her memory, he was a simple and stoic man, whose laidback attitude was perhaps in part responsible for how unruly his wife became.

"Whatever this is? You two better bury it, right now." Mr. Moore swiped his plate of food off of the table in a single violent gesture, sending it against the wall of their living room with a loud *crack,* making both Tabitha and Mrs. Moore flinch.

"I don't care how you do it. You two put everything on the table right now and figure it out. Both of you. Sort this shit out, and put it behind you. For good."

Then he turned and left, striding down the hall to the master bedroom. Mother and daughter alike were stunned silent by what had just happened, and locked eyes with trepidation for a moment before their gazes seemed to repel one another and they looked anywhere else.

"Sorry," Tabitha said quietly, rising out of her seat. *This IS my fault too—I know it is, because nothing like this ever happened in the other life.*

The thought weighed on her. Salad that would have been her father's dinner was all over the floor, and the fajita dressing was sure to stain their worn carpet if she didn't act quickly. To Tabitha's surprise and dismay—she found that the plate had broken.

This is—this is wrong. This plate isn't supposed to break, Tabitha held the dish up in disbelief. She recognized it, because it was one of *her* old plates. Cream-colored ceramic, with a pink floral motif adorning one corner—one of the pieces of tableware she would inherit eventually. It would have been part of her mismatched collection of tableware all throughout college, a familiar, even *sentimental* thing that she still used in regular rotation right up into her sixties. Now it was in two uneven pieces, and would not be joining her on her life journey this time.

Because everything's changing, Tabitha realized, feeling a little shaken. *Things are breaking. It was never like this for them. Daddy never did anything like that. My mother and I never butted heads like this. Everything's way, WAY off course.*

Anything can happen. There aren't any guarantees from last time, Tabitha thought, trying to stop her fingers from shaking as she picked pieces of lettuce off the floor. The new future, which had seemed bright with infinite possibilities for her, also had this darkness of the unknown to it—Tabitha had so focused herself on climbing to new heights that she'd refused to see the depths those heights created.

Knowing that tonight's exchange came about from her actions *terrified her.* She felt smaller, *diminished,* in seeing what she was doing to their family. *Even when I'm trying to make things better, some other things are just going to get worse instead. That's just life. But... is this how it's supposed to be? Or was last life how things should have been?*

———

Sorry. Unlike her daughter, Shannon Moore wasn't able to say it out loud. Her own temper got the best of her, like it always did. Those imperturbable calm eyes and that collected way her Tabitha held herself got deep under her skin, yet again. *I WAS acting like a child. I still am.*

Worse yet, she knew what stress her husband was going through right now. With his brother Danny arrested this past weekend, their entire extended family was in turmoil. They hadn't told Tabitha yet—Alan still wanted them to sit down and explain to her what was happening and what it all meant.

That hadn't happened, only because Shannon was dragging her feet about it. Sitting down and attempting a heart-to-heart with that know-it-all pretty little face was the last thing she could do right now. The very thought of her daughter's lovely but guarded expression evoked undisguised self-loathing and malice that bubbled to the surface like a sickness.

You think that's how easy it is? That's all it takes to become an actress? Mrs. Moore frowned, absentmindedly watching her daughter take the initiative to clean up spots of marinade with the kitchen stash of fast-food napkins. Even facing away from her and crouching down, Tabitha somehow affected a grace to her posture that might as well have been directly mocking her. *You have no idea how hard it is, or what a toll it will take. You're young. You think you know everything, but you have no idea, Tabitha.*

Everyone told me having a daughter would be worse. Mrs. Moore turned and glared angrily at the grilled chicken fajita salad in front of her. She was so hungry that it ached, so furious and ashamed and nauseous all at once that she wanted to throw up. *I never believed them. I never WOULD have believed them 'til just a few months ago.*

The salad was delicious, and she hated salads. It wasn't normal food—there wasn't anything Tabitha made that was normal, period. Making dinner for the family took the girl almost an hour every day, and *that* wasn't normal. Everything they ate was amazing, took obvious effort to prepare, and was supposedly even healthy fare. Shannon hated it.

Somehow or other, this past summer, Tabitha had learned how to push all of her buttons. All of them at once; she pushed them and then held them down, until it felt like she was going berserk. Mother and teenage daughter; deadlocked in a futile struggle through every nuance of their interaction.

Even the guarded look Tabitha wore when she was in her presence was equivalent to a line drawn in the sand. The girl was working out the scheme of her overall life alone, and the very fact that she was at it alone, that it was all kept secret made it evident to her that she was not a part of that future. Changing everything around in their little trailer was the rebellious teen's way of trying to assert dominance, and taking up cooking for the family was a challenge; open provocation to Mrs. Moore's position to their family.

Shannon knew that Grandma Laurie must have been behind some of those attacks—because they were done without the subtlety of a thirteen-year-old girl, yet each and every one seemed to catch her completely off guard all the same. When had the grandmother and daughter even colluded to put all of this into action? None of it had made any sense—even with practice and instruction, the Tabitha *she thought she knew* wouldn't have the sheer drive to keep at something like this for more than a day or two. Certainly not for months on end like she had been. It didn't add up to Mrs. Moore at all.

Until she found out Tabitha had seen the little blue album, that is.

Mrs. Moore was watching her daughter again when Tabitha turned her head and looked over at her. That composed expression, the subtle smug look—weren't there.

Looking into Tabitha's eyes, she just looked lost and alone. Vulnerable. A hollow, defeated look on those familiar features, a look Mrs. Moore had seen exactly once before—staring at herself in the mirror some fourteen years ago when she'd discovered she was pregnant and the ignorant dreams she'd had for the future turned into smoke.

The revelation stung her, and she couldn't help but think that for so many years, Tabitha had followed in her own current image —soft-bodied and slothful. The girl's absurd transformation, this *look* in her eyes, it was like watching her own life play out in reverse. The redhead with the brilliant smile beaming out in those beauty pageant photos, the glamour shots she'd collected for her portfolio haunted her; they represented the future that would never be. Shannon felt further removed from her naive past self than she'd ever been, and it felt like the distance between her and her daughter was growing even further distant still.

"Tabitha, I..." Mrs. Moore began listlessly.

Her beautiful daughter went still at hearing her speak, however, and the look of caution settling into the young girl's expression might as well have been a door slamming closed in her face.

"Tabitha..."

9
BRINGING A FRIEND HOME FROM SCHOOL

"Uhhh. Is this the right stop?" Alicia hesitated on the steps off of the school bus. She'd been chatting with Tabitha about designs for her goblin story and somehow entirely lost track of the surroundings passing by the bus windows outside.

"Yep, this is our stop," Tabitha confirmed, waving Alicia forward with an excited smile.

"This... is a trailer park," Alicia pointed out, uneasily stepping down from the school bus.

It wasn't a nice-looking trailer park either. Alicia had an aunt that lived in a mobile home lot in Georgia, but those ones were all new homes, painted uniformly and arranged neatly onto their picture-perfect manicured little lawns. *This* lot that Tabitha had taken her to was as close as Springton had to a ghetto, the sort of slummy, broken-down place that spoke of a lifetime of mistakes.

Dilapidated trailers were packed together in claustrophobic rows, stretching on down the hill behind a gas station and a liquor store. Garbage was everywhere; discarded trash, sagging water-logged fast food cartons and cups, unidentifiable broken pieces of plastic, and rusting metal parts littered the sides of street. Lawns consisting of clumps of weeds seemed popular, while bare, sunbaked dirt patches scattered with cigarette butts and gravel were also apparently in vogue in this neighborhood.

The trailers themselves were obviously, *visibly* run-down. Some had doors boarded up with plywood already black with mold, others sported roofs covered with tarps or trash bags. Broken glass in windows, with duct tape applied haphazardly across the spiderweb of cracks. There were trailers with sagging paneling, trailers filthy with grime, and even an abandoned, gutted one that looked like it had become a playhouse for neighborhood kids. Or possibly drug addicts.

"You... live in a trailer park?" Alicia asked, turning to cast a doubtful look in Tabitha's direction.

"Surprised?" Tabitha gave her a knowing smile.

"Yeah. I mean, kinda." Alicia took another look around. "You're for real? Not messing around?"

"Oh, c'mon, it's not *that* bad," Tabitha teased. "Now hurry up, let's get inside—I don't wanna get mugged today."

"Har, har." Alicia gave her a sarcastic snort. She stopped in place a moment later, giving Tabitha an unsure look. "...Has anyone here ever actually mugged you?"

"Of course not." Tabitha laughed. "I've lived here my whole life —well, *sorta,* anyways—so everyone here already knows I'm dirt poor. I don't have anything worth taking."

"Um. You're still *a pretty young lady,* though... you know?" Alicia said in a pointed tone. *Be a little self-aware of what could happen to you, please? Mom might not even want to drive in here to pick me up. This whole place screams all kinds of bad news.*

"Damn, you're right," Tabitha said sheepishly, and the redhead smacked her forehead into her palm. "I keep forgetting about that."

"Please be careful." Alicia let out a nervous chuckle as she looked around, not sure if they were joking or not.

"Yeah, no kidding." Tabitha nodded. "Hah. C'mon, this way."

Still. Dirt poor, huh? Thumbs hooked into the straps of her backpack, Alicia couldn't help but reevaluate Tabitha as she followed the redhead down the narrow lane between the rows of trailers. Nothing at all she thought she knew about the girl had ever hinted that Tabitha grew up in *this* sort of poverty. *The most beautiful white girl in all of Springton High comes home every day... to THIS? This is the rest of her life?*

"Here we are," Tabitha said, heading up the steps of a rather nondescript trailer.

...Huh. It looked as shabby as the others, and Alicia awkwardly wondered if she was expected to remark on how nice it was, make some sort of polite observation. Unable to think of anything to say, Alicia pressed her lips into the thin line of a forced smile and followed her friend up the concrete steps and into the worn-down mobile home.

"Dad? Mother? As we discussed yesterday, I've brought a friend home with me from school," Tabitha announced. "Her name is Alicia Brooks. Please treat her respectfully, and make her feel at home."

That's... a weird way to phrase it? Alicia tried not to feel on edge. *'As we discussed?'*

The interior of the double-wide wasn't as bad as Alicia feared. Their living room was a neat, tidy area, without any of the cluttered furnishings or mess she'd expected. Worn but well-cared-for furniture, sparse but tasteful decor, a recently cleaned carpet, and wide-open window views gave the illusion of having a much larger open space.

Tabitha's parents were both home today and sitting around the TV—an older man with a forgettable face who looked like a blue-collar extra in a movie, and a fat, rather unfriendly-looking wife.

"Hi." Alicia gave Mr. and Mrs. Moore a meek wave. *Oh shit. I thought they would seem more like Tabitha, or something. They look like... generic rednecks? Racist maybe? Is my skin color gonna be a weird issue?*

"Nice to meet you, Alicia." The father got up out of his seat to shake her hand.

"Hello." Mrs. Moore didn't rise out of her seat on the sofa, instead giving Alicia a lingering glance before turning to give Tabitha a scathing look.

Oh shit. Oh shit.

"Here," Tabitha called, pulling two chairs out at their dining room table. "I'm sorry there aren't more places to sit. Would you like anything to drink?"

"I'm good, thanks," Alicia said, placing her bag on the table and settling into the seat. Nothing about this visit had gone like she thought it would—she'd pictured a nice, upscale house in a suburb somewhere. Good-looking parents, maybe ones with some light-hearted sense of humor to help put their daughter's friend at ease and make her feel more welcome. *Why can't anything ever be like it is on TV?*

Mr. Moore returned to his chair, and the trailer went quiet.

"I, uh, I read through that whole masonry book you gave me last night," Alicia spoke up. Even if tense silence was situation normal for this family, it felt incredibly straining on her as their guest. "*Art of the Stonemason.* Well, kinda. I definitely didn't *read* any of it, but I studied all the diagrams and everything."

"Oh?" Tabitha's eyes lit up with interest. "Was it helpful at all?"

"Oh my God, yes." Alicia nodded emphatically. "I was... well, you know. I draw people and expressions mostly. I was never interested in drawing walls—until now.

"If slaves are doing all the actual labor, they wouldn't have the, uh, *modern,* perfectly-squared off bricks that fit all nicely together. They'd have to take each random rock, chip away all the weak parts, protrusions or what-have-you, and then fit all these different-sized pieces together somehow with mortar so that it's structurally sound.

"There's so many aspects I'd have never even thought about 'til going through that book. Thinking about it in terms of structure, figuring abutments, springers, and a keystone when you form stone arches—and you're gonna want arches—thinking about using longer stones as corbels to support weight, that kinda thing. Here, look at my new doodles," Alicia said, opening up her current sketchpad and sliding it across the table.

"These are amazing," Tabitha praised, tracing her fingers along the paper with reverence. "They look so much more... *real*."

"Right? That book really helped me start thinking of each piece as its own three-dimensional thing. Like, it's made of all of these mismatched components, but everything still fits together in a certain special way. Matching up rubble with uneven joins so that they're all in their courses, spacing out what they call perpend stones, or through-stones, to keep the pilings from shifting away from one another... there's so many little details that got put into stuff back then that you just don't see with boring cinderblock kinda stuff today—I never realized how cool this kinda thing would be to design and draw.

"I mean, I was always doing that generic, boring, *flat surface with overlapping rectangles* brick pattern for things 'til just last night, when I read through that book. Is there gonna be a whole lot of this kinda stuff in your story?"

"There is!" Tabitha nodded. "The second book will feature stone-working throughout its plot! The mages, they had their goblins build up these labyrinths around the leylines—labyrinths designed in a specific way, so that everything from the mana spring gets focused and channeled along onto this one singular, specific path.

"But the free goblins hide out there, break down some walls and build up others, messing everything up and turning the labyrinth into this huge, sprawling maze. So, not only do the mages have to deal with navigating this underground deathtrap full of rebel goblins, they have to figure out which exact walls to repair and which to tear down to restore the proper magic flow."

"I understand less an' less o' that conversation the more I over-hear," Tabitha's father commented, turning from his seat to give each of the girls a baffled look. "What's all this about goblins, now?"

"They're, you know—they're part of Tabitha's story?" Alicia tilted her head and gave the man a quizzical smile.

"Her what, now?" For some reason, he looked more confused than ever.

Does Tabitha never talk about her interests with them? Alicia looked from Tabitha to the girl's parents and back again, hoping she hadn't committed some sort of unknowing faux pas.

"Oh, um. Yes, I'm working on writing a novel," Tabitha admitted.

"*Hah.*" Tabitha's mother barked out a short, humorless laugh. "Of course she is."

Before anyone else could say anything, Mrs. Moore heaved herself up from the sofa and left the room, shaking her head and muttering under her breath. The woman had looked agitated to begin with, but Alicia couldn't piece together exactly what had happened, or what particular choice of words had suddenly set her off.

So—okay, what the hell? Alicia turned to her friend for answers, but all she saw was a conflicted look as Tabitha bit her lower lip in frustration.

"You're writing a story with goblins?" Mr. Moore sounded like this was news to him. "I tried reading that *Hobbit* book when I was 'round your age, but I couldn't make heads nor tails of it. That stuff sure is popular as all get out, though—fellow that wrote that must be a bigshot millionaire by now."

"That would be John Ronald Reuel Tolkien," Tabitha clarified in a wistful voice. "He passed away in 1973. I've been a longtime admirer of his work—I would kill to possess even *one-hundredth* of his talent."

"Huh... is that right?" Her father nodded, already distracting himself with the television in front of him again.

...Are these people actually even related to Tabitha? Alicia blinked in disbelief. *Is this really her family?* There didn't seem to be a single shared trait between them. While Alicia felt uncomfortably out of place in this weird, kinda messed-up situation, what struck her the most was that Tabitha seemed *even more* out of place.

"You're a very strange girl," Alicia blurted out before she could stop herself. *Ah, crap.*

"Oh?" Tabitha winced and gave her an apologetic smile. "Yeah... sorry."

"She sure is." Mr. Moore chuckled. "But we love 'er anyways."

Well, at least one of you does, Alicia thought, glancing over to the hallway Mrs. Moore had disappeared down.

"Um... anyways, I've been spending every day this month practicing martial arts, over in the empty area on the other end of the trailer park." Tabitha forcibly changed topics. "Do you want to come see?"

"You know martial arts?" Alicia asked, raising her eyebrows. She wasn't sure if any random new thing this girl said should surprise her anymore.

"Yes," Tabitha said, looking embarrassed. "I mean, I practice a little bit."

"Sounds like you're gonna be my volunteer model for whenever I need a cool action pose, then," Alicia decided, grinning and flipping her sketchbook to a fresh page. "Perfect, I've got my camera in my bag today too!"

———

A pair of teenage girls loitered around on an empty stretch of grass beside the parking spaces at the end of Lower Park mobile home lot. The first girl was pale, a fine-featured young lady with lovely red hair wearing an elaborate sleeveless blouse, while the second was a rather smart-looking dark-skinned young woman with glasses and her hair drawn up in a business-like bun.

"You promise you won't laugh?" Tabitha asked with a nervous expression.

"I promise nothing." Alicia gave her a snarky look. "C'mon— let's see it."

"Um... yeah, okay." Tabitha sighed. "The best *action pose* I think I can do for you is—well, it's called a butterfly kick. It's very... cinematic? But I'm not sure it will work for a static drawing. Maybe I can just run through like, one of the basic forms?"

"Well, let's see it!" Alicia prodded.

Alicia held her disposable camera against her face like a mask, turning it this way and that. Looking out at the world through the narrow viewfinder, she tried to imagine each of the rather stilted action scenes before her as a captured photo. It was a Kodak Max, a small but expensive contraption of black plastic and yellow cardboard, and almost all of the film within had already been spent on family beach photos. The handful of remaining shots, however, her mother had said that their young *artiste* could take however she pleased, because they were getting them developed soon.

She'd already taken a photo of herself earlier, in her artsiest getup and presenting what she hoped would be a mesmerizing look off into the distance, and when it was developed, she was going to use it to draw a glamorous self-portrait. Now, Alicia wanted a photo of Tabitha.

Super weird thing to just ask for outta the blue, though, Alicia thought, feeling guilty for some reason. She didn't want just any random picture of her strange school friend like this—she wanted the absolute BEST angle of her, one that captured Tabitha's surprisingly beautiful features in just the right way. A reference she could use, to portray the girl just the way she wanted for this big goblin project of hers. The idea was growing on her.

WOOP-WOOP!

The brief sound of a police car toggling his siren interrupted the teenagers, and they looked up in unison to see a white car being pulled over by a cop car across the empty stretch of grass from them. The lone driver being stopped cussed loudly, slamming his hand against the side of his steering wheel in frustration.

"Uh-oh—somebody's in trouble!" Alicia chuckled. The dark-skinned girl was looking over with interest when something strange about Tabitha's awkward stance had Alicia do a double-take.

"Y-yeah," Tabitha mumbled uneasily. The young woman had frozen up at the sight of the guy being pulled over, and when she abruptly turned away from them, she was wearing a rather strained smile.

What's this? Alicia arched an eyebrow at her friend. *Guilty conscience? Maybe there's some story there, or maybe she just gets real nervous around cops?* As an artist, she was a fair study of body language, and as Tabitha's friend, her intuition told her that something had her friend very ill-at-ease. There was raw apprehension there, a strained sort of jittery look, as if Tabitha was clenching her jaw.

"Uh, sorry. Someone you know?" Alicia asked, looking back over as the police officer got out of his car and sauntered up to lean over the window of the man he'd pulled over.

"No. I—um. No," Tabitha said distractedly, stealing a glance over in their direction herself.

The cop was asking the man to step outside of his vehicle. When the door opened, the guy stepping out had a narrow face and sharp, angular features. He had short, messy hair, wore a distinctly unwashed-looking shirt, a pair of gym shorts, and no shoes at all. Tabitha quickly looked away.

Okay...? Lately, something had been weighing heavily on Alicia's strange school friend. Each day in class or at lunch, Tabitha seemed progressively more high-strung and on edge. Despite both subtle prodding and even direct interrogation, the girl wouldn't reveal why.

Well. I can make plenty of guesses, Alicia mused, quirking her lip. *Maybe it's a boy I don't know about? And then there's her weird family thing she has going on. Also, sure, she says it doesn't bother her, but all the things those girls at school keep saying about—*

A thundering *crack* sounded out, impossibly loud, louder than anything Alicia remembered hearing before, and she flinched in response, hunching her shoulders and wincing. It sounded like a gunshot from a movie or on TV, but at such an incredible, exaggerated volume that Alicia couldn't help but swear out loud. The dark-skinned girl whirled, searching for the source of the disturbance.

She looked just past Tabitha—who was also turning to see what had happened—to see the police officer collapsing backwards onto the ground on the median. The man he'd pulled over made a mad dash back to his car and he dove into the driver's seat, peeling out before he'd even gotten the door closed again after him. Seconds later, the white car was practically gone, quickly disappearing down the road and out of sight.

What. Was that? Alicia was still frozen in place, staring at the scene in shock when Tabitha bolted forward toward the downed police officer. That was when it hit her, and Alicia realized—the cop lying right there just a few dozen yards in front of them *had just been shot.* This wasn't something staged for a movie, or a game some kids were playing.

He just got shot!

In her stunned disbelief and confusion, she took a few hesitant steps after Tabitha before realizing she was still clutching her disposable camera in both hands, right in front of her. Realizing how stupid she was, missing this once-in-a-lifetime opportunity, Alicia hurriedly raised the camera up and snapped a quick shot.

Shit! Fuck! Alicia cursed to herself, realizing she hadn't been holding the thing steady. She tried immediately snapping another shot, but this time, there was no click. Staggering to a halt, she belatedly remembered to wind the film for the next shot and carefully brought the camera up again. *Damnit, Alicia, don't waste it...*

She took the photo just as the running Tabitha was reaching the police officer, and it looked like a pretty good picture. The subjects were a little too far away for it to be ideal, but Alicia didn't have any more time to think about shot composition—she quickly jammed the disposable camera into the back pocket of her jeans and rushed over toward them.

Oh my God...

The police officer was a clean-cut-looking man in his thirties with an old-fashioned taper haircut and rather rugged features that were just beginning to droop. A handsome man just a little past his prime, he looked like a stereotypical *Dad,* one that might have just walked off the set of some white family sitcom. Except, he was dying.

It wasn't poignant and serene, nor was it dramatic—something about the scene unfolding before her eyes was just so *real* that horror and instinctive revulsion rolled through her uncontrollably. His eyes were mostly closed and slightly fluttering, his body was jerking and slightly twisting as he struggled for consciousness, and she could see blood, a deep, dark wet spreading out across the dark blue of the man's uniform. She could smell it, even; a metallic, somehow sticky smell.

"... No, no, *no no no!*" Tabitha cried out, dropping down beside the officer. She snatched up the officer's handset from the man's belt, and her young voice rang out back to them from the radio within the nearby squad car. "Officer down! We have an officer down at 1322 South Main Street. He's shot, he's—he's bleeding everywhere."

There were several strained seconds of tense silence before a response crackled back over the radio.

"Hello, can you repeat that address?"

"Thirteen twenty-two South Main Street; it's the lower trailer park. One, three, two, two, South Main," Tabitha repeated, nervously stretching out a trembling hand above the policeman. "Lower trailer park."

"Help is on the way; they should be with you shortly. Is the shooter still at that location?" the dispatcher asked.

"No, he's—the shooter drove off," Tabitha answered. "I need, um, sorry, I have to stop the bleeding."

"Hold on, I need you to stay on the line," the dispatcher insisted. "Honey? I need you to stay with me on the line."

Ignoring the dispatcher, Tabitha tossed the radio to Alicia and scrambled back to the downed officer. Alicia caught the handset awkwardly in both hands, nearly fumbling the thing as Tabitha inhaled sharply through her nose and then clamped both palms right down into the man's blood-soaked chest in an effort to stem the bleeding.

"Are you still there?"

"Hello?" Alicia asked into the radio. She couldn't hear herself over the car radio like she had when Tabitha had spoken through it; she wasn't getting through. In a panic, she tried again, squeezing down one of the buttons on the side. "Hello? H-hello?"

"Hello, we have help on the way, but I need you to sit tight for me if you can do that. Has anyone else been hurt?"

"No," Alicia answered.

"Can you describe the shooter?"

"Caucasian male in his mid-twenties," Tabitha called over. "He was headed southbound on South Main, driving a white Lincoln Continental with West Virginia plates."

"Uh... uh... *what?*" Alicia froze as she looked over to see Tabitha pressing both hands firmly down to pin the officer to the pavement. Her hands were covered in blood, and blood had soaked a large swath down the side of the officer's uniform and onto the pavement. *How-how does she know what to—*

"Are you still there?" the police dispatcher asked.

"Th-the shooter was a white male, in his, uh, in his twenties," Alicia reported over the handset. "He was going, uh, he was—"

"Southbound on South Main, in a white Lincoln Continental with West Virginia plates," Tabitha said again. The slender girl sounded composed, but she was wearing an extremely grim expression as errant locks of red hair fell down across her face, not daring to take her eyes off of the wound she was clamping down on.

"Southbound on South Main, he's in—he's in a Lincoln Continental with West Virginia plates," Alicia blurted frantically into the receiver. "White, a white Lincoln Continental."

"That's southbound, in a white Lincoln Continental?" the dispatcher asked.

"Yes."

"Okay, thank you. Just sit tight, please; we have an ambulance on the way there to you now."

"Okay."

All at once and in several different directions, the town erupted into warbling siren wails, a cacophony of dogged noise. Alicia hadn't been sure if they would even be taken seriously with that *officer down*—after all, they were just teenage girls. It turned out, however, they were taken *extremely* seriously, as what must have been every police car in Springton seemed to immediately mobilize to full alert.

"You said the officer is bleeding?" the dispatcher returned.

"I'm—uhh. I'm gonna let you talk to her again," Alicia said, hurrying over to hold the radio up to Tabitha for her.

"I'm sorry, what was that?" the dispatcher asked amid a burst of static.

"We have an entry wound about an inch, inch-and-a-half left of his sternum," Tabitha reported, leaning toward the offered handset. "That's, um, my left, his right. He's still breathing, he's breathing in tiny little breaths. He's, uh. He's lost a lot of blood. I'm applying pressure, but he's lost a lot of blood."

"Okay, keep on applying pressure, please. Emergency medical is on the way."

"Whatever you're sending, send it faster," Tabitha insisted with an edge of urgency to her tone.

"Emergency medical is getting there as fast as they can. We just need you to stay calm and keep applying pressure to the wound."

Alicia saw Tabitha's form hunched over the officer's body blur as tears filled her vision. The initial stunned shock of the moment had abruptly worn off, and a whirlwind of emotion was suddenly overwhelming her. Clamping a hand over her mouth to stifle her sobs so as not to startle Tabitha, Alicia stood there rigidly beside the police car, looking across the horrific scene and crying.

Short moments later, the siren sounds drew painfully close and a vehicle flashing brilliant blue and red light screeched to a halt. To their disappointment, it was another cop car, rather than the much-desired ambulance. A uniformed police officer jumped out, radio in hand, leaving his car running in the middle of the street.

"Thirty-six to dispatch, I'm confirming officer down at one three two two South Main," the officer reported as he ran forward. "Request urgent medical."

"Ten-four," the dispatcher acknowledged. "Stay there; ambulance is on the way."

"Shit." The officer took a knee beside Tabitha and the fallen officer. "Ahh, shit, *shit.*"

He was a stocky, clean-shaven white man with a crew cut and a no-nonsense expression. The brass nameplate he wore above his breast pocket read *WILLIAMS,* prompting Alicia to realize she'd never looked down to see the fallen police officer's name. Now, she was afraid to.

"Let's get that ambulance rolling," Officer Williams barked into his radio. "C'mon, c'mon, c'mon."

"Ten-four, ambulance is on the way," the dispatcher helplessly repeated again.

"Are you girls alright?" The officer stowed his handset and leaned in, hesitant to jeopardize the downed officer by taking sudden action. "You want me to take over there, Miss?"

"I'm not releasing pressure until the ambulance is here," Tabitha promised in a resolute voice. She was paler than ever, and her eyes were wet, but she wasn't crying. "We were over there on the side of the road when it happened—we saw everything."

"Good—okay, good, good, you're doin' great, just keep putting on pressure," Officer Williams told her, pulling a pair of latex gloves out of his belt pouch and hurriedly putting them on. As carefully as he could, he opened the fallen officer's eyes one by one, shining a small diagnostic flashlight into them.

"Is he gonna be okay?" Alicia blurted out, hoping the cop could tell them something.

"Uh, I don't know, hun," the man admitted regretfully, surveying the copious amount of blood that had already spilled. "I really don't know."

"He's going to be okay," Tabitha decided, gritting her teeth and staring back down at her bloody hands pressed against the officer's chest. "He's going to make it."

How do you know that? Alicia wiped tears from her face with the back of her hand, staring at Tabitha incredulously. *How did she know what to do?*

The answer, surprisingly, came to mind right away, and many things all at once seemed to fall into place. *Of course—Tabitha read about all of it, in the school library. All those books. Specifically. Is it a coincidence? Everything was like, tailored for this situation, preparing her for exactly this.*

Her steadily increasing anxiety. Her not wanting to be alone today. Her wanting to hang out around here, right here, for no apparent reason... waiting for something? Alicia's eyes widened as she regarded Tabitha in shock. It seemed impossible.

She knew this was going to happen.

10

KEEPING A GIRL IN THE DARK

"Tabs? You still awake?" Alicia asked, twisting on the narrow mattress toward her friend on the floor. "Uh, is it cool if I call you Tabs?"

The past several hours had been a whirlwind of sirens and blood and concerned parents, a news van, and the police officers, and nightfall had seemed to creep up on them all at once. It was hard to focus on her mother's terrified expression as she arrived and nearly tackled her into a stranglehold of a hug, and Alicia didn't remember much of what she'd said to those policemen or reporters. There were too many *questions* burning on Alicia's mind.

"Yeah," Tabitha answered, sounding exhausted. "Call me whatever you want. Tab, Tabby, Tabitha."

Alicia had refused to part after the ordeal they'd been through, pleading to sleep over in Tabitha's tiny room in that worn-down mobile home of theirs. She was offered the tiny single bed, while Tabitha gathered up blankets and stretched out on the floor. Alicia's mother sat out in the dining room with Mr. and Mrs. Moore, still exchanging words in hushed voices.

"Doesn't bother you if I use 'Tabby?'"

"No."

"Okay. Um. You prolly know what I'm gonna ask, right?"

"What?"

"How did you know?"

The dark bedroom was dead silent for a few long moments before Alicia heard her friend let out a long sigh.

"I didn't... *exactly* know," Tabitha muttered. "Didn't think it would happen on the first of October. Just sometime in October."

"But, you *did* know?" Alicia quickly sat up.

"...Yeah," Tabitha admitted.

The room went silent again.

"Okay. Tabitha. Can you understand why that would freak me the hell out?" Alicia blinked, trying to make out the other girl's expression. "I know this is gonna sound shitty, but if we're gonna be friends—you need to fucking tell me what's going on."

For possibly the first time in her life, Alicia felt *shaken.* Witnessing the shooting, stammering out responses to the emergency dispatcher, even simply standing by while Tabitha and the other officer struggled to stem the bleeding had been an incredibly taxing experience on her. The implications of Tabitha possibly having advance knowledge of all of this weighed heavily on her, and she knew she wouldn't be getting any sleep until she addressed things.

"I..." Tabitha struggled out. "I don't know what I should say. How *much* I should say, right now."

"Was it, like, planned out?" Alicia asked in a flat voice. "Premeditated? Was this like, a set-up and planned out cop killing?"

"No!" Tabitha exclaimed, and from the rustle of blanket, it sounded like she'd sat up as well. "No, no."

"What, did you get, um, like, a vision of the future? Dreams?" Alicia guessed. "I dunno, prophecy sorta stuff?"

"Not exactly."

"Time travel?"

Tabitha didn't answer.

"Time travel?" Alicia prompted again. "Tabitha?"

"Kind of...?" Tabitha whispered in a weak voice. "But not exactly?"

Time travel? Alicia frowned. The dark bedroom seemed to spin with fantastical scenarios for a moment. *Yeah, right.*

"Okay, um. Time travel. What else do you know? What can you say that can like, prove it for me? What do you mean 'not exactly?'"

"I... ugh," Tabitha made a sound that Alicia guessed was the girl slapping her own forehead, and then she heard the girl fall heavily back down onto the comforters arranged on the floor. "I don't even know where to start."

"Time travel?" Alicia suggested. She tried to settle back down on the bed, but the events of the day and the sudden introduction of the topic had her too amped up. "Start at time travel? What, was there a time machine?"

"I don't think so," Tabitha said quietly. "I lived out my life, and then somehow I came back to *this* point in my life. Er, I came back to right toward the end of middle school."

"Wait, so did you die? In the future, I mean? How far in the future? Does anything big happen?" Alicia didn't really buy into what Tabitha was saying, but she couldn't help herself from blurting out questions all the same. "Did you die?"

"No." Tabitha sounded unsure now. "I... I don't think so. I don't remember dying, at least. I was in the hospital, getting my headaches checked out."

"How far in the future?" Alicia prompted.

"Forty-seven years," Tabitha answered in a quiet voice. "The year 2045."

She's actually going there? Alicia frowned. *She's seriously gonna try to sell this bullshit story to me? I know she's imaginative and all, but I'm still legit freaked out here—this isn't the time or place to play around like this. Is this her own way of coping with shit? Should I NOT just poke a bunch of holes in her stupid time travel thing?*

"Okay—so, the future," Alicia splayed out her hand in the dark and began ticking off fingers, "is there flying cars? Robots? Teleporters? Or aliens?"

"Sort of, sort of, no, and no." Tabitha chuckled sadly.

"Okay, back up, back up to those two 'sort ofs.'" Alicia laughed. "Explain. Flying cars?"

"There's always been flying cars," Tabitha said. "Probably even in these times—in the late nineties. It's the kind of tech project that'll make the cover of *Popular Mechanics,* maybe, but never ever gets mainstream."

"Lame and boring answer." Alicia rolled her eyes. "Why not? What's a future without flying cars?"

There was a long, drawn-out silence, and Alicia was sure Tabitha had given up on her time-traveling charade.

"The *common-sense* answer is that they're expensive. A compromise between a street legal vehicle and one capable of flight also really sacrifices the better points of each." Tabitha's voice was odd—it was somehow too tired and world-weary. "But that's not the *real* reason they'll never be a thing."

"Oh yeah?" Alicia sat up on one elbow, interested.

"There's a terrorist attack," Tabitha murmured. "It's... *the* terrorist attack. They hijack four flights from the Boston airport and... fly them into buildings. I think it's Boston. Either Boston or Baltimore. Two of the planes hit the twin towers; the World Trade Center. A lot of people die. Another one hits the Pentagon. The last one crashes in a field in Pennsylvania; it was heading for the White House, but... who knows what happened."

"Okay, kinda not funny anymore." Alicia let out an uneasy laugh.

"The economy tanks right away, and things stay bad for years. People are afraid to fly, airport security changes forever. Airlines need government bailout money to keep operating. It was... there got to be this sort of... mass hysteria in the background of our culture, a paranoia that certain people in office use to—"

"Robots?" Alicia interrupted, feeling a little unsettled. "Robots was your other 'sorta?'"

"They don't act like humans and walk around." Tabitha sighed. "The common *everyday* ones are just automated janitors and groundskeepers, really. They mop floors or mow lawns for whatever area they're programmed for, and return to their dock to recharge. They don't look like people; they look like vacuums and mowers, but without the handle stuff."

"Your future sucks," Alicia said. "I guess at least everything's all magically clean everywhere, though, right?"

"It's not really any different than things are now," Tabitha replied sadly. "It's just... buying a smart-cleaner rather than paying a night janitor to mop the floors."

"Lame," Alicia decided. "Do robots take a lot of jobs, then? Fast food?"

"Yes, actually," Tabitha said. "Well, it's technology, but not exactly robots. Nobody behind the counter taking orders anymore —it's all touch screens, or through your phone. Actual people still make the food, but I'm sure that'll eventually change, too."

"Through your phone?" Alicia laughed. "So what, you have to call ahead and order if you want fast food?"

"A phone in the future is... a very different concept than a phone in 1998." Tabitha sighed. "They start out as portable phones, but then they're also cameras, personal computers, and 3D scanners and projectors and eventually your wallet and ID all rolled into one, I guess."

"That's... kind of a big game-changer," Alicia said, leaning out over the bed. "Tabitha? How serious about all of this are you?"

"...I'm not going to ever admit to anyone else that I've been to *a* future," Tabitha said carefully. "I understand that you're skeptical, and we can drop it as a joke for now. I'd just like you to... keep it in the back of your mind as a possibility, when I seem to know things in advance from now on that I shouldn't. If that's all right."

"But you *did* know about the police officer getting shot," Alicia pointed out. "What happened with that in your future?"

"He died," Tabitha said.

"So, this time through, he doesn't die? What does that change? What happens?" Alicia asked, interested.

"I... don't know if he *will* make it yet, if that's, um, something that I can change or not. I won't know until we hear what happens. I tried, though," Tabitha managed to say, her voice dropping down to a whisper. "I tried?"

"No, no, I'm not saying you didn't try—you were amazing— you did everything you could with saving him, and all. But, just, like... *why?*" Alicia wondered. "Not to sound heartless, but... why put yourself through all of *that?*"

"Because, I have to try?" Tabitha answered in that quiet voice. "It's all so... complicated. I have to change things, if I'm going to survive. Because I know I can't go through life like I did before all over again. *I'd rather die.* But then changing everything is so terrifying, sometimes so much *worse* than it was before! I feel like... like I'm losing my grip on who I was in the first place—or who I'm supposed to be—or what I wanted? What I'm doing?"

"So... you're—"

"The Julia from my last life would understand that I can't save everyone. I think she'd be cross at me for putting that burden on myself, for even trying. B-but the things that happened that *made* Julia think like that—that made Julia the way she is—I-I can't let them happen to her. *I'm not ever going to let them happen to her.*

"So the Julie in *this* lifetime will never be the Julie I knew. And maybe I'm robbing her of everything that defined her, everything that made her... her? She'll never understand my writing, understand *me* the way she did, and I don't even know if I'm *saving* her anymore or... erasing her real existence?"

Who the hell is Julie? Alicia's head felt like it was spinning at the sudden detour onto what sounded like a really heavy topic. *Or, is it Julia?*

"What would the past, er, your future Julia want you to do? The one you knew?" Alicia asked.

"She would... choose not to exist," Tabitha's voice was wavering now, on the edge of tears. "Yeah. That's exactly what she did. I just—I *can't*—I don't want things to be that way! I'm not going to let those things happen to her, I *won't ever* let those things happen to her, but then that also probably means my Julie, the Julie *I knew* really is gone forever! And, then it's like, what's the fucking point of any of this?! I never—"

"Tabitha. Tabitha!" Alicia urged, clambering down from the bed as Tabitha's voice continued to rise. She could tell her increasingly bewildering friend was working herself up into some kind of hysteria now, and she didn't want the adults running over to check on them.

"Th-the first thing I did?" Tabitha bawled. "When I realized what the fuck happened to me, that I was back in time? I broke down and started crying. Just like this. Because it *sucks*. You were right about that. The future—my future—repeating all of this, is lame and it sucks. And I hate it. *I hate it.*"

"Ssh, shh, it's okay! It's okay, I believe you." Alicia awkwardly pulled Tabitha into a hug to try to comfort her. She heard footsteps coming down the narrow hallway of the mobile home. "Everything's gonna be okay."

"It's not." Tabitha's body was racked with sobs. "It's not okay! I'm—"

"You girls okay in here?" Mr. Moore opened the door partway, sending a narrow band of light from the hall stabbing across Tabitha's tiny bedroom. "Tabitha?"

"She's just—" Alicia turned to give him a worried look, but was thankful he didn't enter. She was just in her underwear and a borrowed oversized shirt to sleep in. Despite the unusual circumstances, Mr. Moore was practically still a stranger to her. "It's... been a long day? We just need a little time."

"...Okay." Mr. Moore hesitated. "You two need anything at all, don't be 'fraid to just holler. We're all right out in the other room."

"Thank you," Alicia gave him a weak smile.

Tabitha refused to raise her head.

"You've both been up on Channel 7 twice now, already," he reported. "Last news was, Officer MacIntire got life-flighted from Springton General to Louisville. Still in critical condition, and... well, you girls did everything you could, and we're so proud of the both of you. He's in all our prayers."

"Thank you," Alicia said again, trying not to start tearing up herself.

Tabitha's crying seemed to redouble in intensity, and after giving the girls a pained look, Mr. Moore quietly closed the door to give the girls their privacy. Muffled sobs sounded out in the small enclosure of Tabitha's dark room for several long minutes, and all Alicia could think to do was hold her friend in a tight hug, wondering what the hell she could do.

"All of it *for nothing*," Tabitha cried. "Nothing's changed. Nothing *really* changes. Knew I couldn't. Knew I couldn't change anything—"

"Ssh ssh sshh, we don't know anything for sure yet," Alicia whispered, cradling Tabitha's head against her shoulder. "We're going to figure everything out, okay?"

She's not crazy. It's just—a lot happened today, with the shooting. She's... out of sorts. Who wouldn't be? Maybe more than just today—a lot happened over a lot of days, and her stress just has her jumping to weird conclusions in her head? Alicia didn't want to believe any of Tabitha's claims, because they seemed awful dark. Ominous. The more she thought about them, the less she liked the time travel idea. Which was a problem, because Tabitha's act was getting pretty convincing.

"Hey, Tabitha?" Alicia asked in a whisper, gently rocking the crying girl back and forth. "Did you know me, in the future?"

Still shedding tears and letting out tiny sniffling sobs, Tabitha simply shook her head from side to side, answering in the negative.

"Really?" Alicia was a little surprised. "That was one of the things I kept thinking was weird, though. You kind of singled me out back then in school."

"—rd about you," Tabitha said.

"What?"

"Heard about you," Tabitha repeated. "You became a big artist. Drew stuff for magazines. You were from Springton."

"I do?" Alicia blinked in the darkness, surprised. "Big? Like, *big* big? Famous?"

"Not *big* big." Tabitha shook her head. "I don't think. Just. Successful? Wanted you to draw goblins for me."

"Oh." Alicia didn't know if she should be disappointed or elated. "Tell me something else, then. What do I gotta invest in, to make big bucks in the future?"

"Alphaco," Tabitha said into her shoulder.

"What's that?"

"Alphaco." Tabitha pulled away, wiping her nose on the back of her hand. "Alphabet corporation. Sorry. I'm sorry for... losing it like that."

"It's fine, it's fine," Alicia patted the girl's arm reassuringly. "I cried today too. I lost it, like, right in the middle of everything happening back there right at the scene. Remember?"

"Alphabet Corporation," Tabitha said again. "They make a search engine called Google. Named after googol—ten to the hundredth power."

"Googol? A—a *search engine?*"

"For the web. The internet. Indexes everything on the inter-net," Tabitha explained in a weak voice, rubbing her wet eyes. "You ask Google what you're looking for, and it finds whatever. Everyone uses it."

"*Everyone* uses it?" Alicia tried not to sound doubtful. "And, that makes money in the future?"

"Yeah." Tabitha nodded. "Advertisements, tracking data. Companies want to know what you search, profile you. Then ads you see are always related to what you want. Money. Lots of money."

"That sounds... clever?" Alicia admitted. That scary thing was happening again, where the things Tabitha said were somehow more thought-out and convincing than they ought to be. "Is that legal?"

"It's all in fine print somewhere or other." Tabitha shrugged with a sniffle.

"Wait, are *you* investing in stuff?" Alicia asked.

"I guess?" Tabitha shrugged again. "Someday? Completely broke now. So, not soon. Most of the big companies that are still around in 2045 don't even exist yet. Alphaco should have their IPO a couple years after we graduate, though. I think? Was going to have us put whatever we had into that."

"What's an IPO?"

"Initial public offering. So that we can buy stocks. Maybe a hundred dollars a share? Something like that?"

"Tabitha... if you're from the future and know that ahead of time, then you're already basically super rich? Or, you will be?"

"Maybe in twenty years, yeah." Tabitha gave Alicia a helpless look. "Won't help us much when we actually need it—and getting enough shares at all isn't going to be easy. It's a popular stock. Or, it will be."

"Tabitha." Alicia took a deep breath. "I can barely even see you, but can you like, look me right in my eyes, one hundred percent dead serious and swear on someone's grave that you're actually from the future?"

"Yeah."

"Okay. I still don't think I actually believe you, not deep down," Alicia admitted. "But I really want to. You're either from the future or some kind of smart that's kinda scary. Do you have anything that can like, prove things beyond any doubt?"

"Nine-eleven," Tabitha sighed, hanging her head until her face fell into her hands. "The big terrorist thing. It happens September eleventh, and pretty soon. I know it was Bush and not Clinton in office, but it's somewhere right after the year 2000. You won't have to worry about Y2K."

"Wait—I think my parents are putting money in a Y2K."

"Probably a 401k. Y2K's a computer bug that has to do with the millennium, but it turns out to be this big false alarm. Nothing major happens."

Finally, found a little hole in her story, Alicia thought to herself, torn between feeling relieved and feeling disappointed. *Bush was the president BEFORE Clinton, not the one after. That was scary—she was starting to actually get me going with all of this. But... she's going through a lot. I can play along.*

"Oh, yeah. That might be it, 401k." Alicia nodded agreeably. "Sorry. So, is there any way to prevent the big terrorist thing?"

"Um." Tabitha seemed at a loss. "Not... that I can think of. I mean, I haven't thought about it much, because I've been focused on the here and now, but... anything off the top of my head I could try will get me in very, very serious trouble. I also wouldn't have any proof or explanation. Also, then the terrorists will probably just plan something else that I *don't* know about."

"If you know who the terrorists are—maybe just tell the cops about them beforehand?"

"It's... complicated." Tabitha shook her head. "Bigger than that. From what I remember, it took us years to catch up with them regardless. Years, and a lot of military deployment. They're not in a good place for us to get to."

"Russia?" Alicia guessed.

"The Middle East," Tabitha explained.

"Ah. Don't know much about them." Alicia looked thoughtful. "What's their beef in the first place?"

"It's a long story," Tabitha said, letting herself fall back onto the spread of sheets on the floor. "And... I think I might pass out before I get anywhere with it."

"Oh! Yeah, totally fine," Alicia said, climbing up off the floor to sit back on the edge of Tabitha's bed. "Um. I know it's not much, but... I'm weirdly believing you more and more?"

"Thanks?"

Alicia felt a little guilty comforting her friend with what now seemed like totally empty platitudes, but tonight didn't seem like the time nor place to flatten Tabitha's coping mechanism. At the same time, however, she was incredibly frustrated not knowing how Tabitha *actually* knew the shooting was going to happen. She couldn't even tell anymore if Tabitha completely bought into this, or if it was all an increasingly roundabout way of avoiding having to give her real answers.

"Although, if you *are* really a time traveler, you're just about the worst at covering up details and keeping it all secret and all," Alicia prodded. "I mean, you were checking out all of those books regarding bullet wounds and emergency medical stuff, and then you're *coincidentally* caught up in all this? People could connect that."

"Didn't actually check out any of those books." Tabitha yawned. "They never left the library."

"Oh. Well, still—like, *I* noticed it."

"You're the only one who ever came over and saw," Tabitha said with a self-deprecating laugh. "Just like last time through—I have no friends. Nothing much has changed, no matter what I do."

"Wait, why didn't you hide all of it from me, then?" Alicia chuckled. "Sorry. I swear I'll let you sleep. I just, I have so many questions..."

"Wanted you to notice," Tabitha murmured. "Needed you to, if you were ever gonna believe me."

"So, you were gonna tell me about all of this?"

"Yeah. Soon as you asked."

"*Why?*"

"Because... I really wanted to not... do all of this alone," Tabitha admitted reluctantly. "Wanted a friend."

"Why me, though? I'm just fourteen. If everything you've said is true, you're like, actually this ninety-year-old grandma."

"I'm thirteen. Turn fourteen in December," Tabitha mumbled. "I just have... extra memories, or something. I don't know. Definitely feel thirteen instead of sixty. Not even just my body. I have my thirteen-year-old mind, but then also with things I shouldn't remember. Because they haven't happened yet? Can tell the difference."

"Okay," Alicia said, leaning forward in the darkness. "Then. I want you to know, that whether or not you're somehow making all of this up, we're definitely friends. Okay?"

"Thanks."

"No, not 'thanks.' You say 'okay.'"

"Okay."

They didn't speak any more after that, but there was no way Alicia was going to be able to fall asleep. She really *did* seriously consider Tabitha her friend, and that was what made all of this so complicated and impossible to work her mind around. Whether she was lying about this or not, Tabitha was different; interesting. Even if nothing else tonight was real, the raw emotion her friend revealed didn't seem feigned at all.

Maybe she's just fuckin' crazy? Alicia thought to herself, staring toward the ceiling with a perplexed smile. *I don't even really care. Not like I had the guts to tell her I don't have any other friends either.*

11

MAKING NEW FRIENDS

"Good morning everyone! I'm Tom Bradshaw with Channel 7 News—live, local and late-breaking news you can trust covering the Fairfield, Springton, and Sandboro areas. We have new information today on yesterday's Springton *South Main shooting,* where multiple police officers were locked in a *deadly gun battle* with a man identified as Jeremy Redford of West Virginia. Two officers were injured, and one remains in critical condition. We take you now to our own Channel 7's Kathy Anderson with more on this story."

"Isn't that just crazy?" Mrs. Seelbaugh grabbed the remote off the kitchen counter and turned the volume on their TV up several green bars. "That happened right here in town."

"Uh-huh." Sharing her mother's long legs, blonde hair and striking good looks, fourteen-year-old Elena Seelbaugh was perched on one of their bar stools for breakfast at the counter in their expensively furnished kitchen.

Like her mother, she woke up early every morning and tackled each day *with a plan.* She'd already finished deciding her outfit for school, styled her hair, and applied light makeup to accentuate her best features. When Elena turned her attention to their kitchen television set, aerial footage from the Channel 7 News helicopter was showing the familiar parking lot of a nearby Springton strip mall, filled with police cruisers and an ambulance.

"I know where that is," Elena remarked, glancing from the TV back to the puzzle on the back of her cereal box. "That's over by where we used to go for soccer practice. Right?"

"Yeah, South Main Street," Mrs. Seelbaugh replied. "That's *close*, though, that's just a few blocks down from where—"

"—Thank you, Tom." Channel 7's view cut to an inoffensive mid-thirties woman in a blazer, standing beside a small two-lane street. Behind the reporter, a hillside of rather decrepit mobile homes rose up to meet a gas station and a liquor store.

"Wait, where is *that?*" Elena made a face.

"Officer Darren MacIntire of Springton first pulled the suspect over here, in what residents call the *Lower Park* of Sunset Estates, for what should have been a routine stop." The camera panned across a well-trodden roadside median of weeds and gravel blocked off with yellow tape.

"Shortly after stepping out of his vehicle, however, Officer MacIntire was taken surprise by gunfire—he was shot in the chest at close range and then left for dead, right here beside the road." The screen then snapped back to frame the reporter woman.

"Officer MacIntire was just entering his ninth year with Springton PD, and remains in critical condition after being life-flighted to the University of Louisville Hospital. We now have the police dispatch recording of the two Springton High students who *may* have saved this officer's life."

"Springton High kids?" Mrs. Seelbaugh repeated in surprise, turning to her daughter. "Did you hear that?"

"Yeah," Elena replied, sitting up and watching their television set with new interest. "I'm listening."

A somewhat fuzzy audio file began to play, with dialogue

presented sentence by sentence in white lettering beneath two different yearbook photos. The first picture was 'Alicia Brooks,' a softly-smiling scrawny black girl Elena didn't recognize, but the second one...

"Officer down!" It was the clear voice of a young teenage girl. "We have an officer down at 1322 South Main Street. He's shot, he's—he's bleeding everywhere."

"Hello, can you repeat that address?" an adult voice, presumably the dispatcher, responded.

No effing way. Elena dropped her spoon beside her bowl of cereal with a clatter, scattering droplets of milk. The second picture was the unsmiling wide face of *Tubby Tabby,* in the terribly unflattering 8th grade yearbook photo from Laurel Middle. The caption beneath the picture even confirmed it—'Tabitha Moore.' Leaning forward over the countertop on her stool, Elena listened in disbelief as the recording played out.

"Thirteen twenty-two South Main Street, it's the lower trailer park. One, three, two, two, South Main. Lower trailer park."

"Help is on the way; they should be with you shortly. Is the shooter still at that location?"

"No, he's—the shooter drove off. I need, um, sorry, I have to stop the bleeding."

"Hold on, I need you to stay on the line. Honey? I need you to stay with me on the line. Are you still there?"

Tabitha Moore, Elena thought, swiping her spoon off of the countertop and turning to grab a napkin from the holder. *The whole school's going to go crazy. This is a huge deal!*

An individual was usually only the talk of Springton High for a week at most before becoming forgotten, old news. Tabitha, however, was a unique topic that seemed to always linger on everyone's minds. She was an extraordinarily visible beauty, while at the same time, she was inexplicably socially disconnected from the general student populace.

No one seemed to know anything concrete about her—except

that she was incredibly attractive—and that made her the fantasy dream girl for boys, whose imaginations were all too happy to fill in any of the blanks. The girls, for the most part, despised her. Spiteful new stories about her were constantly being started by drama diva *agitators,* but there was no one close to Tabitha to offer counter statements or put out any of the fires. As a result, the gossip always seemed to run on unchecked and grow out of proportion with each retelling. Eventually, they became tall tales so absurd that nobody really believed any of them.

"Hello? H-hello?" A different girl's voice, this time. Elena wondered which one was Alicia and which was Tabby.

"Hello, we have help on the way, but I need you to sit tight for me if you can do that. Has anyone else been hurt?"

"No."

"Can you describe the shooter? Are you still there?"

"Th-the shooter was a white male, in his, uh, in his twenties. He was going, uh, he was—Southbound on South Main, he's in— he's in a Lincoln Continental with West Virginia plates. White, a white Lincoln Continental."

"That's southbound, in a white Lincoln Continental?"

"Yes."

"Okay, thank you. Just sit tight, please; we have an ambulance on the way there to you now."

"These two brave young girls remained at the scene with the downed officer, and were able to stabilize his condition until paramedics arrived at the scene," Kathy Anderson continued. "Their detailed description of the suspect vehicle may have been instrumental in the resolution of what we're now calling the *South Main Shooting.*"

The view then changed to what Elena assumed was footage from yesterday, of Tabitha—the 'new' Tabitha, lithe and effortlessly beautiful—being interviewed along with that scrawny black girl. Evening had apparently fallen and it was getting dark out in the picture, but dozens of bystanders from the trailer park and uniformed policemen were milling about in the background. Tabitha's red hair was a little more tangled than usual, and while she was wearing one of those expensive designer blouses of hers, it was now dirtied, spotted with little dark flecks.

Oh my God. Is that blood?

"Were you two scared, seeing all of this go down right in front of you?" the man offering the microphone asked the girls.

"Yeah," the black girl blurted out in response, looking a little shell-shocked from the ordeal. "I was. I was so scared."

"I was terrified." Tabitha gave a weak smile, not quite looking at the camera. She managed to look amazing, *poignant* somehow, captivating even when she was bedraggled and exhausted. There was a certain serene sadness to her that was picturesque.

"I'm still terrified. I don't know that I'll feel any less scared until I know that the officer's going to be okay."

"Well, our thoughts and prayers are all going out to Officer MacIntire and his family, hoping for his quick recovery," Tom Bradshaw concluded as the screen snapped back to the studio view.

She saved a cop? Elena's blue eyes narrowed as the shifting implications whirled through her head. *This is gonna change everything. In a town this small, it's gonna change what people can say about her—and, to who.* For instance, Elena was still just a freshman, but she had her sights set on Matthew Williams, who was indisputably the cutest sophomore guy. Everyone knew that Matt's dad was a cop.

I think it's time Tabitha and I have a talk, Elena quickly decided. Currently, the consensus around school was that Tabitha was an exchange student from California, but Elena knew she was actually *Tubby Tabby* from Laurel Middle, but had gotten liposuction and plastic surgery. After making the news like this, soon everyone would know.

Tabitha Moore... the trailer trash girl, Elena remembered, quirking her lip. Back in Laurel, that was how everyone had known the girl, and her *Lower Park* heritage still featured prominently in the ongoing topics of gossip around Springton High.

Word was that Tabitha's parents supposedly owned the entire Sunset Estates trailer park; they were rich upstarts. Alternatively, there was the story that they *used* to be rich, and were forced to live in poverty due to any number of possible circumstances— drugs, gambling, malpractice lawsuits—and now, Tabitha would do anything for money.

Or, maybe Tabitha lived with her twenty-two-year-old boyfriend in Sunset Estates, and there were no parents in the picture at all. Possibly, Tabitha came out as a lesbian to her rich parents and was then disowned; now she had to live on her own in a terrible mobile home with just a tiny stipend to get by on.

"Oh my word." Mrs. Seelbaugh cupped her hand over her mouth, turning to her daughter in shock. "Do you know either of those girls?"

"Yeah," Elena replied, snapping out of her thoughts. "Sorta. One of them's in my first period class. Marine Science. Tabitha Moore."

"Wait, *that* Tabitha? The one who was caught doing things with the teacher?" Mrs. Seelbaugh frowned in disapproval.

"Uh, I guess she wasn't. It turns out." Elena shrugged, trying to remember what hearsay she'd already passed on to her mom over the weeks of the first semester. Now that her stance on Tabitha was about to change, she regretted saying anything back then at all.

"One of the deans caught wind of the rumor and people got called up to the office, had to talk to the counselors. I think the story was made up? It got narrowed down to this one junior and three sophomore girls who were just trying to start shit."

"Start *stuff,*" Mrs. Seelbaugh absentmindedly corrected.

"Yeah, start *stuff.*" Elena rolled her eyes dramatically. *I'm almost fifteen now. Jesus.*

"Well, the one with the red hair, she's the spitting image of Shannon Delain." Mrs. Seelbaugh crossed around the counter and into the living room, where she opened up the bottom cabinet below the entertainment center. "Girl *I* went to school with."

"Shannon... Delain?" Elena asked. She didn't actually care, but her mother's habit of gabbing away was always easiest to manage when she feigned appropriate interest in all of those old news *ancient history* stories of hers as if they would ever be relevant.

"Yeah, Shannon Delain." Mrs. Seelbaugh slid out a dusty scrapbook and cracked it open. "If she did have a daughter, though, she wouldn't be your age. I don't think? When I was first pregnant with you, Shannon was headin' off to be this big-shot Hollywood actress."

"That's... uh, cool?" Elena responded distractedly.

"The resemblance is just uncanny, though," Mrs. Seelbaugh muttered, pawing through the scrapbook pages. "I wonder what-ever happened to her—we were good friends."

Maybe Tabitha is finally the friend I need, Elena thought, taking a sip of orange juice as she idly watched commercials flash by. *The leverage I need.*

Her group of girls from Laurel had been broken up into different courses and classes in Springton, and some of them—Carrie in particular—had sold out, toadying up instead to some of the older sophomore and junior cliques. Elena was prepared, she was outgoing, she had all the looks and attitude of a winner, but starting as a freshman at the bottom rung of Springton's hierarchy had still been an enormous setback for her. Now, this girl, this new Tabby who'd seemed like too much of a gamble before could be her ticket to regain all of that lost social traction.

———

Tabitha felt sick. Her red hair was pulled into a ponytail, which bobbed with each plodding step of her daily morning exercise. She wasn't in very good form today—as the sun began to rise, she was seeing the nauseating reminder of a taped-off crime scene at the lower end of her jogging loop around the trailer park. There was vomit in one of the living room waste baskets shortly after checking the local news, and she planned on skipping breakfast because that urge to retch and dry heave just wasn't going away.

Jeremy Redford died because of me. Tabitha grimaced and her pace awkwardly slackened again. Oddly enough, she realized she hadn't ever put much thought into the *shooter* these past months, just the *shooting*. He'd existed in her head somewhat as a plot device, rather than a person. A faceless criminal who'd never been identified, one who quickly disappeared into the annals of history in her last life. Except, this time—because of her actions—his white Lincoln Continental was spotted a little over a mile down South Main, where it led police cruisers on a surprisingly brief high-speed chase.

Which ended abruptly when a cruiser traveling on a perpendicular route *T-boned* the Continental, violently forcing it out of an intersection, through a curb, sidewalk, and concrete divider, and finally into several parked cars in a shopping plaza. Springton PD had been *out for blood,* and when that Jeremy Redford of West Virginia stumbled out of his car and fired several wild shots... he was immediately put down in what could only be called a hail of gunfire.

Oooph. Tabitha paled. She felt her throat constrict and she almost threw up again just thinking about it. Their local news on Channel 7 didn't normally have big, exciting stories, and unsurprisingly, they were running variations of the *South Main Shooting* every hour.

She knew, in a detached way, that exchanging the criminal's life for the police officer's was potentially the best outcome. There hadn't been much of any consideration past that, really. It was the clear-cut right thing to do, in her mind. *Despite* deciding that, however, feeling directly responsible for the death of the man weighed on her in all the wrong ways, a formless and nauseating pressure. If the police officer had died again, then that was one thing, because maybe that was just what was originally supposed to happen. Jeremy Redford died specifically because of what she'd done.

That's not even what I should be worried about... Tabitha lurched to a stop and stood on the sidewalk in the early morning light, stooping over with her hands resting on her knees. She wasn't even winded by her running routine anymore—no, instead, she felt like she'd been punched in the gut.

Alicia knows everything now. I WAS open about all those library books on purpose, Tabitha told herself, trying to steady her breathing and calm herself down. *I DID want her to slowly piece it all together. Then she'd eventually confront me, and it'd be this big cool reveal. The talk that happened last night was... not cool, it was impulsive and emotional. It was dumb. God, it was so dumb.*

Tabitha kicked off, surging back into the angry motion of a sprint to bleed off some of these intense feelings. She hadn't actually expected Alicia to figure anything out while she was this young. Now she knew the truth but didn't really believe it, which was worst-case scenario. If Alicia didn't completely buy into what had happened to her with coming from the future—well, *a* future, anyway—she wouldn't have the seriousness, the *gravity* of the situation to compel her to keep it secret no matter what.

This could get messy. Tabitha forced herself to lower the pace and measure her footsteps again. *No. It IS messy. I knew it would be. But... I tried my best? Officer MacIntire's still in critical condition, but that's certainly better than bleeding out en route to the hospital, like last time.*

Probably? Probably better. Tabitha winced. *How long is it safe to be in 'critical condition' for? Hours? Days? What defines the condition as not being critical anymore?*

While the overall result was better than she'd feared, looking back on it in hindsight, a lot of her planning had evaporated right out of her head in the heat of the moment. She'd intended to recite the Continental's license plate number back then when she'd tossed Alicia the radio handset—only to realize that she'd completely missed catching it, and the car was obviously already long gone. For over a month, she'd been drilling herself on a plan of specifics, but when it finally happened—her nerves were so taut, she never even thought to spare a glance at the license plate.

Likewise, most of the emergency first-aid instruction she'd so carefully studied seemed to vanish like smoke when she'd grasped for them, and only after Officer Williams arrived and began running through basic steps did Tabitha begin to remember. Looking back on it now, there was a certain surreal quality to it all, like watching herself in a dream.

But, it's whatever. Crisis is over, everything's done and past now. Tabitha swallowed, trying to settle her feeling of unease. *It's whatever. Over and done with.*

————

To her surprise, stepping off of the school bus with Alicia and nervously entering Springton High's campus commons... nothing out of the ordinary happened at all. No one was eyeing her any more than usual, and none of the other students approached her. Despite wanting it to be *over and done with,* Tabitha couldn't help but feel like the fallout from this ordeal was still lingering overhead, sure to come down on her at any moment.

Of course they wouldn't know or even notice! Tabitha realized, almost wanting to laugh at herself. *It's the year 1998. There's no social media. No Myspace or Facebook or Alphapage where everyone's seeing a story pop up instantly in their feeds. Teenagers aren't particularly predilected to watch boring news channels in the first place.*

If anything, dozens of eyes were on *Alicia* this time. Tabitha had gifted her friend one of the blouse prototypes that had been put together over the summer. This particular project started as a short-sleeve cream-colored cocktail dress, that featured a rather lovely lace motif along the neckline and midsection. Though Tabitha absolutely adored the design, it would just never be a color she could wear.

Blouses in shades of cream and tan weren't, in her opinion, for girls with a skin tone as dreadfully pale white as hers. Grandma Laurie had insisted it was fine, that she'd find a look she was comfortable wearing it with, but honestly, it looked so much more amazing on Alicia, like it had been made for her. The girl's dark skin stood out, directly contrasting the cream lace and embroidery, being at the opposite end of the same natural palette of colors.

"So, is everyone here like, little kids to you?" Alicia leaned in and whispered, sharing a conspiratorial grin. "Since you're this old lady?" She was sticking close to Tabitha now, awkward and fidgeting excitedly like a skittish young doe at everyone's new attention to her appearance.

"I'm not an old lady," Tabitha insisted.

"You are on the inside, though, right?" Alicia pressed. "Sixty-year-old granny?"

"I..." Tabitha paused, uncomfortable. *I wasn't a grandma. Or even ever a mom.* "I did feel that way at first with everything, felt this sort of age gap. Thought of my dad as a young man, felt like the high-schoolers here were just so dreadfully young. But that's... been going away."

"Going away like, *disappearing?*" Alicia blinked at her. "Like, *Marty McFly fading out of photos because the future changes* kind of disappearing?"

"No, not like that." Tabitha shook her head, furrowing her brow in concentration. "Or maybe... only a little like that? It's more like the old lady I was, and the unhappy tubby little trailer trash girl—they're not who I am anymore. I'm... something I've never been before? A new direction, a new, different person...?"

"Huh," Alicia said, looking around. It seemed like she was in a playful, teasing mood, but she didn't have a joke to commit to that one.

I have a friend, Tabitha thought, feeling a little surprised. While she and Alicia had been walking rather aimlessly around the quad area's patio tables, where dozens of students were chatting before first bell, Tabitha only now realized how things must look.

I mean. We were friends before, I think? Hanging out and talking in the library at lunch. But now, we LOOK like we're friends, to other people. I've been wearing these DIY dress tops to school for a while now, and now we're both wearing them—and people are noticing that. People are noticing I'm not alone, for once.

It was such a trivial distinction, but it shocked Tabitha with how much it meant to her. How far this feeling went in suppressing that ever-present sense of loneliness and *not belonging* that continued to cling to her despite after everything she'd done to improve herself before the school year.

"You alright?" Alicia seemed to notice Tabitha's change in expression. "Yesterday was super crazy."

"Yeah." Tabitha gave the girl a genuine smile. Then she sighed heavily, still feeling exhausted. "And... yeah."

"Just to check—you do still have all of your future memories, right?" Alicia asked, still grinning. "Nothing suddenly disappeared or anything?"

"Not that I can tell." Tabitha shook her head. "But I think my local knowledge is going to be a little off from here on out, on account of the butterfly effect."

"Uh, *butterfly* effect?"

"Uh, yeah." Tabitha hesitated, frowning. "It's a time travel thing, fairly well known in the future. I guess the butterfly effect movie isn't out for another few years, huh? Ashton Kutcher. It's about how these tiny differences can potentially snowball into big changes in the future."

"Ashton Kutcher? Isn't he the idiot guy on *That 70's Show?*" Alicia raised an eyebrow. "Kelso?"

"*That 70's Show?*" Tabitha turned her head toward her friend suddenly with a muddled look of confusion. "That. Shouldn't be out yet for a few more years... right?"

"It's been airing for a while now," Alicia informed her, giving her a look. "It's on Fox. Eight thirty."

"Maybe I just never saw it until later, when I was older?" Tabitha guessed, giving her friend a sheepish look. "Sorry."

"You're a terrible time-traveler," Alicia chuckled, shaking her head in dismay, "and *butterfly effect* is a line from the chaos theory thing in the first *Jurassic Park*, just so you know. Didn't have anything to do with time travel. You're not gonna beat me on movie trivia! I'm gonna head over to my class. See you at lunch, Tabs. Thanks again for the shirt!"

"Yeah." Tabitha made a weak smile. "See you."

I AM a terrible time-traveler, Tabitha thought, suppressing a groan of frustration. The exchange with Alicia was all helping, though; anything to keep her mind off the man who'd been killed, and the police officer who was likely dying a long, drawn-out death because of her meddling.

I may have seen all nine Jurassic Park movies at some point or another over the years, but I've never been able to keep all of the details straight. Didn't even watch them in order. Trudging on alone to her first period Marine Science class, Tabitha racked her brain trying to recall the movie trivia of her last life. *If I can think of something REALLY good, it'll help Alicia believe me.*

Nothing sprang to mind.

I DO remember reading an article once, about how on average, there's a thousand films with major theatrical releases every year in the US. Even assuming that number's probably halved all the way back here in '98, the sheer VOLUME is so daunting that—

"Hey," a tall blonde girl perked up as soon as Tabitha rounded the corner to arrive at her Marine Science class. She recognized the girl, sort of—they'd exchanged words briefly once, on one of the very first days of school.

"...Hi." Tabitha froze in place, giving the girl a wary look.

"Tabitha? Tubby Tabby?" The girl laughed, showing her a playful smile. "We had a couple random classes together back in Laurel. I'm Elena—Elena Seelbaugh."

12

GETTING THE NEWS

"I remember you," Tabitha said, deciding to display a polite, somewhat distant smile. "We spoke, back on the first day of school."

"Uh, yeah!" Elena flashed her a cheery smile.

Forty-five years ago, Tabitha would have been both frightened and enthralled by the sudden attention of one of her peers in this situation. In a lot of ways, she wished she still was that naive. The forced enthusiasm she was able to discern in Elena's expression now was yet another wet blanket cast atop Tabitha's already dampened spirits today.

"We haven't talked since then," Tabitha pointed out, maintaining her courteous mask.

"Hah, uh, well... yeah." Elena offered her an exaggerated wince, and then the girl's eyes shifted away in apparent guilt.

Whatever, Tabitha inwardly groaned. The additional perspective Tabitha possessed made Elena's overacting seem particularly *unsubtle,* and she wasn't sure how she was supposed to react. *Am I expected to call her out on it? Is this some ham-fisted litmus test of my social viability? Whatever, I just... whatever. Not today. I'm not up for games.*

"It's okay—I get it." Tabitha quirked her lip. *I now tacitly agree that we should gloss over my awkward standing within Springton High. Let's please move on to whatever topic is at hand. Don't bother to fabricate excuses—I'll start to resent you for real.* "Guess you were watching the news last night?"

"Caught the whole story this morning, actually," Elena's sheepish smile seemed slightly more genuine, this time. "Did everything really happen like that? I mean, yeah—I know it did—'cause they played the dispatch and everything, but like... *wow.* What was it like?"

Immediately surfacing in Tabitha's mind was this morning's footage of Jeremy Redford, stumbling out of his Lincoln Continental after it'd been forcibly smashed off the road by police cruisers. His face was mercifully not visible to the camera, but the *panic* in the way he attempted to level his firearm upon his pursuers was clear. Disoriented, he fired his gun, once into the hood of his own car, and then once into the windshield of the cruiser just beyond it. It was *desperation,* a cornered animal fearfully baring its fangs, and finally—

"...It was bloody," Tabitha admitted, feeling sweat on her palms. She anxiously crossed her arms in front of herself to stop from fidgeting. She wasn't about to forget the actual blood she'd seen yesterday either, of course. After the paramedic had taken over her position above the fallen officer, Tabitha had simply stared in horror at her own bloody hands, unsure of what to do with them. Officer Williams noticed her predicament and rushed to her assistance with a gallon jug of water and some towels from the trunk of his vehicle.

"*Bloody?*" Elena repeated, both awe and disbelief in her voice. "Whoa."

Tabitha could still picture Jeremy Redford in the moment right after he'd been pulled over, the man swearing loudly and slamming his hand against the side of his steering wheel in frustration.

You tried to kill a cop. I don't need to feel sorry for you, Tabitha told herself.

"Yeah," Tabitha finally said, not wanting to talk about it any further. "Bloody."

"Well, it was real cool what you did." Elena seemed to take the hint and not press for details. "Just wanted to tell you that I saw the news, and all. We should hang out sometime. Where do you eat lunch?"

"I don't really eat anymore." Tabitha put on a wry smile. *Not at school anyways.*

"Yeah!" Elena exclaimed, her eyes lighting up at another topic to latch on to. "Definitely noticed that too. They put up your old Laurel school picture, and then had your little interview thing right after, and it's like—*is that even the same person?*"

"Almost doesn't seem like it, does it?" Tabitha uneasily chuckled.

"You definitely look amazing now." Elena giggled. The tall blonde's hesitant facade was already gone, and she'd deftly switched tacks into a familiar act, as if the two of them were old friends. "So—what's your secret?"

Stomach ulcers, Tabitha was tempted to say. *A dietician. Time travel. Taekwondo. Nutrition, meal-planning. Forty-some odd years of learning how to plan and structure goals for myself. Having a REASON to even try; magically being in this thirteen-year-old body again, having this impossible second chance at my entire life.*

"Um—" Elena noticed Tabitha's awkward pause.

But yeah, most of all, it's just the time travel.

"G'morning, ladies." Mr. Simmons brushed past them, loudly jangling his lanyard of keys to unlock the portable their Marine Science class was held in. "'Scuse me, watch out, comin' through, hot coffee here, watch it."

"Mornin'." Elena nodded her head.

"Good morning," Tabitha greeted.

"You two hear 'bout that shooting last night?" Mr. Simmons asked, opening the door and stepping back to let the girls through. "Happened right here in town."

"Yeah, I saw the news this morning." Elena beamed, shooting Tabitha a pleased look.

Tabitha mustered a weak smile, feeling unsettled as Elena followed her into the classroom. She made her way across the aisles of empty desks and settled into her assigned seat, trying not to feel self-conscious.

"Scary stuff, scary stuff," Mr. Simmons grunted, shuffling on past them up to his desk at the front of the room. "Happens every other year or so in Sandboro, but here in Springton? Very unusual."

"We should talk, after third period," Elena proposed in a whisper, pausing beside Tabitha's desk and presenting her with a confidential smile. "Where do you normally chill during lunch?"

"I'll be in the library today," Tabitha answered, giving the other girl an appraising look. *Now it's supposed to be like we're sharing a secret, and we have this special bond between us?* "I was gonna meet up with my friend Alicia."

"That other girl that was on the news?" Elena's voice was full of feigned excitement. "Awesome! Meet you guys there, then. Cool."

So, Elena really wants to be buddies, now? Tabitha mused, withdrawing her textbook from her bag and flipping it open. The timely nature of this teen's approach wasn't much of a coincidence, which made the friendly effort seem rather... lacking in sincerity. *But... it's not exactly like I didn't have ulterior motives when I first introduced myself to Alicia. Who am I to talk?*

———

Just a few hours later, Elena was checking out their surroundings in Springton High's library, looking across the rows of books at the lunchtime regulars sitting in the central computer lab in thinly-disguised disapproval. *Not a fan of* Oregon Trail *and* Carmen Sandiego? *Or, is it that we're not as VISIBLE to the general student populace when we hang out in here?*

"Hi! I'm Elena," Elena said, giving Alicia a small wave despite them already being close enough to shake hands. "Alicia, right? Saw you on the news too. I love your blouse!"

Do high school girls not give each other handshakes? Tabitha wondered with a tired smile as they sat down at one of the study tables. *Is that the wrong common sense to use here? Maybe I spent too many years in a professional setting?*

"Uh. Yeah. Hi?" Alicia said warily, looking from Elena to Tabitha for explanation.

"This... is my new friend, Elena," Tabitha gestured. "She used to bully me in middle school."

"*What?*" Elena gave Tabitha a shocked look and playfully slapped at her shoulder as if to say *you sure know how to kid around.* "I totally did not! You said you didn't even remember me!"

"It's okay." Tabitha shrugged. "Everyone bullied me. I'm getting past it."

"*I* didn't pick on you, though," Elena insisted, looking personally aggrieved. "I didn't! Name one mean thing I ever said to you."

"Like I said, it's okay." Tabitha chuckled. "I get it. Just wanted Alicia to have some perspective."

"Is this... supposed to happen?" Alicia broke into a nervous grin and looked at Tabitha. "What's the story, here?"

"I don't know." Tabitha sighed. "I think I only got two hours of sleep—I'm just trying to keep up with everything, at this point. Don't even remember what I'm supposed to have read last night for AP English."

"You're in AP English?" Elena asked in disbelief. "You can't be. *I'm* in AP English."

"Then you probably have the other teacher, Mr. Cooke," Tabitha said. "There's two freshman AP English classes; I'm in Mrs. Albertson's AP English."

"But... like, I remember you from Mrs. Hodge's Lang Arts class before," Elena said, her brow furrowing in apparent confusion. "Your grades weren't *that* good."

"Got a recommendation from the school board, because of the essay I wrote for the Language Arts final," Tabitha revealed. "Part of the essay got published in the *Tribune* over the summer."

"Are you serious?" Elena's mouth fell open in surprise. "What was it about?"

"Small world, then, huh?" Alicia commented, giving them both a suspicious look. "Old classmates? What a coincidence. Let me guess, Tabitha—was your essay about *the future?* Can I read it?"

"Small *town.* Small towns are like this; it's not that unusual. And... it was about the future, yes," Tabitha grudgingly admitted. "The essay's called *Social Media.* Mrs. Albertson has a full copy of it printed out somewhere, if you want to read it."

"I want to read it!" Elena jumped back into the conversation. "Social Media, you said? I'm planning to be a journalist, once I—"

"Are you one of the girls spreading rumors about Tabs?" Alicia interrupted, leaning over to rest her chin on her knuckle as she observed Elena. "There's a lot of real ignorant talk going around."

"Of course not!" Elena appeared indignant. "That was all Kaylee. Her and her little cronies that're in Marine Sci with Tabby and me. They already got called up to the office and got a warning. Oh, and Carrie. Tabby, do you remember Carrie? She was with us in Laurel too. Carrie's always been talking shit about you."

"I wonder why?" Tabitha frowned. "I don't even remember what she looks like."

"It's 'cause she feels threatened?" Elena shrugged dismissively. "Because of the way you look now? She sure remembers you."

"No." Tabitha shook her head. "I don't think that's it. It would've been the same either way—they'd still find some reason to pick on me, some new angle. I just don't understand *why*, really. Back then, I was bullied directly. I wasn't a person; I was a goblin, a *concept,* I was the metric of person that defined the bottom of their power hierarchy. I didn't like it—I don't like it—but, I understand it.

"As far as I can tell, the way I'm bullied *now* is very different. Indirect, this time. I'm being intentionally excluded, others are being pressured not to become friends with me. Malicious rumors are spread about me; attempting to embarrass me, to harm my perceived reputation. It's never been like this."

"That's just what it's like being a normal teenage girl?" Elena spread her hands in a helpless gesture. "Hah. Welcome to the club?"

"People don't treat *me* that way," Alicia argued.

"You're invisible, no offense." Elena gave the dark-skinned girl a false smile. "You don't wear makeup, you don't dress up—before today anyways—and, you don't talk to anyone."

"I wear makeup," Alicia growled back. "Anyways, speaking of all that, Tabitha—these two girls in my second period class were asking how I knew you today."

"How you know me?" Tabitha blinked.

"Probably just from me wearing this," Alicia added, tugging at the collar of the cream-colored blouse for emphasis. "It's like... I went from innocent bystander, to enemy in their midst in like, zero seconds flat. They were all pissed off; now they have to whisper instead of just bullshitting out loud like they usually do."

"Which girls, who asked you?" Elena asked, leaning forward with interest. "What'd you tell them?"

"The truth, of course." Alicia smirked at Elena. "What's it to you?"

"I'm just trying to be friends with you guys," Elena said defensively, turning to Tabitha for support. "C'mon, what's your problem?"

"She doesn't trust you." Tabitha smiled.

"Can you, like, say something to her, then?" Elena growled. "Geez."

"Elena—I trust you even less than she does." Tabitha gave the blonde an amused look. "Listen, what do you really want from us?"

"I just wanna be friends," Elena explained in exasperation. "I want to hang out with you guys, do *friend stuff,* have each other's backs, you know? Is that so much to ask?"

"I don't think I like you, though," Alicia stated with a smile.

"You don't even know me yet!" Elena gave her a frustrated look. "That's not super fair of you, now is it?"

"I don't care?"

"Hold on." Tabitha held up a hand. "I'm sure Elena has some sort of reason for coming to us—let her explain."

"It's Carrie," Elena blurted, as if sensing this was her last chance to win them over. "Carrie and I used to be best friends. Back in middle school. Like, we were a team. Slumber parties, traded diaries, practically sisters, and all that. But now, we don't have a single class together, and she's too busy sucking up to all the juniors and sophomores to even say 'hey, what's up' when we pass in the hall. She's this total... backstabber sell-out. Now it's starting to be like everyone hates me and school's going to really suck."

"Sounds rough." Alicia rolled her eyes. "So, you and Carrie used to bully Tabitha, am I right?"

"Sounds like you're being very rude." Elena folded her arms across her chest. "I don't *bully* people."

"I sympathize with you, Elena." Tabitha sighed. "Really. Losing a friend is hard. But I don't know what you expect from pariahs like us. I don't imagine we have a lot in common, and I doubt we're the social capital I think you're looking for either."

"You *are,* though," Elena argued, not dissuaded in the least, "and, we have plenty in common. You're in AP? I'm in AP. We have Marine Science together, we had classes together in Laurel. I'm pretty popular—or, I was—and, you're more popular than you think. You're this ugly duckling gone all swan. Everyone loves that kind of story—"

"Apparently, *someone* in Springton High doesn't," Alicia interrupted. "Maybe a lot of someones? *Apparently?*"

"—You wear all these amazing tops, and no one can figure out where you even buy them from. You're apparently top of the class in more than just Mr. Simmons', and you just saved a cop's life, probably. You were on the news, so everyone's gonna know about that, soon."

"All of that's just about *me*, though." Tabitha's eyebrows rose. "No wonder Alicia doesn't like you."

"I wasn't tryin' to dis you with any of that, Alicia." Elena turned and held up a hand to forestall Alicia's response. "Just, like —I don't really know anything about you at all. Okay?"

"Easily remedied," Tabitha said, tugging her backpack off the table and out of the way. "Alicia—show her your new portfolio."

"*Tsk.*" Alicia made a playful face, sticking out her tongue at them. "Do I have to?"

Grudgingly, Alicia took her art book out of her bag and slid it across the table to Elena. The slender blonde opened it and respectfully flipped from page to page in silence, enduring Alicia's teasing stare for several minutes. Finally, she closed the book and passed it back.

"Those are beyond amazing," Elena admitted bluntly. "You have a lot of talent, and if you're in art electives—well, everyone's gonna know it soon. I want to be your friend just as much as I want to be Tabby's friend, okay? I like, never meant for it to seem like I was brushing you off or anything."

"I still don't like you, though," Alicia said in a flat voice. "Sorry."

"Fine, whatever." Elena helplessly threw up her hands. "What do you guys want me to do?"

"Apologize for bullying Tabitha back in middle school," Alicia decided. "For starters."

"I *didn't* bully her in middle school, though," Elena exclaimed, rolling her eyes.

"Yeah, uhh—I don't buy it," Alicia countered, crossing her arms. "At all. Seems to me like you just had a falling out with this girl Carrie, who decided to be all against Tabs. And now, in *your* head, that makes us friends. But—we're not. To me, you're exactly the same as all those other girls who're always talking shit about Tabitha."

"It's okay, Alicia," Tabitha said, glancing from Alicia to Elena and back again in surprise. *I never thought there would be so much contention between the two.* "I really don't mind what anyone says about me anymore."

"Well, *I* do." Alicia scowled. "Elena... look us in the eyes and tell us that coming and talking to us has nothing to do with your stupid little prom queen power games."

———

The day rolled on, detail and definition escaping Tabitha's attention as she floundered her way forward in a distracted daze. Tabitha attended her classes, filled in her worksheets, trudged to her bus when the final bell rang, and rode it home. She *had* been hoping these past few weeks that a girl like Elena would reach out to her at some point—but *today,* of all days? She felt unprepared, off-balance, mired in an exhausting mental struggle between guilt she didn't think she deserved and the search for any shred of affirmation that she'd actually done the right thing.

But there is no RIGHT thing, not to them, Tabitha sighed. *They don't have the context; no one else knows how things were supposed to go. No one but me; it's just me here with my dirty little secret...*

The phone rang several times before she snapped out of her

reverie and she stared at it, reluctant to answer. Her parents weren't home when she got back from school, but now she couldn't remember why that was. With a tinge of superstitious fear she found incredibly silly, she finally stepped into the kitchen and picked up the receiver.

"Moore residence," Tabitha spoke slowly into the handset, "this is Tabitha speaking."

"Tabitha!"

"Hi, Grandma Laurie." Tabitha's shoulders relaxed from a hunched posture that she didn't realize she'd been holding.

"We heard the news last night," Grandma Laurie said. "I wanted to make sure I called you as soon as you got home from school. Are you okay? Have you heard anything about the police officer?"

"I'll be okay." Tabitha slumped down across the kitchen counter and exhaled slowly. "I just didn't sleep much—it was hard to calm myself down."

"You don't know how proud I am of you, sweetie!" Grandma Laurie exclaimed. "I was going to drive over last night, but I figured with all the fuss going on over there you didn't need me being a bother too. Are you okay? I almost had a heart attack when I saw that you were involved in all that mess."

"You're never a bother, Grandma," Tabitha said. "I'd love to see you soon."

"Was that colored girl that was on the news with you one of your friends from school? Or does she live in the park there too?"

That COLORED girl?

"Alicia. She's a friend from school that was hanging out with me," Tabitha explained, slapping a palm to her own face in embarrassment. "Uh, Grandma—please don't call her a colored girl, or a person of color, or anything like that. She's just a teenager like me; you don't have to make any sort of racial distinction. Please."

Mr. Moore had once related a conversation he'd had with

Uncle Danny to her, with her father certain that African-Americans preferred being called *blacks* and Uncle Danny insisting that it was more politically correct to call them *negroes*. Tabitha remembered it being a discomforting topic back then, and it was many times more mortifying now. Her family wasn't *actually* racist—well, maybe Uncle Danny was—but the casual remarks they made out of ignorance were all the more difficult to bear after experiencing the next four decades of American culture.

"Sorry, sweetie. I'm so glad you're making friends at school! And that you weren't alone for all of that nonsense! Did you say her name was Alyssa?"

"Alicia," Tabitha corrected with a wry smile. "She's an artist."

"I can't wait to meet her. Both of you are safe and sound and everything? Are you okay?"

"I'm... yeah. I'm just, sorta... waiting for the other shoe to drop," Tabitha admitted, rubbing her face in a bleary way. "They don't know if Officer MacIntire's going to make it or not. Critical condition, still."

"Oh, honey. I'm sure that he's in good hands, and that they're doing everything they can."

"Yeah." Tabitha gave a helpless sigh. "I guess."

"Well, it'll be just me and the boys over here for a good long while Danny's in county waitin' on his court date. We'd love to see you some weekend! The boys really got attached to you over the summer. You were such a big help."

"*Court date?*" Tabitha went stiff.

"Yes, his—didn't your parents say anything to you?" Grandma Laurie asked in surprise. "Danny was arrested a week and a half ago."

"No. They didn't say anything to me." Tabitha gritted her teeth. "At all."

I was supposed to be ready for this. I even knew in advance that it was happening sometime around this year, and it STILL just slipped right on by me! Why the hell didn't they tell me about it? I remember them sitting down and us having 'a talk' about it last life. Is there too much distance between my parents and me this time?! What's the God damned point of being back in time if I miss out on fixing the things that matter?!

"Well, they caught your Uncle Danny on surveillance cameras, stealing electronics from a pallet in the back of that Service Merchandise department store. Over in the Sandboro mall," Grandma Laurie explained with a heavy sigh. "Thirty-thousand dollars' worth of IBM, Compaq, and Toshiba personal computers. He doesn't know a damned thing about computers! I don't know what on God's green earth was going through that mind of his."

"Are the boys okay?" Tabitha asked, trying to swallow down her frustration.

"They're all little troopers; we'll be alright over here," Grandma Laurie assured her. "So long as I can keep them away from their momma—Lisa keeps trying to twist things around and tell them *'oh, it's a victimless crime,'* and *'your daddy did right because he was doing it for us,'* which is all just *nonsense*. Right's right and wrong's wrong, not a one of those computers belonged to him. Stealing's stealing, and that's all there is to it. Sorry, hun, I'm sure you don't want to hear me ramble on right now."

"No—no, you're absolutely right," Tabitha said. "Try to keep them away from Aunt Lisa. I'll think of something."

I barely even remember Aunt Lisa, but I know she's going to ditch her incarcerated husband AND all four of her sons in short order for some new boyfriend. And, I don't think we ever hear from her again, Tabitha thought to herself with a frown. *Should I try to go meet her, talk to her? I don't even know her. I never did. How the hell am I supposed to salvage this?*

"You'll think of something?" Grandma Laurie sounded confused. "Honey..."

"I—yeah, tell the boys I'm going to take them out to the park playground this weekend, so we can all catch up," Tabitha said. She felt a headache coming on. "I'll think of something."

"I'll tell them, but... well, I don't want you to go thinking you have to try to fix everything yourself, okay, honey?"

"I—I should probably at least *try*, though. Right?" Tabitha said. "If I don't, then... then what's the point?"

"Tabitha—"

"I've gotta go, Grandma. Love you. Don't forget to tell the boys, alright? This weekend."

"Alright, dear. Love you too."

"Bye, Grandma."

"Bye, sweetie."

Although Tabitha managed to keep her composure until the end of the phone call, she couldn't help but pull back her trembling hand, ready to *hurl* their cordless phone handset against the wall. She stood there in the kitchen, poised to throw, for several long, tense moments before turning and clapping the device back into the phone dock.

"Fuck," Tabitha sniffled, swiping angrily at her watering eyes. *"Fuck!"*

All these second chances, these opportunities to make things right, and I'm just mucking them all up. Tabitha swayed on her feet as she strode forward, almost stumbling. She needed *out*—out of the kitchen, out of the trailer, out of this town and this time period and away from everything for a breather.

I lost weight. Tried so hard to look nice and be pretty—and high school finds new ways to make me miserable instead. I try to play hero, change the whole shooting event thing, MAKE A DIFFERENCE, and someone else gets killed instead. Maybe the cop even dies anyways! It's all just getting worse!

She left her mobile home behind, pacing past the aging trailers lined up beneath the waning October sun. Taekwondo practice didn't look like it was happening today, and she instead absent-mindedly watched cigarette butts and clumps of weeds pass beneath her feet with each directionless step she took. Before she realized what she was doing, Tabitha found herself standing in front of yesterday's crime scene, a small section of parking lot and roadside median sectioned off with driveway markers and yellow tape.

Blabber everything to Alicia like an idiot, so of course now she thinks I'm a mental case. My mother avoids me like I'm diseased; we haven't spoken in what—days? Weeks? I start getting close to my cousins, because I want to be a part of their life, to be there for them, and where the hell am I when they need me the most? Going back in time, doing all of this over again—what's the point? Where's the damn meaning in this? Why am I even—

"Tabby! Hey, *Tabby!*" Mike yelled out, hurriedly braking to a stop next to her on his bicycle and sending pieces of gravel skittering across the asphalt. As always, the boy was barefoot.

"Hey, you okay?"

Tabitha reluctantly turned to look at him, a little ashamed to find her eyes were wet all over again.

"Mom saw you and told me to run out and tell you right away —the police officer made it, the TV said his condition's stable," Mike blurted out in a single breath. "And that means he's not gonna die."

"He's okay?" Tabitha tried to blink away her tears. *He's okay.*

"He's okay, yeah," Mike confirmed, nodding. "Are *you* okay? You're crying."

He's okay, Tabitha felt stunned. *He made it. He MADE IT!*

With a lunge, she stepped forward and wrapped Mike up in a fierce hug, nearly toppling the eleven-year-old boy off of his bike.

"Ah, geez!" Mike protested, trying to squirm his way out of Tabitha's embrace. "Hey, cut it out, lady! I have a girlfriend already."

He's alive. Yeah, I feel like I'm running myself ragged, and like nothing's ever working, but—but he's alive, Tabitha told herself, letting warm tears roll down her cheeks. *Like in that parable. Encountering the boy on the beach, the boy who's picking up the starfish who've washed ashore, and then throwing them back into the ocean.*

'*Thousands of starfish dry up and die here on the sand every day, and there's only one of you,*' *the man says.* '*You're not making a difference.*'

The boy picks up another starfish, throws it out into the waves, and says—'*Well, it sure made a difference to that one.*'

13
TABITHA'S IN TROUBLE

After giving Mike one last teary-eyed hug, and ruffling his hair to his even louder protests, Tabitha went home. It felt like something big had changed deep inside of her, something she hadn't felt in all the months since time-tripping back to 1998. For once, that tense, almost frantic compulsion to do everything she possibly could, all at once, was gone—and in its wake, there was only exhaustion. She felt her shoulders go slack as she re-entered her family's mobile home, forgetting for a moment that her parents were—well, somewhere else. She had no idea where they were today.

Still aching from this morning's run, Tabitha realized, letting herself collapse onto the couch of their living room and sink deep into the cushions. Pain had been such a constant for all this time that it'd been shoved into a throbbing backdrop in her mind. The trailer was quiet, and she idly wondered to herself how she'd even managed to get this far. She was tired, more mentally spent than she'd ever realized, and it finally—*finally* felt like she was allowed to rest.

Cleaned and organized everything, lost all that weight. Made a real friend at school, maybe more friends soon. Saved the officer's life, Tabitha thought, letting out a slow breath.

No Taekwondo, not for today. I can take it easy, just for a little while. I don't need to run and practice forms every single day. She was already in trim shape, and unlike where she'd been at this age in her previous life, she didn't suffer much in the way of cravings for food. After living through stomach ulcers that had hospitalized her more than once, she first associated eating with debilitating pain and nausea, rather than satisfaction.

She'd almost drifted off to sleep right there on the sofa when the phone began to ring, momentarily startling her. Combing errant red strands of hair out of her face, she wearily clambered up off the couch and found her way over to pick up the phone. *Probably Grandma Laurie again, just getting the news.*

"Moore residence, this is Tabitha speaking," she said. "How may I help you?"

"Tabitha Moore?" A woman's voice, and not one she recognized. "My name is Sandy—Sandra MacIntire. Rob found me your number, but I didn't—I wasn't, um, I'm so sorry for not getting a hold of you until now. You saved my husband's life. You saved my husband's life, and I can't ever, ever thank you enough."

Mrs. MacIntire's voice was awash with emotion, and it sounded like she was beginning to cry over the phone, bringing tears back to Tabitha's eyes and making her choke up.

"It's okay," Tabitha managed. "I just heard it was on the news, myself. I'm really glad he's going to be okay. I, um. Wasn't doing okay at all myself, until I knew for sure."

"I wasn't either." Mrs. MacIntire tried to chuckle but had to stifle a sob instead. "Oh, honey, I wasn't either. B-but they say he's, he's going to be alright now. That it's just going to be some time before—before he's back on his feet, and up and around again and everything. Thank you so much. I can't ever thank you enough. If there's anything you ever need—"

"I just need him to be okay," Tabitha explained, sniffling into the back of her hand. "I'd like to come visit him, if that's alright. I've been having... bad dreams."

One long, bad dream, where your husband bleeds to death on the way to the hospital, because no one was there to help him in time. A bad dream where the little trailer trash girl hears the gunshot and just goes back to watching TV. A dream where she grows up callous to his death, and starts to resent him for the way people treat her for being from the Lower Park neighborhood.

Except, it wasn't a dream, really. It was a total fucking nightmare.

"Oh, of course you can, honey—I'm sure Rob would be happy to drive you out here to Louisville. Rob Williams, he was the officer first at the scene there with you, he told me everything you girls did. Thank you so much. I really—I don't know what I would have done, what I was going to do, if. If."

"He's going to be okay," Tabitha reminded her, wiping her eyes. "I can't wait to meet you both, and see for myself."

After profusely thanking Tabitha again, promising her that Officer Williams would be in touch with her parents about a trip to Louisville this Sunday, and suggesting they all share a meal together over Thanksgiving when her husband was fully recovered, Tabitha was finally able to say her goodbyes and hang up the phone. Not a moment too soon, she would discover—because several vehicles were pulling up to loudly park out front.

Stepping over to the window with no small amount of trepidation... she discovered Uncle Danny's car had arrived. Tabitha couldn't help but slump forward and knock her forehead against the glass in frustration. In her head, the vaguely-remembered events of her past life were supposed to follow some sort of episodic narrative, where the next chapter would begin only after the current one had concluded. In reality, however, occurrences overlapped in such a way that now she felt like she'd already missed out the first half of this *Uncle Danny going to prison* story, and completely lost any opportunity to take preventative measures.

Swallowing down her frustrations, she opened the door and strode down the steps to see what she already knew was going on. The familiar car was finally here; no doubt to find its near-permanent resting place up on cinder blocks on their lot. To artfully complete that last missing piece of their long anticipated trailer trash decor. Both of her parents had followed behind in her father's truck, likely in case Uncle Danny's car broke down again en route.

Looking over it now, she saw the thing was a relic. Already a full decade old even here in this time—Uncle Danny's car was a sun-bleached and faded black two-door coupe; a 1988 Oldsmobile Cutlass Supreme Classic, perhaps one of the last fumbling grasps automakers made with gigantic boxy, rigid-looking notchback designs of the era. The loud but wheezy-sounding motor finally sputtered off, and Tabitha turned her attention to its driver as she disembarked, a sleazy-looking young woman with peroxide-blonde hair and uncomfortably revealing clothing.

There's no way that can be Aunt Lisa... right? Tabitha found herself dumbfounded, forced to run the math in her head. Her aunt didn't look to be even twenty-five years old, but the eldest of her four cousins was Sam—and he was eight or nine years old. The woman wore a low-cut tank top that didn't seem to cover up her bra at all, and crammed herself into cut-off jeans tight enough that they pinched her midsection into a noticeable muffin-top. The princesses of pop—Britney Spears, Jessica Simpson, and Christina Aguilera—wouldn't emerge until next year, but Aunt Lisa already seemed ahead of that trashy late-nineties fashion curve.

"Oh my wooord, Tabby, is that you, darlin'?" Aunt Lisa crooned in mock surprise. "Goodness sakes, I wouldn'ta recognized you one bit if not for you havin' yer momma's hair! Jus' look at you!"

"Hi, Aunt Lisa." Tabitha weakly waved.

"Why, I'm surprised you even 'member me. You were just a little thing last time we met." Aunt Lisa seemed pleased, and she slapped the roof of Uncle Danny's car. "Well, you go on and thank yer Daddy, 'cause he just bought you a car for when you turn yer sweet sixteen! Soon as y'all get a new battery in there, it'll be good to go!"

"Oh wow," Tabitha tried to mask her disappointment with a look of shock. *What a waste of money.*

Over the next fifteen years, she remembered they would discover it was a problem with the alternator and not the battery, that there was a fuel line leak, and that both the electronic control module and controller for the idle air intake were shot, causing the engine to stall if the vehicle idled for a little bit too long... amongst other problems. By the time Tabitha had given up on finishing her Goblin Princess novels and started working at the safety plant, her parents decided the cost of getting the rusty old thing running ever again wasn't worth it. Eventually, they paid to get it hauled to a junkyard in Sandboro.

"How are the boys?" Tabitha asked, trying to rein in the anger she was feeling rise up at this hussy.

Aunt Lisa ignored her question, instead turning away from her with a blank look on her face toward Mr. and Mrs. Moore as they climbed out of the pickup.

"You're a lifesaver, Al!" Aunt Lisa squealed in a chipper voice. "Thank you so much. This li'l bit of cash is gonna get us through some of these hard times. You sure you're okay with swingin' me by over to Shelbyville?"

And we never saw her again, Tabitha thought to herself. Sam, Aiden, Nick and Joshua wouldn't see her again either for years and years. This woman was about to ghost all of them and start a new life elsewhere, now that Uncle Danny was locked up. To her own surprise, Tabitha realized... she actually felt no compunction to speak up or try to stop Aunt Lisa from disappearing.

It's going to be hard on you boys, but you're better off without her, Tabitha decided, her previous anger settling deep into the pit of her stomach in a cold feeling. *Grandma Laurie takes better care of you anyways, and this time, I'm going to be over there looking out for you as much as I can. I know it hurts, and I know it's not fair, but...*

She watched on with that icy feeling in her gut as Aunt Lisa said goodbyes to Mrs. Moore, sent Tabitha a cheerful parting wave, and then left, chauffeured away by her father in his pickup. When Mrs. Moore finally approached her silently staring daughter, the fat woman actually had the decency to wear a guilty look.

"I'm... sure you have some questions," Mrs. Moore managed, not making eye contact with her. "'Bout what's going on with your Uncle Danny."

NOW you say something?! What the fuck am I supposed to do about all of this now? It's too late. It's too late to figure out how to keep Uncle Danny's nose clean. Too late to talk Aunt Lisa into remembering she's a fucking mother of four, and needs to fucking act like it. It's too late for me to trust you—and that's what really makes this all so tiresome. Because I probably could have figured something out. Or, at least tried. Everything's too late, Mom.

"Questions? No," Tabitha said flatly, turning to head back inside. "I don't."

———

"What're you doin' for Halloween?" Alicia asked. She was sitting on one of the planter ledges alongside Springton High's quad area, while Tabitha sat on the bench of a nearby table. It was a crisp morning, and the two girls had taken to hanging out with each other there among the crowds of students before the first bell sounded. Alicia frowned, furrowing her brow, and deftly flicked her pencil over in her hands to quickly erase a few lines of her drawing. "Any big plans?"

"I'm going trick-or-treating," Tabitha said, flashing her friend a genuine smile. "I'm really excited."

"Trick-or-treating?" Alicia scoffed, smirking at Tabitha. "Tsk, tsk. At your age? Shame on you."

"Yeah. I *really* want to, though," Tabitha admitted. "I remember it being awkward and miserable back then. Trick-or-treating stops being a thing in a few more decades, so I want to really experience it properly back in its heyday. Not... awkward and lonely and miserable."

"*What.*" Alicia was forced to slap her drawing down into her lap. "Bullshit. How does *trick-or-treating* stop being a thing?"

"Things change." Tabitha gave her a listless shrug. "Stops being acceptable to let your kids run around free range like that, even on Halloween. Whole different social dynamic, with the helicopter parenting thing."

"Helicopter parenting?" Alicia rolled her eyes and chuckled, returning to her drawing. "Okay, I do believe you just made that up."

"It's when parents just kind of hover over their kids for their entire lives, making a lot of noise." Tabitha grinned. "You can't even leave your kids in the car while you grab groceries, in the future. They could get heat stroke, so other parents'll call the cops on you."

"Speaking from experience, I guess?"

"No. I, uh." Tabitha's expression wavered, and her grin began to disappear. "I never had kids."

Surprised, Alicia looked back up from her drawing just as Tabitha looked away from her.

"Did you ever get married, or anything?"

"No," Tabitha answered in a neutral tone. "Nothing like that."

"Uhh." Alicia cleared her throat. "You're getting real convincing with all that. But maybe quit making every cool future thing into some... monkey's paw wish gone wrong sort of deal, okay? You're bumming me out. Helicopter parenting is when you raise your kids to fly choppers, and nothin's gonna change my mind."

"Choppers?" Tabitha gave her a confused look. "Doesn't chopper mean motorcycle?"

"Since when? Chopper means helicopter, and always will," Alicia bantered back, gnawing on the tip of her pencil distractedly as she examined her half-finished drawing. "Nice try, though. What're you gonna dress up as for Halloween?"

"Um. I want to be Ariel." Tabitha gave her a sheepish look. "Ariel, from the *Little Mermaid*."

"Of course you do. I should've guessed." Alicia arched an eyebrow. "And, you're gonna rock the coconut bra in this weather?"

"No no no, I was planning on doing the human version. Like she wears in the little boat for the *'Kiss the Girl'* scene. Long-sleeved open neck blouse. Bodice, long skirt. Big bow for my hair. I think I might be able to find a really good pattern for everything at the library," Tabitha confided. "And, Ariel wore sea-shells, not coconuts!"

"Yeah, whatever," Alicia conceded with a chuckle. "You'll make a really good Ariel—you're already like, ninety percent there. Lame that they don't have a black Disney princess."

"They will," Tabitha said. "Princess Tiana."

"What?" Alicia blinked, immediately pausing her pencil mid-stroke. "Yeah, who?"

"Princess Tiana, from *The Princess and the Frog*, maybe... ten or so years from now?" Tabitha revealed. "I think it's the last hand-drawn animation they did, before their films were all either computer-animated or live-action."

"Are you for real?" Alicia asked, hugging her open sketchpad against herself defensively. "In ten years? That's a long time. Do you think I could be an animator by then?"

"Um." Tabitha appraised her friend for a moment before giving her honest opinion. "...Yes. I think that you really can; you're incredibly talented. In my last lifetime, I know you drew illustrations for different magazines."

"What kind of illustrations?" Alicia asked. "Like, political cartoon sorta stuff?"

"No, not like that at all." Tabitha shook her head. "Beautiful ones."

"Uh, describe them?"

"The piece that really stood out in my memory was a woman's nude back." Tabitha frowned, trying to recall everything she could. "Her head was turned, so that you could only see the profile of her face. It was like a sketch with the way you had your lines, but not in an... unfinished way, if that makes sense."

Alicia stared hard at Tabitha, still clutching her art pad against herself.

"It didn't seem anatomical, exactly," Tabitha continued, now struggling to put what she'd seen way back then into words. "All of the little muscles and the curls of her hair hanging down were detailed in like... a light map, kind of? The drawing itself was composed of crosshatch in the different shadow areas, to define everything, without putting in solid outlines.."

"Tabby! Alicia!" Elena waved cheerfully as she approached. "Morning! I want to introduce you to some people at lunch today, if that's cool with you guys. Are you both gonna be in the library again?"

"Who?" Alicia scowled, hugging her sketchbook protectively against herself to prevent Elena from catching a peek of her work.

"Matthew Williams, he's a sophomore, and Casey... uh," Elena paused. "I don't remember Casey's last name. She's a junior, and she helps run art club stuff."

"Are they your friends?" Tabitha asked, curious.

"...No, not really," Elena shook her head. "I'm crushing on Matthew, and he's interested in you. Not *interested* interested, I don't think. His dad's a policeman, and he had something to do with the shooting stuff you were involved in."

"Ah." Tabitha nodded in understanding. "Rob Williams. Okay. I was hoping he could drive me down to Louisville this Sunday."

"Have you met Matthew already?" Elena froze.

"No, I don't think so."

"Okay." Elena let out a slow breath, giving Tabitha a wary look. "I really like him."

"I have no interest at all, there," Tabitha assured her with a smile. "Trust me."

"Pfft." Alicia made a point of going back to work on her drawing, disregarding the conversation with an exasperated shake of her head. "Yeah, I wouldn't worry about Tabitha going after *boys* at all."

"Why?" Elena arched an eyebrow at Tabitha. "Are you gay? There were some rumors going around about that."

"I'm not," Tabitha sighed. "I just don't plan on entering into any relationships in the near future."

"Okay, cool." Elena gave her an appraising look. "I don't like gays. I think they're really weird."

It was a struggle for Tabitha not to wince and hide her face in her palms at hearing that. She probably shouldn't have expected a teenage girl in 1998 to be quite as politically correct as she'd grown accustomed to over her previous life, but hearing the girl's thoughts laid out so bluntly was still... unexpectedly jarring. Worse yet, Alicia seemed to find the misunderstanding she'd helped foster incredibly amusing.

Going to have to ease them both into a talk about some things later on, if we're all going to be friends.

"Casey's an artist," Elena continued, turning now to address Alicia. "I don't know how your stuff measures up against the upperclassmen, but I think you can impress her and get in with the art club crowd. She's apparently real close with all of them."

"And what does the art club do?" Alicia challenged, not looking up from her sketch.

"I actually don't know," Elena admitted with a shrug. "I only went to the poetry club open house, and I don't even know that I'll go back. I'm assuming art club meets in one of the art rooms someday after school, and that they organize activities and stuff. It could mean some sort of opportunities for you, I guess."

"Okay," Alicia tried to look indifferent. "Where's Matthew and Casey now?"

"I didn't say anything to them yet," Elena said. "You and Tabitha've pretty much kept to yourselves since school started. Didn't want to intrude on you guys or anything without asking first."

That's... surprisingly thoughtful of her, Tabitha thought, blinking at Elena. She wasn't sure what to make of the long-legged blonde. After returning to 1998 and having almost each and every hour of the day allotted to various planned endeavors, Tabitha could appreciate Elena's aggressive enterprising. The girl was definitely a go-getter, but Tabitha hadn't ever thought to consider nebulous concepts like friendship something you could really plan out. *I suppose we'll just have to see?*

The first bell sounded, a long, ringing warble that prompted the scattered students idling around the patio area to disperse towards their individual classes.

"I'd like to meet them," Tabitha decided, glancing toward Alicia. "What do you think?"

"Sure," Alicia said, feigning total disinterest. "It's whatever. I'm cool with it."

"Great!" Elena's eyes lit up. "Awesome. I'll let 'em know when I see them in class. Library at lunchtime?"

"Yeah," Tabitha said.

"Great," Elena said. "I'll let you two discuss, then. See you in first period, Tabby." The blonde left with a wave, pointedly giving the two some space to talk without her.

"What do you really think?" Tabitha gave Alicia a wry smile.

"I don't know." Alicia dropped her sketchpad back into her lap, no longer pretending to draw. "I still don't really like her. But it *was* cool of her to ask first. I guess."

"Any interest in art club?" Tabitha asked.

"Maybe?" Alicia lifted her hands in a helpless gesture. "I don't know, never really even thought about it. Crap. Should I grab my good portfolio out of my locker before lunch?"

———

"Alicia still doesn't like me," Elena reported, leaning toward Tabitha from her desk a row over in Marine Science. "What do you think I should do?"

"She doesn't really know you yet." Tabitha laughed. *I don't really know you yet either.* "Give her some time. She didn't warm up to me right away."

"Okay," Elena said. "You don't think it's because I'm white, do you?"

"...What?" Tabitha cocked her head, shooting Elena a look of disbelief. She held out a forearm, so pale that she could trace the slight blues and greens of veins along the inside of her wrists when she inspected closely enough. "No? I'm significantly whiter than you."

"No you're not," Elena scoffed, pointing at herself with both fingers. "I have blonde hair."

Tabitha was rendered speechless, tilting her head in confusion even further.

"I'm *kidding,* Tabby." Elena laughed.

"Both of y'all need to get a tan," Amber, the brunette girl who sat in front of Tabitha, spoke up. "Y'all are embarrassing."

"Your face is embarrassing." Elena smirked.

"Your momma's embarrassing," Amber shot back.

"Those shoes are embarrassing." Elena glanced down at Amber's muddy Reeboks with disdain.

"Your outfit is kinda embarrassing," Amber retorted. "Slut."

"Your boyfriend was pretty embarrassing," Elena snorted. "Trust me, I know."

"You sucking up to whore-face back here is what's embarrassing," Amber shot back with a laugh, twisting in her seat to give

Tabitha a skeptical once-over. "What's your whole deal supposed to be anyways? Think this was like, the first time I've even heard you talk to anyone."

"Running your mouth all the time is pretty embarrassing." Elena scowled at Amber. "Fuck off. You don't even know Tabby, and you're already tryin' to jump in and talk shit. Mind your own goddamn business, hoe-bag."

What... is happening? Tabitha looked from girl to girl with wide eyes.

She didn't want to be drawn into the surprisingly childish squabble at all. Having someone else immediately leap to her defense, however, was... different. Tabitha wasn't sure if she felt touched or if she felt alarmed, but it was a very strange experience for her, and when she opened her mouth she realized she had no idea what to say in this situation.

"Bitch, please," Amber spat. "You think I don't—"

"Ladies, ladies!" Mr. Simmons called over helpfully. "Save the Jerry Springer for next period; this is Marine Science. If you girls *absolutely* must bicker, at *least* say you're gonna go subtidal on her beach-face. Something like that—we have appearances to keep, here."

———

Casey was already waiting in the library when Tabitha arrived at lunchtime. With light brown hair cut in a shaggy bob, the girl wore a yellow tee with a summer camp logo emblazoned on it and a rather plain pair of shorts. With her now finely-tuned sense for differentiating the ages of various fellow students, Tabitha could tell she was at least sixteen or seventeen, and Casey was also putting off that flagrant *too-cool-for-school* vibe. The teen was rocking back dangerously in her chair, with her sneakers up on one of the library tables, while she idly played with her smartphone.

Wait. Tabitha lurched to a sudden halt, stunned. *She has a SMARTPHONE...?*

"Oh hey, what's up?" Casey noticed Tabitha's abrupt stop, giving her an enormous grin. "You must be Tabitha, right?"

"Uhh," Tabitha worked to regain her composure. "Yeah, hi. You're Casey? Is that a phone?"

"A phone?" Casey rolled a thumb across a dial on the side of the device, and the distinct sound of electronic chipset music was audible in the library for a moment. "It's a Gameboy Pocket. Cool, huh? I've got *Pokémon Red.* They're coming out with the Gameboy Color sometime this Christmas—I'm *super* stoked."

"Yeah! That's, um. Wow." Tabitha laughed, feeling the knot of unexpected tension slowly loosen itself. *I completely forgot Gameboys were a thing.* "That's really cool. It just runs on double As?"

"Triple A's, actually." Casey smiled. "Crazy how small they can pack it all into now, right?"

"Crazy, yeah," Tabitha agreed. *You have no idea. In just a few years, a smartphone'll have more processing power than all of the Apple II's in this computer lab put together. Forty years from now, a tiny little finger ring'll have more computing power than all of the machines in the world here combined.*

Before she could further ruminate on the bounding leaps of technology, Alicia showed up, her leather-bound art collection under one arm.

"Alicia?" Casey guessed, pulling her feet off the table and arranging herself in a more normal sitting position.

"Yeah. Hi." Alicia stood awkwardly, looking nervous.

"Elena said you're prospective *art club* material, so let's have a looksie at each other's stuff," Casey proposed, setting her Gameboy aside. The upperclassman pulled a worn spiral notebook out of a backpack at her feet and slid it across the table toward them.

Gingerly passing her own portfolio across to Casey, Alicia sat down with Tabitha at the table, and they opened up the offered spiral notebook between them. Within, they discovered each page was packed with squares upon squares of different panels filled with stylized doodle animals and speech bubbles—unlike Alicia, Casey was a cartoonist.

Cocoa Cinnabun was a pet bunny, drawn in a style reminiscent of old Garfield comics. In fact, as Tabitha's eyes flicked down the page, she found the plot of the comic storyboards was collectively something of an amateur homage to Garfield. Cocoa Cinnabun lazing about, Cocoa sometimes chewing through things he wasn't supposed to, or knocking over the waste can in the background, which was drawn as a simplified trapezoid shape.

"*Holy shit,*" Casey whispered as she leafed through Alicia's artbook opposite them. "You drew all of this? This is like, this stuff's *serious.*"

"Those are from last year, yeah," Alicia said. "I have my recent stuff in this one, if you wanna see."

"Gimme it all, I wanna see!" Casey laughed. "This is all like... *wow.* Hah, ashamed that you're looking at my awful garbage now."

"Your stuff isn't bad at all," Alicia said with respect, flipping from page to page. "Just, y'know. Stylized, totally different direction."

"I think Cocoa's really cute!" Tabitha added carefully. "He kind of reminds me of Garfield, Garfield crossed with Hello Kitty."

Wait. Would people in the US know about Hello Kitty, back in '98?

"I *love* Hello Kitty!" Casey broke into a beaming smile, putting Tabitha's concerns to rest. "Oh, hey! Matthew! Elena! You guys've gotta come check this stuff out!"

Tabitha turned in her seat to see Elena ushering a young man through the library's metal detector, and—

A single loop of tension slipped out of the knot she felt earlier and then her anxiety *constricted* the whole thing, forming what felt like a tight noose around her chest that made it difficult to breathe.

Matthew had mesmerizing blue eyes that immediately stole

her full attention, a steely heaven-eyed gaze she could wax poetic about—if not for her mind immediately turning to sugary molasses on her. Besides those unfathomable eyes, Matthew possessed strong, masculine features: distractingly broad shoulders, stern eyebrows and a lovely jawline. His wavy hair was a mottled dirty blond, and playfully swept back in what she thought of as a *surfer cut*. Tabitha felt her heart pound and blood rush to her face.

Goddamnit. You've got to be kidding me...

14

TRUST EXERCISES

Hormones. It's just... teenage hormones. Tabitha fought to school her face into proper composure. She hadn't felt so completely *betrayed* by her own body since first transmigrating back into the past. *He's just a kid. A cute kid, sure. But he's young. Waaay too young. Focus.*

"Hi." Matthew directed a potent smile her way, and Tabitha's wits seemed to scatter in every direction like they were scurrying away from a sudden spotlight. "Tabitha? I think you met my dad a couple days ago—Officer Williams? He was asking me about you."

"Yeah. Uh, whuh-what did you tell him?" Tabitha blurted out anxiously... completely embarrassing herself. Alicia and Elena both turned heads to look at her with interest, and she felt her cheeks go completely red. *No, no, no, no, no this isn't happening. This isn't happening.*

"Hah." Matthew let out a good-natured laugh. "I said you had all kinds of rumors goin' around, but I didn't know what to believe since I hadn't met you myself. My name's Matt—but, everyone calls me Matthew, for some stupid reason."

"There's already too many *Matts*." Casey chuckled, not looking up as she flipped through Alicia's second sketchbook in awe. "If we get another one after you, we're just gonna call him *'Phew.'*"

"I'll call you Matthew, then," Tabitha decided, just barely stopping herself from rising out of her seat to shake his hand. *Highschoolers don't do that!* "Mrs. MacIntire said she might call your dad, um, about driving me out to Louisville this Sunday...?"

"Yeah!" Matthew nodded. "She did. My dad works a shift Sunday, though."

"You could take her, Matthew," Elena chimed in helpfully. "You just got your license, and everything..."

"Sorry, no way." Matthew gave them a sheepish smile. "I've had it for like, just a couple weeks. Not super comfortable driving I-65 on my own yet."

"Oh, that's fine." Tabitha blushed. "I don't want to impose or anything."

Inwardly, she was impressed at his candor—he was uncharacteristically up front about his shortcomings, for a high-schooler. Wouldn't most boys fresh into their license be eager to show off? Matthew seemed laidback and mature in a way that had her start going moon-eyed all over again. *It doesn't help that he's a little, um, easy on the eyes either...*

"Hah, impose?" Matthew shook his head. "Naw, Mr. MacIntire's practically family—he used to go with us on our hunting trips, back when I was, oh... twelve? Thirteen? So, after what you did—"

"I didn't do much at all," Tabitha admitted, embarrassed. "Alicia was there too. All we did was try to stop the bleeding."

"She's lying. She did everything." Alicia sold her out without compunction, grinning widely. "She called it in, and was putting pressure on it like, right away, while I was just standing there bawling like an idiot."

"Y-you were not!" Tabitha argued, giving Alicia an incredulous look. *Alicia!*

"Well, thank you," Matthew said, letting out a slow breath.

"Seriously. You're some kind of hero; you did a great thing. Don't know if you knew, but Mr. MacIntire has a daughter—Hannah— she's just seven years old. We've been looking after her while they're both up in Louisville, and I'm really, *really* glad I didn't have to give her any bad news."

"...Oh," Tabitha replied dumbly, feeling her eyes water.

"If it's cool with you, my mom'll swing by your neighbor- hood this Sunday, take both you and Hannah up to Louisville to visit," Matthew explained. "You're living right there in Sunset Estates?"

"Yeah! It's, uh. Yeah." Tabitha nodded, fighting back tears as she found herself flooded with emotion. "Sorry, I—sorry."

"Uhh—you okay?" Casey was the only one that seemed surprised.

"Just give her a minute," Elena scolded the art club girl. "Are you okay, Tabby?"

Tabitha nodded quickly while hiding her face behind her hands, not trusting herself to give an answer without choking up.

She'd never heard a thing about Officer MacIntire having a daughter. Somehow, it felt like that changed everything. An unknown crisis, averted by bare inches—this little girl Hannah's entire world must have come crashing down in that last life, without Tabitha ever being any the wiser. She felt the knife of guilt in her heart lingering more closely now than ever. *Hannah. Her name's Hannah.*

"Sorry, I should probably leave you girls be," Matthew said, obviously discomforted by Tabitha's sudden tears. "Just wanted to let you know. You should swing by the Quad some lunch and sit with us sometime, at least put all the rumors to rest. Everyone's dyin' to meet you."

"Thanks," Elena spoke up on Tabitha's behalf. "We'll do that."

"Nice to meet you," Alicia added.

"Yeah," Matthew nodded. "Alicia, right? Saw you on the news too."

"Did you see her freaking *art?*" Casey exclaimed, holding up one of Alicia's portfolios. "She's like, half pro."

"Cool, cool." Matthew paused. "Join us in art club; we meet on Fridays. You do any photography?"

"I—uh, oh, wow!" Alicia's eyes went wide, and she slapped her forehead. "I don't. *Normally.* But, on the day of the shooting, I had a camera with me. I completely forgot about it with all the... Tabby stuff going on."

"Were you taking pictures?" Elena pressed.

"I was," Alicia revealed. "I did. Took two right at the crime scene, like, literally just moments after it happened. Shot of Tabby running towards the officer. The one's probably blurry, but the other one should be... decent? Maybe?"

"How do you forget something like that?" Elena asked in disbelief.

"This has all been a lot to deal with, okay?" Alicia shot a scowl at Elena. "I haven't been sleeping at all."

"Where's the camera now?" Casey clapped the sketchbook closed and jolted up to her feet. "If we tell Mr. Peterson, he can develop it right in the art room right away. You said the *crime scene?* Like right there at the parking lot shooting? This is big."

"Um. Still in my bag, I think," Alicia answered. "I left it in class. Tabby and I were there when the first officer got shot, not the big parking lot shooting."

"The first officer?" Casey didn't quite seem to be following.

"With your and Tabby's permission," Elena jumped in, "the Channel 7 people'll probably pay big bucks for that. I can have my mom get in touch with them."

"First thing's first—as acting treasurer, I hereby induct thee into the hallowed ranks of the Springton High Art Club," Casey said solemnly, making the motions of knighting Alicia shoulder to shoulder with the girl's own sketchbook before passing it back to her. "Ten bucks if you want an art club shirt. C'mon, let's go see if we can grab your bag and get to Mr. Peterson before lunch is over."

"O-okay," Alicia agreed, rising out of her seat.

"Guys, guys," Matthew chided them, watching as Tabitha blearily wiped her eyes. "Slow down, give her a moment."

"It's fine, I'm fine," Tabitha sniffed and gave Matthew an appreciative smile. "Sorry. Go for it, yeah. I'm just gonna sit here for a bit. Do your thing, Alicia—I didn't even realize you took a picture."

"I forgot," Alicia admitted, wincing. "Sorry."

Casey pulled Alicia along with her out of the library with Matthew in tow, who waved a casual goodbye, finally leaving a flustered Tabitha sitting alone together with Elena at the library table.

"*Well.*" Elena crossed her arms in front of herself, looking a little too pleased at Tabitha's guilty expression. "You're definitely not gay. What are you doing this Saturday?"

———

"I have to say, I *love* your outfit, Tabitha!" Mrs. Seelbaugh praised, turning from where she sat in the driver's seat for a moment to give the redhead a once-over. Elena's mother was steering their silvery-white family minivan across town toward the apartment where Tabitha's grandmother lived; Elena and Tabby would be looking after Tabitha's cousins for the day. "Where did you find that top?!"

"My grandma helps me put them together," Tabitha answered respectfully. "From thrift store dresses."

"You're *kidding!*" Mrs. Seelbaugh exclaimed, chancing another quick glance away from the road back toward Tabitha's attire. "From the thrift store right here in town?"

"Yes, ma'am."

"I'm a *mom*, not a *ma'am*," Mrs. Seelbaugh chided playfully.

"Wait—Tabitha, even the one you're wearing right now?"

Elena couldn't help but twist from the passenger's seat to scrutinize her pretty new friend.

"This was originally a prom dress," Tabitha explained. "We just removed the cups, stitched it overtop a plain white shirt, and then hemmed them together at the waist.

Blinking in disbelief at the ensemble for a moment, Elena could actually see it. What looked at first glance to be an extraordinarily well-fitted vest and shirt combination was actually just the upper portion of a black A-line prom dress—one with an extraordinarily plunging neckline—on top of a long-sleeved white shirt. Once the secret was revealed, she couldn't *unsee* it.

"That's amazing," Elena found herself blurting out. "Are you planning on selling them?"

"Selling them?" Tabitha shook her head. "Maybe someday. I know we'll need the money. For now, it's just something I love doing with my Grandma Laurie."

"That's so sweet!" Mrs. Seelbaugh said with a smile, sparing Elena a meaningful look.

Yeah... I want in on that, Elena thought with a small grin. *What teenage girl DOESN'T dream of launching their own fashion line? Even the business model is perfect! The thrift store material costs are negligible in the face of the price tags we can put on these.*

For an awkward moment, she'd already begun to mentally exclude her new friend Tabitha from her new plan to model her own business out of these blouses. With a pang of guilt, she murdered those ambitions while they were still in the cradle—she actually *liked* Tabitha. The girl was different, interesting. She was transparent emotionally in a manner no teen should be, and yet in other ways completely, utterly unfathomable. She was, to coin one of her mother's favorite phrases, a riddle, wrapped up in a mystery, inside an enigma.

"I want to try making one," Elena decided to admit. "I really love your tops."

Besides, that's not the kind of friend I want to be. If she continued to foster another such mercenary mindset—one based loosely on coinciding mutual interest alone—it would be her situation with Carrie all over again. Elena wanted beautiful friendships built on love and trust, ones that she'd be able to look back on fondly for the rest of her life. But, at the same time, it was difficult for her personally to set aside her competitive nature and pragmatic cynicism to make those happen *properly*.

When she'd talked it over with her mom, she'd been blanketed with assurances that she was perfectly normal, that friendships weren't picture-perfect in the way television made them out to be, and that in no time at all, she'd find close friends and confidants again to replace the middle school ones she'd grown away from. She knew her mother was right—her mom was always right—but at the same time... something about the answer didn't completely satisfy.

"We can show you how we do it, if you'd like—the next time we visit," Tabitha offered. "I was hoping we could spend most of this time with my cousins. I'm really worried about them."

"How old are your cousins?" Elena asked. Her growing anticipation for the afternoon fell a good deal at being reminded about the cousins. *Next time, I suppose.* "Grade school, or middle school?"

"Grade school," Tabitha answered. "Sam's the oldest; he's in fourth grade."

So it's babysitting little kids. Elena tried to swallow down her disappointment.

Their budding friendship was going swimmingly, however, and Elena at least felt relieved to finally be on an organized outing with someone again. She hadn't done anything important with a friend since the Six Flags trip with Carrie in the middle of summer —now, it felt like she had to blot out those mistakes by making as many new, *better* memories as she could.

This is okay. It doesn't have to be anything huge right at first, Elena thought, striving to focus on the positive. *Babysitting's a perfectly normal thing for girls our age to do—maybe we'll talk, find something cool to bond over. That's what matters—even if it's not big and exciting.*

Elena smiled faintly to herself as she watched the scenery pass by her window, mercifully oblivious to what she was about to experience.

"This is it up ahead," Tabitha called softly. "Those are my cousins playing there."

The silvery-white minivan performed her indicated turn onto the upcoming side street, and then pulled up several lots to where a group of young boys appeared to be taking turns running and crashing into a large pile of autumn leaves. They looked *rowdy,* the kind of boys Elena had avoided like the plague when she'd been at that age. Each of Tabitha's cousins had the same closely cropped haircut, making it difficult to tell them apart. Leaves and twigs stuck to their clothes, and dirty brownish grass stains were apparent on the knees of their pants from slides into the leaf pile.

"Give me a ring whenever you two're ready to be picked up." Mrs. Seelbaugh smiled. "Love you, Elena. Have fun, girls!"

"Yeah. Love you, Mom."

"Thank you, Mrs. Seelbaugh."

"Hey, *Tabby's here!*" a boy cried out, and all at once, they were scrambling out of the leaves with crunching footsteps and running toward them. Elena grimaced, mentally bracing herself for an entire afternoon corralling rambunctious little hooligans.

"Boys, come over here," Tabitha instructed, gesturing them forward.

At a closer look—Elena confirmed they were all completely filthy. Each boy appeared to be emulating the character Pigpen from the Peanuts comic strip, liberally covered with dirt and dead plant debris from playing outside. It was an amusing contrast, seeing Tabitha in her lovely fashion-wear gently scolding this line-up of little rascals, dusting them off in frustration and picking bits of leaves off of their heads.

What Elena hadn't prepared herself to see was Tabby drop down to her knees and pull all four boys at once into a giant hug, disregarding her own custom-designed attire and the mess they might make of it. Even more surprising—the cousins weren't resisting. There was no aggravated struggle free from her arms, no exasperated laughter or groaning; the oldest-looking one spared Elena an embarrassed glance, but they all dutifully returned Tabitha's embrace.

"Boys... I'm so sorry about your parents," Tabitha said in a quiet voice. "I wish I'd done something. I'm so sorry."

"It's okay," one of the boys spoke up. "Mom said she's coming back."

"Yeah," another one agreed. "She's coming back soon. She said just a few days."

"No." Tabitha shook her head slowly, locking eyes with each of them and giving them a firm look. "I'm sorry. She's not coming back. But Grandma Laurie and I are going to do our best to take care of all of you."

...*What?* Elena awkwardly stood by, dumbfounded by the unexpected heavy atmosphere. *She said they were going through a rough time or something, but I never really thought... oh my God, what happened—did their parents just pass away? Or worse, divorce?*

"Mom said she was coming back." The smallest one pulled back from Tabitha with a cross look. "In a few days."

"I know she did, Joshua," Tabitha replied gravely. "But she's not. She's not coming back."

"I don't care," the oldest one scoffed. "We don't even need her anyways."

When the quartet of young cousins were awkwardly released from Tabitha's hold, they exchanged looks with each other and stole glances back at Tabitha. Their initial childlike demeanor had clouded over, and they were all quiet, *solemn*. The littlest boy Tabitha had called Joshua looked sullen, while two of the other brothers had their brows furrowed in thought at receiving the horrible news, and then the oldest of them just looked disappointed and angry.

Should... I even be here? Elena forced herself not to fidget.

"This is my friend Elena—I want you to treat her with the same respect you treat me," Tabitha told them, rising back to her feet and patting the leaves off her knees. "We're taking you to the playground to play."

————

"Has everyone been doing their stretches?" Tabitha asked, lining up the boys in a row along the dead grass beside the playground. "Who can get down the farthest?"

The four cousins slowly shimmied down, legs spreading apart in an attempt at a split. Joshua had the most success, nearly reaching the ground, while the other three struggled, their legs forming different degrees of obtuse angles. *She's going to run them through... gymnastics?*

The playground itself was a small chain-link fence enclosed affair attached to the nearby neighborhood, with several wooden risers and staircases constructed into a covered central fort. An enclosed hard plastic spiral slide featured on one end of the fort and an open slide on the other, separated by the wobbling clatter bridge. Radiating away from the structure were the expected allotment of swing sets, animal-shaped rocker seats situated on thick springs, and benches for parents to sit. On an October Saturday, the area was nearly deserted, entirely empty save for a pair of very young girls attempting to climb up the plastic spiral slide from within, watched over in the distance by a sitting mother.

The boys were unexpectedly *obedient,* Elena had discovered on the short walk over. Not quite docile—as they were quick to pick fights with each other and bicker pointlessly over the tiniest things—but she was fascinated to see that at a stern word from Tabitha, they immediately bowed to her apparent authority. At school, Tabitha was something of a withdrawn, shy-seeming girl who sequestered herself in the library of all places, so this contrasting, *commanding* presence was incredibly interesting.

"Why're you having them stretch?" Elena leaned in and asked. *I thought they were just going to play tag or hide-and-seek or something.*

"Stretches help keep them limber, and give them higher kicks," Tabitha explained, turning to Elena with a smile. "I promised them last time that I'd teach them a few moves."

The redhead demonstrated, tilting her upper body to one side and drawing one knee up into the air all the way to the level of her chest. There was something smooth and powerful in the unhurried ease with which she seemed to ready her kick that was startling, the young woman's balance not wavering in the slightest.

She snapped out a kick impossibly high in the air, quick and crisp, before immediately returning her foot to its tucked position up in the air—poised to strike. Two more kicks flashed out, each faster than the last, and then Tabitha relaxed, returning her foot to where it belonged on the ground.

Whoa, whoa. Elena blinked, struggling to reevaluate everything she thought she knew about Tabitha. *She's like, a martial artist?*

"Show her the thing with the pop can!" one of the boys suggested.

"Yeah, show her, show her!" another one quickly joined in.

"We don't have one." Tabitha looked around helplessly. "Sorry, boys."

Not ones to be dissuaded, all four of Tabitha's cousins quickly abandoned stretching practice to dash every which way across the playground, canvassing the area in search of an empty soda can. When they finally discovered one—a discarded Pepsi can sporting that dramatic new *blue* look Elena had yet to grow accustomed to —the boys immediately fought over it as they all ran back over.

No way. Elena grew a little alarmed. If she didn't know any better, their struggle appeared to be a contest of which of the two taller boys would be balancing the empty can on his head. *What, she's been playing karate-kick William Tell with them? That can't be safe. What if one of them nails the other one right in the head?*

"Behave yourselves." Tabitha laughed, striding amidst the cousins to pluck the can away from the boys. "Elena's here with us today." Before Elena caught on to her meaning, Tabitha had already stepped up right in front of her and was gingerly attempting to balance the empty Pepsi can on top of Elena's blonde head.

"You can't be serious." Elena laughed nervously, not even bothering to keep still enough for Tabby to balance the can. "I'm a lot taller than you."

"That's what makes it good exercise," Tabitha countered with a grin, steadying Elena's shoulders so that she could perfectly place the pop can atop her head. "And, for you—you can think of it as a trust exercise."

"No way." Elena froze, uneasy at the way the boys were gathering around them in anticipation. "Tabitha, no way—what if you kick me in the face? I'm way taller than you anyways; you can't even reach."

"Do you trust me?" Tabitha challenged her. "I can reach."

No—obviously no, please don't even think about it! Elena bit back her response with a terrified look. The situation was deteriorating at incredible speed, and all of her previous efforts to befriend this girl weren't going to count for anything at all if she got kicked in the face right now. Friends didn't kick each other in the face, not even by accident. Elena drew the line there, and it was not something she was willing to compromise on.

But, wait, no. She said it's a trust EXERCISE—this is just a test. She was never ACTUALLY going to—Before the girl could even finish her own relieved thought, Tabitha *leapt* up into the air, leg suddenly exploding forward in an unbelievable flash of force just inches above Elena. The tiny weight perched atop the crown of Elena's head disappeared with a hollow *clank* as the can was sent flying, and then Tabitha calmly landed back on her feet.

Oh my fuck. Fucking fuck. Fuck. Elena was still completely tense and frozen in place as her mind caught up with what happened.

Somewhere behind her, she could hear the empty can clattering across the pavement in the distance—it had crossed the entire stretch of lawn and landed in the parking spaces in front of the playground. The sound of the four cousins cheering and jumping up and down in excitement was muted to nothing but distracting noise as she struggled to collect herself.

That would have taken my head clean off—I felt the wind of it move my fucking hair! Elena stared at Tabitha with wide eyes. *Oh my God. Oh my God, I can't breathe.*

"Thank you for trusting me," Tabitha said, offering her a shy smile. "It's really not as scary as it seems—my control's pretty good now."

Still standing, she neatly brought her foot up into the air again and perfectly traced the outline of Elena's shoulder, and then overtop her head—Tabitha straining on her tiptoes to reach—without the edge of the girl's shoe ever actually touching her. There was a steely gracefulness to the motion, and Tabby finished drawing the silhouette of Elena's opposite shoulder before casually bringing her leg back to the ground.

"Okay." Elena swallowed slowly. "Okay, how do you do that?"

"I've been kinda-sorta teaching myself Taekwondo," Tabitha revealed. "Over the summer."

"Teaching... yourself?" Elena raised an eyebrow. "From what? How?"

"You really wouldn't believe me if I told you." Tabitha gave her a sheepish smile. "Seriously. I was actually just about to show Alicia my butterfly kicks last week, when all of that business with the police officer went down. Like, right in front of us."

"Show her your flips!" one of the cousins called out.

"She can do backflips, and walk on walls," another boasted.

What is she supposed to be, a Power Ranger? Elena wanted to laugh at how ridiculous all of this was getting. *Spiderman? Human beings don't walk on walls.*

"Get back to your stretches, or none of you little heathens are ever doing any of this." Tabitha chuckled, giving the boys a stern look. "We're playing tag in a bit, and I want you all warmed up. No sissy excuses later on!"

The four children reluctantly returned to stretching their legs and grudgingly twisting their bodies through warm-up movements.

"Can you really do a backflip?" Elena asked, her mind sprinting through the possibilities of what they could do with all of these emerging new factors. *But what is Tabitha really capable of?*

"Don't listen to them. I'm really not great at it," Tabitha admitted. "I don't like doing backflips unless I'm starting on top of something that's up off the ground a bit. To give me that extra room, that clearance space. Oh—I can do back hand-springs easy, though."

With that, Tabitha leaned back, arching her body, and reached backwards for the ground behind her. Before her hand was even planted, her legs rose up in the air, and with baffling ease, her body simply flipped through the air to land right-side-up again.

"But yeah, that's kind of cheating," Tabitha said. "Even the boys can already do cartwheels just fine."

"...Do you want to try out for the cheerleading team together?" Elena blurted out.

"I don't... think so?" Tabitha shook her head. "I'm sorry, I never had much enthusiasm for sports. Were you going to try out?"

"No, I'm just thinking out loud—you're really amazing." Elena laughed, shaking her head. *Does Springton High have a gymnastics team, or something like that?* "I was planning on going for girls' varsity basketball... right until I saw this. Now I don't know what I want to do. What are you going to do?"

"Do you like to run?" Tabitha asked. "I run a lot, but, just on my own. For a while now, I've been thinking I should try doing it with other people, be more... uh—get more involved?"

"I can run!" Elena's eyes lit up. "My mom runs—I've run a 5k with her before. Were you looking into joining the track team?"

"I hadn't thought about it, really." Tabitha shrugged. "Should I? I was just wishing I had someone to jog with me in the early mornings... but I don't think anyone who lives near me is the slightest bit interested, hah ha."

She didn't get liposuction over the summer, Elena realized, wanting to slap herself for ever believing that rumor. *She's obviously been at this for a while—there'd have been like, some sort of RECOVERY period, where you can't be jumping and running around after a surgery. She actually lost all of the weight for real, just doing this —exercising, and running, and stuff.*

Her new understanding of Tabitha felt like a long-missing puzzle piece was falling into place for Elena, personally. One of the hallmark traits Elena had always looked for in her peers—up until now—was a certain sense of *ambition.* Now, it felt like she'd been just slightly off the mark all along—what she really desired was a best friend that was *driven,* motivated toward her pursuits in the same dogged way that she was. *The same way Mom always has been.*

In way of contrast, Carrie's ideology had always been to just leverage every possible advantage she could squeeze out of any given situation. While Elena still largely agreed with that line of thought... in hindsight, that wasn't *exactly* who she wanted to be, and certainly not what she wanted in a best friend anymore.

"I don't know how yet, but I am absolutely going to be your jogging partner," Elena decided with a grin. "You run every morning? Should I be doing stretches? Can you teach me how to do karate?"

15
THE LEGACY OF SHANNON DELAIN

Five hours later

Gasping for breath, Elena scrambled up the exterior of the playground fort, frantically grabbing for every available handhold across the wooden edifice and scuffing her new sneakers into every foothold she could cram them in. She hauled herself up over the railing and dropped heavily into that uppermost section featuring the long plastic spiral slide, the fort's tower.

This is... so much fun!? Elena thought, feeling a little bewildered as she struggled to draw in lungsful of chilly autumn air.

If someone had told her earlier that she would be covered in sweat and panting with exertion from playing a *game of tag with children,* Elena wouldn't have believed a word of it. They'd been playing for hours and hours now, though, and it was already getting dark out. Her hands felt raw from clambering around the playground, she had *splinters* in the side of her arm she'd yet to pluck out, and her elbows were scratched up from a tumble she'd taken across the mulch. She didn't even want to think about what she'd done to her nice white shoes.

Their game began in an incredibly lopsided five-against-one, with Elena roped into joining all of the little cousins to oppose Tabitha's purported 'dominance' of the game. To win, Tabitha had to tag out their entire team—with the caveat of not allowing those she'd tagged to in turn tag her, which reset the round, forcing Tabitha to start tagging them all out all over again.

The tables turned back and forth as the day progressed. Each game—with the exception of one particularly unfortunate instance—began with Elena's team hurriedly dispersing in every direction to put as much distance as possible between them and Tabitha. Then, one by one, they would form back up into a hunting party to pursue Tabby as they were each tagged out.

No two rounds played out alike, and the dynamic within each round could and often did change in a heartbeat. If you hadn't been tagged, you were frantically fleeing Tabitha's approach, and if you'd already been tagged, you were racing after her to try to catch her before she tagged the rest of the group. Sometimes, Elena and the four boys formed a cohesive group; other times, they split up with an every-kid-for-themselves attitude. Many of the rounds ended with Elena leading the tagged-out pursuers in close coordination to defend the last remaining untagged cousin from Tabitha.

The first two rounds had both been shocking losses, with Tabitha dispatching all four cousins and Elena in a handful of minutes. Although she could hardly believe she was starting to take a game of playground tag seriously, Elena felt her competitive spirit rise to match the circumstances and she started giving it her all. In the third round, Elena coaxed and cajoled the boys into attempting some semblance of a strategy—clustering up together for mutual support.

If we all stick real close together, one of us can just tag her back right away, Elena remembered, shaking her head in disbelief at her own naiveté. *Yeah, right.*

Tabitha had lunged fearlessly into their midst, tagging each of the boys with a healthy shove that sent them sprawling back out of retaliatory range. Weaving and ducking past clumsily outstretched arms, the fiery-haired girl struck them out with practiced precision, and it was the shortest round ever. Their entire group of five was overturned in a handful of seconds.

That wasn't to say Elena didn't have fun—there was something incredibly *uninhibited* about this whole experience, a refreshing simplicity to today that she wouldn't have ever imagined, and didn't think she could recreate. The four cousins hadn't spoken a word to her when she was just *Elena,* an outgoing but somewhat unknown quantity here to babysit them with Tabitha, this total outsider. As an aloof older teen, she in turn hadn't really had any particular interest in them either. Once they started playing, however, their different perceived roles fell out of relevance and were quickly forgotten.

The boys—she recognized them individually as Sam, Nick, Aiden, and Joshua now—were young enough that they weren't *boys,* weren't this complicated different gender dynamic she was forced to be aware of. In playing alongside each other, they somehow ceased to be part of the social rhetoric that dictated how Elena acted and how she treated them, and something about it all was incredibly straightforward and liberating. They were just all kids having fun together—except Tabitha, of course. Tabitha was some kind of monster.

Tabitha... Elena immediately grew alert. The idea of *Tabitha* had been imbued with several new flavors throughout the course of the day, and the name rolled back and forth over her tongue unspoken, something she couldn't quite adjust to.

Am I ever gonna be able to see her like I used to again? Hunkering herself down into a crouch, Elena turned to peek through the wooden bars of the fort at the chaos below. Aiden was dashing frantically by in the waning October light, but she wasn't sure if he was in pursuit or retreat. One of the three newcomers to the game, a taller neighborhood boy who the boys were calling Kenny, ran past as well.

Whatever else she thought the girl was in Marine Science or in the school library, this seemingly shy and reserved classmate of hers was the undisputed *apex predator* on this playground. The previously unassuming redhead became an unstoppable juggernaut, an invincible tyrant whose shock and awe blitzes regularly sent all four cousins scattering with yelped shrieks and panicked laughter. The very sight of Tabitha's agile figure darting about the playground after them—or worse, closing in instead on her—filled Elena with a thrilling sense of fear. Although their team of five did win several games, victories were few and far between enough that every win felt like an enormous accomplishment.

Throughout the game, Elena had witnessed Tabitha perform incredible feats of acrobatics. The girl was *fast*, and had no qualms committing herself to hand-springs, diving lunges or running slides to tag someone out or avoid pursuit. She was fearless in both scaling up the playground equipment and then jumping off of them as the situation demanded, and wasn't shy about rolling across the mulch as she scrambled back up to her feet to avoid a tag.

The different terrain was used to full effect against her opponents—the animal-shaped rocker seats and park benches she could leap over and clear entirely, a feat impossible for the much younger boys to imitate. At a full sprint, Tabby would grab the posts of the playground fort or the swing set bars to sharply swing her entire body in a new direction, while those chasing after were forced to patter to a skidding stop in the mulch to bleed off momentum.

Elena's long legs enabled her to outpace Tabitha briefly in the open spaces—but in the fenced enclosure of the playground, there really wasn't anywhere for her to go. Instead, they endlessly traversed the trifecta of grounds between the fort itself, a giant tree that shaded the area, and the detached set of monkey bars. The cousins constantly gravitated toward the playground fort, ready to make a quick escape on one of the slides or at one of the series of riser exits the moment Tabitha began to capture the fort. After all, she could only cut off one of them at a time. Usually, anyway.

Elena was just in the middle of determining her preferred getaway route from the fort... when she noticed her mother's silvery-white minivan parked in front of playground.

Oh my God! Alarmed, Elena abruptly stood up, struggling to shift mental tracks back to normalcy. They'd been playing for— how many hours now? It was dark already, and not heading back to call had been an uncharacteristic and irresponsible lapse on her part. Her mother had obviously checked in at Tabitha's grandma's place when she was worried, and then been directed here. When Elena saw Tabitha run up the risers toward her position, she felt torn between the game mindset and this sudden return to reality.

"My mom's here," Elena blurted out with a grin, holding up her hands.

"Yeah. She's been watching for a while," Tabitha revealed, and the petite redhead continued her ruthless advance. "At the bench over by the tree."

"...Oh." Elena was embarrassed not to have noticed.

It felt like a standoff showdown atop the fort, and each of the teenage girls eyed each other warily under the unspoken agreement of *one last tag.* There was only the stretch of the clatter bridge and a small landing of risers between them. The spiral slide was just beside Elena, but its exit down below was practically facing the fort where Tabitha stood, and it would only be a short hop down for Tabitha to catch her. That felt... *anticlimactic.*

In a moment of inspired courage, Elena shot Tabitha a grin and vaulted over the railing of the fort tower and dropped— almost eight feet all the way to the ground. She landed gracelessly on her hands and feet, but it felt heroic, *adventurous,* and the surprise she got from Tabitha, the surprise she felt *herself* was the sort of satisfaction she couldn't get from a roller coaster at Six Flags. That an innocuous game of tag would so easily eclipse their big summer trip as a personal experience for her was exhilarating, and Elena had to chuckle to herself as Tabitha landed beside her.

"Good game?" Elena laughed, brushing off her palms.

"Yeah." Tabitha nodded with a wry smile. "Good game."

Letting the cousins and other assorted neighborhood children continue to run amok for a moment, the two girls crossed over to the bench where Mrs. Seelbaugh was waiting.

"You girls look like you've been having fun!" Elena's mother remarked, giving them both a curious look.

"Sorry, Mom. Totally lost track of time," Elena admitted sheepishly, working to reconcile herself with the more mature Elena of earlier today, the one who didn't play on playgrounds like a child. She could tell her mother was thrilled that she'd had such a good time, ready to inundate her with questions about what had happened as soon as they were alone together.

"No worries! *Hakuna matata.*" Mrs. Seelbaugh laughed. "I got to talking about those lovely thrift store blouse designs with Tabitha's grammy for longer than I intended, myself. Are you girls ready for me to take you home? I can give the boys a lift down the street so they don't have to walk."

"That'd be great, Mrs. Seelbaugh," Tabitha said. "Thank you."

"Oh, I meant to ask you earlier, Tabitha," Mrs. Seelbaugh said, rising up off the bench and stretching. "It's been on my mind since this morning, the resemblance is so crazy—by any chance is your mother's maiden name *Shannon Delain?*"

Tabitha's smile seemed to go rigid at hearing the name.

"Yes, ma'am," Tabitha finally answered in a quiet voice. "That's my mother. She's Shannon Moore now."

"I thought for sure she must be!" Mrs. Seelbaugh exclaimed in excitement. "We were good friends, we went to Springton High together! Where has she been all these years—did your family just move back to the area? I can't wait to tell the other moms; we all still talk about her! Is she home, do you think—"

"I'm sorry, Mrs. Seelbaugh." Tabitha winced. "She's home, but... you can't see her."

"Oh—I'm so sorry, just listen to me going on," Elena's mother apologized in a fluster. "Did something happen. Is everything alright?"

"If she saw you now..." Tabitha said with some difficulty, "it would fundamentally break her."

"What?" Mrs. Seelbaugh froze. "Break her?"

"I'm thirteen," Tabitha explained, glancing at the bewildered Elena beside her. "I turn fourteen in December. From that timetable alone, you should be able to tell that something went terribly wrong with Shannon Delain's... big plans, her dream."

"Oh, honey." Mrs. Seelbaugh gave her an apologetic wince. "I wouldn't say *wrong,* I just wondered if—"

"Everything that could go wrong for her all those years ago, did go wrong," Tabitha interrupted with finality.

What? Elena blinked in surprise at the sudden and unexpected direction the conversation had taken.

"Starting with me," Tabitha explained in a quiet voice. She looked down and brushed the edge of her sneaker across an errant tuft of mulch. "You picked me up from the Lower Park, so you've seen how... well, you've seen where we are now. It's so much worse than you think, and... I don't think she's in a state where she can stand to be seen by you, not now. Maybe not for a long time. I'm sorry."

"Oh my word." Mrs. Seelbaugh looked taken aback. "I'm so sorry, I don't mean to make anything difficult, or, or cause any problems. Can you just tell your mom that I remember her? That I'd love to get together and catch up sometime, whenever she's comfortable with that? Would that be alright?"

Mom knows Tabby's mom, and something real bad happened? Watching the entire exchange with increasing unease, Elena turned from her mother's anxious expression to Tabitha's frown in confusion.

"I'll tell her that you asked about her," Tabitha decided, letting out a slow breath and giving them a helpless shrug. "But I don't think it will go over well. We're hardly on speaking terms anymore."

———

They dropped off the boys with their grandmother, and then drove Tabitha over to Sunset Estates, awkwardly seeing her off in front of a worn-down, dilapidated mobile home. Mrs. Seelbaugh finally pulled their silvery-white minivan up the hill and parked at the gas station overlooking Tabitha's neighborhood. They'd never filled their tank here—her father remarked that the gasoline quality here was awful—yet another black mark signifying that difference in social status that set this area of town apart from the rest of Springton.

The casual questions and light-hearted small talk had given way to an uncomfortable silence once Tabitha left, and Elena looked at her mother with concern. They weren't stopped here for gas, and it didn't look like Mrs. Seelbaugh was going to run into the attached convenience store and buy anything either.

"Mom?" Elena asked. "Everything okay?"

"I don't know!" Mrs. Seelbaugh gave her daughter an exasperated laugh, shaking her head. "I really don't know."

"Is it the thing with Tabitha's mom?" Elena prodded.

"Yeah." Her mother seemed at a loss for words, looking off somewhere into the darkness outside. Moths and other assorted little insects were flicking about beneath the overhead lights of the gas station in a frenzied swarm.

"Shannon Delain was... well, the gals and I, we still talk about her all the time, even after all these years. *Shannon Delain.* I had no idea she was right here in town! No idea that she..." Mrs. Seelbaugh tried to explain. "Cindy, Melissa and I, we were some of the cool kids, but Shannon was the real popular one, in this whole different league.

"She was going places, was gonna be someone, move out to Hollywood and... y'know, *be someone,* and everybody knew it. But we never heard a thing. Cindy was always so sure she was gonna pop up in a movie, or a TV show, or a magazine somewhere. Then there's Melissa, insisting Shannon must've found a rich husband somewhere, became a—you know, the Malibu trophy wife. Hah."

"What did you think happened to her?" Elena asked, only interested in the opinion that mattered.

"Modeling for advertisements. Maybe little parts for commercials?" Mrs. Seelbaugh mused. "She was so pretty. I always thought it'd be neat to find her in something, to be able to say, look, that's Shannon Delain—we went to school together."

That would be cool, Elena agreed, picturing an older version of Tabitha, starring in some sort of big action movie blockbuster.

"But she's been here all along, I suppose," Mrs. Seelbaugh realized, her expression falling. "All these years. *Shannon Delain*—it was like she was the one to strive for, the one who dared to dream big. All these years feeling like we were chasing after her tailfeathers, and it's like... it's like..."

Her mother struggled to find the right words.

"Like she must've fallen right out of the sky the very moment she was out of sight. All of us still lookin' up after her all this time, when instead she was really... um. She's really been *down there.* In the last place we'd ever look."

They both stared down the hill. Sporadic streetlights revealed cramped rows of battered mobile homes where the lowest-income families eked out a difficult existence. The glow of passing headlights from the busy street just beyond demarcated the distant boundary of the trailer park, a residential area bordered on all sides by commercial zones of questionable property value.

There was an ABC liquor store next door, and then the Springton Auto-Repair Center. A strip of small, rundown offices, containing a tax specialist, an orthodontist, and a small law firm. Another gas station, a smaller one. The old American Fidelity Bank and Trust, which had been boarded up for the last two years, shared a parking lot with a rather seedy-looking Hardee's. The surroundings painted a very different perspective than the suburb the Seelbaughs lived in, which was picturesque by comparison.

"Are you gonna call Aunt Cindy and them tonight, about this?" Elena asked. "Have a girls' night?"

"I *really* want to, but... no, no—it's already so late." Mrs. Seelbaugh worried her lip, glancing at the digital numbers of the clock on the dash. "Don't even know what I want to say, just yet. I can rein in your Aunt Cindy, but Mrs. Melissa was always... a teensy bit jealous of Shannon. So she'd be just dying to come over here and see sometime, stir up some kind of drama."

"Was it—is it that bad?" Elena's eyes widened at the thought. "I don't wanna make problems for Tabitha."

"Sounds like you're good friends already." Mrs. Seelbaugh's troubled look fell away, and she beamed with pride for her daughter. "Guess we're just gonna havta keep the whole story between me and you, then, this time. You know what that means!"

"Two glasses of wine?" Elena guessed with a hopeful grin. "I've gotta tell you all about tag with Tabitha."

"Just one glass for you, I think." Mrs. Seelbaugh let out a laugh, shifting the vehicle out of park and checking her mirrors. "I'm really glad you had fun today, Kiddo. But, after *this* kind of news, I feel like I'm gonna need three or four."

———

Mr. Moore was pacing back and forth through the narrow trailer hallway with the telephone handset pressed to his ear when Tabitha came home. He greeted her with a forced smile and a nod, still listening to the tinny voice of the speaker on the other end of the line. She wasn't sure who he might be conferring with this late, but she thought she caught the name *Daniel Moore,* so it surely had something to do with the recent incident.

Removing her dirty shoes in their small linoleum entranceway, she wearily stepped over into their living room. There Mrs. Moore sat, illuminated only by the glow of their television set, bloated bulk situated in her usual spot upon the sofa. Her mother registered her presence with an annoyed glare for a moment, before turning back to the TV with indifference. There was no *do you realize how late it is,* or *where on God's green Earth have you been,* not anymore.

"My friend's mother took us out to the park," Tabitha hesitantly broached the subject. "She asked about you."

"Oh, *now* it's any of my business what all you get up to," Mrs. Moore scoffed, shooting her daughter another dirty look. "Tabby, if you're not gonna listen to a damned thing I say anyhow, don't go makin' anything seem like—"

"Allow me to correct myself," Tabitha interrupted, gritting her teeth. "She didn't ask about you in the capacity of you being my mother. Mrs. Seelbaugh asked if you were formerly Shannon Delain, whom she'd gone to school with. I was told the resemblance was striking."

Mrs. Moore seemed to show no reaction to that, but Tabitha could tell that though the corpulent woman continued to vacantly stare in that direction, her eyes weren't quite fixed on the TV anymore. No longer expecting a response, Tabitha decided to continue.

"I told her that you were indisposed, and would not be able to meet her," Tabitha reported. "Was that what I should've told her?"

Her mother reacted to that, snapping around to face her with a *look* in her eyes. Tabitha wasn't sure what she saw there— anxiety, fear, and maybe a little bit of hate. Maybe a lot. There was a *haunted* look dancing in the depths of those pale green eyes, and for the first time, Tabitha had a real sense of how trapped her mother felt, trapped in this life she didn't want, with this daughter she couldn't deal with, in that fat body she couldn't escape from, the limp red hair framing that perpetual scowl.

The suffocating feeling she saw in her mother's expression was so painfully familiar to Tabitha that she wavered on her feet, wanting nothing more than to *immediately leave.* She didn't want to be in this situation, didn't want to even try to finish this conversation, felt like she never should have brought it up. Didn't want her mother to look at her like—

"Tabitha—sit down," Mrs. Moore asked, breaking eye contact. "We need to... we have to talk. *Please.*"

The urge to flee intensified, but Tabitha found herself instead mechanically moving to sit in her father's chair across from the sofa. It felt like *a talk* was treading dangerous new ground, and she didn't see any possible positive outcomes to this conversation. From the moment she relegated herself to a seat across from her mother, wasn't she setting herself up for another fruitless and destructive confrontation? She had no idea where else *a talk* could even take them now, but she didn't imagine it would be anywhere she remotely wanted to explore.

To her surprise, Mrs. Moore first heaved forward in her seat, reaching down and lifting the upholstered skirting panel of the sofa front below her. Where normally they would slide out their tray of VHS tapes from beneath—Mrs. Moore instead withdrew that familiar blue album. Tabitha watched on in growing horror as her mother hefted the scrapbook of photos in her hands, as if feeling the terrible weight of the bright and beautiful dreams within. Dreams that would never come to fruition.

It felt surreal seeing *her mother,* of all people, take that thing out from wherever she'd had it hidden away. It was in so many ways the Moore household *taboo,* the most sensitive contraband she should never be caught peeking at, worse in some ways than that nudie magazine of her father's she would discover in the bathroom years from now.

"You know what this is," Mrs. Moore said in a gruff voice, gripping the album in both hands. "You've seen what's inside."

"Yes," Tabitha answered, feeling herself tense up.

Beauty pageant photos. Modeling pictures. An impossibly gorgeous young woman with a brilliant, confident smile who somehow or other turned into YOU. Tabitha clenched her teeth, remembering all those many years ago when she'd flipped through the pages of that scrapbook in shock and stunned disbelief.

But then I came along, and I took all of that away from you. You didn't hate me for that last time, at least. This time, though... when I lost the weight and started making the effort, you started seeing yourself again in me—that's what really broke you, isn't it?

"I know what you must think about me," Mrs. Moore began. "I realize. But I don't want you thinking that you were a mistake, honey. Because... you weren't. You were a blessing."

"...Was I?" Tabitha's eyebrows shot up. She fought to keep from a dozen different snide remarks before one finally won out and slipped past her lips. "Forgive me, Mother, but you don't seem very blessed."

"No, I don't," Mrs. Moore agreed, her hands tightening on the album until the blue jacket began to twist in her hands. "But there are... things. Things that didn't get—that would never be put in this album. That you don't know. I'm just afraid that you've... jumped to conclusions."

"You didn't give up your dream because of me?" Tabitha asked, feeling her heart leap into her throat at so abruptly voicing the question. "B-because of having me?"

"No," Mrs. Moore's red-rimmed eyes met her gaze with more conviction than Tabitha had expected. "No, I didn't."

You... didn't? In disbelief, Tabitha opened her mouth, but closed it again just as quickly. She didn't know how to respond to that.

"I was going to be a model, and an actress," Mrs. Moore explained, rubbing a thumb along the edge of the album but not daring to open it. "Flew out to Los Angeles, did photoshoots and videos for... stupid little things. Toothpaste. Deodorant ads, hah—not even perfume; competition was too crazy for perfume. Bit parts in a few sitcoms, even if they were just one appearance and a single spoken line. When I finally passed an audition for an acting role, a *real* role, it was for the movie *Lucas*. It was going to be my big debut."

Lucas? Tabitha's mind was reeling, searching through her sixty years of memories for the title and drawing a complete blank. Whatever the movie was, it hadn't made any noticeable waves or cultural impact in her last lifetime that she was aware of.

"I had the role for Maggie," Mrs. Moore remembered with a small laugh, as if she could scarcely believe it herself. "I would've kissed Charlie Sheen. Instead, I ran away. I ran away, and wound up here. I had you, I became... this."

"You ran away... and *then* had me?" Tabitha asked for clarification. From her mother's phrasing, she couldn't tell whether the two events were related to one another or not.

"Yes." Mrs. Moore nodded sadly. "I disappeared. Broke contract and ran away, two months into filming. They had us out in Lake Ellyn Park, Illinois for shooting. Just some five hours away from here. I called Alan—he was the only one I could trust—and he drove me back to Springton, without ever asking why. Bawled my eyes out the whole trip.

"My parents covered the penalty fee. They were... furious. Didn't understand, thought I was just... I don't know what they thought, but I couldn't tell them the truth. My agent with Fox Studios... wasn't happy, I wouldn't even speak with her. Kerri Green took the role of Maggie in the end, was nominated *Exceptional Performance by a Young Actress in a Feature Film*. It was a good role."

"Wait—couldn't tell your parents *what truth?*" Tabitha asked with trepidation. "What happened?"

"Things," Mrs. Moore said with difficulty, shaking her head. "I... I can't tell you either. I won't. The whole industry, acting, modeling, *show business;* it's all filthy, Tabitha. It's all filthy, and it was making me filthy."

"...What?" Alarmed, Tabitha bolted upright from her seat. "Are you saying—is, um, what you're saying—is Dad not my real dad?!"

"No! *No!*" Mrs. Moore hushed her with a startled glare. "No. There was... there were things, but not *that.* Absolutely not that. There were things that I'm not going to ever be able to explain to you, and they're things that I'm ashamed of, but never *that.* I thought I was strong enough, that I'd do anything to be a movie star, whatever it took. I'm not. Thank the Lord up in Heaven, I'm not."

Shocked, Tabitha felt herself numbly fall back down onto the cushion of the chair. Astonishment, revulsion, and finally—*anger,* white-hot anger rolled through her consciousness in waves as she struggled to grasp the implications of what her mother was now revealing.

Mom was the victim of... something terrible? Tabitha didn't want to believe it because it was awful, but also wanted it to be true, if only it meant her mother didn't blame her for ruining her life. That previous assumption would be almost silly, then, and although she wasn't sure it exactly excused their current *difficulties,* her mother's overblown oppositional stance to every effort she made—

"Your father, he's an honest man," Mrs. Moore went on. "A simple, honest man, and he's... what I needed, after all of that. I didn't give up on my dream, the dream; it... it wasn't what I thought it was. It was wrong. God help me, I know I've been bitter all this time, especially since you've gone and grown up so fast. I'm sorry for that. I haven't been a good mother to you. *You* didn't ruin my life, Tabitha."

"You need to, to come forward with all of that," Tabitha blurted out, her mind still racing. "With everything. Everything that happened. Whatever they did to you. To the police. To the media. *Someone.* Explain what—"

"They *know,* Tabitha," Mrs. Moore shook her head, anguished tears appearing in her eyes. "Everyone who's a part of it knows. I wasn't even the only one that—that things happened to, on that set. They're all either in on it, or, or they don't care, or they can't do anything—you don't come out and talk about it. They'll bury you in whatever dirt they can find. There's always dirt. On everyone."

"I don't care!" Tabitha exclaimed in indignation. "You have to try. What about the next poor girl who doesn't know any better, what's going to keep her from—"

"Tabitha, *stop!*" Mrs. Moore sobbed. "They all knew. *I knew.* I just didn't care, thought that I could... that I could make it work anyways. I'm just as fucking guilty as any of them. God just gave me the strength to step away—and stay away. He brought me back here, and he gave me you."

A handful of rebuttals choked in her throat, and Tabitha's thoughts whirled, trying to keep up. The *#metoo* movement exposing predatory filmmakers and producers was still decades away, she realized. The film industry in the eighties would've been the figurative dark ages for that sort of behavior, a terrible place for naive young Shannon Delain. Regulatory framework built up to protect young actresses like that from sexual abuse wouldn't even be put into place until after—

"None of this is anything I ever wanted to tell you," Mrs. Moore cut through Tabitha's thoughts with a bitter laugh, tears rolling down her cheeks. "I'm ashamed of it all. It's just... when I started to see what all of this with you has been about, it just tore me up inside, Tabby.

"Losing all of that weight so fast, tryin' so hard to be pretty, to look just like *I* did, back then... do you understand why you wantin' to be an actress would do this to me? Why it would make things like this, between us?"

"I... what?" Tabitha mumbled out dumbly, staring at her mother in a daze. *What?*

"Well, I'm through fighting you on it, I suppose." Mrs. Moore tossed the blue album to the carpet in defeat, wiping moisture from her eyes with the backs of her hands. "I can't anymore. I just can't.

"If this is what you've set yourself on, what you and that Grandma Laurie have decided—I'm going to help keep you safe," she continued. "I can teach you more about acting, about the industry than she ever could, and I can at least... I can keep you safe from all of the nonsense. I *will* keep you safe. I'll teach you everything, if you'll just let me."

When did I EVER want to be an actress?! Tabitha found herself confused and caught totally flatfooted by the sheer scope of apparent misunderstanding between them. *I...I just want to write my Goblin Princess books! To adopt Julia when I'm old enough. And to never, ever be the old me again! I never once thought about—*

"Well?" Mrs. Moore sniffled, anxiously searching Tabitha's features for a reaction. "S-say something, Tabitha."

This is the mom I always wanted. Tabitha's heart fell at the realization. *The Shannon Moore who'd really CONNECT with me on something, stand TOGETHER with me, instead of standing in my way. The fantasy dreamland mom who'd have a place in the rest of my life.*

But—I don't care about acting or modeling bullshit at all! I can already see her breaking, turning even further away. It's just. I'm sorry, Mom, but I have my writing. I have my own plans for my life, and I can't just... Tabitha bit her lip with indecision. She watched her mother's expression falter, saw that last sliver of hope disappear from her eyes, replaced now with more tears.

Fuck. All too suddenly, it felt like she was strangling a possibility that she couldn't afford to ever let die. *Fuck it. You only live once or twice, right?*

"Okay," Tabitha decided, steeling her nerves. "Teach me."

16

TRIP TO LOUISVILLE

"You don't have to hold back on my account," Mrs. Moore huffed with difficulty, laboring for breath. "I can jog for a little bit."

"No." Tabitha shook her head. "Let's just walk together."

It was a clear and crisp-feeling October morning, and Tabitha had woken up to the unlikeliest of partners for her morning run. There was something particularly surreal about seeing her mother in the morning light, *outside,* and she wasn't able to stop herself from sneaking glances over to ensure that yes, this was really happening. Her mother had pulled on a sweatshirt and her hair was askew from waking up so early, but it was her eyes that stood out—they were wide and darted around with apprehension, as if fearful someone would notice she wasn't where she was supposed to be.

In Tabitha's previous life, she'd accepted that her mother had some form of agoraphobia—she kept the windows covered and rarely, if ever, ventured outside. Hiding from the world, fearful of being seen, being *judged*, had shrunk the size of that woman's whole world to the cramped and cluttered prison of their mobile home. Tabitha was frankly shocked when her mother agreed—no, *insisted*—on trying to perform her daily morning run with her.

In actuality, what they did was at best a power-walk together, and Tabitha discreetly diverged from her normal route so they were instead headed downhill first. They managed for about six minutes before her mother was out of steam, and then their pace reduced to normal walking speed. She wasn't embarrassed or surprised at how out of shape her mother was, because she'd been fighting to push those same limitations just this past summer.

Right now, she was regretting not donning a sweatshirt herself. While she didn't mind taking a day off from actual running, she was ill-prepared for a walk; usually, she kept away the chill by staying in constant motion to keep her body temperature up.

"I don't want to hold you back," Mrs. Moore wheezed in frustration, trying to lurch forward faster. "Go on, run if you have to. I'll get there."

"Mother—Mom," Tabitha spoke softly. "Don't push yourself, please. You're not ready for that yet, and hurting your knees or ankles will be more of a setback than any exercise you get today."

"I don't want to hold you back," her mother repeated, staggering to a stop and sagging forward to rest her hands on her knees.

"You're not," Tabitha promised. "If you're willing to do this with me, I'd rather walk with you than run ahead alone, okay? Do you need a minute?"

"Didn't think it'd be this bad," Mrs. Moore admitted with difficulty, heaving herself back into motion again. "The uphill's just... dreadful. Things are tough when you get this old."

"You're not old," Tabitha had to speak very carefully to not sound patronizing. "You just haven't been taking care of yourself. You're carrying around all that extra sugar you've ever dumped into that sweet tea, right now. Among other things. I don't know that I have time to prepare the rest of your meals, but... we're going to think up a meal plan. Or something."

"No more sweet tea," Mrs. Moore agreed, trying not to gasp for breath as they walked up the hill at what felt like a rather sedate crawl.

"Sweet tea is... fine," Tabitha managed, unsure of how much she should sugarcoat her words, so to speak. "But, the jugs we buy are *already* sweet tea. Please don't dump in cups of sugar to sweeten them, Mom. They're really killing you."

"*This* is killing me." Her mother tried an uneasy laugh between breaths. "I don't know how you do this every day."

"It's the worst just starting out," Tabitha assured her. "These are the hardest steps you'll take."

"I know," Mrs. Moore said. "I'm... trying, Tabitha,"

"You're doing more than trying," Tabitha said. "This is... this might be the closest we've been, the most we've talked in years?"

"It is." Mrs. Moore sounded surprised. "You're not talking like a robot anymore either."

"I—I wasn't talking like a robot." Tabitha flushed with embarrassment and gave her a weak smile. "I was just... speaking with proper diction."

"On the contrary, my dear." Mrs. Moore's tone changed. "I was referring not to your elocution, but rather the *manner* in which you articulated your ridiculous speech."

Oh, wow. Tabitha was stunned. *She's... way better at that than I am? This is MY mother? Since when can she talk without sounding like trailer trash?*

"Your lines were lovely, but they didn't feel like *yours*," Mrs. Moore explained, reverting back to her normal way of speaking. "Honestly, thought you were just mocking me, *tryin'* to come off as a bad actress. We're gonna work on that, Tabby."

"I..." Tabitha swallowed, feeling ashamed. "Yeah. After a while, I *was* just doing it to piss you off. But I think it all started because I needed something to change. To set us apart, to remind myself, to... um. Get some distance. From you, and from who I was then."

"Well," Mrs. Moore paused for breath, "it worked."

"Yeah, I just... I'm sorry," Tabitha said with sincerity. "I was so caught up in... things, so focused on me, that I didn't care what it did to you. I'm sorry, I haven't been a great daughter."

"Now we're here, so I guess it's good that you did," Mrs. Moore said. "Do you want to get started on the basics today?"

"Um." Tabitha blushed. "I... actually have plans for today—some friends are driving me out to Louisville."

"*What?*" Mrs. Moore actually stumbled. "Tabitha—you're thirteen years old, you can't just go traipsing across the state without saying a word. I know you've... grown up a little, and it's like you have it all together, but..."

———

"Karen Williams," the heavyset woman introduced herself, offering a hand to Tabitha's father. "You must be the Moores!"

Mrs. Williams was a stout-figured but fashionable mother figure, clad in a what appeared to be summer wear despite the current season—a sleeveless floral-patterned blouse paired with white capris. Her blonde hair was worn in a short bob, and she was awash with jewelry—dangling earrings, a brooch necklace hanging above visible cleavage, and bangle bracelets. They looked more *interesting* than *expensive,* the kind of ornamentation that struck Tabitha as conversation pieces rather than a way to flaunt her wealth. In fact, the first, overwhelming impression the woman made was that she was an aggressively *social* suburban mother, and that any awkward conversation made during the long car-ride to Louisville would become her gossip for the week.

"Yes, ma'am." Alan gave her a firm handshake. "Alan Moore, and this is my wife Shannon."

Mrs. Moore watched them both with a weak smile, looking decidedly uncomfortable with this strange woman in her home.

"And, you're Tabitha!" Mrs. Williams deduced, eschewing a handshake for her and instead wrapping her into a hug. "Can't tell you how grateful I am for what you did, honey—Sandy's just been a wreck this whole time."

"I'm just glad we were so close when it all happened," Tabitha said, gingerly returning the woman's hug. "It was lucky."

"Well, both of the *Williams men* are quite taken with you." Mrs. Williams gave Tabitha a squeeze and then pulled her out to arm's length so she could take a better look at her. "I was *halfway* to convincin' Matthew to ride along with us. But now—I think we'll have more fun with just us girls!"

"Matthew said the MacIntires' daughter was coming with us?" Tabitha asked, trying not to fidget at the thinly-disguised inspection.

"Oh, Hannah's out in the car; didn't want her to be a handful," Mrs. Williams admitted in a hushed voice. "We, um. We weren't sure how bad things were going to be, so she doesn't know much specific about *you know*—about what happened. She just knows her dad got hurt, and that we're going to go see him today."

"How old is she?" Mr. Moore asked.

"Just in first grade." Mrs. Williams sighed, shaking her head. "She's quite the little terror, has both the *Williams men* wrapped around her little finger. Well. Are you ready to take off, Miss Tabitha?"

———

Mrs. Williams was driving a brand new 1998 dark blue Ford Taurus, a model of car so ubiquitous to Tabitha that she realized it wouldn't be an uncommon sight on the roads even forty years into the future. It looked terribly out of place here in the shabby presence of the trailer park now, of course. A dark-haired little girl was buckled into the backseat, peering with interest through her window at the dingy surroundings.

"Did you want to sit up front with me, or in the back with Hannah?" Mrs. Williams asked.

"I'd love to sit with Hannah, if she's okay with that." Tabitha smiled, stealing a peek over at the girl.

"Oh, she's fine—hop right on in and we can hit the road. Sure hope you love the Beatles!"

On closer inspection, Hannah was... *adorable.* She was small for a seven-year-old, and looked positively tiny wrapped up in what she assumed was Matthew's blue-and-white varsity jacket, emblazoned with the Springton *S.* She had large green eyes, cute round baby fat cheeks and dark, wispy hair loosely gathered into a long ponytail. The first-grader watched from the back seat with trepidation as Mrs. Williams led Tabitha out toward the car.

Love at first sight—I don't think I've ever wanted a daughter so badly! Tabitha felt a surge of emotion overtake her. *Would the MacIntires let me babysit, maybe? There's years yet until Julie's even born.*

"Hannah honey, this is Tabitha," Mrs. Williams called into the vehicle as she opened her door. "She's coming along with us to visit your dad at the hospital, so don't you dare pick on her!"

Tabitha opened the rear door and nervously took a seat across from the girl. The interior of the car was still pristine, the *new car* smell battling it out with vanilla scent from a dangling pine-tree-shaped air freshener.

"Hi," Tabitha said. "You can call me Tabby, if you want."

"Do you *live* here?" Hannah blinked, looking past Tabitha at the mobile homes behind her in trepidation.

"*Hannah,* mind your manners," Mrs. Williams scolded in exasperation, turning to give Tabitha an embarrassed look. "I'm so sorry—like I said, she's just a little terror; don't mind any nonsense she says. Say hello to Tabitha, Hannah honey."

"Hello to Tabitha," the smarty pants echoed, shooting Tabitha a cheeky smile but holding out her little hand. "Tabby sounds way better."

"Hello to Hannah." Tabitha obliged her handshake. "I only met your dad once, and it was when he got hurt—so I'm a little nervous about going out to meet him now."

"...That's okay," Hannah decided after looking her over for a moment. "I'll vouch for you."

You'll vouch for me? Tabitha couldn't help but smile. *Who did you pick that up from?*

"So, do you have a boyfriend, Tabitha?" Mrs. Williams asked, turning the key in the ignition and starting the car. Heat roared from the vents, and as promised, "Oh Darling!" by the Beatles began to play from the CD player built into the dash.

We're not even out of the trailer park yet. Tabitha winced, putting on a sheepish grin for the woman to see in her glances toward the rear-view mirror. *And already we're failing the Bechdel test...*

"Matthew is my husband," Hannah declared, eyeing Tabitha warily. "We're going to get married."

"Not 'til you're both at least thirteen." Mrs. Williams laughed. "You'll have to let my son play the field a bit until then, Hannah honey."

"Thirteen is *way* too far away," Hannah groaned. "I'm only eight."

"Seven, Hannah," Mrs. Williams reminded her. "You're seven years old. I've been to all seven of your birthday parties."

"...Seven," Hannah reluctantly corrected herself, looking back to Tabitha. "Almost eight, though. *Mostly* eight. Eight enough."

"I feel like I'm too young to start dating," Tabitha finally answered with a grin, enjoying the comedy exchange between the duo. "I'm younger than I look."

"Oh? Fifteen? *Fourteen?*" Mrs. Williams guessed. "I thought for sure you were around Matthew's age."

"Thirteen," Tabitha admitted with a weak smile. "My birthday's this December. I'm just a freshman."

"Thirteen?!" Hannah gasped in apparent alarm. "That's old enough to marry Matthew!"

"I've also only met Matthew once, at school," Tabitha reassured her before breaking into a devious smile. "My friend Elena is very interested in him, though!"

"Elena—who's Elena?!" To Tabitha's surprise, it was Mrs. Williams jumping in with an exaggerated reaction rather than Hannah. The woman shifted into drive and slowly pulled up the hill to leave the Lower Park. "What's her last name? Is she a sophomore?"

————

The drive to Louisville didn't seem long with two enthusiastic chatterboxes to occupy her attention. Hannah was going to be Mulan for Halloween, right up until she heard Tabitha's plans to be Ariel—the seven-year-old immediately decided that she was then also going to be Ariel. Mrs. Williams and Hannah alike both groaned when Tabitha told them that the four cousins she was taking trick-or-treating intended to dress as the *South Park* cast, prompting an animated discussion on all the better alternatives.

It was Mrs. Williams that suggested the boys should dress to match Tabitha's *Little Mermaid* theme, but Tabitha struggled to remember the names of male characters they could be beyond Sebastian and Prince Eric. To her surprise, Hannah happened to be a preeminent authority on the film, enthusiastically detailing Flounder and Scuttle for her—as well as Prince Eric's manservant Grimsby, his dog Max, the singing chef Louis, and even Ursula's eels Flotsam and Jetsam.

This little girl's memory retention is... alarming! Tabitha thought to herself with a grin. Hannah's encyclopedic knowledge of the film impressed her enough that she decided the girl would have a place helping her spin the ever-growing notebook of compiled Goblin Princess details and ideas into a proper story.

"Hannah, honey, don't chew on your hair, please," Mrs. Williams reminded the young girl. "Leave that to your hairdresser."

Well... in a few more years, Tabitha thought with a smile, reaching over and pulling Hannah's ponytail out of the girl's mouth and straightening her hair. The enthusiastic conversation seemed to have run out of steam and Hannah was busy marveling out the window at the sights of downtown Louisville. *Don't think I'll ever find a more perfect beta reader than her!*

Mrs. Williams, for her part, had seemed keen on pitching their family's big Halloween party held this year at their lake house throughout the duration of the car ride. Between several neighborhood families in regular attendance, Matthew's youth group from their First Methodist church, and the various friends of his from school that were invited, it was a big event—a teenage social soiree carefully orchestrated by none other than this fearsome Mrs. Williams herself.

Equally excited and trepidatious of making her *debut,* as Mrs. Williams put it, Tabitha remained politely interested, but ultimately noncommittal in promising her attendance. She'd only met Matthew once, after all, and her feelings were... complicated. It was a discussion to test out with Elena and Alicia first, and there was no time to ponder it over more right now—they were already pulling into the University of Louisville Hospital's parking lot.

The place looked positively *ancient,* like something out of a 1980s film. The Cardiovascular Innovation Institute building, a marvel of curved silvery panels and glass... did not exist yet, and nor did the stark geometric flared lines of the Clinical Translational Research building, or several of the other modern structures Tabitha remembered appreciating but not quite recalling the names of. She'd navigated her own lonely way around the area just months ago, when getting her chronic migraines examined.

That... was really me, Tabitha thought, almost numb to the fact by now. *I lived a life in the future—I was RIGHT HERE, sort of, but in*

2045. It wasn't even that long ago, was it? That strange MRI machine... and what was that nice young nurse's name?

Mrs. Williams clucked her tongue in annoyance at the cold air when she stepped out of the Ford Taurus. She quickly crossed around the vehicle to fuss with Hannah's borrowed jacket and make sure it was buttoned up properly.

"You ready, Miss Tabitha?" Mrs. Williams asked, noticing Tabitha's hesitation.

"Yeah." Tabitha nodded, trying to stop from staring at everything. "Sorry."

Holding hands with everyone while crossing through parking lots was proper protocol for Hannah, and she diligently took Mrs. Williams on one side and Tabitha on the other as they walked past the rows of cars in their parking area. They'd parked across from the Cancer Center, one of the few buildings Tabitha still recognized—although in 1998, the sign emblazoned across the building instead read a full name: *James Graham Brown Cancer Center.*

When they entered through one of the nearby double-doors together, she tried to stifle her sense of discomfort at realizing she didn't have her bracelet PC on her—having her ID and all of her insurance information keyed into the thing wouldn't have done much to help her here anyway. Everything was out of place from how she remembered, but that lingering sense of *didn't I forget something* persisted as they navigated the halls, following the series of information placards with arrows posted regularly upon the walls.

"Mom!" Hannah broke away from them and ran at full tilt through a quiet hospital waiting area upon first sight of her mother.

"Aww—c'mere, my baby girl," Mrs. MacIntire said with a doting smile, grabbing Hannah and hoisting her up with some difficulty to hold her in a tight hug. "Ooph—what's she been feeding you, you little butterball! You've gotten so heavy!"

"Macaroni and cheese!" Hannah gleefully reported. "With ketchup on top!"

"That's... disgusting!" Mrs. MacIntire turned to throw the approaching Mrs. Williams a skeptical look. "Ketchup? I hope you're kidding."

"The acidity helps bring out the flavor!" Mrs. Williams argued with a laugh. "*My* recipe calls for fresh-cut tomatoes, but Hannah wasn't having any of that."

"Tomatoes, ew!" Hannah wrinkled her little nose in distaste, looking up toward Mrs. MacIntire with a giggle. "Where's Dad?"

"He's still resting now; we'll go and see him in a bit," Mrs. MacIntire promised, setting Hannah down to stand on one of the nearby waiting room seats. "Thank you so much for looking after her, Karen. I know she can be a handful."

"Two handfuls! But just say the word and we'll keep her forever," Mrs. Williams said, taking Tabitha by the shoulders and presenting her forward. "This—is Tabitha Moore!"

...Mrs. Crow?! Tabitha froze, feeling her insides seize up in recognition.

There had been a nagging *familiar sense* at seeing this woman. She had dark hair, but there were almost no facial similarities to her daughter at all—Hannah took after her father, while Sandra MacIntire had somewhat prominent cheekbones and sharp, narrow features, giving her a distinct, *intense* sort of beauty. Tabitha knew this woman with the piercing gaze in the future... but not under the *MacIntire* name.

This was—or would be, would have been someday, under different circumstances—the gaunt, hatchet-faced Mrs. Crow, from the office at the safety plant. A woman whose resting bitch-face was only broken by disapproving sneers, who barked out demands and criticisms and was always, *always* giving her the dirtiest looks.

Of course she hated me. Tabitha felt her stomach lurch and twist up with guilt. *She knew I was from Sunset Estates. That we let her husband die. Oh, God... what did we do to you back then?*

Time had been very cruel to the woman in that timeline, because back here in 1998, even her hawkish features were softer, more fleshed out. She was pretty in her own unique way, had a face that could *smile*, one full of love and adoration for her daughter. The Mrs. Crow she remembered from 2014 onwards had a hooked and angular face, with deep lines that were etched into a perpetual scowl.

But, no! No, this isn't her. Not exactly, not yet. No, it WON'T EVER be her; she never lost her husband, never had to remarry, Tabitha tried to tell herself. *Such a crazy coincidence, though! I never realized she was from Springton. I mean, the safety plant's over in Fairfield, and—oh Jesus, they're all staring. I need to say something.*

"H-hello," Tabitha said quickly, swallowing and trying to keep her calm after that awkward pause. "Hi. It's, um, it's nice to finally meet you."

Without saying a word, Mrs. MacIntire crossed over and wrapped Tabitha up in a fierce hug. Before Tabitha could fumble out what to say, she realized from the minute tremors that Mrs. MacIntire had already begun to quietly cry. The sentiment was infectious, because moments later, Tabitha felt her own unbidden tears rise up, and she clutched at the near-stranger just as tightly as this woman did to her.

"Thank you," Mrs. MacIntire laughed out with a sniffle. "Thank you. What you did means so much to me."

"How about I head out and grab you some real food?" Mrs. Williams proposed. "Sandy, you look *dreadful.* Your usual southwestern salad?"

"A giant cheeseburger—something greasy and just smothered in bacon." Mrs. MacIntire reluctantly disengaged from Tabitha while wiping her eyes. "Lots of fries. Coffee? Thank you so much, Karen. Were you able to grab those papers?"

"I was!" Mrs. Williams dug into her purse and withdrew

several folded newspaper sections, giving Tabitha a meaningful look. "Cheeseburgers for you, Miss Tabitha? I know Hannah is strictly ketchup and pickle only."

"Happy Meal with ketchup and pickle only, please!" Hannah eagerly chimed in.

"Um." Tabitha hurriedly dug out the five-dollar bill from her pocket she'd prepared for emergencies. "A salad would be lovely..."

"Oh, Sandy, you're gonna love this girl," Mrs. Williams muttered, casually swatting away the offered five in amusement. "Listen to her—a salad, at her age. What's this world coming to?"

"You should get a Happy Meal!" Hannah agreed. "They come with the Ronald and pals' *Haunted Halloween.* I'm missing Fry Kid, and Birdie!"

"Fry Kid and Birdie, I'll remember to ask," Mrs. Williams promised with an indulgent smile. "Back in a bit, then. I'll leave you ladies be!"

"Thank you again, Karen," Mrs. MacIntire said with emotion as they watched the chubby woman depart. "Phew. Okay. Hannah sweetie—I'd like to sit down with you and talk to you about what happened."

They moved over to the corner of the waiting room, situating Hannah to sit between them. Mrs. MacIntire nervously took daughter's hand, awkwardly spreading the newspaper sections Mrs. Williams had brought her across her lap. *Officer in Critical Condition After Springton Shooting,* a headline stood out in bold lettering, but thankfully, Hannah didn't seem able to read well enough to catch that at a single glance.

"Honey... your daddy was shot, while he was out being a policeman," Mrs. MacIntire revealed.

"Shot?" Hannah asked, her animated smile dropping away. "Shot like... with a gun?"

"Yes, a bad person shot him, and he almost died," Mrs. MacIntire said. "It was very, *very* close. He—he only just started getting better."

The seven-year-old girl went very quiet and extremely still as Mrs. MacIntire began to pass her the sections of newspaper. Several featured aerial photos of the squad car that had smashed Jeremy Redford's white Continental off the road, along with photos of Mr. MacIntire. Tiny fingers held the paper carefully in front of her and Hannah's eyes narrowed in concentration as she struggled to decipher some of the words.

"They said he would have died, if not for Tabitha, here," Mrs. MacIntire said, handing over the section she'd saved for last. "She was right there when it happened, went up right away to go give your daddy first aid. Th-they said—um, they said, if she hadn't been there to stop the bleeding, your daddy wouldn't have made it."

Springton Teen Saves Life of Police Officer, the story claimed, and beneath was an enormous picture of—

Oh my God, that's ME, Tabitha realized, eyes going wide. *This is the picture Alicia took? When did this come out?*

Everything in the photo seemed bright and distracting compared to the tunnel-vision she'd experienced that afternoon, but the foreground was taken up by *her,* rushing to rescue the downed officer. He was laid out across the gravel beside the road, several yards in front of his police cruiser, looking smaller, more diminished than she remembered. The photo was blurred and imperfect, but the way Tabitha's red hair tangled in the wind behind her and her posture leaning into her forward dash made it all look incredibly dramatic.

Hannah looked up at Tabitha in shock, eyes already wet, before looking back at the newspaper, then back again to Tabitha as if to compare them. The little girl's breathing accelerated, and then began to hitch in her throat as she began to lose control and start crying. Heart caught in her throat, Tabitha took Hannah's hand to comfort her, and the little girl immediately squeezed back tightly.

"Wh-what happened?" Hannah demanded angrily between

sobs, letting the newspaper sections slide out of her lap and across the floor. "What happened to the bad guy?"

Mrs. MacIntire's head snapped up, looking toward Tabitha with a difficult expression, and once again, it was hard for Tabitha to reconcile her with the image she had of the despised *Mrs. Crow* from the future.

"They caught the bad guy," Tabitha answered quietly, gnawing on her lip as she glanced from Mrs. MacIntire to her daughter. "The other policeman caught him, and... sent him away for a very long time, because he was in so much trouble."

17

NO GOOD DEED GOES UNPUNISHED

"Well, what happened next?" Alicia asked, leaning forward over the library table with interest. Inwardly, she was feeling pretty thrilled hearing about the way Tabitha got her first look at the photo she'd snapped—sharing a big moment with the people who were most affected by that whole incident like that was amazing.

"That was... pretty much it." Tabitha shrugged, looking helplessly from Alicia to Elena. "We went in and saw Mr. MacIntire twice before we left, but he was conked out both times. No one wanted to wake him up or disturb his rest—he still looked terrible."

"What?!" Alicia made an incredulous face. "You didn't even get to talk to him?"

"What would I have even said?" Tabitha chuckled. "Still, I'm glad I went. Hannah's *adorable,* and her mother Mrs. MacIntire was... really struggling to keep it together. They even invited me to have Thanksgiving with them!"

"Huh," Alicia huffed. Spending Thanksgiving with people who weren't your family seemed surreal to her. But, then again, the

Moores seemed to have a pretty tense relationship, and she felt a pang of sympathy for her friend.

While Tabitha had gone gallivanting off to Louisville over the past weekend, Alicia had been mulling over the rather spectacular art club meeting she'd attended on Friday. Mr. Peterson introduced her by way of a giant print of her *Tabitha in Motion* picture, informing everyone that it was already being published in a paper. As if that hadn't *wowed* them enough, Alicia then revealed her portfolios of drawings, which managed to impress even more. General consensus was that her work as a freshman was on a college level, something only two other members—both painters—could claim.

Casey and Matthew were the only art club people she knew so far, but typical meetings were ostensibly just free time in the art building to practice their craft rather than social get-togethers. Later in the year, they'd supposedly run an art show, and at some point or another, the Springton High administration was going to task them with painting a new school mural over the old one. Alicia wasn't the best at fitting in and making new friends, but she found herself surprisingly optimistic about the whole *art club* thing.

"That's not *all* you got invited to, though, is it, Tabitha?" Elena spoke up, giving Tabitha a look of challenge. "Word through the grapevine is that yesterday, Matthew *personally* invited you to his big Halloween party on the lake."

"Um. No, he didn't." Tabitha shook her head with a wry smile. "Mrs. Williams tried to convince me I should go, during the drive up. Don't know if I will, though. I've never been to that sort of thing."

"His *mom* tried convincing you?" Elena gave her a skeptical look. "What about him—what did he say, during the trip?"

"Matthew wasn't there," Tabitha explained. "It was just his mother, Hannah and I."

"...Huh," Elena frowned, narrowing her eyes in suspicion. "That's not how it went in the story I heard, at all."

"Rumors spreading around again?" Alicia remarked in amusement.

"Maybe," Elena sighed. "I spend one Saturday with her, and *I'm* about to start spreading rumors already. I want to tell everyone, but I feel like no one'll believe me."

"Why?" Alicia quirked an eyebrow. "Saturday? What happened?"

"Nothing happened," Tabitha rolled her eyes. "We were looking after my cousins."

"Yeah, right, *looking after your cousins,*" Elena retorted with a laugh. "Tabby—you know *kung fu.* I saw it with my own eyes."

"Kung fu?" Alicia turned an expectant smile toward Tabitha.

"I don't know kung fu!" Tabitha protested. "It's taekwondo. It's not some *mysterious,* profound thing like in movies either— there's a taekwondo place in downtown Springton, for crying out loud."

"You mean the dojo or whatever in the plaza across from Food Lion?" Alicia asked. "Sign says 'Martial Arts?' I see it on the bus ride home."

"You said you were self-taught, though, Tabitha," Elena remembered, tapping her lip. "So you didn't learn there?"

"No, that place—it's, um. Expensive," Tabitha mumbled. "For us anyways. Even if we could afford it, there's a lot of more important things to put money towards right now."

Like what, stock investments? Alicia gave Tabitha an appraising look. *Hey, maybe she picked up taekwondo somewhere in the future, and just brought that knowledge back with her?*

Alicia's prior certainty that Tabitha's *time travel* story had been completely made up was experiencing a slight crisis of faith. Tabitha had proven both imaginative and intelligent, so it was understandable if the redhead's educated guesswork could paint a believable future—*except* when it came to Alicia's private artwork.

Stashed in the gap between her bed and the wall, Alicia had a folder of borderline erotic drawings hidden, and absolute complete confidence that *no one* else knew about them. Even if someone were to discover them, they would remark on the boobs —Alicia admittedly practiced drawing a lot of boobs in secret, because they needed to look just right. There was only a single drawing of a woman's naked back.

One that Tabitha had described in eerie detail last week.

There was just no way anyone would guess that it was Alicia's favorite, her *muse,* something she'd scrawled out in a mesmerized moment of inspiration, some accidentally amazing thing that filled her with powerful emotion each and every time she brought it out to admire. If there was any one concept that Alicia was absolutely determined to realize into a masterpiece someday in the future—it was exactly that one.

She once again found herself carefully watching Tabitha, the girl who was casually penciling out algebra equations while simultaneously engaging them in conversation. *Is she filling out that worksheet suspiciously fast, or... do I just suck at math?*

"So she leaps up into the air like the Karate Kid, and kicks this soda can *right off the top of my freaking head,*" Elena recounted. "Tabitha's like—she was doing *backflips* and stuff during a game of tag with little kids."

"She's exaggerating; don't listen to her." Tabitha shook her head with a smile. "It was a teeny bit of taekwondo, and then a couple hand-springs to show off for the boys. They love seeing anything remotely acrobatic—they're still in elementary."

"*Everyone* loves acrobatics, Tabby," Elena insisted. "You can make JV cheerleading with those moves easy, tryout season or not. I think you should."

"Sorry." Tabitha winced. "I just don't have the interest—or the time. My mother has it in her head now that she's going to personally teach me how to act and model and whatever."

"She *what?!*" Elena demanded, planting both hands on the

tabletop and dropping her voice to a grave whisper. "Your mom said that? Are you gonna switch to theater electives?"

"At the end of the semester I think, yeah." Tabitha sighed. "Was hoping to take creative writing instead."

"Is this how things were *supposed* to go?" Alicia asked, giving Tabitha a meaningful glance. "If you know what I mean?"

"*Supposed to go?*" Elena repeated, looking from Alicia to Tabitha for answers.

"They…" Tabitha gave them a weak smile. "No, it isn't. They were *supposed* to go… poorly. The acting thing isn't what I thought I wanted, but… my mother's really trying, and I want to see where this goes."

"So, we're off course, or…?" Alicia looked surprised.

"Way off course," Tabitha groaned, dropped her face into her hands. "Just making it all up as I go now. She's gonna start teaching me today after school. I'm pretty much dreading it."

"Sure wish *I* wasn't excluded from whatever your plans are," Elena said, looking put out. "So that, y'know, maybe I could be a part of them?"

"Yeah, nice try," Alicia playfully scoffed. "It's a big secret—and you've only known her for like, one week."

"So there's really a big secret?" Elena perked up again almost immediately, presenting an interested smile.

For all of her talent and foresight, Tabitha was pretty terrible at guarding her expression, and Alicia couldn't help but grin, because the girl's face gave everything away.

———

"Hey, did you hear Matthew Williams asked that Tabitha girl out?"

Um—he what? Tabitha had been busy adjusting the outline of the *Goblina* novel with some of her new ideas when she discovered her name once again seemed to be on everyone's lips. That cabal of popular girls loosely grouped in the center of the class was putting on a show of speaking a little too loudly again, and the other surrounding students had already gone quiet.

"Ew, Tubby Tabby? Why *her?*"

"He's supposedly all head over heels for her now; it's this whole big thing. Mrs. Albertson was going on and on about her, has this article clipping that makes it look all like Tabitha was *running right in to the rescue,* yeah, har har. So Matthew drove her to up Louisville yesterday to see his dad, who I think's one of those police officers who got shot? He asked her out and I think they kissed."

Kissed?! Matthew... never even asked me out, though? He didn't take me to Louisville either! Tabitha's pencil lead snapped at the pressure she was applying to the notebook page, and she swiped the broken lead away with the back of her hand in aggravation. *I may have... okay, like a tiny little crush on him. But it was super evident the other day that he was just being polite with me. Where is all this even coming from—are they purposely conflating Officer MacIntire and Officer Williams?*

"She's so fucking fake," a third voice insisted. "I can't stand her. Like, Matthew's dad *almost died,* right? Have some goddamn decency. There's *no way* she did anything for that cop but spout bullshit way afterwards. We'd have *known.*"

"Yeah, did she really even do anything?" one of the girls scoffed. "She lives in that trailer park. Bet she hears sirens and then just *happens* to be right there when the news van pulls in. So that she can spin whatever story she wants. *So* sick of hearing everyone stuck on that whole stupid shooting thing anyways. Like, yeah, okay, it happened—now, can we move on?"

"Can someone speak up to Matthew, though?" a girl griped. "As if the shooting thing wasn't bad enough. Now it's like she's totally just taking advantage of him, when he's in grief or whatever and isn't thinking straight."

"Y'all are full of shit," a tall boy spoke up—the one Tabitha mentally thought of as *the redneck kid* for his white shirt and tight blue jeans paired with cowboy boots. "Matt's dad was in my drive-thru late last night for coffee—seemed pretty fuckin' healthy to me."

"Shut the fuck up, Bobby," one of the girls spat back with vehemence. "You don't even get what we're talking about."

"We're talking about *Matthew's* dad," another girl retorted. "Matthew Williams. Not one of the other Matts."

"Yeah—you're talkin' 'bout Officer Williams? I know him waaay better'n any of you bitches," Bobby boasted. "Busted me an' my brother with a joint back behind the Minit Mart, but he had us stand there and finish smoking the whole thing first 'fore he took us in. Ain't never forgettin' that—I always say what's up when I see him."

"Mind your own damned business, Bobby, *geez.*" The first girl glowered. "This isn't even about you. Asshole."

———

"It's an honor to meet you, *Mr. Wilcott.* Thank you for coming in on such short notice," Mrs. Moore said from her seat on the sofa, picking up the half-dozen sheets of blank paper on the worn coffee table in front of her and aligning them together into a perfect stack with a crisp tap of the edges on her makeshift 'desk.'

"Please, call me John," Tabitha blurted out, speaking a little too quickly.

Directly after arriving home from school, her mother had taken her by the shoulders without a word and directed her into the living room, where they sat across from each other as if they were about to have another serious talk. Instead, by best guess, it was a theatre exercise—the first of what would likely be many constituting this nervously anticipated mother-to-daughter crash course in becoming an actress.

She hadn't known what to expect, but to Tabitha, the current situation felt ridiculous to the point of becoming surreal.

"Alright then, John." Mrs. Moore turned a disinterested glance from the blank papers in front of her back to Tabitha. "We pulled your resume out of a rather large pool of candidates with better qualifications than you—can you guess why that is?"

"The reason for that is..." Tabitha's paused to gather her thoughts. *Resume—okay, so this is supposed to be a job interview. I'm Mr. Wilcott, please call me John, and I really need this job.*

"Because the qualified candidates you've brought in haven't met your expectations," Tabitha elaborated without missing a beat, deciding to punctuate her sentences with what she imagined were masculine gestures.

Apparently, her first acting lesson was being thrown in the deep end without warning. Improvisation exercises, and while Tabitha thought herself fairly adept at thinking on her feet, she struggled to stop thinking of the situation in terms of what her mother wanted from her in an acting lesson, and instead what this interviewer expected to hear from Mr. Wilcott.

"Oh?" Mrs. Moore—no, the human resources director at *Employment Corporation* challenged, arching an eyebrow. "What makes you say that?"

"The only thing I can imagine setting me apart from my peers —hah, aside from lacking a degree, of course—is that I have some actual experience in the field, even if it's not *exactly* related. I believe you need experience, connections, and hands-on know-how more than you need a fancy frame on the wall behind my desk, Ms.—?"

"*Mr.* Goldstein," Mrs. Moore introduced herself with a frown.

"Mr. Goldstein, excuse me." Tabitha tried to cover her wince with an awkward smile. "Yes, I'm of the mind you chose me over candidates with better qualifications because you believe I can give you results, and I can."

"Hmm." Mrs. Moore made a disapproving frown. "I definitely don't agree with that."

The mock interview went on for almost ten rather excruciating minutes, with Tabitha choosing to plaster a rather uncharacteristic smarmy smile across her face for the whole thing. The point of the game seemed to be to act out a character under pressure, and Mrs. Moore playing the part of the stern interviewer was pulling no punches.

"Moving on—" Mrs. Moore wrapped up the session with an attitude of scarcely concealed disdain. "When we contacted your previous employer, we were informed of certain... circumstances regarding your termination. Would you care to elaborate on the nature of those circumstances?"

"That is, well." Tabitha finally frowned and adjusted the collar of the imaginary business attire Mr. Wilcott was wearing. "Hah, you know how this industry is, Mr. Goldenstein. It's *competitive*. As soon as I'm not working for them, I'm working for someone else, working *against* them. Do you understand? You see, when a man with my skills—"

"I'm disappointed." Mrs. Moore sighed and dropped the blank papers back onto the coffee table. "That's not what I wanted to hear, Mr. Wilcott."

"Please, call me John," Tabitha insisted with a nervous laugh. "Now, whatever's been said about me, surely there's—"

"Yes, yes, we'll be in touch with you if we have any further questions, Mr. Wilcott." Mrs. Moore sighed again, rising up from her seat on the sofa and offering her hand.

"Of course, of course." Tabitha stood up with a strained expression and shook hands. "Thank you for the opportunity."

"You didn't freeze up, Tabitha." Mrs. Moore broke character and grinned at her daughter, not releasing her grip. "Thought for sure you would. That *please, call me John*, came out right away. You pulled it off so fast, it's like you already knew what we were going to be playing."

"Thank you." Tabitha exhaled slowly, dropping the fake smile and working to relax the not-quite-feigned tension in her shoulders.

"Let's talk 'bout how that interview went." Mrs. Moore dropped back down onto the sofa with a pleased smile. "I'm very impressed with your ad-libbing! You came up with great answers, out of nowhere."

"Thank you." Tabitha nodded again, returning to her seat.

"The gestures were a nice try—I didn't expect those either—but you really need to practice them. I didn't think you'd attempt any body language on a surprise first pop quiz, so it was a good effort, but they came off as very stiff and unpracticed."

"For the record," Tabitha cleared her throat, "a pop quiz is to determine how much knowledge I've retained without any fore-warning to study. As you *haven't actually started to teach me yet*, I had nothing to retain. I recognize your criticism, but feel it is rather undeserved. There was no chance I would have known any of these things."

"There you go talking like a robot again." Mrs. Moore rolled her eyes. "Don't speak with proper diction anymore if you're not going to put some character into it—yer flat delivery really isn't doin' you any favors, Tabby."

"Noted," Tabitha grunted, giving her mother a cool look and crossing her arms.

"Moving on, your answers were surprisingly well-thought, but overall, you were speaking too fast," Mrs. Moore explained. "You never found your rhythm. That you can think everything up on the fly like that is impressive, but try to mind your pace a bit more. Put your speech into a cadence that fits the character and the situation."

"...Okay," Tabitha said after a moment of reflection. "Got it."

"Now, what can you tell me about your character?" Mrs. Moore mused, momentarily slipping back into her interviewing voice. "Your impression of the role you took."

"He *really* needed that job," Tabitha said. "I could feel the sweat forming on his brow. I think there were consequences looming over him, and he was prepared to lie or cheat to try to land the position."

"Then why didn't you?" Mrs. Moore gave Tabitha a curious glance.

"Didn't I?" Tabitha returned the look with a mystifying one of her own.

"Touché!" Mrs. Moore smiled, a beaming, proud smile that for a strange moment Tabitha connected to the lovely Shannon Moore she'd seen in photos from the past. "I was never, *ever* going to give you the job anyways. Of course."

"Of course." Tabitha showed her mother a shy smile. "Um. Are all of our lessons going to be like that? On the spot?"

"Not all of them." Mrs. Moore chuckled. "I'm gonna run you through all the exercises I remember helped me the most, though. I always *hated* the improv ones, but I see it turns out they'll be the easiest for you."

"That makes sense." Tabitha nodded, feeling herself shrink up and shrivel inside. *That came off as EASY?*

"I think it's the emotional ones you'll struggle with." Mrs. Moore tapped her lip, deep in thought. "Channeling actual furious anger so you can shout and scream, breaking down into tears, and all the lovely things between. But—we'll work up to those."

"...Great," Tabitha deadpanned, unable to hide her lack of enthusiasm.

———

"Yeah, apparently, she already came out and admitted to making the whole thing up," a dark-haired teen in a Backstreet Boys tee said, rearranging a pile of textbooks in her open locker.

"She admitted it herself?" a short girl with her hair pulled up in a series of butterfly clips waiting beside her asked.

"Yeah," the dark-haired girl affirmed. "Guess she was afraid the police were gonna come down on her for all of her bullshit? Can you believe the newspaper actually put—"

What.

"Hey—are you talking about Tabitha?" Elena interrupted, approaching the students with a frown. She wasn't feeling shy at all about inviting herself over to stand in their personal space along the busy locker-lined corridor. "Tabitha Moore?"

"Yeah, why?" The first girl paused, sizing Elena up.

"Tabitha Moore admitted to making up the story about saving that cop?" Elena pressed.

"Yeah?"

"When?" Elena challenged. "To who?"

"I dunno, her friends, I guess? Then, after that, word just spread?"

"No, she didn't—that's *bullshit.*" Elena scowled. "I'm one of her friends—she really saved that cop's life."

"That's not what everybody's saying." The dark-haired girl laughed, shrugging it off.

"So, what, that picture in the paper's fake?" Elena retorted.

"Pssh, uh *yeah.* Obviously. All newspapers and tabloids have programs that can doctor stuff like that, easy. Corel PaintShop Pro, or Adobe Fireworks. Y'know?"

"Then, her calling it in over the police dispatch, that was fake too?"

"What police dispatch?" The girl gave her a doubtful look. "Umm, probably? I don't think they're even allowed to release those. Like, legally."

"It was all over the news last week, though," Elena refuted. "Waaay before that new article with the photo came out."

"Yeah, okay, if you say so?" the dark-haired teen snorted. "*I* didn't hear anything about it. Couldn't have been very big news?"

"So... you're saying Matthew Williams' dad is a liar?"

"What?"

"He was the officer first responding to the scene. Apparently, *he* thinks Tabitha was there saving the other cop's life."

"Who told you that?"

"Matthew Williams himself."

"I didn't say anyone was a liar—I'm just tellin' what I heard," the girl groused, looking toward her short friend for a helping word in frustration. "Matthew's like, biased now anyways if him and her are a thing now, right? And, if Tabitha's not guilty, why'd she tell her friends she made it all up, then. Huh?"

"Oh, well you see." Elena smiled through gritted teeth. "*She didn't.* I'm one of Tabitha's friends, and that's not what she told us, *at all.* I'm Matthew's friend too—he never asked her out. I'd just *love* to hear where you bitches got *your* fucking story from."

"*Excuse me?*"

"Maybe don't run your mouths if you don't know what you're talking about?" Elena suggested cheerfully, reaching between them to slam the girl's locker closed and then brushing past them. "Makes you all sound pretty fucking stupid, in my opinion."

Jesus... Elena let out a slow breath of frustration as she strode down the hallway.

She was exhausted, repeatedly throwing herself onto the front lines to hotly contest every single false word about Tabitha she overheard. It was only Tuesday, but the amount of conversations she'd forced her way into already was dizzying. She couldn't be everywhere at once—she didn't even have time to chill with Tabitha and Alicia at lunch today—but in broad strokes, a bigger picture was forming.

The Tabitha gossip disseminating throughout Springton High wasn't random, and it always seemed to originate from sophomores, rather than their fellow freshman. Elena didn't know many tenth-grade girls—that was Carrie's crowd now. But the narrative, from the sophomore's responses, was definitely evolving in specific reaction to Elena's own efforts to stamp out the rumors everywhere.

Yeah? Elena smirked. *Well, bring it.*

She'd taken a firm side on this and was adamant in her stance, blood running hot as she went from each conversation and verbal spat with fistfuls of facts and counter arguments. Her immediate reputation was battered and beaten—more than half of the girls in her classes were pissed at her, to say nothing of everyone else... but that was going to be a temporary thing.

Probably.

———

"Do you think that's one of the girls talking shit about you?" Alicia asked in a low voice, leaning in toward Tabitha so that no one else would overhear. Though the school seemed divided on the Tabitha issue, several of the art club people had voiced their support.

Despite Elena finally convincing them to stop spending their lunch periods in the library, their friend was nowhere to be found today. Regardless, their attempt at staking their claim on a good location in the quad area was turning a lot of heads. Though they were getting a lot of stares, Tabitha seemed particularly distracted, her gaze consistently turning toward a particular table of girls across from them.

They definitely looked over here when we sat down—are they talking about her?

"What?" Tabitha asked with a distracted laugh. "What? No, that girl keeps moving her hands when she talks."

"Moving her hands...?" Alicia peered over toward the other table.

"I'm supposed to practice my gestures," Tabitha explained, turning toward Alicia and raising one hand. "But, soon as I start keeping an eye out for people with expressive body language, it's like they're nowhere to be found. That girl over there's the best one I've seen yet today."

"Best at... what?" Alicia arched an eyebrow.

"Physical expressions. It's like she's physically grasping onto the conversation," Tabitha said. "She does these little pantomiming waves to illustrate the flow of whatever she's saying —at least, that's how I think of it. Then, when she wants someone's response, she indicates it with this gesture like she's actually passing the reins of the conversation to them."

Tabitha splayed out her hand open-palmed toward Alicia to demonstrate, putting her on the spot.

"Umm." Alicia blinked. "Yeah, I mean, I get it? One of the *how to draw* books I have has a thing on gestures, if you wanna check it out. Seems super weird when you do it, though."

"Sorry." Tabitha laughed. "It's just—it's not something that I ever do myself naturally, so when I try to practice it, it feels incredibly... silly? Exaggerated? Some people are just naturally very animated when they're speaking. It's something I'm supposed to be able to imitate."

"It's definitely a little weird on you," Alicia admitted. "I don't think it works with your serious expression. You gotta pair it with like, one of those big, fake smiles that they do."

"I think it goes just as well with a serious expression." Tabitha frowned, imitating a flap of the hand as she watched the other table. "But then, I need to slow down the movements to... match the mood?"

One of the girls over there caught sight of Tabitha's hand movement and immediately scowled, hunching in toward the other girls at that table to whisper something.

"Uhh, or people'll think you're mocking them?" Alicia struggled to hide a grin with the back of her hand.

"I-I'm not, though!" Tabitha immediately dropped both of her hands to the table and quickly hid her face. "I was just—"

"Like, wooow." Alicia shook her head in amusement. "As if you needed to stir up any more drama than you already have?"

"Alicia, th-that's not funny!"

Ohhh my goodness. Elena thought giddily to herself. *He's way too hot!*

She'd stoically planted herself right in the path of Matthew Williams himself, and she was struggling to maintain her disapproving frown. Final bell had rung and the school day was over, but while Matthew had his own car, she had a narrow window of time to take care of this before she had to make a dash for the bus loop.

"Hey, 'Lena." Matthew smiled, pausing in the hall with one thumb hooked casually into the backpack strap at his shoulder. "What's up?"

"Yeah, hi." Elena scowled, crossing her arms. "Were you talking about Tabitha to anyone yesterday morning?"

"Uhh, yeah?" Those dreamy eyes of his looked perplexed. "Why?"

"Don't know what you actually said, but word's going around everywhere that you asked her out when you drove her to Louisville on Sunday."

"That's... not true." Matthew blanched. "Think all I said was, like, how my mom was trying to embarrass me to her. I didn't even *go* with—"

"I heard the real story from Tabitha already," Elena interrupted impatiently. "But *you* need to fix this. Whoever's been spreading all the dumb rumors about her all this time has to be someone close to you. Like, one of the sophomores."

"Hey," Matthew protested. "I don't think it means—"

"You're making things awkward for Tabitha," Elena talked over him, giving him a disappointed look along with an ultimatum. "Either figure out who the problem is, or just don't ever bring up Tabitha at all. 'Kay? *Thanks.*"

She brushed past him without giving him a chance to speak, storming away in apparent anger. Several surprised students turned heads in the hallway at the dramatic departure, watching the long-legged freshman girl who dared to chew out Matthew Williams.

Adopting the overprotective friend approach and keeping him on the back foot, however, made everything a breeze! Elena thought to herself in satisfaction. The best-looking sophomore guy was intimidating to talk to, even for a girl of her caliber. Now their encounter would be memorable, it'd make him subconsciously want to appease her, and even more importantly, establish her in his mind as someone who was loyal to a fault.

Her mother had been eager to reminisce about her own high school days over a few glasses of wine this past weekend, so she couldn't take full credit for the idea, of course. Even just a few months ago, those old stories had bored Elena to death—now, though, she was fully realizing just how incredible her mom's insight and social savvy really was.

Elena's anger wasn't exactly a total charade either—it was more obvious now than ever that the talk flying around about Tabitha was intentionally fabricated, and Matthew was going to help her get to the bottom of it. Someone—Elena was now confident it was one of the sophomores—was hurrying to smear Tabitha's name in light of all the new buzz about her from that photo making the front page.

Springton Teen Saves Life of Police Officer. Almost everyone was talking about it now, with several teachers even proudly showing off the paper to their classes. That *someone,* whoever they were, felt forced to try and suppress the rise of Tabitha's reputation with manufactured drama. *The difference is that now I'M in Tabby's corner —and I'm not gonna just smile and turn the other cheek.*

Tabitha, Alicia and I? We're the real deal, Elena decided, stalking through the bustling school corridor with a predatory glint in her eyes. *Whoever you are, all you have is talk... and eventually, all those loose lips are gonna lead us right to you.*

You REALLY don't know who you're fucking with.

18

CATCHING AN UNEXPECTED BREAK

Don't think I'll ever actually feel compelled to act in anything, Tabitha mused to herself, idly glancing around at the throngs of scattered students boarding their buses.

But the things Mom wants to teach me will still be helpful writing-wise. Simply WRITING a character doesn't quite measure up to actually trying to BECOME one. Actually putting yourself in their shoes and trying to adopt their mannerisms and everything gives you a perspective that's so much... DEEPER.

The school day was over, and Tabitha was standing at the curb along the edge of the bus loop among the small crowd of those still waiting for their bus to arrive. Hers was bus fifteen, and it usually arrived a few minutes late.

The dismissal times of Springton Middle and Springton High were staggered an hour apart because they shared school buses, and her bus made a more meandering trip through the district than most. Bus fifteen would make a dozen stops along the suburbs at the far edge of town before swinging back through Springton's main drag toward her trailer park, seemingly almost as an afterthought.

Tabitha had taken up an interest in people-watching after the abrupt acting lesson her mother had foisted on her yesterday. High school teenagers yelling, chatting, and hurrying amid the row of parked buses had a certain *energy* to them she found fascinating. As a writer, she could simply sum up the general atmosphere with a few words, perhaps describing an air of excitement and relief at the drudgery of the school day finally concluding—but how would she express that as an *actress?* It felt like there were discernible differences in the way everyone carried themselves, but it was difficult to pinpoint what exactly they were.

They're a bit more lively, for sure, Tabitha thought, watching people pass by. *Their gait is a little different too. They walk a little bit more quickly, more freely after final bell. But there's also this tinge of IMPATIENCE to it too, like they don't want to waste another single second—*

With an abrupt and forceful shove, the world around Tabitha whirled as she was thrown forward off of the curb and onto the pavement. There was no time at all to think—she twisted in the air, right arm flailing out on instinct in an impossible attempt to reorient her balance as she fell. For a numb instant, she observed her left-hand flash out in pure reaction to keep her face from smashing into the pavement, and then she landed heavily.

Painfully.

What—The graceless fall *hurt* in a way that shook her bones and completely knocked the breath out of her, and it took a second to collect her thoughts and begin picking herself back up. The curb she'd been poised on was only six inches tall, but the push—

Somebody pushed me!

—The push had sent her sprawling forward so quickly that she'd gone more than horizontal, hit the ground at an angle. Landed on just her chin, her shoulder, and her left hand, her left hand that was in raw agony from the way it'd twisted beneath her—

Fuck it hurts—FUCK. Not good. Not good.

"Oh my God—are you okay?!" The girl who'd been standing nearest scrambled down beside her in a crouch. "Hey, that guy just —*HEY! STOP! STOP THAT DUDE! THAT GUY JUST PUSHED HER!*"

No, no, no, this can't be happening, Tabitha's eyes filled with tears at the sheer blinding pain, working her way up to sit with her knee beneath her while doubled over and clutching her left hand tightly in against herself. *I—I've never broken a bone in my life, never. This—why would anyone—?*

"Hey, are you alright?" A teenage guy was trying to steady her.

Despite herself, all she could manage out in reply was a choked sob. It *hurt,* it hurt so much. She didn't want to cry right now, couldn't cry right here, in front of everyone, but the humiliating tears just kept on coming regardless. The group of people she'd been standing in devolved into further chaos; people were running past them now—*after somebody?*—and highschoolers were actually disembarking back off of the buses they'd gotten on to see what all the commotion was about.

If-if I'd just had, like, ONE SECOND to—to prepare myself, I could've just made that into a handspring, Tabitha thought, furious and ashamed and struggling to awkwardly wipe her face with the inside of her right arm. *But there wasn't one second, it just—it just happened, and I wasn't prepared or paying attention or... or anything. Fuck, FUCK IT HURTS!*

"What happened?"

"It's Tabitha Moore; some dude just came up and—"

"Think she broke her wrist, she's—"

"That guy pushed her, just saw him make a break for—"

"Who was it?"

"Oh shit, they're fighting! Look, he—"

Everyone was talking, people were crouched beside her now, crowding all around her, and someone helped lift her up and back onto unsteady feet. People were still running past, and although she couldn't actually see what was going on over there, Tabitha had a sense that a fight had broken out wherever they'd chased the pusher down to. Only, it *hurt,* and her throat kept constricting, seizing up in tiny sobs that she wasn't able to stifle.

Everyone was looking at her, everyone was gathering, talking, staring, *gawking* at her predicament, and she'd never felt so wretched. *Why? Why would anyone—is it just bullying, anymore, with this? This—it hurts so much. What did I do to anyone?!*

"Check on her." She recognized the stern older voice of what was probably the school dean yell out. He didn't appear, so she assumed he was rushing over toward... whatever was happening over there.

"Excuse me." Another man—*a bus driver?*—pushed through the teens and carefully took her by the shoulder. "Are you alright? Can you let me see it?"

Trying to quickly blink the stinging tears out of her eyes so she could see, Tabitha slowly lifted the hand she'd had cradled up against herself out so the man could see. It was trembling; she couldn't keep it from shaking until the bus driver cautiously took hold of her fingertips, and it looked *wrong.* The silhouette of her pale hand wasn't correct—there was a puffy *wrong*—looking area between her wrist and her pinky. It *hurt.*

"Ooooohh."

"Oh damn."

"Yeah, that's broken."

"Yikes."

"Might be a break, might be a fracture," the bus driver admitted. "Are you hurt anywhere else? What's your name?"

Tabitha shook her head from side to side, trying to clear her throat, trying to *breathe,* but someone answered for her.

"She's Tabitha Moore," one of the nearby guys supplied.

It wasn't anyone she recognized from her classes, she didn't think, and it was a bit overwhelming right now that everyone in Springton High seemed familiar with who she was. All of the sudden sympathy and support might have felt really nice, if not for the circumstances that evoked it all. She'd never been the object of so much attention all at once, not even on the first day of school, and the alarming abruptness of it all felt crushing, made her intensely vulnerable, like her troubles were exposed for everyone's interest and entertainment.

My troubles... Tabitha whimpered to cut off a wail before the rest of it could escape her lips, trying and failing to stiffen her face into a grimace rather than continue losing control and breaking down. Which she did. There was grit on her right palm from when she'd first lifted herself up off the blacktop, so she attempted to hide her crying behind the back of her hand, covering herself with her forearm, smearing it with her unabated tears.

It hurts so much! This—this isn't bullying like it was before. I was— someone ATTACKED me. That's not okay. That's not okay. What did I even do? What did I even DO?! Why? I tried so hard, I tried to be so nice to everyone...

She didn't realize she was being led forward until the dozens of gathered teens surrounding her fell away and were behind her as the bus driver led her back into the school toward the nurse's office.

———

"No, I'm taking her to the fucking hospital *now,* and you all better have some goddamn answers for me when I get back," Mr. Moore swore. "Or you're all fucking *through.* You hear me?"

There was an unbridled fury in her father's quiet voice that made Tabitha flinch in the plastic seat of the tiny waiting area within Springton High's nurse's office. Seeing him like this, witnessing something *cruel* in her typically plain, unassuming dad terrified her on a deep, subconscious level. It was as if these warnings he gave them were just a brief precursor to him actually erupting into violence, and the situation was growing more uncomfortable with each passing second.

She was balancing a large bag of ice atop the hand in her lap, and the intense pain had been subdued to a dulled, aching throb in time with her pulse. The biting cold was spreading up her entire arm, though, and she couldn't help but shiver, gritting her teeth in irritation at how unpleasant it all was.

The initial shock and trauma of the incident had already given way to anger and annoyance, her mood plummeting to rock bottom and then settling in there for a long stay. The tumult of emotions took an enormous, exhausting toll on her, and she just wanted to sit and blankly stare off into the distance by herself for a long time.

"C'mon, sweetie, we're going," Mr. Moore said in a soft tone, helping her up out of her seat with exaggerated care as though she were made out of glass. "Up, up, up, easy does it."

"Thank you," Tabitha murmured, letting him guide her out the door. "Sorry for all this."

"This isn't your fault, sweetie," her father promised. "But it sure as hell is *someone's* fault, and we're gonna get to the bottom of it once and for all. This isn't going to happen ever again, okay?"

"Yeah." She nodded, deciding not to display her doubt and bewilderment. *Maybe. It shouldn't have happened in the first place. I don't even understand why it would ever happen to me.*

His familiar truck was parked right in the staff parking area just outside the school offices, a strange juxtaposition to the eerie sight of the now empty and quiet school grounds. Mr. Moore brushed aside *polite and helpful* and unabashedly went full *overprotective father* on her, not only opening her door for her, but actually lifting her up into the passenger seat of the cab and buckling her in. The sentiment was embarrassing, but also... nice, in a way. A tiny island of contentment in her sea of distraught anxiety.

This broken... hand? Wrist, maybe? Is going to affect everything I do, Tabitha accepted with a sullen sigh. *Guess I'll probably need a cast? For... what, months and months? How am I going to even...?*

Mr. Moore started the vehicle, pulled out of the parking lot, and they rumbled their way through town in tense silence.

Tabitha felt like she needed to think, needed to plan, or figure out solutions, or *something,* but every shake and bounce of the bumps on the road sent distracting pangs up the length of her left arm even despite the bag of ice she was smothering the contusion with.

"This's twice in a row now, Tabitha," her father remarked. "In just a couple months. You gettin' pushed and hurt, me gettin' the call. I don't like it; s'giving me gray hairs. I know you've been keepin' things to yourself, but... honey, I don't like it. Not one bit. You just say the word and we'll transfer you to Fairfield. These girls can't keep treatin' you like this, it's... it's inhuman."

Wait... what?

"I think it was a boy," Tabitha said. Something about what he'd just said still felt *off* to her, though. "They said it was a boy who pushed me."

"Yeah, I'll just bet it was," Mr. Moore grunted, scowling. "What grade's that Taylor girl in by now? Tenth? Eleventh?"

"That... who?" Tabitha turned to give her dad a puzzled look. "What?"

"That Taylor girl, the oldest one," Mr. Moore continued. "Whichever one of them that pushed you off of that trampoline. Courtney? Brittney?"

"Pushed me off of the trampoline?" Tabitha dumbly repeated. *What?* "I thought I... fell?"

"Yeah, *you fell,* okay." Her father sounded genuinely irritated now. "Only promised not to say anythin' on it 'cause you were bawling your eyes out, but, Tabitha... *enough is enough.* You gettin' hurt like this again, the bullying, whatever's going on—this wasn't supposed to happen again. What on God's green earth am I supposed to tell your mother now?"

"I... forgot," Tabitha realized, a sinking sense of dread pervading throughout her as something important, some missing piece she'd been intentionally overlooking for all too long finally fell back into place. "I... didn't fall off the trampoline? Someone—they, they *pushed me.*"

No, I didn't forget! Tabitha's breath hitched, and her heart was racing now. *It wasn't amnesia either, or the concussion. I just... walled it all off, buried it, repressed it, all of it.*

I came back to life as a thirteen-year-old, but I never manage to put an exact face to the girls who pushed me around and called me a goblin? How do I not realize that? How does a big fucking missing gap in my memory like that not stand out, until now? I fell off a FRIEND'S trampoline? Friends, what fucking friends?! Why did I never think to look into them?

Tabitha felt her stomach lurch, and she struggled to keep from vomiting right there onto the dashboard.

The three Taylor girls. The youngest one—Ashley? Ashleigh? Something like Ashley, but spelled a weird way?—was nice, but the older two... were fucking terrible, to both of us. They hit us, hurt us, ABUSED us. Fuck, FUCK. One of them's been here with me in high school all this time—they both fucking HATED me. It's either Erica or Brittney Taylor. And, Ashley—

"I forgot about Ashley," Tabitha blurted out, her eyes watering all over again at the magnitude of her mistake. "I forgot all about Ashley."

"You what?" her father asked, concern evident in his voice. "Ashlee Taylor?"

Oh my God. I forgot all about Ashlee—she's been dealing with them, with this all alone. I never went back. Never went back after the trampoline thing the first time through. I was too scared to go back. Then I just... what, fucking REFUSED TO REMEMBER? To ever think about it? Is that even possible? That poor girl, she must've thought I—no, I DID abandon her. Didn't I? What the FUCK have I done?!

"They made me promise not to say anything," Tabitha stammered out, tears running freely down her face again. "So—so they wouldn't get into *real* trouble. Said they'd hurt Ashlee if I told anyone they pushed me."

"They *what?*" Mr. Moore barked.

"But I told you anyways, made *you* promise," Tabitha finally remembered, feeling her heart sink and sink until it felt like it'd dropped right out of her. "I just, I didn't tell you about Ashlee. I was scared. I—I was her friend, and then I just fucking forgot all about her."

———

"Great to see you again, Miss Tabby," Officer Williams took off his reflective sunglasses and put on a friendly smile, trying not to intimidate the girl. "You sure look a hell of a lot calmer than I'd be, in your shoes."

That scrawny redheaded girl looked even smaller than he'd remembered, sitting now up on the paper sheet of the hospital examining table like this. Though her eyes were puffy, likely from crying earlier, she was seated upright with proper posture like a young lady. There was a certain *stillness* to her, a sense of presence that didn't seem to fit her age at all. She didn't seem like a teenage girl overwrought with emotion and struggling with pain—there was just a wistful, sad sense of resignation as she sat there clutching carefully at her new cast.

"It's the codeine, I'm afraid," Tabitha said with a weak smile. "I'm actually... quite ill at ease."

Quite ill at ease, huh? Officer Williams paused, giving her a second look.

The girl's demeanor had startled him back then when they'd been together trying to stop his idiot buddy Darren from bleeding out. A couple busy weeks had dulled the impression, making him wonder if he'd been overstating things simply due to the nature of the situation and circumstances... but no, this girl was definitely different. He dealt with Springton's youths all the time, hell, he *had his own* kid about this same age whom he considered pretty sharp—but no, none of them were quite like this.

"Mr. Moore, good to see you again," Officer Williams stepped over to shake the man's hand and gave him a perfunctory nod.

"Yeah," Mr. Moore grunted.

"Let's have a looksie; how bad is it?" Officer Williams asked, gesturing toward her brand new cast.

"...Three to five months bad," Tabitha said in a small voice, lifting the hand for his inspection.

The outer shell of the orthopedic cast was a ridged and rigid light shade of blue fiberglass, with softer white bandaging beneath visible at the edges. The big, clunky shape of it all but buried all of the fingers on her left hand, leaving only her thumb somewhat free to wiggle. Although he'd already learned she'd hurt her hand taking that fall, the cast was larger than he'd expected, continuing on down to just a few inches shy of her pale elbow.

"The fifth metacarpal is broken, and then my wrist is fractured —a Colles fracture." Tabitha sighed. "I'm told it was a terribly unlucky fall... and also, that I'm not been getting enough calcium in my diet."

He almost made a careless comment about how she needed to drink her milk every day but tactfully managed to stop himself. They lived in that Lower Park area; this was a pretty poor family— maybe they didn't go out of their way to buy milk, maybe they drank water for breakfast. Who knew where they had to cut corners to save money? Their income and dietary practices really weren't anything it was appropriate for him to say things about.

"Uh-huh. Well—just wanted to get down a few things 'bout what happened real quick, then I'll get out of your hair," Officer Williams finally said, letting her lower her broken hand back into her lap again. "Miss Tabby, the one who pushed you was a kid by the name of Chris Thompson—are you familiar with this boy?"

"No, not at all." Tabitha shook her head. "I'm sorry, I didn't even see what he looks like."

"...Huh. Well, that takes care of my next question too, then." Officer Williams chuckled, clicking his pen out and jotting down *no relationship at all?* into the spiral notebook he'd brought in with him. "Now, I'm to understand all this has somethin' or other to do with my son Matthew, and some sorta misunderstandings that might've been goin' around the school this week?"

"Yes and no." Tabitha frowned, taking a moment to gather her thoughts before she began elaborating. "There was a rumor. Supposedly, your son Matthew grew enamored of me when driving me to Louisville this past weekend and asked me out, kissed me, or some other such variation—which we know is false on all counts, as he wasn't present there with us on that trip."

"Right." Officer Williams nodded. That was actually the main reason he was here in the first place—when he'd offhandedly asked his son if he knew anything about the situation, Matthew had said *Dad... this might actually be my fault somehow, people taking what I said the wrong way or something somehow.*

"However," Tabitha continued. "I'm of the opinion that there was never any credence to the rumor at all; that it was simply another *useful* misunderstanding being leveraged by third parties as part of the ongoing harassment targeting me."

"...Say what, now?" Officer Williams laughed, looking from her to her father and back again.

Our legal guy can't even rattle off stuff like that without reading it off of his paper, he thought, feeling that sense of incongruity grow even further.

The hell's this girl doing growing up in a trailer park? After a few beers those two weeks ago, he'd remarked to his wife that a shit-hole mobile home park like Sunset Estates was no goddamn place for a cop like Darren MacIntire to die—this little girl was *living there* in that shitty place.

Even more recently, his wife had gone on and on about how intelligent the girl was, and apparently, she was great with Hannah too.

I offered to grab some quick McDonald's for everybody, his wife had sighed into her pillow. *Tabitha all politely asks for just A SALAD, and she digs out this crumpled old five-dollar bill for me. Like it was only natural, like of course she'd pay for her own meal—my heart just broke this little bit. You know Hannah—she wasn't shy at all, went on about getting her Happy Meal toys. That's how children should be, not... oh, honey, I don't know. Burdened with so many worries, it's like, whatever it is growing up in a place like that—she carries herself differently, and it's just fascinating and heartbreaking to see.*

"So," Officer Williams cleared his throat, "you think that's what this is about? You've been being bullied?"

"All my life, yes." Tabitha gave him a dry smile. "The school board had to launch an investigation because people were spreading the rumor that I was... engaging in inappropriate activity with a teacher. I was actually hospitalized just a few months earlier, under similar circumstances to these today."

That got his attention in a big way.

"Hospitalized?" He quickly started scrawling out quick notes on a new line—that student/teacher misconduct thing would have to be looked into as well. "Can you tell me what happened there?"

"I was pushed off of a trampoline," Tabitha explained. "By one of the older sisters of a... friend of mine."

"Hairline fracture on her skull," Mr. Moore spoke up, sounding just as angry as he looked. "She got her X-rays here, then they sent her upstate to Emsie Saint Juarez children's hospital for an MRI."

"Yeah, trampolines are dangerous; someone's always gettin' hurt," Officer Williams remarked. "Sure it wasn't just an accident?"

"Just as much of an accident as today's incident was," Tabitha said, looking a little amused. "I was threatened—told that if I spoke up about them pushing me, they'd hurt my friend Ashlee. One or possibly both of those older sisters currently attends Springton High, though I don't think I've run afoul of either of them since."

"You think they're related to this time?" Officer Williams asked.

"I don't know," Tabitha admitted. "Maybe? I don't mean to implicate them in this affair today without cause... but I really don't have any other conjecture at all on why anyone would attack me. I keep to myself, and seldom interact with any of my peers. I have two friends, and... that's it."

"Well, somethin' to look into, in any case," Officer Williams said with a thoughtful frown. "So I'm to assume you've been speaking out about this, that this whole situation is possibly just some escalating drama that got out of hand?"

"No, not at all." Tabitha shook her head. "I've kept my mouth shut—I haven't said a word. In my experience, you *never feed the trolls*. The conventional wisdom is that they're deliberately attempting to provoke an upset or angry response out of me—why should I give them what they want? In time, they'll eventually lose interest and move on to attack someone else."

"Hah, *never feed the trolls,* huh?" Officer Williams chuckled. "Don't think I've ever heard it put that way. I've heard somethin' like playing dead during bear attacks and whatnot, but hell— teenage girls're way meaner than any bear."

"*Trolls* or *bears* is damn right," Mr. Moore grunted. "It's inhuman, the way these kids've treated her."

"But—if you'd spoken up, defended yourself, said—*no, hey, that's not how it happened,* it mighta defused the whole story," Officer Williams pointed out. "Put all those rumors to rest."

"I don't think you really believe that," Tabitha replied with a bitter smile. "None of the talk is ever about what really happened. It's senseless mud-flinging—they'll throw whatever they can get their hands on in hopes that something will stick. I refuse to play into their game, and there's no point dirtying my hands just giving them ammunition to use against me."

"What you're doing is very mature, sweetie," Mr. Moore said.

"Makes me damned proud of you, that you don't stoop to their level."

"When you put it like that, it's hard to see how things went this far," Officer Williams remarked, rubbing his jawline in contemplation. "They don't seem to have, as you say, *lost interest and moved on to someone else,* and this is headin' in the direction of an actual criminal case if we don't do something.

"If there's no connection between you and this Chris Thompson boy, then somebody sure as hell put him up to it, or said *somethin'.* You think it was these girls that pushed you before?"

"I think it's possible." Tabitha shrugged, carefully cradling her cast. "Like I said, I really do keep to myself. I don't know any of those girls, and I can't think of who else it might be."

"Worth looking into, for sure," Officer Williams said. "Could I have their names?"

———

"Brittney and Erica Taylor," Carrie revealed, her voice tinny-sounding and distant through the phone Elena had pinned between her cheek and her shoulder. "They absolutely hate her the most anyways. Tabitha used to go over to their house to play with their li'l sister Ashlee, and I guess *stuff kept coming up missing.* You know what I mean?"

"They're sisters?" Elena asked, furiously writing down the two names as quickly as she could. "Both sophomores?"

"Erica is, Brittney's a senior," Carrie said. "But, did you hear what I just said? You sure you wanna hang with a girl like *Tubby Tabby?* Do you even remember her from back in Laurel? You know she's from that nasty trailer park, right?"

"She's really, completely, totally not whoever she used to be," Elena said with conviction, trying hard not to carry even a hint of anger in her tone. "Like, at all. I mean—Carrie, c'mon, you've seen her."

Calling up Carrie for answers had been extremely hard for her, yet surprisingly, her former friend wasn't being all that antagonistic. It was somehow still so easy to talk to Carrie, but at the same time, this estrangement was now there, and Elena wasn't sure which hurt more—the realization that Carrie had changed so much, or the thought that actually, Carrie hadn't really changed much at all.

"Well, it's gonna be this whole stupid big thing now!" Carrie sighed. "I'd keep my distance, 'Lena, I'm so serious."

"Why? Elena asked slowly, struggling to not immediately leap into the same active defense she'd become so practiced it over the past two days. "Because of Matthew Williams, or just because of some newspaper article?"

"Matthew Williams? Newspaper article?" Carrie sounded bewildered. "Elena—were you on one of the buses that was already gone? Chris Thompson's probably gonna get suspended 'cause of her. Like, I've already heard talk like they're not gonna let him play anymore—so, yeah, um, our whole football team's basically fucked now."

"—What?" Elena abruptly sat up on her bed. "Fuck our football team, Carrie! Chris Thompson, the varsity running back? What happened, what the hell did he say to her?"

"Say to her?" Carrie paused. "Wow. You really don't even know? Elena—please, please, please, quit hanging around with those trailer trash girls and stick with Monica and me and the rest of us from now on? Tabitha's seriously bad news, they're both such bad news. Did you know that black girl friend of hers is the one who made up that photo and sent it in? I heard that—"

"Carrie, what happened?"

19
FRIENDS, FOES, AND FIGHTER JETS

Tabitha lay on the neatly-made bed within her tiny, orderly room and stared blankly up at the ceiling, her healthy tangle of reddish-orange hair strewn across her pillow. She was feeling light-headed from skipping dinner, her hand ached in a dull way, and the codeine tablet she'd taken for the pain made her brain feel fuzzy. More than anything else, though, she felt thoroughly *lost*, despondent and directionless.

Ashlee Taylor. Try as she might, she couldn't conjure a face to associate with that name—honestly, she wouldn't have remembered the name at all if not for her father reminding her. The girl had been an *early* childhood friend, and little more than a vague impression of her remained after forty-some years. *I think she must have been from... fifth or sixth grade?*

The incident with the trampoline happened more than four decades ago—but, she wasn't so sure she could chalk up her lapse in memory entirely to the passage of time.

More likely, I just didn't want to think about it, Tabitha thought, lifting her new cast up into the air and straightening her arm, trying to find a balance point where it took as little effort as possible to maintain it up. The thing was awkward and heavy, but keeping it elevated seemed to lessen the throbbing sensation. For the past few hours, it felt like her hand and wrist were so swollen up, they were straining against the confines of the cast.

I was ashamed, so I tried to never think about it, Tabitha listlessly stared at the cast. *Eventually, over the years, I ACTUALLY started to forget, started to lose the finer details of it. But, deep down, I knew. I kept quiet when a friend was being abused, because I was scared for myself—and no matter how much I put it out of my mind, it was always there, deep down there inside of me. Shaping my life.*

As a writer, she couldn't be any more familiar with character flaws—but, applying that familiarity to herself as a person? That was the work of a counselor, a therapist, maybe a psychologist. She knew by now that throughout life, people would do anything and everything to overlook their own personal shortcomings. It was easier to justify themselves as the victim, or project their flaws onto others, to stonewall themselves into denial, or make any number of excuses.

"Tabitha?" Mrs. Moore's voice called softly through the door. "One of your friends is on the phone for you—an Elena? Are you okay to talk right now?"

"Yes, Mother." Tabitha gingerly lowered her arm and twisted to sit up with her feet over the side of her bed. "Thank you, I'll speak with her now."

The door opened, and her mother stepped inside with the phone. The heavyset woman was wearing a sad, almost timid expression as she offered the cordless handset to her daughter. It seemed like she couldn't help but send glances toward Tabitha's light blue cast, and Tabitha felt an inexplicable urge to hide it or cover it up somehow.

"You're... talking like that again," Mrs. Moore said.

"Yes. I know." Tabitha squeezed her eyes shut in a grimace of frustration and took a deep breath. "I'm sorry. It just—it helps, it keeps everything at some distance. I know it's stupid, but I don't want to be real right now. I don't have the energy, I-I just—I'm just not up for it."

"Okay." Mrs. Moore nodded. "Here for you, if you ever want to talk. About anything."

"Thanks, Mom." Tabitha watched her mother carefully close the bedroom door, and then slowly hunched forward with her elbows on her knees, cradling the phone against her ear. "Hello?"

"Hi, Tabitha? It's Elena," her friend said. "Sorry, I found your number in the phone book. Just found out about what happened from Carrie earlier—are you okay? What really happened?"

I'm fine, Tabitha almost said, but her throat seized up again and her eyes watered. She wasn't exactly sure why her first instinct was to lie, or why she'd wanted to hide the cast from her mother's sight. After all, the vulnerability she was feeling right now didn't have much at all to do with her injury.

"I am," Tabitha let out an unsteady breath, "not okay. At all. But I'm trying. I'm... I'm going to figure this out."

"Tabitha, I-I think it might be my fault," Elena blurted out. "Like, this was pushback. Yesterday and today, I got into it with a few people—everyone was talking bad about you, and like, all of it was just—this completely fabricated *bullshit.* I got in a few arguments, I defended you, but. I didn't think they'd *ever* go this far! Tabitha, I'm so sorry! Everything that's going on, what they're doing, it's all just so totally, completely out of line!"

"Nothing was your fault." Tabitha felt herself smile. *Elena spoke up for me? That feels... weird and surreal and kind of amazing. I don't think I've ever had a girl like her on my side.*

"Do you even know Chris Thompson at all?" Elena asked.

"I'd never even heard of him before today," Tabitha said. "I didn't even see him. It was all too sudden."

"Okay. So, he's Springton's star running back, sorta," Elena elaborated. "How much do you know about football?"

"Um." Tabitha winced. "I only watch the Super Bowl for the commercials."

"I guess you don't really need to know anything anyways," Elena said. "He's a total scumbag. Mom says if you decide to press charges, you can absolutely *destroy* his chance of getting a football scholarship."

"I..." Tabitha paused to settle her thoughts. There *was* an immediate vindictive pang, but she needed her cooler head to prevail. "I don't know how I feel yet. Or what my parents will do. I think that... I just want to speak with him. To understand, to find out *why*."

"Well, I think I've found out who's behind all the rumors going around school, at least," Elena said.

"Brittney and Erica Taylor?" Tabitha guessed, her shoulders slumping. *I'm going to have to figure out how to deal with them.*

"Yeah—" Elena sounded surprised. "How'd you know? You know them?"

"Do you remember back in Laurel, right before the end of the year?" Tabitha sighed. "The concussion I had? That was them— one of them pushed me. I'm not sure which of them it was. Cracked skull and a serious concussion."

"No *fucking* way!" Elena hissed, and then her voice grew faint as though she'd turned away from her phone's receiver. "No, I *won't* watch my language, Mom! Tabitha says those same two girls were the ones who put her in the hospital back in middle school! Yeah, the Taylor girls."

"Sorry." Elena's voice returned to full volume. "Tabitha, are you okay? How bad is it?"

"Three to five months bad, I was told," Tabitha said, slouching even lower, until she was almost hugging her knees. "I'm. Um, it's dumb, but I'm... kind of scared to eat. I don't think I can cook normally, or run, or do my exercises or... really any major activities, for a while. Even with the painkillers. I don't ever want to go back to being the way I was."

"We're going to figure everything out," Elena promised. "One second."

We are? Tabitha wondered. A moment later, however, she could overhear Elena repeating the words *three to five months* and then beginning to paraphrase some of what had been said, presumably for Mrs. Seelbaugh. There was something incredibly heartwarming about how her friend was treating her problems as her own, and the way she jumped in without a second thought to tackle them immediately.

———

"How is she?" Mrs. Williams demanded, crossing their living room with an angry stride.

Shortly after parking his cruiser and coming in the front door, Officer Williams found himself besieged right away by a particularly vengeful-looking housewife, and he couldn't help but let out a long, slow breath. *Day's taxing enough when I'm ON the clock...*

"She'll be fine," Officer Williams tried to reassure her. "She'll just have a cast for a couple months."

She shadowed him as he stepped through their tastefully furnished foyer and into the comfort of the living room. The interior of their suburban home was a warzone of bitter conflicts and grudging compromises when it came to their tastes—he favored comfort and luxury, while she was adamantly fixated on a certain rustic vintage aesthetic. He was responsible for their overstuffed recliner and couch set, as well as their enormous rear-projection TV. She'd absolutely covered the walls in decorative antiques of all kinds, and replaced the rest of their furniture with what he jokingly considered *museum* pieces, because they were strictly for looking—not for touching.

"Well?" Karen Williams still looked absolutely *livid*.

Officer Williams saw his son Matthew awkwardly seated on one end of the sofa, but the kid definitely wasn't just relaxing after school—by all accounts, it looked like he was in the hot seat, like his wife had continued grilling the poor boy ever since he got home from school.

"She's a tough cookie," he grunted. "Broke a bone in her hand, fractured her wrist, and she was still completely calm and able to explain what all she thinks happened."

"She broke her hand," his wife repeated, gritting her teeth at hearing the extent of the girl's injuries. "And fractured her wrist?"

His wife usually had this natural jovial disposition to her that put everyone around her at ease—but when something rubbed her the wrong way, this woman's temper was fierce in a way that made even him want to flinch back away from her.

"Who broke whose hand?" Hannah asked, peeking around the corner of the hallway while clad in her *Rugrats* pajamas.

"Hannah honey, get back to bed right now," Mrs. Williams told her in a stern voice. "Mama Williams is cross right now, and I don't want you to see me when I'm cross. Skedaddle, I'll send Matthew to tuck you back in in a minute."

"Okay." Hannah blinked at them. "Sorry."

"Well," Mrs. Williams continued only after making sure that their ward had scampered back down the hall toward the guest room. "What did Tabitha say?"

"She said she was... what, somethin' like the whole thing was... making her not at ease? Uneasy?" Officer Williams recalled. *Damn, I should've written all of it down, I guess.*

"*Uneasy?*" Mrs. Williams glared. "What does that mean?"

"Something like this happened earlier in the year, so she thinks the same girls might be behind it," Officer Williams admitted, gesturing with the spiral notebook. "I've got all the details down."

"This has happened before? Give me that." She snatched the notebook out of his hands and turned a chilly look over toward her son. "Girls, what girls?"

"Well, the thing is—Tabitha said she'd never even met this boy who pushed her," Officer Williams explained.

"What girls are we talking about?" Karen asked, giving his scrawled notes a dour look. "What's this about student-teacher misconduct?"

"She claims someone at school was spreading rumors that she was involved with one of the teachers."

"That's true," Matthew dared to speak up. "About that rumor spreading, I mean—she didn't actually do anything. Everyone was saying she was fooling around with Mr. Simmons and getting her grades adjusted. The deans had to look into it."

"What a *horrible* thing to say." Mrs. Williams scowled, reading on. "Can't you write notes in complete sentences? Who're Erica and Brittney Taylor? Are they the girls behind all of this?"

"Um. Erica Taylor's one of my friends," Matthew said with a guilty look. "She's coming to the Halloween party."

"We'll see about that," Karen Williams said in a cold voice, stabbing out a finger at her son. "*You* are going to make sure nothing else happens to Tabitha from now on, buster. I don't care who's saying what, or how you got involved—I want this gossip at school about Tabitha to stop. *Now.* Am I making myself understood? I'm calling Mrs. Cribb from the school board about this tonight."

"Um." Matthew grimaced. "I don't know how it started, but they've also all been saying... that Tabitha never actually helped save Mr. MacIntire. That she just made everything up when the news van pulled in, so that she could steal all the credit."

"Say *what*, now?" Officer Williams slowly turned to regard his son.

———

"Mornin,' sweetie," Mr. Moore said, looking out across the wide open space behind their trailer. "Whatcha up to out here so early?"

"I'm going to try to put together an F-22," Tabitha said with determination, wiping machine oil from her hands onto her skirt as she surveyed their junkyard. Piles of military surplus aviation components were heaped everywhere, and she had an incomplete fighter jet chassis propped up on cinderblocks that was going to need a lot of work.

"Based on the Lockheed Martin F-22 Raptor design. A fifth-generation twin-engine, all-weather stealth tactical fighter aircraft."

"*F-22*, huh?" Her father chuckled. "Another one of them future things? What're we gonna even *do* with one, once we've got it?"

"No, it's not for us." Tabitha frowned, looking across the yard in confusion for a moment. Wasn't something... off? Something wasn't right, but she couldn't quite put her finger on what it might be. How long had she been stockpiling old jet parts to even fill the enormous area next to their makeshift machine shop?

"I'm hoping if it goes well... maybe we can get a government contract?" Tabitha said, narrowing her eyes at the mess every-where. *Must be nothing?* "Then you won't have to worry about money anymore."

"Well, try not to make *too much* noise," Mr. Moore said, shaking his head. "You know we're proud of you no matter what you do, honey."

"I think I might have to run the smelter later to try out a new batch of alloys, if that's okay?" Tabitha said, examining the F-22 schematics on her bracelet PC again. She didn't remember exactly why she'd saved the documents in the future, but it was turning out to be lucky that she had.

"Gimme a holler when you're ready, and I'll come out and give ya a hand." Her dad nodded. He still wasn't comfortable with her pouring out the superheated metals by herself yet, even though she was already almost fourteen. "Oh! 'Fore I forget, you got a letter from Julia. Here you go, Hun."

"Julie!" Tabitha exclaimed, perking up right away as she accepted the message and then opened it, greenish-blue hologram text projecting up into the air from her bracelet. *I've missed her! How did she even figure out where I am? WHEN I am?*

She beamed an excited smile as she saw the mail—Julia had written her so much! Paragraph after dense paragraph floated up into the air like a *Star Wars* opening marquee, and the simple fact that she was hearing from her friend again filled her up with joy. Why had it even been so long since they were in touch?

I can't... quite read it, though? Tabitha's smile faltered as she squinted at the blocks of text. She wanted to know what Julia had to say right away, but no matter how hard she tried, she couldn't actually focus in on the words—all she was getting was some sort of *gist* of what Julia meant to say. Something about coming to visit her, here in 1998? *So... frustrating! It's all right THERE! I want to read exactly every little thing she says!*

"Dad, I want to read it, but I can't." Tabitha let out an exasperated sigh of confusion. "Dad?"

Mr. Moore was gone.

"Dad?" Tabitha left the scrapyard behind, trotting up the sun-bleached wooden steps of the back porch to look for him. "Dad, I can't read it..."

A growing sense of discontinuity was tugging at the back of her mind as she looked for her father—but it wasn't strong enough for her to realize that the back porch belonged to an apartment she'd had when she was in her thirties. In the mobile home's living room, she found her mother's massive obese form seated in her typical spot on the sofa. She was gigantic and bloated, far too fat for her to stand under her own power, and her hair was faded and streaked through with gray.

"Mom?" Tabitha blinked. "Where's Dad?"

"Cancer." Mrs. Moore scowled in annoyance at her. "Cancer, Tabitha. He's gone. Weren't you supposed to fix that, this time through? What'd you need 'im for anyways?"

"Right." Tabitha nodded slowly, remembering. "Cancer—the

brain tumor. Sorry. I-I didn't, um, I didn't think it would even *appear* this early, though—when did...?"

"*Hah.*" Mrs. Moore snorted. "Well, make sure you get it taken care of next time, an' I don't care if you have to sit at the table the whole damned night to get it done, if that's what it takes. You hear me? I'm not tellin' you again, Tabitha Anne Moore."

"Yes, Momma." Tabitha lowered her head. Simply saying the words made her feel ugly and fat and vulnerable, that small and helpless thirteen-year-old all over again. "It's just... my friend Julie was gonna come visit. I, um, I wanted to go meet her, when she arrives?"

"Hmmph," Mrs. Moore sneered. "You're not goin' anywhere 'til you clean up that God-awful mess out there, or your father's gonna hear about it. Now go on, *get.*"

"Yes, Momma." Tabitha turned to run back out the—*back out the what?*

Their trailer only had a front door, on the one side. They didn't have anything like a back porch. Embarrassed and confused, she ran out down the front steps and then made her way around to the back of the trailer. There was just grass and weeds, those few feet of patchy landscape between their tiny shed and the neighboring trailer behind them.

I... guess that counts as cleaned up, then? Tabitha decided with one last guilty glance around, unable to place just what was wrong with the situation. *Need to get to the hospital and make sure Julie comes through the MRI okay!*

It was a long drive over to Louisville, and Tabitha knew something was definitely not right. Thankfully, her battered old 2022 Honda Pilot was right where she'd left it after her parents passed away, and someone or other had even refilled her tank. Streets and intersections passed by in a blur as she drove on and on what seemed to be forever and ever, and that pervasive *wrong* sense in the back of her mind had her gripping the steering wheel anxiously with her weathered old hands.

In her mind, it became more and more important that she see Julia right away, *no matter what,* because something wasn't right. There was this feeling of foreboding that she'd never get a chance to see her friend again if she didn't hurry. Tabitha didn't quite remember arriving or even parking, but at some point eventually, she found herself within the University of Louisville Hospital complex, lost somehow in an endless jumble of mislabeled corridors and waiting areas and examination rooms. There wasn't any time to ask anyone for directions!

When she finally, *finally* found the familiar room with that colossal MRI device... it was too late.

"Look, the goblin's finally here!" Brittney and Erica Taylor, Elena Seelbaugh, and two of the other intimidating girls from middle school were standing around the room waiting for her, greeting her arrival with mocking smiles and laughter. When the examination table slid out of the MRI with a whirring noise... it was empty.

"Wh-where's Julia?" Tabitha stammered, feeling crushed.

"She's *nowhere,* now." Brittney Taylor laughed. "It's like, wow —she's even more stupid than you are. She *wasn't even born yet* in '98! Where was her mind gonna go when she doesn't even have a body yet here? Retard. That means she's just gone now, forever."

"No—she can't be gone forever," Tabitha sobbed, furiously shaking her head in denial and clutching at her clothes. "Sh-she can't, she *can't!*"

"Uhh, well, she's not here in the past, and now she's not in the future anymore?" Elena smirked at her. "What'd you even expect? She doesn't belong anywhere anyways—duh, that's why she offed herself. *You* don't belong either."

"She can't be gone!" Tabitha repeated stupidly, feeling herself crumble and break down.

"Yeah, you shouldn't have come back in time." Erica laughed. "What, you think you're *special?* You didn't even remember which stocks to buy up! *We've* only been back in time for a few days, and we already have like, six hundred and fifty thousand dollars in shares."

"They're making me a White House advisor, at fourteen years old," Elena proudly preened. "'Cause I kept track of every little bit of corruption going on throughout the time period. I'm like, *a god* to them."

"I've just been getting laid!" One of the other girls guffawed, cupping her own breasts with her hands and waggling them. "Like, look at me—I'm *a teenager* again, what the hell else am I gonna do first?"

"What have *you* been doing, Tubby Tabby?" Brittney sneered. "You haven't done jack shit. Uh, hello? It's fucking *time travel*. If you can't even accomplish anything, why the fuck are you even *here?*"

"Yeah, are you *stupid?*" another girl chimed in. "Lockheed Martin F-22s debuted in like, 1994—they already have those, here. The design they don't have yet is the F-35 Panther Mark II."

"I'm—I'm," Tabitha cried out, blinking through her tears in disbelief at the empty examining table. The teenage girls surrounding her wore sadistic grins, leering smiles of anticipation, waiting for her to answer. What could she even say? One of them giggled, and Brittney snorted and *shushed* that girl, eyes flicking past Tabitha's shoulder for a brief instant. As if—

Tabitha flinched with her entire body as some hidden figure forcefully shoved her from behind, and then she was wide awake in the darkness of her bedroom with a sudden intake of breath.

She trembled in place on her bed, pressing her face into the pillow to stifle an anguished wail. Her wrist had woken her up, rather than the nightmare—somewhere throughout the night, that first codeine tablet had worn off. She was in blinding, feverish agony. The details of the dream were already starting to evaporate as she clutched at her arm, trying to pin it in place so it wasn't jostled by her racking sobs.

I can't. I just can't. Can't deal with everything all at once like this.

Julie. Dad. How can I even convince Dad to go in for expensive x-rays, when he won't even HAVE those headaches for years yet?

————

Chris Thompson wore a slight grin as he followed after his father into Springton High's administrative office. A five-day suspension was supposed to be a punishment, but he couldn't help but feel pretty pleased with himself. It was hard *not* to feel smug—his 'youthful indiscretion,' as his father put it, meant he didn't actually have to sit through classes today. He now had the entire week before Halloween to relax and goof off, while all these other students loitering around the quad area were stuck in their same daily routine.

Don't even have anything to feel guilty about, Chris thought, running fingers through his closely-cropped hair. *FUCK that Tabitha girl.*

He'd felt pretty ambivalent about Tabitha, at first—even despite all the nasty rumors going around about her. So what if people said she was a bit of a slut? He didn't particularly mind easy girls, and she was pretty cute. In his mind, they'd make a great couple—she was the attractive freshman everyone talked about, and he was the star running back. Tall, good-looking, and with that athletic, rangy stride of his that ate up yards on the football field like magic.

Hey, you guys know that Tabby girl, right? he'd asked some of the sophomore girls in his class yesterday.

Yeah, one of them had scowled. *What of her?*

Ask her what she thinks of me, Chris had proposed with a grin. *I think we'd make a good couple.*

Pfft, uhh yeah, Erica Taylor had laughed. *Well, I think she definitely knows about you...*

She does? Chris had perked up at hearing that.

Yeah—Erica had leaned in to confide in a whisper, and it'd been a struggle not to look down the girl's shirt. *Didn't wanna say nothin' or make a big deal, but... I heard her telling people she thinks you run like a total faggot.*

No, she didn't. Chris had made a face of disbelief.

It's true! another girl had chimed in. *I heard it too. Can you believe that bitch?*

The fuck?! he had erupted. *Who the fuck does she think she is, that she's gonna talk shit about me like that? Runs like a total faggot? God damn—she don't even fuckin' KNOW me!*

Completely blindsided, Chris found himself seeing red for the whole rest of that day. In fact, if Tabitha had been a freshman guy, he would've immediately gone and beat the shit out of her, without any hesitation. The more he dwelled on it, the more infuriating it was—*I was actually interested in her, and instead she's tryin' to just fucking shit all over my reputation? We've never even talked! FUCK this girl! Who's the faggot-ass little bitch now, huh?*

In his opinion, a minor little shove after spotting her at the bus loop was already letting her off lightly. He'd booked it afterwards, of course, in hopes that he'd get away scot-free... but a pair of freshman guys chased after him, probably some of the very same dudes he'd heard Tabitha regularly hooked up with. There wouldn't have been a ghost of a chance of the clowns catching him either, if not for his ill-planned attempt to double back and catch his own bus—when the dean Mr. Shaw caught up, Chris was already caught up in a fight with those two asshole freshman guys amidst a growing crowd of onlookers.

Fucking unbelievable...

"Good morning. My name's Donald Thompson, and I'm here about my son's suspension," his dad said, turning a stern look from the administrative clerk to the teenage son he was firmly gripping by the shoulder. "An apology and a five-day suspension is acceptable. Chris was in the wrong, here, and I've already had a talk with him about it. But you're not going to suspend him from playing games for a whole season for this; that's ridiculous. He has a future ahead of him, and the school's responsible for seeing to that."

"Er…" The woman frowned, turning to look at Chris. "Mr. Thompson—"

"I've heard from my son, as well as parents of other students here—this Tabitha girl's been known to instigate problems," Mr. Thompson cut her off. "I think that things may have been blown way out of proportion. From what I've been told, he gave her a playful shove, and then this fall was purely accidental. Is my understanding correct?"

"I'm sorry, Mr. Thompson, there's nothing I can tell you about it. The—"

"There's nothing you can tell me about it?" Mr. Thompson repeated, sounding annoyed. He leaned over the counter, trying to spot someone in the rear offices with more authority. "Yeah, of course not. Tell me, just who do I need to speak with to resolve this?"

"The district school board," the administrative clerk replied. "Nobody can do anything about the suspension until they meet on Monday, sir. Not while there's civil or criminal action pending. The best you can probably hope for is an expulsion hearing."

"*Criminal*—" Mr. Thompson's voice rose. "Expulsion hearing? You can't be goddamn serious. The district school board? *Criminal* action? For a playground scuffle—a tussle between *children?* What a complete and total crock of shit. Oh, this is the girl from that trailer park, isn't it? Let me guess, I take it her parents are chasing after some enormous, trumped-up cash settlement for damages?"

"No, sir." The clerk shook her head. "Her father sure raised a fuss yesterday, but it was two Springton police officers that came in this morning and filled out the notice of claim—it's already filed with the district."

"Ridiculous," Mr. Thompson scoffed. "After that stunt she pulled with that police officer? I'd be surprised if they're not preparing to press charges against her already, juvenile or not.

Listen, if for some reason *my* son's being implicated in some sort of lawsuit or slander, I'm going to need a copy of the claim immediately."

"Just one moment." The woman nodded, stepping back from the reception desk and disappearing into the back offices.

"I'm not apologizing to Tabitha—she called me a faggot," Chris fumed. "Jesus. Where the hell's *her* suspension?"

"You want to keep playing football, you'll do what you're told," Mr. Thompson instructed. There was anger in his tone, and he hadn't released that iron grip he had on his son's shoulder. "This was goddamn stupid of you, Chris, and you can be sure as hell they'll try to drag all this out kicking and screaming. Goddamn *stupid.*"

"Here we are." The clerk returned, grabbing a stapler so that she could fix a pair of papers together at their upper corner.

Chris caught a glimpse of the form when the woman passed it to Mr. Thompson to read, and there was *a lot* of writing there. To his dismay, he watched his father's expression darken as he read through the document, angrily flipping the paper to read the next page. An anxious, unsettling feeling began to blossom as his father turned the page back and read it over again from the beginning.

"Chris—" Mr. Thompson slapped the claim copy on the reception counter and grabbed his son by the collar. "What *the fuck* have you gotten yourself into?"

20

THE ROAD TO RECOVERY
AND THE PATH TO REVENGE

Like always, Alicia sat by herself on the bus, settling into a comfortable slouch with knees up against the vinyl of the seat in front of her so that she could stare out the window and watch the scenery pass by. The dark-skinned girl wasn't *brooding,* exactly, but nor did she feel like a particularly friendly and talkative morning person. When another kid dropped in beside her, singling her out by asking if she was *that Tabitha girl's* friend, Alicia couldn't suppress her annoyance.

Until the boy—a friend of one of the guys who'd tried to pick a fight with Chris Thompson yesterday—began catching her up on what'd happened in the bus loop yesterday. Alicia listened on in dismay and disbelief, mentally kicking herself for never exchanging phone numbers with Tabitha.

Can't believe I was in the dark about this, Alicia thought to herself, furious. *All this nonsense is finally exploding completely out of control. These kids are fucking unbelievable!*

The trip to school had seemed to take forever, with Alicia sitting up and gripping the top of the seat in front of her impatiently, silently swearing up a storm. When they finally arrived, she burst out of her seat and down the aisle to *run* off of the bus, dashing over to Tabitha immediately upon spotting her slowly trudging along in the distance of the quad area. First bell wouldn't ring for some fifteen minutes, but it felt like there were a million things she needed to ask.

"I'm so sorry! Didn't hear anything 'til just this morning!" Alicia hurried to apologize as she slowed to a stop beside her friend. "Are you okay? Tabs—Jesus, *you look like shit.*"

"Feel like shit," Tabitha admitted with a weak smile. "Didn't sleep much."

"What *happened?*" Alicia asked, stepping closer to examine her friend. The new cast was held up across the girl's chest in a faded nylon sling, and she couldn't help but stare at it.

Alicia really wanted to grab Tabitha into a fierce hug, but the redhead was looking more than just a little under the weather—it looked like she was barely managing to stand upright. The girl's shoulders were stiff and hunched in, and her already pale features had a dreadful *sickly* pallor to them, with bruise-like dark circles under her red-rimmed eyes. It seemed like a stiff breeze could come along and knock this slightly swaying Tabitha completely off her feet.

"Got pushed, fell," Tabitha said with a grimace. "Hurt. Three to five months to heal."

"Are you okay?" Alicia fretted, carefully taking Tabitha by the shoulders to steady her. "Jesus. Did they give you like, painkillers? Tylenols?"

"Yeah, yeah," Tabitha nodded with a strained face. "Codeine. Kinda."

"Kinda?"

"It came back up this morning—couldn't keep it down."

"You... threw up?" Alicia frowned. "Can you try and take another one? Tabitha—"

"It's not as bad as last night," Tabitha refused with a pained expression. "They only gave us so many tablets. I just—I need to sit down for a minute. Please."

More than a few people were watching them as Alicia guided Tabitha over toward one of the nearby concrete planters lining the quad. The decorative foliage within had long since died and been rooted out, and students typically now just used all the planter ledges as seats. When she finally sat Tabitha down, the redhead *folded,* doubling over to clutch at her knees in an alarming way. Alicia dropped to a crouch beside the crumpled girl in concern.

"Tabs?" Alicia asked. "Hah, Tabs, you're scarin' me. You are *not* okay—you shouldn't be in school today. Tabs? Tabitha?"

"I'm okay," Tabitha grunted unconvincingly. "Just. Need a minute."

"Um..." Alicia glanced around for Elena, but it looked like their other friend hadn't arrived yet. "I mean, how'd this even happen? Shouldn't you have known like, just the right moment to dodge, or something, to prevent it from happening? Or the right day to skip takin' the bus? With your, uh, *bein' from the future?*"

"Hah." Tabitha let out a tired laugh, slowly straightening herself to sit upright and carefully adjusting her sling. "I wish. Changed too many things, I guess. Never got pushed, last time through—never broke a bone. This is... a first."

"Oh, shit." Alicia felt stumped. "Guess I never considered that. Uncharted territory? So things are now like, *worse* than they were the first time?"

"No, not worse." Tabitha gave her a bitter smile. "Just... different. Hard. I didn't break anything back then, but also... no one would've cared if I had. This time, I have you. And Elena. Friends."

"Sorry," Alicia blurted out, feeling a wave of guilt wash over her. *Geez, some friend I've been.*

"No, don't be sorr—" Tabitha began, looking troubled.

"Tabitha!" Elena was quickly crossing their way with that long stride of hers. "Hey. My parents talked last night—they're gonna try to do something 'bout all this."

"Try to do something?" Tabitha repeated, blinking.

"Yeah," Elena gave them a serious nod. "My dad thinks that so long as we just apply this little bit of pressure, the school'll cave like, right away."

"Oh. Elena—your family doesn't have to, um," Tabitha said sheepishly. "Do all that on my behalf."

"It's not a problem." Elena frowned. "Tabby, I'm like—I'm *pissed*. Look at what they did to you!"

"She's right." Alicia nodded in support. "This has all got to stop."

Although she completely agreed with Elena's stance, Alicia couldn't help but feel terribly inadequate as a friend. The confident blonde white girl always seemed to be *in the know,* always seemed to have parents or someone to turn to right away for immediate results. She didn't *dislike* Elena for that, not anymore, but there was this helpless frustrating feeling she couldn't shake all the same.

"Tabby... are you gonna be alright?" Elena asked. "You don't look so good, like, at all."

"I'm better, now." Tabitha softly smiled. "Better than I've been in a long while, I think."

"Tabs—I'm gonna get you a marker by lunch period," Alicia promised Tabitha, hopping up to sit beside Tabitha and then gingerly pulling her into a hug. "For you to keep with you."

"A marker?"

"Don't let anyone else sign your cast before I do—I wanna be the first, okay? It's gonna be really cool, I promise."

———

I think... I'm in serious trouble, Tabitha thought, weakly clutching at the edge of her desk with her remaining hand.

The first period Marine Science classroom felt like it was slowly spinning, and she was afraid to meet the worried looks

Elena kept shooting in her direction. Tabitha *knew* she couldn't take today's codeine tablet on an empty stomach, so she'd tried to force down half a banana for breakfast. That had apparently been a mistake, and she'd kneeled over the bathroom toilet retching it right back up shortly afterwards.

Stomach ulcers from her past life made it extremely easy for her to mentally associate hunger with gastric pain, which had been a great help in rapidly losing weight over the summer. Now when she actually *needed* to keep food down, however, it was working against her in a terrible way. Intellectually, she recognized her body was actually famished, that she was practically faint with hunger. But some subconscious part of her brain stubbornly continued to interpret the increasing discomfort as ulcer pain, and her body seemed intent on rejecting everything in a dizzying bout of nausea.

I mean, I also I don't want to gain weight, sure—I'm TERRIFIED of ever gaining weight again. Especially right now, Tabitha slowly winced. *Damn. Am I, what, turning anorexic now?*

The problem was, she just didn't feel like she was hungry at all —instead, it was registering as a steadily deepening pit of stress and pain in her tummy, until the very idea of eating felt absolutely vile. Which meant the last actual meal she'd had was *yesterday's* breakfast, the morning of the day she'd taken that fall. Right now, she felt feeble, like her body was well past *running on fumes* and instead starting to coast to a complete stop.

Didn't work out last night. Didn't sleep much. Didn't do my morning run, or even just a walk with my mother, Tabitha inwardly tallied her recent negligence. *Need to figure out how I'm going to cook dinners with just the one hand, for a while. Start teaching Mom to help? That would—*

"Tabitha Moore? Excuse me, can we speak with Tabitha Moore outside for a moment?"

The adult voice jarred Tabitha out of her thoughts, and she twisted in her seat toward the door of the classroom in confusion.

The entire class had turned to look as well. A rotund older man she recognized as a school administrator of some sort was leaning in through the doorway.

Oh. Okay. She'd paused for a moment in something of a daze, and before she could get up herself, Elena was helping her up out of her seat and down the row of desks. There was another adult waiting outside, along with a teenage boy that Tabitha assumed was a student aid of some sort. She felt Elena's grip on her arm tighten at the sight of them, and when Tabitha looked up, she saw her friend was scowling with such undisguised malice that she was nearly baring her teeth at them.

...What?

"Just Tabitha, please." The administrator waved Elena away.

Ignoring the man, Elena trotted over to grab a plastic chair from the table at the back of the room, carrying it outside the classroom and placing it down for Tabitha. The tall blonde then went back inside, closing the door behind her, and stood there— glaring out at them through the vertical rectangle of glass set in the classroom door with her arms crossed.

"Good morning," the administrator greeted, putting his hand forward. "I'm Principal Edwards, this is Mr. Thompson and his son. We'd like to talk to you about what happened yesterday."

———

Fucking hell, Chris, Mr. Thompson wanted to swear, looking from this scrawny waif of a girl to his tall and athletic son in growing outrage. *You pushed THIS girl? She must weigh ninety pounds soaking wet—just look at her skinny little arms!*

From the rumors and hearsay, he'd expected some sullen, sulking teenage girl, maybe one styling herself after... *damn, who is it nowadays? Madonna? Shania Twain?* Whatever stupid fashionista kids imitated these days. Instead, this Tabitha girl dressed tastefully and had a gentle, somewhat mousy demeanor that seemed completely at odds with all prior assumptions.

The pain the girl was experiencing didn't look feigned in the slightest either—she was unsteady on her feet, her eyes were tight, and she was forgetting her own dangling arm sling to instead protectively hold her cast up high against her own collarbone. Her entire little frame seemed to be *radiating* distress, and it was all he could do not to slap his son stupid at the mere sight of her.

Scoffed at the idea anyone'd break anything just falling down off a curb, Mr. Thompson found himself struggling and failing to rein in the protective instincts that Tabitha naturally aroused. *Looking at her now, seems damn lucky she didn't break more—she got shoved by a running back probably twice her size! Jesus, the cast even looks huge on her. Chris, don't you see how damn bad this ends up looking?*

"Have a seat, please," Principal Edwards said, gesturing toward the chair the girl's surly friend had brought out for her.

"Um." Tabitha hesitated warily for a moment before easing down into the seat. "Thank you."

"This is Chris Thompson." Principal Edwards motioned Chris forward. "He's here to apologize for what happened yesterday."

The girl shrank back in her chair, hunching her shoulders in ever so slightly, as if only now really registering the teenage boy's presence.

"Yeah," Chris reported stiffly, as if reading off a script. "...Sorry."

Donald Thompson turned an incredulous stare at his oaf of a son, but it appeared that was all the boy was willing to say. Before he could resist, he found himself swatting a smack upside the idiot sixteen-year-old's head. In front of them, Tabitha flinched back at the sudden violence, timidly half-rising out of her chair.

"Mr. Thompson—please." Principal Edwards frowned, holding up a hand. "Chris, c'mon now. I know you're a team player and you're a good kid—is that really all you've got to say for yourself?"

"Yep," Chris replied with a stubborn set of his jaw. "Sorry."

"How do you two kids know each other, if you don't mind my asking?" Principal Edwards pressed, looking from Chris to Tabitha for answers. "I'd like to know how things got to this point."

"I'm sorry. I... don't believe we've ever met?" Tabitha turned a perplexed look of her own toward Chris.

"Yeah, right," Chris scoffed, refusing to look her in the eye. "She's been telling everyone I run like a faggot."

"No—I haven't." Tabitha sagged back into her chair, displaying a bitter smile that didn't seem to match her age. "But I suppose one of the Taylor sisters told you that."

"Not really." Chris gave them an unapologetic shrug. "Everyone's been hearing her say it."

"The Taylor sisters?" Mr. Thompson prompted.

"They... put me in the hospital earlier this year," Tabitha explained slowly. "Under similar circumstances. They pushed me when I was visiting their younger sister, Ashlee. Cracked skull, had to be sent up to Louisville for a better MRI. I think they've been... out to make things difficult for me here, ever since I started school."

"No, they're not," Chris sneered. "She's the one always starting shit—ask anyone."

"She *has not*," Elena interrupted, opening the door a crack so that she could speak through. "The Taylors are the ones spreading all the nasty rumors about Tabitha nonstop. Mr. Simmons almost lost his Goddamn job! Hey, Mr. Simmons, come tell them about—"

"Could you go take your seat, please, Miss?" Principal Edwards frowned. "This is a private issue between Tabitha and Chris."

Except... that doesn't seem to be the case? Mr. Thompson coolly turned to appraise the Springton principal. *Seems like some other girls were just using him to harass this girl? This Tabitha girl didn't recognize Chris from Adam when she stepped out here. God DAMNIT, Chris. You've got to be smarter than all this.*

Visibly fuming, Elena slammed the door closed again. She

continued to scowl out the little window at them, refusing to go sit down.

"Did one of these Taylor girls say something to you?" Mr. Thompson pressed, giving his son a cold look.

"I guess?" Chris grudgingly shrugged again. "Everyone's saying it, though."

So that's it, then, Mr. Thompson narrowed his eyes. *You might've just thrown away your whole football future, all because you never stopped to question anything that was said for a single damned second.*

Donald Thompson liked to imagine that his boy was pretty sharp, that Chris had great prospects and a promising athletic career ahead of him. Realizing just how immature and short-sighted his son actually was... had an incredibly sobering effect. This time, he could almost *feel* the gray hairs coming in.

"Tabitha," Mr. Thompson resigned himself to a sigh, looking away from his wayward son. "Has your father said anything about pressing charges? We'd like to cooperate and settle all of this as cleanly as possible, no matter what that ends up meaning."

"No, but. Um." Tabitha hesitated and then winced. "Can I give you our phone number? I don't think my father's insurance likes me being so, um. *Injury-prone.* He hasn't said anything to me, but I'm sure he had to pay mostly out of pocket for the x-rays and cast, this time. If there's... any sort of assistance you could—"

"Consider it all covered," Mr. Thompson agreed immediately. *Right out of Chris' college fund, and he's gonna work his ass off to put it back into shape before the end of the year. For STARTERS.* "That goes without saying. How bad is it?"

"It's..." Tabitha frowned, unconsciously trying to wiggle the cast-encased fingers of her left hand. "The fifth metacarpal is broken, and my wrist is fractured. I'm sorry, I-I don't know how much it all cost."

"We'll take care of it," Mr. Thompson promised, frowning in his son's direction but somehow managing not to hit him again.

"Good, good." Principal Edwards smiled. "I'm glad this was all able to be resolved."

———

"No, this is not *resolved,*" Mrs. Cribb growled in exasperation, digging and hunting through the dish of Halloween candy someone had set back behind the front desk. She threw Principal Edwards a dirty look. "Are you *serious?*"

Wearing a sweater featuring a pumpkin patch atop her more professional button-up blouse and suit pants, forty-nine-year-old Pamela Cribb from the Springton school board couldn't help but think she'd arrived not a moment too soon—the situation here was turning into a total fiasco! Although ostensibly just another member of the school board, in practice Pamela Cribb found herself doing a lot of legwork and oversight between the schools, as their district was considered too small to appoint an actual assistant superintendent.

Resolved? Mrs. Cribb seethed, finally singling out an individually wrapped little Milky Way. *Not damned likely. Mr. Edwards—you don't seem to have any grasp of the SEVERITY of this situation.*

Karen Williams had called her late last night, *angry to the point of tears,* and Mrs. Cribb hadn't had any clue where to even begin placating the woman. They were longtime friends—both members of the Springton United Methodist Church, and they'd been in Women's Fellowship Choir group together for years. Karen Williams was such a *nice,* friendly woman that hearing her so furious, even over the phone, had been more than a little startling. Worse yet, it was *Karen Williams,* and that woman knew everyone.

"Erica Taylor, Brittney Taylor, Kaylee Mendolson." Mrs. Cribb double-checked the names she'd written down. "Pull these girls out of class and have them sent up to the office. They'll all be facing suspension."

"Suspension, based on a *he said, she said?*" Principal Edwards frowned. "When it's just one of these girl's words against another—"

"Yes, suspension—based on the school board's immediate harassment investigation," Mrs. Cribb's anger was rising, and she found it difficult to keep it out of her voice. "Springton police has a county lawyer preparing to press charges, the parent-teacher association's flooding with angry calls already, and we just received a *second* notice of claim, now from the law offices of Seelbaugh and Straub."

"Seelbaugh and Straub?" Principal Edwards began to bluster. "The Thompson family already agreed to cover expenses for—"

"This isn't just about the Thompson boy!" Mrs. Cribb interjected. "Henry—we're being threatened with lawsuits based on information that we, the school board, haven't even begun to collect yet. Everyone's out for blood—if it's going to be ours, I think I'd at least like to know why! Go pull those girls out of class. *Now.*"

She rubbed her temples in vexation as Principal Edwards left with the brief list of names. The heavyset principal had just been so confident that smoothing things over between the Thompson and Moore families would put the entire matter to rest. Mrs. Cribb felt the pressure and urgency, even if the Springton High administration did not—she knew that she needed to get to the bottom of this before things snowballed completely out of control. The situation didn't seem to warrant an emergency school board meeting—yet—but if she didn't get a handle on things quickly, the matter wouldn't end at just a few expulsions.

The last thing we can afford right now is any kind of legal battle!

"Mrs. Clara?" Mrs. Cribb asked, knocking on the door of the rear office. "You have the student record for Miss Tabitha Moore out?"

"Have it here—Ninth grade. Graduated from Laurel, recommended for advanced placement English. Birthday in December. Vaccinations are up to date," Mrs. Clara read from the brief file while shaking her head. "There was the one rumor about inappro-priate conduct with a teacher, but it was just a rumor—we thought it best to handle as quietly as possible. Nothing grade-wise 'til the end of this first term, but Mrs. Albertson's insisted the girl's at the top of her class."

"Top of which class?" Mrs. Cribb asked. "Mrs. Albertson teaches her, what—English?"

"The advanced placement English, yes." Mrs. Clara nodded. "From what I understand, though, she means Miss Moore may be at the top of the entire class, the *entire freshman class*. We have signatures from three teachers, recommending we skip the girl on up another grade level."

"You're kidding," Mrs. Cribb sighed, palm on her forehead. "Freshman, birthday in December? Is she thirteen years old, or fourteen? Fifteen?"

"Looks like..." Mrs. Clara checked the printed date of birth. "Thirteen?"

"Thirteen—that's *way* too damned young for this kind of bullying," Mrs. Cribb growled, letting out a slow breath. "Have either student aides, or a monitor, or *someone* keep a close eye on her—in fact, I don't want this poor girl out of anyone's sight until this is all taken care of. Classes, between classes, at lunch. The bus loop too. Send any problems right here to the office for suspension —worst comes to worst, we pull the whole damned student body into the auditorium and give them all a long talking-to about acceptable conduct."

Thankfully, Mrs. Clara didn't dilly-dally once she had her instructions. The woman gave her a prompt nod and immediately stepped out, off to track down and notify each of Tabitha's teachers.

Our saving grace so far seems to be that the first major incident with that fractured skull didn't happen on school grounds, Mrs. Cribb pursed her lips, leaning across Mrs. Clara's desk for the office phone and pressing for an outside line. *If this does wind up in court,*

I'm gonna make sure it's the parents of these girls answering, not the damned school board.

Punching in the number on record and then dropping down heavily into the office chair, Mrs. Cribb fought the urge to drum impatient fingers across the surface of the desk. She remembered Karen Williams had always been a delight to collaborate with, on anything—be it organizing a fundraiser dinner, a surprise birthday party to celebrate one of the congregation's elderly members, or even putting together a fun trip for the youth group at the last minute, after original plans had fallen through. It was more than a little frightening imagining that smiling woman instead working *against* her, and Mrs. Cribb couldn't help but grit her teeth at the prospect.

"Hello—am I speaking to the parents of Erica and Brittney Taylor?"

———

"Well, both Erica and Brittney got sent home, so *something's* up," Elena deduced. "Everyone's talking about it."

Tabitha was slumped over, leaning up against Alicia at their lunch table. Her left arm was trapped under Alicia's, and even pinned into place, because her artistic friend needed her to be absolutely still so that she could finish drawing on Tabitha's cast. Today, it was easy for Tabitha to obediently lie still and motionless —she felt exhausted and empty.

"Everyone here's *always* talking, about everything," Alicia grumbled. "Don't know how you do it, Elena. I sure couldn't put up with it."

Even though she didn't feel quite all there, Tabitha wasn't blind to the marked difference in the way Springton High treated her today. Students had openly stared, steering a wide berth around her and gawking at her from a distance. The chatty teenage girls in each of Tabitha's classes had fallen into a strained, somehow *angry*-seeming silence in her presence. It seemed foreboding to her, made her glumly suspect that the worst was still yet to come.

Most of the severe stomach pain had faded away throughout the day, and she was now more than content to listlessly watch on as Alicia did her thing. Her friend was carefully creating what looked to be a scrollwork series of swirls and flourishes, according to some larger intricate plan that Tabitha couldn't discern. Each steady touch of fine-point marker embellished the light blue of Tabitha's cast with more and more of the artful pattern, and it was mesmerizing to watch.

Looks like one of those fancy designs from the future, like they'd have in those stress relief coloring books, Tabitha mused to herself. *Maybe we can color it in? Can you paint a cast, or does it need to breathe?*

"Communicating with others is super important, though," Elena argued. "I don't like what they have to say, but you need to be able to hear all of it, you know? Otherwise, it's just, I dunno. Burying your head in the sand, missing out on details and things 'cause you just don't wanna hear them."

"It's okay, Alicia," Tabitha murmured, patting her friend's shoulder. "I'm not good with people either."

"I think you can be." Elena laughed. "You were great with your little cousins; it's like you were this whole different you."

"My cousins aren't... *people,*" Tabitha tried to not make a face. "They're my cousins. My little tribe of goblin warriors."

"Can't believe you'd call them that," Alicia chided with a snort. "Shame on you, Tabs. Calling other people goblins already."

"They're not... *people,* though," Tabitha insisted. "They're my little cousins. Don't you have little cousins?"

"Tabitha... you're pretty out of it," Elena said. "You should probably be at home resting today, or something?"

"My dad said he'd pick me up early if I don't feel any better," Tabitha explained, giving her blonde friend a bleary look. "I just, I don't want to be at home. It's frustrating there."

"You still look terrible," Elena said, pausing and sitting up straight as someone approached their table. "Oh, uh... hey. Tabitha; this is Carrie. Don't know if you remember her from Laurel? We all had stuff together."

Carrie? Tabitha wearily looked up at the new arrival, trying to recall where she'd heard that name before.

An unimpressed-looking teenage girl had walked up to their table, wearing one of those fashionable winter vests that puffed out between the quilted seams. It took her a moment to place the design—the closed vest's three colors made up the *Tommy Hilfiger* logo flag, the first instance of it she'd seen in her second trip through life. *But definitely not the last...*

Carrie had a pretty face, touched up with impressive if *a little over-the-top* makeup. A combination of liberally-applied nineties-style blue eyeshadow and cosmetic glitter gave the girl a frosty ice princess aesthetic, and then her long hair was just a few shades blonde of natural, pinned above the thin arch of her eyebrow on either side with barrettes. Two carefully chosen tendrils of hair were left free to frame her face, and while the look *worked* because she had naturally attractive, youthful features, the placement was so deliberate that it came off as a little pretentious.

"You really *do* look terrible," Carrie appraised, looking Tabitha over in return with a level of scrutiny that made Tabitha distinctly uncomfortable. "They're all saying you're faking it—but like, how do you fake it when you're the one that got pushed, right?"

"Right," Elena nodded in agreement—as if she'd coached Carrie in what topics to broach earlier.

"...Hi, Carrie," Tabitha said with caution, trying to sit up and look a bit more presentable. "I think I do remember you."

"You do?"

Or at least, my subconscious does? Tabitha thought in embarrassment. Last night's feverish dream was hazy now, but she definitely remembered that this Carrie girl had been present—the teen bragging about how she'd been back in time getting laid.

"All that was back in middle school." Carrie shrugged by way of apology, eyeing Tabitha for her reaction as if daring her to say something about it. "We're in high school now, sooo all of that back then was whatever. Right?"

"She means she's sorry," Elena attempted to mediate, throwing Carrie a glance of warning. "And that things are gonna be different from now on."

"It's okay," Tabitha said with an awkward smile. "I've put it all behind me, whether I wanted to or not. That concussion back then did a number on me—everything at Laurel is all just kind of... a big scary blur now."

"Okay, cool." Carrie nodded. "I *am* kinda sorry things were like that. Anyways, 'Lena says you didn't get lipo?"

"*Carrie—*"

"Hey, everybody's been saying things," Carrie held up her hands defensively. "Just wanna know what's for real, alright?"

"It's okay," Tabitha sighed. She carefully shifted her sling until her cast was resting at her shoulder, and then leaned back from the table, peeling her blouse up to reveal bare midsection.

"Uhhh—" Carrie laughed, giving her a skeptical look. "*What are you doing?*"

"It's only been a few months," Tabitha explained. "Scars would be noticeable. Fat reduction surgeries, they make little incisions so they can remove tissue. I'm too young for that kind of procedure anyways, though. Don't think you can get it below the age of eighteen."

"Okay, yeah!" Carrie leaned in for closer inspection, finally looking mollified. "Not a scratch anywhere, cool. You're super pale, though—*yikes.*"

"It's *October,*" Elena said, exasperated. "All of us are gonna be a little pale, okay? 'Cept Alicia, of course."

"*Hey!*" Alicia yelled in mock-indignation.

"*I'm* not that pale," Carrie retorted, looking from girl to girl. "And—Alicia's black."

"I am?!" Alicia held out her hands and gaped at them in feigned shock. "Gee, nobody'd pointed it out for a few minutes, thanks. Sure wouldn't wanna forget!"

"Har har." Carrie made a disgusted face. "Chill out, geez. I have black friends."

"I'm actually just... always pale," Tabitha tried to explain. "I'm pale, or I burn—there isn't any, um. In between, for me."

"You didn't have to show Carrie anything, Tabitha," Elena said. "You don't have to prove yourself to anybody."

"That's dumb," Carrie disagreed, giving Elena a doubtful look. "Like, if she can prove it with that, she should've just shown everybody?"

"S'not what my mom says," Elena refused, crossing her arms. "You shouldn't ever try to appease the people who put you down, for any sort of validation—'cause then from then on, it's like you've given them authority over you."

"That doesn't even make any sense." Carrie rolled her eyes. "Elena, you're turning into a total nerd."

"You're... both a little right," Tabitha said as diplomatically as she could manage, carefully smoothing her blouse back down. "I just... I'm not great with confrontation."

"You're really not," Carrie decided, seeming to have made up her mind. "Like, the more you think about it—there's no way you'd've called Chris Thompson a faggot. Even if he kinda is, like for pushing you and all. Just doesn't really fit with what you'd say, though, y'know?"

"I've never called him anything." Tabitha took a deep breath, squeezing her eyes shut. "I just first met him today. When he came to... apologize."

"Everyone's tryin' to figure out why you've had this big vendetta against him." Carrie grinned. "But you never did, did you? It's all made up, huh?"

"No shit—everything going around about Tabs has been made up," Alicia groused. "She saved that cop; I was fucking *there*. Mr.

Peterson's pissed about all the naysayers too. People keep saying like the photo in that paper was faked—uh, Mr. Peterson developed it himself, right from the negative."

"Yeah, and that whole thing with Mr. Simmons?" Elena chimed in. "Totally bogus. She was in the library every day at lunchtime; they checked. There's a security camera in the ceiling there."

"Okay, yeah. And Matthew didn't ever ask her out." Carrie nodded, casting a glance from Elena to Tabitha to gauge their expressions. "Yeah, I knew that one was fake already—they started it just to try and like, drive a wedge between you two. Since fuckin' everyone knows Elena has the hots for Matthew."

"Not... *everyone* knows." Elena scowled. "Geez."

"You *did* tell both of us you were crushing on him right away," Tabitha pointed out with a slight smile. "Like, the very day we met."

"No, I didn't," Elena denied. "Not like, right away anyways. Besides, he *is* hot. Try to tell me he's not."

"You guys *do* realize he's randomly wandering around right over there, right?" Alicia smirked. "Matthew Williams. He keeps glancing over this way."

"*Duh*, he's been trying to look out for Tabitha." Elena rolled her eyes. "Whatever. Everyone look over at him for a second."

———

Matthew Williams' stride faltered midstep as the table of four girls he was discreetly keeping an eye on all turned in unison, and then pointedly stared in his direction.

Damn. He flashed them a somewhat guilty smile. Abandoning his pretense of idly roaming around the outer area of the quad, Matthew turned and headed over toward them. *How do they DO that?*

His mother's *smooth move, detective* joke for Dad had been

completely beaten to death over the years, and Matthew would be the first one to admit he and his father didn't have any particular proclivity for sneaking around. He *was* relieved to notice he wasn't the only one watching over Tabitha—one of the deans, Mrs. Clara, was sitting at the one out-of-the-way corner table, and hadn't taken her eyes off the girls the entire time.

Guess... I'd better just go say what's up? Matthew Williams ran a hand through his hair. *I can just invite all of them. Mom REALLY wants Tabitha to come to the party, but I don't wanna make it seem weird or anything—especially after that stupid rumor.*

21

WITHDRAWING FROM SCHOOL

"Hey, guys." Matthew Williams gave them a sheepish greeting. "What's up?"

"Hi, Matthew!" Carrie rewarded him with a brilliant smile.

He recognized Carrie as one of Erica Taylor's coterie of freshmen being groomed for a position in Springton High's labyrinthian *pyramid-scheme* of popularity. She'd been pointedly introduced to Matthew several times already, and he was supposed to *know* her, but honestly, this platinum blonde beaming a smile at him had never made any credible impression herself.

So—what's one of Erica's girls doing hanging around Tabitha now? Matthew wondered, sending a questioning glance toward Elena.

"Matthew." Elena acknowledged his presence with a neutral tone, not seeming particularly pleased to see him.

Ahh... fuck, Matthew tried not to wince. *S'all gonna be about taking sides now, huh?*

It wasn't that he wasn't sympathetic toward Tabitha's group —just, with him already implicated in rumors, he had to tread very carefully and watch what he said to them. While also somehow making absolutely sure he invited Tabitha to the

Halloween party, of course. Because his mother would ask him about that.

From what people mentioned, Elena was *interested in him,* which only made things more difficult for everyone. Matthew was discreetly dating Casey, and after a youth retreat last month spent making out and getting handsy with each other beneath a blanket, he was fairly certain that he was going to love her forever. With his art club friends on one side, and the majority of his sophomore peers on the other, getting caught up in the internecine conflict surrounding Tabitha seemed inevitable—he *really* wished he could just not be involved in anything complicated.

"I, uh—well, I got to the bottom of who was spreading that rumor," Matthew joked, presenting a lopsided smile for the girls. By the time he'd arrived at school today, the topic had somehow already disseminated throughout the school and become common knowledge.

"We know," Elena said, crossing her arms.

"We know," Carrie agreed with a chuckle. "Duh."

"Smooth, Sherlock." Alicia glanced up from the cast she was decorating and shot him a teasing grin. "Real smooth."

"You alright, Tabitha?" Matthew asked.

"I've... been better?" Tabitha sighed. She had a dazed, somewhat dreamy look in those pale green eyes today—painkillers, obviously—and despite Matthew's sure future with Casey, that familiar surge of teenage hormones had him wondering what it would be like sharing a blanket with Tabitha.

"Real sorry things got so crazy out of hand like this," Matthew apologized awkwardly, feeling a sharp pang of guilt for his attraction. "Mom was *pissed,* she called the school board. Dad was all trying to calm her down—'til he heard people were saying you made up the whole thing with Officer MacIntire. Then *he* was pissed, and—well, listen, we're all pissed."

"We *are* pissed." Elena nodded in approval, uncrossing her arms and resting them back on the table.

"You letting people sign your cast, Tabitha?" Matthew asked.

"Not 'til I'm finished," Alicia decided, hunching protectively over Tabitha's arm. "And then you're only allowed to sign right where I show you to sign."

"You can't just keep using Tabitha as your art project for everything." Matthew chuckled. Alicia hadn't been shy about telling the club she was using that photo she'd taken as a painting reference as soon as she got into the Art II elective.

"Yes I can—and yes I will." Alicia stuck out her tongue at him, looking pleased with herself.

The dark-skinned girl had been a lot more reserved back at that art club meeting, and it took a moment of Matthew gauging the body language between the different girls to guess why— Alicia was acting playful to prove their familiarity and make Carrie and Elena uneasy.

No, wait—it's really just to put Carrie on edge, Matthew realized. Carrie and Elena seemed cut from the same cloth, but Elena's posture was decidedly guarded, like there was a wall of tension separating her from Carrie. Despite mostly facing him, she never let the other blonde out of her peripheral. Closer observation revealed that yes, the *Erica faction* Carrie was the obvious odd one out, and both Alicia and Elena were sitting protectively to look out for Tabitha.

Gah. I really DO think Elena's cool, Matthew groused to himself as his estimation of Elena rose another notch. *But... I absolutely don't want to get into this. Or seem like I'm leading Elena on, or anything. Definitely don't want to jeopardize things with Casey.*

"Well, anyways, having a big party, the Sunday after Halloween," Matthew announced. "My Grammy and Pawpaw have a big house on the lake, but they hurry down to Florida every winter, so my parents always trash the place throwing all the parties they can."

He meant that to come off as humor, but if last year was any indication...

"Wanted to make sure you're all invited—I can write down the address for you, if you want."

"We're *all* invited?" Elena blurted out, her standoffish demeanor slipping for a moment.

"Yeah, of course," Matthew confirmed. "Any of you free?"

"Is it a costume party?" Alicia looked up from the cast with interest. "Like, a Halloween thing?"

"Yeah, or at least—mostly," Matthew admitted. "Me and some of the guys from my youth group're definitely gonna dress up."

"I'll ask my mom, then." Alicia shared a glance with Tabitha and Elena before looking back to Matthew. "If that's cool?"

"Yeah, awesome." Matthew nodded, eyeing Tabitha for her response.

"...Is *Erica* going?" Carrie inquired with a mischievous smirk, knowing what a loaded question that was.

"Uhhh—well, she *was* invited, yeah," Matthew grimaced. "Like, I'm not gonna go out of my way to *uninvite* her, but with her already—"

"I think you probably *should* uninvite her," Elena cut in with a biting remark. "You know what she's been doing; if she's there, we're not going."

"No, no—it's fine," Tabitha protested weakly. "I don't even know if I can go. If I did—all of us would be there, so things would still be... civil, right?"

"*Right,*" Carrie let out a sarcastic snort. "Civil."

"If Erica's going, Tabitha and us are not," Elena decided in a firm voice. "Like—no way."

"Address, please," Alicia asked cheerfully, drawing out a blank page from the portfolio sitting beneath Tabitha's cast and passing her marker to Matthew. "Uhhh... gimme your phone number too, yeah?"

"Yeah, of course." Matthew nodded, pretending to be oblivious to the way the other girls all turned to stare at Alicia.

REALLY wish I could just put it out there that I'm taken without dumping drama bullshit all over Casey.

It took him a moment to scrawl out the address and then his number beneath it, and Alicia immediately took the paper, quickly folding and putting it away before Carrie could peek at it.

"*Thank you,*" Alicia smiled to herself.

"...Can I borrow a piece of paper?" Carrie asked, giving the black girl a look.

"Uh, shit—sorry, I don't have any blank paper," Alicia lied. "I really don't—even that one already had one of my drawings on the back. Sorry?"

Carrie looked from girl to girl, visibly trying not to scowl as she suspected her apparent exclusion, but there was nothing Matthew could do—it was lunch period, and he didn't carry things on him. *Shit.*

"I'll get the place from you later," Carrie said to Matthew, her tone suggesting the words were not-so-subtly directed at the others. "I really wanna go, and I'm *definitely* gonna be there."

"Uh, cool," Matthew said helplessly, determined to not get involved. "Yeah. Well, I'll catch you all later sometime. Feel better, Tabitha."

"Matthew?" Tabitha spoke up. "Say hi to Hannah for me, please?"

He waved as he turned to go, amused to see Carrie frozen with indecision. For a moment, it had looked like she was also about to walk away from the situation... but when he left the girls behind, he could still faintly overhear her hushed whisper.

"Who the hell's *Hannah?*"

———

After lunch, Tabitha managed to trudge along to her fifth period Algebra I class and settle into her seat to review her *Goblina* notes. Most of the freshman algebra assignments were from a workbook they were given at the beginning of the year, and aside from tests and the odd errant printout, Tabitha had completed all provided work well ahead of time. It was difficult to focus on her broad story outline today—she wanted to imagine what Hannah would make of things, were the spritely little girl to read her story.

Tabitha was feeling beyond haggard, stretched past all of her tolerances and ready to have a breakdown, and only realized it when she'd reread a sentence three times before the actual meaning registered. Her thoughts were wandering all over the place. With a bit of reluctance, she resigned herself to scribbling in her *Goblina* 'ideas' scratchpad section—random thoughts she would review and reorganize into proper outline pages at the end of each week.

Use alternate method of exposition for supporting characters to delineate from heroine? Define by interaction with designated character foils? Explore other contrasts than traditional protagonist/antagonist clichés, experiment with defining abstract character traits using character foils.

Work on splitting exposition prompts (profile pages 3-7, 13, 15) into backstory / narrative hooks, AVOID MYSTERY BOX STORY-TELLING. *Backstory exposition* should always be in unreliable narration to ~~setstablish set up~~ establish the twist for the Goblin Princess book. Other narrative hooks are either character moments or chekhovs guns for setting up key plot points. Consider compiling a reference page of everything remember about Julie's story observations in regard to how Goblina sets up Goblina Princess! Her comments were very helpful. Test out different order of operations for planned exposition for best story fit. Divvy up backstory reveals for both the two book + three book alternate outlines and weigh merit, refer to page 118.

(Page 118 tearing at top. Compare cost of plastic page protectors vs. occasionally rewriting pages w/ new paper when these older pages get crumpled or rip?)

Ask Mrs. Albertson if there are research papers or studies on the best balance of concurrent subplots (by genre, if possible) and/or a technique for resolving subplots in sequence so there is always something satisfying for the reader. (Staple of serial fiction/webfiction, but thorough analysis of those distinctions may still be three decades away.) Ask Mrs. Albertson about research tomorrow, DON'T FORGET.

Practice acting out character ~~manneirsms~~ mannerisms w/ Mom? Helpful, adds insight to characters. Make ref page to explore and define which character traits can/can't be best expressed w/ written mannerisms? Teach Mom cauliflower rice recipe tonight, NEED EAT SOMETHING BEFORE GET WORSE. BRAINSTORM SIMPLE MEAL PREP OPTIONS FOR WEEK? PRIORITY, ASK GRANDMA HELP.

Staring down at her new entries with a strange sense of satisfaction, Tabitha set down her pencil and readjusted the strap of her sling. Her notes were mostly nonsense, but it was still incredibly cathartic putting all those nagging thoughts down onto paper, because then it felt like they were out of her head for good and didn't need to be worried about anymore. Slouching over her desk to rest her cheek on the inside of her arm, she closed her sore eyes for a moment—and before she knew it, she'd completely drifted off.

Tabitha fell asleep for almost thirty-five minutes right in the middle of class, and when she woke up, the binder that she kept her *Goblina* project in was gone.

At first, she was only confused. She'd instinctively sought out the binder almost the moment she was awake and aware again, because it often existed to her as a tangible representation of her thoughts. It was where she *collected* her thoughts, a security blanket in the same sense as Alicia never letting her sketchbook too far out of her sight. Her desk was empty, and a cursory inspection leaning forward revealed it hadn't been nudged off and onto the floor. She knew she hadn't put it in the backpack resting by her side, but she checked anyway.

Thinking perhaps another adjacent student had been curious and was flipping through it on *their* desk caused her to look around, and immediately, several of the neighboring teenage girls sitting nearby purposefully looked away from her in unison, studiously avoiding her gaze.

Tabitha stared back down at her empty desk in total disbelief for a moment.

Oh... OH. Realizing what must have happened was immediately, *intensely* upsetting, and Tabitha glared up at them in furious consternation even as her eyes began to water.

This wasn't *completely* new—Tabitha vaguely remembered classmates having nicked her belongings in her first life, but right now, she felt so angry, hurt, and vulnerable that she was completely beside herself. She was *trying* to be the mature, level-headed Tabitha through each crisis, but she was past the limits of what she could endure right now, and didn't imagine she could weather this without having a breakdown.

I'm so fucking done. I'm so fucking done with all of this.

There was more than disjointed ramblings in that binder, it was a *piece of her soul* she was relearning how to carve out and express to others; it was her struggling—but promising—attempt at breathing new inspiration into the failure of her last life's work. She wanted to *flip out,* she wanted to scream and cry, she wanted to shut down and hug her knees like a child, she wanted to wail and whine about how fucking ridiculously *unfair* all of this was becoming.

Tabitha squeezed her left hand against the confines of its cast, attempting to clench her hand into a fist until it really started to hurt.

But I'm not going to do any of that. Shaking slightly, Tabitha gritted her teeth so hard, her jaw ached, and carefully rose up out of her seat. *Because I'm a GODDAMN adult.*

There was a rush of dizziness and her vision blacked out for a moment as she stood, but that was slight malnourishment, not rage, and helped clear her head a bit. The room was quiet except for Mr. Stern droning on as he drew an example equation on the board at the front of the class, but the silence seemed somehow deafening to her. Students were turning in their seats to see what she was doing.

Slowly—carefully, watching her feet on the chance someone would purposely put out a foot to trip her, because she was *completely* out of trust for her peers right now—Tabitha walked down the aisle of desks to the front of the classroom beside Mr. Stern.

"Yes? Miss Tabitha?" Mr. Stern paused, looking at her with surprise.

"I fell asleep," Tabitha explained quietly. Tears had rolled down her cheeks, but she'd managed to not start actually crying. If she did, there was no way she was going to be able to collect herself anytime soon.

"Yes, I saw that," Mr. Stern admitted awkwardly, glancing over toward her assigned seat. "But you're a fair bit ahead of the class, and with—"

"When I woke up, something on my desk was gone. A binder. It was full of—it had a personal project that was very important to me," Tabitha explained in a low voice. This close to the front of the class, she doubted anyone would be able to overhear, but with how quiet everyone had gone, it seemed like they were all *extremely* interested.

"I'm going home," Tabitha said, giving Mr. Stern a bitter smile. "I don't feel good, and—I don't feel safe here anymore. I don't know if I'm ever going to come back. I'm sorry."

"Stole your notebook? Binder?" Mr. Stern's face became a grimacing frown and he glared out across his students. "I'll make sure that—"

"*Please do,*" Tabitha felt herself begin to choke up. "But—I, I need to go. I'm going to the main office. I'm sorry."

"Robert," Mr. Stern snapped, pointing out the guy Tabitha had thought of as *that redneck kid* and then jerking his thumb back toward her. "See Miss Tabitha here up to the main office. And don't bother her."

"Yessir." Bobby leapt to his feet agreeably, turning a smirk and a side-eyed glance towards the glowering group of girls that seemed out to get Tabitha.

"I'm gonna call this in to the office," Mr. Stern promised her. "Go home and get some rest; we'll make sure this all gets resolved."

————

"Thank you for picking me up, Grandma," Tabitha said with a weak smile. "You got... a Jeep?"

"Belongs to my friend Nancy's daughter. She's being a dear and lettin' me borrow it," Grandma Laurie said, taking Tabitha by the shoulders and anxiously inspecting her. "Certainly better than Danny's old piece of junk. Now, *are you okay?*"

"I'm—no, I'm not okay, Grandma," Tabitha admitted. "I'm so tired and just... so close to giving up, that I don't know what to do anymore. Don't know if I can stay in school. But I have *friends* now, I have—or, I want to try to... I don't know. I just wish..."

"Well, let's not dawdle about *this* awful place," Grandma Laurie insisted, casting a dirty look around the school grounds. "You look fit to faint dead away. Is your hand hurtin' you?"

"A little." Tabitha nodded, letting her grandmother guide her over into the passenger's seat of the Jeep. "I, um. When I took my codeine this morning, it didn't stay down. I threw up."

"Let's get you to my place and get you all the aspirin you need," Grandma Laurie proposed, giving her another worried look. "Unless you think it's bad enough to stop by the hospital, have them take another look at it?"

"No, no." Tabitha shook her head, adjusting her cast and sling so that they weren't pinned uncomfortably by the crossing seat-belt. "Maybe just... aspirin and a nap?"

"I'll scare some quiet into the boys when they get out of school," Grandma Laurie promised, starting up the Jeep. Unlike Mr. Moore's practiced and cautious driving, Grandma Laurie had them jerking forward with a sudden burst of acceleration, and then seemed content to maintain that uncomfortable speed.

"Have you had lunch already?"

"I... I'm not hungry," Tabitha said, mustering a weak smile. "I'll be fine."

———

"You can't *suspend* me!" Clarissa Dole insisted, her face twisting in an exaggerated expression of pure teenage indignation.

"Suspension's just a temporary measure," Mrs. Cribb remarked dryly, giving the girl an unimpressed stare. "To keep you off of school grounds until the expulsion hearing."

What a debacle this is turning into... Having commandeered Principal Edward's office, Pamela Cribb was working to convey the gravity of the current situation by sitting down for a one-on-one with Clarissa —a student who seemed intent on continuing to bully Tabitha Moore.

Was sending those three girls home earlier too subtle a message? I imagined the SIGNIFICANCE would have traveled quickly in whatever social circle these problems are originating from. Was I overestimating them?

Mrs. Cribb had now seen but not spoken to Tabitha Moore herself—who turned out to be a slim young lady with lovely red hair and eyes that reflected a certain melancholy *sadness* that didn't seem to befit her age at all. The girl carried herself with a stiff but troubled kind of poise, carefully safeguarding her new cast close against her body, and looked more than a little unwell— the ongoing ordeals had clearly taken a toll on her.

Though very interested in actually meeting Tabitha for a chat, Mrs. Cribb had been hurrying off to investigate the stolen notebook. By the time she'd returned to the office with a perpetrator, sixth period was nearly over, and Tabitha's grandmother had already picked the poor girl up from school.

"You can't *expulse* me either!" Clarissa exclaimed, jumping out of her seat. "It was just *a joke!*"

"...*Expel you,*" Mrs. Cribb corrected Clarissa. "Sit down, please. We certainly can, and we're making a strong case to the district superintendent to do so. Perhaps you can explain to me just what about this you thought was a joke?"

"All we did was hide her notebook for a bit." Clarissa scowled, dropping back into the chair opposite the desk from Mrs. Cribb. "*God,* it was a joke."

"Ah; '*we.*'" Mrs. Cribb picked up her pen to take down names. "Who is '*we?*'"

"No one," Clarissa quickly frowned. "I'm not telling you anyone!"

"But there were others involved in this?" Mrs. Cribb pressed. "Those friends of yours?"

"...No," Clarissa denied.

"I see." Mrs. Cribb set down her pen. She folded her hands in front of her on the desk and stared at the uncooperative teen in silence for almost a full minute before speaking again.

"Let's go back over your... joke, Miss Dole," Mrs. Cribb finally said, turning in her seat and patting a hand on the recovered evidence—Tabitha's binder. "I'm told that while Tabitha was resting in class, this was stolen from her."

"Resting? She was *asleep,*" Clarissa retorted. "But *oh no,* of course she's not gonna get in trouble for that."

"Another student confirmed that several girls were behaving suspiciously." Mrs. Cribb ignored the interruption. "These girls volunteered to provide their school bags for inspection, and nothing belonging to Tabitha was found. At *that* time, these girls

—including you, I believe—denied taking anything from her. Is that correct?"

Clarissa remained silent, glowering at Mrs. Cribb with her lips pressed into a thin line.

"Mr. Stern then revealed that *you* had been given leave during class to attend to the restroom. Upon searching that restroom—Tabitha's missing notebook was immediately discovered in the waste bin. Tabitha did not visit the restroom. No other students in that period had to visit the restroom. *You* visited the restroom. Correct?"

"But it was just a joke," Clarissa persisted. "We were going to tell her where it was right away."

"There it is again, 'we,'" Mrs. Cribb noted. "Which other girls were in on this '*joke?*'"

"No one," Clarissa eventually decided with a difficult expression. "Just me."

"Right, fine then." Mrs. Cribb sighed in aggravation. "Clarissa—here's the problem with your 'joke' right now. You *did not* tell Tabitha where the missing item was right away. You are not, I'm told, on joking, or even friendly terms with Tabitha. We've been informed by several students that you—and several other girls who'll be questioned and likely also face some form of suspension—have been openly antagonistic toward her. Miss Dole, tell me—*are you* somehow friends with Tabitha Moore?"

"No." Clarissa made a face. "But it was still just a joke; you're not allowed to expel me for it. Jesus. I don't have any warnings or strikes yet or anything like that. I've never done anything wrong!"

"So, stealing isn't wrong?" Mrs. Cribb raised an eyebrow. "Under normal circumstances, it would fall right under our student misconduct code—your parents would be contacted about a five-day minimum suspension, and it would go on your permanent record."

"So... what, why isn't *this* normal circumstances?" Clarissa balked, paling a bit at mention of her permanent record. "That isn't fair."

"You happened to play your little joke during a criminal harassment investigation." Mrs. Cribb smiled coldly, trying to remain patient.

"Last month, false allegations were made that almost cost a teacher his job, and stood to very severely damage Tabitha's reputation. I understand she's endured constant harassment, and been physically harmed twice this year to the point of requiring medical attention. Now, in addition to all of that, we have *this*. I'm told she's at the top of her class here, yet she may be voluntarily withdrawing from Springton High because *she doesn't feel safe here*. I'm now inclined to agree with her—and that's a serious problem.

"The Springton Police department owe her a debt of gratitude —I'm sure you've heard all about that—so, in addition, we have the district attorney and an independent firm preparing legal action to resolve this. We on the school board are going to do everything in our power to assist them, whether it means expulsions, handing students over for arrests, or appearing in court to testify. We are taking this situation *extremely seriously*. Do you understand?"

"...Oh," Clarissa said dumbly, sagging back in her seat. "Shit."

"Yeah," Mrs. Cribb agreed, drumming her fingers against the desktop. "*Oh, shit*. We're going to go over this all again when your parents arrive, but right now, I want you to think good and hard about how cooperative you'd like to be."

Clarissa Dole seemed dazed, lost in thought as Mrs. Cribb continued.

"It seems very likely that you'll be expelled for the duration of the school year. Depending on the ruling of the school board, you may or may not be allowed to enroll in remedial night classes or alternative education within the district. You *will* be assigned a mandatory course addressing your behavior and conduct, that you will be required to pass. Otherwise... you can expect to be restarting ninth grade here at Springton High, next August."

"You're *holding me back a year?!*" Clarissa stammered in disbelief. "You can't be serious! That's not fair—it was just a joke!"

"Doesn't seem very funny to me," Mrs. Cribb said gravely, gesturing her out with a finger. "Take a seat in the outer office while we wait for your parents, please."

Mrs. Cribb followed the student with her eyes as the stunned teen rose out of the chair with a hollow, vacant expression and slowly walked out of the office with heavier steps than she'd entered with. As a member of the school board, Mrs. Cribb didn't particularly like taking the reins with disciplinary action herself— even putting on the stern air of authority was taxing and stressful —but, she just couldn't trust Principal Edwards to not be soft on them.

Spare the rod, spoil the child... Mrs. Cribb let out a slow breath, leaning forward to rest her elbows on the desk and massaging her temples. *Certainly never approved of the paddling WE got if we stepped out of line growing up back then, but seeing this younger generation going astray like this is very... sobering.*

Shaking her head in dismay, the woman glanced back over at Tabitha's binder and then slid it in front of her out of curiosity. It was an inexpensive, rather plain-looking typical blue plastic binder. She found *property of Tabitha Moore* had been helpfully printed in permanent marker on the upper corner of the inside, and the three-ring binder was unexpectedly full—almost over-filled, with reams of content. There were almost no blank pages at all.

Just what class is this for? It's only October; even an advanced placement class wouldn't require this much work already, Pamela Cribb pursed her lips, carefully flipping through page after page of neat, orderly handwriting. *This all looks like... literary analysis?*

She rocked back in her chair, settling the binder in her lap as she leafed through the binder in search of class or assignment headings. There were none. Perplexed, Mrs. Cribb turned back to the front and began to read. Before she even finished the first page, she was thumbing through page after page in surprise to verify a suspicion that beggared belief.

This is... an EXTREMELY in-depth outline, for... a fiction novel? This planning, the way she's organizing the story structure, the thought she's putting into these details... this is put together like university-level work. Not something a high school girl should be capable of—not a thirteen-year-old freshman, at least. Does Mrs. Albertson know about this?

Mrs. Cribb's eyes had gone wide realizing the breadth of insight that had gone into the outline—for a novel apparently titled *Goblina*—and she looked up at the office door Clarissa had left through with a growing sense of horror.

And those girls THREW THIS IN THE TRASH?

———

"Uh-oh," Nick whispered, elbowing Sam in the side and jerking his chin forward. "Look."

"Ow. What?"

"Grandma," Nick said.

The boys had just now disembarked together at the bus stop in their grandmother's neighborhood to see her awaiting their arrival on the porch. The tension in her body language suggested there was trouble, and each of them quickly ran through a mental check of things they might have gotten caught for. After several seconds, they each turned toward each other as they cautiously approached.

"What'd you do?!"

"*I* didn't do anything. It was probably Josh?"

"Shut up, nuh-uh, I didn't!"

"Haha, you're in so much trouble."

"I didn't *do* anything!"

"Maybe the neighbor lady told her about that book on her roof?"

"That was *Nick!* Nick's threw it up there!"

"Yeah, but it was your book—that makes it your fault. You threw it at me first."

"Yeah, and if you tell on him, that makes you a snitch."

"Yeah, he doesn't even have to tell, it's *your* book, retard, so you're in trouble."

"No, I'm not!"

"Whatever. Rain's gonna wash it away anyways, it's probably not even a big deal. Right?"

"Books don't *wash away,* retard."

"Uh, yeah they do, retard—books are just made outta paper."

"You don't *wash* paper. Words wash off, but the paper just gets wet and stays."

"So what happens then? It gets... moldy?"

"That's food. If books got moldy, how are there *libraries,* stupid."

"Oh yeah, libraries."

"What do you know? You just—"

"Wait, so if we leave it up there long enough, all the pages will go blank?"

"Libraries are *dumb.*"

"*You're* dumb!"

"Hey, sssh!"

"Ssshhh!"

"*You* sssh!"

"Boys." Grandma Laurie silenced them all with a single stern word. She put a finger to her lips with one hand and waved them closer forward with the other, lowering her voice. "I told you Tabitha got hurt yesterday, at school? That a boy came up and pushed her from behind?"

All four of them nodded seriously, feeling everything else but anger drain away at the reminder.

"Today, someone stole one of her books," Grandma Laurie revealed in a quiet voice. "She's had enough—she left right in the middle of class, and I brought her here. She's sleeping now on the sofa, but I want all four of you boys to be *absolutely quiet* and not do *anything* to wake her up. She's hurting, she's had a terrible day, a terrible *week,* and she needs to rest some until she's feeling all better. Do you understand?"

They turned to each other, unified in sharing the same look— fury and disbelief. Now the other high schoolers were even *stealing* from Tabitha? Why weren't *they* getting in trouble for this?

"It's *not fair,*" Joshua spat.

"*Sssh,*" Sam admonished him with a glare. "*Quiet for Tabitha.*"

"*We're outside,*" Nick whispered. "*She can't even hear.*"

"*I don't care,*" Sam insisted back in a whisper. "*Quiet.*"

"I know it's not fair," Grandma Laurie sighed, tousling Joshua's hair. "But you boys behave today, okay? I'm going to take apart the sleeve of her Ariel dress so she can fit her cast through it... and maybe she'll still be up for taking you trick-or-treating on Saturday. Alright?"

"She didn't even get to try it on..."

"*Sssh!*"

"*Sorry, geez. She didn't, though.*"

"*Sssh!*"

"*No, YOU sshh!*"

One by one, they tiptoed across the porch and held their breath when Grandma Laurie gently turned the knob and opened the door with exaggerated care. They followed her inside, slowly sneaking into an unusually dark living room where all the curtains had been closed. They couldn't help but gawk with interest at the sleeping Tabitha, and Aiden clamped a hand over Joshua's mouth in warning.

She was curled up on the sofa, half-covered by one of their grandmother's throw blankets. Her tangle of red hair was flipped back from her serene face, there were dark circles under her eyes, and her left hand—now in a blue cast covered in cool swirly designs—was carefully resting on the cushion just by her cheek. Tabitha was always their awesome *action star hero*, the strange athletic big sister figure who was cool and a little scary and always looked out for them.

For the first time now, she looked beautiful in a *girl way* to them: wounded, vulnerable and tragic like a fallen princess. The sight evoked hitherto-unknown feelings of *raw outrage* from deep within, and her cousins realized it once again in each other's eyes as they glared back and forth at one another. Not a word was exchanged, but they were completely united in thought.

Each of the young cousins knew—somehow, someday, they were going to find who did this to their Tabitha, and make them pay.

22

MOORE AND MOORE MEMORIES

Is it possible to boil broccoli for TOO long? Mrs. Moore pursed her lips thoughtfully. *Everyone knows uncooked broccoli has dangerous things like arsenic in it, but I may have been a little... overzealous in boiling them a little EXTRA all the same. Just to be sure.*

When she endeavored to pick up the slack for them tonight and imitate Tabitha's *healthy* cooking, the results were... underwhelming. Whatever she'd done wrong cooking this chicken and broccoli, it was *bland.* It wasn't hard to imagine that her husband was measuring the pace of the unappetizing dinner with constant sips of water just for a little flavor.

No one was touching the rather soggy-looking vegetables, which seemed to have begun to liquefy into grotesque green paste. The family shared an unspoken agreement to simply pretend they didn't exist, to tactfully not mention the too-mushy-looking broccoli florets and the way the stems drooped like runny noodles.

"Well, don't force yourself to eat it if you don't want to," Mrs. Moore chided, gesturing at her daughter with her fork in exasperation.

She'd *meant* that to sound light-hearted and joking—the food really did look terrible—but she was honestly a little upset. Mrs. Moore considered herself no stranger to cooking, but she was also used to preparing meals like the good Lord intended, the way a normal person did. Using the microwave.

"No, I think... I think I need to," Tabitha said, frowning in determination. The girl seemed to be punishing herself by cutting the unseasoned chicken into absurdly tiny portions and working her way through them one by one.

Shannon Moore wanted to put on an affronted look, but even after the nap Tabitha had taken at Grandma Laurie's place, the teenage girl seemed woozy, listless, and completely lacking in energy. The constant ordeals Tabitha had gone through in the past several days were putting Mrs. Moore on edge, and she couldn't help but cast fretful glances at the way her daughter cradled that awful cast against her body.

"Gonna drive up to the school tomorrow and see what they have to say for themselves," Mr. Moore announced, taking another long draw of water. "You did the right thing leavin' when you did, and I'm proud of you. Want you to just concentrate on resting and feeling better for a few days, sweetie."

"I need to be doing all my exercises," Tabitha said in a small voice.

Alan looked like he was about to object, but Mrs. Moore silenced him with a fierce glare.

"Tabby, honey..." Mrs. Moore spoke up softly. "I understand, I really do. But, you really do need to rest, just have a few days off without workin' yourself to death. You're not going to lose your figure just from skipping your routines for this little while, sweetie. Your body needs to recover."

"I—I apologize, I failed to explain myself," Tabitha said, staring down at her plate with bleary eyes as she picked at her food. "The lack of proper exercise was affecting the quality of my sleep. Last night, I..."

Tabitha trailed off with a frown and blinked, seeming to lose her train of thought, and Mrs. Moore shared a worried glance with her husband. This wasn't normal for their daughter at all. Not only was she defaulting again to what Alan had once described as *auto-pilot* Tabitha, where she seemed to retreat way back into her own mind and go through life with mechanical motions—it seemed like even *that* was on the verge of shutting down.

"You look plenty tuckered out to me," Mr. Moore said, sliding his chair out and rising from the table. "Why don't we get you to bed, sweetie?"

"I-I'm sorry," Tabitha choked up. The girl's eyes were wet, and she unsteadily stood and started gathering her plate with her single remaining hand. "I'll put this in the Tupperware."

"You've got nothin' to be sorry for—you leave it be." Mr. Moore took Tabitha by the shoulders and gently guided her away from the table. "We'll clean up. You go and get them teeth brushed and we'll get you settled, okay?"

"Sorry," Tabitha apologized again, retreating down the hall.

Alan watched his daughter leave, then turned and gripped the back of his chair until the wood creaked, glaring vacantly across the table at nothing. When he finally sat down again, he did so heavily, looking like he'd aged ten years over the course of the week.

"Sorry about dinner." Mrs. Moore slid her plate away with the back of her hand, unable to keep up any pretense of interest in the meal.

"Don't you start too." Alan sighed, giving her a weak smile. "Nothin' to be sorry for. It was fine."

"You're full of shit." Mrs. Moore shook her head in dismay. "Really goes to show how spoiled we've gotten with Tabby cooking, huh?"

"It was fine." He chuckled before holding his hands up defensively as she gave him a withering stare. "Alright, alright. The chicken was... a little dry."

"*Thank you,*" Mrs. Moore said, appreciating the honesty if not the truth of the sentiment. *Probably should've just boiled the chicken breasts in with the broccoli instead of microwaving them. That's probably how she'd've done it.* "What are we going to do about Tabitha?"

"Well..." Mr. Moore stewed on his words for a moment. "If she's set on withdrawing from school for good, I've half a mind to let her. I was worried she might get picked on when she started senior high, because she's so... *different,* but this whole nonsense going on is just... it's completely beyond the pale. These other kids, they're goddamn animals. Who knows what they might get up to next?"

Mrs. Moore shifted uncomfortably in her seat, remembering that icy spike of raw *terror* she'd felt when she'd heard about Tabitha getting pushed at school and needing to go to the hospital. That terror struck deep and then began to percolate over the past several days, disturbing all of those long-buried remembrances of her own trauma from all those years ago—when the film producer had insisted on... touching her.

The way Tabitha's peers were mistreating her was already atrocious, but she was also growing into a lovely young girl—the horrible idea that bullying at school could possibly escalate to things like *that* made Mrs. Moore turn sick with rage. What happened on those studio sets all those years ago wasn't something she was ever prepared to discuss with her husband. She'd been worrying herself into nervous fits over how to explain her current fear and paranoia to him without sounding like a crazy person.

"I don't want her at that school," Mrs. Moore finally admitted.

"We need to have a talk with her about it tomorrow." Mr. Moore rubbed a hand across the stubble along his jaw. "She does have friends there. Think it needs to be her decision, and we'll havta support her no matter what she decides. She's... she's just so damned smart that it scares me, and I hate thinkin' of her bein' here at home instead of out getting a proper school education."

Mrs. Moore bit her tongue. She *wanted* to argue that her

Tabitha would thrive with or without school simply because of her single-minded focus and drive for improvement, but she knew that the feeling was mostly likely just her bias as a mother.

"There's... there's somethin' else I haven't told you." Mr. Moore sighed. "Promised Tabby I wouldn't, but... I think it's a part of all this goin' on, think it's *important.*"

Shannon Moore felt herself go stiff with fear, and her grip on the edge of the table tightened until her knuckles went completely white.

"This past summer, Tabby didn't fall off of that trampoline jumper," her husband revealed. "Those Taylor girls, they pushed her. Threatened to make her pay if she told anyone, really put a scare into her. But she told *me.* Made *me* swear not to say anything. She was blubbering and wailing and completely beside herself—I *had* to promise her."

"*What,*" Mrs. Moore bit out.

"I was still gonna look into it anyways," Mr. Moore tried to explain. "Maybe go talk to the parents of those girls. But, then..."

He shook his head in disbelief.

"Then it was like Tabby hit this *critical mass,* this... this point way out past her hysteria an' breakin' down and something changed inside of her. I keep wanting to think it was such a... I don't have the words for it. Such a *transformation,* that it put the fritz on that MRI machine, like the thing just didn't know what to make of the goings-on in her head that night at all. Maybe nobody but Tabitha knows.

"She fainted dead away in there. When we got her out of there and she came to, she wasn't sobbin' and caterwaulin' like when she got in. She came out, and she was so calm, *cold,* distant, there was this... this patient sense of... I don't know, *purpose* to her. You know how she was, that night I brought her home from that. How she's been. It's like, whatever happened, whatever decision she came to that night, she looks around now and sees everything with these new eyes, this completely different perspective."

Mrs. Moore remembered the strange new Tabitha glancing across the dinner table in surprise all those months ago. *'Oh? You didn't know? Everyone calls me tubby Tabby. They always have. I've been made fun of for being fat and smelling bad my whole life.'*

"She was being bullied all along," Mrs. Moore realized, filling with emotion at how stupid she'd been. "All this time. She tried to tell us—she tried to tell us, and I couldn't even listen. Said they were calling her *tubby Tabby,* back then. Didn't she!"

All this time, I thought it must've been Grandma Laurie. But it wasn't—Tabby was DRIVEN to this, she was pushed to this point, Mrs. Moore covered her face as she began to cry, sagging forward over the dinner table. *How totally fucking stuck on myself could I have even been to ever think she was trying to spite me somehow?! This all, this was never about her seeing the album, or thinking I was keeping her from her potential. She NEEDED to change, living as who she used to be was BREAKING HER.*

Just like being who I was broke me, Shannon Moore sobbed. *This whole stupid tragic story played out for my life, and now it's playing right back over itself in reverse for Tabitha. Why can't it all just—what do I have to do to put a STOP to this?*

———

Tabitha always steamed the broccoli. Why did I try to boil it? When Shannon Moore sat up abruptly at two AM to a mobile home of still silence, it felt like her mind was more clear than it'd ever been in her whole life—it was just like she imagined Tabitha had felt coming home from that concussion this past summer. Like she'd been reborn.

The bewildering realizations, epiphanies, and misunderstandings had crashed through her for hours last night like a hurricane, displacing, uprooting, and even destroying the stagnant, ingrained mindset that had become her own prison. Everything after sitting at the dinner table was a blur

—she remembered weeping and weeping beyond her husband's ability to console her, and her muffled tears and choked cries didn't stop until long after he'd managed to bring her to bed.

When's the last time we all WENT somewhere, just to get away from it all? Mrs. Moore glanced around the dark, increasingly claustrophobic enclosure of the trailer's master bedroom. *Taken family pictures together, made new memories? What have I been DOING here, besides being miserable and petty and waiting to die? What's been the point?*

I could go out and start looking for a job—we could use the extra income. Why did we even stay in this trailer park for so goddamn long? Want us all to go somewhere tomorrow, DO something together. Tabby's writing that story of hers—I want to read it. That blue album I had hidden away... I'd forgotten, but there were GOOD memories in there too. So many of them—I want to actually go through and share them all with her. How have I been living?

She turned the covers carefully so as not to wake her husband, and slipped out of bed. In the fourteen years she'd spent holed up in this mobile home, she'd never before felt so *restless,* and as she crept down the narrow hallway and through their tiny kitchen, she found herself staring at all the once-familiar odds-and-ends and random detritus of their time here and seeing nothing but a life never lived.

Tabitha was doing stretches at first. Going on walks. Sit-ups and things like that; she had a whole chart drawn up. I wonder if she still has it?

It didn't seem like enough.

Shannon Moore whirled in place, looking around at the now-stifling walls with a sense of dread. The only reason the tiny chamber of space barely resembled a home at all was because Tabitha had taken down the blankets blocking out the sunlight, then scrubbed the mildew off the ceiling, repositioned the aging furniture, and cleaned the carpet so thoroughly.

How have I been such a fool all this time? I want to wake Tabitha up, just to tell her how much I love her.

———

Tabitha woke up confused and completely disoriented. It took her several moments blinking herself back to full awareness to figure out when she was, *who* she was, and she still needed to sit up in bed and clutch at the rigid encumbrance of the cast on her left hand to be completely sure.

It had been another strange dream—or maybe more accurately described as a very dull nightmare. She'd been seated at the row of bar tack stations at the safety plant, working on some order, but filled with a strange sort of *gnawing dread*. Afraid that someone would notice she didn't belong there, that someone would find out she was lying about being from the future. It made no rational sense, because she only ever worked at the plant in her mid- and late-thirties, which *was* in the future. Also—she *wasn't* lying to herself about being from the future. If she was making it all up, how would she even have memories of the safety plant at all?

...Right? Tabitha blearily ran a hand over her face.

Unfortunately, the logical parts of her mind that would have immediately worked that out had apparently been sound asleep, leaving her subconsciousness to experience the dreary dream while disarmed of reason.

Ugh, the safety plant... Tabitha remembered, making a disgusted face.

Since crossing over into the past, she'd hardly put any thought at all into her time spent at the plant. There were *possibly* aspects she could take advantage of their using her future knowledge and experience—but they were rendered moot, because *she didn't ever want to work there again*. It had paid well, but the production floor was noisy, it smelled terrible, and assembling safety harnesses for eight-hour shifts was unbelievably monotonous tedium.

Plus, I hated everyone there, Tabitha mused as she slipped out of bed. *And they all hated each other.*

The floor of her tiny room was incredibly cold as she got dressed—fuzzy wool socks, sweatpants, the undershirt she'd slept in, and an oversized sweatshirt borrowed from her father. She felt more than a bit lost forgoing both her normal preparations for school as well as her usual morning workout routine. Now, without even her *Goblina* outline to focus on for a welcome distraction, she couldn't help but feel frustrated and directionless. She needed all the distractions she could get right now.

Okay. Safety plant. Safety harnesses. I've... admittedly been trying real hard not to think about them. Rolling back the large sweatshirt sleeve from her cast, she uselessly tried to dig and wiggle a fingertip down the back of her cast toward a persistent tickling itch.

The itch taunted her, remaining just barely out of reach.

Like many of her future memories, her time working at the production plant just didn't seem useful here in 1998—she'd acquired a number of skills there, but they weren't *pertinent* to the life she wanted to lead now. Tabitha knew how to use the cut table to measure and mark nylon material, and the pressurized hot knife to separate nylon pieces and sear the ends to keep them from fraying. She was proficient in operating several different kinds of industrial sewing machines for sewing leather pieces to nylon webbing, and could use the rivet machines to affix leather pieces together.

Which is great, okay, Tabitha grumbled to herself. *But what do I DO with all that?*

As a storyteller—and particularly as someone experiencing something as fantastical as being sent back in time—she sometimes found herself obsessing over everything in terms of *narrative meaning*. Each aspect of her past life, even her time at the safety plant, *should* have been an element that contributed a purpose to her overall story as a whole.

Is that really all just wishful thinking, or... Tabitha frowned, stumbling out of her room and down to the bathroom. *Maybe sunk cost fallacy, driving me to look for a purpose, where there is none? To tell myself that it wasn't ALL a total waste of life?*

Almost five years of her previous life in the 2020's had been spent filling orders for different models of harnesses for line workers—but none of them would have the same specifications back here in the late nineties. The exact measurements and methods of putting together all of the harnesses updated constantly, and they'd often required her to swap out material data sheets in the workstation books for each of them. Multiple times, every year.

Future safety innovations introduced here would potentially save a lot of lives, but they largely relied on technological advancements she had no way of replicating: improved materials that made for tighter, stronger weaves of nylon webbing, rigorously tested new configurations of harness, and bartack machines programmed to spit out complex stitching patterns in seconds, rather than needing to be manually—painstakingly—sewn in with the heavy-duty machines. The job was impossibly boring, yet any momentary lapse in concentration, the machine jamming up mid-stitch, or other simple human error could easily foul up the process and become an aggravating setback.

I could POSSIBLY introduce the basic concept behind the shock-absorbing stitch to one of the engineers there, Tabitha thought as she washed her face and then started brushing her teeth.

It's incredibly simple, and got worked into all the harnesses while I was there. But, in what universe would a guy with an engineering degree listen to the ideas of some dumb thirteen-year-old girl? ESPE-CIALLY regarding safety products customers are going to be relying on. Doubt Mrs. Crow—err, Mrs. MacIntire will even be there in the office this life. Why would she, if her first husband lives, this time through—

"Tabitha?" her mother yelled from the other side of the trailer. "Do I hear you up and about?"

There was something... *different* about her mother's voice, and Tabitha paused in the middle of brushing her teeth, staring blankly at herself in the mirror for a moment as she tried to puzzle out what was off. *She sounds almost... chipper?* Growing concerned, Tabitha quickly spit into the sink and rinsed out her mouth.

"I'm awake," Tabitha called.

"Can you come out here, please?"

"Oh." Tabitha lurched to a stop just at the end of the hallway. "Hello."

"Good morning." There was a woman seated at the kitchen table with her mother, and she was already rising out of her seat to introduce herself. "I'm Pamela Cribb, and I'm here on behalf of the school board."

"It's... a pleasure to meet you." Tabitha found herself mechanically moving forward to shake the woman's hand. "May I call you Mrs. Cribb?"

"Oh, anything's fine." Mrs. Cribb laughed with a careless wave.

Is this... not an official visit? Tabitha might have expected one due to her abrupt departure from class yesterday—but that didn't quite seem to be the case based on how informal the woman was being.

"I apologize—am I interrupting?" Tabitha asked awkwardly. "Or, did I keep you waiting on me?"

"Neither, neither," the woman assured her. "Please, come sit with us, whenever you're ready. I'm glad you were able to get some rest. Your mother was just telling—"

Mrs. Cribb stopped mid-sentence, sucking in a short breath at the sight of Tabitha's hand.

"My word, you're—honey, are you alright?"

"Sorry," Tabitha said quickly, embarrassed, starting to roll her sleeve back down over her cast and hand. "I—wasn't expecting we would have company."

"Nonsense, come let us have a look at that." Mrs. Cribb hurried to stop Tabitha and then guided the girl to the table, even pulling out the chair for her. "Is it hurting, or, ah, do you have enough circulation?"

"It's... fine," Tabitha explained, fidgeting beneath the sudden and intense scrutiny. Last night, a mottled and somewhat sickly shade of yellow had become noticeable along her mostly immobilized pinky and ring finger, but by now, darker purplish-blue shades were becoming apparent along her skin. "Just the bruise spreading."

"This looks like it's too tight—your fingers are all swollen," Mrs. Cribb fretted, carefully turning Tabitha's cast over to examine it. "Is this hurting?"

"It's... um," Tabitha tried to hide her discomfort. "I have codeine tablets for three more days. I'll have one with breakfast. I just... need to keep my hand elevated for a bit after waking up—and not bump into anything."

"Of course, of course," Mrs. Cribb withdrew her hands, looking troubled.

"I'm sorry you had to see that," Tabitha carefully rolled the sleeve back up over her cast and hand.

"No, no, it's..." Mrs. Cribb looked like she was at a loss.

"Could I offer you anything to drink?" Tabitha asked. "Mother, as we have a guest—may I turn the thermostat up to sixty?"

"Oh no, I'm fine," Mrs. Cribb said. "Don't worry about me."

"Sixty sounds perfect." Mrs. Moore gave the woman from the school board an apologetic look. "Normally, we—"

"Please, please, don't worry about me," Mrs. Cribb repeated. "I don't mean to impose at all. Tabitha, I'm—I'm sure you know why I'm here?"

"Yes." Tabitha nodded sadly, finally slipping back into her seat at the table. "I was... *distraught* yesterday when I left school, and remiss in acquiring whatever paperwork might be necessary for my withdrawal from the school system. I'm prepared to justify any absences in the short term while I withdraw, and I'd like to seek accreditation for home schooling before I can be declared truant. I imagine you, or someone else on the school board, could help expedite that process."

Speechless, Mrs. Cribb turned her wide-eyed stare from Tabitha to Mrs. Moore.

"She's like that when she's stressed, and... she's been under a lot of stress." Mrs. Moore sighed. "I *do* agree with her, though."

"Well, before I say anything at all, I'd like to return this to you," Mrs. Cribb said, reaching down to a bag beside her purse and drawing out—

My story notes!

Surges of surprise and relief had her standing up so abruptly that Tabitha's chair nearly toppled over, and when Mrs. Cribb passed it to her, she found her good hand sagging beneath the familiar weight of her blue binder. Relief fell over her like a curtain of exhaustion, and she dropped back down into her chair heavily, hugging the binder tightly against her chest.

It was stupid to start crying over such a little thing, but she did anyway.

The story outline had at some point become a treasure she'd taken for granted, never appreciating what it was to her until it was suddenly and unexpectedly gone. *Goblina* and *Goblin Princess* had been *good* but never *great,* in her past life. Revisiting them in this one had become an endeavor equal parts new perspective and enthusiastic inspiration—many parts she had little confidence in attempting to recreate while in her current mental state.

"Thank you," Tabitha choked out, not daring to look up. "Thank you."

"Well," Mrs. Moore spoke up with forced cheer in her voice. "Let's get some food in you—what can I make you for breakfast?"

"Wh-whatever I had left over from last night is fine," Tabitha managed, trying not to sound alarmed. *Mom... making breakfast?*

"Oh." Her mother had the decency to sound embarrassed. "I'm sorry, sweetie—your father and I—we finished up all of the leftovers."

Either thrown out as completely inedible, or she's too ashamed to have this lady from the school board see the state of her broccoli, Tabitha surmised, suppressing a hapless laugh.

"That's... that's fine." Tabitha nodded. "If the other half of my banana is still on the refrigerator door, that will be more than enough for me."

"Are you sure?" Mrs. Moore sounded disappointed as she stood with the fridge door open. "I'm sure I can whip up... *something?*"

"It's fine, but thank you."

To Tabitha's amusement, their entire exchange seemed to make their visitor Mrs. Cribb visibly uncomfortable. Especially when the half banana—its peel browned enough to be blackened on one side—was placed atop a napkin in front of her, along with a small glass of water and her bottle of pills.

"One of your classmates took your book there while you were distracted," Mrs. Cribb revealed. "Clarissa Dole—she snuck it out when asking for a bathroom break, and tossed it in the trash can of the nearby ladies' room. She's been suspended, pending an expulsion hearing this coming Monday after Halloween—along with Chris Thompson, Kaylee Mendolson, Brittany Taylor, and Erica Taylor."

"I—" Tabitha blinked as she tried to wipe away the last of her tears with her good hand. "I'm sorry, I don't know who Clarissa or Kaylee are."

"Clarissa's in your fifth period class; she admitted to stealing your notebook. The Kaylee girl was guilty of spreading that malicious rumor regarding you and Mr. Simmons."

"Malicious... rumor?" Mrs. Moore's expression darkened.

"Yes, given the intent behind it—Mr. Simmons could have lost his job—and in light of the current circumstances, Kaylee will now be up for expulsion as well." Mrs. Cribb frowned. "Tabitha... I'm very, very sorry for everything that you've been put through. The school board will also have a formal apology for you after the hearing, I'll expect. Springton High's administration acted too little, too late, or not at all in situations which should have been *immediately* addressed with their full attention.

"You're an extremely brilliant young girl, and several of your teachers have recommended we advance you up a grade level. I'm told that the freshman curriculum simply isn't challenging you. We *very* much want you to continue at Springton High, and we're doing everything in our power to make sure it becomes a completely safe environment for you to learn. Would you be interested in returning after a short break, possibly as a sophomore?"

"No, I—no, I'm not brilliant," Tabitha denied, shaking her head in firm refusal. "It's just that—"

"Tabitha," Mrs. Cribb interrupted softly, "I read through what you have in that book—I was very surprised to discover that Mrs. Albertson wasn't aware of your project. Please believe me when I say that you are, in fact, *brilliant.*"

"You... read it?" Tabitha looked completely mortified.

"Yes, I'm sorry if it seems like an invasion of privacy, but..." Mrs. Cribb shook her head. "Honestly, I'm still just completely stunned. What you've compiled there is well beyond what I was capable of as a college graduate—and I majored in Education. If you'll allow it, I'd really like you to share it with some of the better minds in Springton High's English department, so that we can find the best teacher for you—whatever grade level that ends up being."

"You... um. What did you think?" Tabitha asked in a timid voice, furrowing her brows. "When you read it."

"Oh, would you like to discuss it?" Mrs. Cribb smiled. "There's quite a bit I'd love to talk about, if you have time."

"I..." Tabitha stopped and stared at the tabletop for a long moment. "I need to think about that, I'm sorry. I'm not sure if you could tell, but... I want to turn this into fiction."

"Yes, it's one of the most outstanding—"

"No, no. I mean," Tabitha quickly interrupted. "Some of what's most important to the story is... what *isn't* written in here. What

I've been going through, the ways people have treated me, it's *not* fiction, but I've been, I'm trying to, um. This project is to turn *all of that* into fiction. It's... a very personal project."

"I'm so sorry!" Mrs. Cribb covered her mouth in shock and alarm, turning to Mrs. Moore and only seeing confusion and worry on the woman's features. "I hadn't even thought to look at your narrative from that perspective. Of course, it makes so much sense that... oh, Tabitha, I'm—I'm so sorry."

"Thank you for returning it to me," Tabitha said in a slow voice, gripping the binder even more tightly. "I... I really didn't know what I was going to do without it. This book, it's more than just a coping mechanism, it's... I can't explain how important this is to me."

"I'm so glad we were able to find it!" Mrs. Cribb admitted, putting a hand to her chest and looking more anxious than ever. "How about you stay on a leave of absence—rest as much as you need, spend some time recovering—until after these expulsion hearings, and then we can meet up again and discuss what you'd like to do?"

"Please." Tabitha nodded in agreement. "I'd like that. Thank you again for returning it."

"Um." Mrs. Cribb hesitated. "I almost hate to ask, but... several of these girls who were bullying you, they had some unexpectedly serious... *enmity* toward you that I found myself just baffled by. Tabitha... do you have any idea where all of this started?"

The muck of guilt mired deep in her subconscious seemed to suck at Tabitha's feet again, inviting her *deeper,* but she *had to* try. Maybe they would believe her, maybe there was enough gravity to the circumstances that they would really dig into this, and maybe, just *maybe,* this wouldn't all rebound back on an innocent girl in terrible retribution. Tabitha couldn't even remember the face of the childhood friend she'd abandoned, but seeing the discoloration creeping out from under her own cast certainly brought to mind what she *did* remember.

It was long past time to swallow her fears and come clean, *forty-seven years* past time.

I'm not afraid of the bullying anymore. Even if I get hurt again, Tabitha's thoughts were whirling now, and her facade of forced calm began to unhinge itself as repressed things boiled up from deep within her.

What terrifies me now is... the thought of living with what I've done —with what I failed to do—all over again. The trailer I lived in, what I looked like, how people treated me—none of those things are what made me TRASH. Deep down, I've always known what made me trash.

"There's..." Tabitha's eyes watered, and she wet her lips as she struggled for the words she needed. "There's a third Taylor sister."

"A *third* Taylor sister?"

"Yes." Tabitha nodded, unable to look up at the woman. "Ashlee Taylor. I was her friend. *Was* her friend. I—I don't fucking get to call myself that anymore. She—you need to find her, please, I think she should have been a freshman with me, *but she isn't.* I don't know where she is. Can't even picture her face anymore. I was her friend. She was in sixth and seventh grade with me. The same grade as me. She should have been. She, she—"

"Tabitha, honey—"

"Find her, please, and—check beneath her clothes," Tabitha sobbed. "Beneath her clothes, her back, um, under her shirt. Look for—look for bruises. I-I don't know if it's still going on, but—"

"*Excuse me,*" Pamela Cribb shot to her feet with a horrified expression, shoving her chair back out of the way. "Mrs. Moore—I need to use your phone, right now."

23
TRICK-OR-TREATING WITH EVERYONE

Still cut a pretty poor protagonist, I guess. Tabitha sighed to herself. *Which is... unbelievably frustrating. Am I being melodramatic? Are the teenage hormones in control again?*

She couldn't help but feel that she'd been incredibly self-centered and conceited to have expected anything else. This wasn't a teen novel where the police would insist she ride along in their car so that she could be part of the *story resolution* and see them rush to Ashlee's rescue or make some sort of dramatic arrest. In the real world, events simply didn't revolve around thirteen-year-old girls, and she was to have no further involvement—the adults handling the situation hadn't even thought to tell her what was going on, or what was being done.

What seemed like this intense personal watershed moment for Tabitha as a person didn't elicit much of the same reaction from everyone else. Mrs. Cribb had spoken over their phone with someone in a rather heated discussion for several minutes, and said her goodbyes shortly afterwards. Just like before with the shooting incident, Tabitha felt like she was out of the loop; like things went personally unresolved. She wasn't privy to what was going on, and despite asking, information stubbornly remained beyond her reach.

Just focus on resting and recovering. Tabitha couldn't help but scowl at the response they gave her.

Sharing the details about her guilt regarding Ashlee with her mother afterward hadn't gone like Tabitha expected either. Mrs. Moore didn't seem to *get it,* didn't seem to see any issue with her neglecting to speak up.

Well, of course you wouldn't, her mother had tried to console her. *Tabitha—they were threatening to hurt you girls!*

Tabitha didn't know how to feel about that.

Everyone else would naturally treat her as if she was this naive young girl, but she *wasn't,* not exactly, and there wasn't any way to explain her own obligation to hold herself to a higher standard. It was an uncomfortable situation, exacerbated by how strange her mother was acting now. The woman was... different. Friendlier, *motivated* even, she did a loop walking around the neighborhood with Tabitha in the mornings, and asked for assistance in learning some basic daily exercises. In the dismal days that followed, however, Tabitha felt listless and emotionally empty, going through all of the motions of a somewhat normal life without much spirit.

Then Saturday finally arrived, and nine different people showed up to see her.

———

"Sit there and *stay there,*" Grandma Laurie warned the boys as they trooped into the trailer past her. She pointed sternly at the sofa in the Moores' living room. "I hear one more foul word—from *any* of you hooligans—and you can forget about trick-or-treating this year!"

"Have they not been behaving?" Tabitha asked with a wry smile, sharing a look with her mother.

For trick-or-treating, the four cousins were dressed in the brightly-colored winterwear of the main cast from *South Park*, and from their silence and stiff expressions, it seemed as though they'd already gotten themselves into trouble. The only one of them Tabitha could identify with any certainty was the youngest, Joshua, who wore the orange hoodie—the meme character Kenny who died every episode.

The other ones are... Cartman, Eric, and...? She drew a blank what the last character's name might be. Having never actually watched the show herself, everything she knew about it was gleaned by cultural osmosis, and she considered her partial recollection to be not too shabby.

"*Apparently,* that *South Park* cartoon isn't for children," Grandma Laurie sounded exasperated. "They used to sit and watch it with their mother, so I thought it must be okay—but, it's *not* okay, it's just this... mindless, absolute filth!"

Seems to fit perfectly with what I remember about Aunt Lisa. Tabitha refrained from wincing, instead schooling her expression into a tacit look of sympathy for Grandma Laurie's difficult position.

"What did they dress as last year?" Mrs. Moore asked. "The Beatles? I remember they wore those handsome little suits."

"Men in Black." Grandma Laurie shook her head. "Whatever that is. Shining those little toy laser wands in everyone's faces the whole night, 'til I took the batteries away."

"There's no lasers this year, at least," Tabitha reassured her with a slight smile. "I'll look after them, Grandma."

"Well, I wish I'd known about this *South Park* earlier, then they wouldn't be wearing these," Grandma Laurie griped. "It's not even a proper cartoon! They're paper doll cutouts, and all they do is swear at each other and make vulgar jokes. I want to get the boys watching *proper* cartoons like *Felix the Cat*, *Porky Pig*, and *Betty Boop*, but I can't find tapes for them anywhere."

"...I'll talk with them about it," Tabitha promised, looking at each of the boys in turn. "I know of a few series that—"

A knock at the door interrupted. Perplexed, Tabitha crossed over to the door and cautiously opened it, revealing her friend Elena. The tall blonde was dressed rather conspicuously in black slacks and a long-sleeved black shirt... and nervously glancing around the area as though she were a cat burglar.

"Hi!" Elena said, stepping forward to grab the surprised Tabitha in a quick hug. "We missed you this week! Did Alicia talk to you about trick-or-treating? Is she here yet?"

"Hi!" Tabitha laughed. "No? Er, were you guys wanting to—"

"Oh, we definitely are," Elena nodded, hefting up a large handbag. "Got everything here. Mom's waiting out in the van, though. Um... is it cool if she talks to your mother?"

"Uh—" Tabitha began.

"I'll go out and see her." Mrs. Moore had already overheard, patting Tabitha on the head. "I invited some of your friends, Tabitha. Thank you so much for coming, Elena."

"Thank you having us, Mrs. Moore," Elena said politely.

Mom—what? Tabitha was stunned enough to be unable to process the news immediately. *You invited my friends? Wait, WHAT?*

It was great news, and *she was thrilled,* but the surprise came so far out of left field that she was blindsided into wide-eyed silence. Her mother was a reclusive and bitter woman. Or, at least—she was, she used to be. Mrs. Moore certainly wasn't someone who took the initiative to make social calls on her daughter's behalf.

Did... did something I do accidentally set this off? Tabitha struggled to come to terms and adjust to the new outlook. *Is this really all just from agreeing to let her teach me to be an actress? We only even did practice exercises twice since I withdrew from school!*

"Tabitha?" Grandma Laurie called over from the bathroom. "Tabitha honey, we need to get started on your hair!"

"Um." Tabitha remained flabbergasted.

"Go ahead!" Elena said with a smile, stepping over into the living room to set down her bag. "Joshua. Nicholas. Aiden. Samuel. Very cool costumes, guys! I'll be taking over the trick-or-treating mission this year, so I'd like to begin our strategy meeting."

The Moore household had never had so many people visiting all at once, and Tabitha was able to persuade Grandma Laurie to instead plug in the straightening iron and set up her bag of hair products in the kitchen, so as not to inconvenience anyone needing to use their bathroom. Standing as still as she could in front of the kitchen sink, Tabitha watched over the counter in amazement as Elena managed to gather the four cousins into an obedient huddle.

"Okay! We are *here* right now." Elena unfolded a black and white photocopy of a Springton map on their coffee table, and was marking notations on it in pink, blue, and yellow highlighter. "The playground where we had that game of tag is over... *here.* By these streets. Can one of you show me where you live?"

"Here." Sam, wearing a red sweatshirt and a blue-and-yellow ski cap, tapped a finger at the map. "Grandma's place is right here."

"Thank you! Now, I don't know what route you all had planned, but I'd like to suggest the course I used to take back when I used to go trick-or-treating. Mom helped us plan a Springton route based on population density and median neighborhood income—if no one dawdles, we should be able to hit these eleven different neighborhoods marked in yellow before people start turning off their lights!"

This got... unexpectedly serious? Tabitha couldn't help but smile as her grandmother gently ran a comb through her hair.

"For this one, and this one, we're going to have to double back after getting to the end of a street," Elena continued. "Then, these three areas are too far apart for us on foot—Mom's going to follow us with the van to shuttle us across. Each of you should bring an extra pillowcase or grocery bag or something for candy. If our hauls are anything like Carrie and I got in '95 and '96... each of us should be filling two whole bags."

"*Two whole bags?!*"

"Is that even possible?!

"Ohhh my gosh... how many pounds is a bag?"

"Two bags of *good* candy?"

Elena's apparent commitment to help them collect the largest volume of candy physically possible impressed the boys beyond measure, and none of them dreamed of questioning her sudden imposition of authority over their prior plans. Sam, Nick, and Aiden immediately swore oaths to follow Elena's every command for the night's mission, and each of them warned Joshua to never lag behind or complain about all the walking.

I was going to divide up my spoils for the boys after each house, based on how well they listened to me. Tabitha watched them interact with her friend in amusement. *My carrot and stick approach really can't hold a candle to Elena's.*

Then Grandma Laurie's hand carefully covered Tabitha's eyes, using enough hairspray on her to choke the trailer with the acrid smell of Aquanet. Ariel had voluminous, gravity-defying bangs that swept over her forehead from left to right, and a worn *Little Mermaid* Goldenbook was propped open in the dish drainer for constant picture references. Tabitha's own hair was a more natural shade that was visually more orange than fire-engine red like Ariel's, and she was a little nervous about how the final look would come out.

When Alicia and her mother arrived twenty minutes later, Grandma Laurie had already washed out and towel-dried Tabitha's hair in preparation for a second attempt, this time liberally using bobby pins before adding spray. Everyone was wowed by Alicia's entrance, and all four of the cousins leapt up from the couch to get a better look.

"Holy cow, Alicia." Elena laughed. "Is that what I think it is?"

"Are you... from *Star Wars?*" Tabitha guessed, staring at her dark-skinned friend in surprise.

"I'm Luke Skywalker, and I'm here to rescue you!" Alicia flashed everyone a nervous smile. "C'mon, nobody laugh at me. Please."

Alicia's outfit was an orange jumpsuit with black boots and gloves, complete with all of the appropriate harness straps, air tubes, and sci-fi doodads instantly recognizable as a rebel pilot uniform from *Star Wars*. A toy lightsaber hung from the belt of her flight suit, and Alicia even carried a familiar pilot's helmet in the crook of her arm.

"That. Is. *Awesome!*" Joshua blurted out.

"I wish *I* was Luke," Nick joined in. "I wanna be Luke next year. Or Han Solo."

"You watch *Star Wars?!*" Sam seemed shocked.

"My dad and I *love Star Wars*," Alicia confided, looking a little relieved at their admiration.

"Which do you like better, *Empire* or *Jedi?*" Aiden demanded. "Because *Return of the Jedi* is *way* betterer."

"*'Betterer'* isn't a word, Aiden," Tabitha corrected him in a soft voice.

"Oh, don't even get 'Licia started." Alicia's mother laughed, rolling her eyes. "Sorry we're late—the gloves and boots needed one more coat of spray paint. I wanted to make *absolutely* sure it all dried right before anything got traipsed into someone's carpet."

"You made that?!" Elena asked, eyes going wide. "Alicia— that's amazing."

"Thanks! And yeah, kinda... sorta?" Alicia grinned, awkwardly tugging at her costume. "Started out as this prison jumpsuit costume—which Dad didn't find funny at all, 'til I told him what we could turn it into. White flak vest's cut outta this old shirt I had, wearing my rain boots and some dishwashing gloves. Rest of it's all stuff from the junk drawer in the garage, put together with hot glue. The helmet's my dad's—it's a Don Post replica. I helped repaint it, so it looks more like it does in the movie."

"Can I see your lightsaber?" Joshua begged.

"No, can *I* see your lightsaber?" Aiden chimed in.

"I'm sorry... but this is the weapon of a Jedi knight," Alicia refused with a solemn face. "An elegant weapon, for a more civilized age."

"Can I see your helmet?" Joshua tried.

"Nope!" Alicia grinned. "Dad will *actually* murder me dead if I let anything happen to it. He already started digging a grave—just in case. He said he can have another daughter anytime, but he only has this one helmet."

"Oh, stop," Alicia's mother protested. "It's a toy helmet. Damn thing just sits up on the shelf collecting dust."

"Don't let him hear you say that, or there'll be *two* graves," Alicia joked. "Tabs, you are looking awesome! Did you get the dress to go with that, or are you goin' with the coconut bra tonight?"

"They were *seashells!*" Tabitha said with an indignant laugh. "And no—we have the dress."

"Shame," Alicia snorted. "And, Elena—where's your costume?!"

"Mine's... actually super lame," Elena seemed to realize, gesturing toward her long-sleeved black shirt and black pants. "I have cat ears, a tail, and a bit of face paint to put on for whiskers in my bag... I was just gonna be a black cat. Is that too lame?"

"It... doesn't have to be," Alicia said, carefully passing the pilot's helmet to her mother. "Don't drop this! Elena, I mean, it won't be lame if *I* do your nose and whiskers. If that's cool?"

"I... yeah?" Elena brightened. "You'd do that?"

"Are we friends?" Alicia challenged.

"...Yeah?" Elena sounded more hopeful than confident.

"Then, *duh.*" Alicia smirked, looking around to size up each of the cousins. "I suppose you boys must be Tabitha's warrior tribe?

Elena, if you have a kit with white paint, I can draw them up big round South Park eyes on their faces."

After a round of belated introductions while Alicia was crouched down in front of half of those crowded into the living room to apply face paint, Grandma Laurie finished fussing with Tabitha's hair with a final tie of the enormous blue bow and declared her *perfect*. She was shooed off to her bedroom to put on her Ariel dress, where she finally got a look at her enormous— albeit impressive—*Little Mermaid* hair in her bedroom mirror. *This is just... amazing!*

When she returned, she received a heartwarming round of *oohs* and *aahs* as everyone praised her look. Elena now wore impressive feline face paint, with a painted pink nose adorning the tip of her actual nose, a slender downward line that connected to her upper lip, and a series of dots artfully clustered on the inside of her cheeks that spread out to beautifully painted whiskers along the outside. In contrast, the four boys looked absolutely ridiculous with enormous *South Park* eyes that took up most of their faces. The Rebel Pilot helmet looked a little too big and out-of-proportion when Alicia actually wore it, but everyone agreed her outfit was the most impressive of all.

"Pictures, pictures!" Alicia's mother insisted, pulling a Kodak disposable camera out of her purse. "C'mon, everyone, get together."

"Um—" Tabitha glanced around nervously. "Is... my mother still outside?"

"I think they're all still talkin' out there. Your daddy just pulled in the drive," Grandma Laurie said, stepping over to lean out the open door—while it was a brisk late October afternoon, the hair-spray fumes had been a little too strong. "Alan! Get yer butt in here, we're taking pictures!"

"Pictures?" he called back. "Hold up, wait for me!"

Mr. Moore appeared in the doorway and took in the strange gathering with a big smile. The moment he caught sight of his daughter, he made a tossing motion, lobbing what looked like a yellow pillow toward her in an underhand throw. Surprised, Tabitha clumsily fumbled it between her hand and her cast, dropping the thing before she could grab it. A boy darted forward beneath her hands and caught it before it hit the ground.

"Thank you, Aiden," Tabitha said sheepishly, accepting the pillow to take closer look—it was a large stuffed plush doll in the shape of a familiar large-eyed yellow guppy with blue markings.

"Oh my God—it's Flounder!" Elena exclaimed. "That's so cute!"

"Coworker 'cross town mentioned his kids had it," Alan said proudly. "Glad I caught you girls before you headed out! You girls all look lovely—er, Miss Alicia, are you from *Star Wars?*"

"I'm Luke Skywalker," Alicia answered with a beaming smile.

"You look great," Mr. Moore said. "Boys, good to see you all again. Mrs. Brooks, thank you so much for comin' on out."

"It's my pleasure!" Alicia's mother replied. "You're just in time for pictures!"

Her four cousins crouched down in a row on their knees to better emulate the squat forms of their *South Park* characters, and then Tabitha was jostled back and forth until it was decided she would be situated in the center. Elena in her kitty-cat makeup stood on one side of her, and Alicia in the orange pilot uniform posed on the other side, flicking out the toy lightsaber to extend the blue plastic blade.

Hugging the Flounder pillow tightly against her chest and looking into the camera lens with a bashful smile, Tabitha didn't think she'd ever been so happy in her life.

———

"Trick or treat!" Tabitha joined in saying as yet another door opened.

"Holy guacamole, look at you all!" the woman said, taken aback by the small crowd at her doorstep.

They'd arrived in full force, with the four boys packed in close and the taller girls arrayed behind them on the porch stoop of a suburban Springton home—the fiftieth or sixtieth of the fourth neighborhood they were canvassing. It was fun, in an exhilarating but somehow embarrassing way that still had Tabitha's cheeks burning. There had been a brief, completely dissonant thought that candy from all the way back in *1998* should be terribly expired by now, but Tabitha was able to quickly snuff it out. The woman dropped a handful of treats into each of their outstretched bags.

"Thank you!" the four cousins answered in chipper unison. They'd done so without any prompting after only the second house of their very first neighborhood, and Tabitha felt proud that they'd made it a habit so quickly.

"Thank you, and—Happy Halloween!" Tabitha smiled at the woman.

"Happy Halloween." The woman waved. "You all look great!"

Elena's long legs carried her back out to the sidewalk first, and like eager ducklings Sam, Nick, Aiden and Joshua trooped after her. She no longer needed to gesture them on past her toward the next house, simply guiding them on in the same well-practiced motion she had the entire evening.

"It's already *heavy*," Nick boasted, hefting up his bag of candy.

"I know!" Aiden said gleefully, swinging his own.

"Less talking, more walking!" Elena playfully scolded them. "Do you want everyone to give out all the candy before we get there?!"

Although she'd said it a few times tonight already, it still had the same effect—the boys double-timed it to the next porch, arranging themselves in a proper side-by-side line. Like well-trained dogs with a biscuit balanced upon their nose, they all hungrily stared at the faint light of the doorbell, but none jumped over to press it. Elena had decided that was her job, and with her pressing their trick-or-treating routine into clockwork efficiency, none of them seemed inclined to squabble with her for the honor.

Tabitha and Alicia caught up—Tabitha was actually feeling a little out of breath—Elena nodded at their arrival, and she pressed the doorbell.

"Trick or treat!" they joined together in a sing-song voice as the door opened.

"My word." An elderly woman stepped into view with a festive orange bowl of candy. "You all look lovely. Who are you all supposed to be?"

"Ma'am," Elena spoke up, "This is Eric, Stan, Kyle, and Kenny. Alicia is Luke Skywalker, Tabitha is Princess Ariel, and I'm a kitty-cat!"

"Goodness." the old woman chuckled, offering her bowl for each of them to grab a handful.

Back when they'd piled into Mrs. Seelbaugh's van for the short drive between the first neighborhood and the second, Elena had given them an updated briefing—she was appointing herself to field any and all questions regarding what costumes the group was wearing.

All of us trying to answer at once is setting us precious seconds behind schedule! Elena admonished them, making an exaggerated stern face.

Yes, drill sergeant! Alicia had snapped a joking salute.

The girls—Mrs. Seelbaugh included—had all laughed about it and poked fun at the military efficiency they were trying to squeeze out of the holiday, while the boys didn't find anything ironic about it. They had been peeking in their surprisingly over-stuffed bags with looks of naked greed.

As much fun as they were all having trooping quickly from door to door through block after block, Tabitha was starting to feel winded. The sun had gone down, but the neighborhoods at night were alive with activity, with dozens of other roving bands of costumed children interspersed with the occasional adult shepherding some kids along. There were power rangers and Disney princesses, toddlers waddling along dressed as Raggedy Ann dolls and young boys dashing around in Batman capes.

"Elena," Tabitha finally called out. "I'm, um. Go on ahead with the boys, and I'll catch up. I don't want to slow you all down."

"We can slow down some." Elena paused. "We've been making good time. Are you alright?"

To Tabitha's surprise, the quartet of her cousins who had been marching like highly-motivated soldiers all lurched to a stop. A moment later, it was like they'd lost all interest in trick-or-treating for the night, abandoning their beeline for the next house and gathering quietly around her. It was... moving, in a way that almost had Tabitha choke up. It felt like she'd done so little for them in this life, considering their circumstances, that seeing them care about her, *care about her more than candy,* made her a little misty-eyed.

"I'm just... a little tired!" Tabitha let out a weak laugh. "I'll skip a few houses and catch up with you at the end of the street."

"Boys?" Elena asked, shooting an uncertain look from Tabitha to them and back again. "What do you think?"

"Go on," Tabitha urged them. "Go—I'm not in it for the candy anyways. I'm fine."

"I'll stay with her," Alicia promised, waggling her lit lightsaber toy. "Go with Elena."

With a surprising amount of reluctance, the four obeyed, scurrying back into action toward the next house at Elena's discretion.

"You okay?" Alicia asked.

"I'm..." Tabitha smiled. "I don't have a lot of energy, I, um. Haven't been taking great care of myself. It's been hard to eat. This is—this is great, though. This has been one of the best nights of my life, already."

"Huh. Sooo, Tabitha," Alicia said, idly swinging around her lightsaber in the air. "Are you a big *Star Wars* fan at all?"

"No, not really." Tabitha gave her friend a helpless shrug. "The two I liked the most were the ones everyone said were the worst of them. *Phantom Menace* and *Force Awakens*."

"Force Awakens?" Alicia arched an eyebrow.

"I think that one's... ten or twenty years away, still?" Tabitha shrugged. "They come out with a whole bunch of new movies and shows when Disney buys *Star Wars*."

"*Disney* buys *Star Wars*... Jesus. I think I need to sit down or something." Alicia laughed, putting a hand up to adjust the over-sized helmet. "But, uh, yeah. Okay. *Phantom Menace*. I think you pass."

"I pass?" Tabitha quirked her head in confusion.

"Yeah." Alicia nodded gravely. "They just revealed the name of the first prequel on the *Star Wars* official web page. Last month, on the thirtieth. Like, no one but people like my dad seem to have really picked up on it, just yet. *The Phantom Menace*. I... I don't *think* you would have cared enough about *Star Wars* to know that—you don't have a computer, and you didn't seem to ever use them in the library at school. Which means..."

"I didn't even see *Episode One* when it came out," Tabitha admitted sheepishly. "Actually didn't catch any of them in theater until *Force Awakens*—I just had them in a set on DVD."

"Does DVD end up replacing VHS?" Alicia blurted out in alarm. "I—sorry, now it's like, anything and everything you remember could be actually huge and important. Tabitha—you're *for real* from the future."

"I am," Tabitha sighed. "And, DVD does, for about... twenty years? Then they try to push a whole bunch of different high-resolution formats, but none of them really stick. No reason to buy movies when you can stream things in quality from just about anywhere online."

"Okay." Alicia nodded. "Okay, whoa. Stream. Resolution. DVD. I feel like I need to be writing these down now. Should we, uh—do we buy stock in DVD? Or... uh, how would we do that?"

"I have no idea." Tabitha made an apologetic face. "I'm sorry. A lot of the really big things come and go so fast—Amazon, Myspace, Vega Lyrae—it's hard for me to pin them to exact dates. As soon as I'm old enough for some kind of part-time job, I'm just going to set aside everything to invest in Alphaco."

"Alphaco, right." Alicia frowned, furrowing her brow. "I remember you said that. They build the world wide web engine? Or something?"

The girls hesitated, stepping off of the sidewalk as a Buzz Lightyear sprinted past, chased shortly after by a smaller child wearing a Simba mask from the *Lion King*.

"An internet search engine, Google," Tabitha nodded. "I hope you'll invest with me—I think it may be our best shot."

"Are you kidding?!" Alicia snorted. "Of course I am, you're like —Tabitha, you're freakin' *from the future*. Probably would've gone in with you anyways, even if I didn't believe you. Just 'cause we're friends. Okay?"

"Thank you." Tabitha let out a sigh of relief. "You don't know what it means to have someone—"

"No, not 'thank you,'" Alicia scoffed, thwapping her lightly with the lightsaber blade. "You say, 'yeah, we *are* friends!' Alright?"

"Yeah." Tabitha smiled. "We are. Thank you."

"You realize at some point we're going to have to tell Elena, though," Alicia pointed out.

"I... yes, I'm prepared for that," Tabitha said slowly. "But I'm not going to say anything until she figures out enough to ask."

"That's fair," Alicia agreed. "I figured it out first anyways. Hah! I'll keep it secret. We *do* need her in on this eventually, though, okay? Definitely before Alphaco."

"That's still years away," Tabitha said. "I... I haven't even *started* saving money. It's honestly going to be hard to."

"Still." Alicia shrugged. "She'll think of a whole bunch of other stuff we need to do. Probably. Well, if she can even keep a secret from her mom. Don't think we should have too many people know. Right?"

"Yeah." Tabitha nodded. "It, um. I just want to say... it means a lot to me, that you believed me. I really couldn't do this alone."

"I *didn't* believe you, actually," Alicia revealed. "Like, no, not even a little bit. Sorry. Don't think I ever would've believed you at all, 'til you described my artwork in the future."

"Wait—really?" Tabitha looked confused. "But, um. You couldn't have possibly drawn that one here, all the way back in this time...?"

"I haven't." Alicia nodded. "Yet. But I know I will. That one's... an important piece to me. I've tried it a couple times—it's not quite there, yet. Artistically speaking. No one else could've ever known about it, though—it's stashed in with my nudie drawings."

"*Nudie drawings?*" Tabitha asked in surprise.

"Yeah, nudie drawings!" Alicia grinned. "C'mon, Tabs. You're supposed to be the super mature one, here."

"I'm... not sure I am anymore," Tabitha admitted uneasily. "I felt so sure of who I was at first, but lately... I mean, I know some of it's hormones, and getting hurt, and everything going on, yeah, but—I'm kind of a wreck. Feel like I've had an emotional break-down almost every day, for weeks. I make stupid decisions, I'm always crying, my moods are all over the place, I. I just can't..."

"How different is all this from your first time?" Alicia asked.

"Very. Maybe *completely*," Tabitha said. "I was... a very damaged little girl back then, but I rarely ever actually cried. I'm always crying now. Back then, it was all very, um. Everything was at this *distance* from me, all of the bad but then all of the good too. It was... lonely. I hated myself. I wanted things to be different, but I wasn't able to change. I was... trapped."

"Tabitha..." Alicia gave her a long look. "Okay, yeah. You *do* need to talk about all of this, to someone. Either me, or, I dunno, *someone*. Not just future stuff—you need to sort all the *you* out. You know?"

"Yeah." Tabitha gave a bitter nod. "I know."

"Were you ever in love?" Alicia asked.

"I... no, I don't think so," Tabitha admitted. "Nothing like that."

"Are you a virgin?" Alicia asked. "Sorry, but I've gotta know. Are you?"

Am I a virgin? Tabitha tensed up at the unexpected question, but finally nodded.

"Really? Counting both?"

"I'm thirteen," Tabitha said in a small voice.

"Yeah, but—"

"I didn't look like this, last time," Tabitha said. "Ever. I was—I was around the weight my mother is right now. But even shorter. It was more than that, though, I... Alicia, *I hated myself.* I don't know if you understand what that's like, completely. The only way I could even remotely think about... intimate things was by completely removing and detaching the idea of *myself* from the concepts. Making it impersonal. Clinical?"

"Okay, sorry," Alicia said after a moment of consideration. "What are we going to do about that?"

"About love?"

"Love can wait," Alicia said. "I think. I'm just trying to get some perspective on who you are, what you're going for, some basic... general idea. What are we going to do about you hating yourself? You don't *still* hate yourself, do you?"

"Um."

"Tabs, if you don't give me a strong 'no,' I'm going to take it as a 'mostly yes.' Alright?"

"Alright."

"Tabitha—" Alicia stopped and grabbed Tabitha's shoulder, forcing her to a halt as well. "You hate yourself?"

"I... I really didn't get to pick and choose," Tabitha said defensively. "What I brought back with me to this life. I have a thirteen-year-old mind and body, with... a lot of these extra memories. The memories, they have a lot of issues attached to them. Do they still count? I don't know. Are the feelings *real,* now that the timeline's going differently? I don't know. What do I do about them? I, I don't know—I. Fuck, I *never knew.*

"I don't know what to do with all of this inside me. I'm just, kinda... well, I'm here, now. Even when I do better and fix some things—I've still got all this baggage that makes less and less— well, it doesn't really make any sense anymore. Doesn't match up. Cognitive dissonance, in all of these... weird ways. I'm just trying to get through this. I wouldn't have ever chosen to do any of this all over again."

"Okay." Alicia pulled her into a quick hug. "Well, *I'm* glad you're getting the chance to. This is good—this is all a good start. Do you feel any better, getting any of that off your chest?"

"I... don't know."

"You're gonna get through this, and I'm gonna help." Alicia squeezed her tight. "*We're* gonna help. Elena too—together we're gonna work everything out. We're friends. Where do you think we should go from here? What happens next? Anything happening soon?"

"I don't—um. No, I guess I do actually know," Tabitha admitted. "I need to find Ashlee Taylor. Help her, apologize to her. Ask her to forgive me."

"Great!" Alicia clapped Tabitha on the back. "I don't know who that is, but we're gonna track her down. Alright?"

24

TABITHA CHEATS ON HER DIET

Their expedition party had returned triumphant from a trick-or-treating mission that had possibly gone *too* well. After the seventh neighborhood, Mrs. Seelbaugh had asked with a look of amusement if everyone wanted to keep going, and received a resounding and determined affirmative. When they'd completed the eighth and ninth, and each of them had a second bag of candy that was beginning to fill—the boys were using spare pillowcases—they'd all continued to push on despite their aching feet.

I... think I might sit this one out, Tabitha had reluctantly said before their final planned neighborhood on the route. To her surprise, both of her teenage friends and all four of the cousins agreed with enthusiasm and relief. It had been an absurdly successful night, the amount of candy each of them had collected was ridiculous, and everyone seemed more than satisfied with their haul. With everyone unanimously deciding to skip their eleventh area, Mrs. Seelbaugh had instead steered them in the silvery minivan back toward the trailer at Sunset Estates. Once again, the trailer was crowded and bustling with people, more than Tabitha ever remembered seeing inside all at once.

"Tabby—can I talk to you for a second?" Elena asked, regarding Tabitha with a solemn expression. "Privately?"

"Is... something wrong?" Tabitha said carefully, feeling her mouth go dry. *Is she asking about the future already? Did Alicia say something, or did I let something slip?* "Here, let's head into my room."

"Alicia—can you watch the boys for a little bit?" Elena asked.

The request revealed a lot about Elena to Tabitha. Though the night was ostensibly over and they were back in the trailer with all of the adults, Elena never relinquished her unspoken mantle of responsibility to any of the parents present. She'd decided that the teenage girls were going to remain *in charge* of the four younger cousins at all times, was set on affirming this hierarchy, and seemed to take their duties very seriously.

"Yeah, sure." Alicia smiled. "*Boys.* No one's had any candy yet —right?"

"No," they obediently replied. Over the course of the night, they'd become well-trained and were getting pretty good at synchronizing their responses. Joshua's *no* was an eager one, because he thought they were about to get permission to start gorging themselves. Nick's *no* sounded a little sullen and frustrated, while Aiden's was chipper, like he was proud to have not broken a rule this time. Sam's *no* was curious, and he was carefully appraising Alicia from across his open bags of candy.

"Alright." Alicia grinned. "It's a good thing you didn't, because it's time to see which one of you *won.* Everyone—start counting your loot!"

"This way," Tabitha said with a wry smile, leading Elena down the hallway to her tiny room. *I thought I was really good at managing the cousins, but 'Lena and 'Licia are teaching me a lot. It's... actually a little scary how good they are at this.*

Tabitha's bedroom was small, very small, a simple box measuring nine feet along her bare walls in one direction and seven feet in the other, which featured little else but a small window with curtains. She kept her decor rather bare and minimalistic to help provide the illusion that the bedroom wasn't quite as cramped as it actually was, with furnishings likewise extremely spartan. All of the odds and ends of her now *incredibly* distant-seeming prior childhood had been carefully packed into boxes and stacked in the shed. Oddly enough, Tabitha's room had no closet at all—the previous owners of the mobile home had removed it to give the adjacent bathroom a little more space during a remodel. All of her clothing that didn't fit in her battered vintage dresser was hanging up in the back of her parents' closet.

Watching Elena evaluate her living space with an interested look around had Tabitha feeling more anxious than she'd ever imagined, and so she awkwardly sat down on the neatly-made bed to await her friend's verdict. She'd left her bag of candy on the kitchen counter, but was still hugging the Flounder pillow against herself.

"Needs more kitten posters," Elena judged, shooting her a teasing look.

"Yeah," Tabitha said with a nervous smile. "I'll... work on that."

"Good." Elena nodded, sitting down on the other side of the bed. "I'm kidding, it's fine. Okay, um. First of all; how are you feeling?"

"Better," Tabitha answered with a wince. "...And also worse."

"Why worse?" Elena asked. Her tall blonde friend seemed a little too composed, and Tabitha began to suspect that Elena had been planning and preparing for the different ways this conversation might go.

"I feel... out of place," Tabitha said with caution, watching Elena for any clue as to what this talk was about.

"Out of place because you missed school this week?" Elena pressed. "Or, out of place in a... general, social way?"

"...Both, really," Tabitha swallowed uneasily.

"Okay. That's perfectly normal," Elena reassured her. Tabitha could practically hear Mrs. Seelbaugh's kind and patient voice within Elena's. "But, I want us to do something about that."

"Something?" Tabitha echoed.

"Matthew's Halloween party is tomorrow," Elena reminded her. "We were all invited, and I want you to go."

"Okay." Tabitha inwardly let out a sigh of relief. "I thought that was a bad idea. Because Erica might be there."

"I know I said we shouldn't go if she was going to be there, but... I've been thinking about it a lot. Are you willing to hear me out?"

"...I'm listening."

"I *really* like Matthew," Elena said. "Just to be like, completely clear and totally transparent about my... priorities and ulterior motives."

Elena doesn't really sound like a teenage girl at all either, Tabitha mused. *But she's so much better at making it all still sound natural. Her words and mannerisms come off as just being picked up from her parents. In a really strong way. How can I make it start to seem like that when I'm in my... PROPER DICTION mindset?*

"So... I want to go, no matter what," Elena continued. "But *you* going or not is... the big topic. Everyone at school thinks you'll be there."

"You're kidding." Tabitha felt herself go pale.

"Both Erica Taylor and Clarissa Dole are gonna be at the party," Elena revealed. "Clarissa privately approached Matthew and asked if she could go, because people think *you'll* be there and she wants to apologize to you. She legit didn't know what she was getting into with all of this, I think, and will switch to your side in an instant if it means you can put in a good word. So that she doesn't have to repeat a year."

"*Sides?*" Tabitha made a face. "I really don't think—"

"There are sides to this, whether you like it or not," Elena insisted. "You're one of them. The Taylor girls—well, Erica's pretty much the other, right now. It's pretty much confirmed that she's gonna be there, and Matthew's mom is kinda-sorta okay with it—to 'give her a chance to apologize in person.' No one actually thinks that's gonna happen, though. Erica apparently shrugs things off whenever people ask her about it, but word from *Carrie* is that she's still completely trash-talking you, and that actually it's gotten way worse. *Way* worse."

"Then I definitely don't go." Tabitha blinked. "...Right?"

"I really want you to go," Elena repeated. "You'll literally never have these kinds of advantages in a confrontation like, ever again. Matthew and his parents are both on your side, so right off the bat, that's like having a home-ground advantage. *I'll* be there with you, right by your side the whole time. Alicia and Casey will both be there with us—together, they pretty much represent the Art Club people. You're like, *the poster girl* of the whole club right now, 'cause that print of you is literally hung up by the board like a poster, and Mr. Peterson is totally in your corner. All the teachers are, really. It's *bitchy popular girls* versus *everyone with common sense,* at this point."

"Um." Tabitha blanched. "Is it... wrong, or cowardly or something, to admit that I just don't want any kind of confrontation, period?"

"No, it's not." Elena put a hand on Tabitha's shoulder. "I mean that. But, I mean, also, if there ever *is* a confrontation—and there probably will be—this is your best shot ever. Like, the terms'll never be as... favorable? You know what I mean? I really think you need to go. If you go, that makes a statement, and people are going to take it a certain way. If you *don't* go, but Erica does, then everyone'll make these certain... assumptions? Think you're hiding, or have a guilty conscience, or that you're afraid of her. Or afraid of the truth. She can spin things however she wants, if you don't go."

"That doesn't seem very fair." Tabitha frowned.

"I know." Elena gave her a helpless shrug. "I'm just saying. I really want you to go, Tabitha—I think it's in your best interests to go, and... I'll hope that you trust my judgment on that."

"Okay," Tabitha said after a moment of consideration. "I do trust you. We're friends, right?"

"Friends!" Elena promised, lighting up at the word and clasping Tabitha's hand. "Thank you. You'll really go?"

"I'll go. But you don't say 'thank you.'" Tabitha chuckled, thinking back to her prior conversation with Alicia. "You say: 'Definitely. We're friends.'"

"Definitely!" Elena affirmed. "We *are* friends. The party's going to be amazing, and we're all gonna be there with you. Everything's gonna be fine, no matter what Erica tries to pull. There's nothing she *can* even pull, really. It's a costume party, and we're all already set there. Oh—uhhh, we should probably talk about this too. How do you actually feel about Matthew?"

"He's cute. I like him," Tabitha revealed, fidgeting with her cast for a moment. "But I don't *like him,* like him. No... um, conflict of interests, there. He's all yours?"

"Cool." Elena let out a sigh of relief. "I mean—it's totally cool either way, it wouldn't be a problem. Just... I do get competitive, and I don't want things to get weird between us right now. Did Alicia talk to you about dating, who you're interested in?"

"Um." Tabitha remembered the awkward earlier talk. "Kinda? I don't think I'm ready, not for a long while. Years, maybe?"

"Okay. That's perfectly fine too," Elena said, again in that way Tabitha couldn't help but think was in imitation of Mrs. Seelbaugh. "Just, there's been freshman guys at school... expressing interest, and we weren't sure if we should vet them or not. Or, if you're even coming back soon. *Are* you coming back soon?"

"I don't know, right now," Tabitha admitted honestly. "I think... it'll depend on how things go at the big hearing thingy, this coming Monday."

"Okay." Elena nodded again. "Is that gonna be like, at the courthouse or something? Can anyone go and watch? I want to be there with you. Alicia too."

"I think they're normally held at the district office." Tabitha racked her brain for what she remembered from her experiences working in Springton Town Hall. "This one sounds like it involves a lot more people, though, so... they'll meet in one of the local school cafeterias in the evening on Monday. Either Springton Middle, or Springton High—probably Springton High. They might use the auditorium instead, maybe. I'm not sure. I can ask?"

"If we're allowed to go, we want to be there with you," Elena said in a determined voice.

"I really appreciate that," Tabitha said honestly, feeling as if a slight weight was disappearing from her shoulders. "I mean it. Um —actually. I just had a random thought—are you going to be dressed as a cat again for the Halloween party?"

"I... was, yeah." Elena looked down at her outfit. "Is it actually too lame?"

"This might be weird, or super awkward or something—but, we're definitely friends, right?" Tabitha said, sliding off the bed and pulling open one of the drawers of her dresser. "Can I give you one of my blouses, as a—a friendship thing? I mean, it's—"

"We're *definitely* friends!" Elena affirmed, her blue eyes lighting up at the prospect. "I was trying to think up a way to steal one anyways—uhh, because that's what friends do!"

Tabitha carefully lifted a neatly folded pile of shirts—mostly tees or workout clothes—and pulled out a blouse she'd had hidden beneath the pile. It unfolded itself as she held it up, a long-sleeved black affair with rather intricate lace.

"What the fuck," Elena mouthed in surprise, accepting it from her friend and holding it up for a better look. "You never wore this one to school. Tabby—this is *sexy!*"

"Yeah... that's actually the reason I don't think I can wear it, ever," Tabitha said in a weak voice. "It's just not *me*. It was part of a dress that was really, *really* beautiful, but I don't like layering it with anything else I have, and... um. I'm not comfortable showing cleavage, yet. At all."

"Can I try it on real quick?" Elena asked. "Yeah, cleavage is hard to get used to—Mom and I've been over that a lot. We clipped out these two different magazine article guides on it, they're up beside my mirror at home. My comfort zone goes as far as showing two inches, right now—and that's like, only even a recent thing. Don't ever feel pressured to show off more than you're okay with. Damn, are you sure about this, though? Tabby, this is a *really* nice top."

"Try it on, please." Tabitha nodded. "If it fits, I want you to have it. I'm glad we made it, but it wasn't ever really *me*. It'd be really cool if it works with your cat costume."

"I think it will." Elena stepped in front of the mirror and held the slinky garment up in front of herself. "Probably? Tabitha—thank you so much; this is *amazing*."

Slipping out of the bedroom and closing the door to give Elena privacy to change, Tabitha walked back down the hallway toward the living room with a faint smile. It was silly, but it felt *good* giving Elena the black blouse, like there would be a bit of visible solidarity between the three girls in wearing them. *Would it be super weird if we all wore them to school on the same day, or... just together sometime, so we could get a picture of us all looking fancy?*

The living room was still a madhouse of activity—both of her parents and Grandma Laurie were at the table with Mrs. Brooks and Mrs. Seelbaugh, while Alicia and the boys had pushed aside the coffee table and were crowded together in front of the TV amongst their heaping piles of candy.

"Everything okay, sweetie?" Mr. Moore called over.

"Uh-huh." Tabitha nodded. "Who ended up having the most candy?"

"I did," Grandma Laurie joked. "All of the boys' candy is goin' right to me."

"Is *not!*" Joshua took the bait, sounding horrified.

"No way," Sam protested, hunching protectively over his loot.

"I won—I had the most," Aiden boasted proudly. "By *thirty-two* pieces. *Way* ahead of Sam."

"Good job, Aiden," Tabitha praised, feeling a little surprised. *Isn't a thirty-two piece lead several handfuls of candy? They all went to the same doors!* "How do you feel about sharing with your brothers?"

Their side of the room went quiet, and each of the cousins— still with ridiculous smudged *South Park* eyes drawn across their entire faces—regarded each other with narrowed eyes.

"You're all a team," Tabitha explained, grabbing her own bulging bag of candy off of the counter. "You're *my* team. If all four of you boys put your candy together in one big pile, for *all of you to share together*... I'll add my haul in with yours. I really don't want any candy for myself."

"Tabs—it's Halloween," Alicia protested, pulling three lollipops at once out of her mouth so that she could speak clearly. "You're not allowed to have *no* candy. You have to have at least something. It's the law."

"That *is* the law, I'm afraid," Grandma Laurie agreed with a smile. "Rules are rules!"

"It's a Kentucky state statute, I believe," Mrs. Seelbaugh joined in with a wink.

"We'll do it," Sam said with conviction, already pushing and shoving his rather enormous pile of candy across the carpet into the middle. All at once, the other three cousins began nudging and tossing their piles to join the heap.

"You say, '*we accept your proposal*,'" Alicia directed. "But, Tabitha—you *do* have to have a piece. At least *one*, c'mon."

"We accept your proposal," the four cousins said in a chipper chorus, marveling at how humongous the pile of Halloween candy had become when gathered into a single mound.

"I'm... trying not to eat too much sugar," Tabitha protested weakly, looking around at all of the expectant faces.

"It's Halloween," Mr. Moore said. "I'm sorry, sweetie—but the law is what it is."

I don't think I've had any candy in... what, years? Tabitha thought to herself, reluctantly peeking inside the heavy bag. *Since well before the stomach ulcers...*

With no small amount of bashful excitement, she picked out the best thing she spotted—the bright orange wrapper of a pair of large Reese's peanut butter cups, and then passed the rest of her candy to the nearby Joshua. He gleefully poured it out in a rush atop their collected pile, and all four boys marveled at the sheer size of the thing. It was enormous, almost a foot and a half high and with a large, spread-out base made up of hundreds upon hundreds of different colors of wrapped treats.

"Look at that, you're all gonna get diabetes," Grandma Laurie sighed, getting up out of her chair. "Well, come on, then, boys. Gather 'round behind it for a picture."

"What'd you pick?" Mrs. Seelbaugh asked, sending Tabitha a curious look.

"Reese's," Tabitha said. "Um. Mom, if I have one of these cups... would you want the other one?"

"Aww, Tabitha." Mrs. Moore looked moved. "I'd love that!"

"Are those tears I see, Shannon?" Mrs. Seelbaugh teased.

"It's true," Mrs. Moore theatrically wiped away some moisture with her fingertips. "I really do just love Reese's that much."

"Uh-huh." Mr. Moore rolled his eyes.

Tabitha had just begun to tear open the orange packaging when Elena stepped out of her room and pranced down the hallway with an enormous smile. She was still wearing the cat-eared headband, and unlike the boys had managed to keep her face-paint from smudging—but the black blouse she was wearing now looked *incredible,* and when replacing her previous long-sleeved shirt, it added a certain elegance to her entire look. It was low-cut enough to show cleavage, but on Elena's taller figure, it seemed to work. The lines of what had once been a rather sexy party dress were embroidered with a lace pattern, which continued across the mesh of her shoulders and back where the garment was mostly see-through.

"Well—what do you think?" Elena asked, stepping out and giving a twirl to show it off.

"*Ooh la la.*" Mrs. Brooks laughed. "It's lovely—is this another one of Tabitha's?"

"I helped a little with that one!" Grandma Laurie called over.

"She did more than help—she did most of the work," Tabitha corrected with a smile. "*I* was the one who only helped a little bit."

"I like it, it looks great," Mrs. Moore decided. "Daring, but not distasteful. It looks good on you, Miss Elena."

"Thank you!" Elena beamed, turning to Alicia and the boys. "What do you think?"

"It looks really good," Sam said politely, trying not to stare.

"It's cool!" Nick offered.

"Cool," Joshua agreed.

"Me-*ow*," Alicia growled, playfully clawing at the air in an *Austin Powers* imitation.

"It's... *alright.*" Aiden tried to sound unimpressed, but his eyes had gone a little too wide at the sight of her. "I *guess.*"

"Oooh, Aiden's got the hots for Elena?!" Alicia blurted out in mock-surprise. "My, how scandalous!"

"I do not!"

"Aiden and Elena, sittin' in a tree!" Joshua sang. "K-I-S-S-I-N—"

"Oh, shush." Elena rolled her eyes.

"It *does* show a lot of neck, though..." Mrs. Seelbaugh leaned forward with a thoughtful look. "I think you need a necklace to go with it—or, maybe a matching choker?"

"A cat collar, with a little bell!" Alicia proposed. "Maybe we can find one that fits?"

"Ooh, kitty collar, that's a really good idea," Elena said with an appreciative nod. "I think I have a thin little belt at home that could work if I cut it shorter—then, just slip on a jingle bell, I guess?"

"Sure, that'll work. But... c'mon, Elena," Alicia smirked. "Don't keep us in suspense. Did Tabs say yes, or did she say no?"

"She said yes." Elena smiled.

"To the big sleepover tonight—or to the big party tomorrow?" Mrs. Seelbaugh asked for clarification.

...Is everyone here in on this?! Tabitha couldn't help but give them incredulous looks.

"Oh, right!" Elena seemed to remember, twisting to face Tabitha. "Would you want to—"

"Yes!" Tabitha grinned, carefully sliding out one of the peanut butter cups into her good palm—it was awkward holding anything with her left hand trapped in a cast—and passing it to her mother. "Please—can we?"

"Yes, pleeeaase!" the four cousins called out, instead of saying *cheeeese* from where they were posing for a picture huddled together—and almost obscured behind—the gigantic pile of candy.

"Good, good," Mrs. Brooks said with a pleased nod. "We hoped you'd say yes—we went and hid Alicia's sleeping bag and things right outside the door there."

"Cool!" Joshua said. "We can pillow-fight."

"Hah, well—I don't think any of you boys are invited." Grandma Laurie laughed. She took the first picture with a flash of light, and then stooped down lower for one with an even better angle. "I think it's a *girls only* slumber party."

"Yeah—no icky boys allowed!" Alicia teased, wrinkling her nose at the nearby Aiden.

"I'm not icky," Aiden protested.

"You're a little icky," Alicia compromised.

"Whose idea was it to have slumber party?" Tabitha asked in bewilderment, looking from Elena to Alicia.

To her surprise, both of her friends turned their grins toward the table of adults, and from there Mrs. Brooks and Mrs. Seelbaugh turned to pointedly look over at—

"...Mom?" Tabitha felt absolutely stunned.

"Happy Halloween, sweetie," Mrs. Moore said quietly, and there was a sparkle she'd never seen before in her eye as she took a bite of her peanut butter cup.

"Happy Halloween, Mom," Tabitha said, feeling her eyes betray her and tear up again—they'd been doing that too damned often lately. "Happy Halloween, everyone."

"Happy Halloween, honey," her father said softly.

"Happy Halloween!" Grandma Laurie exclaimed.

Tabitha slowly—tentatively—unwrapped her own Reese's cup and put it to her lips. When she bit into it, experiencing the sweet flavor of chocolate and the rich peanut butter, she let out a small noise of appreciation. It should have been a guilty pleasure... but it didn't feel like one, not anymore. Instead, it was the most delicious-tasting thing she'd ever had in either of her lives, and as she took a spot on the floor next to Alicia to sit down, tears rolled down her cheeks.

"Wow," Mrs. Seelbaugh remarked with a wry smile. "Look at you two—you Moore ladies sure do love Reese's, huh?"

"Really?" Elena said, crouching down to open up her bag of candy. "They're alright. Actually, if you'll trade a Snickers for each —wait, *Tabitha!* What happ—why are you crying?!"

———

"These are *really* nice houses out here," Elena observed in an awed tone.

"They really are, aren't they?" Mrs. Seelbaugh sighed, glancing over at her daughter situated in the passenger seat of the minivan, and then at Tabitha and Alicia sitting in the back. "How'd you like to live in one of these someday, girls?"

"*I wish,*" Tabitha chuckled with a small sigh.

Seeing how large and expensive these lake houses were, was a lot more intimidating than she'd prepared herself for. Tabitha had already been a little uncomfortable having Elena over for the night—she knew the Seelbaughs were more affluent than her family, and by more than just a degree or two. When all three teenage girls had been packed into her tiny bedroom for the impromptu slumber party, she couldn't help but keep apologizing for the cramped accommodations. They were friends, and they attended the same school together, but the stark difference in social class was an embarrassment difficult for Tabitha to shake.

All things considered, Tabitha thought of it as more of a *sleepover* than a proper *slumber party,* because it had already been getting pretty late by the time the group returned from trick-or-treating. The girls wound up chatting in the darkness for almost an hour before all falling asleep, mostly just discussing the tense situation at school that followed all of the suspensions. Elena had a finger on the pulse of the Springton student drama, and had been dying to regale Tabitha with all of the stories—Alicia binged her way through her bag of candy while making an occasional clarification or inserting a snarky remark.

It absolutely makes me want us to have a REAL slumber party, Tabitha thought, watching the scenery roll by outside her window with a wistful expression. *Having fun with friends is... beyond amazing. I'd gladly trade my entire previous life for a few hours with them, just giggling over stupid stories in the dark like dumb girls.*

The Williams' Halloween party was a fair distance outside of Springton, in an area sequestered away from commercial districts and busy intersections by miles and miles of forested hills. Even after the lake itself became visible through the trees, it was a fifteen-minute drive skirting around it toward their destination. Each of the lots they passed were enormous, sprawling things with long driveways, featuring opulent structures that didn't quite register to Tabitha as houses—these were *estates,* or possibly even mansions—often complete with their own luxurious-looking boathouses built out onto the water.

"I *will* live someplace like this, someday," Elena decided, smiling out the window.

"Not me." Alicia laughed. "No way. Too far out from everything. This is where like, horror movies take place. Slashers, y'know?"

"Well, you *are* having a party on the lake, and it *is* Halloween," Mrs. Seelbaugh teased, playfully imitating the iconic horror movie sound cue from *Friday the Thirteenth*. "*Ch ch ch, ka ka ka...*"

Alicia and Elena broke into a fit of giggles that was so contagious, Tabitha couldn't help but laugh along with them. As someone only recently in possession of a mother she was on friendly terms with, Tabitha found the relationship between Elena and Mrs. Seelbaugh endlessly fascinating.

Will Mom and I ever be like this? It seems... possible. Things between us have already deviated so much from the original timeline that it's like the story's completely jumped into a different genre.

"It's after the real Halloween, technically. So, I think we're safe." Elena chuckled, twisting in her seat to check on her two friends. "Hey, Tabby—you okay?"

"I'm... yeah. Okay, but also a little nervous," Tabitha admitted, unable to keep from smiling at seeing the elaborate cat makeup once again turned her way.

"Ladies—I think this is it!" Mrs. Seelbaugh announced.

The silvery minivan slowed to a stop at a rustic wooden mailbox with a bundle of Halloween balloons twisting in the wind, and then pulled into a long hedge-lined driveway. The Williams family seemed wealthy even in comparison to the other houses in the area, and Tabitha's discomfort continued to rise.

"Guys... holy cow," Alicia muttered in awe.

The house itself was enormous, a multiple-story affair with a three-car garage connected as a wing to the lower level. A half-dozen other cars were already parked in a large gravel parking area for the party, boxed in on the opposite side by a shed the size of a small barn. An extravagant split-level porch wrapped around the lake house itself, with an upper-level veranda and then broad stairs down to the ground-level porch, which connected to a covered walkway that led all the way out to the lake. Their docks stretched out dozens of yards into the water, where a large pontoon boat was nestled into a berth beneath a roofed enclosure.

"Well, when you get a place like this, Elena... I'm movin' in with you," Mrs. Seelbaugh told her daughter.

"Of course," Elena snorted. "You can babysit the kids while I gallivant around Europe with my rich husband."

"Deal!" Mrs. Seelbaugh grinned. "Alright, girls, have fun! Alicia, take lots of pictures. I'll be back by to pick you all up at midnight, so try not to fall in the lake or anything."

"You're not staying for the party?" Alicia asked, surprised.

"Of course not," Mrs. Seelbaugh said with a gentle smile. "Elena needs to be able to let her hair down, spread her wings, and party with people her own age! Without having to worry about having her boring old mother being there and seeing everything she gets up to."

"You are the coolest mom," Alicia said with wide eyes.

"*Pffft.*" Elena blew a raspberry. "She's lying, it's totally backwards—Dad's taking her to an actual *adult* Halloween party with skimpy costumes and lots of alcohol, and they don't want me there spoiling their fun."

"Well, yeah." Mrs. Seelbaugh's eyes twinkled. "That too."

"You are the coolest mom *ever,*" Alicia remarked.

"Alright, ladies, get out of here." Mrs. Seelbaugh shooed them away with a gesture. "Go on, get! Kiss lots of boys, break lots of hearts."

"Thanks, Mom," Elena said, opening her door and hopping out.

"Thanks, Mrs. Elena's Mom!" Alicia chimed in. "You too!"

"Don't tell her that!" Elena protested.

"Thank you for driving us all the way out here," Tabitha said with a nervous smile. "And for taking us around everywhere trick-or-treating yesterday."

"Anytime, anytime." Mrs. Seelbaugh reached over to pat her shoulder. "Hey. You'll be fine. Just go and have a great time."

"I'll try," Tabitha promised, sliding out after Alicia and carefully closing the door behind her.

The three girls hesitated outside together, staring up at the big lake house as Mrs. Seelbaugh waved and then backed out down the driveway. There were a lot of cars present, but it seemed like everyone was inside for the party. They'd just started walking toward the large front entrance when a pair of French doors on the second-story veranda opened and a small figure scampered out to welcome them.

"Hello to Tabitha!" Hannah squeaked out, just barely lurching to a stop at the edge of the porch and beckoning them forward. "C'mon, this way, this way! Everyone's up here. Ugh, okay, I'll show you."

"Hello to Hannah!" Tabitha called out in return, letting out a small breath of relief at seeing a familiar face.

Hannah MacIntire was just as impossibly adorable as Tabitha remembered, but now the little girl was dressed in a pink and blue *Mulan* Halloween costume, tied at the waist with a bright red sash. The seven-year-old carelessly bunched up the hem of the faux-feudal Chinese dress in tiny fists so she could plod down the steps.

"Say hello to Hannah." Tabitha shared a smile with her friends.

"Hello there!" Elena called out. "Happy Halloween."

"Hello to Hannah." Alicia waved.

"Hi, and hi," Hannah greeted, giving both of them a perfunctory nod before staring at Tabitha. "You got a cast."

"I *do* have a cast," Tabitha said, awkwardly switching the Flounder pillow to her good hand so that she could show off the blue cast to Hannah. "You can sign your name on it later, if anyone here has a marker."

"I'll ask Aunt Karen!" Hannah's cute cheeks lit up in a bright smile. "I'm in first grade. I can already write my name."

"First grade at Springton Elementary?" Tabitha gave her a thoughtful look. "Actually, do you know a Joshua Moore? He's one of my cousins."

"Ummm... I dunno? Joshua?" Hannah hopped off the porch, and then jumped right back up onto it in alarm. "Whoops—I'm not allowed to go off of the porch without shoes. See?"

Hannah lifted up her dress to show them her bare feet.

"...I can see that," Tabitha remarked. "You don't want to step on anything, or get splinters!"

"I've already got splinters before," Hannah scoffed. "They're no big deal. I even got stung by a bee before."

"Well, this is Elena, and this is Alicia." Tabitha introduced her friends as they all stepped up to join her on the porch. "They're friends of both Matthew and me."

"Hi," Hannah said again.

"I hate bees!" Alicia said with a chipper smile. "They're the worst, and they should all die."

"*Alicia!*" Elena scolded, slapping the girl's arm.

"I used to think they were cool, but now I hate bees too." Hannah nodded with understanding. Seeming to bond in the kind of immediate friendship that only a mutual hatred of bees can produce, the cute seven-year-old grabbed Alicia's costume-gloved hand and began to lead them all up the stairs.

"This way, this way! Anyways, I'm Mulan. Tabitha is Ariel from the *Little Mermaid*, she's a black cat, and... what are you supposed to be? A Ghostbuster?"

"I'm from *Star Wars*!" Alicia explained, looking crestfallen.

"Ew, *Star Wars*," Hannah teased, making a face. "Matthew likes *Star Wars*. I think it's dumb, though."

"*Star Wars* isn't dumb!" Alicia cried out in mock-indignation, pulling her hand out of Hannah's little grasp. "Everyone loves *Star Wars*! There's *statistics* that even prove it!"

"I love your dress, Hannah," Elena remarked, swatting Alicia on the shoulder. "I really liked *Mulan*."

"Thanks!" Hannah said. "You're really pretty."

"Um—thank you." Elena laughed.

Entering through the set of French doors, they found themselves in an enormous living room with high ceilings and skylights that faced toward the lake. The carpet was plush, a fireplace was lit, and row upon row of family photos seemed to decorate every wall. A large, somewhat antiquated tube TV built into a wooden cabinet was playing *The Nightmare Before Christmas*.

Aside from the familiar face of Casey standing nearby to watch the movie—wearing a decidedly unfamiliar white bridal gown— there was only a single other lone teenage girl, seated on one of the three couches. Several adults could be seen chatting in the nearby kitchen, but otherwise, there was only the telltale sound of a ping-pong game going on somewhere nearby and occasional interspersed voices in the distance. The Halloween party seemed surprisingly empty.

"I'm gonna bug Aunt Karen for a marker so I can sign your cast —don't go anywhere!" Hannah called, bunching up her Mulan dress again so that she could dash over into the kitchen.

"Oh, hey guys!" Casey waved. "You're early! Pretty much only the youth group's here so far. We all came over right after second service. The guys're all downstairs in the rec room."

"Which church?" Elena asked with interest.

"Springton United Methodist," Casey said. "Wow, you guys look awesome!"

"Aww. My parents are Presbyterian," Elena pouted. "Not enough kids for a youth group, though."

"First United Methodist Church, but over in Fairfield," Alicia said. "I think we just have Youth Choir, hah. Not my thing."

"Oh my gosh, Matthew's gonna *die* when he sees you, 'Licia," Casey exclaimed, marveling at Alicia's rebel pilot costume. "We're both real into *Star Wars*. Both of us have *Shadows of the Empire* for

Nintendo 64. They're actually making an X-wing flying game for 64 this Christmas, called *Rogue Squadron*! Did you buy this outfit?"

"Made everything but the helmet!" Alicia said with pride. "And the lightsaber, I guess."

Incredibly relieved that the conversation had turned in a different direction before anyone thought to ask her what church her family attended, Tabitha sidled over to stand behind one of the couches and idly watched as the familiar scenes of the stop-motion Tim Burton classic played out.

My parents both SEEM religious, so it's hard to call them Godless heathens, but... they definitely never took me to church. Maybe that's something I should ask them about? Even with the miracle or whatever it is that's happened to send me back in time, I don't think I have any strong beliefs one way or another. Getting them involved in some sort of community—Mom especially—might actually help a lot, though. Why didn't I ever think of it?

"There's a Darth Vader downstairs playing ping pong with all of them, but he's just got one of the lame-o store-bought cheap costumes." Casey laughed, turning to see Tabitha and Elena. "I mean, you both look great too! You're like, *spot-on* for Ariel, and Elena—I just love your blouse! I'm guessing Alicia did your face paint?"

"Thank you, and yes." Elena grinned. "Let me guess: you're a run-away bride?"

"Yep, you got it!" Casey said with a mischievous laugh, plucking at a number-emblazoned runner's bib that was safety-pinned overtop the wedding dress. "Got me Nikes on and every-thing! My mom ran a marathon in Lexington, this was her tag thingy-ma-bob."

"Cool!" Elena nodded. "I actually ran a 5K with my mom, once. Tabitha jogs in the mornings. I was thinking about really getting into it so I can run with her."

"You guys thinking about joining the track team?" Casey asked. "One of the dudes in my Geometry class just—"

"—Tabitha? *Tabitha Moore?*" The lone teenage girl who'd been seated on the couch watching the movie jumped to her feet in surprise. She was wearing a very brief dress in surprisingly loud colors made out to resemble the British flag, and her face looked vaguely familiar—but with her strawberry-blonde hair teased out for whatever Halloween costume she wearing, Tabitha couldn't quite place where she'd met her before.

"I took your notebook," the teen blurted out, staring at Tabitha with wide eyes. "I'm so sorry. I didn't even know you, but everyone was *saying things* and I believed them, *but I shouldn't have.* Please don't hate me—I'm so, *so* sorry. I mean it. I didn't know anything about how things with you really were, I just—"

"Clarissa?" Tabitha guessed, examining the erstwhile classmate.

"Yeah. I didn't even think you'd know who I was." Clarissa paled. "We—we never even talked. Tabitha—I'm so, so sorry."

"Um," Tabitha said, reining in a brief surge of emotions. "Is it okay if we all sit here with you?"

"Okay," Clarissa readily agreed. "I really am sorry, though—I mean it."

25

THE BIG HALLOWEEN BASH

The four girls moved to sit in a corner of the living room, with Alicia and Elena joining Tabitha on one couch while Clarissa anxiously took a seat on the adjacent perpendicular one. Several sophomores and juniors from Springton High had arrived that Casey bounced over to talk to, and a few pairs of the youth group boys playing in the room beneath them wandered up the stairs in search of pizza, giving the area a much livelier feel.

"Sooo, why'd you have it out for Tabitha?" Alicia questioned in a catty voice, scowling over at Clarissa. "What'd she ever do to you, huh?"

"She didn't do anything!" Clarissa looked from Alicia to Tabitha with tension in her hunched shoulders. "She just— everyone was saying these things, and I was dumb, and I believed them. I didn't even know you broke your arm for real until afterwards. They were saying like your cast was fake, because it doesn't look like a regular cast. I'm so sorry."

"Fake?!" Alicia demanded. "What, because I drew on it a bit?"

"Uh, it actually looks really pretty!" Clarissa said quickly. "I just thought—uh, we thought that it maybe wasn't..."

"Clarissa," Tabitha took a deep breath, "I appreciate that you're apologizing, and I'm not mad at you. I *am* still feeling very hurt, though. Everything I kept in that binder was important to me—it's a personal project I've been putting a lot of work into. It may seem like I... overreacted, leaving school like that all of the sudden, but I've been under a lot of stress. A lot has been happening, and... having my work stolen on top of everything else just made me feel like I wasn't safe at school anymore."

"No no, you were completely—you didn't overreact at all," Clarissa stammered. "You like, you got your arm broken, you—"

"Fractured her wrist," Elena corrected.

"Right, fractured your wrist, and everyone was being so mean to you, and all the girls were saying just all of these horrible things! You like, didn't overreact at all. I'm so sorry. I wasn't thinking. I didn't even *know* you. They're, uh, they're going to hold me back a year. For what I did. I'm so sorry. I really wish—"

"Holding you back a year?" Alicia laughed, tapping the pilot helmet she set in her lap. "Hah, serves you right!"

"I... don't want you to be held back, Clarissa," Tabitha said, feeling uneasy. "But what you did was very cruel. I need you to understand that."

"I do, I do! What I did was totally messed up, I realize that now," Clarissa said, sounding panicked. "If I could go back and do it all over—I never would. Wish I'd been on your side from the beginning; everyone just—"

If you could go back and do it all over... Tabitha found herself lost in thought at hearing the words and fell into a daze even as Clarissa frantically continued to apologize. *No one else really ever gets to do that. No one but me, I suppose...*

"—Erica Taylor, and then her friends Kaylee and Summer. And, the other sister, uh—Brittney Taylor. They were always saying that you—"

"Clarissa..." Tabitha challenged. "Do you actually think that you and I could be friends?"

The girl froze, shrinking back from Tabitha with a fearful look.

"I'm not saying that to be sarcastic," Tabitha explained. "Or mean. I want you to really think about it. I never wanted any of this to happen. I *don't* want you to be held back a year, and start to resent me for that. All I've ever wanted... was to have a normal high school life, a normal life with lots of friends. That's what I want.

"If you really want to be friends with me—I'd like that. I still feel hurt by what you did, but if you're willing *and we can become friends,* I'd feel a lot better about everything than them holding you back a year for what you did. Them punishing you doesn't help me—I need, um, *friends,* I'm a mess, and I need all the help I can get."

"I *definitely* want to be friends." Clarissa latched on to the idea immediately. "Please, please. If we can—"

"I don't want you to answer right away," Tabitha cautioned, holding her remaining hand up. "I'm serious—I want you to think about this. Not just *react,* or make a decision because you think it'll keep you from getting held back. I'm willing to talk to them about it, but I don't even know if I have a say in anything they decide. If you're just saying things and don't *actually* think that you would in seriousness want to be friends with me—that would end up hurting both of us a lot."

"I want to be friends," Clarissa insisted. "Please—I really mean it."

"Yeah?" Alicia scowled. "Well, there you go; I don't trust her."

"Alicia, shush," Elena said carefully. "I'm... honestly not sure about this either. But, Tabitha—that's a really mature way to look at everything, at all of this. I *do* like that."

It's a lot more mature than I feel, Tabitha thought to herself, rising up off the sofa. *Never thought I'd be so—angry. Bitter. Like, HOW DARE she want forgiveness, after what she did to me. What they all did. I know that's not fair of me. But then, also... I feel guilty too. Because, she DID mess up. And she doesn't get to go back and redo things like I do. Not unless... not unless I personally set aside my griev-ances, and give her that chance.*

Steeling her resolve, Tabitha tossed aside her Flounder plushie and stretched her arms out for a hug.

It was hard to see Clarissa as one of the cruel high school bullies right now. She looked like a terrified teenage girl who'd done something stupid and didn't know what to do about it. The girl nervously stood, stepped forward and awkwardly embraced her. Even though it was a little weird, Tabitha thought she could feel a tiny bit of the *hate* she'd carried with her into this life wick away.

I mean, I already knew Elena was kind of one of the mean girls from Laurel, but... Tabitha thought to herself with a bitter smile. *This feels... good. Better than all those fantasies about GETTING EVEN or making them pay. Feels like—almost like I'm maybe growing out of being the goblin I used to be.*

"I'm so, so sorry," Clarissa said in a small voice.

"I forgive you," Tabitha said, giving her a comforting squeeze and then releasing her. *I really DO forgive her.* "It's okay. Let's just... put it behind us, alright?"

"...Really?" Clarissa gave her a doubtful look. "I mean..."

"On that note... I have to ask." Elena ticked a finger toward Clarissa. "Ginger Spice?"

"Uh, yes. I am." Clarissa shot Elena a thankful look. "For Halloween. This is the Union Jack dress like she wore at the Brit awards last year. I'm, um. I'm a *huge* Spice Girls fan."

"I am too," Elena confided. "Actually a little jealous that I didn't think of doing that for Halloween. My cat idea was super lame; it's just what I had from last year."

"No, no, no," Clarissa said quickly. "You look incredible! I'm not good at creative stuff at all. I just, I already had the dress, and I'm always looking for an excuse to wear it."

Although Alicia continued to look unimpressed, Tabitha felt a strange sort of relief in seeing Elena making an effort to put

Clarissa at ease. The two girls shared *Spice Girls* small talk while they watched Jack Skellington lament over the denizens of Halloween town misunderstanding him, and more and more people showed up for the party. The couch across from them was eventually occupied by a Green Ranger and his girlfriend who was dressed as a traditional witch with a large pointed hat. They also all got their first glimpse of Matthew, who was wearing the iconic *Space Jam* basketball uniform, as more of the group downstairs dispersed in search of other activities.

———

Tabitha wasn't entirely sure how she felt about the Halloween party. It was fun so far, *sort of,* but the enjoyment of sitting here with her friends was offset by her trepidation around all of these other people that she'd never met. While she was a bit curious to walk around and see things, she was even more reluctant to abandon the safe foothold of the living room corner they'd laid claim to. When Alicia shared an uneasy smile with her, Tabitha wanted to giggle, because it was both comforting and vexing seeing that she apparently felt the same way about the situation.

"Oh my Gosh, hey you guys! You all look so great!" Carrie exclaimed with enthusiasm, skipping over toward their couches. "Ugh, *Elena!* You totally stole my idea!"

Tabitha looked up with surprise to see that Carrie was dressed almost exactly like Elena had been when she'd shown up at the trailer yesterday. Black pants and a black long-sleeved shirt, with a cat-ear headband and lackluster whiskers painted on her cheeks. Carrie's chipper smile faltered slightly at seeing that Elena's cat costume now apparently looked a lot better than anticipated.

"Really?" Elena mused, giving Carrie *a look.* "Funny. I was a kitty-cat last year too, though. Remember?"

"Yeah—oh, I guess you were, huh?" Carrie made a teasing face. "Hah, well geez—one of us has to go change now."

"Looks like that'll be you, then," Alicia remarked dryly. "Ours was a group effort—Tabs picked out her new blouse, and I spent a long time doing 'Lena's face paint."

"'Licia helped with the kitty collar too," Elena added, flicking the jingly bell she wore at her throat with one finger.

"Hey, I was just kidding," Carrie snorted. "It's no big deal if we look the same."

"You *don't* look the same, though," Clarissa chimed in, looking from Carrie's costume to Elena's and back again. "Like, at all."

"Why are *you* even here?" Carrie made an ugly face at Clarissa. "Didn't you get expelled? You got caught stealing stuff, or something?"

"She's with us now," Elena said, giving her former friend a chilly look.

"Oh, huh. Well, cool, I guess?" Carrie blinked. "She'll fit right in, hah. Guess I'll catch up with you guys in a bit—I'm gonna go say hi to Matthew, alright?"

"Yeah..." Elena frowned as Carrie strode on past them into the next room. "Alright."

"Sooo—Carrie's definitely *not* with us, right?" Alicia asked, drumming her fingertips on the pilot helmet she held in her lap.

"I guess not." Elena sighed. "Sorry. I was really hoping she'd... I dunno, get over herself, or something."

"She's part of Erica Taylor's posse," Clarissa added. "Like, for sure."

"There's no... *sides*, to this," Tabitha insisted. "Or posses, or cliques, factions, party lines or *whatever*. We're all just teenage girls, okay? This doesn't have to be some big dramatic thing. Some of us can be friends, we don't all *have* to be friends—it doesn't mean someone's *against* us if they don't want to hang out. There's no sides."

"Oh, absolutely!" Alicia agreed, throwing Elena an exaggerated wink. "Right, 'Lena? Definitely no one taking sides. Wouldn't that be silly and childish?"

"Sorry, Tabitha." Elena gave Tabitha a sheepish look. "I *did* try talking with Carrie before, trying to get her to come around. We used to be friends. It's just... Carrie's—"

"No, no—I was being completely serious," Tabitha said in aggravation. "There's no *sides* to this."

"Yeah." Alicia elbowed Tabitha and gave another obnoxious wink. "No one's taking sides—right, guys?"

"*Alicia...*" Tabitha groaned.

"I'm on your guys' side," Clarissa promised. "I swear."

"*Tabitha!* Honey, you're here! I'm so glad you could make it!" Mrs. Williams called out, stepping into the room with a glass of wine in hand and gesturing for someone to follow. "Sandy, Hannah! Look who it is!"

"I *told* you she was here already!" The exasperated seven-year-old Hannah dashed forward, proudly holding up a thick Crayola marker. "We found one! Can I sign?"

"Of course!" Tabitha offered up her left arm.

Hannah hopped up on the couch beside her, tucked her legs beneath her, and popped off the top of the marker so that she could write her name. The expression of *intense focus* the little girl made as she began to draw a small 'H' on Tabitha's cast was precious, and Tabitha couldn't help but smile.

"Tabitha?" Mrs. MacIntire also rounded the corner carrying a glass of wine, and she lit up upon seeing her. "My word, it's so good to see you! Look at you, the Little Mermaid! You look amazing! All of you girls look amazing!"

"Thank you, Mrs. MacIntire," Tabitha said politely, trying not to blush as everyone in the room seemed to look over in her direction. "It's good to see you again. Thank you so much for inviting us!"

The plump Mrs. Williams wore a green and purple medieval gown with a collar and frills, had a dash of lipstick on only the center of her lips, and had her hair brushed up into rather silly-looking bushy piles on top of her head. Mrs. MacIntire, on the other hand, wore her dark hair down and had squeezed her slender figure into a salmon-colored medieval corset dress at least a size too small, worn with a small cape. The tops of her breasts bulged out from her costume, and the woman looked more than a little tipsy.

"This girl saved my husband's life," Mrs. MacIntire boasted, gesturing toward Tabitha with a lift of her wine glass. "She's gonna—they're gonna give her a medal and everything."

"Or at least a special commendation," Mrs. Williams spoke up with a twinkle in her eye. "Maybe not a *medal,* but—"

"No, they're gonna give her a *medal,* or, or I'm gonna throw a fit!" Mrs. MacIntire chuckled softly, taking a quick sip from her glass. "They're gonna throw a big ceremony in her honor, soon as my hubby's transferred back here to Springton."

"I just did what anyone would have done," Tabitha said with a guilty look, quickly turning to Alicia. "Alicia was there too—she helped."

"No, no, no!" Alicia held up her hands. "I mostly just stood there like an idiot."

"You helped talk with the dispatcher!" Tabitha persisted.

"Tabitha did everything. I was just useless," Alicia denied involvement. "I had no idea what to do—I was just standing there, bawling my eyes out."

"Alicia Brooks—I remember you from the news clip." Mrs. MacIntire stepped in to give her a small hug with her free hand. "Thank you for being there. I didn't know what to do either, for *days.* I was just, I was just in complete shock. Don't any of you girls ever marry a policeman!"

"Don't ever marry a policeman," Mrs. Williams agreed, taking another generous sip of wine. "Whenever any trouble happens, that's right where they have to be. It's the worst!"

"It is." Mrs. MacIntire nodded. "It's all just—they're the worst."

"...How much wine have you ladies had tonight?" Tabitha asked.

"Oh, would you like some?" Mrs. Williams beamed at her with rosy cheeks. "We can fetch you a glass. It's non-alcoholic! Practically."

"*Practically!*" Mrs. MacIntire let out a giggle.

"I'll... think about it," Tabitha said with a polite smile. "Thank you."

"So, I've heard through the grapevine that you're taking a breather from school," Mrs. Williams said. "How have things been? We've all been worried sick about you. Are you going to that expulsion hearing tomorrow?"

"I am." Tabitha paused, feeling her shoulders go stiff. "I think... I'm going to request that the school board to be as lenient as possible. To everyone. I don't like that they'd all get in such serious trouble because of me."

The two adult women exchanged glances, and Mrs. Williams took another hearty swig of wine while Mrs. MacIntire scoffed.

"That's real sweet of you," Mrs. MacIntire said cautiously. "But, me? I hope they get the book thrown at them! Especially that quarterback boy—there's no justifying what he did, not no way, no how."

"Running back boy," Mrs. Williams corrected.

"I don't give a damn what he was, he's *a violent criminal.*" Mrs. MacIntire shook her head in consternation and quickly downed the rest of her wine glass. "It's all fine and dandy if he wants to break some boy's bones *playing football,* but—"

"*Running back,* Sandy." Mrs. Williams rolled her eyes in exasperation. "He run run runs, he runs away from the big scary bone-breaking. From what I heard, he even tried to skedaddle away after pushing poor Tabitha."

"Rotten little fucking *weasel,*" Mrs. MacIntire spat fiercely. "They should break *his* fucking—"

"Sandy!" Mrs. Williams cut in, giving her friend a gentle slap on the arm. "Sorry, girls—the situation's just so upsetting, and the *Verona* has *loosened* her *lips!* We just wanted to say that we're both gonna be at the hearing tomorrow, and we'll make sure everyone gets just what's coming to them!"

"And *then some,*" Mrs. MacIntire growled.

"Yes, yes, and then some," Mrs. Williams promised, taking another sip. "Oh, Miss Clarissa—I didn't see you there. I hope you're behaving yourself tonight?"

"...Yes, ma'am," Clarissa said in a quiet voice, having gone very, very still while the two women talked.

"Good, good!" Mrs. Williams had a meaningful gleam in her eye for a moment. "Well, we'll get out of your hair. Come along, Hannah honey. There's all sorts of snacks and pizza and soda in the other room; you girls just help yourselves, of course. Feel free to roam around! There's ping pong downstairs."

"We will," Tabitha promised. "Thank you."

"I'm all done," Hannah reported, wiping imaginary sweat from her brow with the back of her hand in a charming little gesture. "Phew!"

HANNAH MACINTIRE was spelled out in somewhat crooked letters, with part of her last name passing through several of the lines Alicia had drawn because it wouldn't fit without writing over them.

"Good job, Hannah!" Tabitha praised.

"Thanks!" Hannah said with a proud grin, sliding off the couch and running back over to return the borrowed marker to Mrs. Williams.

"Oh—by any chance, did you recognize our costumes?" Mrs. William asked, striking a dainty pose.

"You're the Sanderson sisters?" Alicia blurted out with a grin. "From *Hocus Pocus?*"

"*Thank you.*" Mrs. William laughed, stamping her foot. "Finally, *someone* gets it! Almost makes it worth putting up my stupid hair like this. Alright, girls. Have fun!"

"Hey, Tabby." Carrie trotted over. "Can I see you alone for a sec?"

"What is it?" Tabitha asked.

"It's nothing major." Carrie smiled. "Someone just wants to talk to you, out on the porch."

"Who?" Elena asked with a suspicious scowl, crossing her arms.

"Just someone, okay?" Carrie snorted. "Don't be all nosy. It'll only take a minute."

"...Who is it?" Tabitha asked.

She exchanged glances with Elena, and Clarissa took that as her cue to hop up and step over toward the nearest window, where she could peek out at an angle to see the rest of the lake house's wraparound porch.

"Just someone," Carrie repeated with a shrug. "It's not a huge deal. Can you come talk to them, or not?"

"Uhhh, *are you out of your fucking mind?*" Clarissa called over. "Erica Taylor's out there. With a *fucking baseball bat.*"

"Just someone, huh?" Elena gave Carrie an incredulous look. "*What the fuck,* Carrie?"

"Fucking *waaah,*" Carrie sneered. "Knew you'd pussy out if I told you who it was. Jesus Christ, chill. She just wants to apologize to Tabitha. Alone."

"Apologize to her *with a baseball bat?*" Clarissa hissed. "Carrie, what the fu—"

"It's not a bat, it's a *Louisville Slugger.* Hello? S'part of her costume, dorks." Carrie rolled her eyes. "She's not gonna friggin' *attack* you with it. Look, see? She's a Cardinals player for Halloween, duh. Go fucking talk to her already. God damn, all of you are such pussies."

"Yeah, right!" Clarissa said angrily. "Look at how pissed she looks. Don't go out there, Tabitha."

"Of course she's pissed," Carrie muttered. "She's got *reason* to be pissed."

"Reason? Such as?" Elena arched an eyebrow. "What reason, Carrie?"

"All this bullshit she's going through with Tabitha." Carrie waved a hand dismissively and gave Tabitha a slight smirk. "Are you gonna go talk to her like a grown up, or do I go tell her you're too much of a pussy?"

"Quit saying *pussy*—what are you, twelve?" Elena shook her head. "Tabitha's just fine where she is. If someone wants to discuss anything, she can come in here where we are."

"She wants to talk to her alone," Carrie looked at Elena as if she was an idiot. "Like, *privately.*"

"Yeah, I bet she does," Elena rebuked. "But we don't always get what we want, do we? She can apologize with all of us in here, or she can piss off."

"Hah, *okay,*" Carrie said with a sarcastic laugh, heading back outside to tell Erica. "Whatever, pussy. *Pussies.* Hide out in here all you want, see what happens."

Tabitha stood up and took a hesitant step forward, feeling her body start to go stiff with tension.

"No," Elena said in firm refusal. "No, you're not going out there. If Erica wants to talk, then she can—"

The French doors opened and Erica Taylor stepped inside, stalking forward with a glare locked directly on Tabitha.

She hadn't been reacquainted with any of the Taylor girls since coming back to this life, and didn't quite recognize the teenager, beyond feeling there was something vaguely familiar about the set of her eyes and cant of her nose. Erica had dark brown hair pulled into a ponytail beneath a Cardinals cap, worn with a matching jersey but with white jeans in lieu of baseball pants. A wooden bat was held in hand, and the only other thing anyone would glean from this first new impression was that Erica Taylor's posture, demeanor, and expression were all *extremely fucking hostile.*

This... is bad, Tabitha thought, feeling her heart race. *REALLY bad.*

"What the fuck... is wrong with you?" Erica asked in quiet, vicious voice.

"...Excuse me?" Tabitha managed to say.

Tabitha couldn't imagine how it was even possible, but Erica Taylor was already worked up somehow into a simmering rage, and it was *visibly* clear that her fury was about to boil over and spill out in a horrible way. The taller girl's chest was quickly rising and falling, her nostrils were flaring, and her pupils were dilated, seeming to tremble with whatever scarcely-contained insanity had driven her here. The Louisville Slugger wasn't casually held at her side—it was held low and very still. Like a weapon.

"What the fuck. *Ever.* Gave you the right. To take things from us?" Erica bit out, speaking with gnashes of her teeth and clenches of her jaw.

"I haven't taken anything from you," Tabitha protested, feeling panic starting to rise up from within her. *TAKE things?*

"You didn't fucking take anything from me?!" Erica bared her teeth, her face twisting with hatred.

Erica Taylor stalked forward a step, and the slugger in her hand wavered as the girl wrung the handle in a white-knuckled grip. Although Tabitha wasn't by herself—she didn't even want to imagine being trapped alone in a room with Erica right now—both Alicia and Elena seemed to be frozen with fear, and the other random people throughout the room seemed to be stunned into silence. Clarissa had been lingering nervously at the edge of the room, and Tabitha heard her scurry out of the room, running out and abandoning them.

Not abandoning—she's probably getting one of the adults, Tabitha realized, fighting the urge to not simply bolt herself. *She'll be back with help. I hope.*

"First, it was my makeup," Erica hissed. "Then, Brittney's makeup. Then, it was our *shoes.* My Spanish book. My *favorite fucking jeans.* Brittney's new headphones. The Vera Bradley bag that I got for Christmas—how much did you get for that one? My fucking *shampoo*. Who *the fuck* steals *shampoo?* Peefy Poofy. We had Peefy Poofy since I was like, two fucking years old, and you took him away from me? *For WHAT? WHY?* He was a fucking *stuffed animal;* he wasn't worth anything to anyone but me. But you took him anyways."

What... is she TALKING about?! Tabitha found herself completely bewildered. *Is she—is she bipolar? On drugs?! This is, it's crazy, she's... she needs to calm down, someone needs to calm her down from whatever this is. We can't talk like this. Can we not do this?*

"Ashlee always making excuses for you. Guess what? *IT'S. NOT. EVER. OKAY. TO. TAKE. THINGS. FROM. US.* Don't care how fucking poor you are, or if you're fucking starving—or if your whole fucking trailer trash family's starving to death because you're so fucking poor. You don't get to just *take* things from us, you trailer trash fucking *goblin.*"

"Erica—" Elena started.

"Shut the fuck up and stay out of this," Erica snarled with a vehement glare. *"Fucking. Stay out of it!"*

Oh, no, Tabitha realized in horror as she finally put it all together. *Oh, Ashlee—Ashlee, what have you done?*

There weren't many things she could remember from her childhood, but what Tabitha *did* remember was that both her and Ashlee had been terrified of the older Taylor sisters. She remembered feeling small and helpless all too clearly.

Ashlee was terrified, Tabitha swallowed uneasily. *She was so much smaller, she didn't have any way to fight back. Not in person. But, when they're gone, how easy would it be for Ashlee to exact every little petty revenge? To take and hide their things, or throw them out?*

I was easy to blame. Of course I was—I wasn't there for her anymore. I abandoned her because I was afraid. Then she blamed me for stealing their things, because she was afraid.

What a pair of friends we are.

"And now?" Erica panted with unbridled fury. "NOW—*YOU THINK YOU CAN FUCKING TAKE OUR SISTER AWAY FROM US?"*

They found bruises on Ashlee, then. Tabitha flinched, feeling her throat go dry. *They found bruises, and then of course they separ—*

Erica exploded into violence.

The Louisville Slugger swung at Tabitha so fast that it cut a hissing arc through the air, and out of pure trembling reflex, Tabitha managed to shift into a back stance. She even attempted a Taekwondo block to prevent the wooden bat from slamming into the side of her head—all too late realizing that that actually put her *already-injured hand* right into harm's way. Blinding, white-hot shards of agony jolted up her arm the instant the Louisville Slugger cracked into the blue cast.

Oh no, no, no, stupid you don't TRY TO BLOCK A BAT, her mind raced, but Erica Taylor was already swinging again, and all Tabitha could think to do was backpedal and attempt to keep her arms up in front of her face.

Someone behind her was screaming, *shrieking,* really, and Tabitha was momentarily blinded with pain as the second strike glanced off of her fingertips, again clipping her left hand with the cast. Terrified that they were broken—surely *everything* was broken now—Tabitha continued to stumble backwards, this time tucking her left hand, or whatever was left of it, in close against her chin. Recoiling from the assault in a panic, her back foot encountered the edge of some piece of furniture—she couldn't recall where the couches behind her were positioned anymore, and she lost her balance, unable to retreat.

When the next swing crashed into the side of her head, Tabitha didn't feel anything at all. She simply watched the room spin wildly in a distant, somewhat detached daze. The Green Ranger who'd been sitting across from them had apparently leapt off of his couch and rushed to intercept Erica, but it was already far, far too late to make a difference. Tabitha fell, and her face pressed into a floor. The plush carpet immediately flecked with tiny little beads of blood, and Tabitha fought to wake up enough to remember why that was *a very bad thing* as those spots of blood swimming into and out of focus quickly began to multiply.

There was pain.

It was hard to tell how bad it was, however, with how dizzy and disjointed everything felt, how *wrong* the sensation was. Tabitha let out a single choked sputter, and there was more blood now. Her eyes were watering too much now to keep them open, and she simply squeezed them shut and tried her very best not to exist. The intense, debilitating hurt manifested as a steadily growing *pressure,* as if her head was pinned in place there on the floor by the crushing force of some steel beam.

Her last thought, as her consciousness slipped off into darkness and she fainted was that *she understood.* She understood what had happened, now—why the girls had bullied her—and even though she already knew that it wasn't fair, she wanted another try anyway. *Just one more try.*

Then the bleed on her brain opened up, and all Tabitha Moore could hear was that familiar annoying *whirring* resonation sound of the MRI.

———

Casey was halfway down the stairs to the rec room again with a cheap plastic cup in hand when she heard the screaming. Screaming, and then shouting—the thumps of something being struck, and then *breaking glass* and more screaming. The shrill pitch of some of the shrieking sounded like it was coming from *Hannah,* so Casey hastily turned and dashed back up the landing to see what the hell was going on up there, covering the top of her drink with one hand so soda wouldn't slop everywhere.

It was a scene of utter mayhem.

Everyone seemed to be arriving all at once to see Officer Williams squatting over a screaming teenage girl, with a knee pinning her shoulder to the ground and one hand violently shoving the girl's skull to the floor. Michael was standing beside them, his girlfriend Olivia fretting over a cut on his arm that had ripped his flimsy Green Ranger costume. It was clear that Michael or *someone* had taken Erica Taylor down in some sort of running tackle, that they'd crashed partway into a nearby entertainment center, breaking one of the glass panels that protected an expensive sound system.

Oh—oh my God. What the fuck did she DO?!

The scene *should* have looked silly, because Matthew's dad had chosen to wear a cheap policeman costume for the Halloween party. It had been hilarious to see earlier, with Mr. Williams in a parody facsimile of his normal uniform—but right now, he looked like a one hundred percent deadly serious, extremely pissed-off cop. Beneath him, Erica Taylor was shrieking incoherently and flailing her limbs, trying to buck the stocky and much larger police officer off of her.

What the fuck.

"—beamed her in the head, she's completely out cold. She won't stop bleeding, and—"

"—phone to call 911? I think she's—"

"—Tabitha? Tabitha can you hear me?—"

"—biiithaaa, noooooo!! *Taabbiithaaaa*—"

"—my keys, I'll get her to the hospital right away—"

"Shut up, *everyone shut up!*" Officer Williams roared, and for a brief moment, everyone fell silent but the screaming Erica Taylor and the wailing little girl Hannah. "Hun, you've been drinking, you're not driving anywhere. Where's Matthew?! Sandy—dammit, take Hannah upstairs, get her out of here!"

"I'm here!" Matthew called out, only now just bounding up the stairs. "What the—"

"Get over here, *now,*" Officer Williams commanded. "Hold her to the fucking floor and *keep her there.* Tabitha's hurt."

Tabitha's hurt? Oh—OH SHIT.

It was difficult to notice at first because so many people were standing around staring, but she realized in shock and horror Tabitha was sprawled and unmoving in front of one the couches, with both Elena and Alicia crouched over her. The redhead's left arm was splayed out across the floor, and the orthopedic cast was broken along the side, with tufts of white bandage visible through a split in the fiberglass. There were drips and smears of blood all over the floor, and a smudged baseball bat rolled away as Alicia unknowingly kicked it backwards with her costume boot.

Jesus Christ!

"Yeah. Uh. Where is Ta—" Matthew trailed off, following everyone's line of sight to stare in alarm at the frail-looking unconscious girl. Clarissa brushed past him with the entire napkin-holder from the kitchen, frantically pulling out one napkin after another and passing them over to Elena.

"Do we call 911?" Mrs. Williams stammered. "Or drive her to the hospital ourselves? Rob, a goddamned ambulance'll take half an hour *just to get out here,* and—"

"Let me take a look," her husband grunted, scowling momentarily as Matthew took over pinning Erica Taylor to the floor. The teenage girl was sobbing, but she continued to wildly scream and thrash. "You're never supposed to move someone with head trauma."

"Her nose is bleeding," Alicia reported in a shaky voice. "It-it won't stop bleeding."

"Give me some space." Officer Williams motioned everyone aside and knelt down over Tabitha and began to quickly examine her.

"—even happened? I thought Erica Taylor got suspended, so why is she even—"

"—raving all crazy, she starts *hitting Tabitha with a bat,* so Michael *tackles* her—"

"*Are we fucking calling 911 or not?*" Mrs. Williams yelled.

"No. We need to take her in now," Officer Williams said, frowning. "Someone get a car started."

"I'm on it," Casey said, hurriedly planting her cup on a nearby surface and already shucking off the restrictive wedding dress.

"H-how bad is it?" Mrs. Williams demanded. "How bad is—"

"Severe head trauma—out cold, steady nosebleed," Officer Williams swore under his breath. "She's got one giant pupil and one tiny one—there's a good chance she's hemorrhaging. We need to get her to the emergency room, *now*. Did I see one of you park a Chevy Blazer?"

"That's me!" Casey called over. "Well, uh, I've got a Jimmy. I'll go get her started."

"—okay to move her if she's concussed? I mean, I heard when there's any sort of—"

"—out of nowhere, this bitch completely flipped out, went totally *ballistic*—"

"—or, or maybe use the folding cot downstairs as a medevac litter? If it's not safe to—"

"—Hannah honey, calm down, calm down. Everything's going to be okay, sh-she's—"

With everyone talking over each other, they all seemed too preoccupied to notice that Casey hadn't worn a shirt or a bra beneath the bridal gown costume. Silently cursing to herself, she scrambled to the French doors, stealing Matthew's familiar Wildcats hoodie from the coats hanging there. She awkwardly shrugged it on, scrambling out the door and then taking the porch steps down two at a time. Icy terror was blossoming in her gut as she fumbled to dig her keys out of the track pants she'd been wearing as part of her outfit.

Psycho actually showed up and attacked Tabby WHILE EVERYONE WAS HERE? Casey was off the porch at a dead run, her Nikes crunching across the gravel toward her parked Jimmy. *What the fuck, what the fuck, what the fuck. Who THE FUCK even let Erica Taylor in?*

Her 1992 GMC Jimmy was a midsize SUV—garnet-red, angular, a little boxy-looking, and always altogether beautiful to her. As a sixteen-year-old junior, she absolutely adored her Jimmy with its angel wings decal adorning the tailgate window. It was an extension of herself, the vehicle was the freedom and power to get around anywhere and everywhere she wanted to go. Right now, it would hopefully get Tabitha to some medical attention in time to make a difference. Casey frantically unlocked the door, yanked it open, and jumped inside.

"C'mon, baby, c'mon—you can do it, girl," Casey pleaded as she tried the ignition. The startup grumble sound the engine made was... not good, but probably still okay. She *did* take good care of her vehicle, but some persistent problem with the distributor kept the *check engine* light on no matter what work she had done on it. After a nervous moment or two, the engine obediently purred into a steady rumble.

"That's my girl!" Casey whispered proudly, patting a hand on top of the dash. "C'mon, baby, let's go!"

When she pulled around to idle in front of the lake house, Matthew was already stepping outside onto the veranda, cradling Tabitha's slight figure in a princess carry. Mrs. Williams, Elena, and Alicia were all following him down the steps, and Casey nervously toggled the automatic locks to make sure that they'd be able to open the Jimmy's doors without any delays.

"—over around to the other side, help me get her in—"

"—to call her parents? Do you need me to call *your*—"

"—nose still won't stop bleeding. Gimme all of those; I'll sit with—"

"—squad car isn't here, so there's no safe place to lock her up—"

"Get in, get in," Casey urged, the moment they had one of the rear doors open. "Shove everything anywhere. *Hurry up.*"

"I'm gonna ride with Matthew's dad. We'll be right behind you," Alicia said, pushing Elena forward. "He's gonna have Erica Taylor with him. I want to see her fucking locked up."

"Are you sure? It's—"

"Go, just *go*." Alicia's voice broke, and she shoved her again. "Take care of her. Fuck."

"Is Tabitha okay?" Mrs. MacIntire was climbing unsteadily down the porch stairs after them. "Is she—"

"Climb up in with Tabitha," Mrs. Williams told Matthew, her features taut with tension and wet with tears. "Try to keep her upright while you—yeah. Hold her head. Okay. Okay, like that."

Casey impatiently tapped the driver's wheel, twisting in her seat to watch. The Jimmy rocked slightly as three people climbed in, managing to ease Tabitha into position on the rear bench. The girl was situated across both Matthew and Elena, with Elena holding Tabitha's head and gently blotting the girl's bleeding nose with a handful of napkins. Mrs. Williams opened the passenger-side door and got in, immediately turning to see how they were doing.

"We've got her," Matthew said, hunched over and securing Tabitha to ensure she wasn't jostled too severely. "We're in—go, let's go."

"Be careful," Mrs. MacIntire sobbed, slapping a hand on the window. "Drive safe. Please be okay, Tabitha, *please*—"

Casey eased her foot down on the gas pedal and the Jimmy steadily accelerated away, roaring down the hedge-lined driveway and off into the night.

26

NO WAY FORWARD AND NO WAY BACK

A terrible *screeching* sounded out from the prototype MRI machine in the Emsie St. Juarez Pediatrics ward. The volume of the discordant squeal rose in both pitch and volume until it was an atrocious shriek, physically painful to hear, before muting with an unsettling *pop* as the electrical breaker finally blew out. All of the passersby within a several block vicinity of the facility cringed, many with their hands subconsciously rising up in a gesture to protect their ears—and then the power went out across all of Jefferson county.

Thirteen-year-old Tabitha Moore lay silent and completely still within the device when the backup power came online within the MRI room. A wispy blanket of acrid black smoke poured out of the enormous prototype contraption, and immediately choked the now very warm room—the fire alarm went off a moment later. The intense pain of Tabitha's sudden head trauma had only just begun to subside, and it felt like she'd been staring in a daze at blood droplets dappling the floor of the Williams family lake house only moments ago. Staring now in disbelief at her own now too-plump hands, Tabitha Moore sagged beneath an anguished, horrifying sense of *loss*.

She was back to the beginning all over again.

No—oh no, no, NO! Tabitha sobbed, quaking within the hospital gown she found herself caught in. *No. No. No, no, no. Oh God please, no. You can't—you can't take all of that away from me. I can't do this again. You can't take all of them away from me. YOU CAN'T.*

"Jesus *fricking* Christ!" The door across the copper-lined wall shielding of the room burst open and a technician rushed in, followed by a furious Mr. Moore. Tabitha's ears still rung from the otherworldly clamor of the MRI going berserk, but she still heard her father yelling the same exact words as last time. *"You get her the frick out of there!"*

Every unwelcome sight her teary eyes took in confirmed the worst. The blue orthopedic cast with Alicia's artwork on it—with her close friends signatures on it—had vanished like it never existed at all, revealing a pudgy but unbroken wrist and hand. Gone too were the lean, graceful muscles she'd honed over the summer, her hard-earned trim physique now once again just soft, doughy fat. It was the least of her worries now, but it *still* took all the self-control she could muster to not frantically claw and tear at the excess rolls of blubber with her nails.

I-I can't. I can't. I-I can't DO this again!

Several figures pushed through the swirl of smoke and managed to pull the sliding examination table out of the enormous cylindrical aperture of the prototype MRI. It was unbearably hot now, and to her horror, in the waning light of the smoke-filled room Tabitha discovered that her fingers now appeared *bloated*, looking like stumpy-looking sausage appendages.

In fact, she felt grotesquely swollen all over, her tissues... expanded, like a marshmallow microwaved for too long. Terror took over. Her breath hitched into tiny, useless gasps for air as she began to hyperventilate, and as the people were trying to help sit her up, she realized her entire body was now shrunken, *misshapen*, her center of gravity agreeing that something was terribly wrong with her.

Eyes stinging with tears, Tabitha looked up into the worried face of her father, and quietly began to have a nervous breakdown.

———

There was little for her to say on the trip back home, and much of it passed by Tabitha in a blur. Her existence had only been rolled back by six months this time, but the *significance* of each of those lost moments took a heavier toll than losing the forty-seven years had before. She was shell-shocked and completely disconsolate, and none of her father's increasingly concerned questions or strained assurances could penetrate through the raw trauma of the ordeal. Tabitha shrank over against the passenger door, curled up her loathsome portly body as much as she was able, and wept quietly into her hands for the entire ride.

After they arrived back in Sunset Estate's Lower Park, Mr. Moore parked his truck and then got out, crossing around the vehicle to pull open Tabitha's door and envelop her in a hug. She discovered she was still just *full* of more tears to cry, and she did, sobbing and wailing while she hid her face against his shoulder just in front of their mobile home. The sun was setting by the time she calmed down, but she was reluctant to follow him inside.

It was bad.

The interior of the trailer was the same awful mess it had been the last time; the carpet was dark and greasy, dirty dishes were abandoned everywhere, the air was so stagnant and thick with body odor, it was stifling, and it was *dark*. The windows were once again all covered, all offending outside light smothered out with the blankets Mrs. Moore had tacked up over them. Not only did Tabitha have no motivation to clean everything up all over again

—the feeling of being trapped in here again nearly worked herself up into another crying fit.

Already trapped in this repulsive fucking body again, Tabitha thought, glaring down her fat arm at the hand with its chubby digits with a scowl. *Least my wrist's not fractured anymore. Just... it's so hard to even feel positive about that. And... my head is still pounding. Was my head hurting THIS much from the trampoline fall last time?*

Mrs. Moore looked fifteen pounds heavier than Tabitha remembered, the first obvious indication she'd seen that the future Shannon Moore *had* gradually been losing weight up through Halloween. *Not that it fucking matters now.* Even more so than a bit heavier and dumpier-looking, her mother looked resigned; defeated. The unattractive frown lines in her face just beginning to droop into jowls, and her eyes were dead and uncaring.

It's... it's not fair. The gripping sadness Tabitha felt at seeing her mother back like this again was unbearable, a melancholy so intense that it staggered her, and she forced herself to hurry past Mrs. Moore. *Things were so different. Everything was getting so much better. I'm—I'm gonna lose it. I'm losing it. I can't do this again.*

––––––

Dinner was baked beans and toasted bread.

"Hope you've learned yer lesson 'bout those trampoline jumpers." Mrs. Moore shook her head in dismay. "Yer lucky you didn't break yer neck."

"Yes, Momma." Tabitha nodded, not daring to meet her mother's eyes.

"Hmph." Mrs. Moore let out a disapproving snort and then continued to noisily fork baked beans into her mouth.

Somewhere, buried deep beneath the fatty tissue of this TRAILER TRASH awful HAG of a woman... is a former model and aspiring actress, Tabitha thought. It was difficult to believe. *How did she come TO THIS? Is it like a role she assumed and just kind of lost herself in? Is any of this FEIGNED? Or, is this just the real Shannon Moore, when you've stripped away all of her hopes and dreams, when she's fallen far, far past caring about anything or anyone?*

The prospect was a little sickening, and Tabitha tried not to think about what must have happened to Shannon Moore all those years ago on the film set of *Lucas.* She honestly didn't ever want to think about that, or think about *anything,* right now. A migraine was continuing to grip her head in a phantom vise, and she was completely burnt out, emotionally exhausted from all of the recent misery. Rather than thinking or speaking, Tabitha carefully ate her portion of baked beans.

Each forkful she removed from her helping, however, revealed a familiar cream-colored plate with a pink floral motif—the very same one her father had angrily dashed into a wall what felt like some months ago. The recognition brought her nausea back in full force, and she shoved the plate back from her place at the table and made an awkward run down the hallway toward the toilet to throw up.

I—don't want to do this again, Tabitha thought as she hurled. *I REALLY don't want to do this all again.*

"Tabitha sweetie?" her father called over. "You okay?"

"I threw up," Tabitha reported in a hoarse voice, stumbling toward the sink with her gaze averted. She *refused* to see her reflection in the bathroom mirror right now.

"You threw up? Are you okay?"

"...I threw up," Tabitha repeated in frustration, dabbing water from the faucet across her face and then reaching for her toothbrush. "I'm okay. I just threw up. I don't feel good."

"Well... alright, sweetie." Her father sounded unsure. "You finishing yer dinner?"

Tabitha accidentally looked up into the mirror, and a teary-eyed overweight *goblin* of a little girl glared back at her. It wasn't a face she *ever* wanted to see again, and it took some presence of mind to keep her trembling hands from reaching up and clawing at her fleshy cheeks in dismay. She *hated* seeing this overweight face again, hated it, *HATED IT.*

"*No,*" Tabitha all but snarled out in anger. "I'm not finishing my dinner."

———

Rather than beg off attendance like she had the previous time, Tabitha decided to just go to school the day after her MRI. After all, she was certainly in no hurry to bend over backwards cleaning house all over again. Instead, she got dressed, disinterestedly chewed her way through a bowl of slightly stale, generic-brand Apple Jacks—without milk. The Moore family didn't seem to keep milk stocked in the fridge—and then shuffled off to the bus stop in her grotesque, fat little body. When it arrived, she climbed aboard, unnoticed and ignored by the other middle-schoolers.

How many times am I going to go through this... this fucking FARCE? Tabitha wondered. Her mental state was deteriorating to begin with, and her spirit flagged further as she watched the morning scenery crawl by outside the bus window. The first time she'd left a life behind, Tabitha had been sixty years old—she'd had acquaintances rather than actual *friends,* and she didn't leave behind anyone she was terribly attached to like a pet or a significant other.

This time, the friendships she'd fostered with Alicia and Elena had been painfully torn away from her, as if those experiences never existed. Losing them made her heart *ache* in ways she would never be able to put into words. The difficulties and happenstance she'd gone through getting close to her mother weren't something she thought she could duplicate naturally either, and picking apart their complicated relationship with what she knew now felt... wrong.

I'm... not going to make it, am I? Tabitha thought with a bitter grimace, resting her forehead on the back of the bus seat in front of her. *If this THING I'm caught up in is going to repeat itself over and over, if it's some kind of time loop... I'm not gonna make it. All the fore-knowledge and experience in the world won't spare me from severe clinical depression. Maybe SOMEONE could become hardened enough, jaded or DETACHED enough to cope with all of this—but it won't be ME. Isn't all of this mess way, WAY fucking worse than where I started from last time?*

Her mood continued to plummet upon arriving at Laurel Middle School, and after climbing down off the bus, her unenthusiastic shuffle became totally discouraged plodding. Middle school. *Middle school.* Tabitha slowly picked her way toward the portable where Mrs. Hodge taught Language Arts—by first bell, the other students passing by made her feel like a squat stone stuck in the flow of a lively stream. When she stepped up into the classroom this time, however, she recognized several faces.

An eighth-grade Elena Seelbaugh turned a derisive glance away from her when Tabitha looked over. The blonde teen instead leaned over to whisper something to her friend... Carrie.

Tabitha *knew* it wasn't rational to expect anything else from the situation, but the raw *hurt* that dropped on her was a crushing weight upon her psyche, and then the feeling of betrayal all but buried her. Clenching her teeth and blinking back tears, Tabitha waddled the overweight, *rotund* body *she detested more than anything* over to her assigned seat and climbed into it, gripping the edge of the desk and trying to rein in her emotions.

It was impossible.

Anger and shame rolled over her like waves, crashing again and again into jagged *despair* and sending up the tumultuous surf and spray of agony. Tabitha hadn't quite taken a moment to dwell on the implications of her current situation until now, but she was increasingly sure that she'd been violently murdered by Erica Taylor at the Halloween party. *Violently murdered.* What felt like yesterday to her. The sheer shock and horror of it all weren't something she felt equipped to cope with.

Are lives really so... fragile? A really good hit to the temple with a baseball bat, and it's just... OVER? Just like that? It's suddenly all over? It certainly seemed logical, but she found herself in disbelief and denial all the same. *Hell—I wish it really WAS over. I'd rather it all be over than live through it all a THIRD FUCKING TIME.*

"Good morning, everyone," Mrs. Hodge called out. "After announcements and pledge of allegiance, we're going through the last parts of our review section, and then I'm going to be giving out a Language Arts practice test. The practice test *doesn't* count toward your grade, but it *does* include all the material that'll be on the actual final, so I want you to please take it seriously. Some of you boys still have homework you haven't turned in, so—"

And CARRIE! Tabitha fumed, unable to bring herself to care about eighth grade Language Arts. *Carrie tried to lure me out of the party, to where I'd be alone with Erica! She HAD to have known what Erica was going to do!*

The shock of returning back to May of 1998 again had occupied her until now, but when morning announcements came on over the school intercom, Tabitha was playing the Halloween party back over again in her head.

It should have been safe—the party was SUPPOSED to be a safe place to meet Erica, Tabitha scowled. *A lot of people were there. Officer Williams was there, there was ADULT PRESENCE at the party, even if they were mostly hanging out over in the kitchen and away from us kids. Erica SHOULDN'T have attacked me.*

Frustrated, Tabitha struggled out of her seat to stand for the pledge of allegiance, but she didn't recite the words along with everyone else, or even glance toward the flag.

But... she DID attack me. Assault me. Physically—with a WEAPON, even. Tabitha frowned. It hadn't been expected. Erica had been characterized as petty and vindictive, but always clever, always one to *kill with a borrowed knife,* so to speak. Erica fueled rumors and set others against her, but she never used her own hand, never acted *directly*.

Wait. That's not entirely true. Tabitha's frown deepened. *She DID push me off the trampoline. Either her or her sister did? Damn— wish I could remember more.*

After working the events over in her mind for most of Mrs. Hodge's review session, the only conclusion Tabitha could arrive at... was that there was something serious going on within the Taylor family. Pushing her off the trampoline and threatening her had been done with the intention of separating her from Ashlee—and, they'd been *successful* at that. In her original life, Tabitha never tried to meet up with or hang out with Ashlee again. By the time of her next iteration, she'd barely even remembered the girl, choosing instead to put the uncomfortable situation completely out of her mind and focus on other tasks.

But they kept on bullying me at Springton High, and no one could really figure out WHY, Tabitha thought, her splitting headache only further dampening her already foul mood. *So, when I point Mrs. Cribb in the Taylors' direction, they of course find the bruises all over Ashlee. Since no one was keen on keeping me in the loop, I only have Erica's words to go on—something about me taking Ashlee away from them. But, who actually got involved—who did Mrs. Cribb make that call to?*

Did she contact a social worker associated with her Springton School District stuff, or some small-town branch of child protective services? Tabitha wondered. *Is there a DIFFERENCE, back here in 1998?*

In the future, she'd been on friendly terms with a very put-together woman named Mrs. Bethany at the Springton town hall, who managed those various local programs. Tabitha didn't know who—if anyone—was assigned to that equivalent role back here in this time period. Just like the specifications of safety harnesses at the production plant, every little protocol and bylaw government offices dealt with changed all the time, in seemingly asinine little bureaucratic ways.

If Mrs. Cribb had called the police, Officer Williams would've— or should've—probably had an inkling about Erica having this potentially dangerous reaction. Right? Instead, from what Elena mentioned the night before, and from that look Mrs. Williams gave Clarissa... it's like they were expecting Erica to be... to be cowed, to be eager to apologize, to try and absolve herself of blame before the expulsion hearing.

Which OBVIOUSLY was not the case. Tabitha grimaced. It was getting hard to concentrate with the way her head was pounding. *If Erica had—*

Drops of blood pitter-pattered down upon the print-out of the practice test in front of her. Tabitha froze, staring at them for a long moment, and then touched a hand to her face to discover her nose was bleeding.

What the—? Tabitha stared at her bloody hand in confusion, then cupped it beneath her face to try to catch the flow of red already dripping down her chin. *This didn't happen last time. What did I do differently?*

"Uhhh, Mrs. Hodge?" Elena's hand shot up, interrupting the silence within the classroom. "Tabby's *bleeding!*"

"Oh, *ew!*" someone nearby exclaimed.

"Tabitha?" Mrs. Hodge hurried down the aisle of desks toward her. "Tabitha—are you alright?"

Tabitha glanced up at Mrs. Hodge's concerned expression in a daze, and then over to Elena. For a brief, fleeting moment, it felt like Elena spoke up because she'd been watching her—keeping an eye on her because she cared, because that's what friends did. The blonde didn't look worried about her at all, however. Instead, Elena wore an incredulous look of disgust, and then turned again to share a smirking grin with Carrie and her other middle school friends.

"Um... no," Tabitha finally said, feeling her eyes water as blood filled her palm and then began dotting across her shirt. "*No.* I am not alright."

———

"Momma?" Tabitha asked. "Momma, can I talk to you?"

"What do you want, Tabby?" Mrs. Moore asked with an aggravated sigh, not bothering to glance away from the television set.

"I... want to give up," Tabitha said in a quiet voice.

"Give up?" Mrs. Moore retorted. "Give up on *what?*"

"I think I want to give up on living," Tabitha said, feeling her eyes water. "I just. Momma, I just don't want to live anymore."

"That's not something to ever joke about, Tabitha Anne Moore," Mrs. Moore warned, turning her fat neck to glare toward her daughter. "What on God's green earth brought *this* on, all of the sudden? Just what's happened now?"

"I-I don't want to be here," Tabitha cried softly, covering her face. "I don't want to do this. I don't want to fight you again. *I can't.*"

"Fight me?" her mother said with a deep scowl. "Tabitha, you're not making a lick of sense C'mon then, out with it. What did you do?"

"I spoke with proper diction," Tabitha sniffled. "You said it was awful—that I was talking like a robot. I, I wasn't pretending to be a robot, though. I was trying to be, um, trying to be a *cool* Tabitha. One who, who had it all together. I was just... I'm *awful* at it."

"Robot... ? What are you *talking* about?" Mrs. Moore demanded. "Tabby—"

"I exercised like crazy—had it all planned out," Tabitha sobbed. "It was, it was six hours of exercise, every day. I lost *a third of my body weight* before high school. I was *pretty. Pretty almost like you were.* It wasn't healthy at all—messed up my menstrual cycle, ended up making everything at school *worse somehow,* and it—and it, it made you think *I was trying to become an actress?!* Like you were back then. Momma—how *does anyone really fucking think I could ever be an actress?! Me, an ACTRESS?! It's—it's completely fucking IMPOSSIBLE!*"

"Tabitha—?" Mrs. Moore looked completely bewildered.

"I tried. *I tried,*" Tabitha wailed. "I tried *really* hard, okay? W-with the shooting, and, and with Alicia and Elena. With school. With *you.* And you know what happened? I'm pretty sure *I got murdered.* She—she killed me, I think. Because of... because of Ashlee. I didn't remember Ashlee. I was, I was just going to try to *get by,* to um, to *improve* myself and get by until I could do something about Julie. But—"

A dizzying wave of migraine pain swept through her, and Tabitha put a hand to the side of her head, swaying on her feet, as a trickle of something seeped down out of her nose. Dabbing at her upper lip with her fingertips revealed they were wet with blood again, *a lot of blood,* and Tabitha's eyes went wide. Terrified, she looked past her bloody fingers toward her mother to see—

————

—that Mrs. Moore was facing the other way, looking off toward the TV screen.

"...Mom?" Tabitha asked.

"What do you want, Tabby?" Mrs. Moore asked with an aggravated sigh, not bothering to tear her gaze away from the television set.

"Mom, I'm—d-did you hear anything I just said?" Tabitha asked in disbelief, feeling a foggy sense of *deja vu* ripple through her so strongly that it was almost disorienting. Something was wrong, but it was hard to put her finger on exactly what it was.

"Hear what, now?" Mrs. Moore grunted, still not looking her way.

Confused, Tabitha stared back down at her fingertips. They were clean. There was no blood on them. Rubbing her eyes with both hands—the edge of her orthopedic cast scraping slightly against her eye socket—Tabitha realized that there were no tears anymore either. They'd vanished, as if she'd never been crying at all.

Wait a fucking second! Tabitha reeled, staring incredulously at the familiar blue cast that was back on her left hand.

"This—this isn't real," Tabitha exclaimed, hunching her shoulders in and whirling to double-check her surroundings.

"What?" Mrs. Moore asked in an absentminded tone.

"This is all—*none of this is real,*" Tabitha asserted. "Either it's not real, or I'm dreaming, I've gone crazy, or—it doesn't matter, does it? Am I... what, *am I dead?*"

"What on *God's green earth* are you talking about, all of the sudden?" Mrs. Moore scowled, turning her fat neck to glare toward her daughter. "Tabitha—you're not making a lick of sense."

"W-was *any of it* real?" Tabitha demanded, clutching at her cast. It had split along one side, tufts of bandage were poking out where the rigid fiberglass had broken, and *it hurt.* "Any of it at all? Where did—"

"Tabitha Anne Moore—"

"Okay. *Okay.* Um. Mom, you're not real—you're probably just... memories?" Tabitha rationalized, clutching at her head again as another wave of pain gripped her skull. Blood ran freely down her face again, and parts of the living room flickered and then went dark. "Jumbled up memories. Or—*ow, ow, fuck this hurts*—or something? Impressions, hallucinations? There's, there's fucking inconsistencies everywhere! The windows were all blocked off with blankets just a minute ago—now, they're not."

"Tabitha—"

Ignoring the *dream apparition* that looked like her mother, Tabitha paced back and forth in place, struggling to figure out *what the hell* was going on. It was inordinately difficult to think at all with her head pounding like this. *Dreams aren't this clear, you can't think this clearly in dreams. Brain damage? From getting hit with the bat?*

Tabitha paused, looking around again through the pain. Some of the distant mobile homes outside the window went dark and *disappeared,* like assets dropping out of render distance in a video game. The longer she tried to stare across the street out the window, the worse her headache got—until her eyes painfully unfocused. It was like trying to peer through one of those magic eye illusion pages to see something with depth pop out, but instead of a hidden image appearing, the blankets were tacked back up and covering the windows again.

Oookay, fuck, Tabitha swore, blinking rapidly. *Usually scenery discrepancies happen like, between camera cuts. Or, or at least with a gentle fade effect, or something. Actually catching them just hurts your fucking brain?*

"Th-that's it, then," Tabitha whimpered in a small voice. "I'm already dead, aren't I?"

"You're not *dead*," a soft voice chuckled, "but you're not in a good place either."

Where the kitchen counter should have been, Julia now sat across from her in one of the booths of a familiar family restaurant, clutching at a mug of coffee.

"Julie... ?" Tabitha murmured in breathless surprise.

A moment ago, she'd been in the mobile home at Sunset Estates, but locales had shifted and swirled around her in that dreamlike quality, and now she was sitting in the Perkins off one of the Interstate 265 exits. This was a memory; this was where Tabitha met Julia for the last time, having driven out to meet the woman because Julie happened to be passing through Kentucky on her way to Pennsylvania. It was hard to keep from being emotional at the reunion, even if she knew it likely wasn't real.

"Of course *I'm not real.*" Julie leaned in with an exasperated smile. "What'd you think, that I was gonna impart some touching words, some wisdom or motivation or something from beyond the grave? What kind of cliché is that?"

"Um." Tabitha swallowed. "No, I just... Julie—I really miss you."

"Ah." Julia gave her a sheepish smile and glanced down at her coffee. "Yeah. I *am* sorry about that."

Wearing a stylish black and red motorsports jacket, Julia had a pale, almost sickly complexion, and hair that had been dyed black at some point but now showed several inches of dirty blonde at the roots. The sound of her words always had a unique *Julie* quality to them, ethereal and a little raspy, high enough in vocal register that her voice always seemed right on the edge of cracking. Julie's wide, mischievous smile was her most expressive feature, but the smile never seemed to extend all the way up to her pale blue eyes, which only ever seemed to look tired and listless.

"So, this isn't real," Tabitha said in disappointment. "You're not real."

"Sure seems like a dream to me," Julia observed, gesturing with her mug toward where the dining area of the Perkins transitioned into the living room of the mobile home. "I mean, hell—it *is* great to see you again, though!"

"Yeah." Tabitha nodded slowly. "It's just... yeah. I-I really wanted to save you."

"You *did* save me, Miss Tabby," Julia playfully admonished her. "C'mon, girl—we talked about this, remember?"

"You know what I mean." Tabitha slowly shook her head. "You still... took your own life."

"I did," Julia admitted with a guilty look. "But, listen—that's on *me,* Miss Tabby. You did save me, and because of that, I felt like I had the freedom to... make that choice. You know?"

"*You know?!*" Tabitha retorted, leaning forward with her elbows on the tabletop and wearily rubbing her eyes. "No, I *don't* know, Miss Julie. That's actually... super fucked up, and I wish I'd never heard you say that. You're saying *I enabled you* to commit suicide? Can you like, reassure me again that you're not real, that the *real* Julie would never say that, and that this is all some fucked up nightmare? Please?"

"Okay, yeah." Julia grimaced and took a sip of her coffee. "Let's go with that."

"Julie..." Tabitha growled in frustration.

"Hah, okay. Listen," Julia set the mug down. "You thought of me as some kind of badass chick, because I have *cool stories,* and ride a motorcycle, and write some really dark, fucked-up fantasy shit. Right? But also... I mean, we've talked about the fucked-up stuff my dad did to me growing up. The shitty relationships I got myself into, the way I just sort of crashed from bad decision to bad decision to bad decision my whole life.

"Miss Tabby—you're like, my best friend, and you liked me, liked who I was. But *I didn't like me. I didn't want to be me.* I couldn't anymore. You know? I didn't want to keep living. I didn't want to keep going, or have to deal with any tomorrows. To me, like, I saw a choice between *more of this* or just opting out, and I opted out."

"You're not real, right?" Tabitha asked in a small voice.

"No, not even a little bit." Julia laughed. "I'm like, a manifestation of your subconscious and all that shit."

"Then... I can disregard whatever you say," Tabitha retorted. "Because—I mean, you're not real. You're a phantom of my imagination."

"Yeah, sure," Julia shot back. "If you think it's real healthy neglecting your subconscious, I guess."

"That... seems exactly like what the real Julie would've said," Tabitha grumbled. "You're either like, the ghost of the real Julia, or —what, like, my impression of Julia? Why did you say that I'm not dead earlier?"

"Well, if I'm your subconscious, then it means *subconsciously,* me saying you're not dead means you think that you're still alive," Julia reasoned. "Which is a fairly compelling argument itself, right? I mean, if you're thinking at all, how can you be dead? *I think, therefore I am,* and all that."

"There's... stories that explore that sort of stuff." Tabitha sighed. "There was the book *The Lovely Bones.* And then that Robin Williams movie, *What Dreams May Come.*"

"Yeah, I guess," Julia shrugged. "Whatever. But you don't *really* think this is like that, do you?"

"I don't *want* it to be like that, no, but—" Tabitha began.

"Then think of it as something like a lucid dream?" Julia interrupted. "You'll figure something out. Get out of here, Tabby. Go live a *good* life. Uh, but listen—your nose is bleeding again, and it's about to get back to those bad, nightmary kind of bits."

"Um..." Tabitha said, touching the blood running down her face again in confusion. "Nightmary bits?"

"Yeah." Julia gave her an embarrassed smile. "Like this, for starters—"

Then Julia was gone, leaving Tabitha alone in the booth, and the daylight outside the Perkins windows turned to evening. She remembered this too, and it was one of her more painful memories —after Julia took her own life, Tabitha always made a point to stop at this Perkins whenever she was traveling down I-275. She would sit there, often in the same exact booth where she'd had that last visit with Julia, and sometimes cry a little bit over one of the dinner specials.

"You're still my best friend, Miss Julie," Tabitha whispered, rising up out of her seat. "But I *really* can't fucking stand your sense of humor."

Looking around, the Perkins didn't seem to be associating itself with the mobile home in a slapdash blend of locations anymore. She'd lost all inclination to stay, however, and since she hadn't ordered anything *real* anyway, Tabitha simply got up and walked over to the exit the diner.

Lucid dream, nightmare—whatever, Tabitha thought, stepping out of the Perkins and looking around the parking lot. *How do I GET OUT OF HERE? How do I wake up?*

It took her a few minutes of wandering down the rows of vehicles lined up beneath the widely-spaced parking lot lights to even realize something else was amiss. She couldn't find her Honda Pilot anywhere, sure, but more to the point—the parking lot was *gargantuan,* unending, something a shopping mall or football stadium would have, not a little roadside Perkins. She slowly recognized it as one of her old college nightmares—other people seemed to have nightmares about being in front of everyone at school naked, or in their underwear, but Tabitha had instead had recurring ones about being lost in an enormous parking lot at night, with panic that would creep in as she realized she couldn't find her vehicle.

But—*this isn't real either,* Tabitha realized in frustration. *I'm not going to find my Honda anywhere here, because I NEVER found my car in these ones. I'd look and look and look, but after a while, it was like there were people following me through the parking lot, and then it was like they were chasing me.*

She quickly walked the rest of the way over to the next pole of a parking lot light and tried to steady her breathing. On a whim, she tried to pinch herself on the arm—that's the trope for determining whether one is dreaming or not, isn't it? She wasn't able to. Holding her plump arm up in front of herself to stare at it, Tabitha's blue orthopedic cast swam back into view like a trick of the light.

You've gotta be fucking kidding me.

"You're fucking kidding *yourself,*" Carrie retorted. "You *are* dead. You even had a second chance, and ya *still* fuckin' blew it. *Woooow.*"

Three teenage girls strode out of the darkness between the rows of cars, and Tabitha's breath hitched in her throat. They were completely mismatched—on the right, Carrie was wearing the Tommy Hilfiger vest Tabitha had seen her in at school, on the left, an eighth-grade Elena smirked at her, and in the middle—Erica Taylor in her baseball outfit from the Halloween party. Erica was baring her teeth, her shoulders seemed to tremble with barely-constrained violence, and the Louisville Slugger she dragged along seemed slightly oversized, large enough that it scraped along the asphalt of the parking lot in a menacing way.

"I'm... not scared of you," Tabitha lied, glaring at each of the girls in turn. "You're *not real*."

"Wanna bet?" Elena called in a mocking voice as the girls continued to advance on her. "You know why we're here. You cheated death—got to do *months and months* all over again—and now, it's time to pay it all back. You even got an *extra* day or two, before the bleed on your brain caught up. *Uhh,* did you think all that shit was free? That you wouldn't have to pay the price for it?"

"The... bleed on my brain?" Tabitha echoed in a hollow voice, fighting the urge to backpedal away from them. "I-I didn't ask for any do-overs, didn't want them. Not my fault."

"But you took them anyways," Erica Taylor hissed in a low voice. "*Didn't you?* Doesn't matter *what you wanted,* you took what you didn't deserve—and you don't get to take things away from us."

"So what if I even did?!" Tabitha growled, retreating a step. "You're not the *actual fucking gatekeepers of time and space*—you're not even teenage girls, you're not real. Memories, *shadows*. I don't have to be afraid of you. I know taekwondo, and this is *my* dream."

"Yeah?" Erica Taylor snorted, tapping the baseball bat loudly against the pavement. "*Taekwondo,* huh? How'd that work out for you last time?"

"Oh yeah!" Carrie giggled. "Pretty sure she got her face bashed in?"

"She went down like a little bitch," eighth-grade Elena agreed, sizing Tabitha up with a smug look. "*Like a little bitch.*"

"You know *all* about *this* nightmare too, don't you?" Erica teased, swishing her bat through the air. "You remember. You'll run and run and run, but you can never get away."

"No." Tabitha gritted her teeth. "No, I'm not going to run."

"Fine by me!" Erica flashed a smile full of teeth at her. "Don't run, then—this'll be even more fun."

"I'm not going to run," Tabitha decided. "I'm going to wake up. I'm going to get back to where I was, and I'm going to fix things with Ashlee, and I'm going to save Julie. Going to figure out how to have a *good* life and be happy."

"Julie's *dead,* retard." Carrie laughed. "Ashlee? Doesn't give a flying fuck about you. And you? You're brain dead and dying. You're never *ever* waking up or getting out of here."

"Getting out of here?" Erica seemed infuriated by her defiance, and she lunged forward, swinging the bat through the air toward Tabitha with all of her might. "With what, your *taekwondo?*"

"With a *goddamn F-22,* if I have to!" Tabitha leapt backwards, and the world spun.

The back of her legs tripped implausibly into one of the Williams' sofas from the lake house, and then she tumbled painfully down the stairs of an old apartment's sun-soaked wooden porch and into the junkyard full of aviation parts behind her mobile home.

Disoriented, Tabitha looked up at the teens standing in the middle of the decrepit porch in surprise. It was daytime here— they were just behind the mobile home, the scrapyard full of machinery from her fever dream was *here* somehow, and Carrie, Erica, and Elena looked just as confused by the sudden displace- ment as she was.

"...What the fuck?" Carrie said.

"Tabitha, where the *hell* do you think you're going?" Mrs. Moore howled, attempting to heave the bulk of her bloated body off a nearby couch. The woman was morbidly obese now, with streaks of gray through her wispy hair and made for a disturbing sight. "Don't you dare *think* about leaving this dream before you've done your homework, young lady. You sit your fanny down right this instant before I spank your sorry behind red! *I mean it!*"

"This isn't a real place," Carrie complained, making a face as Elena shot her a sardonic look. "Oh—*you know what I fucking mean!* It's not supposed to be here!"

"I-I love you, Mom!" Tabitha called as she scrambled to her feet. "But I have to go. Somewhere out there—I'm, I'm going to find the real you. The *actual* you, even if I have to start all over from the beginning. *I'm going to save you.* I love you. I'm so sorry."

"No, you're fucking *not!*" Erica screamed, dashing down the porch steps after her.

"Tabiiiithaaaaghh?!!" The upper part of Mrs. Moore's bloated face collapsed in on itself as her mouth distorted wide into a toothy maw, the edge of her lopsided lip peeling all the way down one side of her neck to roar in anger at her daughter.

The scattered heaps and piles of surplus aviation pieces shifted and collapsed behind her as Tabitha sprinted past them, replaced with the silent rows of cars of an endless night time parking lot. Cursing and swearing and screaming at her, each encroaching step the teenage girls took chasing after Tabitha seemed to destabilize the shrinking area of the half-forgotten *F-22 dream* from those weeks ago. In true dream fashion, Tabitha's run felt impossibly slow, as if she were sloughing through molasses, and she tripped and fell as the dream trembled and wavered like a soap bubble about to pop. Frantically climbing back to her feet, she noticed that her left arm had a frail wrist sporting a bracelet-PC one moment, and a familiar blue cast the next.

No time, no time—I have to get OUT of here, Tabitha shook her broken wrist distractedly, and it flickered and phased between different states of being in an uncomfortable blur.

The junkyard was large but also bleeding off territory quickly, and as she dashed around the last heap toward the mostly-finished F-22 resting in the center, Tabitha realized that the bubble of this dream was *almost gone,* that the horrors of the jumbled memories and old nightmares were spilling in from every direction in a dark flood. Once again, it felt like she was running and running but scarcely seemed to be moving forward at all, and with every moment, the scrap piles of machinery were shifting and twisting, sending smaller pieces crashing and tumbling down.

"It's over—it's over and you're *dead!*" one of the pursuing teens screeched after her.

"Fuck, fuck, *fuck!*" Tabitha screamed, refusing to look behind her as she took a running leap for the ladder hanging off the side of the F-22 cockpit.

She made it.

The enormous transparent canopy wasn't fastened shut, but it was much heavier than she'd imagined—*isn't all of this my imagination anyways?!*—and the best she could manage was pushing the fighter jet's canopy up enough for her to frantically clamber inside. When it dropped down behind her and latched into place, the sight just outside stunned her.

The old dream she'd taken refuge in had dwindled down to barely encompass the size of her F-22. Instead, a horrific hellscape of nightmares had replaced the surroundings. Jeremy Redford stood over the fallen form of Officer MacIntire and fired again and again, the policeman's body rocking in spurts of blood with each shot. With a face transformed into a snarling mask of madness, Erica Taylor stepped over the prone form of a Tabitha to bear down on a costumed Alicia and Elena with the baseball bat, slamming and smashing the girls as they let out shrill, helpless screams. Mrs. MacIntire sobbed and Hannah broke down into tears as a faceless officer came to give them the news that Darren MacIntire had died in the line of duty. In the chaos of the bus loop, Chris Thompson pinned Tabitha down after pushing her, straddling her with a sadistic grin and then tearing at her blouse—

Nope. Nope. All of my nope. Noping THE FUCK out of—out of whatever the fuck this is, Tabitha thought in a panic, forcibly turning her eyes away from the cascade of images flashing by outside and frantically starting up the F-22.

Tabitha knew nothing about how to start up a *real* fighter jet, of course. Here the controls were more a vague impression or facsimile of what controls might be than anything else—deciding to go and throwing the *intention* to start the aircraft up seemed to handwave away technical details. Blinking back tears, Tabitha was reluctant to glance down at whatever her hands were doing to operate the controls for fear of breaking the spell.

There was no runway. She didn't know how to fly. From what she dimly recalled, the F-22 in her old fever dream was unfinished and nowhere remotely near flight-worthy, but none of that mattered right now, because *she was getting the fuck out of there.* With a deafening whine of the F-22's engines, the fighter rose up in a hover like she imagined a helicopter or a ship from *Star Wars* might. The last few yards of ground below the aircraft were swallowed up by madness a moment later, and Tabitha was just about to let out a sigh of relief and fire the afterburners to jet away—

When someone grabbed her ankle.

No, no—NO! Tabitha flailed and twisted in disbelief as the whine of the F-22 suddenly became a deafening squeal of scraping metal. Impossibly, she'd been pulled backwards into a prone position within the cockpit, as if the pilot's seat ceased to exist. When she twisted her body to look behind her, she couldn't help but stare in complete shock—the pilot's seat was gone, and she was instead somehow on an examination table. Where the glassy curvature of the fighter craft canopy should have met the fuselage, it instead seamlessly became the cylindrical aperture of the prototype MRI from the University of Louisville Hospital, where medical personnel were already struggling to pull her out of the screeching device.

———

She was old again, she could feel her entire body riddled with age, withered with age, her muscles had gone frail and she was sagging, joints aching. Blood bubbled from her nose as she tried to breathe and dripped down from her face in a mess, creating red spatters all over the interior of the prototype MRI. The machine was making a ballistic noise, scraping and squealing and filling the air with clogging gouts of black smoke.

"Shut it down—*shut it down!*" a doctor's voice yelled over the grinding shriek of what sounded like a turbine engine tearing itself to pieces.

No. No, no, no. I can't come back here. Not NOW, Tabitha felt her heart sink. *Mom, Dad—they're both dead in 2045. Dead for years and years. I have... I have NOTHING there. No one!*

"I-I *did* shut it down!" The familiar pretty young nurse that had helped Tabitha into the machine what felt like so many months ago cried out. "It's—it's fucking unplugged from the wall and it's still getting power somehow!"

"Yeah—well, no shit, the hologram's still on!"

"I can *see* that the fucking hologram's still—"

"Let—let go of me!" Tabitha screamed, kicking in an attempt to dislodge the man who'd grabbed her leg. "*Let go!*"

"Ma'am, *ma'am*—we need you to calm down!" an orderly called out over the noise and confusion. "For your own safety, we need you to—"

"I'm not going back!" Tabitha yelled, her frail hands scrabbling for purchase along the interior of the MRI. "Please, just—*I can't,* just one more chance! I'm sorry! *Just give me one more chance!*"

"*Ma'am—!*"

"—hologram's not responding, magnetic field fried the interface. Every PC in the whole damn wing's at risk of—"

"Help!" Tabitha gasped out, blood freely flowing down her face from both nostrils. "Someone, *please!* Help me!"

"Ma'am, we're *trying* to help, if you can just—"

"*Fucking let go of me! You're—you're not—you're—*"

"Pull her out," The authoritative man's voice was louder now. "*Fuck,* tray-table's shorted out. *Pull her out,* she's gonna hurt herself thrashing around like that—Bill, grab her other ankle!"

"What the hell happened?"

"She's—hell, I don't know!" the nurse said. "One second it's starting up fine, and then the next it's suddenly making this awful noise! She immediately starts screaming—having, like, these fits, or, or, or some kind of seizure—"

"I've got her, I've got her." Someone clamped down on Tabitha's frantically kicking foot. "Just—"

Her head was splitting with pain, and in discordant flashes, Tabitha could see a patch of dreamlike sky lazily spinning just past the far inner side of the MRI enclosure. It looked like the view through the F-22 canopy, as the fighter jet fell backwards through the air in an out-of-control tailspin. This last few slivers of dreamworld seemed to be sputtering now, wildly wavering in an unseen wind like a candle flame on the verge of being blown out.

"...bitha?" The faint voice of a little girl called, difficult to hear over the calamitous din of the prototype MRI tearing itself apart and the yelling of the medical personnel as they attempted to remove her from within it. "*Tabitha?*"

That sounds like—like—!

With her last surge of strength, Tabitha lunged, stretching her aching old muscles forward and desperately reaching for the back of the MRI. Another blood vessel in her brain ruptured, everything went dark all at once, and—

———

—Tabitha had only just begun to plunge into freefall when a small, delicate hand grasped tightly onto hers. She swung for a moment from her mysterious savior in total bewilderment, legs flailing out and encountering nothing, until she finally hung there in the void, her arm jolting painfully at the weight of her entire body.

Dangling in the darkness from only her one hand, Tabitha looked down past her kicking feet in disbelief to watch the F-22 fall away without her. She caught a last receding glimpse inside the cockpit canopy, of a frail sixty-year-old body going still within the circular window of the MRI—and then it was gone. The falling fighter shrank into the distance of the churning maelstrom below her until it disappeared completely, swallowed up by nightmare darkness.

"Haahhh, hahh, hwaaah—" Panting with exertion as she hung from someone's unseen hand in a completely black space of nothingness. "Hello? Well—uh. *Fuck?*"

Her right arm ached supporting her entire body, but she didn't have the strength to attempt reaching up with her left. Trying, and failing, to calm herself down at being trapped in whatever surreal purgatory this was, Tabitha nervously stared down past her own kicking feet into what felt like a bottomless, nightmarish abyss far below.

Tabitha had escaped back into the dream—or what was left of it—but she now had the sinking suspicion that her future self that had been left behind in the year 2045 was now very, very dead.

———

"Mo*mmy*—?!" Hannah called over. "*Mom!* Tabitha's having a bad dream. You said she wouldn't have bad dreams. Mommy, you *promised.*"

"Hannah honey... Tabitha won't have bad dreams or nightmares," Mrs. MacIntire reassured her with a tired smile. "She's... she's just going to sleep peacefully now."

"Because she doesn't have... brain act-tivity?" Hannah frowned as she pronounced the words, looking from where her mother was seated back toward Tabitha on the hospital bed with a look of doubt.

"Yes, honey, because she doesn't have brain activity. Not having any brain activity means... that she won't ever wake up anymore," Mrs. MacIntire explained in a weary but patient voice. "But she won't have any bad dreams or nightmares either. The good Mister Doctor Man said she won't be feeling any pain, or—or any kind of distress at all before she passes on. She's just... resting, honey. Resting like Sleeping Beauty."

"Mommy, no—*she's having a nightmare*," Hannah insisted with a stubborn stamp of her foot. "*Come look!* Tabitha's having a nightmare—she grabbed on to my hand."

"Honey..." Hannah's mother sighed, lifting herself out of her seat to come take a closer look. "I'm sure that—"

Sandra MacIntire froze.

Tabitha Moore had been declared brain dead, and purportedly, there was no chance at all of recovery—she was in a vegetative state and would remain permanently comatose. Tabitha had been the very picture of serenity for several days now, with only the bandages wrapped around her head to indicate anything at all had ever happened. She'd been taken off of life support already, and was receiving her last visitors for a few days while the grief-stricken Moore family waited to see if Tabitha would quietly pass on.

Instead, what should have been a peaceful expression on the teenage girl's features was now an extraordinarily troubled one— Tabitha was jerking slightly, her brow was furrowed, and her eyes were scrunched shut as if in pain. The sedate rise and fall of her chest was speeding up, and Tabitha's pale lips trembled.

"—elp," Tabitha whimpered out in a tiny, barely-audible mumble. "—meone, pl—*help m*—"

"This is... uh. She's—um—*something's happened*," Mrs. MacIntire exclaimed in a panic, quickly leaning in over Tabitha to closely inspect the girl. "She, she can't be *brain dead*, she just—"

"She's having a nightmare!" Hannah repeated. "What do we do? Will she wake up?"

"J-just hold on to her hand tight, Baby, and don't let go!" Mrs. MacIntire dashed toward the door of the private room and peeked out into the hallway. "I'm going to go find somebody!"

"...Tabitha?" Hannah urged, squeezing Tabitha's hand and gently shaking her. "*Tabitha?* Can you... can you wake up? Wake up now, please? Tabitha? *Please?* Please wake up?"

Eyelids fluttering, Tabitha's body stirred in a restless way on the hospital bed as she fought to pull herself back up to consciousness and return to them.

27

TABITHA'S LONG
CONVALESCENCE

"—There we go, think that did the trick," a nonplussed voice from out of nowhere remarked.

Tabitha jolted back to awareness with her sinuses screaming, and caught a blurry glimpse of a hand holding a white paper capsule covered with tiny black text. Her brain wasted no time connecting the overpowering ammonia inhalant in the air to the idea of smelling salts, and being roused back to consciousness in such a manner was a lot more unpleasant than she'd have ever imagined. There were three faces crowded around wherever she was lying, it was *way too bright,* and she felt completely exhausted, too tired to even *dream* about sitting up.

"...Tabitha?" a woman asked.

Tabitha tried to blink the bright blur into defined shapes and shift her position—her body felt stiff and heavily-laden, and her head felt strangely detached, seemingly anchored to reality only by a terrible aching pain that radiated out from the side of her temple. The woman spoke again, but Tabitha's attention was bleary and wandering. All she could make out was that the voice was choked with emotion, and not someone she immediately recognized, which added to the strangeness of her situation.

"Tabby?" Hannah asked in a meek voice. "Hello to Tabitha?"

She knew *that* voice for sure, and it was coming from the smaller face, closer down to the horizon of muddled shapes that she was beginning to realize was her body on a hospital bed. *I'm back. I'm BACK. Only knew Hannah in ONE lifetime, and it's the life I wanted—the life I WANT, the one I was wishing for. Thank you, thank you thank you thank you...*

"Hannah...?" Tabitha managed.

Her own words came out as more of a breathless sigh than audible speech, and Tabitha wondered if anyone would be able to hear her. There simply wasn't any strength in her diaphragm she could intone into her words to project them at any volume. The sheer effort of speaking was so impossibly taxing that it made her feel like she needed to black out and rest all over again.

"She just said '*Hannah*,'" the woman exclaimed. "Hannah— that's my daughter right here's name! Tabitha *recognized*—"

"Quiet, please, quiet, let's not overwhelm the girl," the male voice admonished her. "Miss Tabitha, we've contacted your parents, and they're on their way here right now. Would it be alright if I asked you a few questions?"

"Hurts," Tabitha croaked in her tiny voice. She wasn't *against* answering questions, but her head was splitting and this seemed like a crucial thing to convey to them as quickly as she could.

"Yes, I'd expect so," the doctor murmured. "We took you off of —well, we'll get some morphine in your IV in just a moment. You're a very, very lucky girl—you've been legally dead for two days now. You'll have a very interesting certificate of death to show off. Can you describe your current pain for me on a scale of one to ten, with ten being the highest?"

"Six," Tabitha replied in a low murmur, fighting to keep her eyes open. "On its way to... seven."

"Six, on its way to seven," the doctor repeated. "Good, good. We'll get that taken care of for you. Do you know where you are?"

In light of her recent—and confusing—experiences, that felt like a hell of a loaded question. Tabitha blinked with difficulty again, fighting to glare through the haze of exhaustion and eyeball her surroundings. She realized Hannah was holding her hand in a tight little grip, and it filled her with comfort. Tabitha tried to squeeze back, but there didn't seem to be much strength in her right hand. Or anywhere.

"...Springton General," Tabitha finally answered.

"That's—yes, you're in a hospital, Springton General Hospital." The doctor nodded, seeming pleased with the measure of her faculties. "Can you tell me the last thing you remember?"

Dangling in the darkness from Hannah's voice. Smashing my head into the back of 2045's MRI prototype in the University of Louisville Hospital. Escaping a series of memories and or nightmares via F-22, the Lockheed Martin single-seat, twin-engine, all-weather stealth tactical fighter aircraft of my dreams. Those awful girls, chasing me through the endless parking lot. I remember talking with Julie, and she felt so REAL. So real... There was—there was another timeline that started. Fuck, I think that WAS real, but my brain bleeding or some sort of damage... DISCONNECTED me? I timed out? Brain bleed. Brain bleed, because Erica Taylor—

"Violence," Tabitha mumbled, deciding to tactfully keep some things to herself. "Violence and pain."

"Violence and pain," the doctor echoed, seeming a little taken aback. "If you could describe—"

"Seven now," Tabitha interrupted to report, squeezing her eyes shut and furrowing her brow. "...Eight, soon."

"Alrighty, everything else can certainly wait," the doctor relented. "Giving you some morphine now. You're going to feel very, very drowsy, but you shouldn't be feeling any pain. Oh, and —welcome back."

He wasn't kidding about the feeling—almost instantly,

Tabitha felt like the sharp agony in her head was stifled beneath blanket after blanket of smothering cottony *tiredness* that completely buried her senses. Her waking thought processes slowed to a sluggish, exhausted crawl, sinking into a soporific muddle-headedness that made her surreal dreams from before seem to have been in vivid clarity by contrast. The following conversations occurring right by her bedside seemed to travel enormous distances to reach the semi-aware part of her mind in broken, disjointed sentences, and when the words arrived at all, they did so in a droning, nearly incomprehensible murmur.

"————————————procedures for————"

"————right to alert us as quickly as you————parents here by her side when she————ither medical miracle, or misdiagnosis. They're going to run another battery of tests to————"

"————indication of————————?"

"————————————————"

"————don't want to————ketchup and pickle only, please! Thank y————"

"————————————————recovery ————"

"————ssible that the instruments we have available here weren't sensitive enough to detect brain activity below a certain threshold. There's never been————ell them she was awake and alert, she managed to say a few words. Yes, yes, we————can't tell anything else until————"

"————visitors, until there's————"

"————————?"

"—stop that. Hannah honey, give her some space. She needs to rest—"

"————————————"

"————know what else we can say. Up until this case, this was unprecedented, there was no————"

"——bitha?!————hear me?"

"——Tabitha baby? Tabby, can you hear me? We're all————"

Mrs. Moore wrung the handrail spanning the side of Tabitha's hospital bed in a death grip. Her eyes were still red-rimmed, her lips were pressed into a thin line, and her figure was noticeably thinner than it had been just the week before. Emotionally, mentally, and physically, she felt about as hollowed out as any one person could be. She'd had no appetite since it happened, and she'd spent several insensate days sobbing and screaming herself to the point of weakness and dehydration. Her husband hadn't fared much better, seeming to age several decades in those several days and speaking only in clipped, terse sentences.

Hearing that Tabitha had inexplicably *woken up*—woken up from being *legally brain dead,* was more than she could comprehend right now, and she was still terrified to believe there was any hope, that it might actually be true. Mrs. Moore was empty of everything else and still reeling—she wanted them to force Tabitha awake again just so that she could confirm it with her own eyes, and she also couldn't bear to. She felt her heart breaking at the pain and suffering her daughter was going through.

"Are you gonna be okay?" Mrs. MacIntire asked, giving her a look of concern.

"Soon as I can hear her speak again." Mrs. Moore nodded quickly, tears erupting out of nowhere to stream down her face again. "As soon as I can see her awake again, alive again. Then I'll be great. Perfect. Everything will be..."

"I know exactly what you mean," Mrs. MacIntire patted her hand. "This whole thing terrifies me. I was sitting right there in the chair and didn't realize a thing. If Hannah hadn't happened to notice something was wrong, that Tabitha was having a nightmare—hell, if this brain activity deal was all a *misdiagnosis,* some sort of goddamned malpractice fucking *fuckup*..."

"I don't care," Mrs. Moore blurted out, sniffling and trying to stop her breath from hitching up. "If I can see her again—if we can get her back, I don't care about anything else. I'll care later. I'll be, I'll be *furious* later. Right now, I just, *I just*—"

"She *is* back," Mrs. MacIntire reassured her with a comforting hug. "They diagnosed her as brain dead and instead she wakes up and starts talking! Everything's going to be fine, with a little bit of time. Someone up there's still looking out for Tabitha, and He'll make sure she pulls through this."

"You're right—you're, you're right." Mrs. Moore nodded, wiping distractedly at her tears.

With Sandra's husband Officer MacIntire transferred to Springton General for his recovery and Tabitha admitted to the adjacent wing, Mrs. MacIntire and her seven-year-old daughter had been spending almost all of their free time here visiting in the rooms of either one or the other patients. The harmful *what-ifs* thinking about what would have happened if Tabitha had stirred near consciousness and no one had been there to see... were horrifying to consider. They'd taken her off life support because there'd *supposedly* been absolutely no chance of recovery. Mrs. Moore wasn't feeling the rage and anger about it yet, but it was certainly weighing more on her mind each passing moment.

Alan Moore stood off to the side, simply staring with a vacant expression. He'd been bottling up all of the pain of losing Tabitha internally and had been pushed well past the point of shutting down—Mrs. Moore felt ashamed that she'd been in no position to help him through it. They'd both just been completely struck dumb and absolutely lost—how do any parents *anywhere* cope with loss of this magnitude? They'd missed the Monday expulsion hearing, which came and went with little fanfare—only Chris Thompson was expelled, with the other girls each being released from their suspensions to return to school for a period of 'academic probation.'

Mrs. Moore couldn't really bring herself to care about any of the bastards.

High school bullying had passed well under the local news

station's radar, but assault and battery at a Halloween party that left a pretty teenage girl in a vegetative state did not, and when Channel 7 began connecting the dots, they quickly seemed to realize there was quite a story to run. Tabitha's involvement in the *Springton South Main Shooting* allowed them to dredge up old footage again, and several of the district schools pulled their entire student bodies out of class for a lecture on teen violence and the implementation of new *zero-tolerance* anti-bullying measures in the student code of conduct.

Democratic Kentucky Governor Paul E. Patton released a statement expressing his regret and condolences, touting Bill Clinton's recent *First Annual Report on School Safety*—a study commissioned between the US Department of Justice and the US Department of Education—as well as reiterating last year's talking points regarding the school shooting in West Paducah, Kentucky. Between the political expediency of using the incident as another topic in support of Clinton's School Safety Report and Tabitha Moore's favored *hometown hero* status with the Springton Police... Channel 7 had the local communities at large worked up into a frothing rage at what had happened to Tabitha.

Erica Taylor herself wasn't expelled—the teen was instead *transferred*, to a Juvenile Detention Center all the way over in Breathitt County—unanimously expedited away from the increasingly hostile Springton crowd to await her court date. People were *angry*, and a deluge of supportive phone calls and letters arrived at the Moore household, each fielded and dealt with by Grandma Laurie, who provisionally crowded both herself and the boys into the small trailer day by day to keep an eye on her son and daughter-in-law.

Elena's father, representing the offices of Seelbaugh and Straub, offered his counsel and insisted that with the current circumstances, any and all charges they decided to press were guaranteed to stick. Mrs. Moore had been trying not to think about it—her thoughts wandered into dangerous ideas of murderous revenge whenever she didn't clamp down on them tightly enough. She knew she should appreciate the assistance and attention of so many well-wishing strangers, but she felt *nothing,* nothing but loss and grief and disbelief.

Tabitha CAN'T ever leave us. She—she can't. SHE CAN'T, Mrs. Moore thought, squeezing the hospital bed's handrail until she was clutching the bar in a white-knuckled grip.

Her lovely daughter's head was still wrapped in bandages, and the only indication that she'd ever returned to them at all was that she would now shift slightly in her sleep, gently cant her head to one side as much as the neck brace allowed. Tabitha looked small and frail, a tiny waif of a girl that barely filled out the hospital gown. They'd cut away the broken cast on her left hand without bothering to replace or splint it, leaving the ugly old yellowing bruises on full display. Though supposedly not *brain dead* now, Mrs. Moore stood solemn vigil, watching her with wet eyes. She wouldn't sit down or relax until she'd seen her wake up for herself.

You're not even fourteen yet. Mrs. Moore began to cry again. *Your birthday's next month—you were about to miss your birthday, Tabby. You can't miss your birthday. Fourteen years—there's so much lost time, and I haven't even started making it all up to you properly.*

———

"'Lena? Honey?" Mrs. Seelbaugh's voice called through the bedroom door. "Are you alright? I thought I heard glass breaking."

"You did," Elena bit out. "I'm fine. I'm fine."

The fourteen-year-old blonde hugged herself as she cast a hollow stare past the wreckage of her once-tidy room. She'd had a bit of an *episode,* and after crying and screaming into her pillow behind the locked door for several hours, Elena had decided to… *redecorate.* Posters had all been ripped into papery shreds as she clawed them off of her walls, and she'd crumpled the cut-out magazine sections and old middle-school artwork that had been taped up. Picture frames had been knocked down, she'd torn and thrown every book on her bookshelf, and the little decorative glass angel that normally caught the light on her windowsill had been hurled against the far wall.

"Elena?" Mrs. Seelbaugh prompted again. "Can I... come in?"

"I want to be alone for a while," Elena replied in a flat voice, slowly scratching her fingernails down her arms.

"Okay," Mrs. Seelbaugh replied. "I'm... I'm always here for you. Whenever you need me."

"Yeah," Elena said without emotion.

When she heard her mother reluctantly step back away from her door and leave, Elena slowly exhaled. Her eyes hurt. Her room was a total disaster, without even safe carpet space to step anywhere after she'd finished toppling everything off of her dresser, desk, and shelving unit. Worst of all, she didn't understand *why* she'd done any of it, why the sudden impulse to destroy had suddenly taken hold and refused to let go.

It's not, like, a TANTRUM or anything, Elena glanced around with disinterest and disgust at the trashed remains of a room she'd once been proud of. *It... it just... I don't know?*

Frowning to herself, the teen wasn't sure she could actually rationalize her actions to her parents. Elena had absolutely thrown tantrums before—even as recently as the previous school year, back when she'd still been friends with Carrie. Looking back on it now, tantrums seemed so *childish.* No, this today didn't feel anything like a tantrum. It felt like madness, *horror,* it made her insides sick and her mind turn cold, detached, and bitter.

Screaming hadn't helped; it just made her throat sore. Punching her pillow and mattress was futile. Something about her bedroom itself had suddenly become absolutely abhorrent to her. The room had been too *Elena,* and each of the tastefully-chosen decorations throughout the room, every poster that had been picked out *because of how it reflected her tastes,* every picture of herself smiling with friends or family became a repulsive monument to insipid teenage vanity. Without any warning, all at once and in an overwhelmingly drastic way, Elena *hated* all of it.

All of it needed to be destroyed.

She didn't feel better after the fact, though. Everything still felt wrong, everything still needed *fixed,* but she wasn't sure what that entailed, or what that could even mean anymore. Raking her fingernails down her arms one last time, a brilliant idea came to her—*inspiration.* She stomped and kicked through the mess on her floor, smashing a plastic case filled with her old school supplies beneath her shoe. Crouching down over it, Elena carelessly scattered the purple plastic shards with her fingertips and picked through broken crayons in search of—*there you are.*

Her good pair of scissors.

I can cut off all my hair! Elena decided with glee. *That will—that will help. It will. It will. It needs to go. The old Elena needs to fucking—*

"Elena!" her mother's voice called from across the house. "Mrs. Williams just called—something's happened with Tabitha at the hospital. Can you hurry and get dressed to go?"

No. No no no no no no. Elena felt her throat constrict. *See Tabitha? No, I can't. I can't. I can't.*

She flung the pair of scissors back into the pile of junk pulled out of her desk drawer as if they had bitten her hand, and then backpedaled unsteadily across the mess strewn about her room. Elena slipped on one of the dozens of *Zoobooks* that had spilled off of her lowest bookshelf and stumbled into the corner.

Tabitha. Something happened. She's... she's dead, isn't she? Elena quaked in dread, clutching at her face as the tears returned.

I. I killed her. It's my fault I killed her I told her it was SAFE and convinced her to go EVEN THOUGH SHE DIDN'T EVEN WANT TO GO and now she's—she's. She's dead. All because of me, all because I THOUGHT I FUCKING KNEW BEST. All because I thought getting closer to Matthew and us all having better standing at FUCKING HIGH SCHOOL was more important than her being absolutely fucking safe and away from everything. I—I can't. I can't. I CAN'T.

Elena wasn't aware of how many minutes had passed as she'd curled up in the corner and sobbed into her hands, but the next thing she knew, comforting arms were around her, and her mother was there. She flinched back in surprise at first, but Mrs. Seelbaugh wouldn't let herself be pushed away, instead kneeling in the junk strewn across the carpet and hugging her tight.

Right. Right. Doorknob has that line bit in the middle of it, that you can unlock from the other side with a screwdriver. I should have, should have moved the dresser. Barricaded. She knows what I did, though. Why would she even BOTHER to—?

"We're going to get through this, 'Lena," Mrs. Seelbaugh insisted. "We can do this. I don't know that I made any sense of what Mrs. Williams was saying, but Tabitha hasn't passed away. Okay? Not just yet. She is... she is maybe doing a little better than she was, and I think we should go and see. What do you think?"

"Mom, it's *my fault*—"

"No. *No,*" her mother disagreed. "No, Elena, honey, listen to me. I know how this all must feel, but this is *all* on that Erica Taylor girl. *She* attacked Tabitha. Not you. When you try to take all the culpability for what happened and put it on yourself, you're taking blame off of Erica Taylor. Is that what you want? Do you want her to have any less blame for what she did?"

"...No," Elena said through gritted teeth. She still didn't agree with her mother, but she didn't have the energy to fight her right here on this—her dad was a capable attorney, and *he* had yet to ever win an argument against his wife.

You don't understand. You just don't understand. Mom, you always understand and get everything, but this time, you just DON'T. You don't understand. YOU DON'T UNDERSTAND.

———

The urge and inspiration to create something beautiful, something *mesmerizing,* seemed to thrum through Alicia's fingertips, but every time she put her pencil to the paper, nothing appeared on the blank space. Not so much as a scribble was conjured into being; lately, her ability to create seemed to be completely stopped up. Sometimes, she would stare in frustration at the empty sheet for minutes on end, other days she would put the page away and rifle through her previous drawings in vexation. Today, she threw her pencil across the classroom.

Okay. Okay, I can't deal. Alicia rubbed her eyes with her knuckles. *I need to... to find SOMEONE to talk to. Probably. About all of this.*

A few heads turned, and Mr. Morrison gave her a questioning glance, but Alicia had already slumped back down in her seat, cradling her face in her hands. She hadn't shed a single tear since they all thought they'd lost Tabitha, but the urge to cry persisted just behind her eyes, lingering there, taunting her with an emotional release that just wouldn't come out. It felt like she needed to *bawl,* to cry and scream and cause a fit, but the most she could manage to force out was a few ragged breaths. The sobs were still stuck, as if hung up on something deep down in her throat.

I can't talk to Elena about this. Not now, Alicia decided. *Maybe I could NEVER talk to her about this...*

Elena hadn't been present at school since Tabitha had been attacked. Well, the blonde was *physically* present; Elena attended classes, and her body occupied space within the campus grounds. But she wasn't *there.* Elena had checked out, there was no Elena spark in her at the moment, just an Elena-shaped teenage girl with a vacant expression and monosyllabic responses. Tabitha had become close with Elena, and it was *normal* for Elena to grieve like she was. Alicia's relationship with Tabitha was turning out to have been a lot more hopelessly complicated.

I... maybe have a big crush on Tabitha, Alicia struggled to admit to herself. *Some... I don't know, some weird level of attraction. Affection? I don't think it's SEXUAL or anything like that. Probably. She's just—there's just something special about her to me. Irreplaceable. COMPLETELY irreplaceable, and...*

She'd been fighting to suppress some strange, unbidden feelings for a while now—but given the circumstances, it was just impossible for Alicia *not* to totally fixate on Tabitha. Her red-haired friend was possibly, even *probably* a goddamned time-traveler from the future! In that light, every little thing the lovely teen did demanded Alicia's complete attention. Enormous implications could possibly be gleaned from any trivial little slip of the tongue when hanging out with Tabitha. For weeks and weeks, Alicia had told herself that this was all these feelings were. *Interest.* Because Tabitha might really be from the future.

But there was more—so much more.

Tabitha was beautiful. She had a beauty that seemed to start on the inside and bloom outwards into her actual appearance, some incredible, intangible thing that shone from deep within. *Artistically speaking,* Tabitha had without any doubt become Alicia's muse in every way. The Tabitha in motion photo she'd snapped was her current masterpiece. Drawings of Tabitha's different expressions now populated Alicia's artbook, crowding out anything else she wanted to draw. The old guilty practice scribblings of bare breasts stashed behind her bed frame had been replaced with sketch after sketch of naked shoulders and the slender lines of a lovely neck—all distinctly Tabitha.

That doesn't make me a LESBO, though, Alicia scowled to herself. *Right? Like, no way. I didn't want to BE with her, or like, DO THINGS with her. Except maybe try kissing her. Okay... that's... yeah. That's pretty gay, I guess. Fuck!*

Alicia didn't *want* to be gay, though. Having weird, fluttery warm feelings of nascent attraction for another *girl*—who happened to also be her best friend and in fact one of her *only* friends—was an awful experience. The guilt and self-doubt were compounded by the attack during the Halloween party, and it felt like her already squeezed and constrained emotions clamped down so hard that she was a smooshed mess on the inside. The only reason she was functioning any little bit better than Elena was because she'd been putting up a false front regarding Tabitha for some time now. *That* made her feel awful too.

———

"Princess... everyone hates me," Clarissa confided. "I think I hate them back?"

The limited edition Beanie Baby gazed down upon the teen from her glass case with her usual wisdom and grace, and Clarissa tried to imagine what the purple Bear was trying to tell her. The rows and rows of the other Beanie Babies that filled the wooden curio above her bed seemed to be *judging her,* and Clarissa couldn't bear to look at them right now. She could only trust her Princess Diana Bear right now.

"If they weren't my real friends, then that means *I* wasn't a real friend to them either," Clarissa said, staring up into Princess' solemn dark plastic eyes. "Right?"

The expulsion hearing had gone well for Clarissa. The threat of being held back a year turned out to be posturing on the school board's part, and everyone was released from their suspensions with a stern warning about their behavior. Everyone with the exception of Chris Thompson—but he'd actually physically attacked another student on school grounds. Of course *he* would get expelled. Erica Taylor wasn't mentioned at all, and when questioned about it, her dad had put on a grim face and said that Erica Taylor was being dealt with by people much higher up than some shitty school board meeting. After the stress and terror of being held back turned out to be a slap on the wrist and a scolding, Clarissa had returned to school that very Tuesday almost giddy with relief.

Everything had already changed, though.

The friendships she'd made previously were nowhere to be

found—the other girls seemed *amused* that Clarissa would dare to talk to them, after what she'd done. They laughed at her, *snubbed* her, quickly outed her as the cruel bully who'd stolen that poor Tabitha girl's notebook and gotten caught. As if they all hadn't talked about doing it, as if they hadn't helped *goad* her into doing it. Clarissa watched in indignant disbelief as each of her friendships was tested for the very first time, and each of them, *every single one,* failed.

"Yeah." Clarissa chuckled, lowering her eyes away from Princess Diana Bear. "Right. I hate 'em. Stupid, it was all—it's all so stupid."

———

"Mom?" Tabitha asked in a weak voice, cracking her eyes open.

"I'm here." Mrs. Moore jolted up from the seat at the side of the small room and rushed to her side. "I'm here, sweetie. I'm right here."

Lifting up her right hand—it felt heavy and sluggish—Tabitha immediately felt her mother take it firmly in her hands. It was still a struggle to see, but it was difficult to tell if it was because the small room was too dimly lit or too bright. Impossibly, it seemed to be both at the same time. Mrs. Moore's faintly smiling face was lined with worry as Tabitha looked up at her in a bit of a daze, and despite the circumstances, it was the first time she was really struck with how her mother still had that glimmer of her gorgeous old self within her.

"I love you, Mom," Tabitha croaked out.

She was back where she belonged. This was the mother she was never, ever going to let go of, and although the delusions of that surreal fever dream were beginning to dilute and subside into faded almost-memories, Tabitha's resolve remained firm. *I'm not going to let you go. I'm going to save you. I mean it.*

"I love you too, sweetie," Mrs. Moore whispered. "I love you too. So much. We thought we'd lost you. They said—they said you were *gone*. God gave us a miracle, he brought you back to us. You're a miracle, Tabby sweetie."

"Then," Tabitha said slowly, "let's go to church. Sometime."

"You want to go to church?" Mrs. Moore asked in surprise. "We can do that, we can start going to church."

"Really?" Tabitha blinked.

"Of course, really," Mrs. Moore promised. "If you want us to go to church, then we're all going to church. Every Sunday."

"I figure," Tabitha breathed, "that it can't hurt. Right?"

"You're right, you're absolutely right," Mrs. Moore said quickly, trying to smile. "I don't know why we weren't going. He's—He's been so good to us. We'll find a good church to go to."

"Elena's family. Presbyterian," Tabitha said. "But 'Licia and the Williamses—Methodist."

Speaking in complete sentences somehow seemed like a huge hurdle, and whatever soup of morphine they were feeding into her IV had Tabitha feeling like she was right on the cusp of falling back asleep at any moment. It was incredibly tiresome, but even through the fog of painkillers, the side of her head felt raw, as if they'd sheared off part of her skull to access the bleed on her brain.

No, not a bleed on my brain, Tabitha told herself. *Not for sure. That was just something from my dream. Probably. I'll need to ask what actually happened here sometime soon. Get everything straight.*

"Presbyterian and Methodist?" Mrs. Moore repeated. "We'll go to whichever one you want. We can try them both. Elena, Alicia, the Williamses—everyone's been in to see you. Hannah stops in every day and holds your hand. You woke up for a bit, tried to say something to Elena, but we couldn't figure out what it was before you were out again. You just went out like a light."

"I—" Tabitha frowned, furrowing her brow. "Sorry. Don't remember."

"It's okay, it's okay," her mother quickly reassured her. "You can talk to everyone when you're feeling a little better. Everyone just had to rush back when we got word that you were making a recovery. It really is a miracle, Tabitha. You were so close to—well. It's Heaven-sent, that He gave you back to us. I love you so much, Tabitha. I didn't know what I was ever going to do without you. Frightens me even imagining it. I, I just couldn't—"

"I'm here," Tabitha promised, attempting to squeeze Mrs. Moore's hand with her own. "Can't leave. Too much to do."

"Can't leave—too much to do?" Mrs. Moore repeated, wiping at her eyes. "Oh, sweetie. I love you."

"Love you, Mom," Tabitha mumbled as she drifted back into unconsciousness.

———

"Nothing here either?" Mrs. Seelbaugh failed to hide her disappointment. "Nothing?"

The Sandboro Mall was once again the first place her mother thought of to try to cheer Elena up, some small comfort or semblance of *normalcy* to interrupt the strange gloom her daughter had fallen into. Instead, each of their familiar shopping haunts filled her with disgust and self-loathing, and Elena glared across the racks of flannel and plaid in distaste and crossed her arms at the rows of distressed jeans on mannequin displays.

"Can I just... walk around on my own a bit?" Elena asked.

"Of course you can!" Mrs. Seelbaugh quickly dug into her purse. "Do you want some twenties, or—"

"I don't need to buy anything." Elena shook her head, trying not to get annoyed. She knew her mother was doing anything and everything to help; she knew her mom cared, just right now with her mood... every little thing was an aggravation that seemed to get under her skin. Elena needed some distance for a little while. From a lot of things. "Just want to go around on my own."

"Of course—I understand completely," Mrs. Seelbaugh acknowledged with a slightly pained expression. "I was getting hungry anyways! I'll just grab a pretzel and sit at the bench by the fountain at the intersection there. Will you be—um, will you please try not to go too far down the way? Please? Just the stores in sight of the fountain. Or, you cou—"

"I won't go far," Elena promised, stepping in to give her mother the hug she knew the woman needed—her mom was positively radiating worry and concern. "Thanks, Mom."

For the next thirty minutes, Elena threaded her way through the aisles and racks of the nearby stores with a listless expression, examining the wares with detachment as she fought to distance herself from the *Elena* of before. The jewelry store held less interest for her than ever before, the shop filled with purses, wallets, and watches bored her, and looking at shoes seemed too *old Elena*. The Waldenbooks held promise and she knew there was escape somewhere in the hundreds of books arrayed on those shelves, but a pair of cheery teenage girls were babbling and gossiping there and the compulsion to leave overtook her.

Having no other stores left to explore and with her mother sneaking awkward glances in her direction from the bench by the fountain, Elena trudged reluctantly into the place she didn't belong—the Sandboro Mall's Hot Topic. The despondent blonde almost scowled and walked right back out again—the displays right in the entrance were all *South Park* merchandise and wrestling paraphernalia; black shirts with nWo or Austin 3:16 on them. Glancing around at the walls, she saw band tees for Korn, Sublime, and No Doubt, also all on black shirts.

Why is everything BLACK, though? Elena thought to herself, already turning to leave.

"Yeah, *can I help you?*" the punkish young woman behind the counter asked with annoyance.

The girl looked completely absurd—her hair was a garish shade of neon green and arrayed to taper into six-inch spikes that jutted out from her scalp in every direction. Between the spikes, her roots were growing in a dull, ashy and damaged color.

The Hot Topic employee was glaring daggers at her through eyeliner drawn on so heavily that Elena couldn't help but think of it as *Halloween makeup*, and both her lip and brow sported piercings.

Beside the employee behind the counter was a much older man—perhaps her dad's age, who wore a leather vest over a sleeveless band shirt and had tattoos running down both arms.

"Hah, don't mind her!" the older man barked out in a surprisingly cordial voice. "What can we help ya find, Little Miss?"

"Um." Elena tried not to stare. "I don't know. I'm. I don't know, I'm looking for... a new me?"

"A new you?" The man seemed to light up. "You've come to the right place!"

"No you haven't," the punk girl disagreed in a deadpan monotone that reminded Elena of the MTV *Daria* cartoon. "A *new you* isn't something one *buys* or puts a price tag on. *Mr. Gary's* just trying to make a sale. *Mindless consumerism* is everything that's wrong with—"

"Pardon my *employee* Ziggy here—she gets a little *confused*," the man said with a good-natured chuckle. "I'm sure we have something here that'll be just what you need."

Elena couldn't help but stare at the punk girl's nametag, which did indeed read *'Ziggy.'* Figuring she didn't have anything to lose, she let out a slow breath and decided to lay her cards on the table.

"I don't really know what I'm doing. I just... don't want to be *me* anymore. I don't like who I was, and I want to... *distance myself* from it, as much as possible?" Elena mumbled out in embarrassment, gesturing across the dark apparel on display. "I just. Don't know if all of *this* is me either."

"You're right at that age where you need to figure out your identity." The man—apparently *Mr. Gary*—nodded, stepping out from the central counter kiosk. "Went through it all myself, we all do. The best advice anyone can give you is that *real change comes from within*."

"Don't listen to him," Ziggy muttered under her breath. "He'll use any *bumper sticker sophism* to try to sell you something."

"Ziggy, please." Mr. Gary rolled his eyes. "Go look busy or something, will ya? Anyways, as I was saying—*real change comes from within.* Now, what does that mean, exactly? For other people, I couldn't tell ya. But, for *me,* that always meant *music.*"

"Oh," Elena said, glancing around the aisles. "You sell music?"

"We do sell a bit of music," Mr. Gary admitted, looking up across the wall of band tees on display. "Wouldn't recommend buying anything blind, though. Not at these prices, *hah!* Won't even suggest any bands for ya—my tastes are pretty rooted in the time period I grew up in, and... well, discovering the music that *moves you* is part of your own personal journey."

"Wait, you're looking for music?" Ziggy's affected apathy disappeared. "I can recommend you some—"

"Oh, *now* you want to sell something?!" Mr. Gary waved her off. "Get outta here with your garage-band punko garbage."

"Are you looking for music?" Ziggy ignored her boss to fixate on Elena. "What do you listen to now?"

"I... don't know. Normal stuff from on the radio?" Elena shrugged. Staring at the punk girl's giant green spikes, the sudden impulse to reveal something swept over her. "I was actually thinking about cutting my hair real short, finding a, um. Totally different look. I... don't really know what I'm going to do."

"Well, definitely don't cut off all your hair," Mr. Gary snorted. "You have great—"

"You should shave it all off," Ziggy disagreed with enthusiasm. "Or buzz most of it off, and then put the rest up in a mohawk, or spikes. My girlfriend Monique did my hair. I can write down her number for—"

"Whoa there, slow down, Ziggy." Mr. Gary laughed. "If she ends up hating it, she can't exactly put it all back right away, you know?"

"*Ugh.*" Ziggy let out a long-suffering sigh and rolled her eyes.

"You just don't *get it,* and you'll never *understand.* Don't you have old man stuff to do? Corporate sellout *paperwork* or something in the back?"

"Tell ya what." Mr. Gary this time ignored Ziggy, opening up a plexiglass display case and tossing a small container over to Elena. "For you; on the house."

"*Oh, and now you're GIVING AWAY product?*" Ziggy slapped both hands on the counter. "Oh, so yeah, it's fine when *you* do it, but the second *I* even want to discount a—"

"Ziggy, stuff it—it's my store, I do what I want," Mr. Gary shot back. "Besides, it's more like *an investment.* If she ends up liking it, she'll want stuff to go with the new look, right? Pretty young girl decks herself out in Hot Topic merchandise, then she's a walking billboard for us to all her friends and admirers. Opens up a whole new market."

"Whatever," Ziggy growled with obvious distaste. "You're not even my real dad. You disgust me."

"Go take your smoke break, get outta here," Mr. Gary waved the employee off and turned back toward Elena. "You go to school here in Sandboro? West Martin?"

"Um. Springton," Elena mumbled as she turned the little tub she'd been gifted over in her hands—it read *Manic Panic,* and purported itself to be semi-permanent black hair dye.

Dying her blonde hair black seemed... great, like it would present a whole different Elena in the mirror. Exactly what she needed. She'd never thought of herself drawn to the subculture until this moment, but now the pull felt *strong.* Carrie and so many of the Springton High girls continued to wrap themselves in the *preppie pop princess* aesthetic anyway, adding appeal to the urge to redefine herself from blonde to black.

Maybe... this is what I need?

———

"I'm going to dye my hair," Elena announced, taking the small tub of *Manic Panic* she'd been hiding and planting it on the dinner table.

"Elena..." Mr. Seelbaugh gave the hair dye a dismissive glance and then shot his daughter an incredulous look. "No. No, absolutely not. You're not *dying* your hair."

Mrs. Seelbaugh pursed her lips into a frown, staring at the *Manic Panic* as if she'd been afraid it—or something like it—would make an appearance soon.

"I'm either dying my hair black... or I'm cutting it all off," Elena revealed her ultimatum, taking the pair of scissors she'd nervously balanced across her lap and putting it on the table next to the tub of dye.

The effect it had on her parents wasn't dramatic like she'd hoped. Instead, her dad seemed disappointed, and was shooting his wife a look of consternation. He didn't seem to be taking her seriously, and that immediately put Elena on edge. If he made *any* sort of eye roll or joke or funny remark right now, she would be very, very upset.

"What, have we been spoiling her too much?" Mr. Seelbaugh barked out a stiff laugh. "Does she think that—"

"*Mister Seelbaugh*—I'd like to speak to my client in private for a moment, please," Mrs. Seelbaugh interrupted, folding her hands in front of her on the table.

It was an old family inside-joke, delivered now with little humor. Mr. Seelbaugh looked exasperated as he rose up out of his seat, and sent Elena a look that suggested he wasn't going to budge on the topic of her appearance. The mother and daughter sat in silence for a few long, tense moments after he'd left the room.

"Talk to me," Mrs. Seelbaugh murmured. "What's going on, Elena?"

"I... want to dye my hair," Elena said. "Black."

"Black. That's a big change," Mrs. Seelbaugh pointed out,

gently taking the tub of hair dye so that she could examine its label.

"I want a big change," Elena said. "I need a big change."

Elena watched her mother read and reread the instructions on the semi-permanent hair dye in silence for several long minutes, fighting the urge to fidget or speak up again.

"Are you going to need a new wardrobe?" Mrs. Seelbaugh asked.

"I don't know," Elena replied with a small shrug. "I guess eventually. Not, like, right away or anything. I just—"

"I'll help you dye your hair," Mrs. Seelbaugh decided. "*But.* No tattoos, no cigarettes, no marijuana. *Whatsoever.* You're still going with us to church every week. If you want piercings, or, or things like that, you need to discuss it with me first."

"I... I don't do drugs," Elena blurted out. "At all. Ever. Not interested."

"Alcohol?" Mrs. Seelbaugh challenged.

"Only with you," Elena said. "Whenever we have glasses of wine."

"Okay." Mrs. Seelbaugh seemed to relax slightly and let out a slow breath. "Okay, good. No drugs of any kind, no needles. I want to know who you hang out with from now on, *especially* if any of them are drinking, or smoking, or anything like that. No pills. No huffing paint, or sniffing glue or any of that sort of stuff to get stoned or get high. Still no swearing. No wearing clown makeup."

"*Clown makeup?*" Elena's eyebrows rose in disbelief. "Mom—"

"I don't make this stuff up!" Mrs. Seelbaugh held up her hands in defense. "Melissa's son David, he's all into the *Insane Clown Posse* or PCP or whatever it is with the clown makeup. Marijuana too; he always smells like shit."

"Mom, I just..." Elena's shoulders slumped. "I'm not turning into a bad kid or whatever. I just, I never. I've never *hated* myself before. And, *it hurts.* I can't keep being the same Elena. It makes me *feel sick.* I want to change. The guy at the Hot Topic gave this to me for free, and said I should try listening to different kinds of music. I am, I'm going to try that."

"Oh. Oh, *honey*..." Mrs. Seelbaugh's eyes watered. "What happened with Tabitha, the Halloween party—none of that was your fault. You know that. We've talked about this. We've talked and talked about this. *Nothing* that happened there—"

"Okay. *Okay*," Elena snapped out. "I do know that. I know that. But what I *feel* is that it *was* my fault. And what I feel hasn't changed—isn't going to change. And it makes me hate me, makes me feel sick. Okay?"

Elena had been bracing herself for serious resistance from her parents, had worked out arguments and counter-arguments along with her ultimatum well in advance. What she *hadn't* prepared herself for, however, was her mother bursting into tears across from her at the dinner table.

"Mom..." Elena began.

"Honey?" Mr. Seelbaugh hurried back over into the room at the sound of his wife crying. "What in the—"

"Oh, *piss off!*" Mrs. Seelbaugh sniffled, wiping her face on her sleeve. "I'm going to help dye Elena's hair, because she's got to *reinvent* herself! After that, her and I are going shopping. *Shopping for everything.* If I hear even *one* word out of you, questioning *any* of her choices about any of it, then *I'm* dying my goddamned hair black with her! *Okay?!*"

"Yeah, I, uh—no, everything's fine." Mr. Seelbaugh carefully backed out of the room. "I just—I'll just—"

"*Piss off!*" Mrs. Seelbaugh sobbed. "Just—go piss off!"

———

"How're ya feelin' today, Sweetheart?" Mr. Moore asked, glancing over the moment Tabitha woke up.

"Better," Tabitha said, trying to sit up. "Much better."

"Whoa whoa whoa," Mr. Moore leapt to his feet in alarm and

hurried to gently press her back down onto her pillow. "Not so fast, you needta be takin' it easy still."

"Okay," Tabitha relented, letting her father carefully tuck her back in. "Sorry."

"Nothin' to be sorry for," Mr. Moore reassured her. "I know you're gettin' antsy. Just a few more weeks, they said."

"I know." Tabitha nodded. "Really want to be out of here before my birthday."

"We'll see, sweetie," Mr. Moore said. "You just focus on getting better."

"Too much time to think, not enough time to *do,*" Tabitha gave him a wry smile. "Trying to be patient."

"Well, you *are* a patient right now, so—good," Mr. Moore wise-cracked. "You've thought about what you want to do once you're out and about?"

"Ice cream," Tabitha answered without hesitation. "I want to go out with you and Mom into Louisville somewhere and have ice cream."

"Ice cream?" Mr. Moore said in mock-surprise. "What ever happened to your vegan or vegetarian nutritional diet or whatever?"

"*Vegan—?!*" Tabitha giggled. "Dad. We had chicken *all the time.*"

"Chicken's not vegan?" Mr. Moore's cocked an eyebrow in surprise, but she couldn't tell if he was kidding or not.

"You might be thinking pescatarians—they can include fish in their diet, but not other meat." Tabitha laughed, trying to twist and stretch her limbs.

"Presybterians, okay. I'll remember that." Mr. Moore chuckled. "So which one of 'ems are the ones who eat chicken but are still eating healthy?"

"Us, I guess. Poor people?" Tabitha shrugged. "Frozen chicken breast is really cheap, pound for pound."

"Tabitha... we're not poor," Mr. Moore said after a long, difficult moment of silence. "Or, well, *you're* not poor. There's a fair few cash settlements coming our way in a bit; we're gonna get a college fund set up for you."

"Don't," Tabitha blurted out, struggling to sit up all over again. "Please—don't. Dad, I'm not going to college."

"You need to get yourself a good education," Mr. Moore refused firmly, pressing her shoulder back down onto the hospital bed. "We want you to—"

"I'm being *one hundred percent, deadly serious*—I'm not going to college," Tabitha insisted, clamping her good hand around his wrist. "Listen to me, please. I'm *not* going. Please, please, *please*, don't do anything rash like put any of the settlements into a college fund."

"Honey, you don't underst—" Her father sighed. "Why don't we wait and talk about it again when you're feeling better?"

"No, I *do* understand," Tabitha said. "I know more about rising tuition costs than anyone alive, I know what *I need* to learn to do what I want to do, and putting all that money and more importantly *time* into a degree won't help me at all. It will, in fact, *significantly hurt my future.* Please, please, *please*, trust me on this?"

"Honey..." Mr. Moore frowned. "What brought all this about? Thought for sure you'd be all on board with the college and university thing."

"I appreciate your thoughts." Tabitha gave his wrist a squeeze. "But I'd like it even more if we maintained a dialogue and regularly communicated about anything and everything pertaining to my future."

"There it is. There you go again." Mr. Moore booped her on the nose. "Your momma told me to watch out for you to start talkin' like that again."

"Daaaad," Tabitha growled, swiping at his finger and missing. "I'm so serious—don't put the settlements into a fund, and don't put them into a savings account. We're going to need all that money. And *soon.*"

"Oh my God—*Elena?!*" Alicia mouthed in surprise. "You dyed your hair?"

"Yeah," Elena admitted, looking back at her with an unreadable blank expression.

It was probably the most words they'd exchanged at once since Halloween. With no small amount of trepidation, Alicia awkwardly approached her former friend, who she'd spotted sitting way off by herself away from all of the other students disembarking from their busses and milling about the common areas before first bell. Alicia's recent epiphanies regarding her personal *Tabitha situation* had her feeling more nervous, self-conscious, and guilty to be around Elena than she'd ever been before—she still remembered what Elena had said back then, about not caring much for gays.

"Well... can I see?" Alicia gestured impatiently at the hood of the dark *Nightmare Before Christmas* hoodie her friend had apparently started wearing. "What brought this on?"

With uncharacteristically stiff body language, Elena drew back the hood and stared at the ground, allowing her friend to inspect her new look. *Self-conscious? Since when is ELENA ever self-conscious?*

"Elena?" Alicia repeated. "What brought this on?"

"It's..." Elena muttered, glancing up for a moment before casting her gaze downwards again. "You know."

"Because of what happened?" Alicia asked.

Elena responded only with a mute nod, and the now raven-haired teen hurried to put the hood of her sweatshirt back up.

"It looks good," Alicia said, trying to sound supportive.

In all honesty, it *did* look great on Elena, but Alicia couldn't help but find it completely unsettling. The sudden change in style seemed too *abrupt,* and Alicia couldn't help but feel a little hurt by the apparent distance appearing between them.

Did... our little JOSIE AND THE PUSSYCATS thing break up?

Alicia wondered to herself with a sinking feeling. *She like, just completely changed character. Melody Valentine suddenly switches to being Sabrina the teenage witch out of nowhere. Okay, not OUT OF NOWHERE, I guess. Just. I mean, I don't HATE IT, I just wish... I'd been in the know? I guess we haven't really been talking much at all since...*

"Um." Alicia tried not to fidget. "We're still friends... right?"

Elena *shrugged,* and Alicia learned for the first time that such a nonchalant expression can harm someone just as much, *or more,* than biting words or glares of hatred.

"Uh." Alicia felt stunned enough to rock back on her heels. "Okay. That hurts."

"No, no." Elena looked conflicted. "I mean. Why would you want to be friends with me?"

"Oh, okay—so you're just being stupid," Alicia retorted with a scowl, lunging in to wrap Elena up in a hug. "Fuck. Not cool, 'Lena. Don't ever do that to me. *We are friends.* Okay?"

"Okay," Elena sniffled.

"No, not '*okay,*'—geez, what is it with you two?" Alicia squeezed Elena as hard as she could. "No '*thank you*' or '*okay.*' You say, '*yeah, we're friends.*' That's how this works. *Duh.*"

"Sorry," Elena squeaked out in a tiny voice, finally returning her hug. "I've been a shitty friend."

"Shut the fuck up." Alicia felt herself start to smile. "No, you haven't. *I've* been a shitty friend. Things have been bad, and. I was just a little—I didn't know if. I was, you know, surprised. Almost didn't recognize you now that you've gone all *Lydia Deetz* on me. I *do* still look for you every morning, you know... I just thought you needed some space. You closed up."

"Lydia Deetz?" Elena asked.

"From Beetlejuice. You know," Alicia released her friend and leaned back to take a closer look at Elena's features. "Lydia Deetz. '*My whole life is a darkroom. One big. Dark. Room.*' Actually—why aren't you wearing any makeup?"

"Um." Elena shrugged. "Tried a little. Didn't like it."

"Can I give you some eyeliner?" Alicia asked. "Just wanna try and see how it looks. Promise I'll be fast, we have like, five, six-ish minutes before first bell?"

"I guess," Elena said. "Whatever."

"Are you gonna be alright?" Alicia wondered out loud. "Ugh, stupid question. I mean; you're on this whole different... everything, now. Whole different dynamic. Tabby gets us into crazy hijinks, I'm supposed to be the snarky artistic weirdo girl. You were gonna be the one with social savvy, I guess, who like, could talk to people and had that *in* with the popular crowd. Now, you have this sudden goth makeover."

"What would—" Elena frowned, making a frustrated face at Alicia for a moment before turning her eyes back toward the ground. "What would you do if your art hurt someone? *Really* hurt someone, someone that you care about? How would you react then?"

"Your having... *social savvy* or whatever isn't what got Tabitha hurt," Alicia refuted in a firm voice. "Elena—"

"I made her go," Elena gave another of her expressive shrugs. "She didn't want to. I made her go. She shouldn't have been there at all. It's my fault."

"No. No. *No.*" Alicia shook her head, unapologetically beginning to rummage through Elena's backpack. "Stuff was going on. *Things.* Between Tabitha and Erica. It's complicated and Tabitha has a *big* secret that makes it all weird and I think I probably need to talk to you about my *own* stupid secret that makes it all even more fucked up and where even *is* your little makeup bag thingie? *Elena, did you even bring it today?!*"

"Big secret?" Elena asked, staring at Alicia. "Sorry. Outside pocket. New makeup case."

"Your stuff's all gonna get smashed if you leave it in the outside pock—oh, it's in a little tin now. This is cool, I like this one. All the little skulls—awesome. Hot Topic?"

"Alicia," Elena warned in a grave voice. "...what *secret?*"

28

EXPLAINING EVERYTHING TO ELENA

Elena didn't know what to think when Mrs. Seelbaugh dropped off her and Alicia at Springton General Hospital to visit with Tabitha for a few hours. There wasn't any *secret* Elena could think of that would justify what had happened, nothing that could absolve Elena of her own wrongdoing. But, against her better judgment, she hadn't pressed the subject, instead allowing Alicia to defer the explanation to Tabitha.

"*Sorry! I can't say any more—I really can't,*" Alicia had said, holding up her hands in a helpless gesture. "*Not my secret to spill. I'm sorry. We DEFINITELY do need to talk with her about this real soon, though. Maybe your mom can take us after school today?*"

So Elena stalked after Alicia down the bright hallway of the hospital ward dressed in her new black attire. She didn't *walk* anymore; she *stalked*. Simply walking was *old Elena*. She wasn't quite sure yet how everything she did was redefining her, but it was helpful discovering and exploring the new outlook. People looked at her differently, an entirely different person was reflected in their eyes as they glanced at her. Even if it was just curiosity, even if they were just bored receptionists at Springton General, or the people idling about in the waiting room. What Elena wore and how she looked was making a statement about who she was.

She just needed to figure out what exactly that meant.

"Do you think she's gonna freak when she sees you?" Alicia asked, giving Elena a look of excitement as they closed in on Tabitha's room.

"I don't know." Elena tried to keep her voice in a neutral tone. "If she does, she does."

Tabitha had still been groggy and delirious the last time they'd visited, so Elena couldn't help but fill with unbridled terror at the thought of confronting her now for real. Her mind was made up, however, and even if Tabitha held nothing but hatred for her now, it was her responsibility to bear it.

However she reacts—I need to face it. Elena took a deep breath and steeled her resolve. *I'm just as responsible for putting her in here as Erica Taylor. I was the one who put her at risk. I—*

"Knock, knock," Alicia called, rapping her knuckle on the already open door of Tabitha's room and then leading Elena inside. "You still alive and kickin' in here, Tabs?"

"Oh! Hi, you guys! I wasn't expecting any—uhhh, *Elena?!*" Tabitha exclaimed.

Against all expectations, Tabitha completely lit up into a brilliant smile upon seeing them, possibly the happiest and most exuberant expression Elena remembered seeing on the girl ever. Elena had braced herself for any level of condemnation, she'd prepared herself to be berated or even screamed at, she'd readied her emotions to see raw hurt and anger written all over Tabitha's face. What she'd failed to do was prepare herself for an eventuality where Tabitha was *thrilled to see her,* and Elena drew a total blank on what to do.

"Oh my God, Elena!" Tabitha's eyes seemed to dance as she admired Elena's new look. "You look *amazing!* When did you do all this?! I thought the whole emo thing was—um, well, I wasn't expecting to see anything like this so soon!"

"Right?!" Alicia smirked, shooting Elena a patent *I told you so* look. "You're lookin' pretty great yourself, Tabs. I see they already took away your snake-charmer turban!"

"Oh my gosh." Tabitha grinned, raising a hand to the remaining headband of bandage that wrapped around her head in a self-conscious way. "Can't believe you all saw me when my head was all wrapped up like that—so embarrassing!"

"If you think that was embarrassing, you should've heard yourself trying to babble out nonsense when they had you all doped up." Alicia laughed. "I like you better this way, though. I'm... Tabitha, I'm so glad you're doing better."

"Yeah, I—it was a pretty close call, I think, hah." Tabitha let out a nervous laugh. "Um. I didn't... totally ruin the Halloween party, did I?"

"You... *what?*" Elena blinked, totally dumbfounded. "No, no you didn't *ruin it,* Tabitha—Tabitha, no one cares about the party! *You almost died.*"

"I *did* die!" Tabitha said in a chipper voice, twisting on the hospital bed and leaning over to grab a framed certificate from the nearby end table. "Sorta. I won a certificate and everything. Legally dead, hah ha. Mrs. Williams and my mom hate it, but Hannah thinks it's really cool."

"Oh wow," Alicia mouthed, accepting the frame from Tabitha. "This is awesome. They'll really let you keep this? Don't they have to, like, invalidate it, or shred it or something?"

"Well, it'll be valid *someday.*" Tabitha chuckled, giving her friends a cheeky smile. "They'll just have to adjust the date, 'cause it's not gonna be soon. I've got way too much to do!"

The growing dissonance between Elena's expectations for this meeting and the current playful mood was a chasm yawning wide that all of her lines of thought were dropping down into. She couldn't help but stare in disbelief at the completely nonchalant way Tabitha was brushing off everything that had happened. It was *frustrating,* the situation was making her feel increasingly uncomfortable, and the now raven-haired teenager felt so jarringly out of place that she had no idea what to do.

"Elena?" Tabitha's bright expression began to falter. "What's wrong?"

"What's wrong?" Elena repeated, feeling stupid. "Tabitha. I—I almost got you fucking killed."

"What?" Tabitha looked utterly perplexed by the assertion. "How? What?"

"She thinks it's her fault that all that happened," Alicia carefully mediated. "For like, convincing you to go to the party."

"I *made her* go," Elena corrected. "She didn't even want to. I *made* her. I—"

"No, no—*Elena.*" Tabitha put on an exasperated smile. "You were completely right about the party, I had a lot of fun!"

"What?" Elena uttered.

"I mean, not counting what happened with Erica, obviously." Tabitha rolled her eyes. "The rest of it, the dressing up and going with you guys, just, *being there,* it was great. I loved it."

"What?" Elena said again.

To her credit, Alicia didn't make any comment, but the *I told you so* look that reappeared spoke volumes. Elena looked from Tabitha to Alicia and back again, but the discomforting sense of alienation just intensified. No one blamed her, no one at all. But how was that possible? How were the feelings of guilt and grief that felt so *true* and real supposed to be invalidated? She opened her mouth to say something, but she had no idea what to say.

"It... it was my fault," Elena finally insisted, shaking her head. "What happened was my fault. You were at risk. You shouldn't have even been there."

"No." Tabitha refused her claims without pause. "No, it wasn't your fault. If Erica didn't find me at the party, she would've just found me at home, or out alone on one of my walks, or something. Can you imagine how bad it would've been if she attacked me when hardly anyone else was around?"

"No, I—no," Elena argued. "You can't know that. She—"

"Tabitha—you need to tell her," Alicia said, giving the redhead a meaningful look. "Your big secret. I've already been through this with her, and like, nothing gets through at all. This whole thing is really messing her up."

"Um," Tabitha squeaked, her expression turning apprehensive. "Has she... guessed anything?"

"No, not really, but—I mean, just look at her!" Alicia gestured dramatically at Elena's new fashion choices. "This is like, *affecting* her!"

What secret can she even have? Elena frowned, watching Tabitha carefully. *Was she... actually stealing stuff from the Taylors? That doesn't seem like it fits her, like it fits what Tabitha would do at all.*

"I... thought that we were going to be careful about this?" Tabitha protested in a weak voice.

"Yeah, well, we were gonna—*you were* gonna have to tell her eventually anyways!" Alicia countered. "Better sooner rather than later, right? The longer you let the lie go on—"

"—I haven't *lied* about anything," Tabitha interrupted. "Not exactly. I just—"

"—Oh, *come on*," Alicia retorted. "You know what I'm—"

"—I just haven't been open about certain unbelievable things that would necessitate lengthy explanations," Tabitha finished with difficulty.

"We need to tell her," Alicia insisted firmly. "This is hurting her, and she needs to know. What happened at the party—that absolutely wasn't Elena's fault, right?"

"Of course it wasn't Elena's fault," Tabitha said, turning her gaze from Alicia to Elena. "Elena, you—"

"It was. I made you go," Elena said with a difficult shrug. "You didn't want to. I practically made you. Talked you into it, all because—"

"*See?*" Alicia waved her hands. "She thinks it was her fault. But it wasn't, right?"

"Elena," Tabitha started to say. "What happened *wasn't* your—

"Don't," Elena warned, shaking her head. "Don't. Just... don't. I've heard it. I've heard everybody tell me that."

"Yeah, maybe 'cause it *wasn't* your—" Alicia started.

"I can make up my own mind," Elena replied, crossing her arms and trying not to choke up, "on whether or not I deserve blame. For what I did. I convinced Tabitha to go, when she shouldn't have been there. Mostly for selfish reasons. Okay? I was trying to, like, build us up as this thing. As part of—as this little group, taking advantage of Tabitha's momentum. And then, when she withdrew from school—I didn't know what to do. I was desperate for... leverage. Needed to feel in control of the social situation. It was selfish. Selfish, stupid games. Tabitha didn't need to go to that party, *I* needed Tabitha to go to that party."

"Elena—" Tabitha tried.

"—And you know what?" Elena bit out as tears formed in her eyes. "It didn't even matter. *It didn't even matter!* Matthew was already with Casey. For a long while, maybe, I just, I didn't want to see or, or didn't care, or didn't want to notice. The school situation is—it's fucking stupid and *trivial* and even thinking about it now makes me feel sick. Us going there, us *being there* to make a point, it wasn't going to do anything—nothing was going to change with us being there. It would have been fine, you *would have been safe,* if, if—"

"Elena, stop." Tabitha held out her good hand. "Come here."

"No, I—no." Withdrawing a step, Elena shook her head in refusal, hugging her arms closer to herself and beginning to cry.

"Elena, *come here,*" Tabitha repeated, gesturing again. "I'm not supposed to get up. But I will, if you make me."

"No." Elena shook her head. "No, no, Tabitha, Tabitha, I'm—"

"Oh, *c'mon.*" Alicia stepped forward, taking Elena by the arm and trying to force the unbudging girl over toward Tabitha's hospital bed. "Both of you—Tabitha, *you need to tell her.*"

"You blame me too, Tabitha!" Elena stammered, trying to pull her arm out of Alicia's grasp. "Tabitha, you asked me *which Elena are you*, when we came in last time. When, when you were, you were delirious from your painkillers or whatever. I said to everyone, I told them I couldn't make out what you were saying. But I heard. You asked me, *which Elena are you?* That's when I knew—"

"Alicia... let go of her." Tabitha sighed, slowly settling herself back on the bed. "They'll flip out if they catch you two rough-housing in here. Pull up the chairs closer, please, and we'll—we all need to talk."

"There's nothing to talk about," Elena said in a bitter voice as Alicia hurried to rearrange the chairs in the small room. "I know what—"

"If you were ever my friend, Elena, you'll at least listen to what I have to say," Tabitha decided. "I won't ask you to believe me. I just—please, will you listen?"

"*Was* I ever really your friend?" Elena challenged. "What does anything I've ever even—"

"Yes, Elena, you are my friend." Tabitha reached over to pat the armrest of the first chair as Alicia placed it beside the head of her bed. "Now come here. Sit."

Feeling ashamed and furious at herself and unsettled all at once, Elena reluctantly stepped over to the offered chair and slowly—uneasily—sat down.

"Elena... I've already lived out a different life, one that went past 1998," Tabitha revealed in a slow voice.

"She's from the future!" Alicia blurted out, scooting the other chair up closer to them.

"I'm from... *a* future," Tabitha corrected. "A different future. This time through is significantly different, because of things I've tried to change."

"She's from the future!" Alicia said again. "Like, she's *for real* from the future. She knows things that nobody else could ever, *ever* know. She knew about the shooting, she—"

"Alicia, whoa," Tabitha chided her friend, holding up a hand.

"Not all at once. Let's let her process this bit by bit—it's a lot to take in."

"Sorry," Alicia said with a sheepish smile. "It's true, though. She's from the future."

"You're... from the future," Elena echoed in a flat voice, staring at Tabitha.

"I'm from the future." Tabitha nodded, wearing an unsure smile as she attempted to gauge Elena's reaction.

In all honesty, Elena felt no reaction at all. She registered the words her two friends were saying, but all the same, they didn't seem to parse at all. The meaning behind what they were trying to convey just wasn't processing, and Elena didn't find herself to be particularly in the mood to puzzle out what they were actually trying to tell her. Instead, she simply stared at Tabitha, waiting for the girl to explain herself.

"Okay, here goes..." Tabitha took a deep breath and began to recount her story.

"In my first life, I was *Tubby Tabby*. I was an overweight little... trailer trash girl, who grew up in a very low-income neighborhood. After some circumstances with the older sisters of a friend of mine —the Taylors—and then some *comparatively* minor bullying incidents, I developed this rather crippling case of social anxiety. Kept to myself throughout school, my hobbies were just, like, watching TV and reading. Staying home. I didn't have friends. I didn't have either of you.

"Enrolled in the community college in Elizabethtown, eventually later transferred to Northern Kentucky University. My college years were all... still a mess. I was fat. Hated myself. Really struggled to interact with people. The major I was pursuing, secondary education English—at first I thought I wanted to be a teacher, but it—it.. well, it wasn't for me. The more I learned, just... the more I realized it wasn't for me.

"My actual social development basically started throughout that time period, during my last years at Springton High and my first years at college. At least, if you could even call it development; I spent my time online. Livejournal. Fanfiction dot net. *Gaia online,* even. Dozens of little proboards forums, geocities webrings, messenger friends, *mIRC*—"

"Wait, wait, wait." Alicia scrabbled to retrieve her sketchpad and pencil. "Lemme write these down."

"Please don't." Tabitha looked mildly alarmed. "Please don't. I —listen, I'm not proud of my history there. I was going through a difficult time, and there were a lot of internet communities for... those of us who were also going through difficult times."

"That doesn't sound *bad* or anything," Alicia tried to reassure her as she began writing furiously. "These are website addresses? Live journal, fan fiction something, and guy online? My dad pays for a web service, so—"

"You don't—" Tabitha made a face. "Well. You'll understand when we all get there. It *was* bad, it was this total cringeworthy... I can't explain. *I won't* explain. All my posts are gone like they never existed now, so I can safely pretend my dark past there just never ever was."

"...Go on," Elena prompted.

"Yeah, anyways," Tabitha said with reluctance. "At some point, I thought I could be the next Rowling or Meyer, become *the next big thing* writing young adult fiction. Gave up on teaching and finished school with just my English major. Tried to write my Goblin Princess trilogy, got through the first two books with this Canadian publisher before all of that fell through. Was deep, *deep* in debt from school, because I wasn't on scholarship, and also hadn't been working.

"So, after Northern Kentucky U, I just came back home and got a job at the safety plant. The one in Fairfield. Worked there for... years and years. Tried dating, because I was terrified of winding up alone, and, um. Well, dating was worse than being alone. I wasn't comfortable being in my own body, let alone uh, sharing intimacy with another person. Let alone the kind of person who—

uh, *okay* yeah, I'm actually not ready to get back into all of that right now.

"Time went on. I got older, fatter, and more miserable. Just like my—well, uh. Moved out of the trailer when things got bad between my mother and me, and... um, she died not long after. We weren't on *horrible* terms or anything when it happened. Things had just been... difficult between us. She saw too much of herself in me, or... I don't know. Complicated. *Really* complicated now, with some of this new perspective. Uh, anyways. My dad died— cancer, brain tumor. My one close writer friend died—suicide, actually. Started working at the Springton Town Hall when I got older—well, I was just old, really.

"I was sixty years old, and I'd been having these persistent migraines—concerning, after what happened to Dad—and all Springton did was keep freaking prescribing different medications at the problem. When I eventually put my foot down, because I'm starting to miss work because of these headaches, they send me to Louisville for a more thorough check. I get into this big custom MRI machine... and something happens. It sends my mind back in time, where I'm in the same machine, but just a little girl getting her concussion looked at. The concussion from being pushed off of that trampoline, all the way back in middle school. Here in 1998."

"So, the MRI's really a time machine!" Alicia gasped at the reveal. "Tabitha—oh my God!"

"Maybe?" Tabitha nodded. "It sent my mind back, at least. I'm not sure how useful that is, though—I think the caveat was that my past self had to have interacted with the machine here, in this time."

"Wait, wait." Alicia slapped her sketchpad on her knees. "Have you like, *investigated* it or anything? What's special about that MRI, who made it? Has it sent anyone else back? If we get into that same machine here in 1998, isn't there a chance our future selves could, uh, bridge through into our bodies here?"

"Um... it's possible," Tabitha admitted. "I suppose. I thought about it a little bit, but I'm not sure what would happen. The MRI would maybe have to do the crazy screeching scraping metal freaking out thing, I think. And then, you'd... wake up with your mind overwritten by *future you?* Maybe. I'm not sure how it exactly works, and the apparent mechanics of it might be a matter of... perspective?"

"Tabitha... how serious are you about all of this?" Elena asked, trying to be as tactful as possible.

"Very." Tabitha winced. "Completely. I *do* realize how crazy it sounds."

"I didn't believe it at first," Alicia admitted. "But like, she will fucking convince you. Back when I met her in the first weeks of school, she was in the school library at lunch every day, reading up on treating emergency gunshot wounds and police response stuff. Then, out of the blue, she knows right where to be to save Officer MacIntire."

"That was... actually a fair amount of luck." Tabitha let out a slow breath. "I only remembered that it was after school early-ish October, so my plan was to be out there at that spot every day. And, I didn't *save* him, I just... managed to get it called in a little earlier and prevented some of the blood loss."

"You saved him," Alicia refuted. "Literally. Like, he was supposed to die, and then because you intervened, he didn't. Right? That's literally you saving his life."

"I mean... I guess," Tabitha said with an uneasy expression.

"He was supposed to die?" Elena asked.

"I can't speak for what was *supposed* to happen, but... he did die in my first lifetime," Tabitha said. "I was watching TV and heard the gunshot, but I didn't go outside to see what happened, or anything. I heard he bled out in the ambulance en route to the hospital, and... they couldn't resuscitate him. He passed away."

"But, this time, *he didn't,*" Alicia said with excitement. "Because Tabs here was ready and waiting, right there when it was about to happen. She ran up and knew what to do right away, was shouting all the medical whatever to me to tell the dispatcher, the—"

"—I wasn't *shouting* at you—"

"—make and model of the shooter's getaway car and everything," Alicia continued. "'Cause Tabitha knew it was gonna happen, and she'd been holed up in the library every day researching the like, gunshot wound trauma and stuff. Like, I *knew*. Somehow, I *knew* that she knew about it in advance. It was just too convenient."

"Elena?" Tabitha prompted, apparently noticing Elena's terrible expression. "Are you okay?"

"No, I'm not." Elena let out a bitter chuckle. "I just—I don't get it. It's not funny, and I don't like it. After how worried I've been, and how much this whole thing with us has been tearing me apart —I just. I don't get it. The people who I *thought* you were wouldn't do this to me. Did the both of you think it would be, what, funny? It's, it's *not* fucking funny, and if—"

"Elena." Tabitha's expression began to fall. "It's... it's true. We're not making this up, and it's not a joke. I really, honestly, *truly* did come back in time, from the year 2045."

"Bullshit." Elena shook her head. "I... I honestly can't believe you'd try to pull this on me right now. This bullshit."

"I wouldn't try to pull anything on you," Tabitha prompted with an encouraging smile. "I think you know that. But I don't blame you for being skeptical. Ask anything, please, and I'll answer as best as I can."

"Okay," Elena scoffed, crossing her arms in front of herself. "What do I invest in to become a billionaire?"

"Well, Alicia and I will be investing in Alphabet Incorporated," Tabitha explained. "The initial public offering for their stock should be in either 2004 or 2005, at about a hundred dollars a share. I think."

"Not oil? Or silver?" Elena pressed. "Not *electronic frontier* stuff, like IBM or Microsoft?"

"Oil prices should spike up in the next year or two because of the war in Iraq," Tabitha admitted. "Well, the next few years. 2002? But, Alphabet Inc's *Google* becomes one of the most successful internet services, and I'm putting all of my money on it."

"*Google,*" Elena repeated, trying out the word for size. "It sounds... just even the name sounds really dumb and made up, Tabitha. You could've gone with, I dunno, *Max Corporation,* or *MicroTech Enterprises—*"

"—Omni-Corp, InGen," Alicia threw in helpfully. "Uhhh, *Umbrella Corporation—*"

"—but instead, you go with *Goo ga ga?*" Elena ridiculed. "Like, really? *That's* what you're going with? Someone in the future's gonna have a huge, successful company and it's gonna be called *Googily Moogily?*"

"You'll both get used to it." Tabitha gave them both a helpless shrug. "*Google.* Everyone and anyone uses it. It's so common it turns into its own common verb, becomes a facet of our culture."

"Becomes its own verb?" Elena couldn't keep the doubt out of her voice. "*Google* becomes a common verb, that everyone uses? Do you... realize how stupid that sounds?"

"So, like, I would *google* Elena in the face? Or, something?" Alicia grinned. "That's verbs, right—action words? I'm so bad with English stuff."

"If you were to google Elena, it would mean you searched for her name online," Tabitha explained. "Google could present you with her information, photos of her, links to her profile or accounts on different major websites."

"Uh-huh." Elena sounded unconvinced. "And people are going to do that a lot, apparently?"

Something about this conversation was starting to not feel right to Elena. As she carefully studied the frail-seeming redheaded teen that was sitting up in the hospital bed... Tabitha seemed a little too composed. Elena knew all about mentally preparing for a debate, covering her bases and readying herself for potential arguments her opponent might pose to her. Tabitha wasn't really the type. But, this girl also didn't seem to have grown tense or on the edge of becoming flustered by running into an inevitable question she wouldn't be able to answer. Instead, her friend seemed... serene and almost a little wistful, and the disparity between that and Elena's expectations almost lent a tiny sliver of credence to the absurdity of Tabitha's claims.

But it's impossible. It's a stupid, pointless FARCE to even consider it, and I don't understand why we're even...

"Sometimes," Tabitha answered with a small shrug, "to *google* something means to search for information on the internet, so it's more broad than just looking someone up. Google is where you'd go if you had a question about anything—or even if you don't know how to properly phrase what you want to ask, because it will have this autocomplete field.

"You would google a recipe if you were interested in trying to make something new, you'd google the route to the airport and then your phone would verbally guide you to your destination, by comparing your current GPS location to online maps of the area. I used Google daily when I was writing, because it's basically a thesaurus, dictionary, and Wikipe—uhm, encyclopedia all at once. Or, at least, it's connected to all of them."

"Wait, *Wikipeep,* what's *Wikipeep?*" Alicia laughed. "What were you about to say?"

"Err... Wikipedia," Tabitha said, making a face. "Yes, I realize how silly that must sound now too. The whole internet concept is... a rabbit hole that really leads all the way down into wonderland. People search for what they're interested in. Movies, pictures, research, studying, celebrities, fashion, finance, current events, cultural trends, *funny pictures of cats,* videos to watch, and... yeah, a whole lot of pornography."

"*Ooh la la!*" Alicia waggled her eyebrows suggestively. "Funny pictures of cats, you say? Go on. Tell us more."

"I'm going to actually have to try to explain what memes are." Tabitha sagged back on the bed, covering her face with her good hand. "Jesus. How do I even...?!"

"How much does *Google* cost to use?" Elena asked.

"For searchers? Nothing," Tabitha said. "But, by profiling both the individual searchers and the overall market trend, companies can make an obscene amount of money via ad revenue, targeted advertising and all that."

"Commercials?" Alicia guessed. "You're saying they basically run commercials?"

"Pop-up ads," Elena corrected. "That's what they are on the internet. We have our own computer at home. *I have my own email address,* Tabitha. You're not going to be able to—"

"Not... exactly pop-ups." Tabitha winced. "But you're close. Pop-ups and spam emails were an early internet thing; they were too obnoxious to be effective for long. Malware blocking addons, intuitive spam filters. Google algorithms are a lot more subtle. Say a searcher has googled information on baby care; maybe a young mother wants to know about... teething tips, or when to wean them off baby food, or something like that. Google *remembers* their search, and from that point onwards, the ads this searcher sees— on Google itself or on any number of sites that use Google's advertising—will be all the cutest baby clothes, the hottest best-selling baby toys, or parenting books *guaranteed to impact their child's development.*"

Okay, now she's even trying to double down on things by actually trying to use it as a verb and a noun...? Elena narrowed her eyes. *Does she not somehow realize how stupid the Googly name sounds?*

"Likewise, a guy searching for how to fix his engine problem would get ads related to his make and model of car, local auto services, cheap car parts, accessories, et cetera. A *Star Wars* fan Googling *Star Wars* stuff would get—you know, advertisements for toys and memorabilia, I guess. Google figures out what you're looking for, and then profits by presenting advertisements, articles, and whatnot based on what you've clicked on in the past. They're *very* good at getting clicks. The whole clickbait culture gets frankly absurd after a while."

"*Clickbait. Culture.*" Alicia spread her hands out in the air. "It's crazy how she does this—all of these sound like they could be totally real things, right? Once you get her going, she's completely full of this stuff. Like, I don't think she could keep making these up nonstop, Elena."

"Okay then," Elena sighed. "What's 'clickbait culture,' exactly?"

"That's... oof," Tabitha made a face. "It's a whole thing. Resorting to certain kinds of sensationalism to bait people into clicking on links. Headlines that promise to reveal something interesting—like, say, *college professors HATE it when students use this one simple trick!* Or, a purported list of *fifteen student tricks that college professors HATE!*

"Tricks, tips, secrets, life hacks, reveals, or even just framing a set of information as something that *shocked* other people, or made their jaws hit the floor. Media sites on the internet will resort to just about anything to get you clicking on their link and earning them their fractions of a penny in advertisement revenue. They'll lie and slander, frame opinion editorials as fact, extrapolate crazy stories from skewed, completely misleading, or downright fabricated statistics."

"Okay, like tabloids, then." Alicia laughed. "Like the *Sun* or the *Enquirer* you'd see at a checkout line."

"Yes! A lot like tabloids." Tabitha nodded quickly. "I'd forgotten about them. Only, when in the privacy of their own home and at no apparent cost to them, people are a *lot* more likely to carelessly click on things like that. It's the same for porn—they might not go out of their way to buy it in real life, but when they have free and anonymous access to it through the internet..."

"That's gross." Alicia looked thoughtful. "But, yeah, I'd believe it."

"Setting... all of that aside," Elena decided to return to their earlier subject. "How much will this Google stock be worth in the future?"

"Twenty years should turn each hundred dollars we put into Alphabet Inc... into about three grand," Tabitha said. "I know it keeps going up after that, but I'm hazy on the amounts, because all of this was from some random article I remember reading at some point, and... the value of a dollar becomes a whole lot more variable as time goes on."

"A hundred bucks becomes three grand—*three thousand dollars?*" Alicia exclaimed. "Tabitha—holy fuck!"

"Over twenty years," Tabitha cautioned. "But, yes. It's not by any means the best investment, or even the highest payoff, probably. But it's a good one, and it's the one I'm absolutely sure of."

"Then, you're set for life, basically," Elena asserted. "If you already know you're going to have this unlimited amount of money."

"Not unlimited." Tabitha shook her head. "You can't make money without first investing money, which I don't have yet right now. I think Google will be a popular stock, and I don't remember at all how many shares will be available, or how much their price will fluctuate early on. The cost of buying property is going to quadruple in the near future, both of you are likely going to face a steep rise in tuition costs, and there's an economic depression coming up with nine-eleven."

"...Nine-eleven?" Elena repeated.

"It's... a large-scale terrorist attack coming up soon," Tabitha revealed with a grimace.

"The one with the airplanes, right," Alicia remembered, turning to Elena. "It's not Russia either, this time."

"Alicia," Tabitha groaned. "You're really not helping."

"Sorry!" Alicia smiled. "I'm just excited. I've—we've both really missed hanging out with you, Tabs. Everything around you gets just absolutely crazy."

"...Okay," Elena said slowly. "Tabitha. I think you should—um, have you been keeping a notebook of these supposed major events that we'll be seeing? A diary? I feel like if you *are* actually trying to be serious about this, you need to sort out future events by their... significance."

"I thought it would be dangerous, so I wasn't really writing things down." Tabitha shrugged. "It's *still* dangerous, kinda, but... I almost died for good, there. I think it's important to have both of you know what I know, or at least as much as I can remember. Just in case... something happens to me."

"Yeah, or we could just make sure nothing happens to you?" Alicia scowled. "I know it's like, the elephant in the room or whatever, but *holy fuck, Tabitha*. You almost died, it's a big fucking deal, and it affects all of us in a big way. Okay?"

"Right. That's... that is right." Tabitha looked down at her hands in a slightly guilty way. "Sorry. None of this happened in my first life. I've been... kind of sticking my nose in some events this time, and getting... unexpectedly severe reactions."

Absentmindedly letting her gaze travel from Tabitha's hands to the folds of the blanket that covered the girl's legs, Elena for the first time started to see how this whole *claiming to be from the future* thing Tabby was espousing connected to the events of the Halloween party. *But why, literally WHY? Why make all of THIS up? Why run with this unbelievable and impossibly convoluted tall tale? If I don't buy it, there's no way any of the adults ever will. It doesn't make sense. None of it makes sense.*

"Tabitha." Elena looked up at her friend. "Why exactly was Erica Taylor so out to get you?"

"Well," Tabitha hesitated, appearing for the first time to be gathering her thoughts. "Erica and Brittney Taylor have a younger sister, Ashlee. She should be our age. In fifth or sixth grade, she was... she was like me, like I was. Kind of a social outcast. I was overweight and... well, my clothes probably smelled like body odor and I had no clue how to interact with other people; they terrified me. Ashlee Taylor, on the other hand, was a *very pretty young girl,* except... she had this mild case of amblyopia. I... yeah, I think that's how you're supposed to refer to it."

"Uhhh, pretend real quick that we have no idea what that means," Alicia prompted after a glance toward Elena.

"Amblyopia is... when one eye doesn't develop quite properly," Tabitha explained. "One of Ashlee's eyes was—only very slightly —misaligned, but everyone treated her like she was—"

"*Ashlee,* with the lazy eye," Elena suddenly remembered. "From Laurel Middle, I remember her. Wait, she was the Taylors' *sister?*"

"Okay, lazy eye." Alicia nodded. "That's—yeah, okay. This kid Norman in Fairfield had that, eyes that pointed in different directions. People were mean to him, always called him *crazy eyes,* they—"

"*Amblyopia,*" Tabitha insisted firmly. "Don't call it *lazy eye,* that's not... listen—I know we're in 1998 right now, but please just call it amblyopia. Please."

"So—what." Elena couldn't help but cast a skeptical look at her friend. "You're saying being politically correct about everything actually gets to be a thing in the future?"

"Short answer; yes," Tabitha answered bluntly. "Long answer... that gets extremely complicated with how societal norms ended up progressing over time. I mean, Elena. Just put yourself in her shoes. Imagine growing up disadvantaged, growing up with people constantly saying cruel things about you, for something you have absolutely no control over. Imagine how often she gets reminded of being different from everyone else."

If Ashlee's sisters are actually Erica and Brittney Taylor, I imagine the reminders are constant, painful, and... yeah, downright abusive, Elena thought, feeling a pang of guilt. *I... wasn't exactly nice to her back then either.*

"Okay, so this Ashlee has amblyphobia," Alicia summed up. "How exactly does that—"

"Amblyopia," Tabitha corrected. "And, yeah. Anyways, Ashlee and I were friends. Friends, by virtue of the fact that no one else would ever be our friends. I kid you not, not only were we the *last two picked* whenever the class had to form teams in Laurel, but when the choices got down to the two of us, the *teams stopped wanting to pick anyone.*"

"Jesus," Alicia snorted, quickly covering her mouth and immediately looking horrified. "Oh, I—sorry, I didn't mean it like that. It's actually not funny."

"...It turned out the Taylors lived nearby to my trailer park," Tabitha pressed on. "We didn't ride the same bus, but they lived in the neighborhood just behind that Hardees near Sunset Estates, close enough for me to walk to. They were, um. This Taylor family was... things were bad. I didn't realize it back then, but when I look back on it with the hindsight of living a fairly long life...

"I think all three of the Taylor girls were living in fear. Ashlee, she got the worst of it because of her sisters. She, uh, she couldn't let herself be touched without flinching back and recoiling. I asked her one day if she was okay, she gets evasive, I was a dumb kid who didn't read social cues and kept asking about it, and... yeah, she finally pulled up her shirt and showed me.

"Bruises. *Really bad* bruises. Fresh ones atop old ones, some of them were so *dark,* and—um. Never where it would show when she was wearing clothing, but—yeah. She was being beaten. Maybe daily. I don't know. I don't even know if the parents were, um, *in on it* or what, I just remember that she was *terrified* of Erica and Brittney."

"Jesus..." Alicia murmured, sharing a concerned look with Elena.

"In my *original timeline,* we were playing on their trampoline when... okay, I'm fuzzy on the specifics after all this time, but Erica and Brittney come out and start being mean, one of them ends up shoving me off the trampoline. Because, I think to them, pushing us around was okay to them, fair game because of who we were.

What we were to them. Only, my fall's unexpectedly bad, *severe head trauma and parents will have questions bad,* so they panic and threaten us into silence about it.

"After forty-seven years, I don't remember a lot of those details so well," Tabitha said in a small voice. "What I *do* remember was that they promised to make life living hell for Ashlee if I didn't stay away and keep my mouth shut. I remember... I remember seeing Ashlee sort of go quiet and withdraw completely into herself, and that was the first time dumb thirteen-year-old me actually connected all the dots in what was going on. How Ashlee always had bruises for no reason, and always acted the way she did.

"Well, it worked," Tabitha admitted in a bitter voice. "I kept what I saw to myself. I didn't go back and see Ashlee ever again—I was terrified. I knew, deep down, how horrible it was to not tell someone about it, but... with who I was back then? I felt like no one would care what *I* had to say about anything. Girls like Erica and Brittney, their words had more weight than mine, parents and adults would believe them first and not me. Never me."

"So, when you came back in time, this time, you did something about it right away?" Alicia guessed.

"I... no, I didn't," Tabitha admitted with difficulty. "Not immediately. I—I know it isn't an excuse for inaction or anything, but... right when I came back to 1998, I was not fucking coping well. With the, um, the transition. Reliving certain horrible, uh, *everything.* I spent the first several months pretty much just obsessively cleaning things and exercising. Trying to, um. Regain any semblance of control around my own body and my immediate environment. I won't blame you if you think less of me for that."

"No, no," Alicia said quickly. "I, uh, I shouldn't have just assumed that—"

"It's okay," Tabitha gave her friend a forced smile. "I, um. A lot of little things came back to bite me because of that. My neglecting interpersonal relationships, and, uh. Private misunderstandings between me and my mother. What happened all those many years ago with Ashlee and them—I honestly had it all just walled off and repressed. Didn't want to think about it. Didn't want to acknowledge it. Wanted to pretend that my *do-over* was this completely fresh new start for me. I mean, isn't that what a do-over's *supposed* to be?"

Elena watched in confusion and disbelief at the regret on Tabitha's face and the guilt she seemed to carry. It wasn't feigned. None of this was making sense to her, because certain nonsensical portions seemed to contain slivers of very real truth to them. Elena could see that now. Time travel was impossible, but it was clear that some of these situations *had* actually happened, or at least Tabitha actually believed they happened.

It's... a coping mechanism? Elena realized. *It has to be. Some of these bad things really happened, but she formed some complex about revealing it to anyone, and it got twisted up in her head into this... fanciful story. But there's TRUTH hidden in there. Whatever happened... it really fucked her up.*

If not for her own recent experiences, Elena didn't think she'd have been able to relate.

"So, um. *This time through,*" Tabitha cleared her throat and continued, "I think it was my new look that changed things. Changed the way the Taylor sisters bullied me. From what I gather, all along, I think Ashlee was hiding their things and blaming it on me. She was too afraid to directly confront them, and it might have also been... kind of retribution, for me abandoning her. Originally, I was bullied in high school maybe because Erica and Brittney thought I'd taken some of their things. This time, it got worse, because now they thought, I don't know, that stealing things from them this time was really benefiting me. To the extent that I looked different, acted with more confidence, could apparently afford new clothes."

"They felt threatened," Elena agreed. "I can see now why they had a more personal stake in needing to take you down a notch with the rumors and everything."

"*Take her down a notch?!*" Alicia spat out. "Fucking hell, they did a lot more than—"

"I know, I know," Elena gave the girl an expressive shrug to illustrate her helpless agreement. "I'm just saying."

"It wasn't that extreme at the start, though." Tabitha shrugged. "I think the tiny little differences in timelines were enough of a change for the situation to... *escalate,* this time through. After getting pushed on the bus loop and getting the fracture, I faced some realities about myself I didn't really ever want to face. Decided to come clean about some things. When this woman from the school board dropped by about my withdrawing from school, I told her about Ashlee's bruises.

"I'm guessing they discovered them right away, and someone or other separated Ashlee from her family while they sorted out what's going on," Tabitha said. "Erica in particular panicked, showed up at the Halloween party where I'm supposed to be—"

"You weren't *supposed* to be there." Elena grimaced. "I—I shouldn't have ever told everyone you were going to go. I just thought that—"

"'*You think you can fucking take our sister away from us?!*'" Alicia recalled. "That's what Erica was screaming when she went going ballistic. That didn't make... any goddamn sense to me all this time. Not until just now."

"Yes." Tabitha winced. "That. So, Erica Taylor kills me, and—"

"She didn't kill you," Elena cut in. "Just. Don't ever say that."

"I... I think she actually did," Tabitha said slowly. "Because, I definitely shuffled off my mortal coil somehow. Like, a few seconds after I blacked out there on the floor of the lake house... I started the timeline over again from the waking up in MRI. May of 1998. *Again.*"

"Wait—you *what?!*" Alicia exclaimed.

"I, uh, I didn't handle it well." Tabitha let out a nervous chuckle. "At all. I, um, I thought I lost all of our moments together. Things and circumstances that came about by happenstance I couldn't recreate. And, I couldn't handle sorting things out with my mother all over again from the beginning, and, well. The way things went, I didn't have to."

"What happened?!" Alicia demanded.

"I'm not sure," Tabitha said after a moment of thought. "Some sort of... damage from the previous timeline—*this* timeline—carried through, somehow. My nose kept bleeding, I had these intense sort of migraine episodes. I'm... pretty sure I ended up having an aneurysm and dying, mid-conversation with my mother. All at once, it was like... like reality *stuttered,* and it went from being a movie about my life to suddenly cutting away to a surreal *making-of* montage. Some behind-the-scenes featurette, with weird dream nonsense stuff mixed in."

Elena stared, an increasingly incredulous expression becoming evident on her face.

"I sat in a Perkins I remember from the future, and talked with my friend Julie," Tabitha went on. "Then, the girls I remember bullying me in middle school and high school, including middle school Elena—that's probably what I meant back when I asked you which Elena you were—chased me through an endless parking lot nightmare. I ended up getting in a junkyard F-22 fighter jet that got mixed in from this *other* fever dream I had once, and tried to escape. I think it worked maybe, because I got pulled back to my *original* timeline, in 2045, where they were trying to pull me out of the MRI that was breaking down."

"Wait, wait, what?" Alicia pressed fingertips to her temples as she tried to follow along. "An... F-22? You went *back to the future?* Were you able to grab more information about things? Lottery numbers, stock market shit? A sports almanac? Did you look me up in the future? Wait, and how do you know which of all that stuff was a dream and which wasn't?"

"I... don't." Tabitha shrugged. "Not for sure. All I have, um, is my interpretation of the experiences to go off of. I felt very confident that the timeline starting over was really happening, but, like

I said... in the middle of talking to my mother, I think I just kind of croaked, or something. Bleed on my brain? Everything after that was *very* inconsistent and dream-like."

"Wait, so you *didn't* go back to the future? Or, no?" Alicia asked.

"I... maybe?" Tabitha held up her hands. "I feel that I did, but I can't say for certain. At the time, I was, um, *freaking the fuck out.* Like, flailing and fighting hospital staff and trying to climb back into the dream, or the other timelines, or anything but being stuck back in 2045 like none of this ever happened. It worked, maybe, because I think my brain was hemorrhaging and it seemed like I watched my future self, um. Pass away. Most of the dream or nightmare or whatever seemed to... drain away and disappear at that point, and I was just kind of hanging in the empty darkness when I heard Hannah calling out to me."

"So... when you put it like that, it's like maybe *all of that* was a coma dream," Alicia suggested. "Right?"

"It's certainly possible." Tabitha spread her hands in a helpless gesture. "But I think certain parts of it were real. The timeline restarting at the MRI, I think all of that—that day and a half, maybe two days of that really happened. I mean, aside from the headaches, I was very cognizant of everything around me. Aware of my surroundings, thinking at my usual capacity, and everything —everything was very real, as real as this is here right now. It was distinctly different from the dream-like portions where—"

"Can I just be real blunt?" Elena interrupted. "I'm not... gonna call you a liar or accuse you of making up this whole wild story, or anything. But, isn't the whole *'time travel'* thing maybe this Uncle Vampire sort of metaphor for you to, uh, express some trauma-tizing situations you wouldn't be able to otherwise?"

"You've read *Uncle Vampire?*" Tabitha asked, eyes lighting up.

"I—uh, yeah," Elena confirmed. "I didn't pick it out. My mom wanted to kind of see how I dealt with more mature reading."

"*Uncle Vampire?*" Alicia asked, throwing each of them a look.

"Is that... anything you two wanna share with the rest of the class?"

"It's a book about a girl who *seems* to think her uncle is a vampire," Elena explained. "But that turns out to be a metaphor for—"

"Wait, wait—don't spoil it!" Tabitha interjected, waving her hands. "Don't spoil it. Alicia, I can find you a copy at the library. I want you to read it for yourself."

"Uhhh, okay," Alicia agreed. "Vampires are cool."

"No, that one wasn't." Elena scowled.

"Let her read it for herself," Tabitha insisted. "But. I see what you're getting at, Elena. No, my situation isn't a metaphor for something else—I have actually, honestly traveled back through time from 2045 to here in 1998."

"Then..." Elena felt her throat go dry as she saw Tabitha's look of resolve. "Then, I can test you. There's like, a million different ways to test your knowledge, on millions of different little things you should know in advance, Tabitha. Are you *really* sure you're ready to get into this with me?"

"Yeah." Tabitha gave her a self-assured smile. "I am. Because you're my friend, and... your trust really is that important to me. Ask me anything, anytime. Whenever you want! Well, maybe not *whenever*. I'd appreciate it if you were a little discreet. I know I won't remember *everything*, but I absolutely remember enough to convince you."

Elena had been riding the ups and downs of an emotional roller coaster for this entire hospital visit. Meeting Tabitha's steady gaze now, an irrational spike of fear jolted up in the pit of Elena's stomach. Fear that against all odds and rationality, her friend Tabitha actually... might be telling the truth.

But there's no way. There's completely no way... right?

29
THE BIRDS AND THE BEES

Several days had passed since revealing her story to Elena, and Tabitha was getting more antsy by the moment. The teenage girl sighed, brushing her red tangle back from her face with her good hand and tucking her hair behind one ear as she surveyed her boring room within Springton General Hospital's inpatient ward. The decor was bright and clean but in a *forced cheer* way, somehow sterile of coziness and comforts to put her mind at ease.

An oversight on their part, to be sure, Tabitha thought to herself with a wry smile. *A big picture of a bunch of corgi puppies on the wall right there would do wonders for my recovery. I'd even settle for a HANG IN THERE, KITTY!*

Her father had brought her a bouquet of chrysanthemums that overflowed from a small vase—reportedly at Grandma Laurie's behest—that failed to combat the strained optimism of the hospital. Sighing with an impatient smile, Tabitha stretched her legs beneath the blanket again, nearly toppling her *Goblina* notebook onto the floor. She'd managed to spend some of her ample free time streamlining her ideas, but her heart just wasn't really in it right now.

I want to DO things, Tabitha thought once again. *Nothing sets your mind on going out and living your life to the fullest quite like an intimate brush with death.*

As her long days of convalescence gave her ample time to mull over her thoughts, Tabitha had come to a number of conclusions about herself. She wasn't making the most of her do-over—her actions since traveling back in time were too timid, too passive, so focused on avoiding some of the specific things she feared that she entrapped herself in a mindset that was even more dreadful; that she was letting so many opportunities slip through her fingers!

I don't mean money either. Tabitha chuckled and shook her head. *After all, as the saying goes—you can't take it with you.*

Her now suddenly gothic friend Elena's questions had more or less all revolved around eking out every possible financial gain using her future knowledge, to the point that Tabitha grew exasperated with the girl's line of thought. As *un-American* as it apparently was, Tabitha knew she had no desire to become obscenely wealthy. Though she'd grown up in poverty and fantasized in her childhood about such a rags-to-riches turn-around, she'd already experienced an adulthood of modest comfort and had the benefit of some rare gems of hindsight on the matter.

I want to fill up my life with moments like when us three girls were just giggling in the dark of my cramped little bedroom for that slumber party. The things that are truly priceless in life are friendships and family; loved ones. Money and EXTRAVAGANCE will honestly just complicate those relationships. I won't allow any of us to be poor enough to suffer hardship because of it, but I also don't think I want us to be rich.

The things I want in life right now are as cheap as an ice cream cone, Tabitha thought wistfully. *To go around Louisville and see the sights and people, to hold hands with my mom and dad on either side like I'm a little kid again. Maybe go swimming somewhere, when it's warm again. Go camping. Watch movies together in the living room. To do all the FAMILY things we never ever did in my past life. Want to go somewhere scenic with them, watch a sunset maybe, while we have ice cream cones.*

Tabitha *really* wanted ice cream.

Money is necessary to an extent, of course—but what I want to focus on is MAKING MEMORIES, Tabitha had decided. *Pursuing a fortune just isn't something I feel called to. I remember a bigger TV screen just made me feel smaller when I watched things. A more spacious, fanciful apartment would just be even emptier space—it's scary to even think that I'll probably be able to afford my own house in this lifetime.*

The point her mind kept returning to was the Williams family lake house. It was nice in a rather extravagant way and she loved visiting, but she didn't think she'd ever want to actually *live there.* It was alien to her, and a place like that would never feel like *home.* In contrast, Elena had seemed to immediately internalize the experience of seeing the mansion on the lake as a sort of personal goal. Dwelling over their differences in perspective was a fruitless endeavor, however, because her thoughts always returned to the current rift between her and Elena.

She doesn't believe me. Of course she wouldn't—we talked and argued and debated, but honestly, how COULD she believe me? It really just is too absurd. It's probably crazier that Alicia accepts it already.

Tabitha didn't regret telling her the truth, though. Getting everything off her chest felt *amazing,* and wherever their friendship went from here, their interactions wouldn't be slowly poisoned by the uncomfortable knowledge of everything she was withholding from Elena. *Agghh, I just wish that there was some way to—*

"Knock, knock, Tabitha!" a cheerful woman's voice called out. "Are you accepting visitors?"

"Good morning, Mrs. Williams!" Tabitha's face lit up.

"What do you mean?" Mrs. Williams joked. "Do you wish me a good morning, or mean that it is a good morning whether I want it or not, Miss Tabitha? Or, is it that you feel good this morning?"

"You've—you've read Tolkien," Tabitha observed in a breathless voice, feeling a little more floored than she should have.

"Of course I have, dear; everyone my age has," Mrs. Williams tut-tutted, bustling into the room wielding a fruit basket. "Look, I've brought you fruit. Doesn't it just look like something out of a high school art painting? Tacky! The grapes looked delicious, though, and I thought, oh, Tabitha's been cooped up in here with nothing but—"

"My parents haven't," Tabitha confided with a bitter smile. "Read Tolkien, I mean. Dad doesn't read, and Mom just... doesn't feel passionate about reading the way I do."

"Ugh, I know just what you mean—hubby dearest and even my Matthew are terribly uncultured bores in that regard," Mrs. Williams griped as she plopped down in the chair beside Tabitha's bed and began unfastening the plastic of the gift basket. "*Football.* Basketball, dreadful *action movie* nonsense on TV, anything *Schwarzenegger* with shooting and explosions and all that."

"What else have you read?" Tabitha sat up with interest.

"Goodness—promise you won't make fun?" Mrs. Williams tore away the last of the wrapping and presented the basket to Tabitha.

"Anne Rice?" Tabitha guessed with a chuckle. "Laurell K. Hamilton?"

"*Tabitha*—my word, you're a touch young to be reading those, aren't you?" Mrs. Williams looked startled for a moment before erupting into boisterous laughter. "You've caught this old lady red-handed. I do enjoy my Anita Blake. I gave the Anne Rice stuff a try, but it was just too dry for me. Sometimes she just goes on and on and on!"

"She does, sometimes," Tabitha agreed. "Stephen King?"

"Oh, I have to be in the mood for him." Mrs. Williams waved a dismissive hand. "The man's a brilliant writer and I love a good visit, but his books aren't someplace I want to *live,* you know?"

"I loved his book *The Talisman,*" Tabitha confessed. "It was my favorite book, for a long time."

"That *was* a good one!" Mrs. Williams exclaimed, leaning forward to steal a grape. "Just listen to you—*a long time,* hah, you're still so young! Have you read any Anne McCaffrey, or Barbara Hambly?"

"I've read *Dragonriders of Pern,*" Tabitha nodded. "I haven't even heard of Hambly—what does she write?"

"I didn't care for the dragon rider stuff," Mrs. Williams admitted. "But McCaffrey wrote a different series *I just adore,* the Crystal Singer trilogy. Barbara Hambly writes these fantasy books with Sunwolf and Starhawk—oh, I'll just have to lend them to you. I don't want to spoil anything!"

"Please!" Tabitha nodded eagerly. "I'd love that—I don't know how long they'll keep me here."

"*Well.*" Mrs. Williams leaned in and gave Tabitha a conspiratorial look. "We have this *unofficial* little book club between some of us old hens at the church group. I think you'd just love some of the... *now wait a minute,* you're just fourteen years old! We can hardly be pressing John Varley books into your hands and just insisting you read! It's honestly scandalous to think you've read Anita Blake at your age!"

"I always preferred Meredith Gentry to Anita Blake." Tabitha chuckled. "And, I'm actually still thirteen. My birthday's in December."

"Meredith Gentry?" Mrs. Williams pursed her lips in thought for a moment. "Are they much like Anita Blake? Who writes them?"

Ah. Right, Tabitha remembered, sheepishly reining in some of her wayward enthusiasm. *It's still 1998. Probably can't mention* Neverwhere *or* American Gods—*and I guess Laurell K. Hamilton hasn't started writing Meredith Gentry yet. I'm too fuzzy on book release dates. At best, I'd only remember when in my life *I* read them, not when they actually came out.*

"I... I don't remember the author," Tabitha lied with an apologetic face. "They just seemed, um, similar in writing style to the Anita Blake ones. I think."

"I'll have to look them up!" Mrs. Williams said. "As you can imagine, quite a few of us church ladies just love the Blake books. Don't you go telling anyone, though!"

"I won't," Tabitha promised with a grin. "Um. Actually... I've been trying to talk my parents into joining a church. I want them to be part of a community, to—"

"We'd love to have you!" Mrs. Williams gushed. "My word, I already go on and on about you to all the women in choir. Are your parents Methodist?"

"My father was raised Baptist, but I don't think he's been to a service since he was little," Tabitha said. "They both believe, they just... never got into attending services and being part of something bigger. I'd *really* like them to, though. I think it'd be good for them."

"Just listen to you," Mrs. Williams remarked, rocking back in her seat. "Shouldn't *they* be the ones looking out for *you?* Tabitha, you're just fourteen years old!"

"Thirteen," Tabitha corrected again with a wince. "Thirteen, but... I dream big. Actually, I've been working on writing my own novels! This here's the outline I've been putting together; I keep all my thoughts and ideas right here in this binder. I think by next year, I should—"

"Hello in there," a nurse interrupted, pushing a wheelchair in through the doorway. "Oh, you have company! Looks like things weren't so bad in the X-rays, but we do still need to get a proper cast back on your wrist for a few months so we can be sure your hand heals correctly. I'm here to bring you over—but your mother's welcome to accompany us!"

"Oh, I'm actually not—" Mrs. Williams began in a fluster.

"She's *one of* my moms," Tabitha quickly insisted, shooting Mrs. Williams a smile. "I mean, you don't have to if you're busy... but I'd love if you came with."

———

After a short session and some mild discomfort with a doctor gently examining her wrist and hand, Tabitha's temporary brace was replaced with another cast. The weight of it was almost familiar, it was fragrant in that peculiar way only new casts are, and at her request, it was once again blue. The only complaint she had about it was how *bare* it looked—completely bereft of her friend's signatures. That would be fixed as soon as she could find someone with a marker and see everyone again.

"It's so dreadful thinking what happened!" Mrs. Williams sighed. "That awful girl. What she did to you. How close we all were to losing you!"

The heavyset woman had waved away the nurse who'd intended to wheel Tabitha back to her room, insisting she take Tabitha herself. She seemed to have been touched by Tabitha's willingness to consider her *one of her moms,* and determined to play her part in the role to the fullest at the first opportunity.

"I'm just sorry I ruined your party," Tabitha said. "It really was a great—"

"Oh, don't you ever say that!" Mrs. Williams fussed. "*You* were an absolute doll, *you* didn't ruin anything. I can't believe we didn't get a polaroid of you in your Ariel costume—you looked so pretty!"

"You know what I mean." Tabitha smiled. "I'm sorry that things happened like that and ruined it for everyone."

"I think we really need to talk about your priorities," Mrs. Williams retorted. "Didn't you just tell me you have a December birthday? It seems to me like we should be planning a big party for you!"

"That..." Tabitha's reflexive refusal stuck in her throat. "Might be what I've always wanted more than anything in the world."

"Really?" Mrs. Williams' voice rose in excitement. "Well, hm hm hmm. Don't you worry your pretty little head about *that,* Missy. You let Mama Williams take care of everything."

"You really don't have to." Tabitha laughed. "God only knows what would go wrong this time. Some new crazy person'll climb out of the woodworks to make a big mess of it."

"We'll pack the whole place full of angry cops," Mrs. Williams insisted. "Wall to wall. I'll make sure they're all armed to the teeth and on the lookout to shoot up anything that so much as looks at you funny."

"Goodness," Tabitha remarked, shaking her head. "It'll sure be a loud party, then."

"You know, we really weren't kidding back then," Mrs. Williams said. "They want to have a big ceremony and give you some kind of award—they were really only waiting on our good friend Mr. MacIntire to be up and on his feet again for it! Do you want to roll on by and see if he's awake? I remember I took you all the way out to that Louisville hospital to visit him, and he didn't even have the good decency to be conscious so you two could talk!"

"Not exactly his fault," Tabitha replied with a wry smile. "I'd love to actually meet him, though. Mrs. MacIntire and Hannah come in almost every day to see me."

"I still haven't figured out how to break it to the MacIntires that Hannah's too good for them and that I'll have to just keep her all to myself." Mrs. Williams laughed as she slowly guided Tabitha's chair down the hospital hallway. "Did you know the other day Hannah said she prefers *Mama Williams'* cooking over her mother's? That's how you always win them over, you know."

"I'm just fortunate that my parents have tolerated my cooking." Tabitha laughed. "Trying to get them to eat healthy is like pulling teeth, sometimes."

"Aw, that's so sweet!" Mrs. Williams patted her shoulder. "You even cook for your family?"

"Well... not lately, no." Tabitha sighed. "With everything happening. I really hope they've been eating okay."

"Just listen to you," Mrs. Williams said, sounding exasperated again. "You're going to be a great mom someday, I can tell."

"Me, a mom?" Tabitha retorted. "Yeah, right. As if."

"Well, I've never been wrong about anything before," Mrs. Williams joked. "Ask my husband! But, who knows? I'm sure there's a first time for everything. Maybe, just maybe, I'll be wrong someday—that'll be something."

"I bet." Tabitha wore an amused smile as she let the woman whisk her down the corridor towards the ward where Officer MacIntire was staying.

"Knock, knock, knock!" Mrs. Williams called into the room before entering. "I brought you a visitor, you ungrateful dirtbag—make yourself decent so I can wheel her in!"

"Yeah, right—just let me shower and shave real quick," a male voice called back. "You know how it is getting halfway presentable around here."

They were apparently joking, because Mrs. Williams abruptly pushed Tabitha's wheelchair into the room. It was almost identical to the layout of Tabitha's own hospital room, although she noted that Officer MacIntire still had one of those tall rolling stands from which an IV bag hung just beside his bed. The man himself wasn't like Tabitha remembered from that fateful day over a month ago, nor did he resemble the clean-cut photograph they'd put up on the news channel so often.

He sported a beard now, which made him look older, and the ordeal he'd been through seemed to have added additional age lines along his face. Officer MacIntire was still *handsome,* though; he still had the rugged if slightly drooping good looks one expected to see from an actor, and Tabitha could see why he'd made such a presentable poster boy for the media to flaunt in the weeks following the shooting.

"*This* is Tabitha Moore." Mrs. Williams presented the wheelchair forward a little too proudly. "Tabby honey—meet Darren MacIntire."

"Hi," Tabitha said with an embarrassed wave.

"Oh, wow, hi." Officer MacIntire seemed startled but pleased to see her. "It's great to finally meet you—it's an honor. The girls tell me about you every day, and I can't thank you enough for what you did for me back then."

"It—it was nothing," Tabitha said. "Really. Anyone would have—"

"Oh shush, you," Mrs. Williams scolded her. "You're a hero, and we're getting you a medal, and that's final."

"I'd just gotten transferred here to Springton General when we got word here what happened to you at that party," Officer MacIntire said. "Everyone was completely heartbroken when we thought you weren't going to make it. I'm really, honestly glad you pulled through. Look at you, they're already letting you roam around! I keep telling them I'm fine, but no one will let me out of bed. I'm ready to face the galloping hordes, fight a thousand bad guys with swords!"

"That sounds suspiciously like yet another Disney song," Mrs. Williams remarked.

"It's all I know anymore! They have me trapped in here, at Hannah's mercy, all day every day." Officer MacIntire chuckled. "You've gotta get me out of here!"

"As you can see, Tabitha, he's doing just fine." Mrs. Williams rolled her eyes.

"It is really nice to finally meet you," Tabitha said politely. "I'm glad you're feeling better. Hannah has been just amazing; she visits me all the time."

"She thinks the world of you." Officer MacIntire gave her a handsome smile. "I do too. We all do. What you did was amazing."

"It, it really wasn't," Tabitha denied in a fluster. "I just helped a tiny bit; the paramedics did all the actual—"

"No, she's in fact the most incredible young woman I've ever met," Mrs. Williams interrupted again.

"I can tell!" Officer MacIntire nodded with a slight grin. "Actually, Karen here tells me you might just have an Oldsmobile Cutlass Supreme at your place that might need a bit of work. I love cars. I'd be more than happy to spend some time working on it while the force has me off-duty. Honestly, you'd be doing me a favor—I'm already going nuts cooped up all the time with nothing to do."

"I... appreciate the thought." Tabitha smiled. "But I think that Uncle Danny's old car is headed straight to the junkyard. I really wouldn't want to trouble you with something that just can't be fixed."

"Can't hurt to take a look." Officer MacIntire seemed undaunted. "I don't mean to brag, and Karen'll vouch for how gosh-darned *humble* I am—"

"*Uh-huh,*" Mrs. Williams snorted.

"—but I do have a way with machines," Officer MacIntire finished. "Back when I was in my teens, I was big into rebuilding classic cars. Whenever a friend of ours needs something looked at, they always take it to me first."

"I heard it was something with the battery," Mrs. Williams spoke up. "But they swapped it out for another one, and it still wasn't working right?"

"Could be an issue with the alternator, then," Officer MacIntire surmised. "Easy way to tell—disconnect the positive terminal and see if the engine quits."

"It's a problem with the alternator." Tabitha nodded, taking a deep breath, "...and a small leak in the fuel line. It needs new tires, the brakes need replaced. The controller for the idle air intake and the entire electronic control module itself are both shot. Even if we could find junkyard replacement PROM chips for a ten-year-old control module computer, they'd need to be reprogrammed. As far as I'm aware, only General Motors can do that—and they wouldn't do it for cheap. Considering all the costs involved in getting it running again, it's really just not worth the effort."

Darren MacIntire blinked, seeming to reevaluate his first

impression of Tabitha, and then turned to throw Mrs. Williams a look with an arched eyebrow.

"That's—well—" Mrs. Williams looked speechless. "Your parents didn't say anything about any of that!"

"I know." Tabitha winced. "I, um. Secretly had a... *neighbor* look into what it would take to get it running again. I really don't want the car rusting in our yard forever. It makes us look like trailer trash."

"You are *not* trailer trash," Mrs. Williams insisted.

"Trying really hard not to be," Tabitha said with a weak smile. "Dad felt obligated to buy the Oldsmobile to help out our Aunt Lisa, because Uncle Danny's headed to jail. But, as soon as she had the money... she walked out on her four kids and just disappeared. It's... yeah, no matter how you look at it, it's all a pretty trashy story."

"She *what?*" Mrs. Williams exclaimed, looking personally affronted. "Surely there's some way of contacting her?"

"None that she's answered," Tabitha said with an uneasy shrug. "We mostly don't talk about it. It's a sore subject for Dad, and I don't ever want to make Grandma Laurie upset. She's the one who's taking care of those four cousins right now."

"That's terrible!" Mrs. Williams shot Officer MacIntire a glare. "There has to be some way for *authorities* to track her down right away."

"No." Tabitha shook her head. "Please don't. I, um, I know it sounds cruel of me to say, but Aunt Lisa wasn't a good mother, and I hope we never find her. Anyone who'll abandon their children isn't someone I can trust with them, and the boys deserve better than her."

"Well—she can still be *held accountable,*" Mrs. Williams fumed, unwilling to let it go. "I'm sorry, I'm sorry. Let's not talk about this now. I didn't mean to bring everything down today with all of this. I'll speak to your parents about it later."

"I really do want to take a look under the hood of that Cutlass

Supreme now." Officer MacIntire tactfully changed the subject. "I've never run into a problem I couldn't fix, and hey, you never know—maybe whoever checked it out before was exaggerating the damage."

"Maybe?" Tabitha nodded, trying not to sound too doubtful.

"I'm really in your debt, Miss Tabitha," Officer MacIntire said with a determined smile. "There's gotta be *some* way I can start to pay you back a little. Heck, between us cops and Karen here, you wouldn't believe the kind of pull we have around town."

"Look at you being humble again!" Mrs. Williams huffed, putting her hands on her hips. "I really don't know how Sandy puts up with your ego."

"There... *is* something important you can do for me," Tabitha said after a moment of thought. "I want you to be the best dad ever for Hannah. She almost lost you forever, an-and it terrifies me imagining what that would have done to her. How things would have been without you for her and Mrs. MacIntire. For the Williams family, for all of the people who care about you."

Officer MacIntire shared another meaningful look with Mrs. Williams for a moment before turning back toward Tabitha to regard her with a solemn look for several moments.

"I can absolutely promise you that," he finally said.

———

After exchanging some parting pleasantries with the recovering cop, Mrs. Williams took Tabitha on a bit of a stroll—or at least, a roll—aimlessly meandering through the building. Anything to get the poor thing out and about and away from the cloying cabin fever of her room for a bit! The redheaded teen seemed to enjoy seeing even the lackluster sights around Springton General Hospital, but Mrs. Williams wasn't content to allow them to lapse into contemplative silence—she still had a mission to perform.

"Since you've read Anita Blake, I should *probably* assume... but oh, I've just got to ask anyways." Karen Williams let out an easy-going laugh. "You're thirteen years old—has your mother had... *the talk* with you? About the little birds and the little bees?"

Steering the conversation in that direction felt dishonest, because Karen knew Mrs. Moore had *not* sat down for that particular discussion with Tabitha. The flustered Mrs. Moore had in fact asked Karen to make this discreet inquiry on her behalf! Extraordinary change was on the horizon for the Moore family, and there was apparently some awkward distance between parents and daughter that needed to be very carefully addressed before the big topic would be broached.

"She has not," Tabitha replied in good humor, tilting her head back to give the woman behind her an amused grin. "I believe I have a firm idea of the, um, *the mechanics* of it, but I don't have any *personal* understanding of that, and don't intend to for some time."

"Okay, *phew*." Mrs. Williams pantomimed wiping sweat off her brow in relief. "I'm so sorry, dear—it really is just such a dreadful thing to come out and ask a young woman!"

"It is," Tabitha agreed with a chuckle. "And it *is* dreadful. I've really been... struggling to wrap my mind around a lot of those ideas, lately."

"Oh?" Mrs. Williams prompted, lighting up with interest.

"I think... I'd given up on all of that," Tabitha mused. "For a long time, I honestly didn't see personal intimacy in my future at all. Ever. Then, I worked out so hard and fixed my diet and *transformed* for high school, and... well, I don't know what I expected. My body's *attractive* now, apparently, but I feel like I already missed out on getting the user manual for how to deal with that, or... I don't know. Maybe I changed too fast, and I just can't keep up?

"There's this..." Tabitha trailed off as she struggled to find the words to express herself. "*Gap*, I guess, in my formative... um. It's like, expressing interest in boys, and what to do with *their interest in me*—it's, it's like I don't even know what to do with it.

"In my first month at school, I'd get compliments from guys, and—" Tabitha cupped her hands out in front of her as if she'd been handed something unexpected, "—I don't know what to *do* with compliments."

The teen shifted in the wheelchair uncomfortably.

"It feels like... an inbox piling up in a department where no one's been manning the desk," Tabitha said. "I know it's not good to just leave it unattended until it becomes a problem, but... I'm leery of picking up the slack over there. Because I'm not trained for that position, and good lord, what if I start getting expected to actually *do* that job in addition to everything else I'm trying to figure out here? That... probably doesn't make any sense, does it?"

"No, no." Mrs. Williams quickly patted the girl's shoulder. "Honestly, Miss Tabitha, you make a lot more sense than you should! At thirteen years old, how are you relating your feelings to *the workplace,* of all things? What are they putting on television for you kids these days?!"

"Yeah." Tabitha blew out a weary sigh that seemed uncharacteristic of a girl her age. "*Television...*"

"So, you have trouble accepting compliments," Mrs. Williams said. "That's not so unusual. Do you feel like you don't deserve the compliments they give you, or are you just uncomfortable with boys being interested right now?"

"I—I don't know," Tabitha admitted. "Both, maybe. I may never manage to get over... this bizarre age dynamic that doesn't make any sense and probably never will. Also, psychologically speaking, I think I have this... *severe* case of imposter syndrome in regard to who I am and who I present myself to be. It may even be totally warranted. I... I don't know anymore. I don't belong with my peers, in *a lot* of ways, and improving my body image may have exacerbated the problem rather than helped it, I think."

"Aw, Tabitha..." Mrs. Williams fretted, momentarily at a loss.

Conventional platitudes and reassurances weren't going to cut it here, and Mrs. Williams felt herself taken aback all over again.

This girl's mind always surprised her, but now Mrs. Williams could see that Tabitha's intellectual development had so far outstripped her emotional growth that the poor thing was completely floundering on the delicate matters of adolescence.

"Sorry, I—sorry," Tabitha apologized. "Weird thing to bring up. I've just been—"

"You stop that," Mrs. Williams chided, patting the girl's shoulder again. "You're fine, don't you ever apologize for needing to talk."

"I... I think I really *have* needed to talk," Tabitha revealed in a quiet voice. "I really didn't mean to bring up the whole *trailer trash* subject or the drama with Aunt Lisa before and make things weird there either. I just... I feel like almost dying changed things for me. Just the other day, I kind of poured my soul out to Elena, and now I'm worried I might have freaked her out a little. Or more than a little. I've spent too much time cooped up in here with my thoughts. Unable to *do* anything about anything, and now there's just, there's just so many things to get off my chest. About everything."

Mrs. Williams paused, guiding the wheelchair to a stop and stepping around in front of it to face Tabitha. Without hesitation, she kneeled down beside the surprised girl so that she could envelop her in a crushing hug.

"Get it all off your chest then, honey," Mrs. Williams said softly. "Whenever you need to—about anything. I'm sure your friend Elena understands, and I'll be here anytime you ever need to vent. I can understand how it could be tough to talk about some of these things with your parents! Well, I can tell you; your family's not trailer trash, *you're* not trailer trash, and I don't think you're any kind of imposter either!"

"Thank you," Tabitha squeaked out. "Mrs. Williams, I—"

"You call me Mom or Momma Williams like Hannah does from now on, okay?" Mrs. Williams huffed. "You're really in luck, because talking about things just so happens to be my favorite thing in the world! About getting that old clunker in your yard fixed up, about introducing you to the church group, about *boys*. I have stories that even make my husband blush!"

"We can talk about your family troubles, or about that story you're writing, about faith; I'll talk your ear off on any subject, and I might even listen to you too! I mean, my word—I can't wait to skedaddle over real quick to pick up some of those novels for you to read! You don't know how thrilled I'll be to have someone new to talk about them with! All Sandy ever reads are those dull old *The Cat Who...* books!"

You're an amazing young woman, Miss Tabitha. Mrs. Williams sighed to herself as she gave Tabitha one last big squeeze. *I don't know why your mother's fussing so much about how you'll react to the news—this really might be just what you needed. You're going to make a GREAT big sister when that little one arrives!*

30

THE GIRL THAT TIME FORGOT

"They completely fucking lobotomized Erica," Brittney revealed in a low voice. "She's fucking brain dead now. *A retard.*"

Ashlee Taylor stared vacantly out the window of her aunt's Toyota Camry and watched as the dull November *dead trees and nothing but dead trees* scenery of US Route 31W rolled by. She didn't want to listen to them fight anymore. Every topic her remaining family brought up simply twisted her guts into new fits of anxiety, but blocking them out or pretending just wasn't really an option anymore.

"Erica isn't retarded," Aunt Kimberly said in a tired voice, "and they didn't lobotomize her. Your Nan doesn't want you swearing, so if you don't start watching what you—"

"They lobotomized her." Brittney shrugged. "She's a retard now. I saw it for myself. *Lobotomized.*"

Lobotomized, like... they removed her brain? Ashlee felt herself pale in horror as yet another wave of drowning guilt began to flood in. *Lobotomized like, YOUNG FRANKENSTEIN lobotomized?*

"Your sister was not *lobotomized*," Aunt Kimberly insisted. "They have her starting on lithium treatments to start stabilizing her moods a little bit. She's *supposed* to be a little loopy at first. It's normal. She's not lobotomized; she's just a little loopy."

Their aunt was once again driving them to *Ireland,* which turned out to be an ugly army hospital a fifty-minute drive outside of Springton rather than the gorgeous green European countryside Ashlee first imagined. It was a trip they made every week now— sometimes with Brittney in tow, sometimes without—visiting some sort of psychiatrist or something to help untangle the complex web of problems that made up the *Taylor family* situation. So far, it was just long, tedious drives, followed by waiting, and then incredibly awkward sessions as the lady tried to prod Ashlee into talking about anything and everything that was wrong.

She hated it. She wanted to be left alone. Ashlee *definitely* didn't want things to go back to the way they were—no way in hell—but the way things were right now weren't any improvement. They were just strange and uncomfortable and scary.

"Fucking lobotomized," Brittney insisted. "She got mind-wiped. It was like trying to talk to a little retarded child. I asked her if she was feeling okay, and she's like *yah I'm okaaay.* I was like, they told me you were crying a few days ago—so what was the issue? She gets all fucking confused and embarrassed. So I ask around, and it turns out she was having trouble *figuring out how to put her pants on right* one morning. Like a fucking toddler. Not even joking."

"They're still adjusting her medications. She's going to be fine," Aunt Kimberly said. "Bipolar disorder isn't something that magically goes away in just a few weeks. It's going to take some time. She's going to get better."

"...Get better at *what?*" Brittney demanded with an incredulous expression. "This isn't *Drop Dead Fred.* There was nothing wrong with her in the first place. This is all bullshit."

"Watch your language, Brittney," Aunt Kimberly warned. "Your sister was diagnosed with a disorder. It was making her do things that she wouldn't normally do, keeping her from thinking right. The lithium is going to help. She just needs to be on it for a while and she's going to be loopy."

Bipolar disorder was their fancy new name for Erica's uncontrollable personality and constant need to lash out at everything around her. Pills were apparently the answer. Ashlee fidgeted in the rear seat of the car, adjusting her seatbelt and then trying—and failing—to find a more comfortable way to situate her legs. Frustration and uneasiness seemed to seep out from everything that was going on and stain every possible aspect of her existence.

Without any warning, an attorney, a social worker, a woman from the school board, and a police officer had showed up on their doorstep one day. With all of them crowding down their house's hallway together, they had seemed like an enormous group. Mrs. Taylor had immediately launched into a suspiciously defensive explanation for Ashlee's truancy, and as her mother grew increasingly more flustered and agitated, Ashlee realized that something was seriously wrong. The social worker, an irritated-looking middle-aged woman with short gray hair and a chain-smoker's voice, had asked to see Ashlee alone in the other room.

Then she'd asked Ashlee if she had any bruises.

Ashlee felt proud and embarrassed and hopeful and terrified as she displayed her naked back to the woman in that other room, all the while the shouting back and forth on the other side of the door grew louder and louder. The bruising then had been getting *bad,* bad enough that Ashlee again had difficulty sleeping because of it, and now finally, *finally* someone had somehow noticed and would maybe do something about things. It was exciting to dare to *dream* of the prospect of change.

Change came immediately.

The social worker left just a few scant minutes after inspecting Ashlee's bruises, taking Ashlee with her. She was brought away with such sudden whirlwind expediency that Ashlee felt completely unprepared for it—looking back, it all felt like something out of a distant, impossible dream. The last thing she remembered seeing was her mother collapsing in a hysterical panic on their front lawn, screaming and shrieking and clawing at the police officer. Ashlee had stared, dumbfounded, through the car window at the once-familiar woman as she receded into the distance behind them.

Ashlee was separated from her immediate family, and after a long talk and a rather mortifying medical evaluation, she spent two nights in a 'halfway house,'—whatever that was—and finally was sent to stay with her distant Aunt Kimberly on the other side of Springton. Ever since then, bombshell after enormous bomb-shell news seemed to drop, one after another. Erica completely lost it and attempted to murder a girl. Police and social services were both investigating their family. Dad was getting locked up forever, Mom was filing for divorce. Brittney got shuttled off to live with Nana, and Erica got shipped off to a loony bin for juveniles and then apparently *lobotomized.*

For attempting to murder my friend, Ashlee remembered in a daze. *Tabby. The girl I blamed for everything I did. I did this.*

All of the sudden changes were more than just disorienting; they were *terrifying.* Every other day, it seemed like a therapist or counselor or caseworker from somewhere was interviewing her with discomforting questions, and nobody seemed particularly satisfied with the answers she gave them. Most of the big red flags weren't even related to Ashlee herself—apparently, some of her father's methods for dealing with Erica were capital letters NOT OKAY. Not okay, teetering all the way past a normal parent punishing an unruly teen and over into sexual abuse—child molestation.

It wasn't easy to keep playing dumb about everything when the adults were so pointlessly persistent, and there wasn't much to tell them anyways. *He never touched ME. Don't even really know what he did to them. Not for sure.*

The topic was a sore subject for Ashlee in a lot of ways. Several years ago, a very young Ashlee had blundered upon her sisters hiding out in the big bushes by the fence in the very rear of their backyard. Curiosity at what they were doing back there turned into complete bafflement as she discovered that Erica was bawling her eyes out while Brittney attempted to comfort her. Erica *didn't ever cry*. It was not something that she ever did, and in ten-year-old Ashlee's eyes, not something that she would ever do.

"*Leave us alone, Ashlee,*" Brittney had warned her in a hard voice. "*Go play somewhere else. NOW.*"

Ashlee had started to scramble away in fright, because surely seeing Erica at a vulnerable moment was some sort of taboo and there would be repercussions for her intrusion here later on—but, to her surprise, Erica had called out to her, stopping Ashlee in her tracks.

"*Ashlee,*" Erica's voice had been thick with emotion and that made her seem even *more* dangerous than usual, "*if Dad. If Dad EVER touches you. Anywhere. Ever. You need to come tell me. You come tell me, and—and if he ever touches you, I'm going to murder him. I'll just. I'll murder him in his sleep. I'll cut his throat.*"

Fleeing the scene back then, Ashlee hadn't understood—she'd simply been terrified that Erica would try to kill their dad, and hadn't connected the *why*. It was even something she could see happening, because sometimes young Erica just *did* things.

Fly into a ballistic fit of rage at someone's poor choice of words, bite one of her classmates at school during a scuffle—the girl's forearm required stitches—or just walk out the door with a backpack because she'd suddenly decided to run away from home. Police picked Erica up all the way out in Fairfield, and everyone had been flabbergasted that a little girl managed to get so far.

The idea that Erica was being abused—that both Erica and Brittney were being abused—had never really occurred to Ashlee. Seeing either of them as victims of anything took quite a bit of mental gymnastics on her part, because to Ashlee, that just wasn't who her sisters were. Sometimes Brittney and Erica would sit off somewhere and speak in low voices while forbidding Ashlee come near, but there had never been any indication that their bond was anything but that normal sort of *popular pretty girl* solidarity that Ashlee hated.

Aside from that one single instance where she'd seen Erica in tears, of course.

In light of the new circumstances as they were revealed, Ashlee could almost imagine Erica had been *protective* and *sisterly* back then in that moment. Which felt weird and unnatural, but was somehow also a sentiment so alluring that she just couldn't discard it no matter how implausible she thought it was.

After all, Ashlee only ever hated her father because he never protected her from her sisters and always took their side on everything, which made the revelations of abuse even *more* confusing. Mr. Taylor had never laid a finger on Ashlee. He always seemed more unnerved than most by her—people often had trouble socially connecting to her, because the orientation of her eyes made it difficult to read where she was looking.

He could probably never adjust, Ashlee thought with a bitter smile. *I mean, other than my eyes, I look just exactly like my sisters. Dark hair, okay face. PRETTY—almost. Makes the difference worse, makes the problem stand out so much more.*

Some rare people never even seemed to notice her lazy eye— like her best friend Tabby, too mired in her own troubles and misery to really look past them. Ashlee liked that. She could appreciate that. Ashlee's own sisters called her *Eyegor,* from the infamous comedy character played by Marty Feldman. Other kids were weirded out by her, or made fun of her, or pitied her like the teachers, and each of them inevitably became distant in different ways.

If I just kept my eyes closed all the time, people would maybe treat me normally, Ashlee thought. *But then I'd never be able to see it happen. All I can do is keep staring and pushing them all away.*

All of these new authority figures in her life also seemed mystified as to why Ashlee had been pulled out of the school system to be homeschooled. They now told her that she had *not* actually been homeschooled, because she wasn't being given any curriculum by her parents or anything to study. Registration and packets of coursework were eventually discovered at the house, but Ashlee had never been aware of them.

Ashlee realized *why* this was, but none of these people seemed to accept *'I was really bad at school and they were tired of putting up with it'* as an acceptable answer. Her mother had never bothered— Ashlee never did schoolwork, and she was too difficult to deal with. It was almost comical to her how aghast and horrified everyone was by that.

As if that wasn't completely normal life for Ashlee.

Suddenly, her mother's knowledge of the bruises itself became a crime—she was now somehow complicit in her sister's misdeeds. Ashlee had always struggled how terribly unfair life seemed, but for the situation to be so suddenly and violently corrected was still completely jarring and overwhelming. She wasn't even sure if she hated her mother. Not completely, at least.

"*Yah, okaaay,*" Brittney mocked, bringing Ashlee's attention back to the moment. "Whatever. Erica's a total retard now. I think it's like a revenge thing. An eye-for-an-eye, for her giving Tubby Tabby brain damage or whatever."

"It's not revenge, stop it." Aunt Kimberly shook her head. "That's not how things work; this has nothing to do with that. Your sister was out of control, and now she's getting help."

"Yeah," Brittney scoffed, shooting Ashlee a meaningful look. "*Help,* huh."

"She was completely out of control," Aunt Kimberly said again, this time in a tone that brooked no further argument. "Can we just stop? Let's just drop it, okay?"

"Right, yeah. Better leave all the bitching for time with the therapists. That's what they get paid for." Brittney rolled her eyes. "You know, they're gonna make you take pills too, Ash. For your ADD. Make sure they don't give you the retard pills."

Icy fear blossomed in Ashlee's gut again, because she *had* indeed overheard them talking about possible medications. They were discussing putting her on something called Ritalin, to hopefully help her focus on things like school work again. *I didn't want any of this. I didn't want ANY OF THIS. Why is it like this? Why did everything go this way? Why is all of this happening to us?*

In her mind, Erica maybe *did* deserve some of what was happening. Not to be *lobotomized,* of course—that was beyond the pale. But Ashlee had always wished Erica would face *some* comeuppance, some sort of consequences for her violent actions. The fact that her sister was dangerous and out of control was something Ashlee had known forever, since she was little. It was only recently that everyone else was seeming shocked by this 'sudden revelation.' Brittney was mean too, of course, and sometimes Ashlee thought that she was the more cruel sister... but Erica could be *terrifying.* Unpredictable, unhinged. *Crazy.*

Ashlee wasn't allowed to describe her sister as crazy to the psychologist or anyone at Ireland, even if her sister was obviously crazy. Instead, it was their dad's fault for molesting Brittney and Erica. It was the bipolar disorder to blame, rather than Erica simply being a psychopath. It was an unfortunate blend of situations and circumstances that caused her sister to unexpectedly commit a serious crime. Everyone seemed so keen on *figuring things out* and *making things right,* but Ashlee didn't think any manner or perspective of comparing all of these wrongs was ever going to make a right.

It's all just... fucked, Ashlee thought as she slumped to rest her cheek against the rumbling window of the car. *Fucked up for good. There aren't any rights, only wrongs. It can't be sorted out or fixed or set straight. It's fucked. Totally fucked. And all of this happened because of me.*

She broke into an unhappy smile again at the thought.

———

"You say that this Tabby girl *was* your friend," Mrs. McDonnell observed. "You're using past tense—do you not think of her as a friend anymore?"

The child psychologist's room was several floors up but didn't contain any windows, and because of the nature of her patients, the decor was a strange mish-mash of toys and kiddie posters that seemed at odds with the professional-looking business attire of the woman sitting across from her. There was even a molded green plastic sandbox shaped like a turtle on one side of the room, filled with actual sand and the occasional bright plastic of a pre-schooler toy. It was *weird* seeing a sandbox inside, and Ashlee couldn't help but wonder whether sand got all over the carpets here in a big mess.

"I don't know." Ashlee shrugged, trying not to make a face.

Sometimes it felt like the adults were grasping for any loose thread they could tug on to hopefully unravel some big story out of her, and they never seemed to care how uncomfortable that made her feel. She didn't want to talk about Tabby. She didn't even want to think about Tabby lately.

"You've said that when your sisters threatened her, she never came back to visit again," Mrs. McDonnell remembered. "Can we talk about how that made you feel?"

"I don't know." Ashlee shrugged with all the indifference she could muster, hoping the woman would take the hint and stop pressing for answers.

"Did that make you angry at Tabby?" Mrs. McDonnell pressed for answers.

"Not really." Ashlee frowned. "It was smart of her. I guess."

"Because you thought your sisters were dangerous?" Mrs. McDonnell prompted.

"Yeah." Ashlee nodded. "I guess. I knew how mean they can be."

"Siblings can be very mean," Mrs. McDonnell said, scribbling something in on her clipboard. For some reason, Ashlee found it incredibly irritating. "Did you think Tabby was in danger?"

"I don't know," Ashlee said, groping for whatever the right answer might be. "Yes?"

"It's okay for you to feel upset with her," the woman explained in that annoying *always patient* tone of hers. "Even if she's not at fault. Her leaving and not coming back after that day, that may have made you feel like she was giving your sisters even more power over you—like they were given control of who could and who couldn't be friends with you. Do you think that's how you feel?"

"I don't know," Ashlee muttered, trying her hardest not to think about it. "What does it matter?"

"How you feel about it matters a lot," Mrs. McDonnell explained in a gentle voice. "My job's to help you work through how you feel about things."

"Or, what?" Ashlee asked. "I'll get lobotomized?"

"No, we won't lobotomize you," Mrs. McDonnell replied with a good-natured laugh.

"They gave Erica pills that lobotomized her," Ashlee said. "Because of what she did."

"I don't think that's what's happening." Mrs. McDonnell seemed amused, and flipped back to a previous page on her clipboard. "I'm guessing this was something... Brittney said to you?"

"Yeah," Ashlee admitted.

Deflecting the topic to Brittney and getting her sister in trouble for one of her sessions had been her plan, but maybe her execution wasn't quite as subtle as she thought it was. Clever adults were bad. Adults who remembered how clever children could be were always worse.

"I'm sure that's something I'll talk about privately with Brittney," Mrs. McDonnell promised. "Would you like me to bring it up another day when we're all having session together?"

"I don't know." Ashlee gave yet another repetitive shrug.

"Okay." Mrs. McDonnell jotted down another note. "Can I tell you what I think?"

"Sure."

"I think Brittney is very uncomfortable about Erica's treatment," Mrs. McDonnell said. "She knew her sister as one person, and now therapy and medication is making Erica seem like another, different person—that's going to be upsetting."

Well, DUH, Ashlee wanted to retort, barely holding it in and instead simply staring. *She said they were forcing her to become retarded!*

"When Brittney's upset, I think she isn't comfortable showing it," Mrs. McDonnell continued. "Because that makes her feel less in control. So, instead, she vents her frustrations to *you* in a way she thinks will upset you—then, you can be upset in her place. She can have an outlet for all of those feelings she doesn't like, by passing them over onto you."

That one wasn't quite an obvious *duh* thing to say, and Ashlee's gaze wandered to the carpeting as she considered it. The idea made sense, but she was really struggling to apply it so that it fit with her idea of Brittney. *Maybe Brittney's just really different around Mrs. McDonnell? She acts more mellow around most adults. More courteous, watches what she says. Not like Erica.*

"So—so, what?" Ashlee asked. "Am I not supposed to get upset?"

"That's not up to anyone but you," Mrs. McDonnell answered in typical cryptic fashion. "How *do* you feel about Erica right now?"

———

"Did you ask them for some retard pills?" Brittney asked as they drove back from Ireland Army Hospital. "For your ADD?"

"Brittney—drop it," Aunt Kimberly warned. "Please. Enough."

"She said Ritalin is the *opposite* of retard pills," Ashlee retorted with all the confidence she could muster. "That they would make it *easier* to think. Get less distracted."

"I bet she did," Brittney snorted. "They probably told Erica the same thing for her stuff. Doctors are all in cahoots with all the big pharmaceutical conglomerates. Getting you on pills is just like selling a car to them. Cash commission, right into their pocket."

Ashlee didn't trust Brittney's words over Mrs. McDonnell's, but she knew that the seeds of doubt her sister planted would sour her impression of prescription medicine all the same. On the one hand, she hated how easy to manipulate her feelings on the matter were, but then on the other—distrusting someone or something always seemed to speak to her on a deeper level. Because that's how things always really were.

"Mrs. McDonnell's a total quack case." Brittney laughed. "Did you ask her how much money she makes for just sitting there going *'hmm, yes, and how does that make you FEEL?'* while she plays tic tac toe on her little clipboard? *How do I feel? Seriously?* Uh, pissed off, mostly? Erica wasn't even in the wrong, really. *Someone* needed to beat the shit out of Tubby Tabby for all that shit she was getting away with. Things only turned out like this because the little bitch got herself all cozy with the cops—you saw how they were treating her. They were totally biased, and *for what?"*

"Please don't start again," Aunt Kimberly snapped. "Just— drop it. Okay? We're not going through this again. You don't talk about that girl to anyone anymore, you don't try to talk *to* her— just drop it, completely drop it, forget about whatever you think happened, and stay away from her so we can all put this behind us and move on with our lives."

"I'm not *Erica,* I wasn't actually gonna do anything." Brittney rolled her eyes. "I can talk about it all I want, though. It's a free country."

"Well, you're in *my* car, and I don't want to hear it anymore," Aunt Kimberly growled. "Alright? Brittney?"

"Am... *I* allowed to talk to Tabby?" Ashlee spoke up. "Ever again?"

The Toyota Camry rolled down US 31W in particularly strained silence for several moments.

"Mrs. Cribb from the school board... did bring that up," Aunt Kimberly admitted. "I wanted to wait and see what you thought. Do you want me to call her?"

What?! Ashlee's mouth fell open as she glared at her aunt. *Why the hell didn't somebody say something to ME about it?! You all just had me assuming it wasn't even an option!*

"Uh, *yeah*," Ashlee said in frustration, ignoring the withering stare she received from her sister. "Is Tabby still in the hospital?"

"I hope so," Brittney made a disgusted sound, crossing her arms and looking off out the window. "She'd better be."

"I'll phone Mrs. Cribb as soon as we get back, then," Aunt Kimberly said with a sigh. "We'll see how things go, alright?"

————

"I can drive you over to see her today!" Mrs. Cribb exclaimed over the telephone's handset receiver held to Ashlee's ear. "She doesn't get enough visitors. I bet she's just going to be tickled pink to see how much better you're doing."

How much...BETTER I'm doing? Ashlee wanted to scowl at the woman's cheery mood.

Just because the marks were fading away didn't ever make them gone. They would *always* be there. Ashlee knew she was probably going to carry them in some form or another for the rest of her life. Some jolly old lady wouldn't understand what that was like, though. The psychiatrists and therapists couldn't understand either. Not really. They saw the bruises but didn't understand why they hurt. The only one who maybe *would* get it was Tabby. Tabitha had seen first-hand what it was like for Ashlee trying to survive in the Taylor family. She knew.

"Today?" Ashlee repeated.

"Yes, of course. I'll make sure that works out with your aunt, whenever you can put her back on," Mrs. Cribb said. "Tabitha's out of school for a while now; I don't know if you'd heard—I was hoping you two girls would be interested in studying together. With Tabitha's help, I think you'll be able to test in as a sophomore without any problem."

"As sopho—as a *tenth grader?*" Ashlee blurted out. It sounded too good to be true. "I didn't go to ninth grade. I mean, I'm not now. I'm not enrolled."

"Oh, I know, sweetie," Mrs. Cribb assured her. "There's a fair bit of English and Math for you to catch up on, but I don't see that being a problem if you and Tabitha put your heads together for a few months."

"A few months?" Ashlee echoed. "You think... I can just go back to school? Aren't I behind on... a lot?" *Like, a whole grade? A lot more than just English and Math?*

It honestly didn't sound like fun—Ashlee still hated school. At the same time, *not* going to school for the past year had continued to fill her with a formless sort of fear she wasn't able to shake. Fear that she was falling further and further behind her peers and would never catch up, never be *normal.* As much as she hated getting picked on and being unpopular, simply not going to school at all was just as bad or maybe even worse, because then she felt like she was missing out on all the important *growing up* stuff promised by shows like *Sweet Valley High, Teen Angel,* and *Party of Five.*

"I'm going to make sure we have everything you need for that," Mrs. Cribb promised. "We'll make sure you both get all squared away and up to speed for your K-PREP assessment, and I'll be there to help you girls make sure you take care of all your other requirements."

"Uh. Okay," Ashlee said, unsure of whether or not this woman was bending the rules for them. "Thanks. I'm gonna put on my aunt."

"Thank you, dear," Mrs. Cribb said. "See you in a few!"

———

Ashlee didn't know how to feel as Mrs. Cribb led her down a corridor of Springton General Hospital toward the room where her friend was in recovery. It was weird that she'd spent most of her day either going to or in different hospitals, and the atmosphere was beginning to wear on her. At the same time, she wanted to see if meeting Tabby again after so long—it had been months—would dispel the strange, surreal sense Ashlee had been caught up in ever since being separated from her parents.

"She's right in here," Mrs. Cribb gestured, leaning ahead of her through the door. "Tabitha? Hello! Your friend Ashlee's here to see you! I'll let you two talk in some privacy."

Turning back toward Ashlee, Mrs. Cribb gave her a smile and ushered her forward. "Go on, go on. I'll be waiting just down the hall with a newspaper. I'm so happy to be able to get you two reunited like this. Have fun!"

The teenage girl hadn't realized how reluctant she actually felt until Mrs. Cribb was actually pushing her inside the bright little room, and once there, all she could do was stare. Mrs. Cribb was saying something in a polite tone, a redhead wearing a headband of bandaging smiled back and replied, but Ashlee wasn't paying attention to anything that was being said.

Is this... some sort of mistake? Ashlee's mouth went dry as she realized Mrs. Cribb was already leaving, rushing out to give the girls some personal time. *Is this a joke?*

"Hello." The girl on the hospital bed gave her an uncertain little wave. "Ashlee. It's... it's been a while. Feels like forever."

The girl was slender, almost frail-looking, with pale white skin and reddish-orange hair. She possessed delicate features, wore a kindly smile, and held herself with a graceful sort of poise that immediately set Ashlee on edge.

"You... aren't Tabby," Ashlee said, staring at the redhead in bewilderment. "Who are you?"

"Um." The girl claiming to be Tabitha Moore seemed taken aback. "Well. I understand that I *do* look very different, but—"

"No, you're not her," Ashlee insisted, stepping backwards as her sense of alarm grew. "*Who are you?*"

This wasn't even *about* looks.

Appearance-wise, this girl did have some features that were vaguely reminiscent of the Tabitha she knew. The similarities only made the *wrongness* stand out even more, make it seem more severe, though. Ashlee had always instinctively felt comfortable and familiar around her best friend Tabby, because at a glance, she could tell they were kindred spirits. *This* person was not Tabitha Moore. The presence she exuded was completely different. It was a slapdash alien facsimile.

Why would they have someone replace Tabby?! Ashlee's mind raced with possibilities, each more paranoid and panicked than the last. *Did Erica actually kill the real Tabby, and they didn't want that to get out? Or, something? No, that would never work—that's impossible. Doesn't make any sense.*

Maybe this stupid setup was just for me? The therapists, or the psychiatrist or somebody thought this would fool me? That I'd snap like my sister did, if I found out what really happened? Does this mean the real Tabby's really dead? My sister's actually a murderer? Erica murdered someone because of those things I said, and everyone knows but didn't want me to find out? Why THIS, though? Who would ever think I'd buy into—

"I lost a significant amount of weight over the summer," the girl in the hospital bed tried to explain with an awkward expression. "I know that I *seem* very—"

"Stop. You can't fool me," Ashlee snapped, feeling her throat close up with terror. "You're not her. I *know* Tabby. *She's my best friend*. You're not her. I don't know *who* you are. Or what you're even doing here. Why are you pretending to be Tabby?"

She did look *a bit* like Tabitha, but the differences in the girl's expression and demeanor were not minute, and grew into uncrossable chasms the longer Ashlee stared. Maybe this was some distant cousin or relative of similar age from the Moore family, but this was *definitely* not Tabby. The real Tabby had an indescribable muddled tension to the posture of her stillness that Ashlee had always found intimately familiar—when this *fake* Tabby was still, there was only an underlying calmness and clarity that was completely, totally out of place. The way she spoke was off, the words this fake chose were wrong, and the patterns of thought they drew from were completely foreign and didn't match the Tabitha she knew in the slightest.

"Where's *my* Tabby?" Ashlee demanded, unstoppable tears forming in her eyes as she felt herself breaking down. "What happened to her? Is she, is—*is she dead?* What's going on? You're *not* Tabby. *Where's Tabby?!*"

"Uhhh." The imposter pretending to be her best friend winced and brought a hand up to her brow in consternation. Like she knew her cover had obviously been blown. "Well, shit."

31
RELEASED FROM THE HOSPITAL

"Ashlee... can we talk about this?" Tabitha tried to muster a hopeful look, but it was a struggle for her to meet the girl's eyes.

"Talk about this?! I don't have anything to talk about with you!" Ashlee spat. "I don't even know who you are!"

Each of Ashlee's accusations felt like a blow to Tabitha, like this forgotten specter from her distant past had finally found a means to haunt her. It was easy for her to read the outbursts as Ashlee saying *my REAL best friend wouldn't have abandoned me,* even when she knew Ashlee was simply failing to recognize her with all of her changes.

"You're not her," Ashlee repeated, accepting Tabitha's silence as tacit confirmation. "You're not her."

The young girl's glare hardened, growing guarded and distant. She wiped the brief tears that had formed and turned to storm out of the room with a resolute set of her jaw.

"Shit." Tabitha clapped her hands over her face in vexation. "Shit, shit, *shit.*"

She's not even unfounded in that basis, Tabitha rationalized to herself. *She's RIGHT to disassociate the current me from that Tabitha.*

I'm NOT the Tabby she last saw on that trampoline. My memories have an almost fifty-year difference, my body is fifty pounds lighter, puberty seems to be affecting me in a different way, my diet and metabolism and energy and body chemistry are all different. Those are all the SMALL changes—I have so many friends and family now. I'm a different person.

Tabitha had been proud of how much she'd grown in these past six months, how much she'd learned, assumptions she'd overturned and new perspectives gained. Her development since incarnating into her past self had been *meteoric,* and by contrast, Ashlee had of course not changed at all—she'd been left behind and abandoned again, now in an entire additional new context. After seeing the hurt and confusion in Ashlee's eyes, Tabitha had never found her own impossibly unfair second chance at life so bittersweet.

She's rightfully angry—and in a lot of ways, Tabitha's mind raced. *She knows me—KNEW me, she isn't going to buy any excuse I can cook up. I don't think she'd believe the truth either. No one would. And no one will believe Ashlee when she says I'm not me, even though... she's right. Technically. As if all of this needs to be any more cruel and unfair to her.*

"Tabitha?" Mrs. Cribb stepped into the room with a bewildered expression, not even remembering to knock. "What on earth happened?"

"She... became upset," Tabitha replied with an apologetic expression. "She's—please don't hold it against her. She's been going through so much. And. Well. I've changed. Quite a bit. From the girl she remembers me being."

"She just stomps out here and says you're not Tabitha," Mrs. Cribb said with wide eyes. "She sat down out there in the waiting room and now I can't get her to say anything at all! What happened?!"

"I think she needs some time," Tabitha pleaded. "Please don't hold it against her. I know she's been through a lot."

"Yes, but—did you say something?" Mrs. Cribb asked. "Are *you* okay? I'm just completely—I don't know what to think, where all this came from."

"I'm okay," Tabitha said with a weak smile. "Can you make sure she's okay? And, um, tell her I'm sorry, if I said anything wrong?"

"Of course, of course." Mrs. Cribb nodded, pausing again in the door. "You're okay?"

"I'm okay," Tabitha promised again.

"Okay," Mrs. Cribb murmured. "I'm so sorry about all of this— I don't know what this is all about."

"It's really not her fault," Tabitha said. "She just... can you give her some time?"

"I will—we will," Mrs. Cribb fretted. "We're going to take good care of her. Sorry for disturbing you with all of this today. I was glad to see you seem to be doing so much better! I'll stop by again in the next week, if they haven't released you yet by then."

"Thank you," Tabitha said. "It was good to see you."

"Take care, Hun," Mrs. Cribb said, finally hurrying back down the hallway toward the ward's reception area.

"Ugggh." Tabitha let out a noise of exasperation the moment she was sure Mrs. Cribb was well out of earshot. She let herself fall back heavily onto her pillow and covered her face, completely at a loss as to what she should do about Ashlee. "This can't be happening."

———

"Hey," Alicia said, standing over the corner table out in the quad Elena had sequestered herself to.

High school as a loner was new to Elena, but wrapping herself in a certain amount of distance from everyone else helped bolster her new goth persona. She wasn't like Tabitha, who'd hidden herself away completely unseen in the library at lunch, because

Elena wasn't intending to be socially invisible. Elena positioned herself on the far outer periphery of everyone else, because that was the statement she wanted to make.

Her present lack of social engagement also may have given her too much time to reflect on such things.

"Hey." Elena looked up at Alicia with a neutral stare, neither intent on continuing conversation nor inviting the other girl to sit with her.

"Can we talk?" Alicia asked.

"Sure," Elena said with indifference.

"Okay." Alicia planted the sketchpad and three-ring binder she was holding onto the table and then climbed over the bench to take a seat. "Are you okay?"

"Why wouldn't I be?" Elena asked.

"I'm serious—are you okay?" Alicia pressed. "Like, are *we* okay? If this is part of your whole new thing, then fine. That's fine and cool. I don't want you to be all upset about the Tabitha thing, if that's what this is about."

Elena looked down at the table for a moment, weighing her words and trying to figure out what she wanted to say. After a few strained seconds, she looked back up, simply deciding her friend deserved the truth.

"I'm *really* upset about the Tabitha thing."

"Okay—thank you." Alicia sagged slightly, trying to study Elena's now intentionally difficult-to-read expression. "You don't have to believe her. Us. You don't have to believe us, we said that's fine. That's okay. But can we talk about it, or...?"

"I..." Elena frowned, staring at Alicia and trying to choose her words carefully. "I don't think there's anything to talk about? Really?"

"Okay," Alicia said, casting a nervous glance around and fidgeting with her binder and portfolio. "We don't have to talk. But can you listen to me for a bit?"

Elena shifted uncomfortably in the seat opposite her friend, fighting the urge to quibble over how listening to Alicia talk *would* be them talking, and how she didn't want to talk about this. With a sigh of frustration and pointed disinterest in her eyes, Elena waved her hand, gesturing for Alicia to get it over with.

"I know time travel's impossible," Alicia said. "But, somehow or other, Tabs *does* know things that she can't know. About the shooting, about movies that haven't come out yet, about—stuff. The way future stuff is. I know you don't believe her and that you're not gonna be convinced, but can I just like, lay out why *I'm* convinced, so that things aren't all weird between us?"

"Okay," Elena said, a little more coldly than she'd intended.

"Tabitha knew I was an artist on the first day of school," Alicia began. "Like, she knew beforehand. I had a paper out and I was *doodling,* not drawing, when she came up to me. Didn't have my art out, no one had seen it. I went to Fairfield Middle, you guys went to Laurel. So, on that first day, she's asking if I draw, wants to see my art, wants to get to know me."

"What were you doodling?" Elena asked.

"Nothing!" Alicia held her hands up. "Just like, lines. Eyeballs. Shapes. Normal, *every person does this* doodles, not even like effort or skill or anything. Just ordinary bored scribbling. But she was suspiciously convinced that I was an artist."

"That doesn't seem suspicious, though," Elena countered. "What seems like normal doodles to you is probably amazing to the average person. You're an artist."

"It's—no, it's not even like that," Alicia said in frustration. "*Anyways.* I get to know her, she turns out to be different than I first thought. We're kinda sorta friends then, I guess. She asks if I want to hang out after school so we can talk about drawings and ideas and stuff, I'm like, *yeah, cool.* The shooting thing happens. I connect it to her looking up first aid and gun shot trauma stuff because she was doing that in the library all the time and *that* was weird. Suspicious. She tells me about the time travel. I don't believe her."

"With you so far," Elena commented in a deadpan voice.

"Yeah. Well." Alicia picked at the edge of her portfolio. "I kinda, I dunno, kid her about it over the days after that. 'Cause I can't tell how serious she really is about all of it. I happen to bring up how, yeah, she must've known me in her first life, and ask her about that stuff. She gets like... *guilty*. She didn't know me, not even from school. We'd like, never interacted in her first life, I guess, and she only recognized me from me getting famous for my art. Kinda wanted to—well, not *take advantage* of that, exactly, but wanted to have a sorta partnership sorta thing going on with me. My drawings, her writing. Like that."

"Okay," Elena said, her interest starting to pique in spite of herself.

"So I ask her about *that,* and Tabitha describes a specific piece of unfinished artwork in here," Alicia slid her portfolio aside and jabbed a finger at the three-ring binder. "I've never *ever* shown anybody these ones. No one knows about them, never brought them to school. My parents would freak out on me if they found them—I've had them hidden in my room at home. *They've never left my room.* Tabitha tells me, in detail, this *specific* one that's super special to me, like it has huge personal significance to me as an artist. *As a person.* There's absolutely, completely no fucking way she could've known about it."

"Could've been a lucky guess." Elena shrugged. "Based on—"

"It's not," Alicia insisted. "Trust me. It's not. I'm going to show these to you now, so don't freak out. Okay? I've never shown anyone these. Not art teachers or friends or anyone I know—nobody. Not even Tabitha."

"Alright," Elena said, curiosity getting the better of her.

With what could only be described as extreme reluctance, Alicia slowly slid the binder across the table to Elena. Intrigued as to what special secret drawings were so important that Alicia kept them hidden away, Elena opened the binder—and immediately slapped it closed again upon seeing the first drawing.

"Is this porn?" Elena mouthed, glancing around them to see if anyone had been looking.

"It's not porn," Alicia said, wrapping her arms around herself and making a face and looking incredibly discomforted at having shown anyone the secret binder. "It's art. Okay? Stuff I have to practice to get good at it, but I can't show anyone because of what they'd say. Okay?! You don't get good at drawing everything without practicing. It's not porn."

Narrowing her eyes, Elena carefully slid the binder off the table and tilted it partway into her lap so that no one else nearby would accidentally see what she was looking at. Upon opening the binder, she again saw the first drawing—a pair of boobs hanging below a pair of shoulders and a neck. Flipping the plastic page protector—another pair of boobs, smaller, different-looking ones from a slightly different angle. The next page, more boobs. The next, boobs again.

Holding her place between binder pages with her fingers, she flipped it closed again so she could shoot Alicia an incredulous look.

"It's art!" Alicia protested, covering her face. "Don't judge me!"

"Are there penises too?" Elena remarked in a dry voice, opening the binder to skim through the pages.

"Ew, no. I'm not drawing penises!" Alicia seemed aghast. "That's disgusting!"

"Alicia—what, are you gay?" Elena asked, looking from one sketch of naked breasts to the next in disbelief. "These are all boobs."

"It's *an art thing,* oh my God," Alicia hissed defensively. "The naked female form is full of *artistic* beauty that I really want to be able to express. Okay?! It's not super sexual or anything, but yeah, okay, *of course* that's the conclusion everyone's just gonna jump to right away. So, you see why I never show these ever, *ever?*"

"Yeah," Elena said, impassively examining the depictions of

naked women drawn from the side, and drawings of them in various contorted positions. "Some of these are really good."

"Yeah?" Alicia squeaked.

"But, then a lot of them look really weird," Elena remarked.

"Weird," Alicia repeated. "Weird how?"

"Like..." Elena went back several pages until she found a particular drawing again. "Like, here. Between her boob and her arm, it looks weird, see? And then the boobs look pressed together like she's wearing something, when she's not. This boob would be out... here, like in this direction. But you drew her with cleavage."

"Uhhh okay, yeah, that one is super messed up," Alicia admitted. "I know the boob position on that one's wrong, but the way the shape turned out was nice, so I had to save it for that."

"You did it again with this one," Elena pointed out, rifling through the pages. "And this one. On the ones where you draw where the bottom rib stands out a bit, it's down too low on her torso. Like the proportions are off, so she looks wrong."

"Okay, okay, okay!" Alicia groused. "Now you totally see why it's something I have to practice, then! And a lot of these are old drawings anyways, geez! I just keep all of the nudie ones together like this; some of these are from forever ago."

"Just don't draw on the nipples, and these won't all be gross." Elena made a slightly disgusted face. "If you'd add in a few lines to give them clothing, it's less... weird and like porn, and you wouldn't have to keep these secret."

"You wouldn't get it." Alicia sighed.

"Yeah, I guess," Elena said, casually flipping through the rest of the pages. "Which one's the one you think Tabitha knew of?"

"...Very last page," Alicia said with a hint of trepidation.

Wasting no time, Elena turned to the very end.

"Okay," Elena said, staring at it intently.

"Okay what?" Alicia prompted, squirming in her seat.

"Okay, this one's different," Elena remarked, letting her eyes search up and down the drawing as she tried to put it into words. "This one's really good. Who's she supposed to be?"

The final drawing stood apart from the rest in that it seemed to convey something larger than the sum of its lines. Rather than the shock value explicit and *in-your-face* drawings of tits, this was a woman's naked back, with only a hint of breast visible on one side. The musculature of the woman's posture hinted at context, the detailing in each tangled curl of hair traveling down her neck and across one shoulder seemed significant somehow, and something about the way it was drawn was simply *moving*.

"I don't know!" Alicia whispered. "I've no idea. This one just kinda came to me. Inspiration. The anatomy's not exactly accurate. But this one was totally free-hand and without any references, and it still came out looking like a billion times better than anything I've ever drawn."

"I don't think it's better than your new stuff," Elena pursed her lips in doubt as she examined the piece.

"It is," Alicia insisted. "It completely is. The others look good, but this *is* good. It has better feeling. It's *more*. I've tried to draw this one a bunch of other times and they never carry even like a tiny fraction of what this one has."

"I don't really get it," Elena said. *But then, maybe I also kinda do?*

"What Tabitha described to me," Alicia leaned in close to whisper, "was the future perfect dream version of this that I *know* I'm going to manage to do someday. She put into words like, exactly how I want her back, how I want to have these parts here just defined by light and shadow so they're a little more subtle— she *knew*. Because, I think she'd seen it. The finished version."

"There's other explanations," Elena said.

"No one else even knows about this crappy version here!" Alicia insisted. "Let alone what it'll be when it's complete. It's not like I sit there and draw leaning back 'gainst my bedroom window so people outside can all see what I work on."

"Okay," Elena couldn't help but slightly concede in the face of

Alicia's apparent conviction. "But that doesn't mean Tabitha's from the future. That's still, like, the least likely explanation ever."

"Maybe." Alicia shrugged, keeping her shoulders hunched in close. "I don't know. She knows *a lot* of future stuff, 'Lena."

"Stuff that we can't verify," Elena pointed out.

"Not yet," Alicia agreed. "But, eventually? What are you gonna do if she turns out to be right about a lot of big things?"

"Invest," Elena said simply, closing the three-ring binder and sliding it back across the table toward Alicia. "Make money."

"Okay," Alicia sighed. "Maybe there'll never be a point where you totally believe her all the way. I guess. But can you at least start believing *in* her? Like, you don't have to believe she's from the future, but can you at least believe that *we* believe that? That we're not lying to you, that this isn't a mean prank and you don't need to be pissed at us? You can just think we're totally fucking stupid, if you want."

"I don't have stupid friends," Elena said, unable to hide her annoyance. "So... don't go saying you guys are stupid, ever. Okay?"

Elena couldn't help but become even more annoyed as Alicia's smile grew.

———

"E-town's... a really long drive," Casey muttered, doing her very best not to scowl into the hand she was resting her cheek on as she doodled. "Like... *ugh.*"

"I know." Alicia winced. "I have gas money. And—you know, money money. I can pay you. I *really* need to get to Elizabethtown before December."

Alicia always gravitated toward the older girl now whenever she was in Mr. Peterson's class for her Drawing elective. As a student assistant, Casey frequented the art room throughout several different periods. Whenever she wasn't toiling away over at the sinks muttering obscenities under her breath at all of the students who neglected to properly clean their paintbrushes, Casey could be found loitering at one of the tables drawing cartoon bunnies.

"What for?" Casey glanced her way with suspicion, peeking over at Alicia's binder and artbooks.

"Uhh." Alicia protectively pulled the binder closer when she remembered it was her *nudie* folder that normally never ever left her hiding spot at home. "It's a secret. Top secret, can't say."

"Top secret, huh?" Casey pouted, drumming her fingertips on the scarred and paint-flecked surface of the art room table. "Okay... did you buy an art club shirt?"

"I did." Alicia nodded. "Gonna wear it soon, I promise. Hasn't been washed yet. I can buy another one, if you need me to."

"Wear your shirt every Thursday for art club meetings," Casey negotiated, pursing her lips. "I'll need gas money. Annnnd I want you to be art club treasurer."

"*You're* art club treasurer," Alicia pointed out.

"Acting treasurer." Casey made a face. "And now also... acting president."

"...Oh." Alicia gave her a sympathetic look. "Sorry."

"It's a small school." Casey shrugged. "Mr. Peterson says some years the art club just doesn't really make it, even if it starts off real strong. We had twenty-seven people at the start of the year, and now it's already basically down to just six. *Counting me.* Me, you, Matthew, Bill, Mike, and Ethan. And Mike and Ethan—they're flakey."

"Sorry," Alicia apologized again. "I can... *probably* be treasurer. Is that just like, handling money? Accounting stuff?"

"Accounting stuff?" Casey blinked. "We're a high school art club—your job's to sell art club t-shirts."

"...To *who?*" Alicia asked, raising her eyebrows. "No one comes to art club anymore."

"You want me to drive you to E-town, or not?" Casey gave her a withering look.

"Uhhh, I can guilt-trip my dad into buying a shirt?" Alicia gave her a weak smile. "And stuff? I mean, I can be treasurer, but— listen, I'm not really a people person. I don't think I can get people to buy stuff. Matthew didn't want to do it?"

"He's... kinda already only showing up at meetings to hang out with me," Casey revealed with a sigh. "Not so much into the whole *art* thing."

"*Ah.*" Alicia gave her an awkward nod. "Yeah. I did... hear about you guys."

"'Bout me and Matthew?" Casey gave her another glance before returning to her doodle. "Shit. Yeah. I knew your one friend had a crush on him, and now she's all... she seems to be taking it really hard. I totally wasn't trying to rub her face in it that night or anything; it was just super stressful and—"

"I think Elena's big makeover thing has more to do with Tabitha than with the Matthew thing," Alicia admitted.

"I feel like shit about it," Casey said. "By the time I even thought of it, Matthew'd already been holding me for a while there in the hospital waiting area. And I was like, wearing his hoodie and all over him and... usually, I'm way better about stuff with, uh. Keeping things discreet and all. Especially there in front of his mom! That was just... a horrible night."

"Really appreciated that you were there for us, then," Alicia said. "I can... talk to Elena about the Matthew thing, if you want?"

"What, in exchange for a trip to Etown?" Casey chuckled as she colored in the large round eyes of her Cocoa Cinnabun drawing.

"No, of course not," Alicia said with an aghast expression. "Buuut, also yes; if it'll get you to drive me out there?"

———

"So, why *did* you have to keep your relationship all secret?" Alicia asked with interest.

Elizabethtown was a fair drive away, and Casey's garnet GMC

Jimmy was hurtling down the road. Both girls wore jackets despite the rush of air from the heaters, and LeAnn Rimes sang out a breathy melody of heartache from Casey's less-than-capable speakers as additional background noise. Alicia didn't mind any of it—she was too excited to get to their destination.

"It's this whole stupid thing." Casey grimaced. "There's like, a bajillion reasons. We're technically the same age, but because our birthdays are far enough apart, I'm a year ahead of him in school, so now all of the sudden, I'm this *cradle-robber* to some people."

"Oh, wow," Alicia remarked. "So, it's like pressure from the other juniors? Or the sophomores? I thought it was to keep away from the jealousy drama stuff, since Matthew's... popular."

"The jealousy drama stuff is at least a majillion of the bajillion reasons, yeah," Casey admitted. "Everyone gets *so* stupid about it."

"A *majillion*, huh?" Alicia laughed.

"And then, also... nah I can't tell you that part," Casey teased.

"Tell me what part?!" Alicia jumped at the bait with enthusiasm.

"Well..." Casey smiled, pretending to be reluctant. "Also it's that if people knew we were a thing, there's *no way* they'd let us run around unsupervised together at all the youth group events our church has."

"Oh. *Ohhhh.*" Alicia covered her mouth in surprise to hide her huge smile. "*I see.*"

"It's not even what you think." Casey shrugged shamelessly. "Not exactly. We make out a lot, and that's pretty much it."

"That's enough, though," Alicia said. "Sounds really awesome just with that."

"Did you have a crush on Matthew?" Casey asked. "Do you think I'm some sort of cradle robber?"

"No, no." Alicia laughed. "The... person I like is... also a little bit younger than me. We're still in the same grade though, at least."

"The person you like?!" Casey exclaimed in surprise. "Who?"

"I'm not telling," Alicia scoffed.

"Is it a boy, or a girl?" Casey asked.

"*What?*" Alicia snapped. "Why would it be a girl?"

"I don't know, I just thought—" Casey laughed, although she faltered into an awkward expression the moment she noticed Alicia's glare. "Uhhh, I was actually just messing with you. None of my business. Totally cool if you're into whoever you're into, so long as it's not Matthew."

"It's not Matthew."

"Okay, cool."

"Cool."

"Is it anyone I know?" Casey prodded, holding up a hand before Alicia could deliver a retort. "Just askin', 'cause like, a great way for you to get closer to your crush? Bring him to art club every Thursday."

"Casey..." Alicia growled.

"No, no, it's totally legit, because you can just say you're asking him 'cause art club is so desperate for people right now!" Casey arched an eyebrow. "Getting extra time to hang out with him would just be icing on the cake for you. Right?"

"You're unbelievable." Alicia made a noise of mock disgust and shook her head in dismay. "Actually, I *was* thinking about art club, a bit. I think Elena would be perfect for treasurer."

"So, it's Elena," Casey decided. "You like Elena. That's cool, she's cute."

"That's not funny," Alicia said. "What I mean is, like, I'm an artist. Not a... business-minded person. If Elena was treasurer, she would go in with a plan and stuff. Set goals, talk to people. Meet... quotas? Agendas? She'd probably get a bunch of people joining and attending art club."

"Wait, are you being serious?" Casey's playful smile faded away. "Wouldn't that be—is she even into art stuff? Wouldn't that be weird because of the whole Matthew and me thing?"

"No clue." Alicia shrugged. "I'm not gettin' into all that stuff. S'none of my business."

"Do you think she'd even go for it?" Casey wondered out loud.

"Before, I'd have said no," Alicia said. "Now—it's a maybe? She's really trying to set herself apart from who she was and be *different* now, and art's all about expression. Right? Elena could be the brooding art club goth girl."

"Fuck," Casey swore. "You're right, I can already picture it. She'd be perfect; she was in good with a lot of the freshman people. But... then, how do I make sure she keeps her grubby little freshman paws off of my Matthew?!"

"*Grubby little freshman paws?* You know what, Casey? I think the whole love triangle drama thing'll be a big draw, actually." Alicia relished her chance to tease Casey for a change. "*Great* angle for convincing her to join the club. We'll get Matthew to ask her!"

"That's not funny," Casey said, making a face. "Wait... do you think that'd *work?*"

———

"Ughhhh, you've gotta be fucking kidding me!" Casey groaned as they finally pulled into an empty parking space. "Seriously. *Seriously?!*"

"This isn't even *on* Dixie Avenue!" Alicia complained loudly in agreement, feeling a mixture of guilt and irritation. "They *said* they were on Dixie Avenue. I swear. They totally lied. It's way back in here."

Although the storefront they'd been searching for in Elizabeth-town was nestled in the very back of a small shopping center and somewhat removed from the main road, it *did* feature a tacky sign out in the streetside marquee that said HOBBY STATION in simple blocky letters. Between griping about the drama queens at Springton High and blaring the radio, however, the girls had somehow both missed it on their first pass and gone nearly six miles before realizing they'd overshot their destination.

"This place looks... small," Casey said with a dour look. "You're *absolutely* sure whatever secret thing you need isn't something the mall in Sandboro would've had?"

"Absolutely sure," Alicia lied with a straight face. "We called and checked literally everywhere. Do you want me to just run in real quick?"

"No way," Casey refused, turning off the engine and unbuckling her seatbelt. "After all this way? There's no way whatever you're getting stays a secret."

"It stays a secret." Alicia grinned, freeing herself from her seatbelt and opening her door.

The two teens left the GMC Jimmy and stepped out into the chilly November air of Elizabethtown, hurrying over into the barn-like decor of Hobby Station. Something about the structure seemed less comic book shop and more utilitarian, like the building might have been designed as an agricultural shed. Tiny decals of model trains lined the window set in the tiny door, and a bell jangled as they entered. The interior was somewhat stuffy with very welcome heat.

"Hello, there." The apparent proprietor was a nondescript middle-aged man rather than a kindly grandpa figure like Alicia thought he should have been, and Alicia stepped over to the counter while Casey was immediately distracted by a large and overly intricate display of model trains.

Sure, it's a cool diorama and all—but, you're supposed to be a junior in high school!

"Um. Hi!" Alicia squeaked out, hurrying to unfold a piece of notebook paper from her pocket. "My mom called ahead. I'm looking for... a *Dragon Models YF-22 Lightning 2?* They said you had it in stock here?"

"Dragon models?" Casey said with interest, immediately nosing her way back over toward them. "You have dragon models?"

"Not literal dragon models, I'm afraid," the man said with a good-natured laugh. "S'a brand. Dragon Models makes military model kits. I was the one who took that call the other day, had one set aside here for ya."

The man pulled a small box from an area behind the counter and placed it in front of Alicia before she could conceal the design on the front from Casey.

"It's... a fighter jet toy." Casey looked confused. "You needed a little fighter jet? From *here?*"

"It's a specific *model,* not a toy!" Alicia cried out in exasperation. She gave her friend a pointed look as if to indicate she should worry about offending the salesman here, but the man just chuckled again as he punched the price into the register.

"Comes to twenty-three ninety-nine," the man said. "We don't sell a lot of these ones, actually. Everyone wants to build the F-18 models after seeing that *Independence Day* movie with the aliens."

"*Independence Day?*" Alicia echoed, glancing down at the fighter jet artwork on the model kit box. It looked—pretty cool, with a streamlined simplicity that seemed futuristic somehow. The fighter boasted an attractive elongated *star* shape, like a five-pointed star that had been stretched out slightly to become more aerodynamic. The twin tail fins jaunting out at angles somehow just made it look even cooler.

"Uhhh, yeah out of curiosity, are F-22s like this in any big movies or shows? Where would someone have even seen F-22s?"

"F-22s?" The man paused to think. "Something on the news, maybe? Nowhere else I can think of... no, nothing really comes to mind. *Independence Day* had F-18s. I know those *Iron Eagle* movies had F-16s. The F-14 kits with the sweep wing like from *Top Gun* are still real popular, of course. Can't say as many collectors are interested in the F-22 models, just yet."

"That's... interesting," Alicia said with a small smile. "Huh."

"Twenty-four bucks, for a fighter jet model," Casey hissed in an exaggerated whisper. "Who wanted this?"

"It's a surprise, for someone's birthday," Alicia gave the salesman an apologetic smile on Casey's behalf while she pulled out a twenty-dollar bill and then singled some ones out of a little blue velcro wallet. "I'm gonna put it together and paint it for them."

"Is he like, in the air force, or...?" Casey gave Alicia a searching look.

"It's a best friend thing; you wouldn't get it." Alicia rolled her eyes. "It's symbolic. It symbolizes trust between me and—well, you wouldn't get it."

"If you say so?" Casey said with a doubtful smile. "Best friend, huh? Just seems kinda... weird?"

"Yeah, so?" Alicia smiled. "We're weird friends."

"Is he *cute?*" Casey elbowed Alicia.

"Um." Alicia couldn't help but look flustered. "Yeah? Kinda?"

———

"Time to wake up, sweetie," Mr. Moore called softly, rousing Tabitha from her sleep.

"I was just... resting my eyes," Tabitha protested groggily, twisting up onto one elbow from the softness of her pillow. After a moment of blinking herself awake, Tabitha saw the empty cardboard box her father was holding and her eyes lit up. "Is it time?!"

"It's time," Mr. Moore confirmed. "We just had our talk with the warden, and they've decided to let you out early on good behavior."

"*Finally!*" Tabitha exclaimed, sitting the whole way up and starting to swivel off the bed.

"Hup-hup-hup, hold your horses, little lady." Mr. Moore held up a hand. "We've gotta talk about good behavior, first."

"Okay." Tabitha grinned up at him. "I'm listening."

"The doctor said no running," Mr. Moore began. "No strenuous exercise. No working out—that's no jumpin' jacks, no sit-em-ups, no pushups of no kind, not no way, no how. For the next few weeks or so, maybe more."

"Okay," Tabitha readily agreed.

"No long walks by yourself—nothing unsupervised at all, period," Mr. Moore said. "No standing up for showers; you can take baths in the tub for a while. No playing tag with your cousins. No rough-horsing."

"Rough-housing," Tabitha corrected.

"That neither." Mr. Moore nodded. "The doc said to keep any physical activity to an absolute minimum. An' then, *just to be mean,* he also said you've also gotta take it easy on your noggin'. No more than an hour of TV at a time, same for readin'. Frequent breaks, whenever you're doin' anything that'll make you concentrate or focus or work that head of yours too much. No *hard thinking,* doctor's orders."

"Okay," Tabitha said with less enthusiasm, casting a guilty glance at *The Unschooled Wizard,* a Barbara Hambly book borrowed from Mrs. Williams that was resting on the bedside table.

"Doc says lots of rest," Mr. Moore continued. "Naps every day, lots of quiet time. They had you walkin' around a little bit okay, but you have any problems with your balance, or even if you just feel tired, you sit your butt right down and call for help. The boys got you a dinosaur to press for when you need anything. You need anything, and your mother'll be right there."

"A dinosaur," Tabitha repeated.

"Makes a dinosaur noise when you press the button," Mr. Moore nodded. "I'm told it is *'way cooler than a stupid little jingly bell.'*"

"...Okay," Tabitha said with some reluctance.

"You're not allowed to skip any meals, we've gotta make sure you eat everything on your plate. No using big words anymore or talking like a robot. You're not allowed to talk back to your mother. You're *never* allowed to talk to boys, and—"

"*Dad.*" Tabitha rolled her eyes and shook her head as her smile surfaced again. "Hand, please."

Mr. Moore obediently assisted, holding her hand as she

stretched her legs down all the way to the floor and carefully slid out of the bed. It took more conscious effort than she liked to steady herself, and after spending so much time as an invalid, she felt physically weak in a way that made her heart sink. *I'm not sure if I put on weight or lost it here, but… I've DEFINITELY lost muscle mass. Worst of all, I won't be able to get it back for a while, seems like.*

"Easy does it," Mr. Moore said.

"I can stand on my own," Tabitha assured him, attempting to tug her hand free.

"Nuh-uh, not 'til you're eighteen and grown you can't," Mr. Moore joked, not letting go of her. "Seems like just yesterday you were first tryin' to stand up all on your own like a big girl."

"Just yesterday, huh?" Tabitha gave him a wry smile, but stopped trying to free her hand. "Seems like quite a few yesterdays ago to me."

"You're *also* not allowed to grow up so damned fast," Mr. Moore cautioned. "The doctor was very clear on that. Wrote it down in all capital letters and underlined it an' everything. You need to slow yourself way down, Missy."

"Uh-huh," Tabitha indulged him. "Guess I've got no choice but to take it easy then, this time."

"'Fraid so." Mr. Moore nodded, setting the cardboard box down on the bed she'd just vacated.

"Is that… real people clothing?" Tabitha asked with excitement. "You've gotta let me go so I can change, at least."

"Your Grandma Laurie made you a dress to wear," Mr. Moore said. "You hold your peace and wait 'til your mother's here to help you get it on."

"I don't need help to change," Tabitha promised. "The little bathroom has handrails everywhere. Look—by the door, by the commode, everywhere. I won't let go of them."

"Hmm…" Mr. Moore gave the attached tiny bathroom enclosure a doubtful glance.

"*Dad*, I've been getting up to go to the bathroom by myself for days," Tabitha pressed. "Ever since they let me try to stand up."

"Well... alright, go on, then." Mr. Moore frowned. "Keep a hand on a rail. You so much as wobble, and you're grounded here to the hospital for a couple more weeks."

"I'll be fine," Tabitha assured him, lifting the dress up out of the box.

Pulling it up revealed a rather plain light gray *fit and flare* dress made out of surprisingly heavy fabric she imagined was perfect for these winter months. It had a modest neckline that wouldn't make her uncomfortable, long sleeves, and it looked like it would fall down just past her knee. A set of undies and familiar bra from home had even thoughtfully been placed at the bottom of the box. Tabitha found herself so enamored with the dress that when she gathered up everything and took an absentminded step in the direction of the little bathroom, she almost lost her footing.

"Sweetie..." Mr. Moore warned, taking her by the arm for a moment.

Didn't, though! Tabitha showed her father a sheepish smile. *Didn't lose my balance. Just wavered a tiny bit. Not gonna let myself get distracted. Slow, careful steps.*

After stepping in and closing the door behind her, she *did* reach out and take hold of the nearest rails, if only to confirm their position. Falling down for real would be no laughing matter, after all. Holding up the dress, she grew more and more pleased with it, and after admiring it for a few seconds more, she gently draped it over the sink and quickly discarded her flimsy hospital gown. Wearing real undergarments again was an enormous relief, the first step to being a person with agency again.

The dress had no zipper or buttons, and Tabitha had to heave the whole thing up over her head and climb her way up into it. The fitted waist was difficult to squeeze her shoulders past, but once her arms swam up into the sleeves and she managed her head through the collar to wear it properly, it was a remarkably comfortable fit. Regarding herself in the tiny ten-by-twelve inch afterthought of a mirror the little enclosure was provisioned with, Tabitha smiled to herself and carefully pulled her tangle of reddish orange hair through the neckline. When she arranged things just right, the shaved portion along the one side of her head wasn't even visible.

I look... frail. Tabitha quirked her lip at herself. *Pale, way more pale than usual. But, the dress is very nice! Has quite a bit of weight to it too.*

"You let her go in there by herself?!" Her mother's voice sounded along with a hearty smack. "Are you out of your mind?!"

Tabitha quickly opened the door only to discover Mrs. Moore had mostly been teasing—her mother wore an enormous smile at seeing her up and about and dressed. The small vase of flowers, Tabitha's binder, the small teddy bear from the boys, the borrowed novel, and the somewhat morbid framed *certificate of death* she'd earned had already been collected into the cardboard box. Her parents stood there, waiting to bring her back out into the world with scarcely-concealed anticipation.

"Aw, just look at you!" Mrs. Moore sighed. "Here you are—your socks and shoes. How does it fit? You look just lovely."

"It's perfect." Tabitha blushed. "Thank you."

"Are we ready to go home?" Mrs. Moore asked, taking her by the elbow and leading her over toward one of the nearby chairs so she could don her footwear.

"I'm *very* ready to get out of here," Tabitha admitted as she bent over to tug on her first sock. "I'm ready... for ice cream. I want to go out into town somewhere—with my mom and dad—and just have ice cream. As a family. I think... I think that's all I've ever really wanted."

"Phew, that's a tall order in the middle of November." Mr. Moore chuckled. "And I remember both you *and* your momma are tryin' to watch your girlish figures now, so—"

"No, we're having ice cream." Tabitha shook her head in curt refusal. "We're having ice cream, and that's final."

"You heard her, Alan," Mrs. Moore gave her daughter a supportive glance. "Ice cream. Family. *That's final.*"

"Alright, ice cream it is, then," Mr. Moore shook his head before looking back to Mrs. Moore. "Did your talk go okay?"

"*Ssh!*" Mrs. Moore glared, raising a finger to her lips. "We'll get into that later."

Intrigued but not overly suspicious, Tabitha carefully tied one shoe and then the other, slowly sitting back up and then holding her hands out for support. Her father shifted the box under one arm and took one of her hands, and Mrs. Moore went for the other —quickly correcting herself after seeing the sleeve straining around the circumference of Tabitha's new cast—and taking her by the upper arm instead. With her parents' help, Tabitha drew herself up to a standing position, feeling better than she had in years.

"Let's stop by and say goodbye to Mr. MacIntire," Tabitha proposed. "Thank him for letting Hannah visit me every day. Let them know I'm being released."

"Hmm." Mr. Moore frowned. "I don't know that we want you doin' a whole lot of extra walking around just yet."

"It's on the way out, almost," Tabitha pleaded. "Please?"

"Well, of course we can stop by," Mrs. Moore said with finality. "Alan—whatever my daughter says, goes."

Tabitha turned a beaming smile up toward her dad, melting away the last of his exasperated expression in a heartbeat. She felt great, Tabitha felt *motivated,* despite knowing her arduous period of recovery wasn't quite done with yet. Getting better enough to be out of the hospital was more than good enough for now—and Tabitha was realizing she'd been looking forward to sharing moments with her parents like this for *a lot* longer than she'd thought. Maybe her entire life.

We're going to have ice cream!

32
RETURNING TO WHERE SHE BELONGS

"I call shenanigans!" Mr. MacIntire complained with a wide smile. "Not fair, absolutely not fair. Hannah Banana, you tell them Miss Tabitha's not allowed to leave the hospital yet. I've put in *waaay* more hospital time already, but somehow *I* still don't get to leave!"

The exaggerated pout the grown man put on when his seven-year-old daughter was here was absolutely adorable, and Tabitha couldn't help but grin at seeing him in this new light. Both Mrs. MacIntire and Hannah happened to be visiting with him when they stopped by and the little hospital room was crowded, so the Moore parents lingered by the door while Tabitha came in to say her goodbyes. As eager as she was to leave the hospital behind, she *would* miss getting to see Hannah every day.

"She can leave if she wants to." Hannah put her little fists on her hips and gave her dad the cutest *stern* look she could muster. "She just got better faster."

"Why don't you tell your father about my operation," Tabitha suggested with an amused smile. "Hannah knows all about it!"

"Tabby got... a third ventriloquist," Hannah explained with a serious expression. "A third ventriloquist is, um... it's like when..."

Mrs. MacIntire turned away and covered her mouth, but not before everyone heard her *snrrk* of laughter escape.

"An *endoscopic third ventriculostomy* is when doctors open up..." Tabitha helped.

"Yeah, an *endoscopal third ventriloquist*," Hannah continued to liberally paraphrase while making a shape with her hand as though she was holding something big. "It's when doctors open up a bit of Tabby's head, like they're carving a pumpkin. Then they take out some of the seeds and pumpkin stuff. To make it so that there's not too much."

"Oh, lordy." Mrs. Moore laughed from the doorway.

"Seeds and pumpkin stuff, huh?" Mr. MacIntire grinned, glancing from Hannah over to her mother, who was still struggling to suppress her own laughter. "Hopefully nothing too important?"

"Cerebrospinal fluid was removed to help reduce swelling from the trauma." Tabitha assisted Hannah's storytelling with a gentle smile. "They didn't *quite* turn me into a jack-o-lantern; they just made a few incisions and lifted back the tiny portion of bone that had been impacted where my skull was cracked. I'm told I was very fortunate in that regard at least—compared to what you went through, I think it was a much more minor operation."

The bleed on her brain had clotted before even arriving at the hospital—which she was told was common—but the clot itself had been extremely dangerous, and with her swollen tissues from the head trauma, the clot was in a position considered unfavorable for a more invasive operation. An endoscope was used through a small incision, the surgical bypass successfully helped drain some excess fluid, after which she'd been placed under observation to determine what would happen with the clot. The blood clot *did* disappear, but it did so along with all of Tabitha's apparent brain activity, so everyone had naturally feared the worst.

Think I only survived at all because of my abnormal circumstance, Tabitha thought to herself, suppressing a wistful smile. *But... who*

would ever believe it? If whatever electrical or neural signals that consti-
tute my memories can somehow transmit backwards in time, is it
possible for damage to be dispersed that way? I want to say that logi-
cally, no that's not even realistic, but then on the other hand—neither is
fucking time travel. It definitely DID seem like I carried that blood clot
into the other timeline and left it there. Sorry, other timeline.

"Yeah, *you got shot!*" Hannah said, looking at her father in consternation. "On TV, when people get shot, they *die.*"

"Not *always,*" Mr. MacIntire protested. "I'm the hero—I'm like James Bond, a bullet here and there won't even barely slow me down."

"Yeah, you're the hero, huh?" Mrs. MacIntire shook her head in exasperation. "I think from now on, no more letting Hannah sneak out of bed to watch Bond movies with you, okay?"

"Well, *obviously,* I'm the hero," Mr. MacIntire grunted, reaching over ruffle Hannah's hair. "Besides, how can you have late night father-daughter *bonding* without *Bond?* Right, Hannah Banana?"

"No, Tabby's the hero!" Hannah insisted, struggling to fight off her dad's hand with both of hers. "'Cause—she's the one that saved you!"

"Then that makes Hannah the *real* hero, because she's the one who saved me," Tabitha said, slowly dropping into a crouch and opening her arms.

"Yeah!" Hannah's eyes lit up and she escaped Mr. MacIntire's grasp and rushed over to envelop Tabitha in a hug.

"Whoa—careful careful, Hannah." Mrs. MacIntire stepped forward in alarm. "Careful with Tabitha."

"She's okay," Tabitha assured her, wrapping her arms around Hannah. "She's fine. She's my hero! She grabbed my hand when I was lost in a very, very bad dream, and that's how I found my way back. It was tough!"

"Really?" Hannah leaned back far enough to search Tabitha's expression.

"Really," Tabitha confirmed with a nod, booping her on the

nose. "Thank you. How about, in the future, whenever your parents are busy or need some time to themselves, I can come over to your house so that you can babysit me."

"Really?" Hannah's eyes lit up. "I can babysit you?"

"Of course," Tabitha said. "I need you to look after me— because you're my hero."

"Mom, can I babysit Tabitha?" Hannah twisted in Tabitha's arms to throw her mother a look of excitement. "In case for uh, for whenever she needs someone to look after her?"

"We'll see." Mrs. MacIntire chuckled, giving Tabitha a look. "We'll see how Tabitha's feeling when she's a little better."

"Soon as you get better, I'm going to babysit!" Hannah said.

"I'll learn all of Momma Williams' recipes you like," Tabitha promised. "We'll cook a big dinner together, and then get cozy under a blanket and watch Disney movies. How does that sound?"

"Hey, wait a minute!" Mr. MacIntire made himself sound extra indignant. "What about movie nights with Daddy?!"

"*Daddy's movies are BORING!*" Hannah confided to Tabitha in a whisper that was more than loud enough for everyone present to hear.

"They most certainly *are not!*" Mr. MacIntire said in a childish tone. "There's nothing boring about James Bond movies!"

"Boooring!" Hannah giggled.

I don't think my favorite movie SPIRITED AWAY *is out yet, but I'm sure* Totoro *and* Kiki's Delivery Service *are on home video here already,* Tabitha thought to herself, pulling Hannah back in close for another hug. *If I can only find them—it's not like I can just order them online. I wonder if she's seen* The Thief and the Cobbler?

"C'mon, Pumpkin," Mr. Moore spoke up. "Let's go and get you home and restin'."

"*Ugh.*" Mrs. Moore thwapped him with the back of her hand. "Geez, Alan—don't call her Pumpkin, not *now.* Not while I still have those images in my head."

"Yeah, not after they carved 'er open and took out all of the seeds and pumpkin stuff!" Mr. MacIntire laughed from where he was reclining on the hospital bed.

"Oh, don't you even get him started!" Mrs. Moore rolled her eyes. "C'mon, Tabby honey. Let's leave them be. Officer MacIntire here will be fine—he has Hannah here to babysit him."

"Thank you so much for stopping by," Mrs. MacIntire said, gently pulling Hannah out of the way and assisting Tabitha back up to her feet so that she could give her a hug of her own.

"No, no," Tabitha said quickly. "Thank you guys for spending so much time visiting me. If you two hadn't been there on that day... I think I would've been in trouble. To say the least."

"Open invitation for you all to join us for Thanksgiving," Mrs. MacIntire said. "I'm making a big feast to celebrate when this stupid lunk finally gets released, but he won't even be able to eat solids for a while, so..."

"Mm-mmm, turkey milkshake!" Mr. MacIntire chimed in, patting his tummy and spurring another fit of giggles out of Hannah. "My favorite."

"You laugh now while you can, buddy—we've got a blender," Mrs. MacIntire teased, shooting her husband a look before turning back to the Moores. "It was great to see you all. Take care and drive safely!"

"Keep an eye on this guy." Tabitha ushered Hannah back toward Mr. MacIntire. "He's a troublemaker."

"I will," Hannah promised with a serious nod. "Bye, Tabby!"

"See you later, Hannah."

———

The wailing keen of ambulance sirens and flashing lights cut through the November air like a knife, and the sparse traffic along the road dutifully slowed and pulled toward the median to let the emergency vehicle pass.

"Tsk, terribly inconsiderate." Mrs. Moore made a dour face. "Honestly. We're trying to take our daughter home, here!"

"We're on the main road that leads right to the hospital," Tabitha reminded her with an amused expression. "I think that's fair odds for encountering an ambulance."

"Always hated the things." Mrs. Moore shook her head, seemingly determined to be unreasonable. "They always mean something bad's happened; it's like they're this dreadful... I don't know, *omen* or something."

"All a matter of perspective." Tabitha smiled. "I'm sure when you really need one, the arrival of an ambulance is a very welcome sight."

"Well, we won't be needing one of those any time soon," Mr. Moore said. "I think we're done and through with them things for a good long while, okay?"

"Okay," Tabitha readily agreed with a nod. *I wasn't even conscious for whatever ambulance took me in from the party.*

Normally, being situated in between her mother and father in the tight confines of the truck cab was unpleasant, but right now, Tabitha felt comforted to be surrounded by her family. She'd been in sore need of a change of scenery, and more than anything, the seductive call of freedom and personal agency had been beckoning for far too long. It was inordinately frustrating sitting there cooped up in a hospital room simply *waiting* to get better, and no amount of trifling distractions would ever be able to change that.

Tabitha needed to *do* things.

I'm going to set up a garden, Tabitha decided. *Always meant to, but just never made time. I can't actually PLANT anything until spring, but I can certainly—wait, I don't even need to keep this to myself, do I?*

"Mom? Dad?" Tabitha asked, breaking into a grin. "Can I clear space for a garden?"

"In November?" Mr. Moore laughed.

"Yes, in November!" Tabitha beamed. "I want to weed the yard so our grass looks better anyways. Spend time out in the sun, feel

the wind on my face. Get my hands in the soil. By the time everything's ready and set up, spring will be here."

"Tabitha—the ground's practically frozen; you'll catch cold
out there in the yard!" Mrs. Moore objected. "What sort of flowers
were you wanting to plant next year?"

"Cucumbers, tomatoes, peas," Tabitha said. "Peppers, maybe? I
don't know just yet."

"Don't sound much like flowers to me." Mr. Moore gave his
daughter a wry smile before turning his attention back to the road.

"Flowers... are only nice to look at," Tabitha pointed out.
"Vegetables can be nice to look at *and* good to eat. We already
took just about everything from Grandma Laurie's garden this
year—I'd really like to be the one bringing her things, for a
change."

"That's very thoughtful of you, sweetie."

"My birthday's next month!" Tabitha's eyes lit up as she
remembered. "For my birthday, I'd like a big bucket for us to start
composting with. And a pair of gardening gloves. If I can use some
of those old bricks we already have in the shed, I can mark out an
area the size of—"

"You're not getting *a bucket* for your birthday!" Mrs. Moore
seemed aghast at the idea. "Tabitha—"

"It's not expensive!" Tabitha promised. "Even just a tall plastic
bucket will do. I want to see if we can—"

"We can get you a bucket, but not for your birthday!" Mrs.
Moore seemed rattled. "Can you just imagine it, *a bucket,* all
wrapped up in wrapping paper on the table with a big pretty bow?
What would everyone think?!"

"Oh, well, you don't have to wrap it." Tabitha blinked. "You
can just—"

"How 'bout we get you fixed up with a whole gardening set?"
Mr. Moore proposed. "Getcha some gloves, a little spade, trowel,
garden rake—you name it."

"I don't know that I'd use all of them," Tabitha admitted.

"How about... a bucket, some gardening gloves, and... three or four tomato cages?"

"Why don't we talk about *ice cream?*" Mrs. Moore suggested, rolling her eyes. "You've been talking about wanting yourself some ice cream for weeks. What kind did you have in mind?"

"I *have* been wanting ice cream," Tabitha remembered with a dreamy smile. "Very much so, yes."

"But *what kind?*" Mrs. Moore asked.

"All of the kinds!" Tabitha giggled. "I want all of the ice cream. All of it. Every kind. All of the ice cream."

Not favoring their chances at the local McDonald's soft serve machine being operational—it had become rather infamous around town for never working—Mr. Moore instead steered his battered pickup into the parking lot of the Food Lion so that they could buy a small tub of ice cream to take home and enjoy. The air was crisp and cool, so the two parents strong-armed their daughter into wearing Mr. Moore's oversized hoodie overtop her dress and carefully guided her down off the cab's bench seat until her sneakers crunched down onto dry fall leaves.

Being with her parents had felt restrictive and terrifying to her back in May, and Tabitha remembered feeling *trapped* by the loss of agency. As she linked arms with her mother and father to stride together down the rows of cars to enter the grocery store now, however, she simply felt *happy*. Sharing simple moments like this with her family wasn't reliving a fond memory—it was treading new ground entirely. Tabitha wore a wry smile and couldn't help but wonder to herself if it really took such a bewildering series of traumatic events to get to here.

I don't know if I can say it was worth it, exactly... but I AM glad to be here like this.

Walking through Springton's Food Lion was one of those surreal experiences that always seemed to pointedly remind Tabitha that she really was in 1998. The overhead strips of fluorescent bulbs were bright, but were they as bright as supermarket lighting she remembered from the future? Were they dimmer by a few shades? As they slowly stepped down the aisles and Tabitha marveled at the tightly packed shelves of product with all of their outward-facing brand logos, the familiar brands were rendered unfamiliar in some strange, subtle and difficult-to-place way. It was hard not to think of the store and everything in it as a veritable time capsule collection of days gone by, and she couldn't help but search for things that stood out to her.

Maybe the colors are different? Or, the font the different brands use have all changed over the years and I'm not used to them like this? Maybe there's less fine print? Maybe not? As Louis said in Interview with a Vampire—*the world changed, yet stayed the same. I guess this feeling really can't be described properly.*

There was a magical feeling in traipsing down the aisles with her parents—after all, this wasn't *like* waltzing through the grocery store from her childhood. It literally *was* the grocery store from her childhood. Just for today, a bit of that almost forgotten novelty and excitement had returned, the feel of being a kid again, where her parents just might be persuaded to buy her something really nice. After forty-some years of this, shopping would become the mundane; a matter of routine and nothing more.

Tabitha was intent on cherishing this with every fiber of her being.

The grocery store's selection of ice cream was arrayed behind glass doors in the frozen section, partially obscured by foggy condensation and a glittering of frost. The different depictions of ice cream on each of the little tubs looked more than absolutely delicious; they sang a sweet serenade to her very soul and every single one made her mouth water with excitement. The picture of scoops of butter pecan ice cream conjured into being every memory of the flavor, until she could almost taste the dessert on her tongue again. The soft green of the mint with chocolate chips made her want to sigh with appreciation, and the cookies n' creme likewise thrilled her with the simple possibility that she might be enjoying it soon. They even had *bubblegum* flavored ice cream—but, she hated that stuff.

Some things just shouldn't have ever come to be. Science was a mistake.

"Lotta tough decisions," Mr. Moore spoke up in amusement, seemingly having read her mind. "You need any help there, sweetie?"

"We can get more than one!" Mrs. Moore spoke up. "We have room in the freezer."

"This one." Tabitha made her decision, swinging open the freezer door. "If it's okay, I'd like us to get this one."

Vanilla with peanut butter cup and fudge swirls; the paper tub was numbing cold in her good hand, and had more heft to it than she'd expected. *Is this... too much?*

"Is that gonna be enough?" Mr. Moore asked. "How much is it?"

"It's two dollars and thirty-nine cents," Tabitha looked up with a pleading expression. She'd forsaken the more expensive *Breyer's* and *Ben & Jerry's* in favor of Food Lion's cheaper generic brand ice cream, and it surely *seemed* like a good price by her modern sensibilities, but—

"No no, I mean—is that there gonna be enough ice cream for all of us, or should we get another tub or two?"

"I... thought you were just kidding about that," Tabitha said, feeling stunned. "It's—um, it's a quart? Oh, a quart and half."

"Pick another one, honey," Mrs. Moore encouraged. "Grandma Laurie and the boys'll be there at home waiting for us, I'm sure they could eat that whole tub in a single setting."

"Oh!" Tabitha blushed, passing her father the tub of *Vanilla with peanut butter cup and fudge swirls* so that she wasn't awkwardly managing it with her hand that was still in a cast. "Right. Okay."

She didn't know the boys' preferences for ice cream, so she

played it safe and chose the combined vanilla, chocolate, and strawberry stripe of a neapolitan for them.

"I've got forty dollars here; you go and get all the ice cream you want," Mr. Moore said, gesturing across the freezer doors again.

"This is enough!" Tabitha smiled. "More than enough. This is just for tonight—I don't want us to have any leftover, or to make this a habit. I want us to keep eating healthy, and then have ice cream only on very special occasions. To help keep ice cream sacred and special."

"*Sacred,* just listen to her." Mrs. Moore chuckled.

The Moore family walked up to the nearest checkout counter to wait while the customer in front of them finished writing out a check. The nearby newsstand display featured a *Time* magazine with the ominous text *The Fall of Newt* above the face of Newton Gingrich, who was currently Speaker of the House of Representatives, almost prompting Tabitha to reach over and examine it. She paused for a moment, made a face, and finally withdrew her hand. Temptation was always greatest here, and she was both interested in what was going on in the wider world stage here in '98... and repelled by the thought of getting caught up in constant thoughts about the timeline and her place in it.

Definitely not tonight—I just want to enjoy being a teenage girl tonight. I feel like I never got to do that the first time, so... so this is fine, I can give all the serious thinking a rest for a bit longer. I'm not ACTU-ALLY mentally regressing. Right? At least, I hope I'm not. I mean, Mom and Dad certainly never cared about world events, so it's not like—

She turned to regard her parents for a moment, and did an immediate double-take, her mind completely blanking from whatever thought she'd been having.

Her parents were making out.

What the actual fuck. Tabitha's eyes went wide and she felt disoriented for a moment, even double-checking to ensure that yes, these were in fact her parents.

Alan and Shannon Moore didn't *kiss.* In her memory, that

wasn't something that would ever even happen behind closed doors—let alone in a shocking public display of affection here in a checkout line! They were parents, not horny teenagers! Their relationship was supposed to be completely platonic. She knew that, *in theory,* they had somehow conceived her into being, but that— that was in distant eons past!

What the—what the fuck. Tabitha quickly looked away, feeling shell-shocked and lightheaded. *This is... this is... new? This never... uh. What the fuck? When did...?!*

Studiously examining the texture of the checkout's conveyor belt and not daring to look up, Tabitha politely cleared her throat when the man in front of them finished and was walking away with his bags. They all shuffled forward, and Mr. Moore passed the tubs of ice cream over her shoulder and onto the counter.

Okay. Okay, they're done. That was... weird.

"Grandma Laurie's gonna kill us for getting the boys ice cream." Tabitha's mother laughed, certainly *sounding* like she was in higher spirits all of the sudden. "I really can't believe they finished off all that Halloween candy so fast."

"Wait, *what?!*" Tabitha's head snapped back to her parents in consternation. "They *what?!* They can't possibly have eaten all of that. There was so much! How long was I out of everything?! It's— it's just barely November, right?!"

"Honey... we weren't sure how to break it to you," Mr. Moore said with a somber expression. "It *is* November—but of *1999*. You were zonked out for a whole year."

"That's—that can't be—" Tabitha hurried to grab for the nearest magazine and then fumbled to find the publication date. "It is *not!* It says right here 1998. I can't believe you would—that's not funny! *That's not funny!*"

The Food Lion cashier couldn't help but give them an amused glance as he rung up the two tubs of ice cream, because both parents were laughing while their redheaded daughter ineffectually swatted at them both with her one good hand.

"That's *so* not funny! I can't believe you would say that! I'm gonna get you for that!"

―――――

They were welcomed home by Grandma Laurie and all four cousins, and for a while, the trailer seemed like a madhouse of activity as the boys struggled to contain their excitement. Raised voices echoed throughout the living room despite their grandmother's attempts to get them to lower their volume, and if not for Mrs. Moore protectively hovering over Tabitha, they would have crowded in and smothered her with questions and attention.

"Did you really die?" Joshua asked.

"We missed you, Tabitha!" Aiden exclaimed.

"Did you see a white tunnel to heaven?"

"It's *white light,* not *white tunnel,* doofus."

"Does it still hurt? How hard did it hurt when you got hit?"

"Yeah, how would there be a tunnel to heaven? It'd be a tunnel only if it was to hell. Because hell's underground, like a thousand feet down."

"Um..." Tabitha's body was feeling heavier and heavier and she was already looking for a place to sit down and rest with anticipation.

"You were on the news. Grammy got it on the new tape we bought. Do you want to see?"

"Can we see your stitches? How many stitches did you get?"

"We saved you some candy."

"Yeah—you like Reese's, we saved all the Reese's!"

"All the rest is gone."

"You... can't have possibly finished off the rest of that Halloween candy," Tabitha said with an incredulous smile, carefully dropping herself down into the cushions of the chair beside the sofa. "Even with four of you. There was so much!"

"We did."

"Yeah, we did."

"There wasn't even that much candy to begin with, honestly."

"Yeah."

"Josh ate most of it. I barely got any."

"*Liar.* You took almost all the gum."

"Yeah, but gum doesn't count. It's *gum.*"

"We went over to where the Taylors used to live and threw eggs at their back door!"

"Yeah, we threw eggs, but they weren't even bad and rotten yet."

"Yeah, but the policeman said they didn't even live there anymore."

"Yeah, the grass wasn't even mowed."

"We didn't even get in real trouble, though!"

"Do you want your shoes off? I can take your shoes off."

"We're gonna find out where the Taylors went, and then—"

"Ssshhh, don't tell them that. We'll get in trouble."

"Aiden, stop, geez—you can untie the other one. I'm untying this one. She has two shoes, *idiot.*"

"I know, *duh.*"

"Do you want a Reese's? Josh, go grab the candy we put in her room."

"Boys, boys." Grandma Laurie shooed them back to give Tabitha some space and grabbed Tabitha's left shoe out of Samuel's hand. "Give her some air, for crying out loud. She can't get a word in. Why don't you boys go get the dinosaur you prepared for her?"

"It's not a *dinosaur,* Grandma, geez."

"Right!"

"Yeah!"

"Sorry. Here's your other shoe."

The 'dinosaur' they had acquired for Tabitha in place of a bell to ring for assistance turned out to be a foot-tall square-jawed Godzilla toy from the American *Godzilla* movie that had premiered earlier that same year. When a small button on his chest was pressed, the iconic *Godzilla* roar would play, albeit in that tinny, distorted way that electronic sound effects built into cheap toys sounded back in 1998. Tabitha turned it over in her hands with a wry smile before looking up at her expectant cousins.

"Isn't it way betterer than a stupid bell?!" Joshua asked. "It's way betterer."

"*Better,*" Grandma Laurie corrected.

"Yeah, better."

"*Best.*"

"Well—thank you." Tabitha paused, taking a moment to search for something appropriate to say. "It's very... um. *Cool.* Whenever I look at it, I'll definitely be reminded of you boys."

"We just put in new batteries," Sam said. "It was the only toy we had that was loud enough."

"Sometimes it just randomly roars, though, even if you *don't* push the button!" Nick added.

"Yeah, it does that all the time," Aiden said. "But we put in new double-As!"

"Press it again, press it again!"

"Yes, I'll... thank you, cherish it," Tabitha said with a weak smile, looking to her grandmother for help.

"Alright, alright, that's enough excitement for Tabby for one day!" Grandma Laurie began to corral the boys. "She needs her rest. Tabby, *just in case the batteries in that awful thing die out,* there's a tiny little hand bell in beside your bed. You give your father a ring and he'll come wait on you hand and foot. Won't you, Alan?"

"Hand and foot." Mr. Moore nodded. "Room service for Tabitha."

"Don't use the bell—that's lame!" Aiden protested. "This is *Godzilla!*"

"Thank you for everything, Grandma," Tabitha said. "You too, boys."

"I'm sorry I didn't come out to see you when you were cooped up in the hospital," Grandma Laurie sighed. "The boys have been a handful here, and you've been getting a lot of calls. You even have a few letters. I set them in on your dresser. You go in and lie down. We'll be back by here to see you tomorrow. Love you, sweetie!"

"I love you." Tabitha gave her grandmother a hug and accepted a kiss on the forehead.

"Get some rest—you look dead on your feet, girl."

"Well, wait—we *did* buy a bunch of ice cream for everyone," Mr. Moore reminded Tabitha.

"Ice cream?!!"

"Ice cream! We get ice cream!"

"Wait what kind?"

"*Ssh*, who cares, it's ice cream."

"Shush, you hooligans!" Grandma Laurie barked, giving Tabitha a look of concern. "Do you want to have some ice cream now, or do you want to wait and we'll have an ice cream party tomorrow? You look like you're slippin' in and out, honey."

"Um." Tabitha gave the boys an apologetic wince. "I think that... why don't we have an ice cream party tomorrow? Sorry, everyone."

Despite her earlier enthusiasm to celebrate her freedom, Tabitha indeed found her energy was already flagging in a big way. It seemed silly to her to look forward to a serious nap after spending so long in a hospital bed, but there was something incredibly alluring about being able to tuck into the comfort and privacy of her own bed, in her own room. Simply being *home* was a relief all in its own.

After saying her goodbyes and seeing her grandmother and cousins out the door, the mobile home filled with peaceful silence and the call of cozy blankets beckoned to her. Tabitha passed the Godzilla toy to her mother with a wry smile and carefully crept down the hallway toward her room, keeping one hand on the wall for balance. Tabitha's room was quiet and still, and in her absence, someone had tidied up and neatly made her bed. The forgotten yellow Flounder stuffed animal rested on her dresser, and her Ariel costume hung from a hanger in front of the mirror.

Tabitha traced her fingertips down across the outfit in surprise —she hadn't expected to see it again. The dress was intact, but as she examined more closely, she found several new seams and lines of stitches where panels of fabric had clearly been replaced.

Of course, I was wearing it that night—paramedics must have cut it apart, Tabitha surmised. *Grandma, you didn't have to put it all back together...*

A large pile of individually-wrapped Reese's peanut butter cups from the boys' candy stash was sitting atop some mail on her dresser like a heap of treasure. Some of the half-buried envelopes had that *squarish* look that signified they might be Get Well cards, while others were rectangular and suggested people had actually written her. Tabitha was very interested in going through them, but the slowly-mounting exhaustion won out and she stepped over to sit heavily on her bed.

Home. Finally, home.

She sleepily struggled out of her new dress, half-heartedly folded the garment, and managed to land it on her dresser on her first toss—her bedroom was tiny. Tabitha tugged back the covers, slipped her bare legs in along the clean linen, distractedly combed her hair back from her face, and then gingerly rested her head down on the pillow so that she wasn't lying on her stitches. Tabitha let out a long, slow breath, and was asleep in moments, with the faint roar of Godzilla out in the living room not even able to rouse her.

33
GETTING THE BIG NEWS

This place doesn't have to be trashy, Tabitha thought as she knelt on the edge of the street, picking pieces of garbage out of the weeds and tucking them into the plastic bag by her knees.

Wearing a pair of jeans over her flannel pajamas and bundled up again in her father's oversized sweatshirt, Tabitha's efforts began just outside the steps of her trailer in their sparse yard, where she filled a little grocery bag up with weeds as she painstakingly tugged them up one by one. It hadn't been easy—each stubborn thing had to be pried from the cold, hard ground and often simply trying to pull them up with her fingers rewarded her with only a fistful of ripped out plant matter, while the actual root of the weed remained firmly planted and unyielding. Tabitha didn't have a spade yet, but she *did* discover a forgotten and somewhat rusty flathead screwdriver in the shed when she was pulling out bricks to examine. Stabbing and scraping into the frigid November soil saw many of the weeds destroyed, and the ones that weren't were certain to have a terrible winter.

Nothing was really growing this late in the year, but Mr. Moore had been remiss in keeping up with the yardwork throughout fall and then apparently content to leave things be through the winter. The sentiment was reflected throughout the entire neighborhood of the lower park, which made it difficult to fault her father for it. Any casual glance at the lots just on either side of them or across the street showed the same trifecta of scraggly undergrowth, littered garbage and random ugly bald patches of bare earth that stood out. The Moores didn't have a *bad* yard, in her opinion—it was simply neglected. Neglect characterized the state of the entire trailer park, and to an extent, the people who made their homes here. The relationship between a person's state of mind and their immediate environment was interlinked in a lot of ways. Cleaning out the inside of their trailer those months ago had done wonders for her.

I don't have to be trailer trash! This can just be a... you know, a community of manufactured homes. It doesn't HAVE to be trashy. I don't know how things even got this bad around here, but like with me... with just a little bit of work, things can be better.

Tabitha gritted her teeth as she fished out a piece of trash—a soiled bit of cloth from something or other—and gingerly dropped it into her bag. She wasn't sure if it had been someone's discarded shirt left out by the side of the road for who knows how long or what, and in truth didn't find herself keen on investigating further.

I don't think I can clean up the entire park, though. Tabitha couldn't help but grimace at the prospect. *Probably? Or, maybe I can, just yard by yard? Yep, that's me, community service volunteer grounds-keeping and maintenance for Sunset Estates! I'm gonna go stir-crazy cooped up inside and I want to DO something—it might as well be something productive. Right?*

Unfortunately, as she'd expected in recovering from an operation, Tabitha found her energy quickly flagged. She had the drive and she had the motivation to *do* things, but there just wasn't enough in her tank right now; she was coasting on fumes. Before she'd even finished weeding around to the other side of the trailer, she found herself feeling listless and more often than not simply crouched in the cold, staring across their small and somewhat ugly plot of grass.

Ughhh, or maybe not, I guess? Tabitha wanted to take it upon herself to make a difference, but her enthusiasm was at a deadlock with her exhaustion. With a long, slow sigh that became visible vapor in the air before her, she resumed her thankless task, this time moving slowly and with more deliberation to each of her movements.

For the next half hour, she hunkered down at the edge of their side of the little road in front of each of her neighbors' mobile homes, slowly filling up a second little shopping bag with trash. Tabitha's broken hand remained tucked into the front pocket of her father's sweatshirt, but her free glove found cigarette butts—so many cigarette butts—along with unidentifiable scraps of mushy paper that may have once been fast food cardboard of some kind. A few smelly discarded beer cans had been crumpled and forgotten, and twisted bits of wire that looked to have been the frame of one of those campaign signs people plant in front of their house—the sign itself was long gone.

Creeping along the length of yards beside the street she retrieved pebble-sized chunks of broken glass, pages of junk mail advertisements that had been left out in the weather, and dozens of tiny bits of blue plastic she couldn't quite place. Until she discovered a blue action figure leg, the rest of the toy having been apparently abandoned to be run over by cars, smashed and forgotten.

There were small pieces of metal. Splintered chunks of wood that must have broken off of someone's porch steps, with a scrap of outdoor carpeting still tacked to them. A mashed and rotting styrofoam takeout container, leaking bright orange fluid she hypothesized might have been hot sauce from someone's order of wings. A broken disposable medical syringe that Tabitha refused to touch, instead gingerly scraping it into the mouth of her collection bag with one of the moldering pieces of discarded mail. Another beer can. *Two more beer cans.* More cigarette butts, so many cigarette butts, the soggy stubs of mushy paper were so ever-present throughout the wild crabgrass that one could be led to believe the things *grew* from the unwelcome vegetation.

Progress was slow, but less because the task was *difficult,* and more simply because Tabitha was taking her time and pacing herself in a methodical manner. Cleaning up the area wasn't fun or pleasant, but it was rewarding in a certain sense—she felt like she was accomplishing something. She'd *craved* that in her time spent recovering in the hospital ward, and finally, she could *do* something and feel productive again.

There was something inherently satisfying in the weight of the plastic bag as she crept her way along and filled it with plant matter, garbage, and the miscellaneous trailer park curiosities that painted low-income Americana in colorful strokes. The weight of her bag represented her determination, and glancing back across the stretch of street to compare their little yard against the neighbors, it *did* look a lot better.

Not by much, but you CAN tell if you're looking, Tabitha decided with a faint smile. *Every little bit helps! Every little bit contributes. In some small way.*

When her ears were stinging from the cold, Tabitha finally—carefully—stood back up, stretching her back and releasing a huff of contentment, her breath still visible in the air. She hadn't finished the area—not quite—but a good deal of the lots on their side of the street were tidied up, and her second bag was almost full to the brim. She'd balked before at being told she was only allowed to take baths instead of showers, but now after even just some forty or so minutes here out in the chill, taking a nice warm soak right now sounded positively decadent.

Tabitha trudged the short distance back home, weary and feeling hollow but at the very least not discouraged. She'd made visible progress at something, and now when she rested for the rest of the day, it would feel earned. *I think that's what I really needed.*

"Momma?" Tabitha called out immediately upon returning to the heat inside the trailer. "I'm gonna take a bath in a bit to warm up—would you take a quick little look with me outside, first? I did a bit of weeding and tidying up. I want to show you."

"Is *that* what you were up to out here?!" Mrs. Moore asked. "Peeked out to check on you earlier and couldn't figure out what on God's green earth you were up to. Tabitha, you can't clean up the entire neighborhood."

"If I don't, then who will?" Tabitha chuckled.

"Tabitha..." her mother warned. "I know you mean well, but what if our neighbors don't *appreciate* you poking around their private property?"

"I'm sure some of them won't," Tabitha said with a wry smile before dropping her voice down into a low, gravelly range. *"This is MY pile of garbage, asshole. Back off!"*

"You watch your mouth," Mrs. Moore said, but she was rolling her eyes and wore an exasperated smile.

They had resumed practice sessions where Tabitha attempted to act, and although she didn't have much natural talent for expressing mannerisms or controlling her facial expressions, Tabitha did have a knack for creating natural-seeming personas and staying in character.

She was cheating, somewhat, in that she had sixty years of experience to draw from and therefore quite a range of memorable personalities from future films, shows, podcasts, and even memes to draw from. For the most part, Tabitha would either attempt to portray an impersonation or spin her own little distinctive character up on the fly, and her mother would critique her performance and teach her specific ways to improve.

I just need to be careful to never ever do it around Alicia, because she'll probably be able to catch me quoting something familiar, Tabitha thought. *Or, wait—maybe that's even more of a reason to do it?*

"Tabitha—I know you've been bored these past few days, but I'd much rather you were here inside writing your book thinga-majig while you recover. You're liable to catch a cold out there!"

"It's just in our little area," Tabitha said with a faint smile. "I didn't go far, and I paced myself and stopped as soon as I felt like it was time to stop. I really just... want everything to be a little nicer. And I have the time. I have *nothing* but time right now."

With some motherly consternation that Tabitha found surprisingly pleasant in comparison to their bitter quarreling earlier in the year, Mrs. Moore fussed over her daughter's winter attire for a few moments before consenting to allow Tabitha back outside. The woman's efforts still seemed silly to Tabitha after having been out there and left to her own devices for so long, but it was honestly a *good* kind of silly.

In the early morning today, she'd begged for permission to spend some time out getting fresh air without being under strict supervision. Only her exemplary behavior in the days following her return home had given cause for her mother to finally relent. Tabitha had been forced to promise not to push herself too hard or do anything *outrageous* like stroll around on her normal exercise loop around the neighborhood. In hindsight, Tabitha thought she could have probably snuck away to enjoy a long peaceful walk instead of how she'd spent her morning. *Weeding was probably even more strenuous!*

But—I didn't go on a light jog, or even a power walk for some exercise, Tabitha mused to herself as Mrs. Moore finally found a scarf for her to wear. *Before, I would have. With the way things were between Mom and me.*

"Tabitha Anne Moore, just you look at this—your cheeks are completely red; you're practically frozen!"

"That's just the honey glow in my cheeks!" Tabitha grinned.

"Oh, you think you're so funny." Mrs. Moore tightened the scarf around her daughter with a good-natured grumble. "You're a real comedian."

I wasn't REBELLIOUS or striking out against her authority or anything—just, I didn't care to obey. Her words didn't use to mean anything, we didn't have this, this... trust. Now, it's like just because I know she cares, it MEANS something. It meant I wouldn't just go on my exercise loop anyways, even if I really, really want to be getting back into things.

Shannon Moore donned a shabby old winter blazer herself and then made sure to hold Tabitha's hand as they opened the door and went down the steps. Being bundled up at this point seemed like a quintessential *too little, too late* gesture, but it was a gesture all the same and Tabitha was rapidly discovering that ever since the evening of trick-or-treating—or maybe even a little before that —she absolutely *loved* any indication of appreciation or heartfelt care her parents had in them to express. It felt childish and embarrassing to have gone from her fierce push for stoic independence back in May to now desperately craving any attention her parents had to spare, but Tabitha couldn't help it.

This is just the way my feelings are now, Tabitha told herself as she eagerly guided her mother to the middle of the street so that she could see all that she'd gotten done. *It's not mental regression, it's... emotional growth. Right? Whatever, I'm thirteen for now—I'm allowed to act like it!*

"Well, it does look very nice." Mrs. Moore sighed as she surveyed the now slightly cleaner trailer park and clucked her tongue. "And I'm proud of you. But I didn't think you'd be getting up to all this out here for so long—it's always *something* with you —and I don't want you out here *toiling away* in the cold, or thinking any of this is your responsibility. Your *only* responsibility is getting your rest and recovering."

"Kneeling down and picking things up isn't exactly *toiling.*" Tabitha smiled. "I think it's just about all I can do with how woozy I feel still."

"Tabitha—if you're feeling woozy, then we're getting you

inside and right into the tub!" Mrs. Moore frowned. "Look at you, you're practically turning blue!"

"Mom. It's *forty-three degrees.*" Tabitha rolled her eyes like the teenage girl she currently was. It was even more fun than she expected. "In Canada, they still wear shorts and tee shirts in this kind of weather."

"Well, this isn't Canada; it's *America!*" Mrs. Moore fumed, giving Tabitha a gentle swat. "You get your butt right back inside this instant!"

"*Yes, Momma.*"

————

Her long soak in the bath was every bit as decadent as she imagined, and Tabitha nearly dozed off as she reclined back in the tub. The warmth of the water stung at first, but after a few minutes, the heat permeated through her skin and seemed to soften up the chill from her muscles until she was positively basking in the steaming bathwater. Adding a folded water-soaked towel to help cushion her back against the less forgiving angle of their mobile home tub helped her relax, and she kept her left hand up resting on the lip of the basin, the plastic bag from a delivered newspaper affixed over her cast with a rubber band.

In the entirety of her past life, Tabitha had only taken a handful of actual baths, instead preferring the expediency of standing up for a shower to wash her hair and scrub herself. As someone who'd been ashamed and disgusted of her own body for most of her life, she'd always tried to see as little of it as possible. That had changed in a big way with her dramatic weight loss here, and Tabitha enjoyed seeing herself naked more than she wanted to admit.

Never quite got to getting a COMPLETELY trim stomach with visible abs, or anything, Tabitha thought as she inspected her tummy. *But I was definitely getting there. Before the big setback. My arms are still looking great, my legs look pretty amazing. I never really appreciated toned and athletic legs, until I got myself a pair. I've already tried shaving them a few times; it's not so bad. Just kind of tedious. Maybe this spring, I'll start experimenting with showing them off a bit? Shorts, maybe. I'm not ready for skirts, no way.*

Her boobs? They were still there. Existing. She didn't know what to do with them.

Sometimes she would stare at them in the mirror—they were a curiosity, and Tabitha was never completely sure how she felt about them, or how they looked. Sometimes, their shape looked surprisingly nice, sometimes they just seemed completely foreign and weird, and there were also many times she just wished she simply didn't have them or have to deal with fitting them into bras. They were probably around the same size as they had been in her first life, maybe even a little smaller, but with the majority of her body fat sloughed off of her frame to drastically change her figure, these oddities now seemed *proportionately* much, much larger than she was used to.

For as much as I hated being the invisible fat girl last time through, going to high school this time, as a slender teenage girl—one with BREASTS? Absolutely mortifying, at times. Too many times. Whew boy, was I not ready for that. At all. Freshman boys weren't careful about where their eyes went, and that level of even accidental, um. SCRU-TINY. Wasn't something I was prepared for. Honestly, I'd always thought the 'hey, my eyes are up here' thing was a joke, or a flex, or something. IT'S NOT.

I wouldn't mind being thought of as attractive! The PRETTY girl. That'd be kinda nice. Or, so I thought. Actually, getting THAT level of attention right off the bat from the first day wasn't something I knew how to deal with, at all. That definitely impacted my initial plans to socialize and be normal... and instead had me hiding away in the library for that first few weeks. Maybe something I should talk about with Elena?

To date, she'd had little conversation about her breasts in this life, so far really only with Grandma Laurie when they were trying out different dresses to turn into blouses for her. Well, even calling them conversations might be a stretch, as they'd consisted entirely of an embarrassed Tabitha just shaking her head and looking completely mortified each time a *too-revealing* design was offered. Much to her grandmother's amusement.

Tabitha wore a wistful smile at the memory, idly plunking a fingertip down across the surface of the water in repetition just to hear the noise it made. There were so many strange moments like that that she was growing to appreciate more and more. After she was all grown up, those situations just didn't really happen. She'd been worrying for the past few weeks over mental regression, or even *brain damage,* and whether or not her mind was actually reverting back to that of a pubescent teenage girl, but if she really was—so what? The added perspective of a lonely and miserable adult life seemed to only serve to make all the experiences of growing up this time more and more intoxicating to her. These happy times with everyone probably weren't going to last forever, and she needed to make the most of them.

After relaxing in the bath until her fingertips were pruny and the water became only lukewarm, Tabitha finally decided it was time to get out. She toweled herself off, then brushed her hair with care—leaning in toward the mirror to examine the stitches along the side of her head as she did so. A little time was spent checking herself out naked in the mirror, turning this way and that. In her own admittedly biased opinion, she simultaneously looked lovely and gross. Her features were pleasing, and her body had a form that was pretty nice to look at, but what had previously just been pale was now a ghastly white. She could see her veins in too many places, there were all sorts of bruises and weird marks, and parting her hair in the different way to make sure it covered the shaved part of her head made her look a little weird.

But, still. Mom's right—a lot of beauty isn't really in any of those things. Tabitha tried to turn her hesitant smile into a beaming one in the mirror. So far, it was still awkward.

It's in the eyes, it's in the way I need to carry myself. My body language and my posture and the amount of attention I put into my expressions. I'd heard of having 'resting bitch-face,' but what I've had until now was honestly 'resting BLANK-FACE.' Now Mom has me learning to let myself emote more, and that sort of confidence won't come naturally, not at first. You have to grow into that. I'm growing into it for the first time, and she's learning how to come back to it. And we're doing it together, which is even more important.

Tabitha stepped out of the bathroom and padded down the short trailer hallway into her room. She dressed in new pajamas, climbed into bed where she could protect that glow of warmth from her bath under winter blankets, and hugged her pillow against herself so that she was completely cozy.

She'd earned this nap.

———

"Honey... I have something important I want to talk about with you," Mrs. Moore said with a nervous expression, letting her spoon clink against the porcelain of her teacup.

"I have something important too!" Tabitha revealed, easing her own teacup and saucer back so that she could slide her notebook in from where it had been off to the side.

It was now late evening, and the mother and daughter were finishing off the remaining ice cream together at the dining room table. At Tabitha's insistence, they only enjoyed dessert from these tiny teacups normally buried in the back of a box in the closet, both because it kept their portion size down to very small increments, and because Grandma Laurie's old tea set was dainty and cute.

"Well, in that case—you go on," her mother insisted. "You go first."

"Okay." Tabitha tried not to give her mother a wary look. "I think I've more or less finalized what I want my story to be, and—I want you to read it. My goblin story that I've been working on all this time."

She pushed the notebook across the table toward her mother.

"Are you sure?" Mrs. Moore accepted the binder and then hefted it up gingerly in her hands. "I know when you got this back from that woman from the school board, you mentioned that this was very... personal."

"It is." Tabitha nodded. "I've been wanting to share it with you because of that. For *months*. Just, it never all quite felt ready until now. I'm really dying to know what you think of it—in how it pertains to me and my life, and just as a story on its own. Right now, this is like how your blue album is for you, but for me."

"Thank you," Mrs. Moore said. "I *have* been very... curious."

"Just, please promise me you'll let me know what you think," Tabitha pleaded. "Like, don't even wait until you're through the whole thing, give me all the feedback you have, whenever it pops into your mind. About any of it. Anything."

"Okay, okay." Mrs. Moore chuckled. "I will."

"Okay." Tabitha let out a breath she didn't realize she'd been holding in. "Thank you. Now it's your turn—what did you want to say?"

"Tabitha, I've... I've been meaning to have a big talk with you," Mrs. Moore said after a long moment of hesitation. The plump woman fidgeted, taking the stem of her spoon pointing up out of her teacup and fiddling with it.

"Now that you're home, and things are... getting back to normal. Somewhat. For our family. We'd been waiting to tell you some big news, and... and your father's been a big baby about it, since he doesn't know how to talk to you about this, and I don't either, so I'm just going to come out and say it. Because I want you to know."

"Okay..." Tabitha said, giving her mother a curious look and feeling herself fill with tension all over again. "I'm listening. What is it?"

"Tabitha—" Mrs. Moore paused. "You're... going to be a big sister."

Tabitha froze, staring across the table at her mother in disbelief.

"I'm going to be... a big sister?"

"Yes, honey."

"I'm... going to be a big sister," Tabitha repeated with a blank look. "You're—what, you're having a baby? *You're having a baby?!*"

"Yes, honey."

Shock didn't quite begin to describe what she was feeling— her mother having another child was impossible; it had never happened before and could in *no way* conceivably happen now. Her parents couldn't *have sex.* It was a series of concepts that didn't fit together in any way, shape, or form. Suspension of disbelief was broken forever. *What the fuck. What the fuck.*

"You're... having a baby?" Tabitha said again. "*Are you sure?*"

"Yes, I'm very sure." Mrs. Moore let out a nervous chuckle. "I was just as surprised as you are!"

Somehow... I doubt that. Tabitha took a deep breath and raised her good hand to her forehead as she frantically tried to think. *This is... this came about from my actions, somehow. Somehow. Changes have consequences. Jesuuus do they ever have consequences.*

Mom's lost weight. No, not even just the weight—her mentality has changed. A lot. I guess I didn't even realize how much until Halloween. Last lifetime, she was just totally swollen up with self-loathing and bitchiness and petty spite and she's been gradually... deflating from that. Her and Dad are a lot more, um. They're...

I mean, I knew Mom and Dad weren't really usually, uh, TRADI-TIONALLY INTIMATE, not for a long time, I guess, so I just assumed they were always going to stay that way. Big psychological blind spot, and—yeah, I don't even want to think about it now, either. Ever. Ew. EW, EW, EW. But. She's having a baby. A BABY. I'M GOING TO BE A

BIG SISTER. Not just a cool older cousin, A BIG SISTER. That's—it's—this is completely different. Who'd have ever even thought? I mean, sure, yeah, she was super young when she had me, but isn't a thirteen-year difference in siblings pretty—

"Tabitha?" Mrs. Moore sounded worried.

"Sorry, um." Tabitha floundered for words. "This is just... you're *really* sure?"

"I'm really sure." Mrs. Moore nodded.

"Okay. *Okay,*" Tabitha breathed, taking the initiative to reach across the table and clasp her mother's hand before the nervous parent could grow any more uneasy. "This... this changes everything. What are we going to do? Are we moving to a bigger place? *What are we going to do?!*"

"Whatever you want to do," Mrs. Moore said, squeezing Tabitha's hand. "We have settlement money coming in—the Seelbaughs helped with that. Everyone did. But that's, it's *your* money, for your future. Your father wanted to set up a college fund for you, but—"

"I'm not going to college." Tabitha shook her head as she disengaged. "I have—well I *had*—other plans. Not college."

"Okay," Mrs. Moore agreed. "Whatever you want. The money —it's a lot of money, Tabby honey. If you want us to move, we'll move. If you want to go to school in a different district, we'll do that. Whatever you want to do, we'll make it happen. I was just— we were just, we don't want to pressure you, or make you think you need to make any big decisions when—"

"We're staying here," Tabitha decided immediately. "I want a few thousand dollars for immediate expenses, and the rest kept available for me to invest in stocks in the next several years."

"That's fine," Mrs. Moore assured her. "Investing is smart! If that's what you want to do, that's—"

"Can Dad take some time off from work?" Tabitha asked. "There's so much for us to do. I'll pay to get Uncle Danny's Oldsmobile hauled to the junkyard; we don't have space for it. I'd like you to call the management of Sunset Estates and get them to approve some changes to the property, and I'll need someone to take me to Springton town hall so we can file for a construction permit. For just a few thousand dollars, we can get a simple deck add-on built and covered and turned into an extension of the trailer. The Jamesons down the street did it, super cheap way of adding an extra room, and we need—"

"The Jamesons added a room onto their trailer?" Mrs. Moore looked up in surprise, leaning forward at the table slightly to cast a look out the window and down the darkened street. "When?"

"Err—no." Tabitha carefully winced, clamping her mouth closed for a second. "They, uh, they *will*, though, they were talking about getting it done. I think maybe they've done it before, some-where else? They sounded very, um, it's a pretty certain thing. Just trust me."

"When have you spoken to the Jamesons?" Mrs. Moore asked, giving her daughter a doubtful look. "You were in the hospital for—"

"Before that! I talked to people, sometimes, back when I did my morning runs," Tabitha said quickly. "I know Mike and his family, kind of. And others. Some people were, um, up and about early in the mornings back when I did my morning routine. Basically."

"Oh."

"*Anyways,* we need permits first, and we need them fast, before it gets any colder. I think I'd like to get a little fence around our lot as well—if memory serves, Sunshine Estates used to let the Upper Park homes have fences. We can get it installed, and then if we plant some thuja green or leyland cypress now, we'll have several feet of privacy shrub coming up by the time the baby's here. If we need the roof sealed, any flooring or windows or electrical replaced, I want you and Dad to tell me now so we can get it done sooner rather than later. We'll have our hands full when he—or she—is born, and I don't want us putting anything off."

"Tabitha honey—do you think it's wise sinkin' more money into the trailer instead of us just up and finding a better place to live?"

"Yes, and no." Tabitha frowned. "I'll do some more research for a more thorough cost-benefit analysis, but the key to take away from this, is that settlement money is just a one-time windfall. Our actual flow of income isn't changing, so when you consider—"

"Okay, okay!" Mrs. Moore chuckled, holding up her free hand in defeat. "It's your money right now anyways. Whatever you want to do with it is fine. Just, please sit down and have a talk with us about everything first, some of these things—well, like taking your Uncle Danny's car to the junkyard. We wouldn't have to pay for that. The junkyard would pay *us* for however much in parts it's worth. If you want it gone, we can get it gone; we won't waste any of your money on it."

"Right. *Right.*" Tabitha laughed to herself. "Guess I forgot what —uh, what kind of times we live in here. Of course they'd pay us— they can still use the scrap. In these times."

"...Yes?" Mrs. Moore said with an unsure laugh. "Of course they can?"

"I was just thinking, *in the long view,* where the automotive salvage industry will someday have to deal with—no, you know what? It doesn't matter. *You're having a baby. I'm going to be a big sister!* There's so many more important things to think about, right now!"

"So, you're excited?" Mrs. Moore asked.

"Of course I am!" Tabitha gave her mother a quizzical smile. "Why would you think I wouldn't be?"

"Just, with the, um. Timing, of everything that's happened," Mrs. Moore said with a difficult expression. "We weren't sure how you'd feel about it, or if you'd feel that we were trying to replace you, or—"

"Wouldn't even blame you if that was the case, and I know it's not." Tabitha squeezed her mother's hand again in a show of support. "Honestly, this might be the best news I've gotten in a long, long long long time. Thank you. I needed this right now."

"Well, that's a relief, then." Mrs. Moore smiled.

"Also, I'll need both of you parents really distracted with something for a couple years." Tabitha laughed. "My late teenage years are going to be *super* suspicious. So, this is perfect!"

"I... don't even know how to respond to that." Tabitha's mother laughed, shaking her head and rolling her eyes.

Mom, I'm actually Tabitha from the future, Tabitha thought with a small smile. *I came back in time.*

I'm just gonna keep layin' down this breadcrumb trail of not-so-subtle slips and misspoken words until you can get to wondering, and HOPEFULLY maybe more receptive to the truth, someday. This is what I should have done with Alicia and Elena. It's just—frustrating. And, I'm still a terrible actress. Maybe that'll make it stand out even more to you?

"You know, you haven't even asked how big the settlements were," Mrs. Moore chuckled.

"I haven't," Tabitha said. "I've just been really focused on, you know, enjoying the fact that I'm still alive. Which is great just by itself! Why, how much was the settlement?"

"Settlements," Mrs. Moore corrected her with a smile. "Plural! Don't forget about that Thompson boy and what he did! And, in light of the near *medical diagnosis mishap* and some people being thrown under the proverbial bus, the fees for your surgical procedure and hospital stay have become... very agreeable. The law offices of Seelbaugh and Straub—your friend Elena's father; he's apparently a very scary man. Having the police and the school board behind you here in town is support that runs deeper than you know. Things have been... *surprising.*"

"I've been very lucky, and very unlucky," Tabitha said, taking a deep breath. "I think that's just how things are going to be, from now on. With little in between. How much do the settlements come out to in the end?"

Mrs. Moore told her the number, and Tabitha felt her eyes go wide as the teacups full of melting ice cream, the table, her mother across from her and their quaintly furnished mobile home around her all suddenly felt distant and unreal.

Uhhh. Okay, wow. My conservative guesstimation was off by an entire zero. Wow, just... wow. Holy fucking shit. THAT much, in 1998?

34
THE MUSIC JUST RIGHT FOR ELENA

"*Well?!* What did you think?" Ziggy asked, leaning in close over the Hot Topic counter. "How many of them did you get through?"

This was Elena's fourth visit to the dark haunt of Sandboro Mall's Hot Topic store, and in essence, this trip was solidifying her shaky friendship with Ziggy, the mall's other resident *goth chick*. Conversing with the older teen was still awkward for Elena, both because of the five-year gap in their ages, and because crossing the boundary between customer and employee like this just felt weird. Ziggy had seemed eager to connect with her ever since she'd come back with her dyed hair and Hot Topic apparel, and Elena definitely also had mixed feelings about that.

"I listened to all of them," Elena said, setting the borrowed plastic cassette cases on the surface between them. "But... I don't know if any of it's for me."

Rather than starting to feel more comfortable in her gothic persona, Elena was beginning to feel like this part of her life was just an unbearable ongoing identity crisis. She was stubborn enough that she refused to see it as a passing phase, but there was just something big and important missing here, and it was honestly making her unhappy. The other day after school, she'd been lying in bed and simply started crying because she realized she was sad—*that* wasn't normal.

Things had been fine at first, because there had been a dramatic makeover into the new subculture fashion. Setting herself up in diametric opposition to the *preppy* girls she despised like her former friend Carrie and... yes, her own former self; all of that felt right. But, shortly after that, everything seemed to fall apart because there wasn't a plan. There weren't really any other goths at Springton High, there was no one to socialize with, and as cool as the loner aesthetic she'd built up was, it was also, well, *lonely*.

As difficult as it was to admit, Elena wasn't sure she was equipped to deal with that.

In the gothic poetry she'd started writing, she described her previous self, the *old Elena,* as being full of petty ambition. It was objectively true no matter which way she considered it—but, once she'd decided to set aside those petty ambitions—then what? What was she supposed to do with herself now? Goth culture existed as a complete outlier to the social hierarchies she was familiar with climbing. Elena was the coolest goth girl in school and also the only goth girl there. It felt like no matter how much work she put into assembling the perfect Hot Topic look and how carefully she did her new style of makeup, her victories would remain hollow and ultimately pointless.

Am I just SUPPOSED to be sad? Elena wondered. *All the time? I feel like gothic culture has a lot of merit in the alternative way they— no, the way WE—express ourselves, but also... I really don't fucking want to be unhappy and alone and crying by myself all the time. I can't stand it. What do I even DO from here?*

"Really?" Ziggy seemed incredulous. "Nirvana didn't do *anything* for you? Pearl Jam? Soundgarden?"

Elena had at first been hesitant to interrupt the girl's work, but then Ziggy also made a point to be as unprofessional as she could

get away with while on the clock, to 'express her rebellious indi-
viduality' and 'stick it to the man.' It certainly helped that the
store owner Mr. Gary was her stepdad, a genuinely nice older guy
who seemed to see their socializing as some sort of subculture
networking that would be great for business.

"I liked Soundgarden, kinda?" Elena tried to compromise.
"Nirvana didn't really... uh, speak to me, I guess. I didn't like Alice
in Chains at all."

"I mean, well duh, you can't *not* love Soundgarden," When
Ziggy shook her head in disbelief, the green spikes of gelled hair
adorning her head swayed back and forth. "But you don't like
Nirvana?"

"It's just—I dunno?" Elena shifted uncomfortably on her feet.
"Didn't really feel anything."

"Okay then, what about the *poser* bands?" Ziggy challenged.
"On that second tape—Candlebox, Bush. Collective Soul. Were
they more your speed?"

"They were alright, I guess?" Elena shrugged. "Just, none of it
like, jumped out at me, or anything? It was just kinda there. I don't
know."

"Well, you're definitely not ready for any of the bitchin' local
bands, then." Ziggy frowned, leaning back and crossing her arms.
"Level with me, here—what kinda music did you listen to before?
Like, what CDs do you own?"

"I don't have a lot of CDs," Elena admitted. "Most of the ones
we have are my parents' stuff."

"Spice Girls?" Ziggy made a face. "*Hanson?* Madonna?"

"Um." Elena winced. "Spice Girls, yeah. LeAnn Rimes, Jewel.
Avalon, Point of Grace, Mariah Carey..."

"Okay—stop, stop, *stop.*" Ziggy quickly motioned Elena to stop
and took a quick glance around to make sure no one had overheard
her apparent blasphemies. "All of those are like the absolute worst.
I mean, Avalon? Jesus, isn't that *Christian* music? Throw all of

those out. Break the disks into pieces first before you put them in the trash."

"Okay, yeah." Elena gave a noncommittal shrug. She wasn't actually going to do that. She felt indifferent about most of that music now, having moved her small collection of CDs out into the living room and putting them in her parents' CD rack already.

"I mean, geez—from remembering how you looked that first day we met, I figured you'd at least be into like, No Doubt, Smashing Pumpkins, or—"

"I do have Smashing Pumpkins," Elena protested weakly.

"Well, whatever. Your mom still said no way on getting into Marilyn Manson?" Ziggy inquired with a mischievous look, tapping a lacquered black fingernail against one of the tape cases.

"Yeah, still no on Manson." Elena nodded. "I listened to it anyways, but yeah... he seems like a bit too... I don't know. It's not for me."

"Doesn't that make you like him *even more,* though?" Ziggy whispered. "Knowing that she's against it *for no reason* other than her religious brainwashing makes the music more meaningful. I mean, Manson, he's a sexy, badass dude—have you ever seen what he looks like? *His eyes?* The guy once bit off the head of a *live bat* onstage."

"No he didn't!" Mr. Gary called from where he was doing inventory across the store. "Hell, that was Ozzy!"

"Yeah, *okay,*" Ziggy snorted, rolling her eyes. "Like *you* know anything about music, old man."

"Ozzy Osbourne, on his *Diary of a Madman* tour," Mr. Gary yelled over his shoulder. "Actually caught part of that tour, at Freedom Hall over in Louisville. This was back when—"

"No one cares, old man!" Ziggy retorted, turning and flipping him two middle fingers and a look of almost manic glee.

I'm... really not against my parents at all, though, Elena thought to herself, feeling even more alienated than before. *I love my dad, I love my mom—I love my mom more than anything. Does that make me less goth? Or more of a poser? I went for the goth thing because it felt right, and it moved me outside the high school hierarchy bullshit and off into my own thing. It still feels right sometimes, SORT OF, but then sometimes it's like it never fit me at all. And if I don't belong here, then—where the fuck DO I even belong?*

————

That Sunday, the Moore family joined them at the First Presbyterian Church of Springton for the early service. Elena was surprised at how thrilled she was to see her friend, and chasing right after that excitement was guilt, bitterness, and a strange feeling of discomfort that left her feeling speechless. Tabitha was wearing a modest long-sleeved dress that seemed tailor-made for her—both in that it was flattering, and that the sleeve on one side had clearly been altered with healthy allowance for the extra girth of her orthopedic cast.

Mr. Moore looked reserved and polite, but then Tabitha's mother Mrs. Moore managed to look mildly terrified at being around so many other people, failing to hide it behind an unconvincing and very strained smile. Everyone in the congregation was happy to meet them, and family after family stepped forward to introduce themselves and shake hands before everyone took their seats in the pews—except Elena. Elena didn't know what to do.

I should—no, WE should go say hi, Elena turned a helpless look toward her mother. *Right? I mean, we're still friends, but also... I need her to know I'm not okay with her time travel nonsense still, need to express that there's a distance between us there. Distance that I'm not going to just bridge over and forget about. Just... God, is it awkward just standing here, like this.*

Elena found herself filling with tension as the Moore family worked their way a little further down the aisle through the church-goers intent on welcoming them to the community, and didn't feel any relief when they finally chose a pew and sat down.

Tabitha seemed distracted by her mother's anxiety and kept leaning in to whisper something to the woman, but when she did notice Elena on the other side of the church, she offered a wave.

Out of reflex, Elena immediately waved back, feeling more stupid and out of place than ever. Mrs. Seelbaugh gently patted her back as if sensing her troubles, but Elena wasn't able to take any comfort from the gesture.

What... am I DOING? Elena thought, smoothing out the modest floral-print Sunday dress she wore. *Jesus. The MATURE thing to do would have been to just run over and make up with her already. Or at least make some kind of effort. That's what Mom would have done. Not be... stupid and petty about her silly whatever story. Ugh, GOD!*

As per her agreement with her parents, Elena didn't wear anything black or gothic to church, so she felt even more out of her element here bereft of her gothic trappings. Wearing her old dressy church outfit would have felt like a lie, because that just wasn't who she was anymore. But now when she wore her full gothic getup complete with makeup and everything—that felt like a lie too, like she was a poser *mall goth* just going through the motions for appearance's sake alone. Going to school was wrapping herself up in that cold Hot Topic persona to separate herself from who she didn't want to be, but left her at a loss as to who she was anymore.

Mrs. Seelbaugh's hand was still on Elena's back, so she could *feel* the moment her mother's posture grew tense.

"Ah, shit," Mrs. Seelbaugh muttered under her breath.

Shit? Elena looked toward her mother in confusion. *What's wrong?*

A month ago, Elena would have already been ribbing her mom about letting a swearword slip out—especially after the woman had always seemed so keen on policing all of Elena's harmless cursing. Mrs. Seelbaugh didn't swear lightly, and she'd certainly never used bad language in church, even when she was socializing with the church group. The raven-haired teen followed her moth-er's attention over toward two very familiar women shuffling into the pew behind them and her mood immediately soured.

Oh. SHIT.

"Michelle! *Michelle!*" Mrs. Melissa hissed out in a whisper. "You won't *believe* who that woman is!"

"That's *Shannon Delain!*" Aunt Cindy added in the same conspiratorial hushed voice. "Shannon Delain, *you-know-who!*"

"Over there, with the red hair!" Mrs. Melissa turned her body partially away from the congregation to shield the insistent finger she was jabbing in the direction of Tabitha's mother from sight. "With the little girl. Red hair, *that's HER.*"

"She got so *fat!*" Aunt Cindy leaned in to confide.

"I *know!*" Mrs. Melissa agreed with a smirk, shooting another glance over her shoulder. "And, that little girl! Do you think that—"

"Melissa," Mrs. Seelbaugh warned. "Have you gone over and spoken to her?"

"No, but I *know* it's her!" Mrs. Melissa declared. "Look at her *face!* That's definitely her, she's just so *huge* now! All that weight. I mean—*Jesus!*"

"You're being very rude," Elena interjected, crossing her arms and giving her mother's two closest friends a glare.

"Hi, Elena sweetheart! I just *love* your hair!" Mrs. Melissa flashed her a rigid smile before turning back toward Mrs. Seel-baugh. "I just love her hair, Michelle."

You already said that when you saw me last Sunday. Elena did her best to not let her neutral expression sink into a scowl. *It sounds a little less sincere each time I hear it.*

The service began, but Elena was swimming helplessly in her own head. She stood and held the hymn book for songs, she sat and stared during the sermon, and she mechanically bowed her head during prayer, all the while her psyche seemed to be working overtime to disassociate herself from everything she tried—or tried not—to be. *What does that even leave behind, what's left over then? What do you even CALL this kind of crisis?*

————

When it was over and everyone was standing and beginning to file out of the pews, Elena rushed over to join Tabitha as soon as she could. When she stood in front of her friend, however, her mind blanked and she had no earthly idea what she should say.

"Elena honey, why don't you show Tabitha around the church?" Mrs. Seelbaugh supplied, almost as if those borderline supernatural *Mom* senses of hers were once again detecting Elena's distress. "While we talk to her parents for a little bit about some things?"

"Yeah," Elena said.

Tabitha smiled at her, and Elena felt relief and shame tugging at her from different directions. With a small wave, she led her friend out of the Sanctuary away from the crowd and down the hallway toward where the choir rooms, fellowship hall, kitchens and Bible study rooms were. The First Presbyterian Church of Springton was large, but over the past few generations, the congregation had significantly thinned. There were several daycare rooms, but they only kept one in operation, and the youth group had disbanded before Elena was old enough to join it, rendering many of the rooms down one hallway without any purpose. The large building and outlying structures were intended for twice as many people as currently attended, and each year, the church areas seemed a little more empty than the last.

"Are you still mad at me?" Tabitha finally asked, glancing around at everything with interest.

"I—no," Elena said, scrunching up her face. "Sorry, if I seem standoffish. I still don't believe you about the whole... *thing*. Just, I don't know what to do about that. I'm not mad. I don't know what I am."

"Okay." Tabby nodded. "How can I help?"

"Uhh." Elena offered her an expressive shrug. "I don't know. You seem kinda different since the hospital."

"I am different." Tabitha grinned. "I *feel* different. Everything's changing!"

"Yeah," Elena agreed—but in contrast to Tabitha's new apparent upbeat attitude, all she felt was a formless sort of dread.

Tabitha *was* different too. Before the events of the Halloween party, Tabitha had seemed hesitant and just kind of timid all the time. Now, it was as if that near-death experience had put a bounce in her step, filled Tabitha with focused tenacity and enthusiasm for everything. The pangs of jealousy that appeared at that realization weren't easy to stifle, because before that same transformative series of events, it was *Elena* who had been instilled with purpose and drive.

"So, are CDs still around in the future?" Elena blurted out.

She still didn't believe Tabitha was actually from the future. But Elena decided she needed to understand the story, to have a better grasp of it so that she could figure out what *to do* with it. If it was a fanciful game of make-believe, Elena needed to tear it down so that it didn't continue to cloud the air between them.

If it was a delusional coping mechanism or metaphor for dealing with trauma, then helping Tabitha unravel it would be good for both of them. Posing a question about *CDs,* of all things, wasn't on her prepared collection of weak points to attack, but music had been on her mind a lot lately and popped out of her mouth before Elena could stop herself. After all, music was supposedly some sort of cultural lynchpin that *should* have anchored her to the whole goth thing. At the very least, it would have given her *something* to talk about with Ziggy.

"Hah." Tabitha laughed. "No. Not at all. They're very much a relic of this time period."

"What's next after CDs?" Elena mused, trying not to fidget. "Little microchips?"

"Sorta." Tabitha quirked her lip. "But not like you'd think. Music goes digital pretty soon. In two or three years, you'll be downloading songs onto your computer and loading them into an iPod. Little handheld device. That really kicks off music piracy—Napster and BitTorrent and all of that, which I actually kinda missed out on in my first life and only found out about in retrospect."

"There's music piracy *now*," Elena countered, the memory of Ziggy first waggling a mixtape for her still vivid in memory. "Tape cassettes, CDs. My friend Ziggy knows a guy who pirates CDs with a disk burner. Music piracy is already a big thing."

"Ehhh, no." Tabitha shook her head. "That's not big, not really. What's going on now is just isolated cases, like one or two people out of thousands and thousands. The kind of piracy I'm talking about is *extremely* widespread, something along the lines of forty percent of the entire market basically just deciding to never pay for music ever again. Just download copies from wherever for free, instead."

"That's... okay, that's a lot, I guess." Elena made a face. "Maybe *too much*, in fact? Forty percent? How do they wind up putting a stop to it?"

"The long answer is a complicated mess and I don't remember all of it, and the short answer is; they never really manage to put a stop to it," Tabitha explained. "Nothing effective anyways. Pirating media—movies, games, music—and assets for stuff like 3D printing was still a common everyday thing right up 'til I came back to the past."

3D printing...? Elena wondered. *Seems like another term to note down. I think Mom had an article in one of her magazines about how 3D stuff works—those red and blue lens glasses that make it look like pictures pop out. I can do a bit of research and find a way to corner her on something and finally stump her.*

"Okay." Elena pursed her lips. "So, should I wait? Like, should I not buy music now, and just wait until piracy just makes everything free? Or, is that a real bad thing to do?"

"That's a tough one to answer," Tabitha said. "To be completely honest with you, I don't think I ever bought music in my life, period. When I was this age, we didn't really play the radio or anything at home, and I didn't really get into music until I was in college. You have to remember, I wasn't a 'cool' kid in my first go-through. I didn't know music."

"So you pirated music later, when pirating wasn't illegal anymore?"

"Well, no, pirating's always illegal," Tabitha appeared to be conflicted on how to explain. "But, less like shoplifting, and more like jaywalking? I never pirated anything, though. In college, I had a Pandora account, but I just had the free version, so they played advertisements in between the music. Then most of the rest of my adult life I was just abusing YouTube playlists whenever I wanted to listen to things, and it was free too. Well, free with some ads that would randomly play."

"Then does that mean you've listened to a lot of music?" Elena asked. "Ziggy—my friend—has it in her mind that I need music to build my identity around, or I'm not *really* goth. Like without the music culture parts of it, I'm just a poser. If you're really from the future, you must have a bunch of bands you can recommend to me. Right?"

"Are you kidding me?!" Tabitha lit up. "Absolutely! I was just thinking about this the other day! Well, sorta. When I think *goth* I think Evanescence, but emo music is what I usually associate with the Hot Topic sorta style. Fallout Boy. My Chemical Romance, Panic at the Disco, Paramore."

"Emo music," Elena challenged, giving Tabitha a stare. "I've never even heard of it, or any of those bands."

Alicia was definitely right about Tabitha being a bit too quick with coming up with those believable names and terms, though. Most of them have a kind of legitimate ring to them, all except the disco one—that sounds stupid. She didn't have to pause for a moment to think them up or anything, though. Does she plot these all out beforehand?

"Oh, you won't for a while yet, I don't think," Tabitha said. "Mid-2000's, maybe? We'll have just gotten out of high school by then. I remember there was a group of emo kids that hung out together at the community college in Elizabethtown where I went."

"Why would they hang out at the college?" Elena asked, perplexed.

"Why?" Tabitha blinked. "Uh, they were students there. I'd just sort of see them around campus here and th—"

"If they're emo *kids,* then they wouldn't be in college," Elena argued. "They'd be adults."

"Well, that's a very... high school perspective to have," Tabitha explained. "For instance, when you were in middle school, you'd think of the high schoolers as all *mature* and *grown up,* but then once you get into high school, you realize what an illusion that was. They were all always just dumb kids. That doesn't change when they get older and get into college or universities, and for most of them, it doesn't even change when they get out into real world jobs either."

Elena wanted to retort with a *well duh,* or segue into a *that wasn't what I meant; technically, they're legal adults,* but the arguments stuck in her throat and she gnawed on her lip, simply feeling stifled and frustrated. Tabitha had at the very least put a considerable amount of thought into this roleplay charade she was doing. That she was expending so much effort on her make-believe was incredibly irritating, though, and made Elena want to catch her in a lie more and more.

"Okay, fine," Elena huffed. "Name an 'emo' song."

"Welcome to the Black Parade, by MCR," Tabitha answered without hesitation.

"Then—sing some of it," Elena dared her, crossing her arms.

"If you're from the future, you'd remember at least one super amazing song that stood out and—"

"When I was a young boy"

"My father took me into the city"

"To see a marching band—"

To her consternation, Tabitha again didn't have to pause, and whatever fake lyrics she'd obviously prepared beforehand were even sung in that soft sort of undertone one does when mimicking someone else's much louder performance. The words were even delivered in a kind of steady rhythmic cadence that seemed suspiciously *too* well done. *Tabby's a writer, though, a creative type. She probably has no problem thinking up poems and pentameter and songs and things*

"Okay... you've put a lot of thought into this." Elena shrugged, doing her best to look unimpressed. "Clearly. But you made that up beforehand. It's not *from the future.*"

"Elena, I didn't make that up." Tabitha gave her a teasing smile. "You don't have to believe I'm from the future if you don't want, but don't say that *I* wrote any of that! It feels like you're accusing me of plagiarism then, or like I'm taking credit for other people's work, or something. Makes me uncomfortable."

"Fine then, you didn't write it." Elena shrugged again and looked away in aggravation. "Whatever. I don't care. I still don't believe you about the time travel. It's—it's. I really hate that it's like I have to fight you on something so *stupid* right now. As if I didn't have enough to deal with, with everything else. I don't see the point."

"Well, if you *did* have a friend from the future," Tabitha mused, "maybe they'd be interested in somehow getting you out to see a certain gothic rock group before they make it huge."

"Gothic rock?" Elena sounded skeptical. "Ziggy never mentioned *gothic rock.*"

"They might've categorized things differently back in these times," Tabitha said. "Alternative rock, I guess? Emo is still a few years away, for sure. I mean, I wasn't super proud of it back then... but I can definitely recite pretty much every Evanescence song, and even do the opening bits of 'My Immortal' if we can get access to a piano."

"*Goth rock* makes it huge." Elena couldn't keep the sarcasm out of her voice. "To *who*, exactly?"

As far as she could tell, she was one of only *three* in the entire student body at Springton High who affected any sort of style that could even remotely be construed as dark and brooding, and she was definitely the only freshman. Every interaction she'd had with Ziggy in the Fairfield Hot Topic indicated that their kind were always loners and outcasts. The idea that a goth song would enter mainstream appeal seemed oddly counterintuitive to her, and the more she thought about it, the more certain she became that Tabitha was simply feeding her a line of bullshit.

"Everyone, really." Tabitha couldn't keep the excitement out of her voice. "*Evanescence.* They get huge, and I mean huge like, fifty million albums sold. Well, by 2040-ish, anyways, that's around the time I caught the video about it. They went platinum quite a few times. 'Bring Me to Life' was pretty much freaking *infamous* for being overplayed on the radio back in... '03? Maybe '04? But right now? I don't even think they're on anyone's radar yet."

"Wait, so... they exist *now,* but they're not big yet?" Elena pressed. *If they're a real band, she had to have heard them somewhere. If they don't become famous in the next few years, what, will Tabitha just claim that the timeline must have just changed? Make some sort of excuse? More and more, I'm just doubting EVERYTHING she says. It's all just too suspect.*

"Yeah. Right now, I think they're just performing in tiny little venues in Little Rock, Arkansas," Tabitha revealed. "Tiny like, *coffee shops.* Bars. Maybe still under a different name, I think it was *Childish Intention,* or *Stricken.* Hell, Amy Lee probably isn't much older than us right now. She must be... sixteen, or seventeen, here in '98?"

"Arkansas," Elena repeated, some of her skepticism fading away as the wheels began to turn in her head. "That's... okay, that's not *that* far away. What are you saying, like—if what you're saying is true, then how would we even take advantage of it?"

Tabitha—what's the point of your make-believe story, here?

"We don't," Tabitha said, holding up her hands in a helpless expression. "Absolutely no way. I know it's kinda ironic, in that they're one of the few things I remember well enough that I could like, steal their songs and everything with future knowledge. But, *I'm absolutely not going to.* I *love* Evanescence, and no one else can sing those songs with the kind of *oomph* that Amy Lee put into them."

"I'm not saying steal anything," Elena carefully clarified. "Just, there would have to be some way or some angle to do *something* with future knowledge there, if you already know they're going to have hits. Right? It could probably even benefit them, somehow."

"Why don't we see if you even like them, first?" Tabitha suggested. "We can... make some calls, or something—*ugh,* not having real internet makes everything such a headache. Figure out when and where they play, take a trip down to see Evanescence live sometime soon. Do you want me to try to sing a little bit for you?"

"Sure." Elena jumped at the offer. "Of course. There's a piano over in the fellowship hall we can probably use, even. Over this way."

"Uhh." Tabitha blanched. "Okay. Yeah. Just to warn you, though —I don't *actually* know how to play real piano. Learning to play piano was one of the early hologram gimmicks, honestly, and most of us only messed around with that as a novelty. Just white keys, and I only learned to play random easy catchy bits—the opening bits of 'My Immortal,' the real basic *Swan Lake* riff. Stuff like the super simplified Dojacat's 'Say So,' 'Malaxa' by Arnault, and Tattletale's motif from Worm. Those are the total extent of my piano-playing abilities."

"Which means...?" Elena prodded.

"So, I'm just saying—lower your expectations way, *way* down." Tabitha made a face. "I haven't practiced any of that stuff in years."

"But you can sing it, or not?" Elena questioned. "Come on."

"I think so." Tabitha shrugged. "I wasn't *bad* at singing, per se, but I don't think I was anything special either. Hopefully, I'm good enough for you to get the gist of how things go."

Elena guided her friend into the large community room where the congregation gathered for the much less formal occasions. It was a wide open space today, with dozens of tables folded and wheeled out of the way and several hundred chairs neatly stacked ten high in the nearest corner and a stage area that took up the far wall.

Elena watched with a skeptical look as Tabitha plunked away at the piano keys in an experimental way, making odd but not very musical noise for several minutes.

"Okay... I lied," Tabitha said with a grimace. "It's been too long —I can do the 'My Immortal' opening, and a bit of Tattletale's theme. If I had a few hours, I could probably figure out the *Swan Lake* thing again. 'Malaxa' and 'Say So' are both off the table, I only remember the one started with three fingers here like this, and then with my right hand, I kinda did... something like this? But, I don't remember it all that clearly anymore. Apparently. Hold on, lemme see if..."

"Which one's the goth rock one that's gonna be big?" Elena asked, unable to tell if Tabitha was just stalling or not.

"'My Immortal,'" Tabitha answered, taking a sheepish glance around. "Am I, um. Am I allowed to sing in here? It might get a little loud."

"Just sing it kinda softly." Elena shrugged. "How does it go?"

"Hah." Tabitha shook her head ruefully and awkwardly placed her fingers back on the keys. "Well, I can sing 'My Immortal,' but I can't sing it softly. That's not how ballads work. I can't *not* really yell some of it out."

"Go on, try it then," Elena said, trying not to sound like she was getting impatient as she checked out the room. There were only a few adult women loitering over near the door separating the fellowship hall from the kitchens, and they didn't seem at all interested in what she and Tabitha were getting up to. "If they tell us to stop, we'll stop."

"Okay. *Okay.*" Tabitha took a deep breath. "Here goes!"

Clearing her throat and stretching her slender fingers one last time, the redhead carefully positioned them back on the ivories and began to play. The music wasn't familiar to Elena, but it sounded... good, and Tabitha seemed to be playing with more confidence this time, measuring herself and now taking appropriate pauses that elevated the piece well above those previous practice attempts. *Doesn't sound very ROCK, though, does it? If—*

"I'm so tired of being here—"

The slowly drawn out words sounded across the entire fellowship hall, forcing Elena to do a double take and again mentally reevaluate her friend.

Each syllable felt inexplicably *heavy,* full of sadness and pain, and when they fell in time with the piano notes, any doubt that Tabitha was making up this particular song on the spot vanished. She was definitely drawing knowledge of this from *somewhere,* the lyrics and notes complemented each other too well for this to be any sort of fabrication. Across the room, both of the adult women stopped their conversation and turned toward them. Tabitha was singing at volume already and the change from her normal speaking voice to one she was pouring emotion into was pretty stunning.

"Suppressed by all my childish fears..."

. . .

In the very last few syllables, Tabitha began to really project her voice, and the weight of emotion she'd been infusing into the song was thrown out to fill the air to become *power*. A thrilling tingle traveled through Elena's body that made the tiny hairs on her arms stand up. *THIS is... well...*

"THESE WOUNDS WON'T SEEM TO HEAL, THIS PAIN IS JUST TOO REAL..."

Tabitha had apparently reached the extent of her piano knowledge by this point and simply dropped her hands into her lap as she continued to sing. The piece seemed to carry on well enough without the accompaniment, though, simply because Tabitha was able to put so much of herself into the lyrics, and with so much passion. The girl's eyes were squeezed shut as she focused herself entirely on vocalizing this impressive ballad—and, to Elena at least, it sounded *incredible*.

That somewhat haunting piano melody began again, and Elena realized both of the church ladies had approached. The women wore equally stunned expressions, looking from Tabitha to Elena and back again, neither of them inclined to interrupt the unexpected performance. Across the room and well behind Tabitha's turned back, Elena spotted Mrs. Moore opening the door and poking her head in, seeming just as bewildered.

Elena watched on with her own expression of shock, but for different reasons—the piece Tabitha chose to play *spoke to her,* it gave her chills just hearing it. *Experiencing it.* She understood now what Tabitha meant; this wasn't a song that could be sung casually or in a lowered voice; there was an operatic quality to it. Whatever the song was, whoever it was really by originally, Elena felt a connection to it, the connection she'd hoped to feel spring into place when listening to the mixtapes Ziggy prepared for her. Those bonds had failed to materialize, but this one, *this* song took hold of her soul in that complete embrace she never knew she'd always longed for.

By the time she snapped to her senses, Tabitha had sung through the rest of the song, and Elena stood there for a moment in a daze as Mrs. Moore, the other women from before, and another family that had wandered in at some point were all congratulating Tabitha.

"Well—Elena, what do you think?" Tabitha asked her with a beaming smile. "I think that might've been my best try singing... ever! Still definitely falls well short of Amy Lee, and my piano playing is, uh, yeah, the less said about it the better, but can you kinda get the vibe of—"

"Tabitha... that was *amazing*," Elena carefully emphasized. "Who's the—Amy Lee? How can we get her music? I need to hear it, hear her, hear the original. If *that* just now still fell short..."

Elena drifted away from Tabitha in a daze as the girl played the piano melody again for her parents, with Mrs. Moore joining her on the wooden bench and Mr. Moore hovering over both of them. The sheer force of the lyrics was still echoing in her soul, and Elena needed to engrave them deep, she needed time to digest them, to examine just what magical way they made her feel, how *alive* they felt. *I need to have my tape recorder ready for next time.*

The fellowship hall was gradually filling up with more church goers, and from the looks of it the women's Bible study group that normally followed right after service had momentarily postponed their meeting to excitedly gather around the new family sitting at the piano. The fact that her own mother had missed Tabitha's performance and like most of the others seemed to have no idea of how well the girl could sing seemed... *jarring.* It was almost as if—

Elena stiffened as she overheard a familiar pair of voices.

She turned, and on the opposite side of the room from the

piano was her mother standing with her friends Cindy and Melissa—and looking absolutely pissed at both of them. The transcendent feeling of the music from before ebbed away as Elena started in their direction, but even the absence they left behind felt like it had changed something about her, or revealed something about herself. She wanted some time alone to really sort out how all of it was affecting her, but first, there was something she suddenly felt inspired to do.

"—And she has a little girl!" Aunt Cindy whispered loudly. "Looks to be about 'Lena's age, so Shannon must have gone right out and gotten herself pregnant the moment she—"

"Well, of course she did!" Mrs. Melissa interjected with a sardonic laugh. "I said it. I always said it—the only way she gets herself in Hollywood is lying on her back. Spreading her legs for—"

"*Melissa,*" Mrs. Seelbaugh warned her again. "*Stop.* You don't know what you're talking about. *Please,* just... watch what you're saying when—"

Elena approached directly, and rather than the friendly but polite smile or reserved meekness she'd displayed earlier, she was *staring down* Mrs. Melissa. For her part, Mrs. Melissa seemed like a rabbit caught in headlights, and after making the mistake of making eye contact with Elena, all she could do was awkwardly half-turn toward Aunt Cindy for support.

"Is this going to be a problem?" Elena demanded.

"*Excuse me?*" Mrs. Melissa huffed in disbelief.

"The only problem seems like it's with your attitude, Elena?" Aunt Cindy's eyebrows slightly rose in challenge. "We were speaking to your mother."

"Are you two going to be a problem for my friend's family?" Elena was blunt. "You're the only two out of the entire congregation who hasn't tried to welcome them. At all. Instead, you're over here giving dirty looks and whispering to each other, so—*is there a problem?*"

Arms crossed, Elena immediately stepped over to block their view of the commotion going on over at the piano. Standing between them and the Moores felt like *some* show of solidarity at least, and Elena felt a small surge of surprise and pride as her mother quickly joined her. Her mother was typically *thick as thieves* with Mrs. Melissa and Aunt Cindy, and they seemed taken aback by her clear show of support for this impertinent raven-haired teen. Sensing the dynamic had already shifted out of their favor, Mrs. Melissa's expression darkened as she forcibly reined in a small amount of her indignation, but it was just as obvious that she wasn't going to bend in this situation.

"What in the world gets into your head that makes you think it's okay to speak to me like that?" Mrs. Melissa scolded her, shooting an incredulous glance from Elena to Mrs. Seelbaugh. "You don't know who that woman really is or what she's like, where she's been or what she's done. *You're fourteen years old.* We've been attending this church for *twenty years,* and if you think that just because we don't *rush over there to kiss her feet* that—"

"You think you recognize my friend's mom," Elena cut her off with a fierce look. "You don't. She just wanted to come to worship with her family somewhere without judgment and she *thought* that maybe the Presbyterian Church of Springton was the place for that."

Elena glanced from Mrs. Melissa to Aunt Cindy and back, weighing and measuring them with a cold gaze.

"It looks like she was wrong," Elena decided, her expression going hard as she turned away, not daring to look at her mother. "Maybe one of the other churches in town will give them an actual accepting *Christian* welcome?"

Is this what it feels like, what being REBELLIOUS like I'm supposed to be feels like?

She'd already decided to cast her lot in with Tabitha, and if that meant opposing her mother's friends and causing strife, then so be it. Elena didn't want to see her mom's face right now, because she was terrified she would see some difficult expression or strained tension, that her mom would already be trying to mediate things and cajole her two friends to come around to the situation. That her mom would be frustrated with her or think she was acting juvenile.

Instead, Mrs. Seelbaugh wore a beaming smile of pride that stunned Elena.

Okay... yeah. I have no idea how I'm supposed to feel. Elena tried to keep her face blank to hide her bafflement. *But at least now I know I definitely feel SOMETHING.*

35

MOORE AND MOORE PROBLEMS

It's a tremendous struggle to write someone who's lost their own narrative. How do you even express someone so difficult to define? Depression in young adult fiction is often oversimplified, to such an extent that nuance is lost and it becomes impossible to relate to. BAD HAPPENS; the protagonist is sad about it. The average reader will grow impatient rather than sympathetic.

Depression isn't just sadness. Depression is feeling nothing much at all about the things that once made you feel EVERYTHING. The pursuits you'd once so invested yourself in seem to lose all meaning, even victories feel hollow. You lose your own narrative and fall into this passive state, repeating what doesn't work or becoming secondary to the drive of a more goal-oriented character.

As one of the most prevalent mental illnesses, I find depression personally important to write about... but, it's also just so damned hard to address, because it really is the anathema of engaging, interesting fiction. Real ~~depresi~~ depression is not compelling, real depression is something anyone will do their best to avoid, deny, and escape from. The quick and messy route is to play up the angst angle, throw your protagonist into a moral gray to struggle with. They can persevere for high ground or they can get a little edgy, either is fine—anything but dare to linger on the unpleasant. The alternative seems to be couching everything in metaphor. Your protagonist becomes physically lost in a maze of choices, or an Artax and Atreyu mired in the swamps of sadness. The emotional weight is there (sometimes), and it can be cleverly done—but, some part of me is reluctant to be clever or dishonest about this at all.

Sometimes, a big part of me just wants to write something terrible, some moments that just really, really fucking suck. Something that isn't simplified until it's meaningless, or wrapped in the safety-padding of allegory, or skewed by survivorship bias. But who THE FUCK would ever want to read it! The only

"—Whatcha reading?" Aiden interrupted.

"*Good heavens!*" Mrs. Moore jumped, almost knocking the binder into the bare patch of dirt worn into the mulch by the feet of those who sat at this park bench.

She caught it, just barely, slapping her hands down against the pages of Tabitha's *Goblin Princess* outline before they could slip out of her lap. It was a thick binder, and if she was honest with herself, it seemed to grow a little heavier with each page she read. Sometimes she could only read and helplessly reread her daughter's words over and over again in consternation and disbelief.

"Young man!" Mrs. Moore finally collected her wits about her with an exasperated laugh. "You were 'bout liable to give me a heart attack!"

"*Aiden!*" Tabitha yelled from the other side of the playground. "Please don't bother your Auntie Shannon when she's reading. Say you're sorry and come back over here with your brothers."

"Sorry," Aiden complied, giving Mrs. Moore another glance before trotting back over to the others.

Her heart in her throat, Shannon Moore spent a long moment watching her daughter play with the four cousins. Tabitha had them all lined up and was showing them some dance or another—

Mrs. Moore didn't have the faintest clue about modern dance and couldn't tell whether this was supposed to be the electric slide or the macarena—but she still just looked so *young* that it was all but impossible to reconcile the frail little girl with the one who was capable of writing about all of these dreadful things.

I KNOW that Tabby's sharp, Mrs. Moore watched on with a complicated expression. *But this—? This is beyond her just being a smart kid, this is—I don't know what to do with this. She's putting words to things I've felt for—for a long time. Too long. More than just putting words to them, she UNDERSTANDS them. To her, they're these, these fully-fleshed-out ideas she can turn over and examine in her mind, ideas that she's already figuring out how to fit into other things.*

Mrs. Moore adjusted her parka and drew *Goblin Princess* the rest of the way back up into her lap, cradling it carefully against herself.

As a parent, it's so EASY to underestimate how much she's grown up! She'll always be my little girl, but she's a teenager now. And somehow, she understood. Really understood, that I had completely lost my own narrative. That I thought I was going to be a model, a beautiful Hollywood actress, a star, a SOMEONE, and that I was so set on it, so set on just racing down that path, that once I WASN'T—there was nothing left of me. No spark, no drive, nothing but just complete bitterness.

It was alarming that Tabitha understood so much, alarming that Mrs. Moore could feel that same bitterness rising up from the girl's written words. To such an extent that they stung! She'd never in her life read anything that made her lose her composure so easily—*this* was the daughter she'd so thoroughly failed to connect with in the past summer months of this year. *These* were some of the feelings Tabitha was grappling with and struggling to jot down back then.

Lord help me—raising a teenage daughter sure isn't easy.

Ostensibly, Mrs. Moore was here at the playground to chaperone the boys and keep an eye on Tabitha should she start feeling faint again—which still happened frequently enough to make

Mrs. Moore's insides feel like they were twisting themselves up into knots. But the reality was that she was terrified to allow Tabitha out of her sight.

When Tabitha had set about her little neighborhood weeding project, and both of the times Tabitha went out to work at setting up the garden plot in their yard for spring, Mrs. Moore had stolen up to the window and watched her in secret the entire time. Guilt, relief, and some difficult-to-define sense of dependency were continuing to gnaw at the mother in a maddening way. Her overprotective instincts had kicked in—too little, too late—and she had no earthly idea how to manage them.

At the same time, Mrs. Moore knew Tabitha was already feeling smothered beneath the restrictions placed upon her for the sake of recovery. There were plenty of excuses to hover over the girl when she was cooking or out here with the boys, but there was also the constant compulsion to follow Tabitha everywhere she went, even from room to room in the house, and that was too much. She *couldn't* do that—because while not knowing what her daughter was up to every second of the day stirred up anxiety, the idea that Tabitha would start to resent her presence filled her with absolute dread.

Hypocrite mother that I am. Mrs. Moore couldn't help but steal another glance over at Tabitha. *All of those years when she needed me, I couldn't stand to be around her. Now, she's at the age where she's trying to go out and be her own person, and I can't bear to give her any space.*

"Is... everything okay?" Tabitha called over.

"Oh! Yes, yes." Mrs. Moore forced a smile, looking from Tabitha to the notebook and back again with an incredulous shake of her head. "This is all—well, it's incredible, honey."

"Okay. Keep on reading. If you want to, that is." Even in the distance, she could see Tabitha muster her own nervous smile. "I'll try to keep the boys occupied."

Feeling inexplicably strained, Mrs. Moore forced herself to turn her attention to the next story section of *Goblin Princess*.

"Silence those shackles, mage," Censede warned in a low voice, carefully lifting a weathered hand from his cloak festooned with bones. "We have arrived—this is the silk road."

The goblin sage, the young girl without a name, and their captive mage stood together on the final plateau rise of the Ostskala, taking in the sight of where the barren rocky wastes abruptly gave way to the drop of a sheer precipice. It was like nothing the girl had ever seen—here where they stood was mountainous ground, and then in front of them there was nothing. Nothing, save for a curious twisting white vine of some sort that adhered to the cliff edge before them in a mess of fibrous strings and then was pulled tight by something high up and far, far in the distance. Much further away than she could see.

"You fools," Beon rasped out in a harsh whisper as he stared in horror. "*You two damn fools!* Do you have any idea what this is?!"

"A single strand of the Great Weaver's net that spans the sky," Censede answered in a grave voice.

"It is our path, and we must tread it lightly."

"Tread it lightly? *'Great Weaver?!'* So, even gobs know of such things." Beon let out a bitter laugh and began his frantic struggle with his chains anew. "What a fool's errand. This looks to be one of the mooring lines of a Chimeric Dreadweaver's web. Quite an old Chimeric Dreadweaver, at that. Several centuries, at the very least—see the thickness of this silk! They're calamities. *Calamities.* World-enders. It's been said they can live forever, that the greater ones weave nests between *planets and moons* and ensnare wyverns and dragons and lesser deities and *who-knows-what-else* as though they were insects!"

"Does the silk road lead to the moon?" the girl asked, following the taut band of white with her green eyes as it ascended from the cliff face towards the sky.

The strand was a pale line that stretched out into the air until it became impossible to discern along the distant horizon. It was not quite the width of a narrow footpath, and it seemed as though traveling across it would be no different than carefully stepping across the branch of a tree limb. Although, unlike the gnarled old swamp trees the girl had climbed in the past, this silk road appeared to hang tens and then hundreds and then thousands of feet into the air. She could only pale at imagining crossing such an unfathomable distance at such incredible height.

"No, child," Censede assured her. "Only as high as the northern mountain peaks. Our Great Weaver, he is not yet so old as to reach beyond the clouds."

"*She*," Beon corrected with a bitter laugh. "Your 'Great Weaver,' she's female. Obviously."

"The Great Weaver... is female?" Censede's wizened old face took pause at the notion, unsure as to whether or not this was a blasphemy.

"That's right," Beon said. "The males, they don't spin webs. Or grow quite so terrible in size. Dreadweaver males wouldn't live beyond two or three meters tall, they'd be nothing at all against a company of Mages. It's said the males mostly become food for the female Chimeric Dreadweaver, though—"

"*An entire company* of mages?" The nameless girl's face fell. "You—you can't mean that."

"To kill a male, yes. A female? Hah! *Hah!* We can't walk this 'road,'" Beon swore. "*Gods below,* a Chimeric Dreadweaver. Here. One *this* blighted close to the border. This horrible web must stretch for entire leagues... must stretch across the entire sky over Ostsea like some terrible unseen...! Gods help us. You have to let me free, you *must* let me return. To warn the capital at least, I beg you."

"Warn the enemy? We'll do no such thing," Censede scoffed. "We walk the Silk Road."

"We won't get caught in it?" the girl asked, giving the enormous line of webbing an experimental prod with the toe of her boot.

"No, you imbecile—this is a radial," Beon explained in vexation. "Part of the frame, it won't be sticky. Trapping lines are then built upon this in a capture spiral starting from—no, you know what? It doesn't matter. We can't take this path. We'll die. There's no chance. No chance."

"You've much wisdom, wizard." Censede gave their captive an appraising look. "But so little courage."

"I'm a mage, not a *wizard*," Beon corrected the goblin elder with a sneer. "I suppose you mean to cross from this anchoring line to a bridging thread along the outer edge of the web. Head back down to the ground somewhere on the other side of Ostersjon, bypass the outposts and checkpoints of the Northern Magi. Well, I'm telling you; it won't work. It's madness and suicide and the only destination this 'path' of yours will lead to is right into the maw of a Chimeric Dreadweaver."

"The silk road can be traveled by those with proper reverence," Censede sniffed. "We are very small. If our footsteps are light, the road will not tremble enough to displease the Great One."

"Oh? Really? *Really?*" Beon laughed. "So, you've walked this path before, then?"

"I have," Censede answered with a grave nod. "Long ago, with my Master and three other Goblin apprentices."

"Impossible." Beon shook his head. "No way, there's no way some ignorant gobs blundered across entire leagues of a web like this and somehow survived."

"There were other apprentices underneath your Master?" The girl perked up with interest. "Does that mean—are there other Goblin Sages? Allies we could call upon?"

"Once, there were many apprentices to the great Goblin Sage." The many wrinkles upon Censede's green face folded into a bitter smile. "Now, there is only me. The Silk Road can be traversed, but it is not without danger. The three other apprentices on that journey—each of them bravely fell from the web."

"They bravely... *fell* from the web?" the girl repeated in shock. "But..."

"Yes. Fell, one after another," Censede admitted. "One must step lightly and with utmost care, while standing tall and prepared to die. You cannot doubt yourself, or permit your heart to waver for even an instant—if balance is lost and you begin to fall, you *must* fall! You cannot catch the line and hang from the thread, for the slightest tug will summon the Great Weaver, and thus doom your companions to become its food."

That sounds... just absolutely dreadful! Mrs. Moore couldn't help but glance over at her daughter again.

Each page of the story manuscript itself was written on white notebook paper, which was then followed by Tabitha's commentary put onto yellow legal paper, and sometimes there were as many as three or four yellows for every white page. Mrs. Moore first read a single story page, then she delved into the yellow legal pages wherein Tabitha often explained how the ideas were connected and outlined the purpose they served in the larger narrative. Mrs. Moore read these pages over and over and over again, searching for and studying over every scrap and hint Tabitha was willing to reveal before finally returning to reread the story page with new appreciation.

Though she had of course read screenplays before, Shannon Moore didn't regularly read for fun, and her daughter's writing prowess was honestly intimidating. Some details were easily gleaned from her first casual read-through—the book was intended for an audience of teen readers, after all—but reading the note pages always seemed to shock Mrs. Moore.

Tabby just has so many ideas she puts into these!

A good deal of the process seemed to be Tabitha creating a methodology for herself as she wrote. The girl was attempting to use a regular rotation of sensory exposition—visuals, sounds, smells, tactile sensations, temperature and et cetera—while also utilizing what she called her 'economy of words' stratagem, using increasingly brief references to past descriptors to omit the more lengthy and repetitive description.

The slave irons worn about Beon's wrists had been written in lavish detail in a previous chapter, both because of what they represented to him and because he would rattle and shake his chains simply to annoy his captors—a character moment. Censede's first line of dialogue here in this section immediately conjured that scene from the reader's memory. As the story progressed, Tabitha would ease back and only allude to previous imagery or build ever so slightly upon them, using less words to greater effect each time because the 'set pieces' and 'production value' now already existed in the reader's imagination.

Many of the more complete notes were almost too verbose to follow, but more than the technical difficulty of interpreting it all, there was just something sanitized and clinical about all of this *story authoring* that Mrs. Moore found honestly bewildering. It was the unorganized notes Mrs. Moore adored and kept poring over again and again; most of them were meandering rambles, important abstracts that Tabitha hadn't quite completely organized yet. Each of these seemed like a precious gem that might allow Mrs. Moore to glean better insights into her daughter's actual feelings and thought processes.

She eagerly flipped forward to the next yellow page, completely enthralled.

Giant spiders, such a fantasy cliche! Though I'm loath to follow the common tropes (and yes oh yes, I do personally hate spiders. Don't most people? (Arah arachnophobia to some extent seems very common but then I can fuse that into the fear of heights here too!)) When a big spider is just a giant monster in a story, it seems like it's lost the essence of what makes a spider scary, to me. Spiders should be written more like ambush predators! Just ~~ominiou~~ ominous tension. Hidden and unseen. If the characters can see it, then it's already too late!

I've always been most fascinated by their webs. Spiderwebs are just so beautiful and *interesting* and I never feel like a fiction I've read before has really done them proper justice. The web aspect itself. Not just spiders. How the webs are constructed, how they work, the function and the why. The beautiful natural geometry to them.

But it's not even just all that either. There's something always a little magical about them to me.

When I was very very young (3rd grade? 4th?) I remember we went on this random fun trip to a flea market, and there was this one stand where the artist was selling those airbrushed VAN ART style paintings. Fairies with butterfly wings and spiderwebs on flowers and tigers sitting on mushrooms and rainbow colored smoke that (IN HINDSIGHT) probably represented marijuana clouds or something. Obv don't want to go all in on THAT sort of thing but borrowing from aesthetics that leave a strong impression on people can be vital! Explore alt art styles with Alicia?

ANYWAYS wanted to focus more on the web, scary tightrope-walk sort of thing, and have the spider itself be more of an unseen threat/tension that hangs over them. The trial itself is obv a metaphor, mostly building upon some of the 'goblin' tenets already presented. Protagonist needs to just soak all of that in, and then decide what to adopt and what to overcome. I guess deep down, so do I.

Mrs. Moore rocked back in her seat at the memory of taking a very young little Tabitha to the flea market. It had been a fair drive away across Sandborough, over forty-five minutes, and she only remembered the whole place as being crowded and unpleasant. The rows of stalls had been beneath the roof of a long, covered pavilion, but it was still too sweaty and humid. Their little Tabby had gotten hungry and started whining for one of the disgusting overpriced hot dogs some filthy vendor was selling, and personally, Mrs. Moore been resolved to never allow their family another trip to the flea market. So they'd never visited the place again after that.

But she wrote here that she remembered it was fun. Mrs. Moore seemed flabbergasted. *Never even considered what it might have been like to her little eyes. To her, it wasn't awful, it was just this exciting new experience. Part of her fresh narrative. All these years, and we never ever even talked about the flea market again. Talked about going ANYWHERE. These notes of hers, they're not a diary, but then some- how... they also are.*

There were also sections that Mrs. Moore couldn't make any sense of at all.

At the time of my original first draft, SILK ROAD was pretty much already a buzzword because of the darkweb marketplace thing, but I always appreciated the name recognition of its more historical origins as a trade route. Maybe if my books take off this time, my own silk road will earn a place in the etymology of the term on a wiki page somewhere?

Darkweb marketplace... thing? Shannon repeated to herself, rereading over the phrase again for any context clue she'd missed. *I've never heard of anything like that. Silk road? Wiki? What in the heck is a wiki page?*

Although Tabitha did occasionally misspell things, all of the errors thus far had already been caught and struck through, likely long before this notebook came into Mrs. Moore's hands. Wiki might have instead been shorthand for something—but, she couldn't imagine what it might be. *Wiki?* Her guesses leapt all the way from the city of Wichita in Kansas to bamboo tiki torches, with no concrete way of connecting different possible meanings into something she could make any heads or tails of.

While Tabitha's story itself was written in fairly simple parlance as it was intended for an audience of a certain age range, her unorganized scribbles were often downright strange. Seemingly made-up parlance and methods of expression for who-knows-what were common, and the notes also fell into a strange habit of mixing tenses so incomprehensibly that it was difficult to tell whether they were referencing an occurrence that happened in the past, or one that would perhaps happen someday in the future. Tabitha didn't seem to be able to mentally separate observation from speculation—but, for some reason, none of her casual assertions seemed born from childish naivete either. Something about it all seemed very *off* to Mrs. Moore, but it was difficult for her to put her finger on exactly why.

Also, whenever the word 'goblin' pops up in her notes, there's this STIGMA of inferiority to it. I feel like I should maybe talk with her about that. But then, at the same time—it's like where to even begin? I need someone to have that talk with ME. It's like seeing Tabitha elaborate on all of these concepts really strikes home how many of my own issues I've yet to ever unpack. It's intimidating that she's capable of writing these things out. That she gets herself so intent on not leaving anything out that may be important to her story, her own narrative...

Mrs. Moore's thoughts couldn't help but keep returning to the idea of narrative. Her own book of Shannon Delain had obviously already closed—it was long since over and done with. But after such a long—too long—period of suffering through self-loathing and drowning herself in what she now recognized was severe clinical depression, a *new* narrative was beginning for her. One that began that late night epiphany after she'd cooked that godawful broccoli—or maybe it really started with the unexpected clashes she had arguing with Tabitha over the summer.

Maybe I started into my new identity when I decided to start walking in the mornings, Mrs. Moore mused. That was a big change —feeling resolved about anything at all. Maybe it was the moment I made love to Alan again, after so long. SO damned long! Maybe this real Shannon Moore came about when we thought we'd lost our baby girl, and who knows? Maybe who I'll be, what I'll be all about is some-

thing still up in the air, something that's still undecided, something that's yet to come to pass.

She hadn't actually started considering it all until the Moore family attended that church service. Some of her fears about presenting herself socially again reared up and absolutely suffocated her, while other fears instead seemed to fall away like they'd never existed at all. Was there some sort of dissociation at play? Or, was it because she'd begun to untangle her current narrative from the dead weight of Shannon Delain? It was so *strange* feeling alive again, feeling purpose and drive again after so long, feeling herself transform.

Strange and more than a little terrifying, especially realizing how many years she'd wasted completely. But Mrs. Moore *needed* this change. Her family was growing, and she was determined to be a much better mother. Both Tabitha and their new child deserved so much more than the half-hearted parenting Mrs. Moore had displayed before—they needed a family. All of the children did, even these four brats Tabitha was playing with across the yard. Her nephews had gone from little terrors she couldn't stand to even think about to becoming family.

And they're all LISTENING to her, instead of just running amok, Mrs. Moore thought, shaking her head in amusement as she let herself grow distracted by what the kids were getting up to again. *I just... I can't even fathom what sort of dance that's supposed to be, when she has the boys step and wave around their arms all together like that!*

————

The four young boys were arrayed in a line on the frigid November mulch of the playground, each in identical stances with one fist extended outwards and held in a punch, the other drawn low and tucked in against their body. It felt silly realizing how proud of each of them Tabitha was, and how emotional she got at seeing them now. Today, her four elementary-school cousins were *standing still.*

It seemed like a watershed moment to her, because until this day, no, *until this very hour,* Joshua, Aiden, Samuel, and Nicholas had been restless fidgets, unable to contain the endlessly distracted energy of their own youth. Her own expectations had been set from her time helping wrangle in the little ones at Lee's Taekwondo studio in her past life, and she knew exactly how difficult children were to corral. She'd only even managed to teach the Moore cousins some dozen-odd practice sessions, so it was as if they'd grown more disciplined after her not-so-brief stay of absence when she'd been hospitalized.

"I'm very impressed," Tabitha praised them, striding down the line of stoic boys as though she were a general inspecting her troops. "You've all kept practicing."

"We're gonna be karate masters," Sam revealed. "I figure, since we started out learning real young like this, we'll be martial art masters by the time we're grown up."

"We'll be legendary masters, and *nobody* will be able to beat us," Joshua added with a look of glee. "We'll *always* win, no matter what!"

"Who are you going to be fighting?" Tabitha asked with a wry smile, stepping in and gently correcting Aiden's posture. "Bad guys? Criminal thugs?"

"Monsters," Aiden said.

Amused, Tabitha was tempted for a moment to make a glib remark referencing *Power Rangers* villains, but she realized she didn't remember what the bad guys were called in that show. She wasn't sure that she'd ever known.

"*Sshh,*" Nick hissed. "There's no such thing as monsters. We're gonna be Green Berets and fight in the military."

Their buzz-cuts from the past summer had grown out into shaggy hair that fell upon each of the cousin's foreheads. Grandma Laurie would occasionally single out one of the boys to sit on the stool at the counter and trim away whatever tiny bit was annoying her, but the speed at which they were all growing seemed to outpace the old woman's ability to fuss over them. All four of them were sprouting up like unruly weeds, just like in Tabitha's previous lifetime.

At least in this life, they seem a bit less out-of-control, Tabitha observed. *They all seem a bit neater, more well-behaved—they were obnoxious little hooligans back then. Or, maybe I've just become biased by how much more time I've spent with them? Now they're MY little hooligans.*

"The military," Tabitha repeated in amusement. "You're joining the army, and you'll use taekwondo. To fight against...?"

"The other military," Nick answered. "Special forces. Death squad *commandos.* The bad guys. Germans—you know, the Nazis."

"I think you may be a couple generations too late to storm the beaches, there," Tabitha said. "That was back in World War II."

"Well, there's the Russian Nazis too," Samuel added helpfully. "Like in *Red Dawn.*"

"Those were Soviets, *also* extinct now, and—*Red Dawn,* who let you boys watch *Red Dawn*?!" Tabitha demanded in exasperation. "Aren't you a *little* young for—you're talking about the original *Red Dawn,* with Charlie Sheen and Patrick Swayze?!"

"We have it on tape," Nick shrugged. "The one that starts with all the parachute troopers all landing in at the high school, and then the one like, *shoots all across the windows with an automatic machine gun* and one of the high schoolers watching gets shot, right in the head! You can see him dead right there in the next scene—"

"—And then there's this one bad guy with a rocket launcher," Sam added, "and they're all trying to get away in the one brother's truck—"

"Wolverines!" Aiden cried out, making a *shiiing* noise under his breath as he held out both fists in imitation of the famous X-men character with adamantium claws.

"I... think I may have to go through your VHS tapes at some point," Tabitha decided, shaking her head with a wry expression. "Next stance, please."

The four boys stepped forward as one, drawing back the extended fist in unison and then swiping in their opposite hand in a lateral chop. The two youngest threw themselves into it with a bit too much enthusiasm and ended up with their feet in the wrong stance, so Tabitha patiently oriented herself to face in their direction. One demonstration of the proper distribution of weight was enough for them to pick up on their mistake and right themselves. Turning back around to regard the four boys, that feeling of pride surged up again and it was hard to even be cross at them.

"I suppose at your age, you've seen all kinds of rated-R movies." Tabitha sighed. "Sex, violence? Swearing, nudity?"

All four of them nodded in eager agreement. It was a little jarring—in some ways, Tabitha felt like her cousins treated her like an adult, but in other ways, it was as if she was just a bigger kid, one that it was okay to confide in with things they thought would impress big kids.

"There's a lady with *three boobies* in *Total Recall*," Nicholas boasted.

"Don't tell her that—*Tabby's a girl!*" Samuel hissed his brother silent.

"Oh yeah." Nick clamped his mouth shut. "Sorry."

"Next position," Tabitha instructed, rolling her eyes. "Turn, knee up in the air—hold it there for a moment—now, *side-kick,* and, down into the next stance. Good—good, very good."

To her continued surprise, they *were* doing well, they all kept perfect balance without wavering as they pointed one knee in the air and then flashed out a kick before landing. The kicks themselves weren't quite there yet, their feet didn't quite snap out cleanly or hit with power just yet, but the boys had all come a long way and had clearly been practicing their forms. *I haven't even heard about them hurting each other!*

"I'm definitely going to go through whatever tapes your dad left behind... but I'm not going to take any of them away," Tabitha decided. "You're boys, and all the shooting and blood and explosions and action whatnot will just seem *cool* to you. You're young enough that I don't think you'll really fixate on *boobies,* just yet. So long as you all act appropriately and I don't catch you picking up swear-words, you boys watch whatever you like. Did you know your Auntie Shannon was almost an actress?"

"We know," Sam replied. "Grandma always tells us."

"Tabby—I have a question." Aiden relaxed out of his stance. "If you're so good at karate—uhh, *taekwondo* like this, how did you even get attacked even in the first place?"

"Aiden, God—*shush up.*" Samuel gave the cousin a glare. "You don't ask stuff like that! *Sheesh.*"

"Yeah, the other girl had a baseball bat—what was Tabby supposed to do? You can't beat a baseball bat with your bare hands," Nicholas retorted. "Idiot."

"Shut *up,* both of you," Samuel insisted, casting a wary glance toward Tabitha.

"Why don't we... take a little break," Tabitha suggested after swallowing back a nervous flutter. "I *would* like to talk to all of you about it... clear up some misunderstandings."

Inspecting the patch of earth beneath her for a moment and absentmindedly brushing the skirting of her dress with both hands, Tabitha carefully lowered herself down to the chilly ground and then arranged her legs beside her. The boys, they gracelessly dropped down and clambered over to gather close around her—as little kids, they were as comfortable rolling around in dirty playground mulch as they were their own bedcovers.

"Okay. To begin with—I started learning taekwondo *strictly* for exercise and weight loss," Tabitha explained. "I didn't set out to become some sort of fighter. I never planned on or wanted involved in anything confrontational or dangerous. Never imagined it would ever happen."

All four young cousins stared at her with what she thought of as blank expressions, and once again, she felt the twinge of that massive age gap between them that spanned across decades and decades all the way into the inscrutable future. Culturally, mentally, and even psychologically, it sometimes felt like there was a chasm there between them that simply could not be bridged by any explanations she might ever offer. Perhaps most jarring of all, the ripples of change she affected on the timeline might mean that the era her mindset came about from might in fact never come about quite the same way again.

But, I'll just go crazy if I keep worrying about that. Tabitha tried to fight down her anxiety again. *I can't change the world. Right? I mean, nine-eleven, Afghanistan, and the Iraqi war? They're too big for me. I'm just a teenage girl in Kentucky. The coronavirus pandemic, the One-China war? Somalia getting burned off the map, the liberation of North Korea... I'm just one girl! All I can do is the best I can, for the people I care about.*

"So, of course when something *did* actually happen—I wasn't ready. I completely froze up," Tabitha continued in a solemn voice, looking each of her young cousins in the eye, one by one.

"Knowing all of the moves by heart, being able to go through forms with grace and precision—that doesn't translate into me automatically being some amazing fighter. Actually *applying* what I've learned in real-life situations, I couldn't do that yet. Still can't. It honestly wasn't something I was that prepared for—because I didn't even want to be in a fight, ever. Didn't imagine it happening. As stupid as it sounds now, I *still* don't see it happening."

"To be able to actually *use* taekwondo in real-life practical situations, you need to run through self-defense drills over and over *and over,* until moves become instinct. In the heat of a real-life threat moment, you won't have time to think about them—I know I didn't. You also need practice sparring against another person, to learn how to read an actual opponent and learn to react to what they're doing. I've done neither—I would be the equivalent of a yellow-belt in taekwondo.

"For starters, I've had you boys learning all the taekwondo stances and the moves—I'm not going to have you fighting each other until I can afford protective equipment. *I won't allow you boys to fight each other.* It is *very* easy to get hurt or to hurt someone else, and the rule of the real world... is that getting hurt is expensive and *it sucks.* Okay?"

Tabitha hefted her left arm—still in its cast—for emphasis, but with bitter humor she realized she probably didn't have to. From the reaction of the four boys, the word *expensive* seemed to spook them even more, and that seemed to tell her a lot about their situation of poverty. *I'm working on that too.*

"In the coming year, I'm going to get all four of you enrolled in the Taekwondo place in town," Tabitha announced. "Lee's Martial Arts, next to the Food Lion. I have a bit of money coming in from those lawsuits, and I can afford it if you're all going to take it seriously and not fool around."

The news seemed to thrill the boys, and Tabitha got some small measure of satisfaction in the way they twisted to look at each other with wide eyes before their attention returned to her.

"Your parents..." Tabitha set her jaw for a moment, somewhat unwilling to badmouth those lowlifes in front of the boys. "They aren't really looking out for your future. They're caught up in their own messes, right now. But *you're family,* and you deserve better. Grandma can take care of you, and I'm going to do my best to make sure you have the tools you need to get wherever you want to go in life. Practicing martial arts now, learning discipline and control will be good for your body and mind—if you at some point want to do football instead, or soccer, or find an interest in... I don't know, carpentry, or art, or even if you want to join the military and serve—I'm going to help you. All of you."

She wasn't sure what reactions to expect in the first place, but the boys mostly looked thoughtful—but puzzled. Did they think she was grandstanding, now that she had money coming her way? It was hard for her to tell. Were they too young to really understand their own situation and the significance of what she was saying? Tabitha couldn't really discern that either. *It doesn't really matter. I'm being open with them, and whatever they wind up thinking about it, that's up to them.*

"What do *you* wanna do?" Joshua pressed. "When you grow up. Are you going to go do taekwondo too? Like, with us at the taekwondo place?"

"Do I want to learn more taekwondo? I... honestly don't know," Tabitha admitted. "Whatever you might think of me or see me as, and despite what my mother thinks, I'm not a movie star or novel protagonist with this *iron will* or *limitless grit and determination,* or anything like that. My transformation over this past summer had a lot more to do with my obsessing over my weight and appearance and that turning into... well, something like a compulsive disorder."

"Your taekwondo was... a disorder?" Samuel gave her a look of disbelief.

"I *hated* myself for being fat and unattractive and unpopular, and that hate turned into fear, and that fear motivated me into change. Well, *'motivated.'*" Tabitha bitterly used her fingers to make air-quotes. "But being thinner and prettier didn't magically give me confidence around other people, and it didn't magically make me popular like I thought it would—it just put me in the game, put me at the starting line. Then, it turned out the game isn't actually fun to play once you're in it, the rules are nasty and whether you're winning or losing, it's stressful and *cutthroat* and—"

Tabitha stopped herself and remembered the four cousins who were listening to her without interrupting.

"Okay, sorry. I'm just rambling now." Tabitha winced. "There's so many things I just kind of need to get off my chest and talk about with someone, but they're kinda too embarrassing for me to bring up with Alicia or Elena."

"It's okay," Joshua said. "Yeah, say whatever you want."

"Yeah, you can tell us," Sam encouraged. "Talk about whatever you want. *We* don't care about being popular."

"Popular kids suck," Nick griped. "Like Max, in my class at school, he thinks he's all better than everyone. Popular kids are just all full of themselves—but actually, nobody really even cares. They're just dumb!"

"Yeah, dumb jerks," Aiden agreed.

"I just feel..." Tabitha couldn't help but feel flustered. "It's awkward, I was worried you guys have like, built me up into some *unstoppable super big-sister* figure, and I didn't want to destroy that for you. But I also—I just want to be real with you boys, not have to put on a front or anything. You're family."

"Is Elena popular?" Aiden mused, tapping a finger against his lip. "She seems like that kinda popular person who's all into that."

"Yeah, she's blonde." Nicholas nodded. "Blondes are *always* the most popular. Like cheerleaders and stuff."

"I think it used to be important to her," Tabitha said, idly picking at the mulch with her fingertips and letting a smile play across her face. "When she first approached me, she was—weird. Facetious; I didn't like it. Like she was being friendly but not *really* friendly, like she was going through all the motions but not really... it's hard to put into words. She was treating it like a business agreement? Or an alliance, or something. A mutual agreement to leverage each other for further popularity or... something. Whenever I think I start to understand it, I wish I hadn't."

"Fashefous?" Aiden screwed up his face in puzzlement at the word. "*Leverage?*"

"Beverage," Joshua corrected helpfully.

"Sorry, um. Facetious means being fake, putting on an act," Tabitha explained. "Beverage means something you drink, *leverage* is... I don't even really know how to describe it. Using each other? Utilizing someone or something to best effect?"

"Being fake means you're not really friends," Nick pointed out. "So wait, is she not—are you and Elena not real friends?"

"No, we are now, I think," Tabitha sussed. "It's hard to even put a finger on when it actually happened—it just *did*. She's changed a ton—she's not even blonde anymore actually; she dyed her hair black! I feel like we're both kinda figuring ourselves out together."

"What about Alicia?" Aiden asked. "She's just weird."

"What's weird about Alicia?!" Tabitha put on an affronted look.

"She likes *Star Wars*, and she's weird," Aiden said. "Girls don't like *Star Wars*."

"I like *Star Wars*!" Tabitha argued. "I probably know more about *Star Wars* than all of you combined!"

"What's the name of the desert planet?" Joshua challenged.

"Tattooey," Tabitha answered without hesitation.

"It's *Tatooine*," Joshua said. "*Tatooine*. Luke grew up there. Jabba's castle was there too."

"Whatever, *I knew what it was*—it sounds like Tattooey whenever they say it in the movies."

"Swamp planet," Nick pressed.

"Swamp planet is—Dagobah," Tabitha had even more confidence in that one.

"Ice planet?" Joshua demanded.

"Ice planet is—I don't think the ice planet really had a name," Tabitha confessed. "The Rebel base was Echo base, but it was supposed to be on some uncharted planet way out hidden away from everyone."

"The ice planet is Hoth, but... she *did* know it was Echo base, so she definitely knows more *Star Wars* than a girl." Samuel frowned, seemingly invested in her level of knowledge and authority on the subject.

"But she didn't even know it was Hoth, and *we* all do," Joshua crossed his arms. "So, we know more, actually."

"She's *a girl* and she knew Dagobah and Echo Base, though," Nicholas deliberated. "That's already really good, right?"

"You've seen the teasers on TV for the upcoming *Star Wars* movie by now, right?" Tabitha struggled to suppress a grin. "What if I told you... that I've already seen *Episode One; The Phantom Menace?*"

"How?" Samuel's eyes lit up.

"How—" Joshua jumped up. "When? *Where?!*"

To her surprise, the boys didn't seem skeptical at all. She'd honestly expected them to scoff at her and need some evidence or convincing, but apparently, her image in their minds as an unstoppable superheroine hadn't been shaken down just yet. On the one hand, she still had mixed feelings about them putting her up on a pedestal to revere, but then on the other—when it came to giving them a better future this time, she was willing to become a hero for them.

Last time, only Aiden and Nicholas even graduated high school. Tabitha schooled her expression into a forced smile. *Joshua died somewhere in 2015, I didn't even go to his funeral. Samuel, from what I heard, was doing drugs and in and out of prison his whole life, just like his parents. That's NOT going to happen this time.*

"My friend's dad works for Nintendo," Tabitha answered with a straight face. "We get to sneak in and see a bunch of movies before they come out."

———

Of all things, Mr. Moore thought to himself, *I shouldn't be worried about the money.*

Closing the door of his truck with a half-hearted gesture, he took a moment to appreciate the way their sparse little yard looked now. He'd had mixed feelings about Tabby picking up so much slack around the house in the past half-year. From inside to out, everything was spic and span and up to shape, and some of the pointed questions she'd been asking suggested that if left to her own devices, his daughter would also begin tackling some of electrical and plumbing work.

Having spent years as a handyman and working now as a general contractor, Alan Moore was more than aware of the irony of leaving so many of his own basic home maintenance tasks undone. Many of those in the industry, however, understood— after a long, hard day at work, the very last thing anyone wanted to do was come home to more work. It was rare that he didn't clock out completely exhausted, and failing to relax in his off hours put him in a cycle of punishment he always wound up paying for.

Hands on his hips, Mr. Moore took the time to walk around the lot and survey some of the changes again. Their lawn was currently looking a little threadbare after the weeding, but what remained was all good grass. An area near the back of the yard had been cordoned off with the old bricks from the shed, creating two rectangular areas of bare earth that would apparently be the future site of their vegetable garden; one on either side, with a footpath between them towards the shed doors. Back behind the shed, an additional place had been cleared for their composting heap. Tabitha had dubbed that area the *Moore family F-22 aviation scrapyard*—he'd seen her let slip an almost manic-sounding giggle, and then watched with eyebrows raised as she admonished herself. Put her good hand to her temple and said *'okay, actually not funny, though.'*

Teenage girls continued to mystify him.

He hadn't understood them back when he was a teen, and as the years flew by, he realized it was smart to just assume anything he ever *thought* he knew was miles and miles off the mark. They were strange and often cruel creatures—Tabitha excepted, of course, as his little girl, she was of course both perfect and also an angel. They all seemed to speak in riddles or some sort of code, however, and generally, teenage girls seemed to be a rollercoaster of emotions that never let you figure out what was what.

For better or worse, you were just along for the ride.

Could probably pick up some of that decorative brick I keep walkin' by at Home Depot, Mr. Moore mused as he absentmindedly scuffed the toe of his boot against one of the upturned clods of earth at the edge of the garden. *Bet she'd be tickled pink to have stepping stones for this little path. I can tell her it was just leftover junk from some contracting job and that whoever all was just gettin' rid of it.*

Tabitha in particular was extremely sensitive to costs, seemed to be ever since they'd had that sit-down with her about allowance over this past summer. Money had always been such a touchy subject in their household, and because of that, the big sum of settlement money coming their way was troubling in a lot of ways. Unlike his brother Danny, Alan Moore didn't put much stock in getting rich and living that kind of life. In fact, *because* of his brother's naked greed constantly getting him into awful fixes, Mr. Moore had what he thought of as a deep understanding of the often-overlooked pitfalls of wealth.

This was Kentucky; any of the men he worked with, for instance, would immediately buy a bigger truck with that money, whether or not they needed one. And, as soon as one of them drove up in the newest F-150, well, then suddenly everyone else felt like they needed one too—it was as asinine as a bunch of bickering women compelled to show off those luxury brand purses. Was the F-150 a good truck? Of course it was. But was spending all that ridiculous kind of money on having the newest thing any kind of necessity? Half the value fell right off of the darn things the moment they drove out of the dealer's lot—and what was the point? In another year, there'd be a newer, bigger best truck. And so on, and so forth. Wasn't it more important to learn to appreciate the truck you have?

Mr. Moore frowned, giving the empty garden beds one last

lingering look before he headed inside to see his girls.

What will THIS kind of money comin' in do to a thirteen-year-old girl? Mr. Moore worried. *One who's grown up in—well, I know the place we have here isn't the best. I know she deserves every red cent of it for what all she's been put through, but at the same time, I'm just afraid that...*

He didn't know quite how to articulate his fears.

Money had a way of changing people, and learning not to let it control your life was a hard lesson for anyone to learn. Many *never* learned, and to them, money was the be-all and end-all. The Moores had their own financial ups and downs and hadn't always been poor; Alan Moore's father was a war veteran and they'd in fact been a pretty well-off family, growing up. As the times got leaner, however, that seemed to affect the pair of brothers in completely different ways. Danny began to obsess over money, while Alan—

Well, guess I was too simple to get into all that. Was too busy chasin' after the girl of my dreams. Mr. Moore wore a slight smile as he opened up the door. *Everyone said I was a damned fool with his head up in the clouds, that she was out of my league. And every-a-one of them was right.*

Both his beautiful wife and his adorable little daughter were sitting in the living room together, one in the chair and the other on the sofa. As he stepped inside, the pair of them looked up from their reading and rewarded him with beaming smiles. Constant change had characterized what he thought of as home for the past months, most of it good. The place was bright and open and all cleaned up, his girls seemed happier, and Mrs. Moore even had a *meaningful* look for him instead of ignoring his entrance in favor of staring at the TV like a zombie like she used to for all hours.

The meaningful look was an even more recent development, as his wife getting caught up in Tabby's fitness and dieting craze was somehow bringing the woman's confidence and libido stirring back to life. To him, she'd always been stunning, even with the extra weight, but nowadays, she just seemed to light up and be more *there,* as if she'd been in a fugue for years and years and was only now really coming back to herself. It made her seem young again.

"How're my lovely ladies today?" Mr. Moore asked, shrugging off his coat. "Gettin' up to mischief?"

"We spent the day with the boys," Tabitha answered with a wry smile. "I was very careful. I didn't do any running around, or any hand-springs, or hand-stands, or cartwheels, or back flips, or anything fun, even though I really wanted to. You'd be proud of me."

"That's good to hear, honey." Mr. Moore nodded in approval. "You leave them circus acrobatics to the boys."

"*Circus acrobatics!*" Tabby repeated in an indignant snort, flicking her hair with a turn of her head. "*Hmph!*"

"You just remember the doctor's orders," Mr. Moore chided her. "So don't you be readin' too hard neither. That goes for the both of you!"

""Yes, *Dad,*"" both of the girls answered—although one of them with a very teenage eye roll, and the other with that rather meaningful look in her eye again.

You cool it with those bedroom eyes, Missy—don't you even get me started on that OTHER predicament we've gotten ourselves into!

That issue was even more enormous than the ludicrous settlement money, but still a distant ways off—right now, Mr. Moore's concerns extended as far as his daughter's immediate health and the happiness and mental well-being for both her and his wife.

"Either of you'ns decide what we're gonna do for Thanksgiving?" Mr. Moore probed. "Thanksgivin' with Grammy and the boys, or Thanksgivin' over with the MacIntires?"

"Oof," Tabitha groaned, clutching at her stomach in mock indecision. "I want to say both, but I also don't want to put on weight. Can we... can we have *two* Thanksgivings?"

"Alan, just listen to her!" Mrs. Moore shook her head in

dismay. "Two Thanksgivings, now?!"

"If you're lookin' for me to be the voice of reason here, you've got the wrong guy." Mr. Moore chuckled, holding up his hands. "We really do have about that much to be thankful for this year. Might need two Thanksgivings just to fit it all in."

Women, to him, were social creatures—they thrived on making connections with other people. Friends, family, meeting people and establishing relationships, opening up a dialogue and just talking each other's ears off about this and that helped them actualize themselves in ways that were well over his head. He didn't characterize himself as any sort of social type, really, but he'd seen that his girls opening up so much in the past months had created miracles. He wasn't above helping nudge them along in that direction whenever opportunity arose.

"Two Thanksgivings it is, then!" Tabitha declared with a wistful sigh. "Can't miss out on one with Grandma Laurie and the boys, and then I also can't say no to Hannah. I'm just going to have to be that much more careful with how much I eat."

A part of him wanted to take comfort in knowing that his Tabby had such a damned good head on her shoulders. Surely, she wasn't going to let the incoming settlement money change her— and, if she did? She would still be his daughter, and he would love her no matter what. Careful to not let the matters weighing so heavily on his mind rise up into his expression, Mr. Moore dropped his keys and wallet into the tray on the ledge where he always did, and then began kicking off his boots.

No matter what, it was always good to be home.

————

Loud, insistent banging sounds startled Tabitha awake and she jerked against her covers, staring without comprehension into the darkness of her room. It seemed to be the dead of night, and being so suddenly roused had her blinking in a daze. There was a moment of silence, just long enough for her to doubt what she thought she'd heard, and then—*bang bang bang bang bang,* it resounded out again. This time, she could identify the unpleasant noise. It wasn't a stray cat on the roof again, it wasn't a neighborhood squabble a few doors down, and—heaven forbid—it wasn't even her parents fooling around in the bedroom.

Someone was outside their trailer and knocking insistently on the aluminum of their front door.

At this hour...? Tabitha half-rose, unwilling to throw back the covers once she felt the chill in the air. *What—what time even IS it?*

Again the bang, bang, bang of someone's fist rattled their front door, and Tabitha turned back her covers and sat up in alarm, pulling her legs free and preparing to—she paused as she heard Mr. Moore swearing under his breath and opening the door down the hall. Unfounded fear and a bit of adrenaline wiped away the last traces of her drowsiness, and all at once, Tabitha was completely alert—but frozen in place, straining her ears as she heard her father's footsteps stumble past her door and out toward the living room to see what the late-night commotion was.

Who would bother us this late at night? Tabitha wondered. *The neighbors? The POLICE? Did something bad happen? To who?! What could be so important that—*

Her disoriented mind raced from possibility to possibility. Could one of the boys have gotten hurt somehow? Or had something happened to Grandma Laurie? To Elena, or Alicia? Nothing much stood out in memory from this time period in her last life except Uncle Danny being arrested and the South Main shooting. But that didn't mean anything anymore either—Tabitha blundering around through this timeline had potentially changed anything and everything.

Beneath her bedroom door, a strip of light shone as the living room light was flicked on, and she heard the front door open.

"Oh thank *gawd.*" A grating but somewhat familiar woman's voice jarred Tabitha out of her thoughts. "Christ, Alan, lemme in!

I'm liable to freeze my tits off, out here! Y'all are even lockin' your door, now?! Things sure do change fast!"

"It's—it's almost midnight," Tabitha heard her father say.

"All yer lights were off, I was 'fraid y'all'd packed on up and moved someplace else without tellin' me a word!" the woman complained. "What were y'all doin', didn'cha hear me knocking?! I was fixin' to break a window just to get in! Hold on—I gotta take myself a piss."

To Tabitha's bewilderment, the woman's voice was *closer* now, as if Mr. Moore had let her into the living room. Which surely couldn't be possible. Tabitha couldn't make any sense of what was going on. In her shocked silence, she listened on as unsteady footfalls sounded just outside her bedroom door, and she heard a hand smack against the hallway wall as if someone was using it to catch their balance. *She's—who IS this—she's just letting herself in to use our bathroom?!*

"Lisa, it's almost midnight!" Mr. Moore rebuked the woman in a harsh whisper.

Lisa—AUNT LISA?!! Tabitha leapt to her feet at the realization, immediately overcome by white-hot anger. *This can't be happening. This CAN'T fucking be happening. No. No. No no no no no.*

"Hold on a second, Al, I gotta piss!" Lisa loudly announced.

"Lisa, it's just about—it's eleven forty-five at night." Mr. Moore didn't sound any happier than Tabitha was about the unwelcome intrusion. "You can't just—"

The sound of the toilet seat slamming down had Tabitha gritting her teeth, and hearing the clink of her aunt undoing her belt —it was all too easy to picture the enormous COUNTRY GIRL belt buckle the woman sometimes sported, with its machine-stamped confederate flag motif—threw Tabitha into a fit of rage. *How DARE she come back here. At this time of night, at ANY TIME, EVER!*

"Lisa—Lisa, you realize how late it is?" Tabitha's father was standing just outside the bathroom door and seemed to be struggling to lower his voice.

"What?" Aunt Lisa called back at her same obnoxious volume. "Were y'all asleep?"

Tabitha smashed her good hand into the light switch beside her door, flooding her bedroom with light. The air was frigid, but she didn't feel the cold right now. In the mirror, she saw a teenage girl that she didn't recognize at all, a hateful glare framed by a mussed tangle of reddish-gold hair, the oversized sweatshirt she'd been sleeping in and her winter pajama bottoms. Tabitha searched her tiny room in desperation for a moment for something to *strangle,* and in no time at all settled in the plush Flounder pillow from Halloween. She crushed it awkwardly between her hand and her cast, but it offered no respite.

She's here for the money. Tabitha bit down hard to keep herself from grinding her jaw. *Of course she's back for the money. The newspapers all went on and on about the lawsuits. About the settlements. Why the fuck else would SHE come back? She didn't come back last lifetime, no, not this early. She sure as FUCK didn't come back for her four fucking children. No—she's here for the money. We don't even HAVE it yet, but here she is.*

Cradling Flounder against herself with one arm, Tabitha opened her door and stepped out into the hall. Her father was in long johns and gave her an apologetic look colored by his own aggravation, and past him, Tabitha caught a glimpse down the hall of a furious Mrs. Moore hurriedly changing into a nightshirt. Satisfied that both of her parents were almost as pissed as she was, Tabitha turned on her heel and stalked out toward the living room.

Oh, we're all going to have a lovely talk about this, Tabitha seethed. *This is just like the stories from people who win the lottery—at first, it's all fantastic. Like living a dream, because all of their money problems are over forever. Right? But then comes the greed, the wretched fucking UGLINESS, then the family or friends or what have you come crawling out of the woodworks, expecting generosity. DEMANDING it.*

As if Aunt Lisa is entitled to our good fortune, after she fucking abandoned all of us when we were suffering through hardship. Aban-

doned her own fucking children! It's unforgivable. I KNOW she's only back for the money, because last lifetime, she didn't come back for years and years and years after she left.

Mr. and Mrs. Moore followed her as far as the kitchen, where they paused to speak with each other in harsh whispers, while Tabitha continued on and took a seat on one end of the couch. It wasn't easy to contain her fury, and Flounder once again deformed beneath her squeezing hand as she rushed to put her thoughts into order. Aunt Lisa was here. Aunt Lisa was surely going to play every card in her hand, every dirty trick she could, to worm herself into this family and leech off of their apparent new wealth.

The thought of it made Tabitha so incredibly angry that she thought she might be sick.

"Whew, my damn, it's cold-as-can-be *inside,* even! *BrRrRr!*" Aunt Lisa chuckled as she swung the bathroom door open and plodded down the hall toward the Moore family. "Thought fer sure y'all'd've had some *heat* runnin'. Didn't ch'all come into all that money?!"

Hearing the woman even *mention* money had Tabitha's frown turn into an immediate scowl, and the sight of her aunt almost sent Tabitha into a belligerent rage.

Aunt Lisa was trashy.

Despite the temperatures outside, the peroxide-blonde was wearing a sleeveless top with a plunging neckline that revealed an unhealthy amount of cleavage. As always, the woman's bra cups were visible, and nothing seemed to fit—she had crammed herself into that top, and the ragged blue jeans were pinching her midsection into a pronounced muffin-top. Rather than the confederate flag belt buckle Tabitha recalled seeing Aunt Lisa wear in the past, this was a new one, an oversized buckle featuring two crossed pistols and a tacky assortment of stars.

"Lisa—what's going on?" Mr. Moore demanded.

"Y'all weren't asleepin', were you?!" Aunt Lisa seemed amused as she glanced at each of them. "If I'd've known, I wouldn'ta been hollerin'. Y'all shoulda said somethin'!"

The woman waltzed past Mr. and Mrs. Moore where they stood in the kitchen and helped herself to the living room chair across from Tabitha. The light cast from the lamp here was even less flattering—again, Aunt Lisa was *trashy*.

Her hair looked greasy, pit-stains were visible upon her shirt, her face appeared both oily and caked with makeup at the same time, and a prominent pair of cold sores on her lip weren't quite hidden beneath the cosmetics. She was clutching a handbag against herself with both hands—immediately prompting Tabitha to suspect she'd already stolen something—and the combined smell of body odor, cigarette smoke, and stale urine wafted across the living room, as if someone had left open the door of a truck stop's restroom to air out.

No. No, no, no, no. NO, this is NOT happening, Tabitha was livid, and she pointedly glared daggers toward her parents. *She is NOT family!*

"Well *yeah*, we were all asleep. It's damn near midnight," Mr. Moore groused, putting his hands on his hips. "What on earth's going on, here?"

"My word, I'm so sorry!" Aunt Lisa pursed her lips into a pout. "I woulda been more quieter if-ins I'da known! I didn't reckon y'all'd've gone ta bed *this early!* I heard all 'bout all yer family's troubles from my girl Tiffany in Fairfield, an' I rushed over to come help soon as I could get myself here—sure ain't easy without a car!"

Aunt Lisa turned in her seat and looked Tabitha up and down with that false smile of hers that never failed to draw out revulsion.

"Lookit *you,* though! Tabby girl, you must sure be on the mend, 'cause you look prettier'n I'd a ever thought from all that goin' on on the news! You look prettier than ever! *Just look at you!*"

Please don't. Tabitha carefully schooled her face into a neutral expression so that her disgust wasn't as blatantly obvious. *Please just—don't.*

"I been workin' the Wild Wings up in Shelbyville—good money there! But I up and dropped everythin' the minute I heard the word 'bout all what y'all been through! I'm so sorry it took me so long to get my way here!" Aunt Lisa drawled out. "Tabby, yer damn near famous! You been on the news and everything, even all the way out in Shelbyville we heard about all this nasty business. You gettin' pushed around at school, then this boy attackin' you right there in the middle of a Halloween party?! Unbelievable! *Unbelievable!*"

Tabitha used all of the acting she'd learned in the past few months to approximate a hesitant smile for her aunt.

"Well, y'all don't need to worry 'bout a thing anymore, 'cause yer Auntie Lisa's here!" the woman crooned, taking a moment to check and make sure her handbag was still held in close against her body. "Ain't no one messin' with my baby niece Tabby while I'm around, *no nuh-uh!*"

Now that Tabitha took a closer look, there was a smattering of acne across her aunt's brow, and something about the set of her eyes now made her immediate impression come off as more haggard than Tabitha remembered from seeing her last. The tells were all present—from the unhealthy skin, her slightly-too-loud voice, the *twitchy* way she was completely unable to relinquish her grip on her purse. It only took a moment for Tabitha to remember the rather *storied* end of Aunt Lisa from her past lifetime and spot the puffy pink puncture mark on the inside of her aunt's arm. When she knew what to look for, there was another one too, an obvious scab on the woman's left hand, apparent just between her thumb and forefinger.

Great. Tabitha forced a warm smile as her aunt continued rambling on. *Great! Looks like our uninvited guest is already a heroin addict. She's not staying. She's NOT family—and she's not welcome here. We're getting rid of her.*

36
DILEMMAS AND DELIBERATION

"Sweetie, you're growin' up to bein' just the prettiest li'l *thang!*" Aunt Lisa praised again, reaching over with a visibly sweaty hand to pinch at Tabitha's cheek. "C'mon, now. Yer at 'bout *that age*—you tell yer Aunt Lissie 'bout all them *boys* yer seein'!"

"Can't talk about boys." Tabitha leaned back from her aunt's grasp in a struggle to keep her composure. "We'd fail the Bechdel test."

It was the same joke she'd managed back when first meeting Mrs. Williams, delivered with even less feeling this time. It honestly rankled that the immediate first question some women had for her was whether she was in a relationship, or chasing after a boy, or had herself set on one. *That* was a joke, because it simply wasn't how Tabitha defined herself or her life. Maybe that kind of relationship—with a man or with a woman—would never even be part of her life.

"*Hah!* Beshul test, that's tha Kentucky public school system for ya, ahyup, nothin' but *test test test.*" Lisa guffawed, turning her look of skepticism from Tabitha toward Mrs. Moore. "So, no boys been comin' round at all? Not a single one?!"

"She's... a little young for that still, don't you think?" Mrs. Moore frowned. "She just started high school this year, and between what happened with—"

"Hell, I got mah cherry popped my first year o' high school," Lisa boasted. "Was datin' one of the seniors, mah freshman year! *Kenny Michaels.* He got married an' lives over by Elk Creek, now. Back then, we—"

"I-I believe that's my cue to retire for the night." Tabitha rose from her spot on the living room sofa, still clutching the Flounder pillow against her chest. "Goodnight, Mother. Goodnight Father. Goodnight... *Aunt Lisa.*"

"Ahyup, beddy-by time for Tabby, you go on and get!" Aunt Lisa cackled at Tabitha's manner of speech. "*Retoir for the noight, hah!* Listen to her. What a *hoot!* Nightie-night, girly-girl!"

Another cold chill crept up Tabitha's back as she slowly stepped back down the hallway to her bedroom, being extra careful not to stomp. She *wanted* to stomp, she wanted to throw a fit—she was so *livid* about this whole unexpected junkie mess *that was dumping itself in their lap* that her blood had adrenaline racing throughout her body in a fight or flight response. Lisa's careless laughter and exaggerated Kentucky drawl continued on behind her, and each and every poorly enunciated syllable just kept getting under her skin in a terrible way.

Closing her bedroom door behind her only slightly muffled the woman's voice, because of course, the wall paneling of their mobile home was paper-thin fiberboard. Trying hard to tune out the somewhat-audible sound of Lisa speaking until it was just loathsome trashy noise, Tabitha nudged aside the crumpled flannel of her turned-back bed covers so that she could sit upon the edge of her mattress and regard herself in the mirror.

Okay. Okay. Deep breath, calm way down, Tabitha locked eyes with her reflection and tried to focus on nothing else. *Okay. Okay. OKAY.*

Calm didn't come quickly, but it did eventually come to her, and she hugged Flounder and plucked absently at the edge of her cast while she considered what to do with the situation. Tabitha had never had a good impression of Uncle Danny or Aunt Lisa. Was that *fair*, though? Memories of her own mother from her first lifetime were uneasy at best, and rife with an entire heap of complicated, conflicting feelings otherwise. Initial perception of Elena had been so rotten that a middle-school *phantom* of the girl had shown up in her subconscious to bully her during one of those surreal fever dreams. The four cousins had once upon a time been annoying hooligans she didn't care for at all.

Okay, so yes—some of the anger at Lisa IS warranted. Tabitha blew out a slow breath. *Some of this is... overreaction. My knowledge and experience, my 'software' is arguably a little more advanced, but the hardware it's installed on right now is vintage thirteen-year-old girl, and emotions are dialed up to eleven.*

Even more than that, I'm feeling so helpless because I'm intentionally sinking deeper and deeper into the ROLE of a thirteen-year-old girl. Somewhat. Right? Classic Stanford prison experiment—I've been psychologically conforming to my expected social role here in 1998. I haven't really been fighting that regression, because... being a simple teenage girl makes me happy, while depressing future knowledge mostly just attempts to poison that happiness or monkey's paw me at every turn.

So, my anger right now, how FURIOUS I am at Lisa showing up also feels so INFANTILE—and that just makes me angrier. It's the worst of both worlds—the teen outrage and frustration, and the adult knowledge and sense of responsibility that comes with that. They play off of each other in the worst way, make me feel like I'm slipping down into a tantrum spiral. As a teenager, I'm angry and sullen because I don't have the agency to just DO anything about her. I'm supposed to abide, to treat her like family, when she's actually this white trash junkie, and yeah, I just don't even WANT to ever treat her like family!

As this once-upon-a-time grown up old lady from the future, I'm mostly upset because... now I HAVE to do something about this. I'm going to HAVE to get involved, I'm going to HAVE to be in some ugly confrontation, I'm going to HAVE to raise a fuss, and I hate it. I'm thirteen years old, but by necessity, I'm going to now need a voice, a real say in the family stuff going on, at the level of what adults decide. Just when this fragile, happy little illusion of a simple, NORMAL childhood was finally starting to stabilize into something I could enjoy. I hate it I hate it I hate it. I wish Lisa would just go away. I wish she'd just go back off to whatever truckstop men's room she was probably whoring herself out from, and stay out of my life. Out of all of our lives. Is that so much to fucking ask?!

"Can't do anything about it!" Tabitha grumbled under her breath to herself. "Have to anyways. *Fuck.*"

Staring at the bedraggled and distraught teen reflecting back at her in the mirror, Tabitha let out an aggravated huff and threw Flounder against the far wall. Her actions looked just as silly and immature as they felt, but she *needed* to start venting some things out at times, or she really was going to explode. It was so frustrating—she *needed* someone to talk to, and it already felt like never having anything but identity problems and family drama to dump on Alicia and Elena was going to sour their relationship.

With a dramatic sigh, Tabitha reached up, managed to catch the light switch with the bit of finger her cast exposed, and turned off the lights. The darkness gave her senses nothing to focus in on but the sound of Aunt Lisa still gabbing away out in the living room, and it was hard not to get upset all over again.

So what do I DO about this? I'm not a teenager, exactly. Tabitha eased herself back down onto her pillow and began resituating her covers over top of her. *And, I'm not an old lady anymore either. Right now, I'm just—I don't know what I am. Something I'll have to figure out as I go, right? I'm still changing. Elena's changed a ton. Mom's completely different from who she was, or how she was supposed to be, or whatever.*

I'll give Aunt Lisa a chance to change. I'll try. Try to cut her just enough slack for her to either pull herself up—or hang herself with it. That's the MATURE thing to do, here, right?

———

"So, I was all, *Debra!*" Lisa laughed. "S'like I been done told you— you can't *never* let someone disrespect you like that. Definitely not'n front of yer kids!"

To Tabitha's annoyance and disbelief, she blinked open bleary eyes the next morning to the *continued* grating sound of Aunt Lisa's voice. Their trailer's furnace was blowing hot air in through all the vents at full blast, and her normally cozy morning blankets now felt absolutely stifling. It was hard not to grimace at the sheer waste of running the temperature so high—in late November, wearing a sweatshirt and thermal pajamas around the house was still comfy, and it kept their bill way down.

Surely... surely they weren't up discussing things all night? Tabitha furrowed her brows, squeezed her eyes shut again, and pressed her face back into her pillow for a moment. *Do drug addicts sleep more than normal, or less than normal? Google won't be here to tell me for years and years yet.*

She had never expected Lisa to be an early riser, but the acrid smell of instant coffee and cigarette smoke became apparent as Tabitha finally kicked back her too-warm covers. The wrist inside her cast was likewise balmy with sweat already, and despite her midnight resolution to give the woman a chance to redeem herself, Tabitha could feel that determination eroding a little more each time she heard her aunt open that mouth of hers to say something.

"Don't matter if it was jus' bullshittin' over beer or jus' makin' fun or *nothin'!* So I says, somebody treats you like that, Debra? You get them right by the balls an' make sure they ain't fixin' to *ever* jus' run their mouth off on ya ever again. S'way you gotta do it—I ain't playin' no games."

Letting out her most dramatic teenage sigh, Tabitha rolled out of bed and wrenched open the door to her room so that she could pad down the hallway in her now too-warm wool socks.

"Why is the thermostat so high?" Tabitha asked, immediately twisting the dial from where it read *eighty degrees* all the way down to sixty. *Eighty degrees?! Are you fucking kidding me?*

"S'colder'n a witch's titty out there, that's why!" Lisa guffawed. "It's the dead o' November, little girl."

The peroxide-blonde delinquent mother of four was already sitting across the table from her father, while Tabitha's own mother Mrs. Moore was nowhere to be found, probably still sound asleep back on the other side of the trailer where the larger bedroom was. Though Lisa wasn't smoking right at this moment, the stifling smell of it was present, and a glance up toward the kitchen ceiling confirmed that the smoke detector's cover was hanging open and the nine volt battery had been removed. Further observation revealed Lisa had slopped instant coffee into one of the nice teacups Tabitha had set aside for ice cream in the cabinet, and Tabitha decided she wasn't going to let it get to her—after all, Lisa couldn't have known any better.

No, you know what? Tabitha all but huffed. *It DOES still bother me! I'm honestly going to be heartbroken if her nasty coffee stains my lovely porcelain tea set forever. I don't have many nice things, and the few nice things I DO have need to be cherished.*

"Mornin', Sweetheart," Mr. Moore said.

"Good morning," Tabitha sighed.

"Y'all know I prayed for this, right, Alan?" Aunt Lisa gushed. "I prayed an' prayed—an' I just *knew* HE would answer mah prayers. Yer Tabby baby is a miracle, you know that?"

"Yep," Mr. Moore agreed, frowning over his newspaper. "She is a blessing."

"She's an honest-to-God miracle, and the money—the money from those settlements? Alan, she's *saved* this family. She's like—

she's like our own li'l redheaded guardian angel. Idden that right, honey? Hah!"

ISN'T that right, Tabitha mentally corrected. *I'm not sure which is worse—that her southern REDNECK dialect is so thick that I can barely understand her, or the fact that I CAN still understand her. I wish I couldn't.*

A certain kind of morbid curiosity kept Tabitha fixated on the woman as her Aunt Lisa applied mascara and 'made herself up' for the day. The woman didn't even bring the applicator up to her own eyes, instead carefully turning over each plastic false eyelash in her hands and plucking at it with the black bristles of a little mascara wand. Was she going to apply the falsies afterward? That seemed backward to Tabitha, and the strange preening motions were *grotesque,* because Lisa's fingers and thumbs now sported the curved hot pink of two-inch long acrylic fingernails, which made her digits seem sinister, spidery, and menacing.

Beneath all the beauty product she plasters all over herself, and these feminine odds and ends she glues on—would any of us even recognize her? Tabitha wondered in a bleary daze as she pulled out one of the chairs so that she could sit with them at the dining room table. *Does anyone even know what Lisa actually looks like? Who IS Lisa, really?*

"You like mah look?" Aunt Lisa crooned with a self-indulgent giggle. "Now, I weren't no *movie star* like yer momma was, but oh you *know* yer Aunt Lisa still knows how ta turn heads and drop jaws!"

"Yeah, it's... sure something." Tabitha was trying not to stare, but it was difficult to look away. *Maybe there ISN'T anyone beneath it all.*

The bleached and frazzled bottle-blonde, the plastered-on foundation, the garish red lipstick—it was difficult to imagine what the woman was going to such exaggerated lengths to hide, because each treatment seemed so much worse than whatever flaws they might have concealed. The longer Tabitha spent observing Aunt Lisa, in fact, the less she seemed like a real person. It was as though the woman simply strived to express a stereotype, or a caricature. If she was acting, Tabitha felt sure Mrs. Moore would call it bad acting. But—*she didn't seem to be acting.*

The writer in me wants to say that everyone possesses SOME nuance, some... hidden depth of character. The realist in me, on the other hand, suggests that she's exactly what she presents herself to be. I know some of the trashy old women I worked with at the plant weren't particularly two-dimensional. I already know I'm biased against her. Every word out of her mouth makes me want to condemn her more and more. What am I even looking for? How would I even GO ABOUT giving her a chance to change? Convince her we can send her through rehab?

"Aunt Lisa," Tabitha blurted out before she even really knew what she was asking. "Why... why *did* you come back?"

"Why'd I come back?" Aunt Lisa snorted, cocking an eyebrow. "Well 'cause I don't gotta work at the *Wild Wings* in Shelbyville no more, ain't that right?"

"You mean *isn't that,* and—*is* that right?" Tabitha asked. "Why is that? Why is it that you don't have to work at the Wild Wings anymore?"

"*'Cause now we got all that money,* Sugar," Lisa explained slowly to Tabitha, as though she were speaking to a much younger child. "Our money problems are *over,* ain't a one of us gotta work no more. Isn't that right, Al?"

"Oh?" Tabitha's eyebrows went up in mock surprise. *OUR money problems, huh?* "Dad—you're quitting your job?"

"Hah, o'course he is," Lisa snorted. "Why would he—"

"No, *no,* I'm not quitting my job," Mr. Moore assured his daughter, seemingly startled to have been pulled back into the conversation. "No way in heck, not no way, no how. Not with a little one on the—"

"*Yer NOT?*" Aunt Lisa was the very picture of incredulity. "I mean—wow. *I would.* I did! *Hah!* You sure must love yer job, Al. Workin' when ya don't have to? Not me, no sire. That's crazy talk."

"I don't... think I understand," Tabitha hinted, attempting to convey a clear *it's YOU that doesn't understand.* "Why wouldn't you have to work, Aunt Lisa? The lawsuit and the settlement money, that doesn't have anything to do with you. *Even if it did,* it wouldn't be enou—"

"Of course it has to do with me. I'm yer Aunt Lissie!" Lisa chortled, giving Tabitha a dismissive smirk. "Listen to you! Tryin' to be a selfish li'l shyster an' wantin' to keep that big ol' settlement all fer yerself! You *do* know that bein' too greedy is one o' the deadly mortal sins, don'tcha? There's a *reason* they kicked all them money-grubbin' Jews outta Egypt, that's *in the Bible.* Written 'n black 'n white, an' that's tha God's honest truth. Tabby, honey... yer still a li'l girl, you don't have no place havin' that much money fer yerself—an' what would ya even do with it? Buy dollies and dollhouses? *Hah!* Tabby sweetie, that money's all goin' *to the family,* so we can best decide how to raise you all up right. You think raisin' up a kid is cheap?! Yer Aunt Lissie's got four of 'em!"

That Aunt Lisa had the sheer gall to assert herself as *a parenting figure*—after walking out on her own four children for months on end without a word to anyone—had Tabitha seeing red despite every attempt to maintain her cool. She inhaled deeply as the rage gripped her, and was forced to clench her teeth simply to prevent herself from lashing out thoughtlessly.

Have you even visited them, or did you just beeline straight here for us, where the settlement money would be? You couldn't have been there yet, Grandma Laurie would have called us right away. Do they even know? Your own kids. Your own goddamn kids don't even know that you're back, do they? Now? Now I DON'T WANT THEM TO. I really wanted to try to give you a chance—but fuck it, I can't. I just can't. I just, I just want you gone. Gone and out of our fucking lives.

"Pfffftt—don't get all huffy with me, girl." Aunt Lisa rolled her eyes at Tabitha's smoldering glare as the teenager fought to keep it all in. "Lookin' like someone pissed in yer Cheerios. Jesus H. Christ, Alan, look at *this attitude* on her! Y'all need to get a handle on that big ol' swollen head o' hers, an' raise her up proper. Yah right, like some suit 'n tie lawyer was gonna hand *all that money* to a li'l girl barely inta her pushup bra. O'course it's goin' to us—yer parents. *Hah!*"

"Forgive me, I've indeed lost my composure." Tabitha rose from her seat and gave her father a meaningful look. He should understand by now just how she was feeling when she chose her words so carefully. "Please, excuse me."

"We'll... talk about it when—" Mr. Moore began to promise, but he was cut off by Aunt Lisa's boisterous *mocking* laughter in response to Tabitha's apparent *prim and proper* dialect.

Now not wanting to talk to anyone *at all,* Tabitha stalked on down the hallway toward the bathroom so that she could brush her teeth and wash her face.

Okay. Calm down again, calm down again. CALM DOWN. Why is it so hard for me to calm down?! Tabitha took special care not to slam the bathroom door, despite the urgent motion of it trembling within her arm, desperate to explode out. *She's just this shitty fucking—she's just, just getting under your skin. Keeping you off-balance. I still have all the advantages, here, right? I have all kinds of future knowledge. I have—I just need to... to calm down, to go through and remember anything I can that might be useful with this.*

It was easier said than done.

She swiped her toothbrush out of the holder, glared at the dab of toothpaste she applied atop the bristles, and then bared her teeth in a snarl toward the mirror so that she could angrily brush her teeth. With each passing month, it became more difficult for her to detach herself from situations and manage that numb *robotic* act, where with her eloquent manner of speech, she could pretend she was more of an observer than a participant in this second life. She was involved now, she was *mired* in this *trailer trash shitpile* life, and now she was going to have to get both hands into the muck if she wanted to somehow climb out of it someday.

Furious, Tabitha spat into the sink before she meant to, wasting some of her toothpaste.

Damn. Do I have, what, latent anger management issues I never discovered? Tabitha paused for a moment to regard her foaming-at-the-mouth reflection with a glare and then spat again. *Just never even found out if I had a temper or not last time, because I always kept my head down and shied away from those situations? Maybe?*

Her psychological issues were complicated and increasingly hard to self-diagnose, and she wasn't sure she trusted herself to sort out relevant factors from misleading ones. She knew *why* Aunt Lisa got her so riled up; the woman was one hundred percent pure, undiluted trailer trash. Soon-to-be or already a heroin junkie, and a shameless parasite uncomfortably close to worming her way back into the small group of people she cared a lot about.

At least, I care a lot about them THIS time, Tabitha glowered as she viciously resumed scrubbing her teeth. *Yeah. That's probably it. Probably why I never got angry at much of anything in my last life—I wasn't real close to anyone. Or anything. Not here at this age, at least. To me, me and my immediate family were trailer trash, and then that whole side of the family over there with Uncle Danny and Aunt Lisa were worse, just... garbage, petty criminals. Convicts and drug addicts, and their drug addict and dropout kids.*

Not relatives she wanted to associate with, but ones that certainly lingered on in her mind all throughout her life. Because, while she always personally felt like trailer trash, at least she had these other people in her life to prop up as examples of worse trailer trash.

Okay. Doesn't feel great to admit, but that's what they were to me, I think. Tabitha spat again into the sink. *Uncle Danny, Aunt Lisa, all of the cousins. They weren't FAMILY, they were just... examples, some idea for me to cling to. Because I could look at their lives and then console myself with 'well, I may have always been trailer trash, but at least I was never THAT bad.'*

It was another tough pill to swallow, but since she'd begun to make progress in bettering herself in this life, it was getting easier to recognize her own shortcomings. As for what she was going to *do* about it—Tabitha just had to start drawing lines. Her four cousins were still young, and swerving their paths onto a better future was entirely possible. Uncle Danny was already in jail; that ship had apparently sailed and there was nothing she could do about it. As for Aunt Lisa...

If I'm completely honest with myself, I just don't even WANT to help her. Tabitha made a face as she rinsed her mouth. *I can't stand her, and that's just a fact. Maybe with some kind of brilliant 4D CHESS, JUST AS KEIKAKU plan, I COULD get her to clean up her act and be a proper mother, and maybe that WOULD be the ideal best outcome for the boys. MY mother seemed just as rotten just a few months ago—and look how far she's come.*

I just... Tabitha grimaced at her reflection as the weight of difficult choices seemed to press down and smother her once again. *I'm a planner, but I'm not some kind of super schemer. I don't know if I can put in that kind of effort for Lisa. I mean, I know I could try—but more and more, I don't think I will. I'm a good person, or I try to be, but maybe I'm not THAT good of a person. It's easy for me to be flippant about it, I guess, until I stop and really think about how much NOT helping Lisa change into a different person might cost the boys. But then, on the other hand... some people can't be helped. Right?*

————

Shortly after Aunt Lisa finished applying her falsies and seemed all fancied up to go out somewhere—the woman crashed, settling in on their couch with her newly-made-up face smooshed in against the armrest to sleep. Tabitha could *see* the cosmetics smearing into their worn upholstery, and she regarded the unwelcome guest in their living room with confusion and bewilderment, finally turning toward her father with an *are you seeing this* expression. All she got in return was a slow sigh and him asking her to try to keep her volume down today while her aunt was sleeping. Then, Mr. Moore left for work.

She still stinks too! Tabitha scowled as she quietly crept as close as she could. *So—she didn't shower last night.*

Lisa had passed out with her purse squashed protectively beneath her one armpit, and despite hovering over the woman for a long, tense moment, Tabitha didn't see any way she could tug it out from under her aunt without waking her.

Worst thing is, she maybe DOESN'T have heroin in her purse right now, Tabitha fretted, crossing her arms. *Maybe she's not actually into heroin yet. Maybe she is, but she's already used whatever she had. That seems likely. Heroin probably isn't cheap—or is it? I honestly don't know, and again—no Google here. Maybe she only came to us because she was out of options and couldn't afford to pay her dealer, or whatever.*

There's no way of knowing for sure, and if I cry wolf now and her purse turns out to be empty, it damages my credibility toward further attempts to remove her. And I NEED to remove her sooner rather than later if I'm going to. Or this is all going to become unbelievably messy the further she entangles herself back into the family. Make a choice, Tabitha, make a choice. Help her, or get rid of her. Help her, or get rid of her, c'mon, think, think, think. I don't know how to help her. I also don't know how to get rid of her. Either way, I need to come up with some-thing smart, real soon.

Torn with indecision, Tabitha was still drawing a complete blank as to how she even *could* hypothetically help Aunt Lisa. There didn't seem to be any way to. The woman was crass and stubborn and would laugh off any attempts to get her to turn her life around. In fact, the more she thought about it... if *Aunt Lissie* were to reintegrate into their lives, she would negatively influence everyone in Tabitha's close family—starting with the boys. Under

Aunt Lisa's continued careless 'parenting,' the four cousins' relatively thoughtful and considerate behavior Tabitha had grown proud of would unravel, and in a matter of time, they would revert back to being the absolute shitheads they were in Tabitha's previous life.

Aunt Lisa's reappearance would once again drive a wedge between Mrs. Moore and that entire side of the family, cutting off that fledgling avenue of growth. As an anxious and agoraphobic shut-in weighed down with repressed issues that was only now in early stages of healing and recovery, Tabitha's mother wasn't really psychologically equipped to handle a loud and outspoken personality like Lisa. Grandma Laurie and Mr. Moore would both suffer in silence, bending to Aunt Lisa's whims if they were able to rationalize that it was for the sake of the four boys or whatever excuses Lisa cooked up. After all, those two were used to it, to an extent—just a few months ago, Mrs. Moore had been just about as toxic and intractable.

It's oh so very humbling. Tabitha's stare turned more and more grave the more she considered the implications. *That almost all the changes wrought in the people around me could be undone so easily. All the blood, sweat, and tears, all the STRUGGLE that went into changing things for the better, healing people, mending relationships—and almost all of it can collapse and go back to the way it was with the reappearance of just one Aunt Lisa. Putting aside whether or not it's even POSSIBLE to help her—can I let her presence destroy all of this?*

I think... I think I need to make Aunt Lisa disappear.

The realization—no, the *decision* hit Tabitha like a pang to her stomach, and for a moment, she felt sick. Hugging her arms tight across herself, Tabitha hurried away from her aunt and retreated back down the hallway to her room. It was one thing to be affected by her teenage emotions and feel anger and outrage that made her think some dark thoughts. It was something else entirely to coldly deliberate *removing* someone like that.

I'm not going to kill her! Tabitha wanted to swear at herself, angry all over again at that all-too-familiar wash of nauseating guilt. *It's not like the thing with Jeremy Redford.*

I didn't even kill him! He just, well, he just died and I was technically at fault for it. I was at fault for it because I made it happen, but not like, like, I'm not PERSONALLY to blame. It did happen because of me, but I didn't kill him. He almost murdered a cop anyways, so what if he even DID just happen to get his, his comeuppance this time through? Right? I didn't kill him. Karma came along. I didn't kill him. I'm not going to kill Aunt Lisa either—I just need to, to, I don't know. Make her disappear off somewhere, out of our lives. To prison or somewhere. I don't know. Anywhere but here.

Fuck me, this isn't fair. Tabitha discovered her good hand wouldn't stop shaking, so she crossed her arms tighter about herself and tried to squeeze her arms into stillness. *Why is this so hard?*

———

The morning hours passed by in a whirl of indecision and abortive attempts at rationalizing various courses of action and inaction. Tabitha was upset, and she knew *why* she was upset. All of her hypothetical solutions were unrealistic and oblique to the point that her common sense rejected them. The route for helping Lisa change predicated upon being able to sit down with Lisa for a serious conversation and convince Lisa herself that she was a problem. Which, based on what she knew of Lisa's personality, and the lack of confidence Tabitha possessed for her own persuasive ability and finesse in dealing with the woman in a heated argument... meaningful dialogue with her Aunt Lisa was somewhere between improbable and impossible.

Getting rid of Lisa seemed to require the opposite—convincing her parents that Lisa was a problem, but not *their* problem. Not a burden their family should attempt to shoulder. Tabitha would have to convey the severity of a problem that Lisa had become, and then illustrate to them how their attempts to help or support Lisa would in fact enable Lisa to become more and more of a problem. Paring down her thoughts and feelings on the issue and sorting everything out, however, did remarkably little toward solving anything. To Tabitha's endless frustration, she honestly didn't believe she could convince Lisa or her parents of either narrative. She knew she'd made major strides in this lifetime toward better expressing herself and communicating with others, and having a sense of that progress made it just as clear to her how much she fell short here.

Certainly doesn't help that I'm so AFFECTED by all of this, Tabitha thought, lifting her elbows up and attempting to roll the stiffness out of her shoulders. *Spent most of my morning here just pacing back and forth in my room, going in circles in my head. Yes, I'm smart and I can think things through—eventually—but in the heat of the moment, actually out there with Lisa? My temper flares up right away, and it's like I just get locked out of rational thought. Start to act and speak out on impulse, or get myself caught up in this psychological loop of angry thoughts that doesn't actually go anywhere else. So, in short—I'm stuck.*

It was just as easy to feel trapped in her bedroom with Aunt Lisa snoozing out there in the living room, because Tabitha wasn't well enough yet to do the kind of morning run she needed to help bleed off some of these feelings. Likewise, she wasn't able to power walk around the neighborhood or busy herself over the garden plot like she wanted to. Going outside at all while she was still recovering from surgery wasn't feasible until it was mid-afternoon and sunnier out—late November was cold, colder every day, but mornings were *bitter cold,* with dreary overcast skies and a steady biting wind that would sap her strength.

A completely teenage Tabitha would go out anyways and damn the consequences. Tabitha quirked her lip in a bitter smile. *A completely grown-up Tabitha wouldn't feel so damned ANGSTY cooped up in here waiting for Mom to get up.*

As such, naturally, time appeared to slow to a crawl and

Tabitha stewed in her simmering thoughts for what felt like several eternities before she heard the door to her parents' bedroom finally open. Listening intently, Tabitha found her mother's heavy footsteps were treading slowly down the hall. Unable to help herself, Tabitha cracked open her door and leaned out around it as her mother passed by her room.

"She's sleeping," Tabitha whispered. "Out on the couch. Good morning."

It took Mrs. Moore a moment to register what she was saying, and when she did, the hint of an aggravated scowl was visible across her face for a moment before she was able to hide it. That tiny change in expression was a merciful balm to Tabitha, and she swung her door open the rest of the way and stepped out to hug her mother.

"Alright—and good morning," Mrs. Moore whispered back, giving Tabitha a small squeeze. "Do you know why it's so warm in here?"

"Sometime overnight, she went and turned the thermostat to *eighty!*" Tabitha tattled in a hushed voice. "I already turned it back down to where it should be."

"Hmph," Mrs. Moore grunted, shaking her head. "Well. First things first—I'm giving your Grandma Laurie a call."

"Grandma Laurie?" Tabitha repeated, crashing headlong through a dozen different emotions in quick succession, too fast to individually process. "Do we have to, um—"

"If we're tryin' to have dinner with the MacIntires on Thanksgiving day, we'll have to do whatever little family Thanksgiving we do early, either today or tomorrow," Mrs. Moore explained in a low voice, pausing for a moment. "And... well, I'll need to let her know to set the table for your Aunt Lisa too, now."

Please don't, Tabitha just barely managed to not blurt it out, but from her mother's knowing sigh and pat on the shoulder, she knew it was already written all across her face. It seemed inevitable that Aunt Lisa would be reunited with the boys, but at the same time, the prospect of it filled Tabitha with alarm and had her mind racing in every direction all over again.

After all—isn't it suspect that Aunt Lisa, a mother of four, returns from wherever she was in Shelbyville not to her own children, but instead to the home of a brother-in-law whose daughter happens to be on the receiving end of a large settlement of money? Is everyone just ignoring the apparent motive that could be driving Aunt Lisa's priorities, here? Am I in the wrong for not just giving her the benefit of the doubt because she's family?

———

"Your Grandma Laurie says it's fine with her if we move family Thanksgiving up a bit and have it today," Mrs. Moore said, returning the cordless phone back to its dock. "She already got her shoppin' done for it, so..."

"Did you tell them about our *unexpected guest?*" Tabitha asked in a low voice, glancing past the kitchen counter and dining room table over to where Aunt Lisa was still sprawled out on their couch, but questionably awake now and watching daytime soap operas.

"I did." Mrs. Moore paused. "She said she isn't gonna tell the boys just yet. So they can maybe have a... nice surprise."

"'Nice surprise.' Or, so that they won't have a nasty surprise if she decides not to show," Tabitha pointed out with a sour look. "If she *doesn't* want to see her children again... are we okay with her being here in our home while we're not? Unsupervised? Or, uh, *at all?*"

"I'm sure she'll go with us." Mrs. Moore frowned. "Just—well, we'll see."

"Where's she going to be staying? Sleeping? Our couch? Mom. I don't think we should provide her a place to stay if she isn't going to be a mother and look after her kids." Tabitha's voice dropped to a lower whisper. "She's either their mom or she isn't. And, if she isn't family—then. Well."

"Well, I don't think we should even get into it." Mrs. Moore sighed, resting her hands on the counter. "Bless his heart, your father was... very patient with me when I was going through things. For years. And he's liable to try to do the same for your Aunt Lisa now that she's goin' through her problems. I... Tabitha, I don't have any place to say anything."

Tabitha bit her lip. She didn't like it, but Mrs. Moore's position on this was difficult to refute. Pushing her mother to force things with Lisa toward an ultimatum wasn't going to work, and her father was going to be even harder to convince. As the teenage daughter, she once again didn't have enough traction on swaying complicated family matters. The only clear way to make her case was the drug angle, and for that, she needed some measure of proof. Any and all of the evidence to substantiate that kind of claim, if such evidence existed at all, was likely in the purse that Aunt Lisa was currently half-sitting on. The handbag still protectively tucked beneath one armpit as the woman reclined on the sofa, as though it were another pillow.

"I was thinking we should bring somethin' over with us for Thanksgiving." Mrs. Moore sighed, tugging open the fridge door and surveying what they had to work with. "But we don't really have much of anything here. We do still have half of that bag of potatoes in the cupboard, but just bringin' mashed potatoes doesn't seem like enough."

"How about... scalloped potatoes?" Tabitha suggested, stepping over to take a glance inside the refrigerator as well. "Hmm. Maybe not."

"You think we should go out and buy stuffing or something?" Mrs. Moore fretted. "Normally, you're supposed to at least bring a casserole or something to Thanksgiving. Right? I just, it's... it's been a while since I had a Thanksgiving that was more than just bein' here with you and your father."

"We have cheese. If you can give me two or three dollars, I'll walk up to the gas station and buy a quart of milk," Tabitha said, stooping down to pull a glass dish out from where it was stored in the bottom cabinet. "Preheat the oven at three hundred and fifty, and if you start peeling now, I should be able to help make scalloped potatoes when I get back."

"Okay. Okay, scalloped potatoes are perfect," Mrs. Moore agreed, hefting the bag of potatoes down from their little pantry. "Are these still good? Will we have enough? How many should I—"

"They're fine," Tabitha promised. "I'll help you peel them all."

"Not with that cast on, you're not," Mrs. Moore protested, but it was clear her resolve was weakening. "Let me get you some cash from my purse, and you can—do you want me to go on up with you? I don't want you goin' out all by yourself."

"It's just at the top of the hill, Mom," Tabitha said. "I'll be fine. You start peeling, I'll help you finish once I'm back. I'm okay to take a five from your purse?"

"Of course, sure. You make sure an' wear a sweatshirt and a jacket."

"I'll be fine in just a sweatshirt. It's just a few-minute walk."

Leaving her mother to her own devices with the peeler would be cruel—Mrs. Moore had no culinary talent and even less experience. Tabitha had already began resuming her previous role in preparing meals for the family over this past week. After all, watching her mother attempt to whittle away potato skin in tiny thin slivers at a time was always so painful that Tabitha's patience whittled away faster than the spud. Actually holding on to a potato herself was obnoxious with her cast encompassing as much of her thumb as it did, but even with the awkward grip, Tabitha could peel a potato in a matter of moments using a knife.

"Aunt Lisa?" Tabitha rounded the kitchen counter and carefully treaded out into the living room. "Do you... need anything from the—"

"*Sssh!*" Aunt Lisa all but snarled at her. "I can't even keep up with what all's goin' on here with all yer fussin'!"

Tabitha paused, slowly evaluating the blonde occupying their couch as the gangly heroin addict once again grew absorbed by the ongoing drama of *One Life to Live.* She hadn't actually intended to get the woman anything from the store, of course. A step forward and a snatching movement could maybe wrench the purse Aunt Lisa was safeguarding out from under her—but would she even be able to get away with it, or get it open before Lisa was all over her? The body odor of the woman was still noticeable, and Tabitha could just imagine what those frightening two-inch acrylics would feel like clawing into her.

I can... bide my time, Tabitha told herself, shoving her sudden emotion back down to an angry simmer. *There'll be an opportunity at some point. She'll drop her guard, or... or I'll think of something.*

The whole mess with Aunt Lisa was easier to put out of mind as Tabitha turned and hurried down the hallway to fish a five from her mother's purse where Mrs. Moore kept it in the back bedroom. She of course knew that was the point—her mother could tell the Lisa situation was upsetting her. And so, Mrs. Moore was somewhat play-acting, subtly creating tasks that Tabitha could set her mind to, so that she would feel productive and useful. It did help. She didn't begrudge her mother for it at all, and she thought that both of them were aware that it was on purpose. In the past few months, each of them had discovered the other was a lot more intelligent than they'd ever let on before this year.

She's reading my Goblin Princess *outline,* Tabitha told herself as she stepped into her sneakers.

After fighting her way back into the oversized hoodie, Tabitha opened the door and bustled outside and down the steps, swinging the door shut behind her. It was bright enough that she was forced to blink rapidly and even squint, but also bleak and muted—unlike picturesque, postcard views of Kentucky in late autumn with trees in brilliant oranges and yellows, here in the trailer park, fall colors were simply washed out and dead. The crisp chill to the air was sharp enough that her face stung right away, and she hugged her arms tightly against herself as she marched on up the street at a brisk pace.

She's reading it. Not just skimming through it like I was afraid of— she's really reading it, studying it, and that means the world to me. Everything I know and feel gets put into the project, so if she's reading it, she'll know me. She'll understand. She'll start figuring everything out, piecing together the clues. She has to. Because I don't know what I'm even gonna do if she can't.

———

"Ah, damn," Bobby exclaimed, frowning as he saw some petite chick was tugging open the door of the Minit Mart and the bell jangled. *Where'd SHE come from?*

Checking again through the broad glass windows of the gas station, he confirmed that no cars had pulled up. Bobby was supposed to be keeping an eye out for customers while his older brother Joe—the actual employee on shift right now—abused access to the store phone line here to chat with his girlfriend Kimmie, who'd been forced to travel to Minnesota with her parents over Thanksgiving break. Charges would show up on the store's bill, but *in theory,* so long as she initiated the call, Joe could just tell his boss that some customer called with a bunch of questions, and that he'd had no idea they were calling from long distance.

The girl who'd just entered the convenience store was cute, if a little frazzled-looking, with her uncombed tangle of red hair and how her pale skin seemed to emphasize the dark circles under her eyes. More to the point, however—she was *cute,* and he recognized her. This was the infamous *Tabitha Moore,* the freshman dropout of Springton High, mysterious and inaccessible enough to have grown into her own urban legend throughout the school. When she noticed him and did a double-take, he found himself already sheepishly throwing her a small wave.

Oh shit, she kinda recognizes me. Bobby was a little thrilled.

The girl normally seemed quiet and a little mousy and always kept to herself, but something about her just *really* ruffled the feathers of all those flocks of two-faced harpies that called themselves Springton High girls. In fact—the more all of those buzzard bitches ragged on her, the more Bobby started to like Tabitha. Whatever ran contrary to what the bitch brigade was saying was probably closest to the truth, right? The rumor mill at school spun up into full swing whenever Tabitha got brought up, and although he'd asked around with the few buddies he considered pretty reliable, nobody seemed to know what was really going on.

"Hey—uh, Bobby, right?" Tabitha guessed.

Oh shit, she ACTUALLY remembers me! Bobby's flash of nervous excitement took him by surprise.

"Yeah, yeah." Bobby chuckled. "You remember me?"

"Yeah," Tabitha blinked at him. "We were in a couple of my classes together. You walked me up to the office the day I withdrew from school—when I was that blubbering mess."

"Naw, you weren't *blubberin'* or nothin'," Bobby tried to assure her. "Maybe just a li'l sniffly? Teary-eyed? Hah ha. It's cool. Everyone's really, uh, missed you at school." Bobby couldn't hold back any longer. "You ever wanna hang out or do somethin' sometime? You seein' anyone?"

"*Um,* what?" Tabitha's weary expression showed nothing but surprise and bewilderment. "Hah, no, I'm not *seeing anyone.* You do realize I'm only thirteen years old, right?"

"What?" Bobby scoffed, eyeing her again. "*Thirteen?* No way, I call bullshit. You've gotta be at least fifteen, right? Don'tcha gotta be fourteen to even be in high school?"

"Don't turn fourteen until next month." Tabitha shrugged, stepping past Bobby and walking toward the row of cooler doors that took up the far wall.

Thirteen? No way. She's gotta be messin' with me... right? Bobby couldn't help but stare.

The redhead girl was on the smaller side and had a pretty slight figure, sure, but *thirteen?* That didn't fit with his perception of her at all, the way she carried herself, how collected she seemed to be and how mature she acted with things. She had to be *at least* fifteen, she definitely *seemed* like a fifteen-year-old. Maybe even older. Sixteen? Maybe not sixteen. Bobby watched as Tabitha didn't pause to browse the drink selection, instead immediately grabbing a carton of milk to bring up to the register.

"Uhh." Tabitha looked around. "Where's whoever works here?"

"'EY, JOE-BRO!" Bobby cupped his hands and shouted back behind the counter. "YOU GOTTA CUSTOMER, HERE!"

His brother Joseph ducked out from the back room with a look of consternation, holding a cordless phone's handset against his chest.

"Sorry 'bout that, I'm on the phone with a... customer," Joe lied, quickly bringing the phone up to his ear. "Hey, babe, gotta put you on hold. Yeah, just a sec."

Bobby and Tabitha exchanged a glance at Joe's half-hearted charade.

"*Ahem.* Will this be everything for you today?" Joe asked in his mild-mannered *customer service* voice. He tilted the quart-sized milk carton up so that the scanner could read it with an electronic beep.

Tabitha silently nodded.

"Uhh, hey, sorry if askin' that was weird," Bobby apologized. "Just, everyone at school's always talkin' about you, it's all crazy out there, stories and you don't know to believe, right? I'd much rather just, like, get to know you for real and hear what's up straight from the source, you know? No pressure or anything."

Joe shot his brother a subtle *yo, who's this chick* glance over the counter as he accepted the five-dollar bill from Tabitha and punched the sale into the register.

"They can't..." Tabitha cleared her throat and then let out an uneasy laugh. "They can't still be talking about me, right?"

"Oh, yeah—all the time." Bobby nodded. "I mean, from what I heard, Erica just 'bout knocked your head off, y'know? But nobody really knows *why,* an' that's like, a step or two up from the usual petty bitch stuff, you know?"

Current popular theory on Tabitha Moore was that she'd dropped out because she was pregnant, and that the whole bullying thing was just some flimsy excuse to bail out on school before she started showing. Tabitha stealing a boyfriend and getting knocked up was the only reason anyone could imagine Erica Taylor would go so far as to try to *murder* her—but it was also a point of contention as to whether Erica had even actually been dating anyone. The sophomore girl hadn't been *official* with anyone, or ever really hinted that she might be seeing someone. Assumed availability and showing that extra inch or two of cleavage was part of the leverage Erica Taylor had over the tenth-grade guys, so who would she give that up for? *Matthew Williams?* Some persisted in thinking that, because of his appearance in some of the other rumors, but none of the sophomores Bobby had talked to bought into it.

Nah, no way, Bobby's friend Liam had outright refused to believe it. *Can't tell you who... but Matthew's definitely already seeing this girl, and it's absolutely, one hundred percent not Erica Taylor. Matthew and Erica knew each other, yeah, but there was nothing between them, no spark or anything. No way.*

Bobby wasn't really sure what to think—from everything he'd personally witnessed about the girl in the classes they shared, Tabitha wasn't traditionally social. She hung out with that skinny black girl during lunches, and she was briefly seen interacting with Elena Seelbaugh, before Elena suddenly turned wiccan or lesbo or whatever. *That* was weird, and the introduction of occult nonsense to the gossip surrounding Tabitha had made all the stories floating around pretty wild for a while. Fueling things even more was that whenever a rumor went a little bit too far, or whenever someone had actually tried to mess with Tabitha, like Chris, Kaylee, and Clarissa—they were suspended or expelled. That meant she was actually a *somebody,* that she had important parents or came from a bigshot family or something, which totally torpedoed all those tall tales saying she lived in the trailer park back behind this Minit Mart.

"It... um. It had to do with Erica and Brittney's little sister, Ashlee," Tabitha explained. "Ashlee Taylor and I used to be friends. I stopped going over there to play when one of the sisters pushed me off their trampoline and gave me a concussion, this past summer. Ashlee started hiding her older sister's things—to get back at them for them being, uh, mean to her—and then blaming me for it, as though I were still going over there and just stealing things. When the bullying at school with me escalated, something I said about their situation to one of the school board women apparently prompted them to step in and separate Ashlee from her sisters. Which in turn seemed to further provoke Erica, and... she lashed out at me."

"Oh, wow." Bobby blinked, not having expected her to actually tell him a whole story. "Does—"

"That's the general synopsis of what happened, *from my point of view,* but I'd love to compare it to all the rumors and examine the differences," Tabitha continued, staring at Bobby with a somewhat blank expression. "I want to call it a *comedy of errors,* because that's one of my favorite expressions, but I'm not sure that it actually fits. I think just implying there's a certain dark humor to everything going wrong makes it easier to accept—and life often just feels like this long, continuous crashing chain of things going wrong. Doesn't it?"

"Uhhh—" Bobby began.

"Maybe I *should* start dating?" Tabitha seemed to be looking through him off into the distance and talking to herself now. "I'm, I'm really losing my grip on reality, and I *need* someone to talk to. But I live in constant fear of actually speaking out, of over-whelming those few I'm close to and pushing them away. Maybe what I really need is someone who will listen to me, but doesn't particularly care what I have to say. Is that what having a boyfriend is like? Or, would assuming that be the *real* comedy of errors?"

This time, Bobby opened his mouth but had no idea how to reply to that.

"Sorry," Tabitha seemed to snap back to the present, and she gave him a sad smile. "That was a strange thing to ask?"

"Hell, uhh, I don't mind at all." Bobby mentally set aside her unexpected long discourse to reexamine later and gave her a reas-suring smile. "It really is kinda like that, right? Like I dunno 'xactly what all you just said, but hell—I do like the way you say it."

"Right," Tabitha gave him a bitter smile as she accepted her change from Joe. "It was nice seeing you again, Bobby."

"Would you like a bag for that, ma'am?" Joe offered in his obsequious *customer service voice.*

"Nah, I'm just down the hill there," Tabitha said, pausing for a moment to give the handset phone Joe was still clutching against his chest a look. "I wouldn't dare to trouble you further—do instead extend your every courtesy to the *other* customer you're servicing."

Wait, what? Bobby froze, shooting his brother an incredulous look.

Their overly posh *customer service voice* had become an in-joke between the two brothers—Bobby himself worked part time at the Springton McDonald's.

Ma'am, could I tempt you into adding a side dish of Springton's finest french fries to the main course of your meal? No? Are you certain?! I assure you, these french fries are a Parisian delicacy direct from France! To this day, the closest any of the other teens in town came to appreciating the Anderson brothers' rather nuanced sense of humor was an occasional sarcastic *why thank you, good sir,* from Kimmie and her friend Caitlyn. Where had this Tabitha girl pulled a genuinely good line like that from?

Did Tabitha have a sense of humor?

In class, she hadn't, but then again, she'd been pretty careful during school hours—and with good reason; glares from the freshman and sophomore girls alike made it clear everyone was eager for her to slip up and say something, anything, that could be twisted around and used against her. Did she have some similar in-jokes with her friends, and was that there just some brilliant coincidence where two private jokes from different parties met in a great way? He intended to catch up with Tabitha and get a few more words in, but by the time he realized it, she was already headed out the door.

The electronic door chime sounded, and Bobby watched the attractive redhead walk on past the Minit Mart's glass windows and disappear from sight. Girls at fourteen and fifteen around Springton with an actual decent sense of humor were *rare.* Although many of them laughed all the time, it usually wasn't at anything funny. It was just self-aggrandizing noise, *social lubricant,* as his Grand Nan put it. Keeping up the appearance of their little clique being so great and having so much fun, despising and alienating anyone who didn't laugh along. It was currently one of the reasons he propped up as to why he hadn't had a real girlfriend yet. The thing with Tracy didn't count. That was way back in seventh grade, and they didn't even kiss.

"Hey, was that that Tabitha chick?" Joe asked, pausing for a moment in the door to the back. "Freshman dropout chick everyone's always in a tizzy about? One that got pregnant or whatever? Drama queen chick?"

Bobby had seen quiet, guarded Tabitha keeping to herself at school, he'd seen her being hurt and vulnerable, sobbing quietly into her good hand, and now he'd seen her tired, rambling, and cracking jokes. At first, back then, he'd spoken up to defend her because—well, she was cute. He kept doing it simply because he was a born contrarian; he liked stirring up trouble and ruffling everyone's feathers. He'd been there the day after some sophomore jock pushed her and got her wrist broken, he'd snuck glances over when the beauty had set her head down at her desk and fallen asleep. Bobby *hadn't* actually seen whichever stuffy bitch nicked Tabitha's folder or whatever, but he'd been able to tell from all the hushed whispers and self-satisfied smug looks that they'd done *something*.

When Mr. Stern'd asked Bobby to walk her up to the office—as class clown of sorts, Bobby was often one of the first students teachers remembered by name and subsequently one of the most frequently called upon—of course he'd jumped at the chance. Tabitha had managed to hold back her tears just about until she got out the door. He'd been thrilled, but also a little ruffled— watching a girl cry, up close? It did things to him, it stirred up natural protective instincts, had him feeling confused and contemplative and brooding about it the whole rest of the day. High school drama was something you only enjoyed fucking around with when you didn't have a personal stake in what was going on, after all.

DO I want a stake in it? He'd always been pretty interested, but did he actually *like* Tabitha? Before it was something he'd wondered about, but now it was something he was more and more sure about.

"Naw," Bobby decided, throwing a thoughtful glance back out the storefront. "Forget all that bull-hickey you heard 'bout Tabitha. That's my future wife, right there."

"Uh-huh." Joe gave him an evaluating look and then a solemn nod of understanding and acceptance passed from brother to brother. "Yeah—in your dreams, *dick muncher*. Don't let any more damn customers in, I'm on the phone."

I talked to a boy? Tabitha trudged back down the hill with a small smile. *Sorta?*

It was a very strange feeling. She didn't *like* Bobby—he was just that redneck kid from class. She didn't *like* anyone, really. There were a few freshman boys she'd noticed who were cute or handsome in their own way, but she didn't have a crush on any of them. In her first life, she'd harbored a small hopeless crush on one of her classmates toward the end of high school. To her embarrassment, after forty some years, she didn't even remember his name, now. Maybe it would come to her, if she ever recognized him again. In any case, since being reintroduced to the wilderness of horrors that was 1998, she'd been reeling from her various traumas and identity problems disassociating from things too much to form something like a crush on anyone.

Still, though. Tabitha felt torn between giddiness and weary resignation. *It was cool. Fun. I'm—I don't know. It's a teenage girl thing. Not my fault! Maybe I just get some automatic rush of endorphins or something by talking with a boy. It's so strangely ENGAGING just talking with a boy, getting into conversation, even if it's... well, it was really just me babbling like an idiot, wasn't it? Shit. I don't even remember what I said.*

Boys, and the almost forgotten prospect of dating. She hated that she *didn't* hate it, and despite purposely schooling her expression back into neutrality, the smile crept back in. Being asked about boys by Mrs. Williams or Aunt Lisa was endlessly vexing, so it was with great consternation that Tabitha found herself forced to concede to herself that yes, talking to boys was pretty interesting. Part of the *high school fantasy* she'd clung to over the summer while working herself to the bone was that she'd be loved and accepted by everyone if only she was thin and pretty. The boys would be polite and aim to court her, the girls would all want to be her friend.

Ugh, the sheer fucking naivete. Tabitha's grimace stifled her giddy smile by a notch or two. *The inexperience and sad, deluded wishful thinking that things were as simple and easy as that. The fat unpopular girl just assuming life was easy and convenient if only you were thin and pretty. I don't know that it's WORSE, but it's definitely an entire new spectrum of bad to adjust yourself to, and I wasn't ready.*

The reality of the situation turned out to be more complicated, with other high school girls at best polite and distant, and at their worst openly hostile to her without reason. As for the boys, Tabitha had fended off a few atrocious come-ons, and then been ignored by most of them. At this age, most seemed to be watching and waiting, still—not many throughout the ninth grade were dating or ready to date yet, and the few pairings that did happen were well known and often discussed.

According to Elena, dating was more common throughout the sophomore year, and then if you weren't in or between relationships by your junior or senior year, there was something wrong with you. *That* thought rankled, the thought that peer pressure had an effect on her stung, and she realized that now the idea of being completely unfettered by social mores was—

Fuck! No no no, stop stop stop. Tabitha grimaced. *Rein it in, c'mon, Tabitha. This isn't the time to get distracted by BOYS, or DATING, of all things. It's not gonna happen anyways—probably never will. There's a whole Aunt Lisa situation to deal with, and these damned hormones just have my thoughts careening out of control in every direction but where they should be. Focus, FOCUS.*

"Bobby's not even that good-looking!" Tabitha rationalized to herself. "Just okayish-looking. Maybe kinda charming when he smiles. Charming, but not TOO charming. Right? He's... okay; at best, he's like a scrawnier Heath Ledger. A super young Heath Ledger, but with his hair cut real short."

Her attention remained in deficit for the rest of the walk back down the hill. Before she really remembered that his name was Bobby, he was just that redneck kid from class—why wasn't THAT bothering her? Everything trashy and redneck about Aunt Lisa got under her skin in a big way, but with Bobby, it didn't seem to trouble her. Was some sort of distorted Electra complex providing attraction based on the superficial similarities between Bobby and her father? While that same perceived 'redneck' social standing made her more and more hostile to Aunt Lisa? Did that even make sense?

...*Maybe?* Tabitha felt surprisingly glum about it. *I was completely at odds with Mom back when she was trying to be the trailer trash queen despot of our mobile home. Wasn't until she tried reconnecting with her roots as a would-be-actress and acting less like trailer trash that she actually started reaching me. Shit. Fuck. Definitely maybe something like an Electra complex. Do I need to start reading up on Carl Jung, so that I don't wind up letting this grow into some sort of neurosis down the line? I've got enough of those already as it is. Would a therapist help?*

It was a troubling distraction, and when she got back home and stepped inside, it felt like her thoughts were still pinballing back and forth throughout her head.

"Oven's still preheating," Mrs. Moore fretted. "How much milk did you get?"

"Just a quart." Tabitha placed it on the counter with the arrangement they'd prepared for scalloped potatoes. "Here, your change."

"Don't mind that. You just hang on to it for if you ever need some spendin' money."

"'Kay," Tabitha sighed.

"Are you alright?" Mrs. Moore paused.

"I'm... I'm tryin'," Tabitha promised, giving her mother a weak smile. "C'mon, let's do this."

———

She instructed her mother in how to whisk the milk in with butter and flour to make a cream sauce, trading occasional quiet banter back and forth with Mrs. Moore, who was always uncomfortable following a recipe that didn't provide exact measurements. They peeled potatoes together in silence as *One Life to Live* out in the living room gave way to *General Hospital,* and then the spuds were washed and sliced and carefully arranged in their glass dish beneath a healthy layer of cheese. The dish went into the oven, where it would remain until shortly before they left to have Thanksgiving with Grandma Laurie and the boys.

Hmm. With this much cheese, these might be more potatoes au gratin than scalloped potatoes, but—so sue me. They're gonna be delicious, that's all that matters.

Aunt Lisa remained quiet the entire afternoon, lapsing in and out of consciousness as the TV played away in front of her. Some small respite from dealing with the woman's grating voice suited Tabitha just fine, and after very carefully scrubbing the instant coffee dregs out of her nice tea set with her mother's help, she carried them one by one into her room to hide the pieces away. When the last teacup was turned upside-down and placed on a small towel on her dresser, Tabitha's eyes continued to wander.

A pair of the golden-foil wrapped Reese's peanut butter cups were paperweights upon her school withdrawal papers, and the homeschooling information printouts Mrs. Cribb had sent them. The rest of that small mountain of Reese's from the Halloween haul was hidden in the freezer, where the chocolate wouldn't tempt them with its seductive wiles. She'd kept a few get-well cards and had them propped up, but the Ariel costume had been folded and put away.

Otherwise, her tiny bedroom was still as sparsely decorated as it had been back during Halloween, when the girls had had that sleepover. Tabitha's spartan bedroom seemed to reflect the limbo of her state of being, because it wasn't the place of a budding young girl, cluttered with her hopes and dreams for the future, and it also wasn't the living space of an old woman, full of fond memories and knick-knacks from days gone by. It was some empty in between, without any indication of what direction her life was going in.

I'm happiest when I can just be a normal boring teenage daughter, Tabitha thought, glancing around her room with a listless expression. *When things can just be simple and I can just have the loving family I always wanted. When I can just be the person I always wished I could have been. SHOULD have been. Or work my way toward that, at least.*

Tabitha's identity problems were beginning to reach a sense of actual crisis.

Thirteen was *supposed* to be a time of metamorphosis, but everything for her was completely backwards, a baffling psychological reversal of concepts. Her future adulthood was in the past now, and the childhood she revisited was nothing like she remembered—it was almost all treading entirely new ground. Even despite her mind weathering through all of this reasonably well enough, Tabitha felt she was sometimes *emotionally* regressing in a serious way. All the intelligence in the world wouldn't help her if the way she *felt* about things completely overwhelmed every rational decision she might make.

That, and also... I'm completely off-balance again here because Lisa showed up out of nowhere. Blindsided me. Despite how I'm supposed to know basically what events happen, and generally when. Or, at least know things in a vague way. Unwelcome BUTTERFLY EFFECT surprises that aren't part of my future knowledge at this point start to make me feel real... extremely vulnerable. On edge. Especially after— yeah, after all the nice 'surprises' so far. I'm less and less okay with these kind of surprises each time, BECAUSE IT ALWAYS SUCKS, and, naturally, it's going to happen more and more often, because of the little ripple effect changes spreading outward and changing everything.

Pretty soon, there won't be ANY comfort to be had from future knowledge, and... who even am I at THAT point? I'm not from the future anymore, then. I'm just a crazy person, with almost completely irrelevant knowledge from some... hypothetical divergent timeline that no longer has any bearing on the one we're in here and now. I'm just an actual fucking thirteen-year-old again, but with added crazy. Basically —bottom line—I'm crazy. I'm crazy. GREAT.

Physically, she wasn't faring much better than she was mentally. Her body had still been undergoing puberty when it was suddenly subjected to the extreme flux of weight loss and the repeated shocks to her system—head trauma from being pushed off a trampoline in the first place, the wrist fracture from being shoved off the curb at school, then renewed head trauma from being attacked at the Halloween party more recently. Not for the first time, she wondered if all of her future knowledge maybe really WAS some sort of hyperactive hallucination brought on by some tissue or nerve damage to her brain.

Tabitha turned her head in the mirror so that she could see her stitches. They looked fine, they hadn't been inflamed or irritated or swollen or anything, and the shaved patch there on the side was beginning to grow back in as a downy soft fuzz of red hair. She was still very, very pale.

What a grand delusion this would all be... but once you start doubting, it never really stops, does it?

37
THANKSGIVING WITH FAMILY

A lifetime ago

"Happy Thanksgiving, honey." Grandma Laurie welcomed Tabitha into the apartment with a weary smile.

"Happy Thanksgiving," Mr. Moore greeted, giving his chubby daughter a nudge to prompt her to do the same. "Say Happy Thanksgiving, Tabitha."

"Happy Thanksgiving," Tabitha croaked, fidgeting in the doorway.

"No Shannon this year either?" Grandma Laurie asked, beckoning them inside.

"She's not feelin' too great about leavin' the house right now," Mr. Moore explained with an awkward expression as he shuffled Tabitha inside. "She does wish she could be here with us."

"Well, I hope she feels better." Grandma Laurie gave him a knowing look and patted him on the shoulder. "We'll put together a big dish of leftovers for you to take over, how's that sound?"

"Sounds great," Mr. Moore said. "Love you, Mom."

"Tabby honey—your cousins are all in the bedroom playing

their video game," Grandma Laurie said. "I'm sure you remember all the boys."

"Uh-huh," Tabitha said with reluctance.

Her grandmother's apartment reeked of the unfamiliar—it was too nice. The furnishings were simple but tasteful with curio cabinets, an overstuffed sofa, a modest television set, and old lamps that lit the room with warm light. In contrast to the décor, there was a pile of grubby-looking boys' backpacks in a small heap by the door, worn plastic action figures were strewn about the periphery—Ninja Turtles, a Megazord missing an arm, a Batman sans his cape, a half dozen small Happy Meal Transformers toys that seemed to turn into fries and ice cream cones and sandwiches.

Both extremes made Tabitha uncomfortable. The toys were violent *boys' things* with swords and guns and whatnot. The taste-fully-appointed *Grandma* aspects of the room were an enormous leap from what home was like and that put her on edge even worse.

Do I havta take off my shoes? Can I just sit on the couch and watch TV by myself? Tabitha couldn't help but hunch her shoulders a bit as she glanced around. *I don't want to play with my cousins. Why can't I just stay at home like Momma does? It's not fair that she doesn't havta come for stupid Thanksgiving.*

"They're right on in there, playing their games." Grandma gestured in amusement, apparently of the mind that Tabby would just love to hang out with other kids. "Go on and say hi."

"Okay," Tabitha said with a blank face, mechanically stumbling down the indicated hall.

The hallway was lined with framed photos, mostly of Dad and his brother Uncle Danny when they were younger. There were several pictures of the cousins when they were toddlers, there was an embarrassing blown-up yearbook photo of a pudgy Tabitha attempting a dour smile from last year at Laurel Middle School—and as if to taunt her gross inadequacy, for some reason, there was an astounding beautiful red-haired young woman with a gorgeous smile in the picture frame just above her.

She gave that one a lingering look, wondering just like when she had visited last year who that one was and which side of the family she was on. Maybe one of her mother's relatives? She looked familiar in a weird, difficult-to-place way. Momma didn't talk about her family. It was a bad subject to bring up, and this was probably why—her momma probably felt just as rotten seeing this girl as Tabby did.

Her four cousins were all gathered around the bed in Grandma's room playing a Nintendo 64, and none of them looked up when she came in. The TV screen was split into four different views, each one displaying a hand with a gun in it and dizzying blurs of walls and corridors and stairways and doors as each boy apparently controlled a different character to race around some weird-looking complex in search of something. A blocky polygon person appeared on one of the screens—no, the figures of two different sprinting people with guns appeared, one on each of the diagonal divisions of TV screen, and suddenly the multiplayer game erupted into a cacophony of wild gunfire that made Tabitha want to flinch back.

"Hah! Gotcha, gotcha, gotcha, gotcha!"

"No you—damn, stop, stop—"

"He's cheating, Aiden's screenwatching—"

"Gotcha! Hah-hah, you're dead, *you're dead,* you're—"

"I'm not even *looking* at your stupid—"

"Well, now I'm gonna kill you, though."

"Nuh-uh, you're not."

"I know where you are and your health's like, all gone."

"Ohhh crap. Oh crap, oh crap, oh crap—"

"Hi," Tabitha interrupted with a half-hearted wave.

"It's Tabby." One of the boys—she knew all their names but didn't know who was who—gave her a brief glance before turning back to the game.

"We're playing *Goldeneye*," the youngest one proclaimed. "Do you wanna play?"

"She can't play. There's only four controllers."

"Yeah, stupid. Are you gonna quit so she can play?"

"No, you are."

"Pfft, yeah right. You are."

"Nuh-uh. I have first controller, so I'm first. Nick has fourth controller, so he's last—he should quit."

"*I'm* not gonna quit."

"Whoever dies next has to quit."

"Oh crap *oh crap, wait, oh crap, oh crap—*"

"It's alright." Tabitha frowned. "I don't play... *Goldeneye*."

"Good, 'cause we're already playing."

"Yeah, we're already playing and there's only four controllers anyways."

"We should play *Facility* next."

"No way, *Facility*'s dumb. We should do *Bunker* again next, but with proximity mines."

"*Bunker*'s dumb."

"How can you say *Bunker*'s dumb? You're dumb."

"*Proximity mines* are dumb. They're basically cheating."

"Yeah, you only want proximity mines because you suck at playing!"

"Well, you're just mad because you suck at proximity mines."

"You can't suck at proximity mines. All they do is just blow up."

"Yeah, when you play proximity mines, it's like the proximity mines do all the work."

Having been immediately forgotten about, Tabitha was more than content to fade into the background and be invisible to them. She remained quiet and found an uneasy perch on the far edge of the bed so she could watch. This *Goldeneye* seemed to consist entirely of them just murdering each other over and over again with guns. The screens were tiny, they lit up with olive wreaths of red and blue squares for some reason whenever they were about to die, and trying to keep up with what was going on when everyone was running around so fast felt like it was just going to give her a headache.

Video games, in her mind, were for rich kids—she was interested and curious, but the whole experience was also intimidating and complex and she didn't imagine her parents would ever buy her anything like that. Glancing at the oversized controllers perplexed her even more, because each of the smooth plastic contraptions in her cousins' hands had three handles, a joystick, and an incomprehensible array of different-colored buttons in strange groupings. Tabitha *did* want to try playing a Nintendo 64 sometime, but not here, and not like this. She wanted to play something that looked actually fun, like from the *Banjo Kazooie* commercials that played on TV, or to get into that Pokémon thing that she overheard everyone else at school always talking about.

Tabitha watched on with a bored expression as the younger boys continue to violently murder each other in the game for the better part of an hour. She didn't have to speak up or try to get to know them, so that was nice at least. She was free to sit back by herself with no one paying attention to her and daydream of someday having her own friends to play cool-looking Nintendo 64 games with. After all, someday—someday she'd have a bunch of her own friends to have fun with, and it'd be amazing.

Somewhere in her bitter thirteen-year-old heart, she already knew it was never ever going to happen.

"*Booooys!*" Grandma Laurie yelled over from the kitchen. It sounded as though she was very used to having to holler. "Tabby, boys—turn that thing off and c'mon out, Thanksgiving supper's ready."

Mismatched chairs had been requisitioned and set up for the additional two guests and everyone took places at the table, with Tabitha sitting next to her dad while the boys all clambered haphazardly into their seats. They didn't have much in the way of manners, with two of the cousins rising up to sit on their knees so they could put their hands on the table and peer across the 'lavish' spread of food.

Thanksgiving dinner was baked beans with hot dogs mixed in, as well as instant mashed potatoes, coleslaw, and stuffing. Tabby remembered the year before there had been a big turkey they baked in the oven, but it apparently wasn't worth the effort with Uncle Danny and Aunt Lisa gone to... well, wherever they were. The boys were picky eaters and wouldn't eat turkey, it came right from a roasted dead bird and that was weird. Much like Tabitha, they were raised on processed meats like bologna slices and ninety-nine-cent hot dog packs—actual turkey was too bizarre. Grandma Laurie had done her best to make an occasion of it, but still nothing looked all that appetizing to Tabby.

"I was gonna buy a big ham and carve it up, but..." Grandma Laurie sighed and gave her son an apologetic look. "I figured the boys might not eat it, and I might as well save the extra money for their Christmas instead."

"Everything looks great, Mom," Mr. Moore promised her. "There's more here than we can eat anyways, we've gotta be thankful. Tabby, boys—doesn't everything look great?"

"What's *that?*" One of the boys stabbed a finger at one of the dishes. "It smells gross."

"That's coleslaw; we had it here last year," Grandma Laurie reminded the boy. "You won't eat it—we have beans and hot dogs for you boys."

"Beans, beans, the magical fruit," one of the other boys sang, "the more you eat, the more you toot!"

"Samuel, enough," Grandma Laurie warned. "Sit properly at the table. Do you wanna say grace?"

"No way." The boy made a face. "Nick can say grace."

"I'm not saying grace!"

"Yub-a-dub-dub, thanks for the grub!" the singing boy chimed in again.

"Hey now, we have company." Grandma Laurie sighed. "Behave yourselves."

"Boys, sit," Mr. Moore commanded in a stern voice. "Mom, I'll say grace."

Tabitha obediently bowed her head and clasped her doughy hands together over the swell of her protruding stomach. It was a constant reminder of how fat she felt, especially when they were about to tuck into a big meal like this. Other girls seemed to simply be skinny and it was natural and effortless for them, and the frustration of that made Tabitha just want to shrink back into herself and disappear like always.

"Dear heavenly Father, we thank you for this meal you've given us. We thank you for looking over us—for watching over these boys, for looking after my daughter. We thank you for all of your blessings, and we're thankful that we're able to sit and eat together as a family. *Amen.*"

———

Now

Tabitha sat sandwiched between her mother and father on the bench seat of his truck, staring down at the cast she held on her lap. She was nothing like that Tabitha of old—she was slender enough now that she appeared frail, but she carried herself with confidence and poise. Mrs. Moore was joining them this time, not only having likewise lost weight, but having overcome the crippling agoraphobia that kept her from ever leaving the mobile home last lifetime.

Aunt Lisa was riding along with them, lounging back there behind in the open air bed of the truck with one bony elbow propped up on the side. The sheer amount of differences between this Thanksgiving and what she remembered from her previous life completely overwhelmed whatever scant few similarities remained. So much had changed that there was little point in ruminating over it anymore—there was no meaning to be gleaned from examining subtle changes. There were no *subtle* changes. *Everything* had changed, in drastic ways, from the cast of actors present to their relationships to the present narrative. It wasn't even November twenty-fifth today. They were having their Moore family Thanksgiving a day early, so that the Moores could join the MacIntires on actual Thanksgiving.

"Boys're sure in for a surprise," Mr. Moore remarked. "Seein' their momma again for Thanksgiving."

"Uh-huh." Tabitha stared forward out the windshield, doing her best not to show any emotions.

To her father's apparent dismay, silence once again pervaded the cab of the truck. Whenever Lisa got brought up, Mrs. Moore sealed her lips and held her peace, either because she had nothing to say about the matter or perhaps in show of solidarity with Tabitha's obvious and ever-growing animosity for the woman. Shannon Moore had never had much of a rapport with any of Alan's side of the family, and it was only in recent months that she'd even started to be on better terms with Grandma Laurie.

Tabitha hadn't known any of them well in her first life. Though circumstances here in this one had at first pushed Tabitha toward her grandma—only for help squeezing out from beneath her mother's obstinate thumb—by this point, Tabitha had bridged strong familial connections between both of them. Her mother and father, her grandma, the four cousins—these were all her family now. Uncle Danny and her Aunt Lisa were *not* family. As far as she was concerned, the lines had been drawn, and they just grew more and more solid every time Aunt Lisa opened her mouth and something ignorant popped out.

"*Heeeey booooys!*" Aunt Lisa yelled out the moment Mr. Moore made the final turn through the development and Grandma Laurie's was in sight. The boys were out playing in the yard as usual, and each one of the cousins appeared stunned as Aunt Lisa rose up into a half-standing position in the bed of the moving vehicle so that she could let out a loud wolf whistle.

"*MOM!*" Aiden squealed, breaking into a teary-eyed sprint across Grandma Laurie's front yard toward the truck.

Mr. Moore slowed as the boy ran in front of the truck, and the chassis rocked as Aunt Lisa hopped out of the back, waving proudly with both arms like this was the parade for a returning hero. Aiden ran into his mother with such force that he nearly bowled the woman off her feet, while Tabitha watched on in mounting frustration. *I should have—I don't know what I should have done. Prevented them from meeting again, somehow. Some way.*

"Awww, Aidey Baby!" Lisa crooned, splaying her long false nails and patting the boy's back with her palms so as not to break her acrylics. "Aidey Baby—did you miss yer Momma?!"

Of course he missed his fucking mother, you stupid TWAT, Tabitha seethed as she followed her mother out of the truck and stepped to the curb. *'Mother' is the name for God in the hearts of little children. You're their mom—at that age, you're, you're EVERYTHING to them! And you fucking left!*

How could she prove to her parents that Aunt Lisa was getting into heroin, and that she had only returned for the money? She felt sure that Aunt Lisa had drugs in her purse, and that that was why she was guarding it so closely. Who would believe her if Tabitha claimed to know there was heroin in that purse, though? She still hadn't been into Aunt Lisa's purse—there'd been no opportunity. Aunt Lisa didn't let it out of her sight for a moment. There might not even *be* drugs in the purse, for all she knew Aunt Lisa could just be paranoid about letting anyone near the last of her stash of saved money or something.

Even if I pull a bunch of needles out of her purse and wave them around—how can I prove it's heroin, and not insulin or something? Tabitha gritted her teeth and shifted her weight from foot to foot and then turned and took several steps back and forth to bleed off her restless annoyance. *It'd be my word against hers.*

Me, the emotional teen. Accusing her of being a drug addict out of nowhere, for no discernable reason to them. When they already feel I'm at odds with her. Lisa's slippery, and probably already has alibis and excuses and whatever reasoning thought up for being called out.

Watching Aiden bury his face against that awful woman, and seeing her carefully sink her talons back into him made Tabitha *furious.* Was that a cold, calculative glint in Lisa's wretched eyes, or was it just her imagination getting the best of her? Tabitha had half a mind to stomp over there and separate them, to make some dramatic display of pointed accusation, to *confront* this terrible truth that everyone else must be willingly blinding themselves to.

There were too many gut-wrenching feelings to deal with right now, and more than anything, Tabitha just wanted out, wanted to immediately leave and go back home. She knew it wasn't fair of her to feel betrayed by how her cousins gathered around Aunt Lisa with wet eyes, but Tabitha felt betrayed anyway. She refused to believe she was jealous, she was *not* jealous, but anger at Lisa and sympathy for the boy's terribly misplaced love for their mother wrestled with one another within her, and she didn't stand to benefit from either of them winning out.

"Mom—*Mom.*" Joshua vied for his mother's attention.

"*Mom*—where did you go?!" The hurt in Samuel's eyes seemed to devastate only Tabitha, because everyone else was smiling as if they were touched by the happy reunion.

"Moooommy!" Aiden wailed, refusing to let go of the woman.

It's just me—of course it's just me. Tabitha gritted her teeth. *I'm the only one poisoned by future knowledge. Knowing that she didn't come back for THEM, that she's just, just this filthy fucking parasite scurrying back at the scent of money. I wish I didn't know. I wish I DIDN'T know. Fuck. I need to—I need to calm down. Calm down. Calm down.*

"Well," Mr. Moore let out an uneasy chuckle, looking up past the tearful reunion in the front yard to where Grandma Laurie was stepping out onto the porch. "Surprise?"

"Happy Thanksgiving." Grandma Laurie gave the family a strained smile. "Shannon, it's good to see you. Tabby honey—I'm glad you could make it."

"Happy Thanksgiving, Grandma," Tabitha forced out, trying—and failing—to put on a smile.

"Happy Thanksgiving," Shannon called, pointedly glancing past the scene Lisa was making from her mother-in-law to her daughter and back again as if to ignore some unspoken unpleasant truth.

"Well, o'course it is!" Lisa snorted. "*Momma's back,* aren't ch'all thankful?! We're gon' havta break out the beer an' celebrate Thanksgiving proper this year, you hear me?"

All at once, Tabitha felt like she was completely done with the entire do-over. She was sick and tired of having future knowledge—she just wanted the ignorance and naivety of a thirteen, almost fourteen-year-old girl again. That time in her first life having Thanksgiving with Grandma Laurie and the boys, hadn't that been pretty okay? Had all this baggage from the future *really* made her any happier?

The future sucks. It sucks! It's completely shitty and awful and depressing and I'm, I'm sick of having it just hang over my head! Tabitha scowled, feeling that familiar swelling surge of emotion get the better of her once again.

Sick of having it LOOM over me with inevitability. Everything I want to change for the better seems to just take HERCULEAN effort, shifting any stone of obstruction in the path of my past reveals some serpent sleeping beneath I never knew about. There's so many frustrating things I CAN'T change—and I'm just hurting and exhausted, all of the fucking time. All of the fucking time!

———

Lisa... you're dressed like a street walker, for crying out loud! Laurie's rigid smile felt more strained than ever. *It's Thanksgiving. Is that how you want your kids to see you?*

Laurie sighed, deciding to rest her old bones on the steps while her grandchildren swarmed their mother with tears. She couldn't say she was thrilled to see Lisa. She'd honestly *never* been thrilled to see Lisa. Both her sons seemed to turn soft in the head when confronted with a pretty face, Alan completely enamored by their small town starlet-to-be Shannon, and Daniel falling head-over-heels for—well, Lisa was a harlot. To Laurie's constant consternation, Lisa got pregnant with the first of the boys while still in her teens, and then the girl just kept on getting knocked up, over and over again. Neither Lisa nor Daniel seemed to have the slightest restraint. Neither ever felt inclined to stop and consider the consequences—that each of these children would need raised up and taken care of.

The sour looks Tabitha and Shannon were wearing told her with certainty that Lisa sure wasn't going to be staying with them, and that meant Laurie had yet another mouth to feed. As upsetting for the boys as it had been when Lisa took off without a word and disappeared on them... Laurie couldn't deny that it had been for the best. The woman wasn't *a proper mother,* and often it felt like every cross moment she had with the boys led right back to the same problem—their upbringing with Lisa.

While the four boys had been with Lisa, the woman had made no efforts to keep them out of trouble or teach them right from wrong. She barely paid any attention to them at all, because at her core, Lisa seemed a self-centered woman and everything had to revolve around her. The only times Lisa scolded them at all were when the boys did something that would inconvenience her. Back when Aiden had scraped his knee bloody and was bawling his little heart out, Laurie remembered that Lisa had been *annoyed* rather than concerned.

"*What the fuck were y'all doin'?!* Lisa had snapped. *Sammie—*

why's yer brother bleedin'? Huh? Why aren't you watchin' out for yer brother?!"

———

"Everything looks nice," Tabitha remarked upon surveying her grandmother's apartment.

"Aw, thank you, dear." Grandma Laurie gave her a wry smile and patted the girl's shoulder as if Tabitha was simply being polite.

It really *did* look nice to Tabitha, but with memories of her past life some forty years distant, it was hard to put her finger on exactly what had changed. The atmosphere was very different— Grandma Laurie seemed less frazzled than Tabitha remembered, the four boys seemed a tiny bit better behaved. Or maybe it was just personal bias influencing how she perceived them now that she knew them better?

The apartment was small but cozy, and had been tidied up prior to their arrival for early Thanksgiving, with four children's backpacks hung up next to each other on the pegs of the coat rack. Rather than toys being strewn about the floor everywhere, the carpet was clear and sported the telltale clean lines of having been vacuumed recently. The boys had obviously been put to task with picking up their things, because many of the toys appeared to now be on the bottom shelf of the entertainment center. A fold-out *Bruce Wayne Manor* playset was on one side, and all of their action figures were standing in close formation next to it—power rangers, ninja turtles, and the exaggerated plastic musculature of WWF wrestlers all arranged in display as if waiting for a presidential address from the balcony of the Bat Cave.

"I'm so glad everyone could make it." Grandma Laurie stepped in to accept the glass dish of scalloped potatoes Mrs. Moore had brought. "Oh, this looks lovely, Shannon."

"Tabitha and I made them fresh this afternoon," Mrs. Moore

said. "Well, I mostly just followed her directions; she's still got her arm in that awful cast. Might've baked too long; the cheese turned a little darker than—"

"*It looks lovely,*" Grandma Laurie repeated, "and it smells delicious. Glad I bought that ham now! Don't think baked beans and hot dogs would've been enough for everyone."

"What, we ain't havin' *turkey?*" Aunt Lisa sounded miffed. "Are you for serious? The hell kinda Thanksgivin' is it without turkey?"

"Lisa, you know the boys won't eat turkey," Grandma Laurie reminded her in a soft voice.

"Well, who gives a flying fart what *they* wanna eat?" Aunt Lisa scoffed. "They're *six years old,* they havta eat whatever'n it is we say they do. An' if they don't finish what's on their plate, they can sit there at the table 'til they finish! I ain't raisin' up no picky eaters."

You haven't been RAISING any of them. Tabitha was once again forced to grit her teeth so that she didn't launch into a furious tirade. *None of them are six years old. Sam's almost ELEVEN years old now. Lisa, you're freeloading food, here. You haven't provided anyone ANYTHING. You want turkey, why don't you fucking—*

"Tabitha, boys—why don't you all go on and play your video game in the other room," Grandma Laurie proposed.

From the dirty look the old woman shot Lisa, Tabitha could tell that Grandma Laurie didn't approve of Lisa's assertion or the foul language used in expressing it. Both Mr. and Mrs. Moore looked embarrassed to have brought Lisa here, but also—what else could they have done? This was supposed to be a touching reunion for her and the four boys, but Aunt Lisa was already hopping on the sofa and fishing for the remote control. Samuel, Nicholas, Aiden, and Joshua were milling about beside Tabitha, uncharacteristically quiet and subdued.

"Sure," Tabitha spoke up, fighting to put on a smile for her cousins. "C'mon, guys. Why don't you show me your game?"

The young boys seemed to grasp at someone finally giving

them attention like it was their lifeline, and quickly clamored to tug Tabitha on down the hallway toward Grandma's room where the other TV and their Nintendo 64 was set up. Despite visiting her cousins semi-frequently over the past half-year, Tabitha had yet to sit down and actually watch them play video games. Whenever she came over, she was bringing them to the playground to play. At best, she'd gone in to check and make sure the game console was turned off before they ran outside with her.

Besides enjoying a few random mobile games like *Peggle* back in her college years, Tabitha's only real experience with video games were android ports of Pokémon games, and then later dabbling a bit in 'classic' titles re-released on the Nintendo Magi. Most of that was simply to see what all the fuss was about with the new holographics—once companies were investing upwards of a billion dollars into development, games and gaming supplanted cinema and television as the more common cultural touchstone.

"The only racing game we have is *Ten-Eighty Snowboarding*, so if—"

"*All-star Basketball* or *Goldeneye*. I bet Tabby'd be really good at—"

"We don't have any girl games, but—"

"Tabby's not like a *girly* girl, though," Samuel interjected. "She'd be good at snowboarding."

"No way, we should play wrestling!" Nicholas whined. "*NWO-World Tour* is—"

"What do you want to play?" Joshua asked. "We have four controllers, so—oh, look!"

"Yeah, look," Aiden chimed in. "Gramma put up your picture."

"My picture?" Tabitha asked.

Turning to see the photographs hanging along the hallway wall, Tabitha discovered that beneath the young glamour shot of her mother was a framed picture of herself clipped out from the newspaper—the somewhat fuzzy shot Alicia had somehow managed to take of her running toward Officer MacIntire moments after the shooting. Likewise, Tabitha found another picture beside it of a flushed but skinny-looking Tabitha about to leap down from the playground equipment in the park while two of the boys were fleeing in the foreground with huge grins.

That's me—that's from THIS timeline. For some reason, Tabitha was shocked. *That's the current me. Well, from a few months ago or so maybe, there's no cast. I look... like a pretty cool little brat. When did she even—does Grandma Laurie own a camera?*

No one in this world knew how important the new memories she was making in this life were to Tabitha, but the fact that some of these moments seemed just as important to Grandma Laurie was touching. In her last time through, Tabitha barely even knew this part of her family at all—Grandma Laurie and the cousins only existed at Thanksgiving and Christmas. She hadn't *valued* them; they'd simply been there in the far periphery of her life.

"C'mon, *c'mon.*" Joshua had his arm hooked through her elbow and was trying to pull her back toward the bedroom while his brothers were already turning the game system on back there.

"Coming, sorry," Tabitha murmured with a wistful smile. "Did I hear you say you had a game about snowboarding?"

Unlike last lifetime, and even despite the improbable return of their own mother, Tabitha was the center of their attention. They weren't willing to let her fade quietly into the background sitting on the other side of the bedspread—they sat her down on the edge right in front and pushed a Nintendo 64 controller into her hands as the CRT TV slowly fuzzed to life.

"What the...?" Tabitha turned the plastic controller over in her hands, having a rare moment where she felt completely like an old lady again.

Am I supposed to bop it or twist it? Tabitha joked to herself. *There's three handles here, and I've only got two hands. There's a joystick here where I can't reach it, and buttons and triggers spread all over the place, so how are you supposed to even—*

"You hold it like this," Samuel instructed, correcting her hold on the gray controller. "Ignore this whole side. Except for this button, you need this one."

"Ah, I see," Tabitha nodded in amusement, feeling like a pro gamer already. "When you put it like that—this must be so that left-handed people can use it the other way around?"

"Left-handed people?" Aiden looked confused.

"This way's right, and this way's left," Joshua demonstrated proudly, turning in place to face the other way and pointing the wrong direction each time. "No wait, this way's left, and this way's right. Left is west and right is east. Right?"

"Left-handed people are born using the wrong hand for everything," Samuel explained to his youngest brother. "It's like a disability, or being handicapped sorta. You can get a handicapped parking tag for it when you grow up; one of the kids in my class has it."

Their childish take on everything was refreshing—in the preinternet era, conjecture and misinformation was *situation normal,* and the entire world around them was decorated with tall tales they'd heard from seemingly reliable older kids. Tabitha was still *fish-out-of-water* enough herself that the first association she made with left and right was democrats and republicans—which may as well not even exist to these elementary schoolers—and it helped the last of her anger at their mother drain away.

Their mother, who'd rather sit out there watching Jerry Springer *and* Judge Judy *than spend time with her own kids. Her own children, who she hasn't seen in months and each of them must have a billion things to tell her and show her and go on about. They're growing up fast, and she's missing it—she doesn't even care that she's missing it. All four of them are just DESPERATE for a mother figure, and Grandma Laurie and I can only do so much.*

The boys were louder than ever as they talked over each other attempting to give Tabitha advice as she guided a blocky polygon snowboarder down a snowy half-pipe on the screen. It was fun despite the pixel antialiasing and janky graphics that seemed prehistoric to her, and mostly because of how enthusiastic the boys were to teach her how to play. Samuel was crouched on his knees on the bed behind her, looking over her shoulder and occasionally pointing out which button was which on the controller. Nicholas turned into a chatty backseat driver criticizing her every move, and Joshua and Aiden stood on either side of television gesturing wildly and trying to show her what *cool moves* she could do.

I need to talk to Alicia about games, or maybe even Casey, Tabitha decided, the boys all jumping and cheering as she steered her snowboarder up one side of the curved slope and then mashed buttons until some kind of trick was performed. *It's—wow, that was kinda neat—um, Christmas is coming up, and I want to get the boys each something special.*

I think Casey said the Gameboy Color was coming out soon—there's no way we can afford four of THEM, but surely that means the price of the original, regular Gameboy has gone down. Right? They could each have one of those, and... play Pokémon against each other, or, or... something. I KNOW that Pokémon gets to be really big. You can't put a price tag on memories at this age, on this sheer childlike wonder they have for new things, this excitement. It won't be like this for them forever.

———

"Aiden. You put that on your plate, now you better eat it. No child o' mine's gonna be wastin' food on *Thanksgivin'*—you better eat it, or so help me God," Aunt Lisa threatened, pointing a finger across the table right in her son's face. "That goes for all of you'ns. If them plates ain't clean, none of y'all are gettin' any dessert. You hear me?"

He DIDN'T put the ham on his plate, you did, Tabitha seethed. *My dad asked if they wanted to try any ham, and they each POLITELY refused and I was so proud of their table manners! So, what do you do?*

You yell at them, insist they're insulting Grandma Laurie who made it for them, and slapped a cut of ham on each of their plates. With your filthy fucking unwashed FINGERS, when there's a pair of tongs right there in the dish with the cuts of ham!

"There's dessert?" Aiden dared to raise his head.

"No, there's no dessert—it's *a figure of speech,* Aiden. Don't be a smartass," Aunt Lisa growled. "Jesus H. Christ, y'all act like fuckin' animals. And they wonder why I didn't want y'all around. It's been nothin' but sass and backtalkin' me since right the minute I got here."

There was a clatter of silverware against a dish as Tabitha rose up out of her seat in a blind, sickening rage, and only Grandma Laurie's hand on her shoulder stopped her. Glaring pure venom at Aunt Lisa, Tabitha slowly—reluctantly—eased back down into her seat. Her temper seemed to be on a hair-trigger now, and although she didn't know what she would actually *do* if she dove over and tackled Aunt Lisa, she knew it wouldn't be good.

"Lisa—please," Grandma Laurie tried to mediate. "It's Thanksgiving. Let's just try to—"

"No, *nuh-uh,*" Lisa forked another helping of scalloped potatoes into her mouth and then used the fork to gesture with. "I ain't puttin' up with any shit. You've been mollycoddlin' these boys an' been soft on 'em, but all that shit ends right here, right now. You hear me, boys?"

What a joke—they haven't done anything at all worth scolding them for! Tabitha felt nauseous simply sitting at the same table as her aunt. *You're going WAY out of your way in an attempt to assert dominance, trying to posture your way back into a family hierarchy you have NO fucking place in.*

Tabitha could only look around the table in disbelief, because it appeared to be working. Her father looked uncomfortable and wore a slight frown as he chewed his food, but didn't seem like he was planning on speaking up. Mrs. Moore almost seemed to be glowering but rarely looked up from her plate and seemed to retreat back into the background once any conversation with Lisa started, because of the social anxieties she still seemed crippled with. Grandma Laurie seemed to think it wasn't her place to intervene between the mother and her children and was simply putting up with it.

But—I CAN'T put up with it, Tabitha felt sick, her appetite was gone, and she glared down at her dish and idly rearranged food she no longer intended to eat with her fork. *Seeing each of the boys —MY boys—just taking the abuse, like beaten dogs—I can't. I can't. I'm going to speak up. I'm going to cause a fit. And, and, if no one else takes my side? Then—I, I don't know. But, I can't keep putting up with this. If she says ONE more thing to them—*

"*Nicholas,*" Aunt Lisa snapped. "Use yer *goddamn* napkin, you're gettin' food on your fuckin'—"

"Aunt Lisa—*stop,*" Tabitha shot out of her seat. "What is *wrong* with you?"

"*You sit yer ass down and shut your mouth,*" Lisa's voice rose. "Don't you fuckin' tell me how to raise my goddamn kids—"

"Lisa, please—" Mr. Moore put his fork down onto his plate with a *clenk.*

"You're not their mother!" Tabitha stammered, feeling her throat constrict and fighting back tears of panic—she was NOT adept at these kind of verbal confrontations. "You walked out on them. You walked out on them. You walked out and abandoned them, and th-that means you *forfeit* any say—"

"I did what I hadta do, and now I'm back, *right here where I belong,* because I'm a *great fucking momma!* I'm the best goddamn momma in the world, you hear me, and what do *you* know about being a mother? *Huh?* You sit yer scrawny ass down! You don't know *shit* 'bout what I've had to do, or where I been, *an' it's none o' your business* no matter where I been in the first place!"

"Mom—" Joshua tried to speak up.

"Where, doing what?!" Tabitha demanded. "You didn't even—"

"Alan—I swear to God, you better put her in her place, 'fore I do it for you," Aunt Lisa warned, slapping a hand down on the table loudly enough to make Joshua flinch. "I swear to God I will. Don't think I won't."

"*Mom*—" Joshua tugged at Aunt Lisa's arm.

"Get *offa* me, ya little turd!" Aunt Lisa backhanded him across the cheek with enough force to rock the young boy back in his chair.

Tabitha was so stunned, she didn't realize she'd risen back up to her feet again until she heard her chair tip back and totter down to the ground behind her. Watching her hands grab out at the back of her mother's chair, and then her father's shoulder made her see that she was racing around the table. She was in motion, but she didn't even know what she was *doing*—either making sure Joshua was okay, or tackling his mother to the fucking ground and beating her to a goddamn pulp. She didn't know what she was doing. Rather than thinking or deliberating or planning, Tabitha felt like a puppet that had been yanked up and into jerky, violent motions by strings of white-hot *rage,* because her emotions had completely taken control.

"*Ya don't go all hangin' on people like yer some kinda fuckin' animal*—"

Aunt Lisa was all but snarling into the face of her wet-eyed son when Tabitha stole him away, taking her small cousin awkwardly with her cast and her good hand and lifting him out of his seat into an awkward embrace. It hurt, Joshua was *heavy*—at eight years old, he weighed maybe sixty pounds—but Tabitha's muscles were screaming out in pain to completely deaf ears as she cradled the boy's face against her and hauled him away. She was running away with him—she didn't know where to, and in a blur of motion further distorted by her own tears, Tabitha discovered she'd wound up back in Grandma Laurie's bedroom.

"I'm, I'm okay," Joshua protested, trying to struggle free and down to his feet. "I'm—"

Fumbling with the doorknob quite a bit, as she was not willing to let Joshua out of her arms for even an instant, Tabitha finally managed to move the door and then shoulder it closed behind them. She locked it. Then she carried Joshua over to the edge of the bed and sat.

"I'm okay," Joshua repeated. "It's—don't cry. It's okay. It's okay."

"*It is NOT okay,*" Tabitha managed out before she felt her throat closing up.

"It—it didn't hurt," Joshua insisted. "I'm okay. It didn't even hurt."

Tabitha couldn't argue with him, because anything she would have said was choked out with sobs. She was in no shape to have attempted lifting him and she'd strained what felt like everything in her back, but the nauseating pit of anger and hatred in her stomach overwhelmed anything and everything else she might have felt. She pulled Joshua close and hugged him tight as she cried, and outside the room, the voices of Aunt Lisa and her parents arguing back and forth out in the dining room continued to rise.

————

Forty minutes passed before her father realized he was going to have to unlock the bedroom door from the other side with a screwdriver, and Tabitha watched the knob finally twist open with detached interest. She felt completely drained. She'd cried and cried and cried, and despite whatever tough little Joshua might tell his brothers later, she knew he'd cried too. Most of the heated emotions that had strangled out all rational thought finally did drop away, but as they receded, her mind felt cold, bitter, and hateful.

Her eyes felt swollen and puffy, her throat felt raw and sore, her entire body ached, and Tabitha simply stared at Mr. Moore as he entered Grandma Laurie's bedroom and sat down beside them.

"You okay, Josh?" he asked, tousling the boy's hair.

"I'm okay." Joshua nodded, glancing at Tabitha. "It's—I'm okay."

"Why don't you go on out there in the living room and watch the TV with your brothers," Mr. Moore suggested.

Joshua slid off the edge of the bed, but looked first to Tabitha for permission to leave. She opened her mouth and then closed it again, not knowing what to say and finally simply giving him a nod. When her cousin left, giving her one last lingering look, the room seemed to close in on Tabitha in a crushing way, and she had to hunch up her shoulders and retreat into herself just to fight it back. She was exhausted.

"Tabby honey..." Mr. Moore cleared his throat. "I don't know what got into your Aunt Lisa tonight. We've talked an' talked with her, an' she's out on the porch coolin' her head a bit. I... know you and your Aunt Lisa don't quite really get along, but no matter what—she *is* family."

"Oh, she *is?*" Tabitha stared ahead at the door, refusing to face him. *'Cooling her head a bit?' Please. She's probably out there lounging on the porch swing, smoking a cigarette and feeling QUITE pleased with herself. If she feels anything at all.*

"She is, sweetie," Mr. Moore said in a firm voice. "She's your aunt."

"Family—by marriage," Tabitha pointed out. "So, if an awful or really untrustworthy person marries into the family, they're still family? We just have to, to *stiffen our chin* and put up with them no matter what? Ignore their mistakes, no matter what? Forgive and forget? Give them money, support and enable them to continue being *awful people* who don't ever have to face the consequences of their mistakes? *Because they're family?*"

"Now, sweetie, your Aunt Lisa isn't *awful* or untrus—"

"Dad, she *abandoned* her children," Tabitha said. "She left them. No notice, no heads-up, no contact information—she was just gone. *Gone.* That's not okay. *That's not okay.* That's not something family would do. She's *not* family. I mean, the minute Uncle Danny gets locked up, she just disappears from their life? That's—"

"Tabitha, this whole thing has been hard on your Aunt Lisa," Mr. Moore rebutted. "You know she was having trouble finding work where—"

"She came back for the money." Tabitha gave her father a helpless shrug. "Not for family. She's *not* family, Dad, she just isn't. I don't care whatever fucking sob story she's sold you, or what excuses you make for her. If you want to ask me if I'm okay with her borrowing money from the settlements—I'm not. Period. End of story."

"If this is about your—your I don't know, this phase you're going through—"

"*Dad.*"

"—that gives you a problem with the way she talks or her being a more down-to-earth kind of person—"

"Dad, she struck her child, right in front of us. She's not *down-to-earth. She's fucking trash.* She's a rat who abandoned ship at the first sign of stormy weather, here. She's a parasite, a parasite who only slunk back here for the money. She's a terrible fucking mother, and she's a drug addict. A junkie. *She's doing drugs.*"

"Honey." Mr. Moore let out another slow sigh as he paused to gather his thoughts. "Your Aunt Lisa... isn't doing drugs. You can't say things like that. Just because you think she—"

"She's got heroin in her purse." Tabitha shrugged, satisfied at least that he didn't dare to refute her other points. "She won't let it out of her sight. There's *drug-use puncture marks* at the vein on the inside of her arm. They teach us to watch out for these things in school—that's what the whole D.A.R.E. program is all about, Dad."

"Your Aunt Lisa wouldn't do *heroin,* Tabby." Mr. Moore shook his head in exasperation. "Tabitha... you know she's smarter than that."

"Check her purse," Tabitha insisted, crossing her arms. "Leave some cash lying about, see if it disappears. Again—*check her purse.* Ask her if she's been in our medicine cabinet—you know, I had three of those strong codeine tablets left over in that little orange prescription bottle. Where'd that little pill bottle go, Dad? Why did she come to us, instead of *here,* stopping by to check on the boys first? Her own children? She could have walked over here any time today; it's just a few blocks away."

"Tabitha, stop," Mr. Moore shook his head. "It's more'n a few blocks, and you know she don't have a vehicle to get around no more. The—"

"Sorry, no," Tabitha rejected his excuse. "Grandma Laurie and the boys aren't *that* far away from Sunset Estates. If I can walk over here to visit them, so can she."

"Your Aunt Lisa isn't you, honey," Mr. Moore argued. "She knew we could drive her over there, and, it's not a problem for us to give her a hand. She's family, Tabby. You don't just—"

"*'Family'* isn't some magical free pass, Dad." Tabitha held her ground. "I'm sorry, Dad, it's just not. You're not going to change my mind on this, and, apparently, I'm not going to get through to you. I'm done talking about it, because I'm done with Aunt Lisa. I'm sorry for all the swearing. I—I want to go home, now."

———

"I'm so sorry about all this," Grandma Laurie fretted, hovering over Tabitha and helping straighten the hoodie Tabitha had donned. "I don't know what's gotten into your Aunt Lisa's head, acting that way. I'll make sure to keep a close eye on her."

"No, she's not staying here with the boys," Tabitha stated with finality. "She's coming back to the trailer park with us. You need to tell her there's not enough room, or, or suggest that she stay with us a few more nights because it's crowded here with the boys. Tell her as if you're going to have the boys move around furniture and make space for her here—but don't actually do that. You won't need to. I'm going to take care of everything."

"Tabby, honey..." Grandma Laurie paused.

"I just..." Tabitha's expression was one of resignation. "I hope you won't think less of me for what I have to do."

"Well, of course I won't," Grandma Laurie gave Tabitha's shoulder a squeeze. "But—well, what are you going to do?"

"I love you, Grandma Laurie," Tabitha stepped in to wrap her arms around the old woman. "I love you, and I love the boys—and I'm going to protect my family."

"I love you too, sweetheart," Grandma Laurie sighed. "Please don't make that sound so *ominous,* though. Promise me you won't go an' do anything dramatic, okay? Whatever all how you must think of her now, Lisa *is* still their mother, and with some time, things'll settle back down with everyone to how they used to be. You'll see."

"No." Tabitha shook her head. "No. No, she isn't, and no—they won't. Sorry."

———

"Matthew baby, could you get the *gosh darn* phone?" Karen Williams hollered. "It'd be so *gosh darn* nice if you would, please."

Her husband's mother and sister were here in town with them visiting before Thanksgiving—Granny June and Auntie Carol, while here she herself retained the coveted title of Momma Karen —and that meant sipping wine and gossiping late in the warm light of her tastefully-appointed den late into the night. Mostly, discussion kept wandering back toward Matthew and this young girl he thought he could date in secret, with each of the ladies obviously having their own input and advice and anecdotes to share.

"I just don't like that he'd keep it secret," Granny June shook her head in dismay. "Keepin' it secret certainly means they were up to things they were too ashamed to talk about, and—"

"Mum, it's his first relationship—of course he's not gonna talk *to us* about it," Auntie Carol argued. "You think I kept you in the loop on all the boys I was seein'? Why, when I was that age—"

"Well, of course you did." Granny June tittered, knowing full well how untrue it was. "I raised you up good an' proper, and you weren't courting any boys until Roger. We—"

"*Oh, please.*" Auntie Carol rolled her eyes. "Don't even bring up gosh darn *Roger*. He had his head stuck so far up his ass that he—"

"*Carol,*" Granny June chided her with a half-hearted smack on the forearm. "Watch your gosh darn language."

"Sorry, he had his head stuck so far up his *you know what* that he didn't know which cheeks were which."

The constant *gosh darns* were a joke that never got old—they were drinking and as the night went on and lips loosened, they knew each of the Williams ladies could and would swear like sailors. To poke fun at each other, they'd correct one another with *gosh darns* and giggle at each other like much younger women. Mrs. Williams was only partway into her first glass of wine tonight, and determined to not slip and say her first dirty word in front of her hilarious in-laws. Not after last year, at least—*that* had gotten so out of hand, it'd even made her husband blush.

"Ooh, I never heard about *Roger*." Mrs. Williams leaned in with delight. "I thought your first guy was... gosh darn, what was his name? Jerry? Went on to manage that—"

"My first boyfriend *was* Jerry." Auntie Carol laughed. "I didn't start seeing Roger until—"

"Oh, shush." Granny June waved dismissively before taking another sip from her wine glass. "Roger was the first one that counted. Dating before high school isn't real courting. It's—it's children's games. Like playing at being doctor, it's not real."

"My son *is* in high school, though—he's a sophomore already."

Mrs. Williams sighed. "They grow up so *gosh darn* fast. So, is this with this Casey girl a real thing I should worry about, or is it—"

"Real doesn't mean forever," Auntie Carol snorted. "Now, I don't mean to make light of him an' his feelings, havin' his first puppy love, but if you think about—"

"Real *should* mean forever." Granny June frowned. "I don't like all this playing around at it I see on television. Why, it's just terrible what they teach kids these days, the state they treat relationships these days."

"It *is* the nineties." Mrs. Williams chuckled, taking another sip of her own glass. "The times, they are a'changin'."

"For the worse, if you ask me," Granny June huffed. "Why, if this thickheaded dummy here had married that gosh darn Roger, she'd—"

"*Oh, please.*" Auntie Carol rolled her eyes. "*Married* Roger?! Even if we had, we'd have never lasted. I know you never believed in divorce, but—"

"I don't believe in divorce," Granny June agreed. "It goes against God. Marriage is a sacred institution, and the more people just—"

"Uh, Mom?" Matthew approached to interrupt the older women with reluctance, presenting the cordless phone to his mother. "It's—"

"Who is it, dear?"

"Tabitha Moore," Matthew replied. "She asked for you, said it was an emergency."

"Now I'm not *defending* divorce, but—" Auntie Carol stopped as Mrs. Williams held up a hand.

"Hello?" Mrs. Williams felt her hackles raise up as she imagined what the emergency might be. "Tabitha honey?"

"I... I hate to impose, so close to the holidays," a small voice said through the phone. "But, Mrs. Williams—there's, um. I really need help."

"Honey, what's wrong?" Mrs. Williams demanded, rising up

out of her comfy seat in alarm. "Where are you? Are you okay? What's going on?"

———

"Tabby has it in her head to be all dead-set against Lisa," Mr. Moore grumbled. "Can't seem to even stand the sight of her."

He and his wife were settling into bed after that fiasco of a Thanksgiving dinner at his mother's apartment. Against expectations, Lisa came back with them rather than staying over there with her kids, and that sure didn't help the tense silence between everyone any. True, Lisa had gone a little overboard disciplining her son there right at the table, but he'd never thought seeing it would affect Tabby quite so much. She had to understand that things were different—she'd grown up 'til now as a only child, and a girl, at that. He certainly wasn't gonna raise his hand against her, but she'd mostly always been a good kid. Boys were different, rowdy, and there were four of them. Some loss of patience on Lisa's part and occasional corporal punishment in spanking or smacking them here and there was understandable.

"Hmm." Mrs. Moore let out a thoughtful hum and buried her cheek deeper in the pillow. "Well, Lisa *did* wake us all up at twelve in the morning."

"Twelve at night," Mr. Moore said.

"*That's the same thing,* and you know all of us are cross at her," Mrs. Moore muttered. "So, what is it? What's wrong now?"

"I'm worried about Tabitha," her husband admitted. "'Bout her and... y'know, all that money. That's a whole lotta money to go to a young girl's head all at once."

"You're worried it's gonna go to her head?" Mrs. Moore blinked one eye open.

"Hasn't it already?" Mr. Moore sighed. "She's got it in her head for a while that anything from—well, you know, *humble origins* is all low class, and she gets herself all set against it. Lisa just seems to really rub her the wrong way, and Tabby isn't even willing to give her a chance."

"Alan—you know I'm not exactly thrilled with Lisa either. Hitting her son like that—that was out of line."

"I know, I know," Mr. Moore mumbled. "But she is goin' through a rough patch right now. With Danny bein' where he is and all. And she is family."

"Uh-huh," Mrs. Moore responded with a noncommittal grunt. "So, what are we gonna do about her?"

"Lisa asked for help, and she's family, so... I think we've gotta do what we can to help her."

"She asked for help—she asked for help *how*, exactly?" Mrs. Moore asked, her sleepiness subsiding.

"We're just about to come into more money than we'll know what to do with, and Lisa sure could use some of it to help gettin' back on her feet. Tabitha's hospital bills're already just about all taken care of, and leavin' all that money for a thirteen-year-old girl to do who knows what with—that's irresponsible."

Leaving the money to TABITHA is irresponsible? Shannon Moore said nothing to that, but she was now fully awake and alert. *Tabitha, who was talking me through home repair and all the specific expenses she had planned here? SHE'S irresponsible? According to who? LISA? Did Lisa just repeat TABITHA'S THIRTEEN AND IRRESPON-SIBLE to Alan until he started getting suckered into believing it? TABITHA, IRRESPONSIBLE? Are you fucking kidding me?*

"I think we should take out some to help out Lisa an' the boys, maybe a tiny bit of spending money for Tabby to do whatever she wants with. And the rest? Needs to go into a college fund or a trust fund or somethin' 'til she's older and can right make up her mind on what's best to do with it. When she's older and we explain what we did—she'll understand. Lisa's family. She didn't run off 'cause she *wanted to,* an' she sure as all heck isn't a druggie or anything like that."

"Alan." Mrs. Moore sat up in bed, shucking off the covers so that she could glare at her husband. "What part of our Tabitha is any less responsible than Lisa? Huh?"

"Now you know that's not what I meant." Alan rose up onto one elbow. "Tabitha, she's—she's still a child. *She's thirteen years* old, she doesn't know what from what."

"Fourteen in a little over a week, and you know *damned* well she's more mature than that," Mrs. Moore growled. "She'll always be our baby girl, okay—but, Tabitha is *not* a child anymore. She's a young woman, an' there's no way you can say otherwise! Listen to yourself, Alan. In what freaking world is Lisa *or* your lousy brother Danny more mature and responsible than *our daughter*? Who's to say Lisa *isn't* a druggie? Huh? Who's to say where she's been or what she's been up to these past months?"

"Now, hold on—" Mr. Moore protested. "I've sat down an' talked things through with Lisa. She's been workin' where she can. Things haven't been easy on her, alright? No matter what, she's family, and we've gotta do what we can to look out for her."

"Just a few months ago, we gave her all that money for a car that don't run!" Mrs. Moore pointed out, growing angry. "What all happened to that, huh? We're the ones who look after her boys when your mother doesn't. Where's she been all this time? She kept sayin' she was livin' with a friend—she never made no mention of a name or that it was a woman. Who's to say she isn't living with some other man now that your brother's locked up? Huh?"

"Lisa definitely wouldn't—"

"Alan, I love you to pieces, but *your heart's so much bigger than your head that it's not even funny*." Mrs. Moore let herself fall back against the pillow and then turned onto her side so that she was facing away from her husband. "If Tabitha doesn't wanna support Lisa's mistakes with that settlement money, then that's that. It's Tabitha's money. Not ours. *Not Lisa's*. Our Tabby doesn't owe her one goddamn red cent. Tabby's got no obligation to throw pearls before swine, and as far as I'm concerned, neither do we."

"Mistakes?" Mr. Moore frowned. "That's not what I'd—"

"*Goodnight, Alan,*" Mrs. Moore called over her shoulder.

———

Nervous tension had filled Tabitha's room until it became absolutely suffocating, and it wasn't until after her parents had gone to bed that the sign she'd been waiting for finally came. Her Aunt Lisa started up the shower after having dickered around in the bathroom doing who-knows-what for almost a half hour. Having been pretending to be asleep already, Tabitha had simply been waiting in the darkness for the sound of the shower. Waiting, with the flathead screwdriver from the kitchen's junk drawer in hand, waiting for the right moment to strike.

With her heart in her throat, she quietly opened her bedroom door and tiptoed out into the hall. The only light here was coming from beneath the locked bathroom door, and it was dark enough that she couldn't see the little line in the center of the doorknob— she had to feel it out with the head of the screwdriver. It made a small noise as metal met metal, but Tabitha didn't freeze. The sound of the shower spray in there would drown that out. She was committed now. The tab swiveled, the doorknob turned, it was unlocked. The screwdriver was dropped down to the floor where it would be out of the way, because she only had one good hand, and she was going to need it.

Tabitha opened the door and burst into the bathroom.

"Hey—what the hell?!" Aunt Lisa crowed from the other side of the shower curtain.

There. The woman's purse was up on the counter, yawing wide open and unattended. Beside it was a worn and faded *Batman* thermos, of all things, likely borrowed long ago from one of her son's plastic lunch boxes. On the porcelain lip of the sink lay a disposable lighter, a blackened, filthy spoon, and yes, the real smoking gun itself—a syringe.

"Tabitha?" Aunt Lisa called. "Hey—Jesus, I'm in here a'shower-in', you know?"

The woman pulled back the edge of the shower curtain, just in time to peek around and discover Tabitha hurrying to pluck the syringe up with careful fingers and toss it into the open purse.

"Hey—HEY!" Aunt Lisa shrieked. "*What the fuck do ya think yer doin?!*"

The spoon and the lighter followed the syringe into the purse with the quickest snatching motions she could manage, and then Tabitha grabbed up the Batman thermos and shoved it inside as well. The thermos was one of those squat, cylindrical ones with a little plastic handle for the cap so that it could double as a tiny cup, and thankfully, it had already been screwed shut. She could feel the contents of the thermos shift in the brief instant it was in her hands, but it didn't feel like liquid inside—it was as if Aunt Lisa was keeping clumps of dirt in the thing. Heroin, obviously. Hopefully. If this was her aunt's stash of instant coffee grounds, then—then Tabitha didn't have time to worry about that right now.

"*HEY! WHAT THE FUCK DO YA THINK YER—*" Aunt Lisa yanked the vinyl curtain back hard enough that the several curtain rings separated from the rod.

Completely naked, with wild, frenzied eyes, Aunt Lisa jumped out of the shower and lunged for her.

The plan had been to also gather up Aunt Lisa's abandoned clothing there so as to forestall the woman's pursuit, but there just wasn't enough time. Tabitha bolted out of the small enclosure with the purse pinched closed with her good hand and held against her. She ran down the hallway in what felt like an instant, but she could hear Lisa's heavy footfalls, *chasing her anyway,* and then the light coming from the open bathroom door was blocked and she knew the woman was right behind her.

Oh shit. Oh shit. Oh shit. Oh shit—

Terror and dread were freezing up her movements and locking

them up in raw *panic,* but Tabitha managed to hold the purse against her and wrench open the front door of their trailer. In the periphery of her vision, she saw Aunt Lisa, naked and soaking wet, was just behind her, mere feet from catching up with her at the door.

"HEY!" Aunt Lisa shrieked. "*HEY!*"

To Tabitha's immense relief, a car waiting outside flicked its high beams on as Tabitha raced outside. From the sound of her aunt's continuous hoarse screaming, the trailer trash had paused in the front doorway, unwilling to run out naked into the night air in the midst of November.

I-I made it. It worked. It worked. I have the evidence, I think, and— I made it.

"Get in, *get in!*" Mrs. Williams looked absolutely furious, and the police officer's wife started slamming the horn on her Ford Taurus to drown out Aunt Lisa's screaming and hollering. "Jesus Christ, we're gonna—are you okay? Are you okay?"

"I have it," Tabitha confirmed as she hurried into the vehicle. "I'm okay, just—let's get out of here."

"Close your door, let's go." Mrs. Williams slammed her foot on the gas pedal and they plunged forward and past the trailer down the street, putting Lisa out of sight. "Get your seatbelt, honey."

"I, I—thank you." Tabitha choked up. "I didn't know what to do. I didn't, I didn't know anyone to, to go to about this. All of this. I didn't—"

"Sh-sh-sh-sh, you're fine, you're fine, honey, let's just get you out of here, okay? Are you okay?"

38
ABSCONDING WITH THE EVIDENCE

"Are you okay?" Mrs. Williams asked for what felt like the umpteenth time. "Talk to me, dearie. Was that—was that—"

Lisa? Linda? Whatever deadbeat aunt of yours that you brought up back before? Mrs. Williams felt furious with herself for not nagging her husband to investigate back then. *It's one thing for the woman to be belligerent and screaming—but, she was also completely naked there in the doorway, like some kind of stark raving lunatic!*

"It was my aunt," Tabitha confirmed in a small voice. "My Aunt Lisa."

The poor thing still looked shell-shocked. Tiny and vulnerable, clutching a natty old purse against herself in the passenger's seat. The situation was grave, serious enough that Mrs. Williams didn't even have her *Beatles* hits playing. Her Ford Taurus was only ever this quiet when she was about to give her son a stern talking to, or when she needed to illustrate to her husband how furious she was over something without having to actually spell it out.

"Well, you're safe now, no matter what," Mrs. Williams assured the girl. "Do you need anything? Do you have enough clothes and toiletries in your bag there for an overnight stay, while we figure everything out?"

The streets of Springton were silent and still this far past midnight as the car rolled on down the street. As a small Kentucky town, there was no nightlife to speak of—all of the shops, businesses, and restaurants shut down before ten o'clock, save for a gas station or two. As a self-professed *people person,* Karen Williams always found the late night empty shopping centers and dark storefronts disquieting and eerie.

"Oh, um." Tabitha seemed to snap out of her daze. "No, I don't. I don't have anything at all. This isn't my bag—this is my aunt's purse. That woman that was screaming at us."

"Your aunt's purse?" Mrs. Williams did a double take. "...Why do you have your aunt's purse?"

"I... I was afraid to tell you specifics over the phone, because I wasn't completely sure yet," Tabitha admitted in her quiet voice. "My dad wouldn't believe me, and my mother, she... she can't do anything about it. I think even if my dad *did* believe me, he would cover for her, or try to help her, and just try to take everything on because... she's *family.*"

That last word spoke entire volumes, because there it had become a swear word, there Tabitha's normally soft tone was laced with pain and anger, so suffused with frustration and helplessness that Karen took her eyes off the road for a moment to give the girl a glance. The teen's eyes were wet, but she wasn't crying. Instead, her jaw was set like she was gritting her teeth, and her face was hard, a mask of bitterness that, in her opinion, had no rightful place being on a dainty young woman.

"What *specifics?*" Mrs. Williams gently prompted, eyeing the purse Tabitha held with trepidation now. "Honey... what did you not tell me, when we were on the phone?"

"Heroin," Tabitha said, visibly uncomfortable at the admission. "She was shooting up heroin in our bathroom—I broke in once I could hear she'd moved into the shower and had the water running. I have all the... well, the *evidence,* here."

"*Heroin?!*" Mrs. Williams was so stunned, she subconsciously hit the brakes.

She was already distracted, so she hadn't been driving particularly fast. But still, the sudden lurch to a stop felt like it took the breath out of her as the seatbelt tightened across her chest. It was past midnight, and Springton's streets were deserted, allowing her to let the car sit there in the middle of the road for a moment while she processed the dreadful thing she'd just heard. *HEROIN. Good Lord almighty, I don't think she's joking with me.*

Heroin use had no place in a nice little town like her Springton —heroin was the domain of awful, wretched big city places like Lexington. This wasn't pot or shrooms, this was *heroin!* The fact that substance abuse of *this* severity had crept into their one little low-income neighborhood was another alarming wake-up call, just like the shooting had been. It was so easy to blind herself with Springton's charming small-town daytime veneer and just never look too closely at the little darker corners. She was a valued member of just about every community organization of importance, well-connected to all kinds of gossip, and had always felt like she knew Springton better than anyone else. If someone from her usual circles had mentioned people doing heroin in Springton, she wasn't sure she'd have believed it.

"Heroin," Mrs. Williams repeated in a daze. "You're sure?"

"No," Tabitha was candid with her. "I'm not sure. If I had more confidence, I'd have called the police directly. I, um, I don't have any way of verifying that it's heroin myself. Just, there's a mark at the vein in her arm. Puncture mark. There was a thermos full of... well, *something.* A syringe, a lighter, and a blackened spoon, like she was heating up something in it with the lighter."

"Well, it certainly does sound like drugs of some sort." Mrs. Williams still felt floored. "And you have it right in there? In that purse?" *There's HEROIN in my car?! In the hands of this teenage girl?!*

What kind of FUCKED UP family has it so that hard drugs are within arm's reach of a thirteen-year-old girl?! I hate to even admit that it's possible somewhere, let alone in MY town, to a girl like Miss Tabby here who's a friend of the family!

"Yes. I-it wasn't easy to get," Tabitha blurted out. "She wouldn't let it out of her sight. She even slept on it, with it tucked under her. *To me,* it's definitely heroin, but I, I need that confirmed. Confirmed by people who can do something about it. I need her away from my family. Away from her children. She's—she struck her eight-year-old son across the face, in the middle of our... our early Thanksgiving dinner, we had our family Thanksgiving today. That made up my mind. I-I had to do something. *I had to.*"

"*She struck her own son?*" Mrs. Williams repeated in disbelief.

"Pretty hard." Tabitha gave her a weary nod. "Across the face— it was, it was just because he was annoying her, um, trying to get her attention when she was in the middle of this, this rant. This rant to the rest of us about how she was in charge, or, or how we were too soft on her sons while she was away, something like that."

"Your parents didn't...?" Mrs. Williams was aghast. "*Do some-thing?* Say something, about any of all this?!"

"My parents..." Tabitha trailed off, her expression full of griev-ance. "My mother isn't good with people or people problems. She's getting better, but she's... um, she's still a long way from who she once was. I think she gets severe anxiety around, um. The kind of confrontation that would be needed to... resolve things here. My father has a big heart, but he's just. *He's blind to things.* Blind to this. He's... more than willing to assume the best in people, let people around him take advantage of him. Especially if they're *family.*"

Again, Mrs. Williams noticed that the word *family* was issued out of the girl's mouth like a dirty word. It put her on edge, and certainly soured what little impression she had of the times she'd met Tabitha's parents. She was getting angry just seeing Tabitha in a fluster here, though, and she wasn't sure now was the time to speak her mind on the matter.

"He didn't believe me when I warned him that Aunt Lisa might be on drugs," Tabitha continued in a weary voice. "I-I was also upset, though, so I don't know? Maybe he didn't take me seriously. Maybe it's *better* that he didn't believe me. I think, I think more and more that if he did think she was getting into drugs, he'd take it upon himself, *take it upon us* to shoulder the burden and make sure she got all the support she needed, got into rehab. Since she's *family*. Maybe that's the right choice, even. I, I just, I just—I don't trust her. I *can't* trust her! In my mind, she didn't come back for her children, didn't come to us as family. She only came back to us because she heard about settlement money, came because she's... she's an addict. I don't trust her. *I can't trust her.* Maybe they knew her back before, knew her differently, or remember her some other way, but to me—she's just this drug addict, and, and I, I can't. I can't."

"Okay, okay." Mrs. Williams patted Tabitha's shoulder. "We're gonna be okay, and everything's going to be sorted out. Everything's going to be okay. You did the right thing calling me, I'm proud of you."

"Th-thank you," Tabitha looked emotional. "And—I'm so sorry again."

"Don't you dare be sorry," Mrs. Williams insisted, starting the car forward again to resume her trip home. "You did the right thing. Let's get you safe, and I'll call my husband right away."

"Is he on duty this late?" Tabitha asked.

"Putting in extra time now, so he can be off a bit longer throughout the holidays," Mrs. Williams explained in an exasperated tone. "He'll sleep in tomorrow 'til just before football starts, while all the rest of us'll have been slaving away getting Thanksgiving dinner ready for everyone. And I say *putting in extra time now,* but all that really means is he's goofing off with his dumb cop friends at the station. Darren MacIntire got released, and the boys've all been getting together there to see him."

"That's good," Tabitha remarked. "I was worried he wouldn't be out of the hospital for Thanksgiving. That's actually why we had our Thanksgiving a day early—Mrs. MacIntire wanted us to get together with them, with their family, for their Thanksgiving."

"They'll be thrilled to have you." Mrs. Williams put on a strained smile, somewhat at a loss as to how she could even shift the topic away from the subject of family. "Hannah talks about you all the time, wants to know when she can come over and 'babysit' with you."

"I—I don't know what to do about tomorrow," Tabitha admitted in embarrassment, letting her face drop down into her hand. "What to do about my parents. Having to turn to you about all of this, because they're... well. Incapable. Of acting against my aunt. We, um, we just... *drove off.*"

"I'll call them and explain," Mrs. Williams harrumphed. "Or maybe they'll have explaining to do to me! If they're any kind of parents at all, that big ruckus your aunt was throwing was commotion enough for them to realize something was obviously terribly wrong! You're just going to be *spending the night at a friend's house,* because of that. I'm a friend. A *concerned* friend, and I'd certainly like to hear their thoughts on all of this! Seems to me like they're due for a nice long chat while we get my husband to look through that purse."

"I just... I shouldn't have had to do this." Tabitha's voice was small and sad enough that Mrs. Williams felt her own throat hitching up. "I just... I really can't thank you enough for coming to pick me up. For trusting me, without me even telling you what was going on. It's even so late at night, and—"

"Oh, hush." Mrs. Williams waved away her concerns. "You wouldn't have called and asked for help if it wasn't serious, and this sounds *terribly* serious. Good Lord! It's the same thing I've told my son—if something's happened, and he doesn't feel safe and needs me to pick him up, it doesn't matter what it is or where or what time of night. I'm a mother! He just has to get a hold of me, and I'll be there, no questions, or dilly-dallying, or any of that machismo *you're on your own* bullshit my husband tried pulling with him. If you'll excuse my language.

"Any of that nonsense, any figuring out what's wrong, or who's to blame, or whatever issues it was, that all can be figured out after the fact, once everyone's safe and away from whatever's gone on." Mrs. Williams clarified her position on the matter with a helpless shrug and shake of her head. "I know it's not really my place to say, Tabitha honey, but you living in that trailer park—I don't like it. You being in these situations. It just breaks my heart! Please believe me when I say that heroin has *no place* around children, and nor do people who use heroin. End of story! There's just nothing else to it."

"I agree." Tabitha sighed. "It's why I called. I can't let her remain around my family, my four little cousins. They need away from her. For good, forever. I can't *stand* the thought of h-her, of her *worming* her way back into our family because of the settlement money—and the way she *treats* them, the way she doesn't even care, it's... it's... I can't. I can't. I can't let anything happen to them."

"You did the right thing calling me!" Mrs. Williams said again, feeling her fury build up all over again until she was almost strangling the steering wheel.

"How to actually make this work, when I'm just the *angsty teenage daughter,* I-I don't know," Tabitha said. "But, I thought, if you could help—Mrs. Williams, you're a *somebody*. People will listen to you, you'll make them listen to you."

"You're *damn* right I will," Karen Williams swore, grinding her teeth. "Don't go and call me *Mrs.* Williams, though—if you trust me enough to call me when you need help, I'm Momma Williams to you, alright?"

———

Against all of Tabitha's expectations, the drive was short and ended in a quiet suburban neighborhood just ten minutes across town. Although the street was too dark for her to glean many details, the driveway they pulled into seemed normal and the house was upper-middle class at best. It sported a two-car garage that Mrs. Williams made no motion to open via the remote Tabitha noticed was clipped to the driver's side sun visor, instead simply opting to park in front of the house.

"Here we are!" Mrs. Williams announced, actually reaching over to unbuckle Tabitha's seatbelt for her. "Oh—shoot, sorry. I'm so used to taxiing around little Hannah! You're a grown teenage girl, I'll let you get the door yourself, hah."

"Th-thank you," Tabitha murmured, unsure as to whether she was thanking the woman for getting the seatbelt for her, or thanking her for allowing her autonomy to open her own door. *I guess the house on the lake is a second property? Or, maybe their parents' home? Something like that?*

Juxtaposing this sudden and dramatic shift in social roles had Tabitha feeling like she had to go rigid with respect and politeness. It wasn't even just the jarring disparity in income class between their two families—it was that while her own mom Shannon Moore was a traumatized woman who just incidentally happened to be a mother, Karen Williams was one hundred and ten percent bonafide aggressive suburban *Mom,* with a capital 'M'. Moreover, Mrs. Williams took this identity and then applied it in the community of the entire town, forming all sorts of connections throughout the strata of Springton.

Definitely brings to mind all those observations I made back when I was attending high school all over again, Tabitha reflected. *With those strange hierarchies that form within their little closed systems. Everyone fighting to be the biggest fish in their pool—is this where that all ends up? At Karen Williams?*

It was something to think about as Tabitha opened her door and slipped outside, awkwardly managing to hold the stolen purse against herself with her cast. The neat *orderliness* of the block of homes visible in the streetlight was picturesque, like something out of a sitcom. Textbook tidy little lawns, mailboxes, decorative shrubs. She was almost surprised there wasn't a—nope, there was actually *was* one, an actual white picket fence a few doors down. The pervading silence at this midnight hour made the place seem oppressive; like she had to restrain her voice to a whisper, to mind her manners and make sure she never spoke out of turn.

An inexplicable wave of panic rose up within her again, but Tabitha attributed it to her nerves as she carefully—slowly— eased the passenger door closed behind her so that it wouldn't make a noise.

Is this... is this where I want to be? Tabitha wondered, too frazzled to ruminate on the double-meanings tumbling around inside her head. *Calling Mrs. Williams for help seemed like the only thing I could do, but at the same time... WAS it the right thing to do? I just feel... I don't know. So lost, so in over my head. This entire... EVERYTHING feels so far out of my element.*

Having lived a life before seemed to mean absolutely nothing when that prior life was a passive, sedentary experience that eschewed dealing with conflict whenever possible.

"Tabitha? Oh, honey, here," Mrs. Williams rushed over to grab her up in a motherly embrace. "You're fine, now. You're safe! Everything's going to be alright!"

Mrs. Williams is—she's not just a Mom. She's THE Mom. Tabitha was embarrassed at realizing how much she needed a hug, and flabbergasted at the woman's ability to sense it. *Like Mrs. Seelbaugh, she's just this weird SUPERMOM figure that I guess I never really believed in, because I just didn't have someone like that, for me. Mrs. Williams is, she's, I don't know. Late thirties? Maybe? Younger than I was. Except she's certainly not younger than me, really, in ANY sense. Or—or, I was never OLDER, really, except just in age. And that was just me, I don't know. Waiting out the clock, watching time elapse and waiting for—I don't know what I was waiting for, but I know now in my bones that whatever it was, it was never coming. Life isn't—it's not just going to come to you; you have to reach out and grab it. I guess?*

Mrs. Williams can do that, HAS done that, so her soul is, it's older than mine. It's like the saying—'it's not the years, it's the mileage.' Mrs. Williams has miles and miles that I just never did. Her soul is well-traveled and just has this wealth of, well, WISDOM. Most of my last life was honestly wasted, because I avoided experiencing anything. I didn't GROW.

"You're going to be alright, okay?" Mrs. Williams gave her shoulders a squeeze. "Look at me. Everything's going to be alright."

"I'm—I'm just feeling a little overwhelmed," Tabitha admitted, smiling through her tears. "I'm okay."

"C'mon, it's cold." Mrs. Williams looked like she was getting worked up all over again. "Let's get you inside!"

Do I WANT the kind of life Mrs. Williams has? Tabitha wondered in a daze. *Is this it? American dream, a life in the suburbs? What DO I want, really? Did I ever know? Did growing up the way I did before, without stumbling across real-life actual VALID role models... STUNT me, somehow? Can I be fixed? SHOULD I be fixed? Am I broken? Like my mother? Like AUNT LISA?*

Tabitha let Mrs. Williams usher her forward toward the front door of the residence in a daze, spinning between what felt like six completely different epiphanies and too tired to firmly grasp and realize any of them. Her life was changing right at this moment. It seemed like some indelible barrier had been crossed and she'd stepped off a path that was going nowhere in particular and onto a new one. Invoking *family* in Momma Williams wasn't something she was going to be able to go back on—because every aspect of this interaction continuously laid bare the inadequacy of her actual parents.

There... may really be no going back, after this.

"Alright, we'll try to keep our voices down," Mrs. Williams said as she led Tabitha up the front step and opened the door. "Forgot we have company; my mother-in-law and my sister-in-law're staying with us for Thanksgiving."

It was hard for Tabitha to register what was being said, as she was still blinking in confusion at the open door.

Wasn't even locked, Tabitha realized as she was guided inside. *She's—they—I thought that kind of thing was just naivete, or urban legend or something. Such a nice neighborhood that they really don't lock their doors? I mean, a POLICE OFFICER lives here, so—so, I guess it makes sense. Who would try to break in here, of all places? Just... wow. More culture shock for trailer trash me.*

"Here, honey, kick off your shoes before we go in on the carpet."

Mrs. Williams then bustled a sock-clad Tabitha, who was still reeling from the various circumstances and trying to take in the sudden decor of antiques and vintage furniture all at once, along into an equally well-appointed dining room. Each room seemed to be furnished as if *Martha Stewart* catalog photographers might arrive any minute, with earth tone colors garnished by splashes of orange and red to represent the fall season.

Looking around, it was a lot to take in, and Tabitha couldn't help but think back to Sharon, the Springton Town Hall administrator who had seemed to pour all of her passion into the seasonal displays. Here in the Williams home, woven wicker baskets were filled with artificial pumpkins and gourds, dry garland wreaths were draped in fabric autumn leaves, and rustic candle pieces filled the shelves and curios. Amish-made cloth dolls of man and wife Plymouth settlers and a large collection of painted porcelain Thanksgiving turkeys were nestled together in an intimidating row upon the fireplace mantel.

"It's late, I think everyone was just shuffling off to bed around the time I left the house," Mrs. Williams seemed to say to herself. "We'll try not to wake anyone up!"

Two minutes after getting Tabitha settled at the table, Mrs. Williams then went around the house and to wake everyone up anyway.

First out was another adult woman, still dressed, who seemed to be about Mrs. Williams' age who was then followed by a much older woman in a nightgown, with a face bedecked in wrinkles and folds and sporting a short crop of stiff gray hair. Finally, a door down the hall opened and Matthew joined them as well, the chip-tune music from a video game still faintly audible from his room.

"Alright, everyone—this is Tabitha; she asked me to pick her up because of some situations going on at home," Mrs. Williams said. "Tabitha, this is my mother-in-law and then my sister Carol. You already know Matthew."

"Hi." Tabitha gave them all a weak little wave.

"Uh, hey," Matthew said, looking confused. "Long time no see."

It was hard not to feel mortified at being in this position. She had no idea what to say or how to act when put on the spot like this, and the sudden alarming appearance of *a boy her age* made her incredibly self-conscious in ways she didn't even want to delve into right now. She met each of their curious gazes for a brief moment before feeling defeated and retreating back into herself so that she could stare down at the tabletop.

"So—what all's goin' on?" Matthew asked. "Am I allowed to ask?"

"Well... why don't we see?" Mrs. Williams gestured toward the purse. "Hun, do you want me to...?"

"I'll..." Tabitha swallowed. "I'll do it."

"Alright, then." Mrs. Williams gave her a reassuring squeeze on the shoulder. "Either way—I mean, no matter what's in there, I'm calling my husband right now and we're gonna do *something* about all this, alright?"

"Alright." Tabitha nodded. "Thank you."

With that, Mrs. Williams' face darkened and she stormed off

around the corner into what looked to be the kitchen. They heard her snatch a phone from its dock, heard a single touch-tone as a number was presumably speed-dialed, and then an angry huff as the woman was forced to wait for several seconds for an answer.

"Hi—yeah. It's Karen. Put my husband on, please, there's a situation and, well—" Seemingly mindful of her guests and how stark the words were in the tense silence throughout the rest of the house, Mrs. Williams lowered her voice to continue the rest. Matthew pulled out one of the chairs opposite Tabitha and took a seat, while both of the other women present exchanged glances with each other and then looked toward Tabitha.

Mindful of her audience, Tabitha hefted the bag, arranging it on the table in front of her, and then unsnapped the opening. With trembling fingers, Tabitha took a faded Batman children's thermos from the stolen purse and placed it on the Williams family's dinner table. After a moment of nervous hesitation, Tabitha borrowed several napkins from a ceramic holder at the center of the table—the sculpted piece was shaped like a Turkey—and spread the napkins across the tabletop. Then she extracted the rest, lifting the implements out one by one; a disposable lighter, a blackened spoon, and a used medical syringe.

"Honey—*is that what I think it is?*" Aunt Carol shrank back from the table and put a hand over her mouth.

"What is it?" the elderly woman in the nightgown asked.

"I... believe it's heroin," Tabitha explained with a wince. "I, I think my aunt, my Aunt Lisa was doing heroin in our bathroom, after my parents went to bed. I... grabbed it, and I ran. Mrs. Williams was kind enough to, to be there to pick me up."

"*Heroin?*" The old woman looked aghast.

"Yes, I want you to shoot her on sight!" They all heard Mrs. Williams raise her voice into the phone. "She was *screaming* at us, buck naked! She's some kind of dangerous God damn drug addict, and I was terrified for my life! *Shoot her on sight!*"

"...Good Lord!" Aunt Carol shook her head.

"Well, I *know* you can't actually shoot her, God damnit!" Mrs. Williams bristled, rounding the corner with the handset phone and then glaring furiously at what she saw laid out on the table. "You get out there, and you get her in handcuffs and you lock her away! There's—look, now we have evidence—there's her *illegal drug paraphernalia* on my Goddamn dining room table, for Christ's sake!"

"How do you know this is heroin?" the frail old woman in the nightgown asked, unable to tear her eyes away from the incriminating items arrayed on the napkins.

"I, um. I don't know for sure, I guess," Tabitha made a face. "I don't want to open the thermos."

"Well, no—don't open it." Aunt Carol hurried to assure her with a knock of her knuckle against the mahogany tabletop. "You just leave that for the police, Hun. You did right not to open it. You leave it well alone."

"I'm just saying—she's dangerous!" Mrs. Williams yelled into the phone. "I don't feel safe with her running around my town hopped up on who knows what! You're going to get everyone out to that park and arrest her right this goddamn instant or I'm going to start making phone calls and then *you're* going to start getting phone calls!"

"It looks like heroin to me," Matthew spoke up, immediately holding up his hands as his aunt and grandmother both snapped their heads around to give him stink-eyes of scrutiny.

"I mean—c'mon, I'm not saying I've ever seen it for real before, but they go on and on about it in all those *D.A.R.E.* videos at school. Heroin—but they call it dope or smack, uhh, *'out on the streets.'* Whatever stuff from in the thermos, it goes onto the spoon, you heat the spoon with a lighter to get it so you can draw it up with the syringe, then it goes right into your arm or wherever, and gets you high."

"Matthew—I don't think I even like you knowing all that," his grandmother huffed, looking angry and uncomfortable. "*Good Lord.*"

"Better to be aware of it, at least." Matthew gave her a helpless shrug. "Dad'll know a lot more about it. No one I know at school does anything like this—at high school, it's just harmless little stuff. Pot and beer, stuff you hear about. This is, uh, this is like the heavy stuff, bad dangerous stuff. Like, *real* drugs."

"Yes. *Yes,* I know. I will. Hurry on home, there's drug paraphernalia on our dinner table, and you need to DO something about it! Yes, I love you. Muah. *Bye.*" Mrs. Williams slammed the receiver down, ending the call. "Jesus. Okay, first of all—Tabitha, are you alright?"

"I'm okay," Tabitha croaked. "I mean—I will be. It's better, thinking that this is. *Getting resolved.* I was going out of my mind or uh, going in circles trying to, um, panicking, trying not to panic, panicking anyways, going around in my head just... tearing myself up. It's going to—things are going to get better now. Right?"

"Of course they are. You don't have to worry about anything," Mrs. Williams promised. "We're going to get all of this mess straightened out. Do you need to use the powder room and freshen up or anything? You've eaten? Do you need a glass of water? Matthew, go get her a—"

"Oh no, no, I'm fine," Tabitha assured them, stopping Matthew with a raised hand. "I'm fine. Please."

"*Okay.*" Mrs. Williams fanned her face dramatically for a moment and then put both hands to her temples. "I'm going to make a few more calls. We have both Carol and June in our guest room right now, because they're visiting from Indiana, but I'm sure I can make you comfortable *somewhere.* Tomorrow, we'll get a hold of Sandra, and I know she'll be happy to have you for however long you need to stay. Hannah would be just tickled pink to have you around. Oh! I introduced you to Carol already, I think. This is Granny June, she's sweet as can be."

"Ah, hello." Tabitha gave a small, awkward wave. "It's nice to meet you. Sorry again for the, uh, circumstances."

"It's nice to meet you, dearie." Granny June sighed. "Don't you worry about anything. You did the right thing calling Karen about all this."

"Yeah, I just..." Tabitha still felt shell-shocked. "I hate having to impose."

"You're not imposing at all!" Mrs. Williams hollered, rounding the corner of the table to hug Tabitha again. "That woman was stark raving mad and *dangerous!* Good Lord!"

"I, I know." Tabitha choked up a little. "I just, I hate it. Always just having problems for you. I don't want to—"

"Ssh-ssh-ssh, none of this is your fault." Mrs. Williams rubbed her back. "You did the right thing."

"They're gonna just arrest her, right?" Matthew gestured at the heroin on the table. "I mean, they can just test that it's in her system, and that's enough to put some kind of charges on her. Get her away from Tabitha's family and out of their hair, and all that. Right?"

"Well, they're certainly dragging their feet on everything!" Mrs. Williams scoffed, smacking the edge of the table. "Your father wasn't out and about on patrol tonight; he's just goofing off around the office doing who-knows-what with the rest of those lousy good-for-nothing cops. He said they're sending someone to Sunset Estates to *evaluate the situation,* and then he's on his way home now to take a look at this drug stuff from that woman's purse. This is that same relative you were telling me about, that walked out on her children and disappeared?"

"Yes," Tabitha admitted, struggling to remember what she'd told Mrs. Williams before between the random talks they'd had in the past month, the frantic phone call, and then the nearly incoherent babble of details she'd spouted out on the ride here as she attempted to calm down. "It's my fault she was naked. She wouldn't let her bag out of arm's reach and was very, um, protective of it. I, I thought she was shooting up in our bathroom, so—as soon as I heard her get into the shower, I broke in and I took it and I ran. It's, it's honestly my fault she came back at all."

"Oh, nonsense, none of this was your fault," Mrs. Williams said. "You just wait'll my husband gets home. He'll fix all of this."

———

In the excruciating half-hour wait, both Aunt Carol and June retired back to bed, leaving Matthew to make awkward small talk with Tabitha while Mrs. Williams paced back and forth and swore under her breath. For all their apparent similarity in age, the two teens were barely acquainted at all, and trying to carry a conversation composed of questions without substance and nervous laughter left both of them fumbling to fill the silence. Anything to stave off what felt like growing tension. When Officer Williams did finally arrive, he was bodily hustled in from the front door by his wife before he could even take off his boots.

"Well?!" Mrs. Williams demanded.

He frowned at the spread across the dining room table—the presumed drug stuff front and center on napkins and everything else from makeup and cigarettes to a brush missing a quarter of its teeth and even the woman's wallet. After surveying it all, the cop let out a slow sigh and picked up the worn Batman thermos, unscrewing the lid and taking the first look inside.

Tabitha stared, shoulders tense and raised, unable to even breathe for a moment as she waited for him to draw his conclusion one way or the other.

"Alright, so we've got some good news and there's some bad news, here." Officer Williams tilted the open container and then shifted the contents slightly with a shake of his wrist. "The good news is—you were right on the money, Tabitha. This is heroin."

"Okay." Tabitha let out the breath she'd been holding but

didn't let herself sag back in the seat just yet. "And... the bad news?"

"The *bad* news is, that takin' the evidence away from the woman like you did puts us in a bit of a pickle," the police officer said, twisting the lid back on and then carefully setting the Batman thermos back down on the table. "It'd have been one thing if *I'd* been the one that caught her with it, but as it is... we might have to do some finagling to get anything like possession charges to stick, now."

"That's a bunch of horse shit!" Mrs. Williams bellowed. "Look! Look at this, right here. Her *identification* was right there in the purse with it! Says on her license right there, *LISA. MOORE.* If that's not *incriminating* enough for you boys at the station, then—"

"Listen, I know, I know." Officer Williams held his hands up. "But there's common sense like this and there's the letter of the law, and miles and miles o' wiggle room between the two that's just packed full of lawyers who'll sell you a bridge 'cross it if they can."

"Oh, *baloney!*" Mrs. Williams fumed. "That's just... *ridiculous!*"

"She wasn't caught with it, so what it might come down to is her word against Tabitha's." Officer Williams sighed. "Now, you do seem to have lawyer friends of your own with Seelbaugh and Straub, so that isn't a total hopeless case. Our best bet right now, however, is to get ahold of this Lisa woman in the next few hours, here. We have cause to bring her in for questioning, and we can certainly get her tested for whatever all's in her system.

"*But* it'd need to be sooner rather than later. Opiates have a real quick half-life, and even if she just shot up, it'll be hard to prove it after the first... I dunno, three hours, or so? After that, trace amounts'd still show up in a drug screening for employment or what have you for a couple days, but she could easily pass it off as bein' from just about any prescription painkiller by that point."

"I was... afraid of that." Tabitha's expression fell. "The last of my codeine from breaking my wrist disappeared. I think there were two tablets left over, in a little orange pill container we kept in the medicine cabinet. The container was gone from the cabinet, and it wasn't there in her purse either, so it's just... *missing*. Would a lab be able to differentiate them, if they were both in her system? Heroin and codeine?"

"Hmm, I honestly couldn't tell you." Officer Williams shook his head. "In any case, all this evidence here'll get us started, so I'm gonna get it down to the station. We'll send someone over to pick up this Lisa character for questioning, and we might havta have you piddle in a cup too, just so we can have it clear and down on paper for later that you didn't have anything to do with this nasty stuff."

"Okay." Tabitha sighed. "You're right. That's smart."

"You wouldn't still have any codeine or nothin' still in your system, right?" Officer Williams asked. "I know you were just out of the hospital all over again, yourself."

"I do not, no," Tabitha firmly denied. "Not for days and days, not since right after the operation. Was always terrified of forming any kind of dependence on it, so just like with when I hurt my wrist—I'd rather tough it out for a few nights than ever get hooked on painkillers."

"Well, nothin' to worry about, then. I'll get you a little cup before I head out." Officer Williams nodded, turning then to the rest of his family. "Matthew—I know it's not fair kickin' you out outta the blue at this hour, but why don't you change your bedcovers so we can put Tabitha here up in your room for night and have you out on the sofa."

"Oh, you don't have to do that," Tabitha protested. "I can sleep on the sofa, or the floor or—"

"Nah, it's fine." Matthew waved her off, already heading down the back hall to his room. "Big TV's out here anyways!"

"Har har, very funny," Mrs. Williams huffed, shooting Tabitha an apologetic look. "He'll be fine out here—let's get you settled in for the night, Dearie."

"Th-thank you all so much." Tabitha's voice hitched. "For everything. I, um, I didn't know what else to do, and—"

"Also." Officer Williams paused, giving his wife a look. "I know there were, you know. *Circumstances,* and all. But you do definitely need to get the girl's parents on the line and at least let 'em know where she is—they're probably worrying themselves sick."

"Oh... *fine.*" The frown Mrs. Williams wore deepened into a scowl. "I'll call them."

———

Though he was tired and bewildered by everything going on, Mr. Moore jumped to answer the landline when the phone began to ring. It had been a hell of trying day, he and his wife both needed *answers,* and between the tension of waking up to hollering and screeching out of nowhere and the sensation of terror at realizing their baby girl had run out into the night for some baffling reason, they had no idea what to think! He snatched the phone from it's cradle and issued a brisk *"Moore residence"* into it while holding a hand up to forestall any interruption from his wife.

"Hello, this is Karen Williams," a woman introduced herself in a brisk tone. "We've met before."

"Yes, I—" Mr. Moore frowned.

"Tabitha is safe and sound," Mrs. Williams revealed. "She's here with me right now."

"Oh, thank God." Mr. Moore sagged down to slump against the kitchen counter in relief. "We woke up to all this screaming, and—"

"There was a woman named *Lisa* staying there in the mobile home with you?" Mrs. Williams asked.

"Yeah, yeah," Mr. Moore said. "My sister-in-law, she's staying with us right now. For Thanksgiving."

"Were you aware of any *substance abuse* problems there might have been around this *Lisa* character?" Mrs. Williams pressed. "Anything like that you might remember? Anything at all?"

"No, *no no no,* nothing like that at all," Mr. Moore quickly assured her. "Lisa's not into anything like that."

"*You're sure?*" Mrs. Williams asked again.

"Absolutely," Mr. Moore answered without hesitation. "Lisa would never get into any of that stuff."

Good lord, He felt a massive headache coming on. *What in the hell is Tabby TELLING them? That's the family of a police officer, for Christ's sake! It's one thing to say that to ME when she's a little too angry to think straight, but to go around implicating stuff like that to other people when poor Lisa's—*

"Because Tabitha brought some woman's purse along with her, she says it's her Aunt Lisa's, and it's full of heroin," Mrs. Williams explained in an irritated tone. "So, you don't have any idea where it came from?"

"Heroin?" Mr. Moore repeated, his features scrunching up in disbelief. "That doesn't make any sense. There—there has to be some kind of mistake, or misunderstanding or something, here. Tabitha's telling you that there's drugs in a purse somewhere?"

"Tabitha had a purse with her," Mrs. Williams growled. "When I picked her up. It's here now with us. Tabitha said she thought there was heroin inside of it. We opened it. *There was heroin inside of it.* Just what are we meant to be misunderstanding, here?"

"That's... impossible," Mr. Moore put a hand to his forehead in confusion. "Where would Tabitha have gotten her hands on something like...? You said *heroin?* That, that just doesn't make any sense."

"Well, it was in this Lisa woman's purse, so maybe, *just maybe* it belonged to this Lisa woman!" Mrs. Williams yelled through the phone, furious now. "Where is this woman now?"

"She's not, she—" Mr. Moore looked around the trailer helplessly, knowing she was already gone. "She took off looking for Tabitha, 'cause we're here all worried about what the hell's going on. But there's *definitely* no way Lisa would ever get into drugs or anyth—"

"*Good Lord,* it's like I'm talking to a damned wall," Mrs. Williams hissed. "Is there anyone there with a lick of sense there I can talk to? Let me speak to your wife. Put her on right this instant!"

"She, she wants to—" Mr. Moore had turned to his wife and had lowered the cordless phone handset for a only moment before she snatched it out of his hands.

"Hello? Is Tabitha safe?" Mrs. Moore demanded.

"Tabitha's here safe and sound," Mrs. Williams assured her. "She called me earlier and asked me to pick her up. Now *what the hell is going on over there?*"

"My sister-in-law woke us up screaming and shrieking and hollering about who-knows-what, Tabitha's gone missing, she says Tabitha stole her purse and ran off with it." Mrs. Moore tried to explain everything all at once. "Lisa—my sister-in-law, she was staying with us for Thanksgiving. I *know* our Tabby wouldn't steal anything from her, though, and, and—she shouldn't be out and about running around either. Doctor Conners said she needs to be careful and take it easy, *and she has been,* I don't, I don't—"

"Okay, okay, you calm down and breathe," Mrs. Williams told her. "You're workin' yourself up into a panic attack. Tabitha is safe and sound here and perfectly fine, and I'll let you speak with her in a moment. First of all; where is this Lisa woman right now?"

"She's—" Mrs. Moore frowned. "Out looking for Tabitha. She said. That's what she said. Threw on her clothes in a big hurry and *left the shower running* and everything! She took off in her car, uh, our car now I guess, she sold it to us, b-back some month or so ago? We, we had the keys for it just in the little dish by the door, it—"

"That Cutlass Supreme we talked about before?" Mrs.

Williams asked. "One that was supposed to have a bad alternator?"

"Yes—I mean, I think so." Mrs. Moore tromped past where her husband was hovering over her, smacking and waving him back with her free hand, and peeked out past the curtains. "It's gone for sure. She got it started this time, at least? Lisa's out there somewhere in it."

"I'll call it in and have Springton PD looking for it," Mrs. Williams said.

"Looking for Lisa?" Mrs. Moore felt panic rising up within her all over again. *"What did she do?* What's going on—"

"This Lisa woman was shooting up heroin there in your bathroom," Mrs. Williams said. "Your Tabitha knew *something* was up and called me beforehand, asked if I could pick her up. It's—*no you didn't just SUSPECT, you DID know, Tabby honey, and you were right* —and anyhow, she managed to grab the evidence and get away from there before that woman could stop her. I saw this Lisa woman myself! Buck naked and screaming at us in the doorway of your trailer like she was completely deranged! Good Lord, I'm glad your Tabby was smart enough to call on me, so I could be there to get her the hell out of all that!"

Lisa was doing HEROIN right here IN OUR BATHROOM?! Mrs. Moore was so livid, she felt her eyes watering. *And Tabitha took it on herself to take care of everything and actually DO SOMETHING about it. She had to. SHE HAD TO. What on Earth were WE doing about any of it?! Her useless fucking parents?!*

"Is, i-is, Tabitha, she's okay?" Mrs. Moore choked up. "She's okay?"

Pangs of guilt and rage so strong they felt like they were folding her stomach in on itself nearly doubled her over. Her memory of being there across the table from Lisa when she backhanded her youngest son was still so sharp and vivid that it might as well have been cutting into her. *Everyone but Tabitha* had seemed to be frozen in indecision in response to that. Only Tabitha immediately got up and *did something.*

"Tabitha's safe and sound," Mrs. Williams reiterated in a cold voice. "She's okay now."

She'd been terrified of Lisa's overbearing attitude and shouting and how aggressive the woman was *about everything,* she'd been proud of her daughter for speaking up, and more than anything else, felt the deep weight of shame in her guts for not being able to stand up and take action when it counted. Speaking up about it afterward, after Tabitha had already taken the poor boy off to the back room, it wasn't enough. The moment to *do something when it mattered* had already passed, and all of the so-called *adults* sitting there watching the whole Lisa mess happening had missed it.

"Can I, um." Mrs. Moore tried not to sob. "Can I speak with her? If she wants to talk to us? Can you ask her?"

————

"Hi, Momma," Tabitha called weakly into the phone. "Sorry about... all this mess. I didn't know what else to—"

Mrs. Williams watched the teen pause in mid-sentence as the voice on the other end of the line interrupted her. The girl that was perched on the edge of one of the couch cushions looked awkward and exhausted, with her pretty red hair all frazzled and the dark circles beneath her eyes stark on account of how dreadfully pale she was. The entire bittersweet scene had Mrs. Williams getting riled up all over again—hadn't this poor thing been through enough?!

Just look at her! Mrs. Williams fumed. *Look at her! She still has that dreadful cast on, and everything! I'd hate to say it—I'd HATE TO SAY IT, but it's her so-called FAMILY, it's her parents, it's that entire god-awful neighborhood! Her parents don't seem to give a damn about anything going on around her at all! Bullied the whole way out of school by those wretched cretin kids, almost got goddamn KILLED—at my own Halloween party!—By some trashy girl out to get her, that everyone says should have been on MENTAL ILLNESS MEDICATION, and now Tabitha's even run out of her home because some naked drug addict LUNATIC woman is holed up there?!*

"Okay. I know. I know. I'll... I'll talk to him," Tabitha spoke into the phone, beginning to hunch her shoulders with apparent reluctance. "...Hi, Dad. Sorry about all the big commotion tonight. I—"

When does someone put their foot down and say enough is enough? Mrs. Williams pursed her lips so as not to display the scowl that wanted to appear. *Her father especially, what an IDIOT! If I had a daughter half as nice as Tabitha, I'd be personally laying down the law with each and every one of these 'problems'—and putting myself between her and anyone who dared look at her funny!*

"No, I—Dad, *no*," Tabitha hissed into the phone. "I, I don't care if you believe it or not! *She was shooting up heroin, in our bathroom.* We—*I'm* not letting her near any of the boys if she's going to be—"

Indignant outrage was welling up within her and Mrs. Williams realized her hands had risen up as if she needed to *do something* about this, but found she had no idea what to do. She wanted to snatch the phone away from this poor girl and scream obscenities through it and then hang up on that stupid lout! This wasn't her family issue to stick her nose into, but *she wanted to*, and with Tabitha's phone call for help earlier, she felt like some intangible line had been crossed. Now, invitation was open for her to start *doing something* about all this nonsense!

"*Dad, stop*," Tabitha interrupted whatever her father was saying over the phone. "Stop, stop—I don't care. I don't care, an-and, and *it doesn't matter*. Let's just, can we just let the police deal with this? Let them decide? She's not getting any sympathy from me. I'm sorry. She's not. Sorry. She's not. Not after—"

Despite her every attempt at self control, Karen Williams bit her lip and was forced to take a step forward as Tabitha rose from her seat and stood, the teen appearing increasingly vexed by what-ever *that man* was trying to say to her.

"*She's not!*" Tabitha's voice broke this time. "And—and even if she *was* family, that *isn't a free pass!* This isn't about her being *white trash,* and she IS white trash, it's about her actions! *LOOK AT WHAT SHE'S DONE,* look at the way she—no, no. NO. Dad, I don't care! I—"

She couldn't hear Mr. Moore's side of the conversation, but Mrs. Williams didn't need to, at this point. Being able to see Tabitha's falling expression, how completely *lost* the young girl looked was absolutely heartbreaking enough.

"I... wish you weren't like this," Tabitha finally sobbed into the receiver. "With Lisa. With *us.* Mom being the way she was for so long, me becoming so, so—*wretched,* and hating everything about myself, and you j-just, just *not doing anything about it.* I-I know it's not really your fault, an-and I know I can't put all of that on you and just *blame you* for everything we've gone through, but, but—but at the same time, you just, just *kept letting it all happen!*

"I know you have a huge heart, and I know you're, you're just *blind* to all the bad in people, somehow, and *I love you for that* because I'm a *stupid thirteen-year-old girl!* A-and, I'm terrified of you *ever* changing, o-of you ever being someone else or, or being different. But I, I just—I just—Dad... I can't deal with this anymore!"

Covering her face with her good hand and her forearm in a cast both, Tabitha broke into tears, no longer caring to hold the phone to her ear. Stepping forward in a rush, Mrs. Williams put her arms around the distraught girl as if to try to shield the poor thing from everything. The rage and sympathy and pure *consternation* she felt at having witnessed this sorry scene had her own eyes growing wet, and Mrs. Williams took the cordless handset from her Tabitha and decisively thumbed the call button on it to hang up.

Then she flung the phone aside toward the couch in an angry toss.

Tabitha's staying with us, or living with the MacIntires from now on—I don't know, we'll figure something out. No matter what, she definitely doesn't need to go back THERE until they clean up and figure out their goddamned priorities. GOOD HEAVENS, what a mess.

———

It was well past two in the morning by the time Mrs. Williams decided Tabitha had gotten it all out of her system, and by then, the girl seemed completely wrung out. There was just nothing left to her! Tabitha simply wore a haunted, vacant expression as Mrs. Williams led her into Matthew's room. The new bedding had been set up, but the mother was forced to purse her cheek for a moment at the disastrous state he'd been content to leave everything else in, and he'd certainly be hearing about it tomorrow. Shaking her head, she got Tabitha changed out of her clothes and into a nightshirt, tucked the teen into bed as if she were Hannah, and then sat beside the quiet girl for a long few minutes, not sure what to say.

"It's just..." Mrs. Williams tut-tutted, shaking her head in disbelief. "I can't believe things turned out this way. *Again.* That they *keep* turning out this way. The shooting incident, you getting your wrist broken. All that awful bullying that just wouldn't stop! That girl losing her mind at the Halloween party, and now? Now *this.* It sure seems like it's just been one thing after another with you, from one big terrible thing to the next. Even just seeing it all happen, it's still hard to believe."

"In another life, in some other life, most of these things wouldn't have gone this way," Tabitha remarked in a distant voice. "It wouldn't have been like this."

"What do you mean, dear?" Mrs. Williams perched herself on the edge of the bed and stroked a strand of red hair free from Tabitha's brow. "None of this has been your fault, okay?"

"In another life, a lot of these things would have just—passed on by and gone unnoticed," Tabitha said. "All of these things...

circling around me, they haven't happened on purpose, but they weren't really accidents either. I involve myself in so many things, I express agency where, in some other hypothetical life, I wouldn't have. I'm not supposed to be... like this. Not like this. Things that would have taken their own course, to their, their own various whatever resolutions over time have all gotten... disrupted. Like I've put my hand into flowing water, and then have the gall to be upset that doing so creates ripples, disturbs the current. It's almost silly. Hypocritical."

"Tabitha?" Mrs. Williams couldn't help but grow concerned.

"If I'd only kept to myself, kept my head down, I wouldn't have even appeared on people's radar," Tabitha confessed in a quiet murmur. "If I'd let the shooting happen... but then—Officer MacIntire, he would have died, and because I was able to do something, I had to. Or, it would have been my fault. Getting pushed, a lot of the bullying, it's because I wanted to have my cake and eat it too. Be pretty and popular, be there for once, be *noticed* for once, but without putting forth the effort in socializing, connecting, being a part of it all, making a place for myself in a social setting. I wasn't even supposed to be pretty in the first place to begin with; it just... just wasn't supposed to happen."

"Well, that's a bunch of nonsense," Mrs. Williams hurried to assure her. "Tabby honey, you have every right to be pretty, and no matter what, there's no reason for you to be bullied for it! And the shooting—no one would have blamed you, even if you saw it all happen and didn't do a thing. Not me, not Darren MacIntire, not anyone. Seeing someone shoot a firearm right there out of nowhere, why, *that's terrifying,* it's loud and terrifying and not a single person would have blamed you if you just ran away. You're a teenage girl, you're allowed to act like one."

"I would have blamed me." Tabitha winced. "I'd have blamed myself."

"You go on and blame yourself for everything that goes wrong if you want, but if you do, you've also gotta give yourself credit for everything that goes right! *Huh, how about that?* Tabby, honey, you're a downright *frighteningly* smart young woman, but I deal with the entire Methodist Women's Choir, and I know sophistry when I hear it, okay? From everything I've ever seen, you've always done your best with what you had. That's all any of us can do! I hate seeing you... *overthink* all of these things to death and be down about yourself over it. *You're fine.* Your mind's just grown up too fast, and all your feelings about everything have to catch up some, now."

"Maybe... maybe you're right," Tabitha did her best to stifle a yawn. "I want to... I want to just not think about anything. For a good long while. I feel so burned out, all the time. I can't even—"

"You're gonna set all of your worries off to the side and let them cool off some." Mrs. Williams bent down and kissed Tabitha's forehead. "I say the same thing to my hubby all the time, tell him when he obviously needs to take a break and just go fishing with Matthew, or watch TV and decompress for a while. Tomorrow, you're going to play with Hannah and stuff yourself with good food, and I don't want you to worry about anything bigger than what it is you want to eat next, okay?"

"No, I can't just—" Tabitha finally gave her an exasperated teenage sigh. "You don't understand. *I'll get fat.*"

"It's Thanksgiving; we all get a free pass." Mrs. Williams chuckled. "Thank heavens. You get some sleep for now, Hun. You've had a rough time until now, but all of that's over."

———

"You alright, Miss?" Officer Stephens asked in amusement as he put his cruiser in park and popped open the door of the squad car to step out into the chilly November air.

"Aw hell—*shit,*" the blonde woman swore, her face running through a gamut of different expressions in an instant before a forced smile was pushed to the forefront and she let out an uneasy giggle. "Shit, shit—I mean, not *you*—I mean this piece o' shit, would ya believe it? Hell, I, uh, I might need myself a jump to get 'er back a'goin' again!"

The main streets had all been empty at this hour, and he wouldn't have discovered her if not for checking the smaller back roads where Springton began to bleed into Fairfield and zoning became a lot less distinct. There wasn't much out here besides a barren stretch of road, a long guard rail dividing the roadside from the strip of berm, and then woods. Dead leaves and bare trees as far as the eye can see, what with the deer population having scoured away all the underbrush already.

"What's this, an Oldsmobile?" Stephens let a low whistle as he flicked his flashlight on and swept the beam across the woman's vehicle. "Whoa, Oldsmobile Cutlass Supreme Classic?"

"Wow!" the woman gushed. "You can tell all that jus' from seein' it in the dark? Must sure know yer cars, huh? I bet you have some jumper cables with ya, right?"

"Whelp, *thing is,*" Stephens chuckled, ambling around behind the Oldsmobile so that he could shine his light across the license plate, "if my hunch is right, I don't think jumper cables are gonna do you any good here."

"Wha-whaddya mean," the blonde demanded. "Officer—look, I know I ain't in any kind o' trouble, I just—"

"Yep, just like I thought it was—1988 Oldsmobile Cutlass Supreme Classic. Black paint. Plates match. Jump won't do you no good, Miss. S'not the battery; you got yourself a bum alternator. I had to guess, I'd say both your idle air intake and your electronic control module are both kaput too."

"Well, holy gee smokes you sure do know yer stuff, a'sounds like." The blonde let out a guffaw of obvious release that turned into a wafting cloud of vapor in the frigid air. "For a second there, I thought—"

"Ehh, not really." Stephens chuckled, shaking his head. "Just— you know how it is, us boys 'round the station get to talkin' 'bout these things. We all love cars. Good buddy o' mine's had us all pitching in to help get some replacement chips sorted out, direct from General Motors. S'not real expensive, just a lotta hoops you gotta jump through to get the exact parts you need programmed just the way you need it for a ten-year-old car like this."

"Sure don't sound easy. I wouldn't know a thing 'bout all that mechanical stuff." The woman laughed. "But, hey—if'n you don't think jumper cables'll work, would you mind givin' me a lift? I gotta friend right on the edge o' Fairfield I'm tryin' ta make it to, an' weather sure ain't good for walkin' my way all the way there."

"Well, ma'am, I'd be delighted to," Officer Stephens said with a smile. "So long as you don't mind if I make a, uh, a quick stop at the station first?"

Quick stop, a quick piss test maybe to check for opiates, then a little talk, maybe? Stephens thought to himself—he had never expected apprehending Lisa Moore would be this easy. *Sure as hell seems like this aunty is 'borrowing' that Tabitha girl's clunker. And after Darren was all set on gettin' fixed up for the girl's birthday next month! If they really want to get the woman out of their lives, hell, we can slap grand theft auto on top of possession.*

39
THANKSGIVING WITHOUT FAMILY

Tabitha woke up in a strange bed and unfamiliar room, and for a long, bleary moment she was too disoriented to remember her circumstances. It didn't take long to remember that she'd fled home in the middle of the night. This was a temporary reprieve with the Williams family, and she had been provided accommodations in Matthew William's own bedroom. The bed was *nice*, though, a queen-sized mattress that seemed to stretch on forever and over as she stretched out her legs. It seemed cleaner, nicer, more luxuriant somehow, and in her daze she couldn't help but grope across the surface of the bedspread with her fingers for a moment.

Mmmm. What IS this?

It felt positively decadent to lay on after spending so long on a rather stiff twin-sized bed that had likely been in the Moore family longer than Tabitha had. She wanted to lay here forever, ensconced in that sleepy morning daze somewhere between being too sleepy to start moving and too awake to properly fall asleep. Replacing her own mattress at home with higher quality bedding began to lazily waft up higher and higher on her list of priorities.

Seriously. Is this... a foam mattress topper of some kind? Memory foam padding? Did they have that back in ninety-eight? I thought the pre-two-thousands was like... hmmm, the water-bed era? This definitely isn't one of those.

As her mind slowly came around to waking clarity she stretched out all of her limbs again, this time holding them as far out as she could for a moment until her legs trembled before relaxing back into the clean linen. It seemed more probable that this was simply an ordinary, run-of-the-mill mattress, and hers at home was well past its expected lifespan and little more than a thin prison cot. Comparisons were cruel, and she remembered that in her first few weeks re-living this life she'd been irritated and on edge by how dated and worn everything in the mobile home around her had been.

But then, I just—I just got used to it all, Tabitha rubbed her eyes with her good hand and opened them so she could stare at the unfamiliar ceiling. *I adjusted to everything. I ACCLIMATED. To a lot of things. Some of which I had to—life before internet, the whole weird prehistoric paradigm THAT is—some of which I probably shouldn't have let myself get used to at all. Too many circumstances, too many things with my parents I just should have made a stand on right away.*

Matthew William's room seemed like a different place when seen with daylight casting sunbeams in through his big window. It was bright, spacious, and fairly tidy for a 90's teen room. He had his own little tube TV set on the desk beside the bed, with a Nintendo 64 console stacked on top of it. The far wall featured posters—a large one advertising the special edition release of *The Empire Strikes Back* had the most prominent position, flanked on one side by the tattoo sun-logo of a *Sublime* poster, and with the little girl playing hopscotch upon an exaggerated cliff edge *Korn* poster on the other side.

Above the posters were Cub Scout certificates and Boy Scout awards, a rather grisly photo of what must have been a much younger Matthew in winter attire crouched beside a deer carcass with his father. Several ensemble pictures that might have been little league teams from various years were tacked up with thumbpins, and to Tabitha's surprise—she also noticed a large marker doodle on construction paper of Casey's *Cocoa Cinnabun,* hugging another rabbit while framed by a large, cutesy drawn heart.

Awww. That's so swee—

Without warning the bedroom door burst open, and dark-haired seven-year-old little Hannah Macintire was there. The girl's adorable eyes went wide at seeing Tabitha awake, and—Hannah immediately scampered back the other direction down the hall before a startled Tabitha could even greet her.

"MOOOOM! MOM SHE'S ALREADY AWAKE!"

Having flinched up onto her elbows at the sudden intrusion, Tabitha let out a small laugh and flopped down so that she could sink back into the borrowed pillow for a moment. Which was *also* incredibly nice, it was even a little astounding how much differ-ence a proper pillow made for getting her some amazing sleep. Although her fitful few hours of rest night before last and then staying up far, far past her usual bedtime last night likely contributed to how tired she'd grown. Tabitha hadn't realized just how in need of good rest she was—it was like months of tension building up in her neck and shoulders had bled away in the unstoppable comfiness of finally having quality bedding to sleep on.

"NO! I didn't even wake her up she was ALREADY up!" Hannah's exasperated cry echoed down the corridor. "YES SHE WAS! She—MOM, come see! I AM using my inside voice!"

"Okay, okay, but we're *guests* so let's pretend our inside voice had an inside voice, okay Honey?" Mrs. Macintire's voice could be heard. "Let's just keep our volume waaay, way down."

Mrs. Macintire then appeared in the doorway, and for the first time, Tabitha wasn't able to find any traces of the *Mrs. Crow* from her previous life at all. The same familiar sharp lines of her cheekbones were there, but now the amused quirk of her lip and the look of delight at seeing Tabitha here at the William's house simply lit up her face. Someone appearing genuinely happy just to see her was always uplifting, and Tabitha felt herself smiling back already.

"Hi," Tabitha said with a shy voice and a little wave.

"Good morning," Sandra Macintre said, crossing the room and sitting on the edge of the bed. "I heard you had a busy night!"

"I did," Tabitha chuckled. "I... what time is it? Did I oversleep?"

"You were pretty tuckered out, so we let you rest," Sandra said as Hannah flew back, this time carrying a can of Dr Pepper. "I don't know, are you a Dallas Cowboys fan? No one here's pulling for Minnesota, but either way I don't think you've missed much so far."

"Oh—um, football? No, I'm not really—" Tabitha looked from one Macintire to the other in a fluster, awkwardly accepting the can. "Oh, thank you Hannah!"

"We're allowed to drink as much pop as we want," Hannah reported with the serious intensity only an adorable seven-year-old can muster. "Until six o'clock. Dr Pepper and Root Beer."

Then Hannah ran back out of the room again.

"I'll take that one," Mrs. Macintire chuckled, plucking it out of Tabitha's hand. "Probably'd spray you everywhere with Hannah running around shaking it up. We can get you whatever you like from the fridge."

"I... actually just try to avoid sugars, as much as I can," Tabitha admitted with a nervous smile. "Um... do you happen to know if my Aunt...?"

"They picked her up late last night," Sandra revealed with a grin. "That old cutlass supreme didn't even get her the whole way out of Springton—now we've got it at the impound lot, where the boys can play with it. 'Parently Nick, one of the chucklehead officers, thought he was real clever bringin' her back to the station like he was just givin' her a lift somewhere. She not only passed out right in the passenger seat of his cruiser—she pissed herself!"

"Then, then—" Tabitha stiffened. "She's been arrested?"

"Yup!" The older woman clapped a hand onto Tabitha's shoulder with a giddy expression. "Woke up to her Miranda rights and some handcuffs and a bunch of dumbass cops laughing at Nick. The one squad car's gonna be airing out back behind the station all day! She's gonna be out of your hair for good. Tested positive for opiates, *annnd* they already had her on possession and misdemeanor theft and some other crap over in Shelbyville to begin with, so it's not like she's gonna wiggle out of whatever we're gonna charge her with. Her goose is cooked! State trooper'll be by to pick her up sometime today, CPS will have custody of those cousins of yours sorted out by tomorrow morning. *Should* have been sorted out whenever she got into trouble over in Shelbyville, but—well Honey, sometimes justice moves fast, and sometimes it moves at the speed of paperwork."

"So—it's over," Tabitha sagged in place. "It's over, she's. She's done."

"That whole mess is all over," Mrs. Macintire hurried to give Tabitha a reassuring hug. "Honestly, it should never have even been your problem for you and your family, but that's... well, that's how it is sometimes."

"Yeah," Tabitha sighed.

"And on *that* note," Mrs. Macintire released her grip on Tabitha. "We need to discuss what you'd like to do."

"What I'd like to do?" Tabitha repeated.

"Both for today for Thanksgiving, and, you know, in the... bigger broad picture," Mrs. Macintire said. "I don't know that there's a delicate way to put this. If you'd like to just put this whole episode behind you and have us take you back home to your parents, we can do that. If that's... *not* what you want, you just say the word and Karen and I will do whatever we have to to make other some arrangements for you."

"Oh... *oh,*" Tabitha winced as she realized. "I'd never, um. I hadn't even really considered it as an option. *That,* I mean. I'll need to... can I think about it?"

"Of course," Mrs. Macintire hurried to assure her. "Of course, of course. Karen and I, well... it's not our place to be critical of your parents. But, *if it was*—we would be, you have no idea. Too many awful things are happening around you, here, and no matter which way you connect the dots, it just doesn't seem to make a pretty picture. If there's anything you want to say, or need to say, about anything else going on—I'd like you to come to us about it right away. We are going to have a long sit-down talk with them playing good cop bad cop, and I don't think either of us is gonna be the good cop."

"It's—no, no, I don't think everything's really their fault, exactly," Tabitha said in a fluster. "I, I might have gone too far with what I said last night. I was upset. I was real emotional at the time, and—I needed to get things off my chest. Some of it might have been just overreaction."

"From the way Karen explained things, you told them you thought your Aunt Lisa woman was doing heroin, and then they just ignored that," Sandra Macintire said slowly. "Which is a problem."

"It's—it's not that they ignored it, exactly," Tabitha grimaced. "I *did* tell my Dad. Just, he just didn't believe me, or thought I was just overreacting, being, you know. Melodramatic."

"Except your Aunt Lisa was, in fact, doing heroin," Mrs. Macintire pointed out. "So, in my eyes, in *our* eyes, you were not overreacting. I don't think we can understate here how serious the situation is—heroin should *not* be within arm's reach of children. Period."

"It wasn't, exactly," Tabitha tried to argue. "She was very— protective of it. Her stash, or, whatever it is you call it. I think, um, with the way I tried to explain to my Dad, it was... well, I'd just thrown a. A tantrum. I was upset, I stormed off, it was—it wasn't completely his fault. It wasn't, like, negligence, it was mostly misunderstanding? I like to think? He's not a bad parent or anything, he's just... a very simple person. One-track mind. With things."

"Alright, I understand," Sandra nodded, lifting her fingers to brush a strand of red hair out of Tabitha's face. "They are your parents. Just—think about it, and if there's ever anything you feel the need to tell us, please don't hesitate."

"I won't," Tabitha promised. "I, uh, *I didn't*. As soon as I felt in over my head, I called Mrs. Williams."

"Which is good, that was good," Mrs. Macintire praised her. "You're a smart girl. And—oh, speak of the devil."

"Good morning, Tabitha Honey," Mrs. Williams greeted from the doorway. "Well, *afternoon* now. If you drink coffee, we have coffee. We keep a brand new toothbrush or two in the bathroom medicine cabinet, please feel free to help yourself. Auntie Carol and Grandma June didn't forget theirs. If you want breakfast, I'll make you breakfast, you want lunch, I'll make you lunch. Our thanksgiving dinner's not for another few hours yet, but we got to talking and with everything going on, I decided to pull the Macintires over and have us a big Thanksgiving with both families."

"*It's because I mentioned I wasn't gonna do a turkey this year,*" Mrs. Macintire confided in a low voice.

"Which is just blasphemous, it's Thanksgiving for crying out loud!" Mrs. Williams stamped her foot. "In any case, Tabitha—if you still want to have Thanksgiving with the Macintires and Williams, we would absolutely love to have you here with us. If you'd rather I take you home, or whatever you're more comfortable with, we can do that, too."

"I don't want to be a bother at all," Tabitha said with a smile. "I really couldn't."

"Sweetie, you're not a bother at all!" Mrs. Williams hurried to protest. "We're happy to have you. I've always treated Hannah the same."

"It's true, she spoils her rotten," Mrs. Macintire agreed, patting Tabitha's shoulder.

"No, I mean it's..." Tabitha gave them a wry smile. "I'm really psychologically just unable to. No one's ever done this much for me, and—I feel like I'm taking advantage of you, and you've already assisted me so much... I really just can't ask you for anything more."

"Nonsense!" Mrs. Williams scoffed. "We'll have Hannah come in here and walk you through how to do it! You're a young girl, and you've been through dreadful ordeal after dreadful ordeal one after another, and—"

"Karen—let's not overwhelm her all at once, okay?" Mrs. Macintire intervened. "This has been a rough time for her, and we don't need to make it any more stressful, okay?"

"No, it's okay, just. Um," Tabitha chuckled. "For your Thanksgiving dinner, do you have a potato dish?"

"Of course! We have some 'tatoes out already, come on out and try them!" Mrs. Williams lit up. "Hah, *do we have potatoes*. I whipped up my own actually amazing mashed potatoes, and Sandra brought over her awful mess of bland potato paste, too!"

"Hannah's picky about her potatoes," Mrs. Macintire laughed. "They can't have any *potato chunks* still in it, and, it can't taste too much garlic, and, it can't have icky gravy on it, and so on and so forth."

"Then—if it's not too much trouble, or too out of the way," Tabitha asked, "if someone could drop me off back at the trailer park, I can make my scalloped potatoes, from my recipe. Shower and change and everything while it's in the oven, and then come back here with it for your Thanksgiving dinner. So that I can contribute, too."

"Aw, Honey, of course we can do that!" Mrs. Williams looked

touched. "Scalloped potatoes? I *love* scalloped potatoes, that'll be just perfect!"

"I'll swing you on by now, then," Mrs. Macintire offered. "There was something I was wanting to talk to you about anyways."

———

Since she would be returning in just a few hours, Tabitha only spoke a tiny bit to the veritable crowd that was filling the William's living room right now—the visiting relatives Carol and June, the visiting other family Darren Macintire and Hannah, as well as Mr. and Mrs. Williams themselves along with Matthew. Sandra waved them all off from holding them up with greetings and questions, and simply bustled Tabitha into someone's coat and out the door.

Their ride happened to be a sporty little 1996 Acura Integra, and quite a bit messier inside than the William's much newer Ford Taurus. Compared to many other cars on the road right now, they were both sleek, modern vehicles, which seemed at odds with the perspective of her future experience where the designs became so ubiquitous throughout the 2000s that they seemed like ordinary old cars. This Acura even had a disk changer that could swap out multiple CDs, which Tabitha found herself momentarily baffled by.

Sandra Macintire herself donned a rather *eighties* pair of aviator sunglasses as she slipped into the driver's seat, and all at once Tabitha was struck with the realization. Mrs. Seelbaugh was a cool Mom, and Mrs. Williams was an all-out Mom's Mom, but Mrs. Macintire—she was a *young* Mom. She had sharp features but dressed fashionably for the times, and kept a trim figure that could pass for someone still in college. *Actually, looking at her—she's probably not even thirty yet! Of course she wouldn't be. Hannah's only seven, so...*

As they pulled away from the curb and sped down the suburban streets, Tabitha was given plenty of food for thought. Thinking about the two women in terms or relative age made her reconsider the relationship between apparent close friends Mrs. Williams and Mrs. Macintire. Both were married to police officers here in town, and both were mothers, but perhaps rather than direct peers, it seemed likely that aggressively social Mrs. Williams had taken Sandra Macintire under her wing, so to speak. After all, if the house on the lake was any indication the Williams family was well connected and came from money, while by comparison Sandra was getting there but didn't quite seem to have her life all together yet.

"So—now again, not to overwhelm you or anything, but it *is* something I want to bring up," Sandra said as she guided the Acura into Springton's intersections. "If you prefer to stay with your parents, that's fine. Completely fine. So long as *this whole mess* of a thing never happens again ever, of course."

Tabitha regarded the woman driving with wary eyes.

"But then also, if you *don't* want to do that—well," Mrs. Macintire quirked her lip as she tried to organize her thoughts into words. "I work at an office in Fairfield. When he was up and about, me and my husband, we made it all work. Now that he's in recovery, things with Hannah... well, I can't very well leave her with Karen all the time. I'm sure you've realized, but like I said Karen *can and will* spoil that girl rotten. *Unapologetically.* As if Hannah wasn't already a little terror to begin with. I've looked into hiring a nanny, wasn't really much into that idea.

"But, I think if it's you—hell, I don't even need to get into how grateful my family is to you. *Nuh-uh-uh,* don't even start denying it. Stow it, missy. Hannah just adores you, she really loves you. *I* love you. My husband has it in his mind he's going to magically fix up that car for you, and realistically, what'll probably happen is we get it running right again and then shop around for a trade-in, for some car you actually like. Anyways, what I'm saying is...

"We have a spare bedroom. You've withdrawn from school for the immediate future. I would *really* appreciate a live-in nanny, to help me out with Hannah. And, for the next month or two certainly, it would *really* ease my mind if someone was just there at the house. In case some complication popped up, or Darren fell down trying to stand up and walk around, or lift something like an idiot or—or, anything, really. You *know* how stupid my husband is, he got himself shot pulling someone over for a routine stop. I wouldn't expect you to be responsible for changing his, his piss bottle or whatever you call it, or giving him baths, or waiting on him, or taking care of him, or any of that. That would be weird and completely inappropriate and I wouldn't put any of that on you. Just, you know—in case of emergencies, if someone was always there who could call. That would just be a huge load off my mind. I've already taken *a lot* of time off work, and I don't want finances to start getting tight right at Christmas-time.

"We'll still pay you, of course! It won't be much, but it will be something. And you would be living with us. I understand things at home are... difficult for you, right now. We're all going to sit down and have a talk with your parents about *that*. I know you're just turning fourteen in another week or so, but—Tabitha, you sure as hell don't act like I did when I was your age. Everything I've seen you go through, how you've handled it all? I trust you, more than anyone else in the world right now. You have a good head on your shoulders, and seeing you getting dealt these raw hands again and again, it just... it really bothers me. If you want or need or even just think about you rather being somewhere else than where you are now—our door is open to you. I want you to just know that, and keep it in your mind."

A long moment passed after Mrs. Macintire finished, where they could only hear the sound of the car in motion.

"I—I don't know what to say," Tabitha stammered out,

completely stunned. "I'm honored, and, and very tempted, but I. I'll need to think about it. A part of me wants to *leap* at the opportunity, but then also there's a part of me that is afraid it would just become an excuse to avoid my family. Avoid tense situations and difficult conversations ahead. Avoid working through and resolving issues that *do* need resolved, instead of left alone and ignored."

"You see? That right there," Sandra Macintire took one hand off the wheel so she could lower her sunglasses just enough to stare at Tabitha. "I know you're almost fourteen, but Tabitha... you're *not* like you're almost fourteen."

"H-hah," Tabitha mumbled out. "I actually get that a lot."

––––––

Returning home was a tense affair, and Mrs. Macintire and her little Acura swept her there down the hill and through the clustered little street of mobile homes far more quickly than Tabitha liked. As immature as it sounded, Tabitha just *dreaded* this. All of this. These constant awkward situations, all of the confrontation, it took a massive toll on her, and she just didn't want to deal with it anymore. Not for a long while, if she could help it.

The Moores were waiting for them, and her parent's faces appeared and then reappeared in the window overlooking the street as Tabitha uneasily climbed out of the car. For a moment she was even attempted to just ask Mrs. Macintire to drive her away—anywhere, anywhere else but here. The wheel of fraught teenage emotion was turning about with clumsy motion within her, and she hated it. The guilt she felt towards cutting her parents out of the loop made her angry, the anger revolved back around into fear and self-doubt, which in turn fed right back into those sapping pangs of guilt and continued it all in perpetuity.

Unable at this point to even mind her body language, Tabitha hugged both arms against herself, and followed Mrs. Macintire up the porch step to the door with reluctance. The woman *knocked,* rather than simply ushering Tabitha forward to open it, and then Sandra stepped back and rested a hand on Tabitha's shoulder. The moment felt weird, and she was just turning her mind towards untangling why when the door to the trailer was wrenched open and Mrs. Moore appeared.

"You're back," Mrs. Moore managed to say. "Good, good— come in, please."

Her heavyset mother's eyes were wet and she looked out of sorts, *stricken*. Like she had wanted to rush forward and grab Tabitha up in a hug, but froze up at the sight of Mrs. Macintire. Guilt twinged within her again with such force that Tabitha felt a little sick to her stomach, and she remained in place for a moment, shoulders hunched and arms crossed so that she was holding her cast in front of her. It hurt recognizing that another wheel of suffering seemed to be turning within her mother, and she was afraid to think too much on what familiar ruts that wheel might be falling back into. Or even carving ruts anew—Shannon Moore's old traumas giving way to newer, fresher pain.

I wish things hadn't gotten to this point, Tabitha stepped inside at the invitation, completely unable to shake how fucking *awkward* it was to have everyone she cared about on edge and wary of each other like this. *But, they did get to this point. Here we are. Now we need to deal with it.*

Mr. Moore was waiting for them just inside the living room, and it upset her to realize he didn't appear distraught like her mother did. He simply seemed confused and angry, like he was about to launch into a tirade or demand explanations or dash one of their family plates against the wall.

Please just don't, Tabitha prayed. *Don't start. If you get into it, then I'M going to get into it, and Mrs. Macintire's here and—please PLEASE Dad just don't embarrass me...*

"Tabitha, we need to talk about what all went on last night," Mr. Moore began with a frown. "I'm glad you're safe. *We're* glad you're safe. But, you takin' off like that—at that hour, without sayin' a word to anybody? That's not okay."

"Not okay," Tabitha repeated with a stony face. "Not okay?"

"No, and you know it's not," Mr. Moore shook his head in consternation. "Do you have any idea how worried me and your mother were? We were up all night and worried sick. What if something had happened to you?"

"*You* were worried," Tabitha put a hand to her forehead and took a deep breath. Arguing with him right now was going to be bad, but maybe conceding any ground would be even worse. "Okay. Tell me—what should I have done? Instruct me. What was the best course of action I could have taken, in those circumstances?"

"Well, you wouldn't—" Mr. Moore appeared angry and flustered already. "You shouldn't've run off like that, that's not okay. That's not okay, Tabitha."

"So—I should have called the police, but from here?" Tabitha asked. "Without evidence in hand?"

"No, you shouldn'ta—Tabitha this is something we all should've sat down and discussed through together as family. Not something you just, you just *run out* and go right to *police* for!"

"*Family...?*" Tabitha hissed in a low, quiet voice.

"It's alright, Tabitha," Mrs. Macintire spoke up, stepping closer so that she could take the girl by the shoulders in a show of support. "Everything's going to be okay—I'll take it from here. Mr. Moore, are you suggesting you or your family would have intentionally withheld this Lisa woman's possession of heroin from the authorities?"

"No, I'm not sayin' anything like that," Mr. Moore blustered.

"We don't know what all it might've been, or, or if it could be some misunderstanding, or—"

"Did Tabitha tell you that she suspected this woman's drug abuse?" Mrs. Macintire pressed. "Was anything said that would have raised some red flags for you?"

"No, no, I haven't had any reason to think Lisa would get into any of that stuff," Mr. Moore denied. "She's smarter than that, and she's got four boys for cryin' out loud, she wouldn't—"

"*Yes or no,* did Tabitha say something to you?" Mrs. Macintire cut him off with a wave of her hand—it was clear she was running out of patience for the man. "Anything at all?"

"Tabby was—she was upset," Mr. Moore said. "She didn't mean it. They'd just gotten riled up at each other, and they were cross at each other for a bit, but that doesn't suddenly mean Lisa's a *druggie* or anything like that all the sudden."

"And, if she *was* a 'druggie?'" Mrs. Macintire asked. "You were willing to take that chance?"

"There's no way Lisa was into any of that kind of thing," Mr. Moore refused. "I think once we all have this sorted out, there's—"

"Tabitha Honey, can you excuse us for a moment?" Mrs. Macintire's voice was cold. "To your room, or the bathroom, or— just give us a few minutes, here."

"Oh, um," Tabitha looked between the adults uneasily. "Okay."

———

Sandra Macintire watched Tabitha carefully tread her way past her parents and on down the hallway that spanned the rear of the mobile home. Maintaining a mask of civility was harder than she thought. She wanted to *tear into* this idiot and his wife, and she was sure that if Karen were there, these 'parents' would've been laid into in a vicious way already.

"It's my understanding that you paid cash to transfer the

title of that Cutlass Supreme," Mrs. Macintire began. "If I may ask —how much money did you give her? This Lisa woman."

"We—" Mr. Moore exchanged glances with his wife for a moment. "We didn't transfer the actual title, no. My brother would still have it in there with wherever he kept all his papers. It was just an informal sort of... trade. She needed some money to help get her back on her feet, and she left the car here for us."

"Until she just up and took it again," Mrs. Macintre pointed out. "Can you give me a number? How much money?"

"Sixteen hundred, it's what we had saved," Mr. Moore admitted. "It's what we had at the time."

"That's very interesting," Mrs. Macintire remarked in a cool voice. "Can you guess how much the Springton police department valued the heroin they found in this Lisa woman's purse at?"

Mr. Moore stared across the room in confusion and disbelief at the woman for a long moment, and eventually Mrs. Macintire decided to simply continue.

"There's about eight grams of heroin that we're trying to prove was in her possession," Mrs. Macintire revealed. "There was eight grams in her purse that Tabitha took. An entire gram runs about five hundred dollars 'on the streets,' so this Lisa had on her person about *four grand* worth of heroin."

"*Trying* to prove," Mr. Moore latched on to her phrasing in search of any possible way out. "That don't mean anything but—"

"She tested positive for opiates, had visible puncture marks on her arm from needle use, and she passed out and fucking *pissed herself* on the ride back to the station when one of the officers took her in," Mrs. Macintire went on. "They found out she'd already been charged with possession over in Shelbyville, as well as some other misdemeanors."

Mrs. Moore had the good decency to look absolutely horri-fied, but Mr. Moore remained frozen in place with an incredulous expression. He simply wouldn't—or maybe couldn't—believe what he was hearing. Sandra recognized that stubborn goddamned *willfull ignorance* from having seen it on her own parents faces all those years ago, and if anything running into it again just made her more and more furious.

"I've known an addict or two," Mrs. Macintire said in a low voice. "I'm a city girl, and I grew up in *Ohio,* for Christ's sake. Tabitha has settlement money coming her way, more money than most any family expects to see. In this sort of situation, do you realize how *easy* it would have been for this Lisa woman to get Tabitha hooked on heroin? She's thirteen fucking years old, socially isolated, and *medically vulnerable.* She'd be hooked and have the money—Lisa would control the supply. Doesn't that just sound fucking perfect?"

"That's... ridiculous," Mr. Moore shook his head in denial. "There's no way. Lisa isn't that kind of person to begin with, and there's no way my little girl would go in for anything like drugs."

"You think she'd have a *choice?"* Mrs. Macintire was growing incredulous at his continued naivete. "You think what, Lisa would *explain it all out first? Ask for permission?* Tabitha's just out of the hospital and hurting, Lisa could spin any story she liked. Say 'they gave you this for the pain,' or even 'it's an antibiotic, you have to take it.' Why let her know before it's too late?"

"Why that's bull-malarkey, and you don't know a thing about either of them or any of us or how we are," Mr. Moore argued with a raised voice. "You can't just come in here and, and accuse anyone in this family of this or that nonsense just based on whatever Tabby said when she was in a mood!"

The slight figure of their teenage daughter chose this moment to come on back down the hallway and rejoin them, and Sandra was thrilled to see that the girl was carrying an overstuffed jean schoolbag.

"Dad," Tabitha swallowed. "I'm going to... stay somewhere else for a little while."

"No, you're not," Mr. Moore refused immediately. "Go on back to your room, we're gonna sit down and talk about all this later. You're not runnin' out to who knows where again, absolutely not."

"I'm going," Tabitha repeated in a defeated voice. "I'm sorry."

"You're not," Mr. Moore insisted. "I don't even know how all this got worked up into this, this—this big crazy debacle. We're putting a stop to all this. Please go on back to your room, now. Mrs. Macintire—thank you for bringing Tabby on back, but now I think it's time for you to leave so we can—"

"Honey... why don't we stop and let her speak," Mrs. Moore warned her husband.

"She's been speakin' enough, and that's how this big whole mess got to how it has," Mr. Moore shook his head. "Tabitha—I know Lisa disciplining her son like that really rubbed you the wrong way and had you all worked up into a tiffy. But, she's their mother and that's— it's just part of havin' kids and raisin' them up sometimes. You've always been a good girl, so maybe I think you haven't really seen that kind of thing for yourself. Lisa loves her kids, and she isn't some fairytale wicked stepmother or drug hippie or whatever it is story you've cooked up in your head about her with your imagination. When you're grown up you're gonna be able to understand."

That last sentence seemed to be *exactly the wrong thing to say*, because even through her own outrage and bewildered fascination with Mr. Moore, Mrs Macintire was able to see the dramatic effect those words had on Tabitha. The teenage girl had been worked up with a dozen different emotions and visibly struggling with all of them, and then—nothing. *Nothing.* At the words *when you're all grown up you're gonna be able to understand,* all of the feeling in Tabitha's eyes seemed to simply snuff out all at once and there was just *nothing.*

A shiver went went down Mrs. Macintire's back at witnessing it, and she clenched her car keys with suddenly sweaty hands. Because Jesus H. Christ she was getting this girl *the fuck out of here* and away from this fucking family.

"I'm leaving," Tabitha decided with a small nod to herself. "I'm going to need your permission to stay with the Macintires for... however long that winds up needing to be."

"We're your parents, and you're not allowed to go *any*—" Mr. Moore began.

"You have our permission!" Mrs. Moore interrupted her husband with both of her fists, swinging them one after another in unrestrained bashes and almost knocking the man to the floor. The Moore mother was already breaking down into tears. "You have our permission, and—you stay safe, and—Tabitha I'm so sorry, I—I—"

"I'm sorry, too," Tabitha said in a distant voice. "I—I'm taking the scalloped potatoes. I'll call and check in when I'm—when I become able to. I'm sorry. I love you."

With jerky, almost rigid motions Tabitha walked over to their refrigerator and withdrew a glass dish covered with plastic wrap. Whatever this Tabitha girl had made for the prior Thanksgiving with her own family, there looked to still be two-thirds of the cheesy potatoes still there as leftovers, and Mrs. Macintire actually found herself pissed off that these ingrate parents might have enjoyed any at all. Tabitha clutched the dish against her hip with her good hand, pinning the strap of the backpack she had slung on one shoulder with the other, and took one last look around the tiny mobile home.

"Dad—when you call me and apologize, I'm going to be where I need to be to forgive you," Tabitha stated in a flat voice.

"Maybe don't call too soon."

Sandra held the door for her, and they left in silence. The sudden turnabout of the situation honestly gave her chills. She wanted to hug the girl, because Tabitha was absolutely not okay, but instead she simply accepted the glass dish of potatoes from Tabitha so that she didn't have to struggle with everything. This petite girl with the tangle of red hair wasn't near tears, she wasn't choking up with sobs or angry or needing to vent—Tabitha Moore was somewhere very, very far away right now, and Sandra Macintire was just going to give her all the time and space she needed.

Good Lord up in heaven, what a total mess, Mrs. Macintire sighed. *We cannot get the fuck out of here fast enough. Definitely drinking with Karen later tonight, Rob or Matthew can keep an eye on Hannah, or something. If Tabitha wasn't thirteen, I'd make sure she was right there drinking with us. What does a girl even DO about all of that?*

———

The Thanksgiving dinner was nice.

Mrs. Williams was an accomplished host, and her talents extended from preparing the best dinner Tabitha might have ever had to remaining in subtle control of conversation as everyone around the table talked. The woman sensed that Tabitha was withdrawing back into herself even before Tabitha did, and gently pulled attention back away from her whenever someone tried to engage Tabitha in more than a sentence or two.

"You're in ninth grade, Dear?" Auntie Carol guessed. "Tenth?"

"Let her eat, goodness," Mrs. Williams laughed. "She's just skin and bones. Carol—I take it you're all caught up on *NYPD Blue?* Detective Simone..."

Tabitha wanted to blush at the excuse prepared for her, because after just a short five minutes or so into the meal she'd been unable to eat another single bite. She was absolutely stuffed and had kept her head down, fiddling with her fork in the errant bit of gravy that remained on her plate and doing her best to avoid notice.

"Oh my God, I couldn't even believe it," Auntie Carol took the hint and shifted tracks into the new topic with ease. "How's the show going to even be the same without Jimmy Smits? I mean, when she took the ring, and looks up at him, and Bobby just has tears running down his face? I just *lost it!*"

"If watching that scene doesn't make you choke up every time, why you aren't even human," Mrs. Williams agreed with a bitter smile, shaking her head. "If they don't win an Emmy for that, then well, I can't imagine who will."

"Listen to her, *NYPD Blue,*" Mrs. Macintire snorted. "As if she just can't get her fill of lousy *cop drama* just from around here in town."

"Well, I can't," Mrs. Williams sniffed. "I'll take as much as I can get. You should really try watching sometime, it's just fantastic."

"Ahh, it's all hokey mumbo jumbo," Officer Williams joked. "All of it. *Especially* all the stuff around Springton PD. It's like— who *writes* this garbage?"

"Oh, please," Grandma June rolled her eyes and let out an exasperated laugh.

"I've been sayin' it, I've been sayin' it for years," Officer Macintire joined in. *"Routine stop,* my ass."

"Darren, language," Mrs. Macintire laughed, smacking him across the shoulder. "There's little ones here."

"Cover your ears whenever it looks like your Daddy might say a bad word, Miss Hannah," Mrs. Williams teased.

It was apparently an inside-joke Hannah already knew her part in, because still chewing a mouthful of her mashed potatoes, the little girl quickly dropped her spoon and clamped both hands over her ears. The sight evoked a small smile even from Tabitha, but try as she might to muster her spirits—her heart just wasn't in it.

The food here was divine, and she'd perhaps never eaten so much in a single sitting since re-living her life again here. Tabitha felt *uncomfortably full,* and also completely empty. It wasn't that hollow ache of depression, it wasn't numbness, exactly, it was just *nothing.* As though she'd spent all of her tears and overdrafted her anger, and now all of it was gone and there was nothing left to do but wait until her next emotional paycheck.

I don't even know what that means, Tabitha thought to herself as her smile began to fall. *I guess I—I don't know. I've dealt with everything I can, and processed everything I can process, and now I'm waiting on some other awful revelation to drop, or, still waiting on some kind of resolution, or—I really don't know. It's all just been a lot of things happening at me, really fast, and then when it's like this and everything's done... what happens now? I have no idea. Where I wound up is way outside the framework of what I knew before or anything I planned for. Just. Here I am. I guess. But, I also just can't... immediately adapt to it.*

The topics of discussion shifted around and Tabitha listened with detached interest, too hesitant to contribute and feel the awful weight of everyone's attention turn towards her. The talk was all light and easy to follow—although the Williams family seemed to be central to many of the local communities and their goings-on, Mrs. Williams adjusted direction of the chatting away from that gossip after each shallow foray into it for the benefit of Carol and June, who were visiting from Indiana. Karen Williams was in her element and had an excellent grasp of everyone's differences and commonalities, ensuring that talk swung around naturally so that each of them could participate on their subjects of interest.

Mrs. Williams and her sister-in-law Carol somehow found time to watch a ton of television and kept pace with what must have been ten or twelve different programs. Both of the visiting relatives were eager to hear how Matthew was doing in school, which usually managed to pull Officer William's attention away from talking football with Officer Macintire. Hannah was adorable and asking for the seven year old's opinion on grown-up topics was a constant source of amusement to everyone at the table. Mrs. Macintire in turn *did* actually still work at the safety plant in this timeline, which surprised Tabitha more than it should have. The woman didn't seem to have as high a position in the plant's office as she had when Tabitha knew her as Mrs. Crow, but her working there at all was already outside of expectations.

"They even have me on the production line here and there helping out this winter," Mrs. Macintire let out a sigh of aggravation. "It's such a mess. This is the *slow* season, there just aren't really any orders coming in. So, we cut off all the temp workers, and just have the plant running on this, this *skeleton crew*. In theory just to, you know, get ahead on producing certain parts for harnesses for this summer when we get really slammed. Just, the thing is—you *can't* just pull apart a full production line like that down to seven people. That's not how it works, and I swear most of the office just does not understand that."

"Good lord," Officer Williams shook his head in dismay.

"So, there's *parts* of production getting done, but none of it's connected," Mrs. Macintire threw her hands up. "It's not connecting. It's like a *connect-the-dots* that's supposed to turn into this big picture—but they took most of the 'dots' out to ramp back hours for the slow season—and then they're just *baffled* that what's left over doesn't quite wind up painting the same complete picture. It's unbelievable."

"And then from what you've said, you just can't keep up in the summertime," Mrs. Williams remarked. "Seems like no way to run a business."

"It's always a new batch of temp workers, and they've all gotta be trained up from scratch," Mrs. Macintire complained. "It saves us a ton in not having to pay out proper salaries, but the cost in time and efficiency is just—it's *ridiculous*. It *isn't* any way to run a business. The industry didn't used to be like this."

Hearing her talk about it had Tabitha rising back up and on the edge of her seat, almost burning to give them her own input about the safety plant. But, she couldn't. She'd never worked there in *this* lifetime.

Keeping the plant staffed and operating at all was a total revolving door clusterfuck, Tabitha wanted to say. *Most of the old hands treated the new hires like absolute shit. The girls running stitches on the sewing line actually WORKED maybe two hours of their eight hour shifts, and just milked the clock gossiping and bullshitting and wandering around for coffee or bathroom breaks all day. Plant manager can't get them in line because he's sleeping with so-and-so. Foreman can't say anything because he's fooling around with whoever.*

Tabitha had been hired on full-time on merit, *because there was miles and miles* of slack that needed picked up. It had made the dismissive way everyone there had treated her rankle, it made the nepotism hires that did as little work as possible infuriating, and worst of all— there was no way she could vent about it here. Frustrations and agreement to mirror what Mrs. Macintire was saying filled her mouth, but each and every bit she would have to just swallow back down.

"Well, we've been saying—Matthew wants a car, he's gonna have to work for it," Officer Williams commented. "We'll get him there through that temp agency so he can work through it this summer, give you guys a hand maybe."

"I was thinking more like a pizza place, or Food Lion or something," Matthew appeared to blanch at having his summer decided for him. "Working to stock shelves or something. Like, I *do* want to work, but I'd rather it be with people my own age. No offense or anything, hah."

"Ehh, work a job for teenagers, and you'll get paid like a teenager," Officer Macintire threw in his two cents. "I'd say go for a Midas or Mighty Auto, or Autoshack or Autozone or whatever they are now. Learn your parts, and then go from there into servicing and all that real money."

"That's right," Auntie Carol remarked. "How's Little Caesar's or Pizza Hut going to want to hire you before you get your own car?"

"The place he *really* wants to work—but doesn't wanna

bring up—is Family Video," Mrs. Williams revealed, rolling her eyes.

"No I don't," Matthew denied with a blush. "They don't need anyone else anyways."

"*Family Video?*" Auntie Carol pursed her lips. "Springton doesn't have a proper Blockbuster?"

"His *girlfriend* works there," Mrs. Williams confided in a loud whisper. "She—"

"I don't like Matthew's girlfriend!" Hannah insisted with a pout. "I don't like her."

"Yes, you do," Matthew reminded her. "It's Casey. You like Casey, remember?"

"Oh, *her,*" Hannah paused in realization. "She's... *okay.* I thought you were talking about somebody else."

"Some other girlfriend?" Mrs. Macintire teased.

"You remember Casey bought a Happy Meal with you?" Matthew asked. "You each got Happy Meals, but then she gave you *both* of the toys?"

"She's okay," Hannah admitted with obvious reluctance.

"But only *okay,*" Mrs. Williams chuckled. "He can do way better, right?"

"*Mom—*" Matthew warned.

"I turn thirteen in just a few years," Hannah argued her case. "I'm almost old enough."

"Hannah, Honey," Mrs. Macintire sighed. "You're seven years old! Thirteen is *quite* a few years away."

"Not really," Hannah pouted. "I'm almost eight. And eight's almost thirteen."

"Speaking of which—our Tabitha here has a birthday coming up real soon," Mrs. Williams announced, in a rare moment drawing everyone's attention to their most quiet guest. "December tenth, wasn't it?"

"Yes," Tabitha winced. "I'll be fourteen."

"Huh, that's pretty soon," Officer Macintire remarked.

Tabitha had been so caught up in simply observing the conversation that she hadn't been prepared to suddenly be on the spot participating in it again. It appeared there were limits on how far into the background Mrs. Williams was willing to let Tabitha fade. Still, Tabitha was fine with that—it wasn't as though she was feeling distraught or emotional or anything right now, just out of place and a little lost.

"Hmm, and what does Miss Tabitha want for her birthday?" Mrs. Macintire asked, giving Tabitha an interested look.

"I—" Tabitha's mind went blank. "Um. I don't know. I didn't think that, uh, that I should have any expectations."

The sudden silence around the Thanksgiving dinner table was absolutely deafening, and the strange looks several of the parents exchanged threw Tabitha into an immediate fluster.

"Not, *no,* not in a bad way or like that," Tabitha quickly amended. "I'm well taken care of, and, uh, provided for. I was, I mean. There—it's that there isn't anything I need, or anything."

"It's alright, Honey," Mrs. Williams assured her with a strained smile. "We'll just have to surprise you!"

THANK YOU FOR READING
RE: TRAILER TRASH

We hope you enjoyed it as much as we enjoyed bringing it to you. We just wanted to take a moment to encourage you to review the book.

Every review helps further the author's reach and, ultimately, helps them continue writing fantastic books for us all to enjoy.

Facebook | Instagram | Twitter | Website

You can also join our non-spam mailing list by visiting www. subscribepage.com/AethonReadersGroup and never miss out on future releases. You'll also receive three full books completely Free as our thanks to you.